T0366082

AN "I" FOR ANOTHER "I"

A NOVEL BY

Francis Lis

Order this book online at www.trafford.com
or email orders@trafford.com

Most Trafford titles are also available at major online book retailers.

Printed in the United States of America.

ISBN: 978-1-4669-2891-6 (sc)
ISBN: 978-1-4669-2892-3 (hc)
ISBN: 978-1-4669-2893-0 (e)

Library of Congress Control Number: 2012906334

Trafford rev. 05/17/2012

www.trafford.com

North America & international
toll-free: 1 888 232 4444 (USA & Canada)
phone: 250 383 6864 • fax: 812 355 4082

LIST OF CHARACTERS

LUKE'S JEWISH FRIENDS

Abraham	Joshua	Jerome	Andy

LUKE'S CARD PLAYING FRIENDS

Jim	John	Martin

LUKE'S BOWLING FRIENDS

Charles	Dave	Earl	Jack
Mark	Sam		

LUKE'S OTHER FRIENDS

Adam	Jake	Tom

LUKE'S ATHLETIC FRIENDS

Tim and Tyrone (twins)

Robert	John	Hank	Fred
Dave	Marvin	Roger	Carl
Scott	Brian		

REBECCA'S GIRL FRIENDS

Alice	Martha	Elizabeth	Jessica

LUKE'S SPECIAL JEWISH FRIEND

Joe

REBECCA—LUKE'S WIFE

LUKE THE NARRATOR AND THE HUSBAND OF REBECCA

RACHEL, THE GRANDDAUGHTER

We are being descended upon by the "I" of Islam in order to eliminate the second "I", Israel, through the buying out of America so no Jewish funds can any longer go to Israel, if America is controlled by Islam! This could prove more disastrous though for the American Jew, more than they would ever realize as of yet. The Israelis' Jews have a little of the land of Abraham's land as of now, but that shall eventually change. Amerika's land has been sold to the highest bidder through capitalism and our own government and its officials.

Since I myself am not Jewish, I nonetheless recognize this fact as such and that Aliyah shall soon close from America's shores and the Promised Land, no not Amerika, but Israel shall be only a distant memory to get to let alone send any kind of funds because of the Anglophile elites who will always sell out to the highest bidder.

Scoundrels in all forms and positions are here now with over 86,000 illegal criminal citizens here now ready to do destruction. This Homeland Security is nothing but a facade to wait till Amerika is completely taken over by heathenism.

In regards to me, my name by birth is Luke and as of right now America now is in great trouble, but the citizenry does not care nor do they realize just how bad it is. For this reason I no longer counsel though I really was never a lawyer or psychologist and for good reason. Man must experience everything to the very end and then and only then shall he understand what lies in front of him.

As I contemplate about the future I think to myself, "What shall it be like when I am gone from earth and where shall I spend eternity?" My thoughts run counter to sainthood, or anything near many times as well as some of my actions, but yet His grace and that alone shall save me. With so many relatives who are non Christians, it is discouraging to realize that family life is not what it should be. I have my wife who is wonderful in her spiritual heart, and thank goodness for that, but before that heaven forbid how I felt and acted. Adam and Eve—except Eve was deceived and Adam was not—would just about explain my wife and I and my inner thoughts constantly tell me, "What would it be like, heaven forbid, if she were no longer here on earth?"

As I was saying, or was I, well anyway what is life all about, when there are only little but nonetheless important things in life and yet for most of my life I believed that somehow I would become well known. What an illusion of falsity that my own ego kept saying, "Your turn is next. Wait and see." Well I am now in my mid fifties and guess what. I have not mentioned this or achieved what I thought I would like to achieve by this time in my life even though life earlier seemed more favorable, but maybe because I was younger and seemed to have all the time in the world and now well there is hardly any more time to count one's finger on at least in my own mind and heart. We stay young for quite a long time, but then we get old very quickly and before one knows it winter is here and is calling to another world and I have not done what I felt He wanted me to do even at this age!

What was this mediocrity, I say to myself, that has proved to be nothing even resembling hope for this world where one man can do incredible things through GOD and yet the question is still posed by my own inner thoughts of, "How can it be like this so quickly ? I have not lived the proper life to do much good for anyone including myself?" Others seem content with what they have done in their lives, or so it would appear so. Is this remorse, or is it this age in all of time that is showing that the world is indeed becoming more and more evil just as Jesus said it would?

I can't retract all the negative statements that that weapon, my tongue, has spewed out for all of these years and with free will to oppose, but not free to separate my flesh of the world in me. Is it just Adam's fall, or is it what we mostly choose to do with repeated warning not to do? Who can really smile and say, "Oh, well"? This must be this spirit of the age or the abyss of mundane nonsense that is worth little or nothing in the eternal light of all things.

My father is gone, who I rarely knew or understood and who had little education to understand what things we never talked about that we should have talked about. Mother is very old and at times somewhat bitter to life, and I myself have started a new road unto marriage with no children to leave behind for the future even though I had spent many times with others' children and youth. The fulfillment of never having children, or should I say the failure of never having children, plays upon my heart and mind each and every day, and my wife and I are about past the age of procreation at least for her and oh how sad I am when I think how beautiful our children might have been.

There are natural things in life that come with human nature and of course that means Adam's fall. Power, money, ego, materialism, obsession with sex and vanity, convenience and luxury, not to mention extravagance at least here in America and wherever affluence is the disease. Ignorance also becomes prevalent because the ones who are rich and well-educated cannot see, nor do they want to see the harm they inflict on their fellow man for now is their time to live and just for themselves, meaning also who they favor in this world which has little if anything to do with Christianity because if it did all us Gentiles would be left to ourselves and only the Jews would have been saved! Christianity really begins outside one's own immediate family, which of course means that one must not only provide for one's own family which goes without saying, but always takes care of these truly in need and not in need of government which has to do with Caesar and not with GOD.

The first one, power, basically is the want of the world to do and to have more than one could ever know what to do with and so hence it is based now in some form of socialism which leads to the destruction of mankind. It is a cancer for any one, yes one man to obtain this, except for GOD for He is perfect and knows no sin.

The second one is money, which our main religions have preached over and over again, and is not the love of money the root of all kinds of evil? This is not the barter system which works well for the uneducated and hard working, but for the ones who see this world as the beginning and the end to all things. "What can I do for myself, me and I?" It is the void within one's own spiritual heart, and is not that what GOD looks at only? If the spiritual heart is by grace, then works shall most certainly follow which are by the Holy Spirit and not by education, fame, fortune, talent, etc.

The third one is ego, or love of oneself in a mundane way that excludes all others and is a Me First of what life is all about. Affluence contributes to this sickness of the mind and also the heart and eventually nothing is left and that individual is never remembered ever afterwards, and if they are then it has all to do with evil, which means a total separation from GOD forever. The saints stay on.

The fourth one is materialism where socialism says I must always use my senses and never use faith since one deals in the physical realm and the spiritual realm is totally evil. "Without faith it is impossible to please GOD."

The fifth one is obsession with sex and vanity and is how man sees man or himself, but is not how GOD sees man. GOD sees the spiritual heart of man. "How can I get what I don't ask for and how can I look to deceive others as well as myself to believe that the whole person does not matter but only the external, which also includes the tongue. "It is not what goes in, but what comes out of the mouth that measures the spiritual heart."

The sixth and final and incomplete number which has to do with luxury, convenience and extravagance of which the American Jew, in particular, has the lead in the sixth realm of life and living. The excess luggage and baggage that we feel we all need to have and carry for the status symbol and the status quo and that we give to ourselves in the form of avarice. The convenience part means no suffering for man in the sense that life is a bowl full of cherries and everything else is relative, including the truth. This is the infanticide of 55,000,000 unborn children for the convenience of not to be of bother with things that annoy us or are too much too take care of even if it involves another human being innocent and defenseless! The American Jew more than any other Jew in the world is guilty of this extravagance to the point of absurdity when one looks at the insanity as to what they buy, how they live, what they say and how most of all they get it! So much yet an abyss of Hell that leads probably to luxury which means no aches and pains but pills and more ills and any other inebriated effect that one can achieve not to feel what life is all about, and too much numbness not just our own sinful pain and suffering, but also numbness to GOD! Our barns are full so we have all we need that there is to need except more! We, or one by one as an individual we use individualism as the Deist Forefathers used at, of course, the expense of others who we say we understand, but just for the moment. It should never happen to us, heaven forbid! This leads to the group mentality of "one for all and all for one!"

Let me get on with the story at least at this time. Technology and industrialization or its misuse and obsession with the internet has ruined this earth, but more importantly has destroyed more Christians than all other things in the last 3-4 centuries! The environmentalists continue as they did so in Russia in the 19th century, the same with the confiscation of private property and that all things become legal and that environment alone instead of individual responsibility was the reason for criminal acts. It was also said that America had "ghettoes" instead of just slums when there was no ghetto in America at this time except for slavery, which, in essence, did allow at times for worship as long as one was . . .

The English seemed quite never to be able to work in the fields for a living, but somehow always got others to work the land and hence the industrial revolution saved us from further slavery to many others! This was John Locke's English Enlightenment that brought materialism and nothing spiritual to this age, and hence brought in this anti-GOD atheism even to America, and even our leaders did not know the difference between the Islamic god and the real Messianic Jewish GOD of Abraham, Isaac and Jacob. Capitalism was just another word for unlimited avarice to satisfy the chosen few!

Many times I would enter a store late at night and see the derelicts of criminality that the courts and politicians let loose on the people and used race as a barrier not to prosecute these "underprivileged" criminals. I would intentionally stay in the store to see that no harm came to the cashier as long as I was in the store with them or until they left and decided not to commit a criminal act. Most other males were usually in a hurry because they feared for their lives and did not care what happened to another person that they did not know or even care to know. The Germans and the English were notorious for this and always needed a uniform to stand up for life and liberty, and in some cases it could be another one's life.

We had been invaded by another culture in a matter of a few years without even our consent! We were told this element would be good for America, but what kind of America did they have in mind? Certainly not a Judeo-Christian one? All this so called goodie two shoes who wanted to make a difference and that was the problem, this difference or so called diversity with multi-culturalism because this would indeed dumb down the rest of society since the 60's had already lost their self-respect and self-dignity. To begin with, the earlier generation were usually only concerned that they got their Social Security checks on time and could retire with nothing to worry about except retirement for themselves and save, or better yet turned over the right of authority to the younger generation who knew absolutely nothing about life's experience but yet were running the nation into the ground!

Even our heroes were ignorant about their own heroes. Even if they were Red Communists and had killed or ordered the killing of thousands and millions of people, they nonetheless shook their hands with no reservation about what these criminals had done in high places. We could hardly distinguish between the moderate and the socialists, but then again was there such a difference at all? I knew that at times I would say to myself, "Let me run the country and see what would happen!" Yes, but would I be any different then the rest in power and government always about power and not about the spiritual realm in life!

Since I had no biological children, it was with just cause because of my own temperament even though I loved children,- but could I raise my own children properly would have been the question? I was told I could not time and again and maybe that was true, because of my strict discipline in my later years and of course in my earlier years I would almost always know when to stop or not go through with it to the very end. I grew up with veterans who now did anything that they could to avoid conflict with evil and took life in stride as long as it meant a so called better way of life for them!

Had I totally changed for the worse or could it be that these old friends of mine never did have anything in common with a "peasant" who was self educated and had an excellent mentor besides and not a nutty professor who only knew about socialism and would sell out their own country for luxury and a good paying "job" ? They were not really professionals, but government employees who were mediocre in whatever they did and that is how they got to be where they were. One only had to go along with this not so hard road to oblivion after all it paid handsomely!

In our very own Hollywood, communism turned almost exclusively to Nazism since the atheistic Jews dwelled upon evil they themselves promoted—evil such as cannibalism, emaciated bodies in films, the occult, and obsession with the total destruction of America and the family like the Nazis in Germany who also promoted for many centuries that women were not human and that their so called "equality" of both sexes only meant the very same sex, and this too was "normal" for them. That homosexuality promoted this mindset of superman.

Then also the culture from India that showed how they break their chidlren's legs and arms to go beg for money, to have rat temples to worship, where the swastika came from, the racist caste system came from, where the new Age came from, how Indira Ghandi sold out her own people to the soviets, where arrogance was the norm and avarice, especially from new Delhi showed the same colors in America, and the Nazis would promote all this and more in America and no one would say a thing and our government was being run by Nazis and also communists!

Our own hospitals were being taken over by these other "Aryans", many who were Moslems or Sikhs, and of course the Hindus, but Germany and England promoted it so much that their own countries became dissipated especially because of homosexuality which has no national honor, but only a "brotherhood" of evil. Could it be that since the Germans loved their systems that the Antichrist would come out of either Germany or England but be of Jewish extraction? America had many times shaken the hand of the devil and even Time Magazine made Hitler in 1933 Man Of The Year! Roman Catholicism continued to fall into the abyss from their own avarice and as well as abnormality by "coercing" the abnormality of celibacy to the priesthood that even the homosexual community was drawn to it in the droves since they came in contact with children and youth and Dostoyevsky's "socialism with mysticism or superstition" was what Roman Catholicism was really all about! "Be fruitful and multiply" was not to be among the clergy in Roman Catholicism and so hence abnormality became the "norm" and an unmet sexual obsession that was never fulfilled because it would be normal to get married and have a family.

With the Hispanics came the Aztec and Inca civilization and also the civilization of the conquistadors that only went to Hispanic or Latin America as gold diggers and nothing more and nothing less. Of course also Latin America had much more natural resources than even America, so the rich and well educated from Europe took complete advantage of this and now were bringing this same mentality to America by inserting or importing millions upon millions of Hispanic Americans here any way they possibly could. From the Spanish Inquisition with Christopher Columbus to the German Reformation we had not even the lesser of two evils, and why all the slavery since all they knew was an evil explicitly mentioned by name in the Bible?

This anti-Semitism grew and grew from Europe so that Europe and then the 3rd world nations could promote anti-Semitism to the full and the American Jew was totally oblivious as to what was going on around them, nor did they take the time to care what even happened to their own children or grandchildren, especially in New York City and within the ACLU which was both communist and atheistic and meant to destroy by the devil's means, our courts, the legal mindset of these "Pharasaical Jews" who only saw what Marx and Trotsky saw, a destruction of mankind as well as their own and their own version of "Let somebody else be chosen!"

Since Nazism kept spreading one could see more people in elite positions wearing uniforms to serve the cause. The internationalists even had these homosexuals and Nazi pedophiles on their own closets so no one would know what they were really like. The system was working amongst the Anglo-Saxons and now the Hispanics because of Roman Catholicism. Yet Americans still went to "church" knowing what was going on in Roman Catholicism yet it did not bother them because "opportunity" proved more valuable than even true worship! They would not read Scriptures, but only quote it as Satan does and has and shall continue to do. The ECT Document was just a beginning to make all religions into the one world religion of possibly the Antichrist.

I had no friends except my beautiful wife who had compassion for all and prayed for her worst enemies and was my constant reminder to do the same even though my human nature wanted to do "an eye for an eye" by not praying for their salvation or their healing wherever it was needed and it was needed for all of us at this part of this age!

Our worse enemies were in our very own families which was a concern because it in itself made an accusation of how we failed to raise children or at least how the enemy had discouraged them and was trying to do the same with me.

Almost all the cities everywhere were shaking each others' hands and were almost best of friends and yet seem to say and believe in diametrically opposed systems or mindsets. Scalia shook Ginburg's hands and even attended the parties of Katherine Graham who was the owner of the New York Times. The Pope shook Arafat's hand, Reagan shook Gorbachev's hand who was once head of the KGB and had people murdered. People of the elite were all shaking each others' hands when they should have been prosecuting them to the fullest extent of the law or better yet GOD'S laws for heresy and evil! George W. Bush shook Khadaffi's hands and even Solzhenitsyn shook the Pope's hand that was from the Vatican and also endorsed Allan Ginsburg's member of NAMBLA. Yes one must certainly question everything and that means everything! Sharansky was promoting homosexuality which meant Satan was hard at work on the Jews again to destroy them like never before in man's entire history since Abraham came onto the scene. Motherhood and fatherhood were dead even amongst the young who got married to Soviet daycare and not because of poverty but just the opposite, money and luxury to have more leisure without really raising their own children but having foreigners do it while they themselves paid for it or the government did. Who would now be the scapegoat? All ministries talked about was money, but never put their own lives on the line to protect our children's lives or our youth's.

It was Yalta all over again, but this time it took on a larger portion of the world and all would be happy! Again England lead us into debacle after debacle year after year, and we, like sheep that is our government was very fascinated with the way the English talked no matter the obscenities involved. Self preservation, as had occurred to the cold war, now was with American individuals by the majority. Even the murder of innocent children would not move us to do anything resembling decency and not revenge, but human decency to disobey Satan's laws. What kind of Christians had we become to ignore what we know for sure was going on in our very own society, and this was not yet Nazi Germany where they too supported Islamic Jihad by hiding Nazi war criminals in their own country and had given them alias names, and the Arabs "agreed" too with homosexuality since it played a major role in their own culture or why else abuse their women and girl children just like the Nazis in Germany did. And why the long robes of narrowed minded and perverse men from the Arab countries, and even the "Christians" from those countries felt that Arafat was a wonderful man?

Immigrants now coming to America for the most part hated America. Then one would suppose why come to America? "They want their cake and to eat it too!" The worse of the criminals were at the elite top top! They were in government at all levels and in our own courts and most of all our huge corporations who thought of nothing but power and wealth with wealth coming first. Who would prosecute these rich and well educated criminals since the ultra-conservative, William F. Buckley, Jr. himself wanted to legalize drugs, not medicine mind you, but hard core drugs! This would definitely mean more profits for the elites and government since taxes could then he levied on them and the doctors themselves would make out like bandits from the pharmaceutical companies who would then produce these synthetic drugs for mass destruction. Talk about "weapons" of mass destruction. Who would need to destruct America when it already destroyed itself with affluence and the god of this world?

Why was there even a Civil War in America besides to hold together the union, and second because of slavery was it not? But who brought slavery to our shores as a wholesale enterprise? Was it not again the English who did what the Bible told them explicitly not to do and they still went ahead and done it! Were not the Bibles revised time and again so that one could hardly know the real truth? And as for history, what was the real truth? Who would now bring the real criminals to justice and try them in a court of law when they *were* the law? The incarcerated criminals for the most part admitted that they did commit a crime or crimes, but these would not even relinquish the fact that that was what they truly were, criminals and that is where real criminology came into play. The younger generation of Europeans also were told to be for the underdog to ease their minds and hearts from the vindictiveness that was about to be perpetrated on them and with their incoherent cooperation.

The colleges and universities would be sure to take care that the real enemy was amongst their own people and with the rich and well educated and these disloyal immigrants. Without experience of life how would or could they possibly know the danger and destruction that lay ahead of them and that their benevolence would not be looked upon as such, but as weakness to these foreign people with their foreign religions who did not worship the same Judeo-Christian GOD that only some of them knew about? They started to emulate what was done before in these foreign lands and usually only the rich and well educated came to this land or any other land first to get away from the havoc and destruction that they created, because few if any Christians were allowed into America under the asylum plan, but only immigration which had nothing to do with freedom of religious expression!

The Ivy Leaguers spread their venom as well as Oxford and Cambridge in England for this multiculturalism, and the Pied Piper played his Marxist/Leninist tune and the newly educated followed blindly. Even their own parents followed blindly and the ones that didn't were looked down upon as the enemy from within and the generation gap was nothing more than to hate one's country and one's family as well as the one true GOD.

Satan had certainly blinded many or most in America who were from Europe and should have known better, but how could they? The generation before them thought that communism and Nazism were defeated or did they? It was in their own backyard, but nonetheless till this time let them live for self preservation, but from now on . . .

College graduates now were making less or the same as union workers, but still the students or ex-students believed in the college system no matter what because it gave them the free-for-all mentality. "Do what you want at anytime to anyone as long as it was politically correct. Let heathen foreigners even worse than Europe take over and teach and show you the way!" There were no questions asked, and they followed as if in the military. All these so called generals were nothing more than false iconoclasts who lived off of the fat of the land such as Alexander Haig! Who ran the military in the trenches? The sergeants; high paid government officials that did not represent the soldiers in the field, but their own egos.

Emotional instability had again occurred as it had in the 60's when civil rights was a group mentality as the salt and pepper club was and it showed in the offspring and also in the non-marriage that also occurred with European women and those who came, or their ancestry came, as slaves. It shocked the senses of most of those parents except the ones that did not care about family, but only about politicized or political correctness which had been around or in the world since the father of communism, Lenin, was here.

Even the children in America now were severely affected by the immorality and evilness around them in their own homes, and love was found wanting for them with no regard for who they were as offspring. Soviet daycare was now the common place thing to do since civil rights' socialism took over. Motherhood had died since then and was getting worse and worse and children had no childhood. The Hispanic children got no toys to play with except the grief of their parents' emotional instability. The Hispanic mothers would even steal for their children when it was not required! The same old 60' songs and such worse now filled the airwaves as if it were a religion to be listened to by music alone, which of course was the way Satan liked to come in most cultures barring none. This now almost sets the scene for my story of now and in the present state of affairs in America and with education not being anything of the sort but just political correctness.

We were into the new millennium and so much had happened in our little town that one had to wonder was it that surreal? Our community had changed from a European family mindset to a 3rd World multicultural mindset of anything goes. The entire town had few landowners and most were a sort of tribal tradition according to their own homeland which they said they wanted to leave, yet they did not really love America. People were shot and killed daily, and the Franco-Germanic political philosophy ruled our entire area while the rich and well educated said this would be a new beginning, but as to what for they did not say.

I had gotten much older, and I saw the destruction of morals come as quickly that it was hard to believe, and big business went around as usual except with different faces and many different cultures, but nonetheless the same political philosophy that was here for years, but not the coerced criminality that came with multiculturalism.

Years ago people could walk any street and be relatively safe, but today it was like Hispanic revolutionaries that had taken over here in America like Liberation Theology and we tried like heck to help Nicaragua to overcome this communist manifesto there which was now here as well as its mentality as if Daniel Ortega was living with us in America!

On the job training is what a college degree amounted to. Many ex-students were in debt to our government while others who did not choose to go to college fared much better because government would provide for them or the unions of the Democratic Party.

The immigration policy was the same as in Major League Baseball where player after player went from one team to another in the same year and none were home grown any longer, and the teams were used as advertising agencies. The reserve clause, but most of all the "free agency of baseball" had destroyed where the authority came from and why one loved to play the game and not for avarice and breaking false records for today it was all a new and different "ballgame"!

Young people who had gone to college came out much dumber then when they had gone in, and yet they were spending thousands of dollars for this heresy of so called knowledge and most of all philosophy. Parents of the 60's were coming to their end and now their own mortality was upon their minds as what to do, but kept on doing what they had done in the 60's and that was rebel against all things that would he normal if one could find a normal person, which probably ran one out of millions upon millions or a little less, but not much less!

Every so often Joe would contact me, but not very often because I chose it to be that way. On this day he made a special visit to my home. When he appeared at the door it somewhat took me by surprise, which of course I did not like even though I kept it to myself and did not mention it to Joe himself. I thought, "Now what could Joe want at this unexpected time since he usually calls me?"

"Hello Joe, come on in and make yourself comfortable."

"I came over unexpectedly, I know, just to tell you that you are invited to my wedding which will be next week."

"Well who is the lucky girl?"

"I do not know if you remember the girl that I had dated about 3 years ago?"

As I thought to myself I said, "No this cannot be the one that I am thinking of, heaven forbid."

"Yes I think I remember that fine young lady the tall one, right?

"Yes!"

"How did this come all about all of a sudden?"

"Well we got back together again and started dating and before you know it we started talking about marriage in a serious tone."

"I thought that you said you would never get married."

"Well I can always change my mind, can't I?"

"Oh yes, do not be offended by what I just said. I only meant that you seemed so dead set on not getting married, that's all."

"Well as I just said, I changed my mind."

"Are you sure she is the right girl for you?"

"What makes you ask such a ridiculous question?"

"Do you remember when she went with the Moslem guy before she met you?"

"Yes, but what does that have anything to do with me getting married to her if I love her?"

"Do you really think that you could love such a girl after you know . . . ?"

"What are you implying about her and about my decision to marry her?"

"Well, I just thought that a Jew like you would never marry a Moslem girl being the fact that your family is Orthodox Jewish?"

"For your information they already know about it and have given their blessings and even if they didn't I still would marry her."

"Is she going to convert to Judaism?"

"No, that is not important, but just the fact that we love each other is all that counts!"

"Well each to their own."

"I am tired of your insults and think I will leave for now."

"Joe, I think that is a very good idea, and by the way cancel that invitation to your wedding. I am not interested in mixed marriage."

"You know something, if I didn't know any better I would think that you were prejudice or jealous!"

"Think what you like, but you are beyond all hope!"

"What makes you so high and mighty? I don't see any beauty chasing you?"

"And I am not looking to get married to any American girl, or any Moslem girl, if that answers your silly question?"

"You know something? If I did not know you as well I would punch you right in the nose!"

"Do what you like, but there are laws against that and besides I am in my own house and I did not invite you. You invited yourself here!"

"Goodbye and that is for good!"

"Shalom buddy. You can see yourself out the door just the same way that you came in!"

After he left I thought to myself, "What a jerk that liberal Jew is after what that religion has done to his people!"

Some would say I am prejudice, but then again who cares what they think, they do not pay my bills. I am the way I am and nothing can ever change that for the most part. Who needs friends like that who would betray their own country like that just to be chic?"

Later that night I turned on the television and saw another bombing in Jerusalem and thought to myself, "That Joe is a real pig head! Well he is one less person I have to worry about liking me since I speak the truth."

I kept wondering why the American Jews were so liberal about morality in most things such as infanticide, homosexuality, euthanasia, etc. and only donated to Israel large sums of money, yet it really did nothing since they did not know anything about GOD. The GOD of Abraham, Isaac and Jacob was only words to most Jews in the world even though they celebrated the Feasts and Holidays in the Bible. The New York City Jew probably was the most liberal of all the Jews in America and many real Russian and Polish Jews did not care for what these New York City Jews stood for even though the elites of them wined and dined with them. They had their own or were making their own "Pale of Settlement" in America and creating more anti-Semitism by the way they support the enemies in the Old and New Testaments and time was running short, or so it appeared so, for them to see the truth for what it was.

Their synagogues were just that "sin-agogues", and they continued in their old ways to ignore what even their Gentile friends were trying to tell them in a loving way even though some of us had had enough of their stiff-necked mentality such as the ACLU, Hollywood, the media, and even their most of all and that is their own religions. They were so close yet so very far away and only the ones who lied to them did they seem to believe, and that was the way it so appeared to me.

The next day I went to see a Phillies game in Connie Mack Stadium where the Phillies were going to play the Los Angeles Dodgers and Sandy Koufax, a Jewish pitcher was going against Jim Bunning of the Phillies, and Don Drysdale was going to pitch against Chris Short of the Phillies. This double-header would decide who would win the National League Pennant! This pennant was between the Dodgers and the San Francisco Giants. The first game was pitched by Don Drysdale who used to throw at Frank Robinson's head, because Frank Robinson would hug the plate, and Drysdale was not afraid to throw inside to back him off of the plate. The first game was won by the Dodgers, which meant that if San Francisco won their game they would be tied with the Dodgers since Los Angeles had played one less game than the Giants did and then for sure Sandy Koufax would have to win the second game for the Dodgers to clinch free and clear.

Well up on the old scoreboard in right center field the final score finally came in and San Fran had won their game which meant that the Dodgers and Koufax had to win the second game to take sole possession of first place and win the National League pennant. There was only one division for the entire National and American Leagues so that it meant if they won they could go into the World Series automatically and there were no money making playoffs. This was added also to bore one to death with America's favorite pastime. In the second game, after the Giants had won Sandy Koufax looked up on the scoreboard and saw what he had to do and his curve ball and fast ball were almost indistinguishable from one another and the velocity was tremendous and the black of the plate was where he threw the ball time and again as the umpire knew that they were consistent strikes. The Philly batters were baffled until the 9th inning when the Phillies started to hit the ball for some miraculous reason and had runners on base finally. Up to that time the Phillies had scored absolutely no runs so this made the game very exciting since I myself was a Phillies fan. Would Walter Alston put in a relief pitcher for Koufax or would he let Koufax finish the game since Koufax was known on rare occasions to get wild and sometimes his arm would tighten up on a cool day? Well Alston kept Koufax in the game and Bill White, the old timer originally from St. Louis and who nobody knew his real age not even him, came up and hit a shot off of the wall in right field which brought in the second run and Bill White was a left handed batter and Koufax a left handed pitcher which should have meant that Bill White was at a disadvantage seeing the left handed pitcher from the same side. The fans went wild and were roaring with approval. Now would Alston take out Koufax and was Koufax stiffening up even more after that shot off the wall in right field? Well to my chagrin and most of the ballpark's, Koufax finally retired the side and the Dodgers won the National League Pennant and were going to the World Series. I can still remember though and shall never forget when Koufax saw that the Giants had won and how he just stared at that scoreboard and then went to work on the Philly batters and pitched with perfection until the

9th inning. What competitors both Drysdale and Koufax were whenever they went out on the mound, and I remember one year when Koufax was already 19-5 and no pitcher in either league had even 12 wins! That's how great he was of a pitcher and he was the best that I had ever seen and that included Steve Carlton, Nolan Ryan, in person but none even came close to the consistency that Koufax showed year after year which was what a true professional on the field was plus the fact I had never seen him argue with the umpires and off the field he gave lectures to youth and college students about life. If he had not had an arthritic elbow he would have put up amazing statistics even though that was not what he was all about. I could also remember if the Dodgers would score one run in the early innings on a hit usually by Maury Wills, their shortstop and then would steal second and then score on a single, Koufax usually would need no more than that to win the game.

Well after the baseball season was completely over by October 1st or 2nd and that included the entire World Series, I took my eyes off of sports and focused on my studies. I remember well when in public school when we would recite the Lord's Prayer and all the students in the class would bow their heads in reverence as the teacher lead us in prayer and that would start the day on a good foot. Then the United States Supreme Court went actually insane and for some queer reason made a law banning us to say the prayer by the time I was in senior high school, and did the "demons" come out from everywhere! Of course that time the federal government was filled with all kinds of socialists that were in the federal government, state and county governments, city government and of course the good old school district that did not get paid but was a stepping stone for higher "education" with professional pay and lifetime "royalty". Most Americans had no idea, nor did they really care about what had happened in society.

After 9/11 our own government should have started to deport all Moslems, but then again that would mean that all that oil money would have been lost and the United States Senate would have lost millions of dollars, for most of the United States

Senators were millionaires. Here a certain religion worshipped demons was allowed to buy out America because our very own businessmen as well as our own government allow that to occur because of good old capitalism which was nothing more than avarice. After all capitalism comes socialism which means that materialism rules supreme and has nothing whatsoever to do with free enterprise since big business in America has even been more covert than our own CIA. We continued at our own peril to think that our own government would protect us when they themselves had sold us out some years ago. We no longer had any type of foundation with which to uphold GODLY morals in our nation, and only slogans were used to say we were the greatest or the most powerful nation in the world, but never did it say we were the "second evil empire". We had come to believe in our very own lies and mob rule, or democracy had shown what human nature was all about. Everything had become legal such as child molestation, homosexuality, infanticide, heathenism, barbarism, Nazism, Communism and most of all this New Age occult that most likely would bring in the Antichrist. This was at least the end of a new age and we were embarking on another age that would first start off very violent and then eventually bring on the Messianic Age which would place the Gentile church behind and the Messianic Jews in GODLY authority. America believed that since it had fallen that the world was coming to an end, but that was not so, since America was not Israel, or any part of the real Jewish people and had always been a part of the European empires that Daniel spoke about in the Old Testament. Even within my own lifetime America had fallen so rapidly that those few mortal years almost seemed like a few centuries and the Gentile church was depending on monetary value and not agape love from GOD and the GOD OF ABRAHAM, ISAAC AND JACOB!

My own wife was struggling with the way she was brought up and so I needed to let her see the way a "peasant" lived. When we were growing up in my own family we did not have much to do with the European religions or any other religion that constantly talked about money and materialism.

Some of the very unusual stories that I noticed were as such: couriers that were Moslems and made important deliveries to big corporations; Moslems that ran or owned businesses that involved money and oil, or one or the other; security airport people who also were Moslems; even one case where one man's own son was killed in the World Trade Center's building and was working on the same floor as a Moslem who was in charge. Moslems were in our very own military, something that not even Israel allows with it's small Jewish population, but of course the Moslems had not bought out most of Israel; Moslems that were selling here in America illegal drugs to promote terrorism here and around the world and our own government knew about it and did absolutely nothing to stop it; Moslems that also owned more than one restaurant in our area and were allowed to make a non-profit business and still stay legit; black American Moslems that were never checked out by our own FBI or CIA; chauffeurs that drove important dignitaries to many important buildings in America; over 86,000 illegal citizens that were criminals walking the streets of America who also were mostly Moslems; clerics that wore the attire that represented the Islamic Jihad; drugs that came from Afghanistan and were sold here and in Prague and in Edinborough up to the present date; intermarriage between, Americans and Moslems; black pastors who posed as Christians, but also were in the Million Man March where Moslems were and anti-Semitism plus they wore the garb that was apropos for Moslems; baseball players who carried Moslem names with no questions asked; doctors that were Moslems; and the list could go on and on.

Yes, America had become a haven for "anything goes" no matter how far out it appeared and our own courts and trial lawyers most of which were politicians seemed to enjoy all that was going on and in fact encouraged this violent multiculturalism that was eroding America including the Jewish ACLU that pandered even to Nazism such as in Cicero where Holocaust victims had lived. The American Jew in general became so heathenistic that one could not tell if they were Americans or from a foreign land! They were using their brains for evil and of course extravagance and also self-preservation and did not care in the least about even their own race of people or their own families, which told one how much they also believed in their own country, or even Israel the homeland of the Jews!

America had become so money hungry that many people who never had money now had it and it was destroying them, and to be a millionaire meant nothing since government itself promoted gambling, another one of their outward vices that the socialists in government wanted to promote and did promote to further bring down America to their so called UTOPIANISM! Even the poor in America did not want hand me downs because big brother, or government had already spoiled them in the sense they got what they wanted free from other American taxpayers better known as the redistribution of wealth according to Marx and Engels, but no one ever said that verbally because it sounded too much like the truth, and only euphemisms were used such as to the left or liberal but never socialism or Communism, or atheism. If one was not with them then they had to be against them, right? In this case some would abstain from making any good moral decision, especially the rich and well educated amongst the Anglo-Saxons. They were in fact colonializing America into a 3rd world country and were importing all who were non-Judeo Christian, and asylum was almost ignored, but immigration was in the millions especially from all socialists countries who were more than welcome to come here and allow their own criminals to come here also, such as Cuba. The Constitutional form of government was not working for the long haul because it was not based upon the Biblical precept of a monarch, but of mob rule which eventually would turn into chaos and then totalitarianism. We were eating our cake and enjoying it too, but we nonetheless would not stop to listen to any kind of reason that invaded our evil lifestyle of "eat, drink and be merry" and who more than the American secular Jew did that with their extravagance in everything they did. So that is why they were always for big government because it meant "free money" for them that never ended and just kept coming with no end in sight and because the ACLU really believed that socialism would work the way Mr. Bronstein had believed! We also got forced integration upon us and if we did not cooperate we would be called bigots and prejudiced, which was their lying ways to promote or silence even most conservatives which was not very hard to do since they were for capitalism, or real big business like the merger of Mobil/Exxon that was against all Vietnam vets! It also endorsed homosexuality to the fullest. Capitalism had become Socialism in America and so had the European religions, not to mention innately Islam with its death wish for mankind.

Now back again to my story about how my ex-friend had betrayed his own people by marrying a Moslem woman. Also the fact that India's Indians had become more and more prevalent that even other Jews were working for them and for Islam. A paradox to say the least and one that needed to be seen to be believed since the swastika itself was from India and the New Age Movement which was actually Nazism was endorsed by our own government and our own democracy "of and by the people".

As we grew older, my wife and I came to understand things in a clearer light than we had previously known all of our lives. Rebecca, my wife, was starting to understand just how bad America had become and just how really anti-Semitic it was since Satan had always targeted the Jewish people because of Messiah in the flesh. Jesus was a Jewish man.

Rebecca would ask, "Is Roman Catholicism really that bad?"

My response would be, "It certainly was and is since it did not abide hardly by Biblical Scripture and made up its own rules as it went along, such as celibacy, a Pope, homosexuality, materialism, anti-Semitism and believed itself to be the one and only 'Church' that also replaced Israel!"

Rebecca again would respond with, "You mean to tell me that Roman Catholicism was that evil and had that many millions of followers in the world?"

I said to Rebecca, "Remember that most people in the world are not believers and some who claim to be are not also and the fact that now all religions were leading to this one world religion, the 'she', or harlot, in the Bible!"

"So the world at this present time is actually that bad?"

"Look how bad America is! Now imagine how bad the rest of the world is at this very present time!"

"How bad shall it be for Israel if it is this bad now?"

"It shall certainly get much worse before it shall ever get better since GOD has His own plan that He has told about in Daniel and in the Book of Revelation."

"Shall there be any Jews at all left to be saved in this world?"

"The Bible says that only a remnant shall be saved, which means even with the small number of Jews now in the world even most of them shall not be saved, so one can imagine how bad it shall soon be as we see the end of this age coming so very quickly as it appears to be."

"Will Israel totally be destroyed, or shall some of Israel, the land that is, be spared?"

"The world as we know it shall not be destroyed, but shall be transformed by the will of GOD according first to the world's heathen one-world religion known in the Bible as the harlot. We must be ever aware to read Scripture and to let the Holy Spirit interpret for us, and we also must maintain a close relationship to it by not sinning so that nothing can block the Holy Spirit such as our own sinning."

"So, in other words, I must walk in the spirit so that I maintain the proper relationship, as you just said, and so that my prayers to understand the present situation if understood by me in this ever evil and present age?"

"Yes, we as believers must obey GOD and His Word, which is His will so that we too do not 'fall away', not from grace, but from His Holy presence in the sense we are communicating with a Holy GOD!"

"As one elderly man said to me years ago, 'Obey GOD AND LIVE AND DISOBEY GOD AND DIE!"

"It sounds almost work-like, but I know it is not by works alone, or should I say that it is grace alone that we shall be saved, if we believe in our hearts by grace and grace alone, but that we should not sin nor want to sin any longer since the Holy Spirit is within us."

"The European religions were all anti-Semitic and so one would have to wonder what is it that they had to show for since Jesus was King of the Jews? It again tells us to read Scripture for ourselves and teach our children and grandchildren to do the same and stay away from genealogy and hearsay such as in Roman Catholicism.

"I can see how one can be confused by all these so called Christian religions and the people who sincerely believe that they are truly serving the will of GOD but refuse to read Scripture, or to be witnessed to no matter how much truth you show them since they would rather believe in a lie and not the Word of GOD.

"So it would appear that most people would not be saved because of materialism, which Roman Catholicism preached and made those people feel good about themselves and had absolutely nothing to do with salvation no matter how many times they were witnessed to?"

"Yes Rebecca, they have found their comfort zone so that it would be easier in this life to go on living on the works, or Calvanist type of salvation no matter what. Some confuse the Epistle of James that says, "Faith without works is dead", meaning, to some, that salvation is based on works also, or alone for salvation. They do not realize that what James was really saying was that if one is truly saved by grace alone than their works one would be able to see by the fruits of the Holy Spirit, and again that only grace and not works or anything other would bring one into a saving grace with Jesus whether they were a Gentile or a Jew, and James was a half brother of Jesus."

Afterwards Rebecca left the house because she had promised her best friend Jessica that she would go to her Bible study that evening. I had already decided to stay at home and work on a book that I felt was not too good in all its contents, but nonetheless I would continue to work on it knowing almost full well that it would never be published, since capitalism would impose its avarice hand on anyone, or anybody, that tried to tell the truth about Scripture, since capitalism represented anything but the truth and since John Locke's Enlightenment was nothing but materialism without any regard for the spiritual part of man. This indeed was what most of America was founded upon, the lie of man's interpretation of what man knew best for man!

The very next day the news media had said that America would be ruled mostly by the UN and that America would be much better for it. All it really meant was that world socialism would be spread faster to all the other parts of the world through our own inept government that came to be nothing but puppets that served the wrong god in this universe. How could one interpret this to an affluent, so affluent that even the poor in America were well-to-do as compared to the rest of the world, which, as I said before, was in total chaos which meant totalitarianism, or the one world government, or religion.

I had thought of my wife and how she was refused disability because she did not have enough credits, which meant she would have had to abandon her children so that she could work in order that she could collect full benefits while Hispanics got it for not being able to speak English, or for obese people. Children of Russian Jewish descent were the best at learning the English language when coming to America, but many others even born here could not, such as Ebonic blacks. Generation after generation had been on welfare from the deadbeat dads syndrome, and the Great Society was continuing many years after the redneck Lyndon Johnson had died. Now on this very day there would be in Boston, Massachusetts a National Democratic Socialist Convention to honor their Catholic Jewish nominee, plus a millionaire trial lawyer and also many other socialists who had held political offices, such as the Sodomite, Hillary Clinton, her Marxist/Leninist husband, Bill Clinton, and of course Kennedyism, the American Nazi family.

All would not be lost if the American people could only think and would give up their anti-Semitism, but then that would be like asking a fish to fly like a bird. I knew that socialism in America was getting stronger and stronger since Islam itself was welcomed with open hands after 9/11. The American people had been melted down by 3rd World intermarriage that would dumb down the average American and bring group and tribal mentality to America. What more could the socialists ask for than animosity and diversity? This is what this multiculturalism was all about. More for the derelicts of society so that we would have to have universal health care and redistribution of wealth, which went much further than one's wages, but included all the things that he owned. The government was already confiscating properties from the elderly because they were giving what they had put in to criminals and illegals at that who looked vicious and never smiled and were as arrogant as the blacks had become and who emulated them to the fullest. These groups would at least need one more century to catch up to the Europeans in knowledge, if the government would stay out of it. Everything pointed to Boston, since the Kennedys were there and homosexuality was there just like the Nazis and of course Harvard and Yale, the poison IVY of the rich and well educated who would help control the world of legalities and of course business and governments.

John had called me late one night in regards to playing cards at his house with a few of the other fellows. I told John I would be over in about an hour's time. When I got there, all the guys were already there and we started immediately to play Pinochle by partners with two on each side and a single deck. As we were playing, Jim, an older fellow and very thin like and emaciated looking, was showing that one cannot judge a book by its cover, since Jim's side kept constantly winning and Jim would count not only trump, but all point cards to the very end so one had to be extra careful and not take anything for granted. As the games progressed we switched partners and still the same occurred with Jim now on my side, and I had to know how many points to count out and also how to play my hand and also almost know what was laid out in his hand. Jim was patient, though, unless one threw out a card without thinking at all. It was a challenge to play with a master at Pinochle because in the process one would learn to be a better player by trial and error. As the night wore down we decided to sit at the table and just talk about whatever came to mind.

Jim said that "Back in World War II there had been stories amongst the troops that Roosevelt could not be trusted even though the Army carried out their duties to the end."

I said, "Did he know that after the war Stalin, Roosevelt and Churchill sold us out to world Communism with their English blueblood and that even now we were feeling its affects here in America and also all over Europe?"

John said he knew that Roosevelt was a socialist and that he appointed Joseph Kennedy ambassador to England knowing full well that Joseph Kennedy was a Nazi. And even today Nazism was amongst the Cape Cod group, as well as another kind of socialism called Marxist/Leninism.

I again said, "I knew that Joseph Kennedy was highly anti-Semitic along with Roosevelt and so they dumped the whole load on the Russian peasants with total disregard for what the butcher in the Kremlin would do and Churchill even warned Stalin before 1941 what was about to occur so Stalin left Moscow because of his pusillanemous nature. Stalin was so paranoid that he even had locks by remote control in his rooms with no windows and kept his decanters under lock and key and would take no injections at all. He had good reason though."

Martin, the youngest of us all said he was taught in college that the Democratic Party was the one to vote for always.

I said, "Did you not have suspicions about voting for the same party time and again?"

He said, "I did wonder how one could be so sure of themselves all the time and vote a straight party ticket in the General Election without ever splitting their ticket no matter what!"

Jim said, "Martin, you have to learn to think for yourself and not trust the socialist professors in our very own colleges who had their own agenda, not for the betterment of America or for that matter mankind in general. You have to investigate and question everything, or anything, you have been taught, or told."

John said, "One can lead a horse to water, but cannot make him drink it."

"What is that supposed to mean?"

"Martin," I said, "One must use their own discernment and judgment to make important decisions in the life of one's nation as well as in one's own life, so do not be influenced by what the rich and well educated may tell you because they are benefiting from all of this and know that what they are doing is wrong, but will not own up to the truth because their 'happiness' now is all that matters."

Jim said, "Martin, since you are with us older fellows, we shall try and guide you properly and since you are intelligent enough to know that we are not always right and that we would not intentionally try to deceive you, then you must also realize that the professors are getting paid from our taxpayers' dollars so that they can teach with tenure and also only put in about 12 hours a week, when 37-1/2 hours is what is required in a full professorship. This all started in the 60's, this invasion of socialism into education and then traveled into all the other lower schools in order to deceive since children brought up with this would not know their left from their right."

Martin then asked, "How do I know that what you are saying is true since you too would be partial to your side?"

Jim said, "I have nothing to gain and I am not running for office where politicians want to limit everybody else, but not themselves. I do not have an ax to grind or a hatred for my own country. I do not believe in foreign ideologies, but I do have a belief in GOD. In order to maintain a true balance between good and evil, one must first be able to recognize this difference and find out for themselves, and not on the Internet, but through Scripture just what GOD has to say about all this."

John added this, "Martin, you will have to go through it to the end since I believe man cannot be told or warned about impending doom from other nations such as Russia, Germany, China and Italy. They were all democracies but then turned into totalitarian states overnight and authoritative governments, not once ever having gone over to totalitarianism. Now that is something to think about, and the fact that socialism has an appeal for the young that excites their emotions without any regard to the consequences later in years. It tells how it shall provide for a people who no longer want the worry of bills and responsibility, but not about how brutal and vicious it becomes all the time with no exception. Nazi Germany had socialism just like the Soviets, but theirs was racial, or better known as nationalism and Stalin's was class warfare. Also, Stalin kept secret his deviousness while Hitler advertised his to the fullest . . .

Both these socialisms were to the left. The Western Jews had always had a more vehement opposition since 6 million Jews were exterminated and since there had been pogroms in earlier Russia. It was natural then for these Jews to oppose Hitler even though Stalin only trusted Hitler and not even his very own daughter or his wives, or other close relatives. Stalin was a Georgian and not a Russian at all and liked to suppose he was a Russian since the Russians went so willingly to their deaths. Now your generation must work to stop this type of cancer from spreading worldwide because the next explosion may very well be an implosion in America. Do not believe that Red China will sit still when the pickings are so good that even our very own leaders are in bed with them in so many ways and agree with their type of socialism, which shall most definitely include Nazism or racism on their part since the English had sold them drugs and taught them so much about Lenin's communism from beginning to end even though they differed on one page, or two!"

"This is just too much to absorb in at the present time," Martin said.

"Just remember, Martin, that you have a huge hurdle to go over and even though you shall be telling the truth you shall be opposed on almost all sides because you choose to think for yourself and also that you will not go along with what is evil no matter how much you are losing and they are winning. Remember do not collaborate with evil or it's ideology that says man must be destroyed and that this UTOPIA shall soon come by man's hands."

I then said to Martin, "Here is a short story. Please just listen. In Russia there was this girl who was emotionally disturbed and who would run around the village quite a lot because her loving parents could not control her. One day the village chieftain, or soviet chieftain made her pregnant and he was a Moslem. He did not want to raise the child and she could not. A Russian couple decided with love to take in this child, and as the child got a little older the child innately sat like a Moslem with legs crossed. Remember this child, since almost day one, was brought up in a GOD-fearing Russian home and yet this child, to repeat, sat innately as a Moslem would. There are different traits in all people no matter where they are from. A wolf sheds its fur but not its habits."

"Well guys, I shall call it a night."

"Okay Jim, I guess all of us shall be going home too."

"We shall take Martin home."

"No guys, I need to walk and think a little about what you said tonight so that I do not lose sight of where I am going in my life."

"Are you sure you will be all right, Martin?"

"Yes Luke, I shall be quite all right and we need to do this again very soon, if it is all right with you guys?"

"Well how about next week say about the same time and same day, unless something comes up?"

We all agreed to that unanimously.

It is always encouraging to try to help a young person see a more universal approach to life and not just constitutional government and the courts and of course the avarice of capitalism.

The next day Rebecca and I walked in the park that was not in the city, but out in the countryside since the city park was too dangerous to walk through anytime of the day or the night. Our federal government kept importing foreigners who were hostile to Americans and knew that the government would not prosecute these illegal criminals because they themselves were living in protected areas with security forces all around. They had all been for this criminal element as long as it was not in their neighborhood or schools. Yet the minorities, especially the blacks, kept voting them in and crime kept soaring up and up and fatherless children continued because the government promised them the moon with green cheese. The Anglo-Saxons actually enjoyed controlling people by passing laws that were court made and placing judges in positions that had much authority, and regular Americans could do nothing about it since the elites in government and in business wanted it that way. Always it is the rich who control all of society including the amount of crimes!

Rebecca said to me, “Remember when we used to walk in the park in town and it was so very peaceful and we could enjoy the sounds of nature?”

I said, “I certainly do remember, and then the rich mushroom people, plus other professionals started to bring many Puerto Ricans to the mainland for cheap labor, and soon Hispanics from everywhere and other 3rd World countries appeared overnight and with government approval from both major parties.”

“Why would anyone want to ruin America knowingly with this multiculturalism?”

“It is a lot easier for people to be controlled if they are grouped by socialism and there is only basically one type of candidate to vote for no matter the party.”

“How long do you think we shall survive as a nation as we know of it today?”

“We do not have much more time, and soon our entire governments will come under socialism and the one world government shall then have to be dealt with or else one might even have to leave the country for good. But where could they go?”

“You mean America will basically look the same, but the form of government shall not really be a constitutional form of democracy?”

“Yes Rebecca, we shall look the same, but our spiritual part of the nation shall have changed and for the worse with much more to come. All of America in the public places shall be absent of GOD, or the reminder of GOD and our nation shall no longer have a soul, or a conscience. We shall become like Sodom and Gomorrah in the Old Testament and Nazi Germany’s ideology that was basically pro-infanticide, pro-homosexual, pro-euthanasia, anti-Semitic to the extreme. We shall have lost what our nation fought for and slavery shall be based upon believers and not by race or culture. We shall be our own worse enemy."

"This sounds to horrible to believe."

"Just remember, Rebecca, that our leaders are constantly surrounded by principalities of the air no matter now who is in office. We have gone too far with GOD and now the rain shall fall on the just and the unjust, and GOD shall have removed His shield of protection from America for good. Man shall not listen to reason no matter what and he shall not also listen to experience of life from other nations who fell also so quickly because they thought that they could go it alone without GOD."

After our walk in the park we went home and then went for our granddaughter to watch her for a few hours. Rachel was only 2 years old, but loved her mom mom and grandpop very much. This was our only grandchild that had normal parents. The other 4 grandchildren had parents who were either homosexuals or materialists. This was most disheartening to us as grandparents. One of our sons was molested by a priest when he was young without our knowledge, and our daughter married an Englishman who too was a bisexual. Those grandchildren were kept out of our lives because these children used their children as objects and nothing more and live the lie of deviant sexuality, and our fear was that our grandchildren too would be molested for sure. We did not know really how to approach our two children who got involved with homosexuality since now they were in their middle twenties, but still prayed for them and especially our grandchildren most of all who were innocent to all of this but knew us only as strangers would. This is how bad the Roman Catholic Church had become, so I had long ago repudiated it even before I knew about all this sexual deviancy because it did not know Scripture at all and had a figurehead, the Pope, the Vatican, a businessman organization, no grace, but works and interfered with just about every other nation's worship of GOD and was not really spreading the Gospel since all one could see was Liberation Theology and materialism as the priests and the nuns lived like kings and queens. Rome should have kept it's own worship of GOD in Rome and in Italy and not coerced this ideology since they used "bread" to entice the world with their so called "good works", which was nothing more than recruiting to make their church larger in mostly ignorant and backwards countries. The Irish Catholics had brought this foreign religion to America, plus Halloween, Christmas (Christ's Mass), and canonized saints, not Biblical saints as Paul describes in the Bible and who was a Jew who worshipped like a Jew as well as Messiah. All one could see was the materialism of the parishioners and now homosexuality in America in it kept getting worse. Most Catholics never had even read the Bible and until a few years ago were not allowed to. They even prayed for the dead and to canonized saints when Jesus is all that one needed. My own mother had said that they did not know any better and her relatives were from Rome itself. All I saw growing up and up to now was how much money and wealth one had and their conversations dwell on this time and again and would use this to many relatives so they too would be lost forever without grace, undeserved merit. They or the church had actually called GOD a liar, because in Scripture it plainly says how one is saved such as in Romans 10: 9-10, John 3: 3-7, Psalm 119, Isaiah 53, etc. No matter who witnessed to them they were the hardest to witness to and that even included the Jews and even some KGB agents. Time after time when one hears the Gospel and refuses to accept Jesus or Messiah in their heart their heart becomes harder and harder, and their conscience becomes seared to the point of no return. People who have never even heard of Jesus are usually more open because they are poor and are not relying on their finances or wealth in order to get through life. How many souls have gone to Hell because nobody told them the truth about Jesus and the one way of salvation? Even countries that were not Latin oriented like Poland had followed this religion and so did Orthodoxy. Catholicism, it appeared, was emulating Judaism in the sense that they wanted to be the all, but yet had much anti-Semitism like Pope Pius XII during World War II and praying for the dead.

Yes, America had been sold out as a Christian nation and both candidates were against what America had once stood for. One candidate was much worse than the other was a Catholic Jew which surely meant materialism since Catholicism was materialism given up for the truth, and the American Jew was totally for extravagance. The other candidate was an incumbent who was in bed with the Saudis who had sponsored 9/11, and this candidate could not think for himself without his father's help. His father himself was a President and a New Ager appointed by Ronald Reagan as Vice President. Our nation had no real national leaders who did not promote either materialism or anti-Semitism. Indians from India where the swastika came from were manning our phone lines from India thanks to Bill Gates who was also a New Ager billionaire. This was the other part of the "Aryanism" that had it's systems from the Germans in Germany who also had, along with the English, taken over government and were selling also the Americans down the tube because for them in one case Nazism had never died out and for the other, colonialism.

The church in America was dead as we had known it, and the television ministries were into consumerism and all kinds of financial matters and not preaching the Gospel as we were all told to do. Television had become the "medium" through which the enemy was now working. It appeared at least to me that Satan was now coming for his own in America, but also the believers as few as there were, were being deceived by him and were complacent about their nation as well as the world. Even honest whole American citizens from the 60's were being duped into believing that they could bring this Kingdom to earth starting in America and were also embracing this multiculturalism without even knowing about it because they were not educated enough to know or were always for the underdog while the New Age Nazis were always for the winners.

Foreigners, all mostly from extreme heathen nations, were brought in by these New Agers especially from the highest levels of government and also Hollywood and also the Vatican which all traded in the truth for materialism, better known as "socialism in mysticism". Who would believe a few people or a writer of no notoriety as to the truth in our own nation and in the entire world that seemed to be heading very quickly for a cataclysmic disaster of epidemic proportions?

Civil rights socialism in America had become more than a nuisance now since it involved national security for so called race relations, which was nothing more than the white guilt syndrome of the 60's and the underdog mentality. While Americans were fearful of the "black jihad" including males in America, Islam was amongst them by 30% and was growing. Security had to include all Moslems who were foreign born, or all Moslems period who had to be deported and put in internment camps if need be and no if s, ands, or buts. This was a time to stop whining about civil rights' socialism and ego and a time to unify Americans, whether foreign born or native born, to the deadly infection of Islam and it's doctrine of demons. While the rich and well educated continued to force integration as well as fear on most Americans. they had to work harder to move away from the cities so that they could protect their community since government would not and now could not and continued to be more and more about our own borders where the trouble was coming from and had been since Clinton had opened on ends and allowed, intentionally, terrorists into America. Clinton was a Communist and hated his very own country and had deluged the FBI and CIA with cronies who would ignore or look the other way when there was a clear and present danger. The agents had to be purged out completely, or America would fall quite quickly since Red China, Islam, Germany, England and civil rights' socialism were all merging to defeat America. Who would believe that we had so many close enemies within our own borders who were placed there by the rich and well educated just so that in exchange they could obtain rights to the oil wells that were in Arabic hands no matter the nation or nations. This was a struggle for real huge power and was feeding into the Antichrist who would eventually take all of it without any of the internationalists really understanding that they too would certainly be first to be expendable since they held the power. Incite the masses from within and no one could defeat them since they had believed the lie hook, line and sinker. The American people did no longer care, and if they did it was for self-preservation and materialism, not realizing their lives as well as their nation's life was on the immediate line! Who was I to argue with all the experts in government and in agencies trained for this type of scenario, or were they? This was not paranoia, but good old common sense as when cancer invades the body, all of it then all of the cancerous cells must be destroyed. But again the rich and well educated who always in all societies control the government as well as the society one lives in. These elites do not care in what way they achieve what they believe is beneficial for themselves no matter how many lives had to be sacrificed for their final end. The rain does fall on the just and the unjust, and in fact even the Jews, a majority of them, would see themselves be involved in the promotion of anti-Semitism. As strange as that may seem, it was the truth but to convey this to them one had to remove the blindfold that Satan had over their very own eyes and the deception that to win at all costs was actually to lose at all costs. That is one thing the Jews could not afford to do, since there was only 17,000,000 now in the entire world and there would be much less soon in the months and years to come, since they refused to say, "Blessed is he who comes in the name of the Lord." The Gentile church also had contributed to this by seeking gold with the Jews and not the salvation of their souls.

American had become a dirty word, and ones even born here were believing it too. America had made a deal with the devil and so we ourselves had to understand that the trouble lay with our not trusting in the GOD OF ABRAHAM, ISAAC AND JACOB. It was, for the present every man for himself, and family was becoming obsolete. Children. were part of the state thanks to Soviet daycare in America. And who said Communism could only survive in Russia? We had certainly proven that wrong and felt that we could go back in time, which any normal person knows that that is an impossibility. We were a young nation that had learned too fast what we should have learned slower, that "Rome was not built in a hurry", but while we were building on sand the old structure had been for a while built on solid ground. But now America seemed to have all swampland with no solid ground to build upon.

All education was anti-American, and even the Christian education had turned to please the listening audience and was winning approval for the ever present underdog or the squeaky wheel that would get the oil. Again both major parties were all ideology and had nothing to do with a particular point of view. Parties always did and always will, something Lenin and Trotsky knew years back, but something America had felt could never happen in America. All these democracies and democratic leanings were leading to mob rule because family was dead!

This President thought that after his full term he would never have to contend with Islam, but little did he know that he had incited the Arabs in the Moslem world to a certain type of vendetta towards him for life, as the Sicilians themselves have for centuries shown. Also, most of the news kept repeating itself with no solutions, and the solution that was available was too hard to swallow for the rich and well educated in America and in Europe since it meant loss of profit regardless of loss of life even to them besides to millions of others! Incredible? Not really when one sees how the Anglophiles dealt with Stalin after World War II in giving away so much because they had a hatred of the Russians because the English felt that they were too refined and civilized for the Russians themselves. How foolish again were these English now also in America who were in the White House and felt that Christians had to vote for them since the other side was so socialistic. What a grave mistake they were making, even though they probably win the election, but never again have peace of mind or just plain peace of anything in America since now the Arabs had thought that the American government and the American people were shielding the enemies and trying to take their homeland which was really their homeland and one could also see how violent they had become when they wanted land that was not even theirs! America had taken on more than it could ever possibly handle because it did not have the will to defend its own nation let alone any other nation and that did include Israel.

All of a sudden the Anglos started to bring up the Holocaust again to subterfuge the whole issue of Islamic Jihad. This would be even worse than the Holocaust was since it was almost for certain that more than 6 million Jews would be done away with worldwide including in America. Gypsies from the war were also spoken about. Were these the same gypsies that were in the Gulags that were thieves and criminals who worked for the Communist in power? They were confined for short periods of time in the Gulag system in order to threaten Russian peasants and others guilty of no crime at all, except the "crime" of the conscience which said do not believe the lie. Did not the West more than even tithing do worse in sinning by believing in the lie since it now involved sacrifice of one's own way of life and possibly worse? The churches in the West thought that tithing more than lying was the pertinent thing, but would soon find out that worship of a foreign god by not repudiating from our own land would be okay as far as GOD was concerned. They believed that GOD could only bless America and never curse it! The land would spew us out of its mouth. "Thou shall have no other gods before thee." We had become like Israel in the Old Testament when in Judges everybody did as they wanted to do, but there would be punishment for sin against a holy and just GOD.

Who is the father of all lies? This question we time and again refused to answer or even bring up, but only the fact that tithing and our way of life, whatever that now meant, was most important no matter how the rest of the world was dying for Christ especially in the 1040 Window. We were or had become our own gods, because we felt invincible because of power and not because of the love of the Messiah. Without Messiah we were another decadent nation ready for the rubble to fall down upon us and bury us for good. Warning after warning was given but we did not respond to them no matter how GOD tried to tell us and hold back His anger and wrath from now a heathen nation with spots of Christianity here and there. Our own empire was doomed to the wrecking crew of the New World Order that was starting to take over that part of the world that would belong to the Antichrist. No matter how much one would warn that, even the Christians would not listen and would avoid one by all possible means because it made them feel uncomfortable and depressed them, or they did not want to hear what they already knew to be the truth, or go back in the past to stir up our own sins against GOD.

There were no friends that I could really talk to except GOD and even family would not listen and were caught up in this world of unbelief. Only my wife who would at times oppose me, but not on GODLY issues, but on the fact that I had said so many times before that. I sounded like a broken record, but things each day had to be addressed for time was running short for not only our nation, but also for Satan and he knew it! How many times would we fail to ignore the warning signs because our stomachs were full and our life appeared to be so merry? Who was I talking to?

Why was I concerned about all this when nobody else seemed to care really at all? Questions upon questions such as these came into my mind time and again and I had seen how my own family had turned totally away from GOD, but would I too do the same? GOD would be there always.

Who had ever heard of Jews working for Moslems when Moslems were killing Jews all over the world? It had occurred in a certain corporation where American Jews felt no sense of remorse for what they were doing to destroy their fellow Jew, and by a corporation that also was funded by Nazi funds or the families of Nazis in America during World War II! Incredible as it seems, these New York City Jews were worse to their very own in Israel and could care less if other Jews lived or died, but only that their extravagance would be met as they had once done in the Soviet Union to others who were their allies in faith. Indeed a stiff-necked people to say the least, and now maybe for the first time in all of world history or for most of it, they were not in unison with their fellow Jews and were apathetic to their plight. The money was too good to pass up even though it was Nazi and

Moslem sponsored by the ones up top who also happened to be homosexuals like in Nazi Germany and were at it again along with their cousins, the Anglos in England. Their love of money more than their love of their fellow Jews was what mattered to them at the present time until probably their own lives would be on the line, which they never really thought about in the least because they were lead to believe the lie that it could never ever happen in America—another Holocaust of major proportions and the fact now even Jews were embracing Roman Catholicism for its materialism that too was too good to pass up. They were asleep spiritually and would not awaken until probably it was too late and then they still would believe the lie of avarice and Western materialism. The Jew seemed to adapt to the environment in the sense that if it was affluence they would be there also for an easy dollar regardless of the immorality of their own decisions and even if it help weaken the state of Israel. The New York City Jew was just like Leon Trotsky who also had this constant revolution on his mind, and who Lenin wanted to succeed as dictator in the Soviet Union and not Stalin. But Stalin had the final say about that. As they had wanted another king and not Messiah, they now also wanted any king they thought was by their own choosing to be their real Messiah when in fact it would most likely be the Antichrist who would most likely be a Jew in the flesh, since Satan would emulate to the closest possible with the rider on the white horse in the Book of Revelation. Would the other Jews in the world not also want to believe the lie from Satan that this was their "messiah"? Many Jewish women still felt that they would give birth to this "messiah".

Castro and Hollywood had much in common, since Castro approved of their political movies and even Alexander Solzhenitsyn had called him the butcher. Now certain courses could only be taken by non-white students in college out in California. The poor white European children in America were the ones that were really left behind and not the white American male. America had that Teutonic mentality of "go along with the winner." Some, though, did not agree, because their very nature and their culture were not made that way. It appeared that the American black and the Teutonics had much in common in regard to coldness. The Italians and the Jewish were much more emotional about life and circumstances in general and seemed to care more about the overall view than just their own people or their own culture. Culture was important, but in the sense that it did not control others or dominate over others. The Jews and the Italians were versatile people, so really they did not need laws or civil rights socialism to enforce decrees that were most certainly unAmerican. The Sicilians were the Turks that made it bad for most Italians in America because of their mafioso or La Cosa Nostra. This dialogue with myself would continue until I could interrupt myself to get in a real dialogue with my wife, friends, neighbors, co-workers, etc. America was under demon control since it had yielded to Islam, the worship of demons, no less and no more.

Our generals like Colin Powell, Alexander Haig, etc. were nothing more than glorified knights in shining armor with nothing inside them. Their promotion had been through favors in government and not because of qualifications at all. People now at the top in America had to be politically correct. The sour cream was rising to the top and was spoiling the whole bottle of milk. Where were statesmen in America that were not in Roman Catholicism, or New Age Ideology? Most leaders were materialists who were millionaires and cared more about the union than the love for GOD. Who would run for President could no longer be the question, but which poison was better to take! Capitalism had turned into socialism as it always does even though it is just an economic system. We in America were apathetic because leaders were halfhearted lawyers in politics. We had more lawyers in America than the rest of the entire world had lawyers! I love my country, so I must speak out, at least to myself, in order to know that I shall not go along with the winner. On the other hand I also wanted to avoid the "underdog" syndrome that lead to civil rights socialism.

Why had George Washington worn a wig and a sword, when Jesus said that those who live by the sword die by the sword? Why were some of our Founders deists and scholars who knew hardly anything about hard work and the sweat of their brow? The Anglophiles were always, till this very day, used to colonialism no matter where in the world, but now England itself was under the gun and was trying to use America to get out of their dilemma. Would we again repeat the same mistake over and over again until at last there was nothing left to repeal except destruction, which shall happen one and only one time, and there shall really be no tomorrow, and for pacifists we would be buried from lack of total action to total inaction because apathy was ruling in America, and the wake up call for us was almost over. When would we learn to worship our very own GOD as American Biblicals? We again had lost our own will to even defend our own nation right here in our states. Our own government was much too worried about what a democracy, or mob rule, would say. We had to make a decision and quick, or all would be lost as we know of it today and Islam, let alone Communism, would pick up the pieces. The "Mensheviks", Islam, vs the "Bolsheviks"; Communism would most likely be the two to battle it out and one would know almost for sure who would be the winner because we had not taken care of "home" while we roamed the earth like the English had done for many centuries. Who now ruled the seas? Was it not Red China? As far as Islam was concerned they would almost self-destruct, especially the Arabs, who never got along amongst themselves let alone the Israelis. All these idiotic nations while Israel would still remain . . . No matter if America saw that way or not. We were deceiving ourselves into believing that GOD had abandoned Israel, because it appeared that GOD would not show Himself but wait there would be much more to come for the entire world. This World War would be a real World War amongst all the nations in the world that would be left to fight this Armageddon. The First World War was to subterfuge the scandal of homosexuality in Germany, so Russia came as a first loss, since the Czar believed they had to fight against Germany. He had been deceived. This was not pacifism, but common sense since Germany always had this lust for power for many years and would not give up until it probably destroyed itself the same as the Roman Empire and

Greek Empire had. Yes even a monarch can make an honest mistake since Germany was involved.

Were the Negroes in America repeating the very same mistakes by letting the authority of government rule their thoughts and decisions through foreign education in our own colleges and cities? Would they too exhibit the same kind of rebellion when they found out that they had been lied to by the rich and well educated even amongst some of their very own? It appeared that the American Negro had lost their healthy agricultural base in America and were turning to the socialism of Europeanism that had invaded their private lives with much affluence and also envy since they were given so much so quick and in so short a time without the knowledge of what to do with what they had or would get. They were also lead to believe that this socialism. disguised as freedom was the solution to all their problems and would lead them into a New Age of liberty. Making up about 12% of the entire American population, they were encouraged into certain professions that would lead one into a blind alley since the money was so great, but the education was lacking since it was an education of true socialism like Angela Davis, Ron Dellurns, Jesse Jackson, Sr. and Jr., Martin Luther King, Jr., Carol Mosley Braun, Stokely Carmichael Malcolmn X. Congressman Fattah, Thurgood Marshall, Bobby Scales, Nelson Mendela, Bishop Tutu, etc. They had been bombarded by this socialism. Lenin in 1914 had kept his eye on the American Negro because he knew the diversity of color could always be played upon to create a schism with animosity. It was only one variable in the ideas of multiculturalism. This was this so called "diversity" which really meant to disassimilate from others according in this case to race which would mean class and racial warfare all the time and not always on a battlefield, but in the battlefield of society itself in one nation, America. It was a form of Trotsky's constant revolution without the physical revolution up to this time, but a revolution that would breed animosity and resentment on both sides constantly and which would constantly work to weaken America as a GOD-fearing nation since hatred would be fused with envy and jealousy. It was a never ending war, and Lenin had thought that this would have happened in Switzerland since they too spoke many different languages, but had already occurred in Russia in 1914. Thanks to the Teutonics, it would continue by sending Lenin and his entourage in a sealed train into Moscow and why this? Again the elites in Germany had to cover up their homosexual scandal with the War and when they did, the Germans did . . .

Had the Gentile world been so unforgiving to the Jews that the Jews themselves had turned away from their own true GOD and thought that secular humanism and Judaism could replace GOD in the flesh? What had the Gentile world done to help the poor Jews in the world which were a small number of about 17,000,000 all together in the entire world? Many shall say there are no poor Jews and that would be a lie. In fact many Jews in Russia and in Israel and even in America are poor but Satan has kept that a great secret. Would the Jews have been open to others such as the Gospel if the Gentile religions or Europe would have stayed in their own countries or their own? One will never know for sure, but I myself believe that there would be a great possibility for that to have occurred. The Gentile religions were a transition until GOD was ready to deal with the Jews as a national people in their land of Israel, which extended across Jordan itself. Churchill, who dabbled in the occult, though had other plans through his anti-Semitism by giving that land to the Arabs in about 1928 which was not his to even give up.

England, once again as during World War II, was going to have to defend its own land and this time it would not be to defend world Jewry, such as in the Holocaust, but their appeal to heathen cultures that now had invaded their own country. The English had bitten off more than they could chew. They also had help to destroy Russia and now were doing the very same thing to America, since both nations were fighting for the world market. They had always coerced the integration by others, but now it appeared that that same mentality was now in their own country to try on for size.

America always had to follow England, and this time we appeared to be competing for top dog in the world as far as economic rationale. Capitalism was the poison that would be used to increase the damage in the world and promote socialism more than any other reason one could think of. It lead directly to avarice and materialism, which in essence said, "There is no GOD!" Man would do it all alone, or at least he thought so, but would get principality help that, once accepted, cannot be returned. And now he was coming for his own even in America because of doctrines of demons. The English believed that one size would fit all in regard to governments, but when had America even had a king or a monarch like England or Russia had? We had Greek democracy which was for small countries and not big countries such as Russia and America, and our own age would prove it.

America had been its own worse enemy because it allowed lawyers to make rules and not laws because only GOD can make laws. These go-along-as-you-play rules were nothing more than sin disguised as jurisprudence, when it actuality was nothing more than everything becomes legal. We refused GOD'S help time and again and the born again experience according to America and not to Scripture. Many people who were supposed to be born again did not have their "works", since James and his Epistle had said, "Faith without works is dead." This meant that grace alone did save and was the only way of salvation, but not the kind that Europeanism talked about. The Bible makes no mention of any nationality, except through the Jews is where that salvation came from. Was not Messiah a Jew and not a Gentile? Too many born again people said the prayer, but more than that it had to be in the heart and not the emotions. Some also used the mindset of reason to believe that without faith one could be saved, but faith is the only way to please GOD just like Abraham did. Many nations would come to salvation and not many religions, because religion deals in time and faith in eternity. GOD was the only one who knew just what was saved and nobody else. Much consumerism was in the church and that meant that John Locke's Enlightenment was a direct effect on our age of affluence. Our own poor were so well off that they also saw that materialism was more important than faith. Charity was not needed because government was in the business of playing the role of a god. We would be lead by our noses.

The church was silent on too many moral issues, but Jesus was not. He has always addressed it through the power of the Holy Spirit, and when on earth He Himself addressed them often. The criminal was set free because the other "criminal" in the court should also have been incarcerated, but since they had done worse then how could they sentence any person who had committed a crime? With a clear conscience can one only sentence a criminal since they themselves can see the difference between good vs evil. Lawyers made ideology through the parties, but not morally. They then had gotten into all levels of government, but did not even know the 10 Commandments. If one does a crime themselves, then how can they convict another of a lesser crime? Most criminals will know that they have broken GOD'S law while the other criminal shall never admit that. The log that was in their eye was not seen opposed to the speck in somebody else's eye.

Who was importing all these foreigners into America? It certainly was not because they had a love for their own nation if they had a nation at all. So many were hostile to America that even Americans themselves became hostile to their own nation. Capitalism was always given as the reason for the importation of hostile foreigners and of course the stock market was a barometer for the rich and well educated and had nothing to do with the average Americans until they were tempted to put their life savings into 401 plans and had lost billions of dollars on just hearsay. The Hispanics were basically Roman Catholic, and it appeared that the Vatican had a vested interest in the affairs of America since we were the wealthiest nation in the world, but did not have nearly the most resources like Latin America and Russia or even Canada did. Rockefeller had flown to the Knesset, the Vatican, Washington, DC, Moscow and Peking just to mention a few. These were big internationalists who could care less about even money, but only sought absolute power at the price of others' freedom. It did not matter if the nation had a dictator or not and whether it was a democracy, monarchy, or even a totalitarian state. One President refused to renounce ties to a still terrorist state, yet said he was fighting terrorism all over the world by having our own troops in more than 40 nations at one time. Why were our troops, for instance, in Germany when they could be used to patrol our own borders in America? Even some of his close relatives had Hispanic blood in their veins. Why was our own government sacrificing our soldiers and putting them in harm's way just so that capitalism could grow into socialism? There were so many lawyers now in government that our own government was turning against native born Americans and were giving away the store to foreigners who were coming here and were being told that they could do anything they wanted and would not be prosecuted for it since it involved wealth and absolute raw power.

Alexander Solzhenitsyn was willing to give up his life and the life of his own loving family just so that the truth no longer would be distorted under the guise of socialism. Hostile elements not on the outside, but in the inner thoughts and hearts were taking our nation down and down into where they felt it should be. But was it not these very same internationalists who raped and pillaged their nation, and not the American people? Would anyone here in America be willing to do what Solzhenitsyn had done in order to stand up for the truth without any mention of money or even

"tithing". Everything was based alone on material wealth in America and we kept falling faster and faster since even the believers, or at least a majority of them, wanted to live the life of Riley. Where would all of this end? Our 50 states were so far apart and not in the literal distance of miles, but in culture, such as California that Americans knew less about each other and their own communities than they did of foreign nations. We were fragmented into individualism more and more so that we would not be one nation under GOD and not just any god but the GOD of Abraham, Isaac and Jacob. People were actually within their own families destroying themselves. The intact family was becoming obsolete and the group and tribal mentality was domineering and that is why there were so many gangs in America, because fatherhood was dead and the family, or this "family" was now a gang on the street selling drugs even to small children. But without the internationalists this could never have been made possible. The breakdown came within each individual person since they felt it was government's job alone to keep an eye out for the spirit of America and when had any government ever really done that even in our own history? Children were in daycare and were becoming very hostile to their own parents, and who could blame them when in the Bible it says, "Do not anger your children." Again money, luxury, convenience, and most of all immorality was playing a major part in our own destruction, but nonetheless we continued . . . The Anglo-Saxons followed, as usual, their "leaders" to the end, and this would be the end if it continued to go this way any longer. People were satisfied with what they owned and not with their very own soul and the soul of their children let alone their own nation! We had always survived it before, but then again we were only about 300 years in the making, and that was a very short period of time. Would we wake up from our own slumber and realize that the enemy was from within and that a nation, or any nation does have a soul?

The Vatican needed more and more parishioners in the world, since America was losing its own amount of Roman Catholics. Hispanic-America was one major source and the next Pope would most likely be Hispanic, and the Poles were forever wanting to be kings and queens and would not stand up against this evil that again was permeating the world since it supplied their "needs". This materialism was all that they needed and the Reformation was a branch.

I had met some new friends who were Christian, but whose children were marrying all people that were non-European and I had to wonder as to the why? This was a very kind hearted family, but they still had to clean out some roots from the 60's generation which was what was starting to pull them down, even though on the outside they were still kind and care-giving. Some things are very hard to give up when one is born into them and sees their own parents embracing them all the time. It could only mean that it was the right thing to do so why not follow along with the civil rights' socialism that always said, "Be for the underdog!" This was indeed a very dangerous scenario. Many of my older friends in years past were predominantly of German descent which meant that only their world was important and that working endlessly for one's own was the way to go and following the leader, or that of government. Oh, they were good providers for their families, but when it came to speaking out for the truth, well that was another matter. In fact I cannot remember even one time when any of them had gone to church, opened a Bible, or would even talk about GOD. At the time it never dawned on me that I was doing the very same thing that they were doing, nothing! We were born into an affluent society, so in a way just like one who is born under Communism (not that we were), we did not really know any better, or did we? We had to search for the truth, because GOD had put it there in all of us to search for Him. Just. as Alexander Solzhenitsyn was born under Communism, he too had to really search for the truth and only found it in prison in a camp and was thankful for it. It involved quite a lot of suffering, since we appear to be made that way, or human nature is made that way. Who would save us from this wretched body of ours?

As I was mentioning, my new and wonderful friends—and I shall not mention the word good because only GOD is good—they soon became my family in life next almost to my wife because they too were very benevolent to all, or that is almost all like the rest of us. That all of us had our very own prejudices as part of Adam's fall was no excuse, but was the reality of the situation in all of our lives. We still did sin and were constantly almost always being attacked in our very own spirits by the enemy. We had to let faith alone in GOD work for us, and what GOD required was an obedient mind and heart. We had to choose from good vs evil,

As I was spending some much valuable time with my granddaughter at a fast food place not the best place to eat healthy food, and after having put my granddaughter Rachel in her high chair, I came across a very sad sight of a lonely elderly lady sitting by herself with a large Hispanic family sitting way beyond her. I wondered where were her children and why was she talking to herself while she was sipping on her cup of coffee? The Hispanics paid no attention to her and did not know that she was even alive. They were all talking at one time in a broken dialect and one could see that they were all tied up in their own culture and were laughing when there was really nothing to laugh at. This was indeed a sad sight to see where the poor elderly were no longer wanted in our nation, but only the ones that the rich and well educated could make money off of since many of them bought 6-8 cars in one household alone. This meant that car production and oil products would continually have a demand and that would make the internationalists happy, since now another kind of culture not wise to their antics would be introduced on the American scene so that capitalism could grow and grow into a leviathan which was really socialism. This indeed was a different and non-assimilating culture to say the least, and the rich and well educated wanted it that way, since they could reap the profits off of immorality from people who were at least 2 centuries behind us in education. Their family structure was from the conquistador mentality and not from men who knew what it was to make responsibility their first priority, and not rights. My granddaughter would somehow have to try to live in a culture that had no purpose in life, or in other words. no GOD. When I would not be on this earth, would my granddaughter be wise enough in GOD'S eyes to know the truth and to live by it all the rest of her years on earth? That would mean a very difficult time for all in the world. Today, though 1 would lift up my spirits by spending some time at the playground with Rachel. She loved to play at for hours on all the old fashioned rides. One could see in some of the teenagers' eyes the uselessness of any purpose in life and a boredom in general about whatever it was they were doing. They needed to know something about their GOD, the GOD of America, that American Biblicals lived by. Who would tell them about Him? Yes, how many other children should be there and were not there because our socialist government had murdered them in the womb and were planning more evil things for other children.

Who would be some of my granddaughter's friends as she got older? Would she marry a believer, and would she become a believer, and not just a "born again" "person that only said the words and nothing else, which meant that one must go into serving the Lord and salvation was by grace and grace alone, not by any religion, because no man had that right, but only GOD in the flesh. The Holy Spirit would convict the would be believer if the believer was willing, and of course GOD was calling that particular sheep to salvation. He alone does the saving and from there the road gets very hard to stay on because there are many different ways to go astray from GOD. One of them was to go through the act of believing without really believing. There had to be fruits in the Spirit for one to see in order to know that GOD was allowed through free will to guide that individual in the path of righteousness.

My new friends were mainly a family of Christians, and the father and husband was a high school teacher, which would mean he was probably influenced by the education culture that surrounded him constantly. His wife stayed at home and raised all 4 children by being an at-home mother until they got out of school. Their choice of music was from that terrible era of the 60's, but none of us are perfect, the fact that the down and out, or the underdog, favored with such zeal.

My first home I lived in and remembered was for World War II veterans. After that one move, one after the other moves kept coming because mom and dad had a hard time making ends meet, but continued to do all the things over and over again. At times I had thought maybe my parents never should have had children, since it was always difficult for them to make financial ends meet and to properly discipline their own children. Both parents had addictive personalities and had both found their addiction. Relatives on both sides were all financially better situated than both my parents had ever been and were the black sheep of the family, while all my aunts and uncles were pretty much well-to-do and could care less about others, but only ego. No one even tried to sit down and help my parents understand how my parents should handle their finances. We had always been "peasants" and never really owned our own property ever. My parents were not agriculturally inclined. They were laborers, but mom did stay at home with us children. My dad never had a father image because his dad, my grandfather, was always in the bar.

Now we had a liberal New York City type Jew and an Anglophile, such as England has brought us the atheistic Beatles and all the other liquid manure along with the homosexual Little Richard who was not English but black. Was it not the English who always were for race mixing and not for marriage, or brotherly love, but for sexual pleasure alone, just like the Anglophiles? This forced integration from Boston and the Bostonians who could do no wrong was more than an individual could handle. "Children should be seen and not heard" meant that if one was a minority and were moral they should always remain silent and acquiesce or collaborate with whatever was popular. Did not the British Isles give us much mayhem and violence even in the founding of this nation known as America? The Negro was forced to conform to capitalism, and it almost destroyed all of them since they were an agricultural people and were close to the land. Had not the South had this kind of ignorance about it that reaped with the smell of immorality? Our own head of state was an Anglophile who had those same traits and could not finish anything he started. On the other side it got even worse with New York City Jewry that was liberal and so extravagant that it became ludicrous to see how they live and what they stood for, if anything worthwhile.

People coming to America now were almost turned into praying mantises and would too devour the male image by using socialism to promote feminism so that the woman was "equal", not so much in rights, but more in authority in the home and in the business and government realms. The blacks had become so arrogant that they even thought they had become intelligent through college and they completely forgot what had made them strong in the past in the spiritual realm. They were emulating the Europeanism of Europe, or the Islamic Jihad violence, and their children had no fatherhood. When discipline was applied in the home it could be brutal, so that when they went out on the streets they would destroy anything in sight. The ones brought up by women . . . . But the ones brought up alone by males, which was so rare, could also become harsh and critical on themselves and on others.

The Irish were smart and versatile, but one drink and all was lost to havoc and chaos. The Polish were their own royalty and had an ego and an avarice problem and, like the Germans, could hoard money like a miser, as only they knew how for generations and generations! The Italians were also money crazed and would work till they dropped and would continue to collect and collect money so that they could take it with them, and food and clothing they went nuts over also. Yes, Europeans had been influenced by their own, each culture as well as, in some cases foreign and in other cases non-foreign religions, or inherited religions that constantly sought the easy life of no labor for wealth and riches on the backs of the poor. Now they even collaborated with Islam and had no remorse, or did not even give it a second thought.

In most of George Washington's pictures it looked like he could have never been the type of general that fought in war as most do not, but looks can be deceiving. Israel did not have a constitution and for good reason. We had believed more in the past than in the Biblical precept of the present and to do for today and not dwell on the past or try to predict the future with socialism. People at the top in government and business rose to the top like cream, but also became sour like spoiled cream because one did not have to be qualified to hold a position in life. Mediocrity was ruling supreme, and soon, or so it appeared that like Lenin someone somewhere was ready to take over the entire banking industry in America and in Europe, and at the present time it was England.

Everyone seemed to have new and glossy cars except for the billionaires because to them it is not their status symbol, but raw absolute power that bought out not only a geographical area in business, but also those entire people that lived there, and without their knowledge. So they were in a class all of their own, which did not include the millionaires, their "peasants", because today anybody could win the lottery!

Yes, coerced integration like in South Africa by Nelson Mandela meant it was okay to give up one's belief and dwell on the English past and collaborate and become popular with political correctness. Lenin would be proud!

I would see signs that said "GOD BLESS AMERICA", but often thought which "GOD" had they meant since this head of state saw Islam's god as our own god in America and in England. This did not even involve separation of "church" and state, since Islam was "church and state" being that it was innately socialistic in nature and had a death wish for mankind.

America had to do what the Anglophiles wanted them to do because it would be chic and sophisticated to be in vogue with these scoundrels! Even their women went with Moslems and Arabs at that and in high places and had homosexuality in the royal family and the Greeks, Catholics, Germans, Blacks, Hispanics too were growing fast in incredible numbers! There was no father, or a hatred for the father . . . So the family disintegrated to nothingness, and if only a father raised the children, they could become (especially the girls) mannish and the boys harsh and not understanding. Then to mix these cultures from now all over the world from India's caste system, Islam, Communism (Karl Marx is buried in England and Engels was rich), homosexual Marxism—and in this case homosexual must always precede the word Nazi—would indeed bring disaster such as reprobate minds to America. We would once again be slaves to the British and possibly fight another kind of "revolution" that these English scoundrels did to their own in privacy for years on end.

Would GOD save this king, and would this king be in the world and of this world? Only time would tell as to when it would all occur, but it would occur nonetheless, no matter what. The timing was what nobody knew, but only that it would occur and as months seemed to become as days in time we were moving to a cataclysmic catastrophe worldwide here on earth and from principalities and from GOD Himself who would not be pleased, especially with America and its idol worship.

Friends would become mortal enemies because of GOD, but did not Jesus say that even in one's own household there would be enemies because of HIM? There would be a one-world government draft to serve this one world New Age system and guess who was best at developing systems and seemed to know from birth their niche in life?

All of our beautiful landscape was covered with "debris" and one could not even grow grass or plant flowers any longer. Our rivers and streams were destroyed for good, and ecology was not the same as environmentalism, which was a disease from socialism and communism. Private property was okay as long as one understood its system, but no one could ever own a piece of property ever, because the state always had its hand in taxation without representation. The paid liars, or lawyers, only knew that money and infamy, one for the defense and one for the prosecutor, would be needed, and the jury system was just Russian roulette to be played with.

With the pecking order of homosexuality that was in most major corporations in America, sometimes a higher employee was deathly afraid of a lower employee because the pecking order had been established according to deviancy and to the extremity to which it went. In other words, the more reprobate the mind, the higher in the pecking order. At one place one German woman was in control of many other women, even ones who looked like butches, but she herself was quite feminine, but there was that peculiarity that at least I could discern that she was the real pernicious one who was married to a male and had children, but nonetheless could be extremely cruel. Another woman who had a huge butch as a body guard to entice pretty young girls, especially Hispanic ones into her brothel with, of course, the body guard there for protection and while on duty or at office hours. This indeed was a psychiatric disorder of vast proportions, yet when she looked at one, who knew what she was? You had a problem if they had the problem and not her, and she had a very important position no matter where she was put in the building. She also was German and had a liking for the anatomical male with huge genitals. These were women who had control of millions of dollars in the community and controlled who was hired and who was fired, even though her job was not in personnel. This was this deviant subculture that ruled in corporations with the knowledge of the CEOs. They always received raises and were constantly promoted because they knew how blackmail worked against people who were higher up but who also had a proclivity towards the same sex and was a bi-sexual Sodomite, or in political correct wording, a lesbian. These pillars in the community were looked up to except by ones who were not homosexuals and knew the score as to the pecking order and how they kept their jobs like a civil servant worker no matter how much they slacked. It appeared that young pretty minority women were the object and especially the light-skinned ones, or the mulatto ones. One friend of mine who had probably the darkest skin color once told me that his people were more prejudice than most white people, and the mulatto ones were some of the worst to be around. The dark-skinned Negro would rarely be accepted, but the mulatto would be, even though they would emulate the Caucasian individual in how they dressed and wore their hair and even the cosmetics they used. These were the so called "love child". In the Gulags there were these types also who were gypsies and worked undercover for the Communists and could get away with murder since they had no morals and would be released even if they killed a political in the Gulag under a 58.

Now in America this melting down of America with backwards and foreign cultures was taken on a form of its own because the elites (billionaires) wanted to bring down the intelligence of the average American and with all kinds of drugs, improper diets, preservatives, sex with anyone promoted from Hollywood, etc. This was creating a tribal, or group, mentality. Americans could not relate to a nation, but more to an ideology so that the nation itself they thought would not have a soul and could care less. It was bringing a dog-eat-dog mentality so family was obsolete and people became objects to be bought and sold as slaves in the world of socialism. It was called a democracy, whatever that meant, and probably it meant mob rule. Democracy did not work; for the Greeks it did because they were a small nation. There also was much homosexuality amongst the Greeks who used their philosophies to control their own culture and nation into deviancy and certain people or tribes have a proclivity for homosexuality and some do not.

The "oriental" Greek was not really European and their music sounded almost Arabic. They were not inclusive and stayed to themselves and would send their children to Greece to keep them in their own nationality. Remember the New Testament was written in Greek because GOD knew that that language would transcend to many people the Gospel in that day and age. Also, there were certain words like the word love that had 3 different types of love. The Greeks were very smart, but were extremely envious people even amongst brothers and sisters that to own a business they had to separate. Envy was worse than jealously because it meant that that person wanted what you had and not just to be jealous of what you had. This is what had held their country back for centuries.

Did everybody want civil rights as a minority? No, the Jews, for example, did not, even though they supported it with a zeal like no other group of people in America including the Blacks. The ACLU was a hotbed of Communism in the order of Marx, a German-Jew who despised people and was poor. Just about all famous Jews were non-believers and were lost as to who GOD really was and were confused about the Triune GOD which to them meant that that was 3 gods, but was not. Constantly they would say why do bad things happen to good people, which was a misnomer because as Jesus said while on earth, "No man is good."

"So it was the homosexuality issue that caused both World War I and World War II and 13 million unarmed civilians were brutally murdered, not to mention about 30 million or 40 million more in Stalin's Russia."

"Yes, Tom, that is the sad story that has never really been told about the West that affected millions of other people in the world. While America was doing the fox trot, millions were in the Gulag system since our leaders felt it would be appropriate after we won the war, but to lose the spoils of victory and in turn also to hand it over to a butcher of unprepared proportions that up until now the world has ever known and has set in motion this "big red machine" that would, up and including today, continue to destroy human life."

Adam said, "What a blunder we had committed (that is the West) and now we are being made accountable for the sins that we allowed to occur in the far eastern part of Europe. For years nothing was said by anybody, and that means anybody until one of their own spoke out with risk to life and his family."

"Is it also possible that our own government, at that time up to the present, was subscribing to the same socialism by also destroying our very own of 55,000,000 people and counting plus the fact that America had served its purposes long ago and was no longer a haven for Christians?" said Jake.

I then said, "That is the short summation of it all, and none of us has been the wiser for it. I keep wondering how much longer GOD shall allow our own sins to destroy millions by the way of capitalism or avarice."

"You would think that we would have compassion at least for our own, but since we do not, how could we ever have compassion for our fellow man in other countries in the world by allowing and promoting that which we were diametrically opposed to for many years, or at least that is what our government had been saying," said Tom.

I said, "Illusions of grandeur for this 'Babylon' called America and by the people, for the people, etc. which amounted to nothing more than 'Babel' talk."

"Why should we have lied to ourselves year after year and thought all was well when we knew it was not and vindictiveness would never prove anything except that we had certainly lost our way," said Jake.

"All I can say is that I am now ashamed to say that I am an American for those past memories no matter if they occurred before I was born for I am still part of America whether early in the age or later in the age of our nation," said Adam.

"We now defend the Nazism that was in Nazi Germany by passing laws that promote homosexuality, infanticide, euthanasia, sado-masochism, liquid manure, that says to kill law enforcement officers, and most of our uprofessionals only see luxury, travel and of course money as the root to all 'goodness'," said Tom.

"We sat back and allowed our government to get involved in Korea where MacArthur botched it up and had become almost 'senile' in his attempt to not aggressively pursue the Communists when he had the chance, and in the Vietnam War where our own government destroyed the chance for us to win against the Communists because at that time capitalism was more important than even the will to defeat socialism," Jake said.

"I can say that now we have to reap what we have sown, and it is up to GOD as to the amount of judgment our nation as a whole shall suffer since we too now must be judged since GOD is a fair and just GOD," I said.

"What shall this nation and the world be like for our dear children and grandchildren as well as children and grandchildren all over the world when it was our given responsibility to defend and protect?" said Jake.

"We must now go through it to the very end and not complain about GOD'S judgment upon our own nation, not as an unbelieving nation, but as a once Judeo-Christian nation," I said.

"Well guys, I guess it is time for us to call it an evening until next week when we can continue on this same dialogue," said Tom.

We all left Tom's place with our notes from each other and continued to think more about what we could do, no matter what would happen to our nation or ourselves. We knew we could not collaborate with evil in the world and that now for us there was only one way left. But could we withstand what was coming upon us all, since we failed to heed even the warning of today of 'there is no president left to vote for' since they do not aspire to all the things of GOD and His Word, the Bible?

I went home and told my wife about what we fellows had discussed tonight and she said she would like to start a women's group to also discuss what the present day affairs mean and also how to tell the truth and government or no government, not to go along with the "winner" or the so called "underdog".

Voting would never solve our major problems any longer since it was spiritual and not politics that was bringing us down and that ones in power wanted all of us to forget about a Holy GOD. Not until they got this would they be satisfied and it had nothing to do with left or right, conservative or liberal, but everything to do with good vs. evil, and who was good but GOD Himself and who was evil but Satan. Totalitarianism America was helping to build up since it did not oppose evil openly and since America always had to see results and not by faith, this meant that man had become his own type of god and his ego became inflated, and his heart hard such as Pharaoh's and reprobate minds were multiplying at an incredible rate of speed. We had forgotten all about the Book of Romans, which is the Constitution of the New Testament and that was all that mattered and not something that man had written for a short civilization, but for an eternity.

"To the saints in Rome". What could that possibly mean to us since it was written so many years ago? It did not mean to the Roman Catholic Church, but to the ones who had placed their trust in Messiah. There were not canonized saints, but saints by the grace of GOD who accepted Jesus as their personal Savior and no other conditions or legalities and, of course, no anti-Semitism because even Satan was a strong, or the strongest anti-Semite ever. He knew what that name meant to all who would hear and respond. GOD was not slow in love, but in anger. He was so we as human beings were fortunate, no blessed, to have such a loving GOD, since we continued to get it wrong time and again, but unconditional love was always there and by faith was our way as Christians in pleasing just as Abraham did. "Perfect love cast out all fear." This was GOD'S love and no other and was called agape love from the Greek.

Every time I saw our own granddaughter, Rachel, I thought more and more of how we could share with her about Messiah, the Savior. This would be her only chance to continue in this life and the next, and there was no other way to show love except through Jesus. I had to do for her and not just for her but others so innocent and small all over the world, but what could I alone do ? I could get down on my knees and pray to GOD, "Holy, holy, holy Lord, are you Lord GOD Almighty who was, who is and who is to come and the 24 Elders continuously sang day and night before GOD'S throne while bowing . . .

Many conservatives had looked to one man for their "salvation" in America, but Ronald Reagan was only a man and what he did is what all presidents should have done so since they did not and he did many felt that this was exemplary in our day and age, but then again, as I just said, it appeared that way, since all the other Presidents failed to do what any decent and honorable President should have done and so the "norm" became the absurd. We were staking everything on financial matters such as the stock market that had absolutely nothing to do with the "peasants" in America or for that matter most average Americans since it was just like poker or any other kind of gambling that one might do. Where had Scripture really said that one should get something for nothing without working for it and had not that also created this monster of avarice in the Western World and now was poisoning the rest of the world? No, private enterprise means just that, private and not on the public market to display one's get rich scheme. Since many Americans understood nothing about it, how could it be for the people and by the people? Someone was doing a two step shuffle and not because it was Republican or Democrat, since both subscribed to the "eat, drink and be merry" philosophy. Capitalism is just an economic system and cannot compete without going outside of its borders. Since the opposing influence in the world says let us add an ideology to it we see now this worldwide focus on socialism or pure materialism. As far as dealing with Communists, does not one have to sell out their soul to the devil? How can oil and water possibly mix, even though now we in America, or our leaders, say that Islam is the very same as Judeo-Christianity and again the lie is believed. This tells one also that it must be socialism which, in all essence, is always pointing towards Communism. We refuse to admit that we must deal with socialism in order for America to survive financially because capitalism, all capitalisms, lead to socialism. Did not Karl Marx mention only 6 types of socialism with many more in the offing? As far as the "Soviet Union" or Moscow, they now have at least 10,000 warheads pointed at America, and Vladimir Putin is a communist, so where is the honor in that? Also, Red China is no friend to humanity. In fact communism is anything but humane. So now we can subscribe, as you suppose, that good is evil and evil is good, or why else say that we and they are the better for it? (Just wait till the Red Chinese and let us not confuse the two, the 80% peasantry). Red China has and the fact that the government there, or group of thugs, just gave these peasants water and bread and that was the world to these peasants. Now how do you suppose that technology, another lie, can ever at this time come to help the people, but might in fact make them believe even more now that the entire West is against them since we offer them nothing so that they can live, but only playthings that the West has fun to be fickle? NO, the Red Chinese government is the enemy and not the Chinese people, so we must have a relationship with the people and not thugs. The same goes for Moscow where people also are starving and where Alexander Solzhenitsyn has already explained Communism, so do you suppose that even the Russian people shall once again fight for Marxism? I think not! We are so impetuous in the West and make decisions without any regard for the future that one has to wonder now how shall we get ourselves out of this dead end? Once our leaders have aged some more and have seen their fatal mistakes, it shall be too late then to go back, for now we can only go forward. We are like sheep that have no shepherd and have fallen down and the wolves are ready to pounce on us since we now cannot get up by ourselves. But who shall we blame then but only ourselves?! You speak of 3rd World despots, but what of Moscow and the Red Chinese leaders plus North Korean leaders as well as Cuba? Someone just does not want to see that the road to Armageddon is closer now than perhaps they thought, and how they too must go all the way for they know now that they cannot return to what once was normal. We talk about taxes when we should talk about infanticide or homosexuality. Now for one to quote the World Bank is indeed ludicrous since it was this very financial institution that helped persuade that it was okay to lose in Vietnam for there shall be many more to come, and why not for how could capitalism ever survive without socialism and inherently take on the very form of socialism itself? Robert McNamara, David Rockefeller, Henry Kissinger, Alexander Haig, George McGovern, the Clintons, the Kennedys, the Fords, and the list could go on and on. As you see by the list of names, they come from all parties, since only an individual can have a point of view and a party always has an ideology! We are ideologues since we refuse to believe that one by one people must decide good vs. evil and never can any such group do that. We must hit bottom and then we shall all have to endure it to the final end. This not a very optimistic forecast, but you and others have not given us much to look for in "sunny weather". Even our religions have become consumer driven and main denominations have become, if you will, word of mouth. "Christianity", since Scripture is the last source.

What moral foundation could one possibly mean in this day and age for all are linked to one another, or why deal with communists for any price at any time at any place and anywhere for anybody? It sounds nice, but has no validity to it. "We must provide the same kind of lifestyle for the people in China and Korea and Cuba." Heaven forbid that they too should come to know what avarice and evil are in the context of capitalism! If we would really have had a clash with communism, we never would have allowed it to grow at the Yalta Conference. The time was there and then, but now it is too late, since the West in our shortsightedness, chose the easy way out and made a deal with the devil. Whatever happened to free enterprise? Since the stock market has drowned us into scoundrels, need one ask the above question any longer? Only one can see that we shall either do exactly like England or we shall compete on this market against England for the World Market. Administrations and bureaucracies do nothing to enhance a free people. Russia found that out many years ago and their Duma was doomed and the monarch fell along with the rich and well educated and hence the socialists too also fell to the Bolsheviks who would finish what they started, and today they are about to do just that! "Nothing to fear but fear itself," or better yet, "never, never, never give up". With these two phrases first about fear. Why did he fear the worse at Yalta and why did the other give up at Yalta? Maybe one can ask the ones who paid with their lives that question, since it was them who suffered the unthinkable. We have stained our nearest past with so much self-preservation that now we have only our own self-preservation in materialism which in essence means dog eat dog and "please leave me alone, or I have lived my life and you live yours."

What can all this mean but that we have now given up to the highest bidder, no not our freedom, but our very national soul for the price of mammon. And this big government is almost nothing more than thugs now coming to the surface who want to do it according to ideology, or party politics, and this party shall be one strong party as it has been for some time now, so now we get really only one candidate to vote for this year. Since no election shall solve our major problems, we one-by-one must see that we ourselves do not be come part of the mob which is what democracy is and which was made only for small countries such as Greece and not like countries such as Russia and America. We only see things from one side and fail to take into consideration that some things have many sides as well as angles and the business world has shown us their angles.

"This was a wonderful idea you came up with of having us meet together to discuss this nation's dire consequences since our own government refuses to deal with it as such."

"Alice, this was really my husband's idea, along with some of his close friends who have taken a long look of just how far we have fallen."

"So, we as woman can do something without the so called "feminists" (which is just another word for unfeminine) and radical 60s women who know nothing about family, GOD and nation and would have many American women believe they are in the majority when they are not," Elizabeth said.

"And I believe with you other women that we must really start from the bottom up even though the rich in society always rule whatever country or nation it so happens to be," said Martha.

"We shall try and discuss what the World War II generation and then the 60s generation never would take upon themselves to even think about, as well as now the new generation, with each generation taking in a span of at least 40 years and not 20 as some incorrectly believe," Rebecca said.

"We are to uphold our husbands and fathers and not deadbeat dad syndrome because the rich are just like them in that they do not want to raise their own children, so they send them off to boarding school or some other type of "errand" so others can put up with their shenanigans," said Alice.

"The Jane Fondas, Gloria Steinems, Jocyelyn Elders, Margaret Sangers, Bella Abzugs, the Feinsteins, the Pelosies, the Patty Hearsts, the Carol Mosley Brauns, the Angela Davises—if one would notice, all the above, or most of them, were either from the rich or the well educated elite of the 60s generation and before," said Martha.

"We may not move mountains, but we can help guide our families, friends, neighbors, communities, to the proper road providing they would want to listen, but we must make it important enough for them to want to listen no matter how much materialism and atheism surrounds them daily," said Elizabeth.

"We have a cross-section of real America where the 'squeaky wheel does not get the oil', but where the truth shall remain the truth and shall not change no matter how popular the lie becomes," said Rebecca.

"We are our brothers' keepers and not babysitters, so that they take benevolence for weakness," said Martha.

"Who shall represent not the liberal or conservative, but the Judeo-Christian in our society?" said Alice.

"When conservatives like William F. Buckley, Jr. want to legalize drugs and a Forbes wants to legalize infanticide, one can also see that this side has no morals or absolutes to talk about in reality," Elizabeth said.

"The other side has some people that sound good when they speak but do not have the courage to stand up for what the truth represents," said Martha.

"The women who were the wives of our Founding Forefathers never obstructed or told their husbands what to do, but did help and encourage and not like our present President or even Reagan's wife who would undermine what their husbands were trying to do in the moral sphere," said Rebecca.

"We are here not to serve ourselves or become popular, but to love our nation, but to criticize, no correct it when it has gone astray," said Alice.

"We are held in authority by our husbands and the fathers of our children and not vice versa as the popular iconoclasts think it to be whether it has reason or a purpose, but a rebellion that spells disaster for all in this nation and in other nations of the world since we are the leader in at least our wealth," said Martha.

"The group mentality of one for all and all for one must be avoided by us and the few others who not only express and show concern, but who are willing to even give up one's life for the truth which it appears we all might just have to do in the near future since things have gotten that bad if one peels the skin from the onion far enough to sting the eyes," said Rebecca.

"One nation and not nations as in South Africa is what we are with a common bond and heritage that says that freedom with responsibilities comes first for the other man and not for ourselves," said Elizabeth.

"We must now support our husbands and they should in turn understand that they must support us in order for the family institution to remain as it always has been, a GODLY institution since Adam and Eve," said Alice.

"This shall not be an easy task to say the last since we all have let this go on for much too long and now it shall definitely be an uphill battle of good vs. evil," said Rebecca.

"Groups and organizations are not the Body of Christ which breathes and lives inside of each one."

"Alice, you have said the very thing that has to be said in order for this to translate beyond languages and borders and to share with others this kind of gospel and not the one that has for ages promoted anti-Semitism among the major denominations," said Rebecca.

As a new day was coming in by a new dawn, we all had come to realize the worst possible scenario that could take place was just about to happen with most Americans oblivious of course except the ones who truly loved their own country and the ones who hated it. The in between mediocre middle had nothing to say, or refused to become involved unless it had a direct affect on their own family which was not the way one should think if they had foresight at all. The challenge was not to go along with whatever blew in the wind and also not to live for oneself which is what it appeared most of society had come to believe in. The handwriting was on the wall, and even the elderly would not lead as nature itself has taught them to do with a wise and experienced life or at least the knowledge that as one gets older they should have more to say and do and not the least to say and do, and not to believe that the senior citizen means "I lived my life and you live yours."

The "I" in Islam and also in itself self meant that whatever part of Adam had fallen, and it was all, was the part that would be easiest to follow, but of course there always would be consequences for sin and the ravages of sin to any people or nation, free or unfree. There is one freedom that matters most, and that is the freedom of conscience where one could even be limited in movement and in action and in speech, but the heart and the mind know the truth and shall not trade in the truth for any lie that comes along or . . . . Do not believe the lie and help your fellow man free himself from the bondage of slavery that this world system has now provided for all who want to be a part of it and in fact for those who have had no intention of being a part of it, but somehow have become part of it.

The other "I" is for Israel and to know that Jacob shall not be removed but only punished for a short while, and the church shall be in obedience to what the real Jews, who shall be the leaders, and of course GOD shall say in the millennial reign of Messiah. This is a Jewish faith, if you will, and nothing shall interfere for eternity with the absolute will of GOD including America or any other Gentile empire that man may believe shall reign supreme.

The West has lots its roots from the Judeo in the Judeo-Christian faith and somehow has forgotten.

Since both sides, husbands and wives, would share in this, we would both be jeopardizing our jobs, that is the husbands and fathers, because they were the breadwinners, and the wives were mothers and wives who correlated their rare skills and nurturing 24 hours a day, so we knew that many things would be on the line. Whenever we would talk to even so called conservatives about there is no one to vote for, they would reply "I must vote for Republicans" or "I must never abstain from voting." This type of go along mentality is what got us where we are to day, but no one could convince them no matter how sincerely wrong they were, because money and luxury came first, even over GOD. Once this President made the statement that Islam worships the same GOD, I myself would indeed be too afraid to vote than not to vote because idol worship is the 1st Commandment in the 10 Commandments. This type of shortsightedness was not even sane to think about let alone to vote on it or on any individual who proclaimed such a lie!

There would be little support from those who had and little support from those who wanted to because the grass was always greener on the other side. The other candidate was the worse of two evils. Yes, when one proclaims such insanity and Americans who say they care vote for that individual they are bringing judgment and more of it to our own nation. Who do they suppose gave us all of our liberties and freedoms within the GODLY realm? They see today as only being important to themselves and the future we would worry about that later on if there was to be a real future in our nation. Yes, maybe America was soon to expire because of capitalism, which meant more to the West than GOD even though many spoke about GOD in a loving verbal way.

Abraham, Joshua, Andy and Jerome would also have to be involved in this discussion, since those four were Messianic male Jews, which were so very few. The whole Body had to be there, I believed, in order for some type of blessing, not for us necessarily, but for the ministry that GOD had placed on each of our hearts. Our conviction was immediate, and with constant prayer we knew we always had to seek His way. Another meeting would be held where I would present to all those present that Messianic Jews had to be involved in this GODLY discussion or what would it all be with just Gentiles in the fold and no believing Jews? In all of Scripture there are always believing Jews involved even with Ruth, the Moabite who stayed with Naomi and Boaz, and this was to represent the remnant of the Jewish people's Redeemer that would come in the Second Advent. No, GOD was not done with His people, the Jews.

There was one radio commentator who was Jewish but was constantly condemning a candidate for the National Democratic Socialists, and it made me wonder when he made a few statements that defended the Roman Catholic Church was which so anti-Semitic and the candidate he condemned was himself a Catholic Jew which was as far left as a socialist could get, yet he seemed to have most all people deceived. It had reminded me of a story my mentor, a Russian Jewish man, had told me about that involved a Jewish family where a brother was accused of murder, and in the courtroom his sister would keep yelling out, "You murderer!" When the jury came back from deliberation and read their verdict, they said, "We find so and so Not Guilty of the following charges." Well, much to everyone's surprise the Jewish sister ran across the courtroom and hugged her brother. This same radio announcer was doing the same in order to get votes for the socialist running for President and by inflaming the public to believe he was for the conservative candidate, he was creating more voters to vote for his real candidate, the socialist, since this announcer, as I said before, was Jewish. Whenever Jewish is mentioned, much anti-Semitism arises, and also being the fact that most voters did not know that the Democratic Socialist candidate was a Catholic Jew. There are many ways to win an election, and this is one of the most unscrupulous ways in doing it.

There was a vested interest in capitalism in most of the American Jewish community, so they repeatedly voted for the socialist candidate that usually ran on the Democratic party ticket, because that is were big business and big government lie in bed together. Islam would most likely gain more momentum in America because the New York City Jew was a kind of Trotsky and not at all like the Old Testament saints that believed in GOD, the Father of Abraham, Isaac and Jacob.

Anyone today in America who had a position and was wealthy had to have their hands with the scoundrels whether they acknowledged that or not. This was for keeps, that is the selling out of America and the rich and well educated played the game as they had in Russia before their revolution. The consequence was that communism came into fruition, and also the peasants later came over to Communism, just like most blacks in America had. There also were many homosexuals in top positions in America and the blacks and the Germans seemed to correlate very well together along with the National Socialistic Democratic Party, not to mention the Jews. This had nothing to do with the "changing of the guard" in America (this Presidential election), and surely not by voting or not voting would anything deeply change. It was, if you will, a subliminal change or an aesthetic change that would occur with nothing underneath really occurring because that would have meant we would have to go back in time, which is always an impossibility, ye we as American could only see what we knew as democracy, which was nothing more than mob rule. No one individual could now change what had happened in America, but one by one, individuals could change only themselves, and that would mean a narrow passage for each one who so chose that way. This was an individual thing and not a group thing which all ideologies were about.

Nobody wanted to publish beautiful poems or even the truth about America and its history and that included believers and so called conservatives. All it was about was money and the love of money and luxury and "eat, drink and be merry' and of course wealth, which one could not take with them into Hell. From one to the next generation, money was being given, and it was destroying the moral fabric because the money was never earned either by the predecessors or the next generation. Instead of really helping the poor who did not go through any type of organization, people were giving their excess to such organizations blindly or in order to keep their jobs, and Islam played a major part in that.

Who would have ever guessed that Americans would help and work for the enemy that bombed the two Twin Towers in New York City and would drive themselves beyond belief to obtain the golden ring? This surely was insanity and as for some groups such as the Catholics who were both "opportunists" as well as anti-Semities, no one would be surprised at that since Roman Catholicism never subscribed to Judeo-Christianity and the Crucifix proved that beyond a shadow of a doubt. Jesus had resurrected 2,000 years ago so why was He displayed on a cross? Yes, America would sell out its very soul for the love of money and what it could buy, but one day all the gold in the world with no bread would then show that what good would gold do when one was starving to death from lack of bread?

As I was planning to convene another meeting, this time at my house, I had to remember all the men I had to contact for that evening and make sure that all would be there, and there could be no excuses for not being there. This was hopefully to start something that I felt could at least say to GOD, "You will not destroy the city if there are only righteous men in it would You? We as the Body must meet.

It was the time of Passover where the death, burial and the resurrection occurred that we would shortly have our meeting to discuss the spiritual vacuum in America and its lack of memory for GOD. It was imperative for us to convene as soon as possible so that we could not maybe someday be told "What did you do for the Kingdom?" Not that we would bring in the kingdom, but that we would try to be ready for the Second Advent, since Paul, or Saul, himself seemed to be looking for it daily as he started a different church here and there. It was not done on works alone, but had to have GOD'S grace through Y'eshua first. That made all the difference in the world and these works would not be for salvation at all. We had already become saints through what He did on the cross and not what we would try to do according to the Holy Spirit. That is why GOD had said, "Get away from Me. I never knew you!" This was Holy Spirit power and love, and not done in the flesh so we had to pray and fast for so many days and do it discretely as the Holy Spirit led us to do. This was not man's religion, or religions, but the eternal GODhead of the Triune GOD.

The ones at the meeting were Tom, Adam, Jake, Abraham, Joshua, Jerome, Andy, and myself. These were all believers in Messiah, Jesus, and they knew what the Holy Spirit was all about. We soon would first start to pray to the Father of Abraham, Isaac and Jacob like the Messianic Jews do and then let it be known that if any in the room were unbelievers they should not be there, but this was done in quiet so that we would know whether to proceed or not. When we felt that all present were believers, we continued to worship (not sing) GOD, because that is what GOD wanted us to do first and foremost, and the main denominations had gotten totally away from that. Once we worshipped GOD in the flesh, we then asked for the gift of prophecy and one to interpret it, and also to speak in tongues and one to interpret that also. There was to be no confusion in what GOD wanted us to do, and there could be no type of sin to interfere with our prayers to Him since sin can cause a conflict in the spirit with even one individual. This was an all male gathering with no women at all, so we had not to contend with what some women and men would say was chauvinism or what Paul was accused of falsely: not liking women. There was no time to change GOD'S Word, nor did we want to change or dare to change. This would move mountains if we only would believe what GOD had said, "And ye shall do greater things than this."

"The first shall be last and the last shall be first" told us the Gospel goes to the Jews first.

Many were concerned about the Republican National Convention in New York City because Mayor Giuliani was not there anymore, and they would now have to worry about how they would protect the city because the mob would not be organized to dissipate any power that the Moslems had, knowing full well that the Sicilians were part Turkish and would deal a blow to them immediately. But Bloomberg, being a billionaire Jew, did not have the same contacts as Guiliani, so the Moslems would be much more tempted to attack the convention now. That is why I believe that the mobsters were being rounded up and people from Africa were trying to get on the island of Sicily where no blacks were allowed to divert the Sicilian mob's attention. So far it had not worked and so Islam had to be very careful because what our government failed to do they would surely do and Gotti, from prison, still could orchestrate power to eliminate certain elements in society in America through different channels. Remember when Kennedy himself used John Roselli and the mob to try and remove Castro from Cuba, but failed terribly at the Bay of Pigs?

Anything could happen at any time, even to the Moslem world since Red China and Moscow had enough nuclear power to eliminate all the Moslem countries. But Israel and the Mossad was a different story, and the communists had once before been defeated in the 1967 war and so had egg on their faces. But this was a new generation of thugs in the Kremlin and Peking and even more vicious because they befriended America and our leaders that they were their allies when really they were waiting to attack either America or Israel. The Republican party was pro-Anglo-Saxon and the Democrat Socialist Party was mixed with black socialists, the Marxists ACLU Jews, and of course the Nazism of the Kennedys. None could be trusted to represent the American people which went back since the time of Woodrow Wilson and FDR, who in the first case was a One World Government man, and in the second case a pure blue-blooded socialist who adored Lord Keynes, who had taught FDR at Harvard and who FDR admired and who was a homosexual. The English and the German were cousins in more than one way. The Austrians were also cousins to the Germans, and that is where Hitler came from, but the Austrians were Catholics. Europe had always had anti-Semitism because it was always against the Jews from the Spanish Inquisition in 1492 to the Holocaust and also the Roman Empire that had every emperor that rule who were also homosexuals except possibly one, and the Greeks had bragging rights in this.

As our meeting began, we discussed many of the above things that no church group would ever touch upon because they felt it unimportant to talk about the evil that surrounded us. They wanted to talk about the self-esteem program and how much did one give when in essence all that would mean is that, as Dostoyevsky had said, the pastors in Protestantism lived the lives as kings and queens and the houses and areas they lived in, as well as the cars they drove (a status symbol) showed it. What did all this have to do with Jesus and the Disciples who dressed probably like peasants and had nothing to do with financial matters as far as relying on them to solve all their problems in world? Jesus worshipped as a Jew and not a Gentile and all the major denominations coming from Europe were materialists since that is where the great Renaissance came from. Even the Middle Ages had much more spiritual content in it because John Locke's materialism without faith is what this New Age was all about and one age represented about 500 years in time. "Render unto Caesar the things that are Caesar's and unto GOD the things that are GOD'S." Our own government was doing just the opposite, and in fact most Gentile Christians thought that Romans meant that all governments were to be followed, including communism, or why else allow one's nation to trade with Red China with no opposition from the American churches?

No, we had to continue to discuss what America was really all about, and that was the American Biblical Christian or the original Christian in the sense that either the Irish Catholic had brought to these shores, or either the German Reformation that brought the German culture and also the fact that German was almost chosen and lost by one vote to be the spoken language in America. We had to discuss and bring out all of the truth as to why America never nearly took in its share of Jews before and after the Holocaust as well as other nations who also rescinded what they had said in regard to the Jews and the way the Iron Fist himself (Eisenhower) had felt about the disease and germs that the Jews would have brought to America. But now it was all right for them to bring the 3rd World rich and well-educated Moslems and the people from Hispanic America which started with David Rockefeller's Puerto Rico and led to much more and was a setup to change all of America or the Americans under NAFTA and other so called "treaties" which were not needed but only again for the super rich and the rich would, of course, follow or no longer be rich!

Today in America it was taboo to say anything negative about a certain race of people no matter how much of a socialist they were. Also no one could pronounce the "free enterprise" or capitalism as no longer worthwhile and only about profit and avarice. These were left alone because one might imply that America had a slave mentality and that one would not be for democracy. As in Russia, when Khruschev ruled, the persecution increased even though Khruschev himself was a peasant. When one's origins come from a very low income or of no property, sometimes they are the most brutal because they envy and want what another has. It brings out the human nature in them though at times one can see the poverty they came from by what they intermittently say and do. In America the agricultural people became so modernized that they forgot about GOD and nonetheless were interested in following Europeanism no matter how much they complained about it. They emulated to a T.

In the vast arena of society there was too much going on, so the simplicity in life was forgotten and even breathing fresh and seeing nature was totally ignored at the price of liberty. We as a group could not find one participant from this group that could not keep physical characteristics out of it and maybe so with just cause, but today the "slavery" was worse than ever before because every day they murdered thousands of their own because socialism now told them through party politics that that was what group ideology or so called strength in numbers, was all about. This President had certainly lost his way, and if this was what was our very best, then we were definitely in trouble, since this man was nothing like Adlai Stevenson, a brilliant man who had gotten a divorce and was put into the United Nations just as Alan Keyes was later on in our history. Alan, of course, was a Roman Catholic married to an Indian woman who probably had a lot to do with his conversion, since he knew Scripture like no Catholic I had ever known or run into. There was no interest to read Scripture and, in fact, years ago they were not allowed to read Scripture, which should tell anyone that this was far from Judeo-Christianity, but then again it was as Dostoyevsky had said, "happiness in slavery", or socialism in mysticism. Again, the ism's were coming in multiple numbers. America was too young as a nation to have developed a full personality, and as a youth would not listen to an elder like Russia who turned out to be like Job. The mold was set for whom would run for political office and thug after thug came in so that they could become part of government's mob and even the point of gambling like Al Capone.

Israel itself no longer was listening to America because our own government had lost its power as well as credibility. Israel had to protect itself and could not worry about the anti-Semites in America who were controlled by the internationalists in the world. America would have to contend with GOD about this matter and it appeared as if we would be the worse for such decisions the rich and well educated were making for all of us even though it was not done by referendum. We had lost our voice in America and democracy was exactly what it was said to be "mob rule". The people meaning at all levels were for the financial end and self-preservation so that they could continue to live out their lives with really no concern about our children in the least. America too had been dumbed down so much that even people in high positions were too ignorant to see the disaster that had already occurred. Yes, when was GOD going to judge America if GOD had judged Russia so and that was a monarchy the only Biblical kind of government? Greece was definitely not Biblical in its day, even with the Hellenistic Jews. Kingdom Dominion Theology was ruling that said, "Man would bring in the Millennial Kingdom."

We had too many heathen religions in America, so that what came was a blockage of GOD'S angels like in Daniel's time and Daniel was a GOD-fearing man all of his life. The blood and the water did not mean storms with deluge like waters or the blood from evil doings. It meant a righteous purification because of Messiah. Whenever I said the word Jesus, there was a peace that I could feel in my spirit. As amateur athletes used to train just to be able to compete, such as in the Olympics, so the believers were to do the same.

The saints, or believers, as addressed in Scripture were the ones who knew Jesus or had Jesus in their hearts. The Bible was written for saints, and could only be understood in the context that GOD Himself wanted it to be, because of the work of the Holy Spirit which was always right. Churchgoing, charity etc. did not matter, but only Christ's love which was held in grace and came from the crucifixion, death and resurrection. Other parts of the world were growing spiritually with lack of food and water and medicine, but we had plenty of this world and hardly anything worthwhile from the Holy Spirit and the churches were verbally talking about revival, which seemed to be dead in this nation as a whole.

"The wages of sin are death" and so goes it with a nation that refuses God's eternal love the way He has given it and sometimes this so called happiness is not really anything but sin disguised as 'good'."

"How is it that the American government which we are a part of, has turned into pure Nazism, Luke?"

"All I can say to that, Abraham, is that we have become part of this one world government and with the United Nations on our own soil we are the 'Babylon' that carries with it the wealth, or materialism, of the world and this of all times is not the time to have such materialism to the point of socialism because it translates into evil and violence, since we do murder our very own people daily."

"We all know here that America has taken a wrong route and is being led by Satan to do what he wants us to do as a people which makes up a nation," said Tom

"This is my question. What are we to do with the evil that surrounds us from all sides, besides not be a part of it?" said Joshua.

"We can be what the Bible says what we ought to be no matter the outcome, for tomorrow is promised to no one," said Adam.

"Don't we need more than that to survive or function?" asked Jerome.

"The whole point is that we have been conditioned as such in the West that any kind of suffering or pain, we automatically want to ignore it or repel it, so what does that say about America?" said Jake.

"We must act according to Scripture and not in a passive way which means we shall all be totally silent at all times and shall not take any kind of risk to help the innocent and the poor," said Andy.

I said, "If I can address all to this one thing I have noticed, we all must, one-by-one, take upon ourselves whatever suffering there is to be and rely on GOD and that our inner joy is not a mental state of happiness that is momentary, but a constant joy to know that Jesus is with us according to His Word."

Joshua said, "I would agree with that and add that we are not an organization but a body just like each of us has a body. So, we must understand that because of sin we shall not always get it right, but nonetheless we shall struggle with even death maybe looking us in the eye and not fear for perfect love casts out all fear. Only GOD has that perfect love to fill our hearts and our minds no matter what kind of freedom or lack thereof that occurs."

Adam said," Must not all of us be in prayer so that we lift up one another because the worst is yet to come?"

"GOD is not required to answer our prayers to our wishes but to His good will."

Our faith is given to us by GOD Himself. We are the derelicts of society and shall be looked upon as idiots and imbeciles. We are the ones that shall not even have family or friends, so we must first know that nothing in this world is promised to us because religion says it is. Satan always works in religions. That is why

Jesus never told the Jews or the Pharisees to follow any religion, but to follow Him and Him alone. Of course they were all Jews and some might even say it was understood what He meant, but no, GOD in the flesh had said, "If you have seen Me you have seen the Father. I and the Father are one." Let us not fool ourselves in believing that one religion shall outdo another because GOD is not about religion but about faith in His Son Jesus, or Y'eshua Messiah," said Abraham.

"I am glad that you said that, Abraham, so that we all know that some of the things we take for granted are what is right and that immediately leads us in the wrong path. This path is very narrow, so we must be ever vigilant in our spirits to discern the times as well as the signs that Jesus spoke about," I said.

Jake said, "Do we all truly believe what was just said and also agree that is what the Bible and the Holy Spirit has convicted us of?"

Yes, we all were in agreement according to the Holy Spirit that dwelled in each one of us. We always were very careful who we prayed with since we did not want to pray with unbelievers. Too much was at stake for other ones in the world, as well as ones who would come to know in him and ones who had already let grace enter into them with obedient free will. This was a time for fasting and much prayer so that we could know the important will of GOD. It is not always that easy to discern the will of GOD amongst men because we always, or most always, have a tendency to do what human nature, or Adam's fall, wants us to do, but we are no longer under the curse of Adam or the law, but under grace, undeserved merit. Our nation had definitely made money the worshipping idol. Much responsibility was ours. It was never a majority or a minority, but a Body of believers all over the world that would have to be in constant prayer no matter where we were or what our standing in life was. It was all or nothing. GOD would not share His worship from us to Him with anyone or anybody else. We would be mocked and laughed at and thought to be even insane or not well. The world could not understand what GOD was about, and we had to understand that from now. His love was an agape love which was not momentary but now and forever more. We belonged to Him and so did our bodies.

After about another week had gone by, I visited some old friends again who were not Christians, and we again decided to play pinochle at Jim's house. Our conversation got into some things that I did not plan to discuss.

"I believe that it is your turn to deal, Luke, and speaking of deal, how about the deal that both these candidates are selling us to make us richer?" said Jim.

"Well, what kind of deal are you talking about, and is it the same candidates that I am thinking about?"

"I think Jim is referring to the politics today in a facetious way, and I also feel myself that to this way of thinking one has to somewhat agree with it since it means we will not have to pay for health care at all," said John.

"All I know is that if one today has sex with any woman, one is sure asking for trouble because of the incidence of AIDS and HIV and VD," said Martin.

"Since you brought up that subject, don't you feel that sex outside of marriage makes one more free and independent to do what one wants to do?" said Jim.

I said, "How insane is that to say when all of us know full well that AIDS and HIV first came from the homosexual community and then spread into the heterosexual community through prostitution and infidelity and not only drug use, as we are constantly told."

"So, what do you suggest that we do, change our preference to the same sex since heterosexuals now also carry this HIV virus with them? asked Jim.

"This is like playing Russian roulette when one comes to seriously think about how deviant our entire society has become with no moral conscience of any kind to stop us from acting," I said.

"Jim, you have to understand one is responsible for one's actions and AIDS did not come from the CIA or a rhesus monkey, but from homosexual males who have anal sex many times with many different partners, and they are partners and nothing else, since homosexuality is an addiction to a sin that destroys human life and also preys on small children as well as adolescents. Since we are all much older, we did not have to go through this when we were so very young since Bill and Hillary Clinton started this," Martin said.

Jim then said, "Don't you really feel that is prejudice to say that against a group of people who only want to be treated like human beings?"

"If they wanted to be treated like a human being, then they would act appropriately at all times," said Martin.

"So, you mean to say that you are perfect in all the things that you do and have no faults, right?" said Jim.

"I think what Martin meant was that we must act in a normal way, such as either being single and celibate or being married to one wife for a lifetime with no infidelity," I said.

"What criteria do you get that from since all of us do sin and have our own problems?" Jim said.

"To put it another way, homosexuality is the last of all body sins that will eventually destroy any nation once it takes hold in a society because it destroys the family institution and also makes for pedophilia that is so horrible to describe," I said.

"Well, John, since Martin and Luke are ganging up on me how do you feel about this whole issue?"

"All I can say is let one live their life as they see fit and stay out of the bedroom, or else government shall soon be telling us many other things to do or not to do in our own private lives!"

"Well at least I have another one on my side."

Martin then said, "I am not against you totally, because I too believe the bedroom is a private place and government should not tell me how I must conduct myself at all times."

I then said, "Don't you feel accountable to anyone besides yourself in this world, and how do you base your lives on the truth if you believe in the truth at all?

"Well, each to their own. The slave issue was just the same way, and we conquered that through civil rights," said Jim.

"What we conquered was the fact that we gave certain individuals superior rights and this also again is the case like it was in Nazi Germany with affirmative action," I said.

"Well, you can't win them all, Luke," said John.

"This is not a matter of winning or losing or liking or disliking, but a moral issue between good and evil, and we as a society must stand on solid ground and not sand or else we shall become like Sodom and Gomorrah."

"What the heck is Sodom and Gomorrah?" asked Jim.

I said, "If I have to explain that then you are lost about knowing right from wrong and good vs. evil."

"Well, just make sure you play your hand good. Okay?" said John and Martin.

After our games were done I could see that these guys I could no longer be around because they were blinded by Satan and knew absolutely nothing about the bible. Jim was a Jehovah Witness who really never went to church or talked about GOD. He was retired from an inheritance, so he felt that he had nothing to worry about and was set for life. His family were all divorcees and thought shacking up was a neat thing. Martin was raised Catholic and believed that good works could get one into heaven. He was a gold digger, or opportunist, whenever money was involved and also rarely talked about GOD but only money and food. John was a Protestant who thought that whatever his religion was in the past according to his parents was good enough for him and never ever tried to really find out about the truth at all. He said tradition was the best thing as well as genealogy and the most important thing going in one's life because it dealt with genetics.

One could see that all three were missing the boat on moral issues because they felt that their way and not GOD'S way was the best for all concerned, or in other words, let bygones be bygones. Yes, one belonged to a cult, one to another kind of world cult, and still another to the German Reformation that said, as Dostoyevsky had said, "misery in freedom". One could not, and I would not, argue with them on these issues anymore, and in fact I would not be bothering them again since I had already shared the Gospel one time with them and they just almost laughed at me. I would not bring pearls in front of swine again.

Later that night, when I got home I said to my wife what had occurred and she knew all along that they felt that way but that I had to see that and all we could do now was pray for them. They were 3 lost souls whom the enemy had control of and they never even knew it at all. It was a very sad evening for me since I knew these guys for quite some time, but sometimes people change completely, and it is like we met a different person or could it be that I had met the Lord in my own life? Whatever way, or even if both ways, I knew now that believers in the Old Testament were not to mingle or marry into heathen cultures, and in this case this meant to surround oneself with unbelievers when believers were around and others who had not heard the true Gospel and not from television

I had thought to myself why should our soldiers fight the rich man's war and in fact foreign rich Moslems who did not believe in GOD? Had GOD Himself made us so simple in our minds that we could not discern what and who we really were fighting for? In Russia no one now would ever get them to fight for Marxist/ Leninism and that is why they kept their nuclear warheads near Moscow even though they gave up the usurpation of other nations. The ball and chain for the communists was much too heavy to carry for them and so they condensed what they had into one or two areas that the Communists felt would be the safest near the Kremlin and the City of Moscow and not all the other nations. Socialism had taken its toll, but quite enough because still the West was deceived by what they thought was the end of Communism. Communism by no means was dead and in fact it had become more dangerous than before because it was playing along with the West and not like in the Cold War where they felt they could, through fear, take over. They had become more worldly wise and now knew what the West's weakness was and were going to use that to the fullest extent.

Red China also was one to be contended with even more so. They had the Oriental mindset that once it would start it would not end in defeat even if it meant death, but then again about 1,000 leaders now knew what luxury was but could they stop the momentum that they had built up in the war machine, and even if they wanted to they now could not stop the cataclysmic event that soon would appear on the horizon and the red horse was out and ready to go!

As time went on, the younger whippersnappers would be even worse than their fathers and uncles and would do things that would be beyond belief to millions and millions of people. We in the West played church with consumerism because we really had not gone to war like this one would be. Most likely it would be one at random at first and then would escalate into mini wars that grew into larger wars until the earth would almost itself rumble. We in the West were in a dream world all of our own and refused to believe that the world, and not America especially was ready to go up in flames. The years would seem very long and mortal, but within time as a whole it would be very short and quick. We would be responsible for what was going on because we refused to believe that each one of us had a part in it and each one of us was responsible for what we did, which in turn affected the world. Now with communications so instant, a war could start and we would have to get involved, and with the village and multiculturalism, our own nation became many nations in one. There was so much animosity in this nation once known as America that just about everyone would be at each other's throats.

Savage youth, or adolescents, were so barbaric, but held so many important positions that one could not tell if they were educated or uneducated because education became so barbaric in and of itself that evil was pronounced good in a court of law, and this law was worldwide and the draft would take who it chose from different nations, including America and these soldiers would not fight for sovereignty, but for the one world government that was controlled by the enemy. The young had become like beasts but then again we gave them a world that said one could do anything immoral that one wanted to do just so it was not GODLY. "Those who lived by the sword would die by the sword." Men who refused to fight for the enemy would soon be put to death because they would not fight for evil no matter how many people said it was for good. The world would be out of control and only the Lord Himself could bring an end to this destruction and demise worldwide. How long could one side of the world live in destitution and severe famine and poverty and the other was obese and materialistic to the point of avarice and corrupt absolute power?

Young children would one could say, be hatched in a laboratory without ever knowing who their real parents were and the parents could care less because his time was so very short and he knew it. It was as if gangs worldwide were fighting against each other and not for wealth so much as for food and water and medicine just to stay alive while one part, or section or the world had it all but would not share it with the other parts in the world which soon would create an even more desperate situation in the world. Man would need to eat and if it meant cannibalism then so be it according to multiculturalism which went as far as Hell would take it and that would be the destruction of man and this earth, but GOD would have something to say about that with all kinds of judgment and these were not from man or the enemy, but from a holy and just GOD.

All foods and water would be intentionally hoarded by organizations which were really all part of the New World Order of barbarism. The 4 horsemen then would be out and all hell would break loose.

The Jewish people were much closer to the Word of GOD than the Roman Catholic Church who made up their own manmade rules such as no Scripture reading; a Pope; the actual blood and water; praying to saints that were not in communication with GOD the Father which only Messiah was; using a rosary; works instead of grace; telling one how much to tithe; refusing communion to whoever was not a Roman Catholic even at that person's mother's death; having Christ still on the cross; using the Apocrypha in their Bible; claiming to be the only way; having priests not get married, or nuns; having Cardinals; having a Vatican; going into foreign countries all over the world without being asked to; Liberation Theology; homosexuality in the church with pedophilia and covering it up for many years, etc. With Judaism in Orthodoxy there was at least the Old Testament, which meant that they read the first part of the Bible and Catholics, if ever read any of the Bible and some years ago were forbidden to do so. The Jews understood in Orthodoxy about the real holidays that were Biblical and Jewish and the ones that GOD only spoke about, such as Jesus and the Passover and not Jesus and Easter. Roman Catholicism also brought Hallowe'en, because of All Saints Day and also Christmas, or Christ's mass, which is nowhere mentioned in the Bible. Even the Messianic Jews did not worship in the holidays because there are no words in the Hebrew or the Greek for Christmas or Easter in the Bible.

The Jews also knew that they were the chosen people while the Roman Catholic Church said they were all that was, such as The Church, which would mean only that they were the chosen group which was not Biblical. Soon the world would know that it was for Israel and not for Rome that the new millennium would be for and it would be in Jerusalem and again not in Rome where the seven hills were. No, religion again has a lock on GOD, and since the Jews are mentioned in explicit numbers in the Bible and only the Jews, then one would think how important to GOD they are as a nation and a people that is the remnant. Israel never forced the faith on the Gentiles, even during Jesus' time, so why did the Roman Catholic Church do that? Spreading the gospel meant that each nation would have to find their own GOD, such as in Russian Orthodoxy and not like a world religion that tended to be in mostly Latin cultures even though some, like Poland, took it in. The Jews were Christian in nature, but not the Gentiles unless they were believers or saints. Only Luke in the New Testament was a Gentile of major proportion mentioned there.

Even though both of my parents' sides were Roman Catholic, I knew that I had never really understood who GOD was or anything at all about what the Bible was about. The Bible at that time was a beautifully bound book which would collect dust on it and, in fact, when I told my own father years later about the grace of GOD he just said that I was not a priest, but really knew not the reason why. Tradition, with generation after generation, kept coming in and the more it sunk in the worse it got, because what was believed was what somebody else believed and not what GOD, through the Holy Spirit was saying. As I was growing up there was nothing then that looked anything Christian as I found out later in life. Money on all sides was the only thing that counted, and more of it and so much so that the enemy had taken so many souls along with him. The only one I remember who prayed every day was my grandmother or my dad's mother, every day and lived to be over 100 years old. She was a devout woman and her faith was real. There was no other Catholic I could say that about even up to this very day. The question to be asked was, "What does it take to be a Catholic, or better yet, what does it take to be a good Catholic? Confession was made to a man or a priest when only Christ was the one who could absolve anyone from sin since it was He who died and later rose in the resurrection. Joseph and Mary were both Jewish and not Italian or Catholic, and Peter who also was Jewish, worshipped as a Jew so he could not have been the first Vicar. Jesus and all the disciples worshipped as Jews, and salvation is of the Jews and not of any Gentile religion, even if they would proclaim a true and real witness. Jesus was a Jewish man and not a Gentile, and so that meant that GOD had a very special place in His heart for the nation of Israel and His people. The branches only came in because of the disobedience of the Jews as a nation, and we can be thankful that GOD allowed that to be, so the next time you hear one say, "that Jew", be sure to remember that if it were not for a Jewish man we all would be going to Hell. Y'eshua Messiah was the Savior now for all who came to Him when the Father called them and they heard His voice and no one ever came unless the Father called. Where does Europeanism even fit into this whole picture in regard to Jesus in its origins? Rome was heathen state, and in Daniel it speaks of 4 empires that are evil and they all are Gentile empires. The roots are the Jews and not the Gentiles. Now cults and occults were in America claiming to be GOD, or better than GOD.

Whoever said that they were GOD in the flesh besides Messiah? There was no one. My parents were hardworking and rarely had little of anything, but I remember dad doing many jobs for nothing just to help people when he needed it himself. This was the peasant in dad, and yes my parents had violent fights between themselves, but somehow they showed that childlike forgiveness and benevolence time and again and did not attend church regularly and, in fact, rarely. They taught us not to steal or to sin, and yet they could not read well enough to really understand Scripture. They understood what nation and family meant as far as raising us to be GOD-fearing or else. We would cross ourselves when we went by a church, or kiss a piece of bread if we dropped it on the floor.

Many skirmishes occurred in our home with the authorities, but we as children and teenagers kept in line according somehow to a Scripture that was there from not a religion but from a people, or part of a people that were not educated but knew right from wrong and wanted their children to also know how to act. Whenever we visited people or friends or relatives, we always asked to be allowed to play outside, and we did not roam in another's home or even touch things that did not be long to us. We respected our parents no matter what and that, too, was Biblical as in "Honor Thy Father and Thy Mother or thy days shall be shortened." We did not raise our voices to our parents, and when dad said it one time, we did it. Obedience to one's elders was also very important. No matter if they were wrong, we still respected them. The things we got we took care of because we knew that mom and dad had to work hard, dad at work and mom at home, and I never remember a babysitter ever in my life! Talk about today's ever present and dangerous daycare Soviet style or by the state who would raise one's child the way government saw fit and not the way GOD saw it.

Our relatives were quite rich and always, it would seem, would be fighting about money and would not help others except, of course, one uncle who was an alcoholic and helped many people and would go to work every day. Relatives were alienated because of envy and jealousy and the religion that says go for the gusto! We did not swear as we were growing up, even though we heard it in our own house many times. Foreign languages were spoken, but only in homes or in extreme emergencies when out in the public. This was the respectful and decent thing, though I spoke only English.

The Sabbath was completely ignored in America and few if any really worshipped as a body of believers anymore. Everything seemed to be permitted, and it was not like that when I was a small boy, when almost everything had been closed in respect to GOD and that was even for unbelievers who also knew that GOD was important and a day of rest also was important to one's mental and physical wellbeing. We had gone a long way downward spiraling into a pit. Most Americans had no common knowledge about who GOD really was and did not care to know and remember Him. We had allowed ourselves to do what we wanted to do like in the Old Testament in the Book of Judges when the Israelites did just that. Russia, too, in the 19th and 20th centuries had forgotten about GOD and that had proved to be their doom also, and they were a 1,000-year Christian nation even though the way they worshipped was different from the American Biblical, but nonetheless that was their way of finding GOD through St. Cyril and St. Methodius many centuries ago.

Divorce and infidelity even amongst Christians in America became so prevalent that over 50% of those marriages were ending in divorce. Our nation had allowed materialism or socialism to enter the mainstream and then we wondered why we were having so many catastrophes and unusual weather conditions occurring in America and why so many diseases and insects of all kinds were appearing on the scene as had occurred in Pharaoh's Egypt. We ourselves had allowed the enemy into our nation as well as into our very homes by Hollywood, our pit of Hell, as well as foreign religions and liquid manure that was summoning the demons. People were getting married, even of the same sex, and there was even an insane debate about this when man knew it was evil. Instead of continuing along with what GOD had given us and not what the rich and well educated said they did, we all were doing what we wanted to do, which meant we were sinning so much more. The churches would not speak of Hell, but only about self-esteem and would sing till they were blue and the sermons were timed so that everyone could go home or either talk in church as a "social" gathering. Yes, socialism was indeed in America since we thought not like a nation with a soul, but a group, or groups of people more concerned about idiosyncrasies and fashions.

Retired people became like vagabonds and would travel here and there and did not even stay in one place, and the homes were abandoned as if they had never owned them. Disney World was visited by grownups as if the 60s had never gone away and liquid manure was what they wanted to hear time and again. Everywhere one would go where people were there was constant profanity, even by children and youth. Where had all these "barbarians" come from, since their parents were never with them? Everything that one had we had and the more materialism that came along the more we were free falling into an abyss of Hell. The elderly only thought about Social Security checks and retiring, and some were even raising their own grandchildren while the parents were as they would say, "doing their own thing".

People in positions of power did not know what authority meant because again, they believed that democracy meant freedom was the right to do anything that one wanted to do in life. They also could not lead and would do only what they were told and did not have minds of their own, even if foreigners of heathen religions were ruling them they nonetheless did what was even wrong and sinful, but did not know Scripture so they did anything just so they had security for the moment and self-preservation also for the moment. Even our peasants were being destroyed daily and had lost their foundation since few were left and their memory of GOD was in party ideology and not in Him. they were following in the footsteps of the rich and well educated and not Scripture. The American Jew had become the most materialistic that I believe I had ever seen or even ever read about. Israel itself kept getting more brutal because we as a nation only cared about ourselves and used our freedom to do just what we wanted to do and not what GOD wanted us to do and required, yes required, us to do for others first and with the heart.

Even our athletes were out of shape and wore earrings and set the worst kind of example for our children and youth and were no better than Hollywood. If we could not see it then we did not want to believe it was possible. America had become the savage youth because our years in existence were 3 and a little more. One day, though, "Babylon" would fall and all this materialism would make Americans panic and not necessarily a war, or even a foreign religion because if we removed all obstacles to GOD we still would be rebellious as in the 60s but even worse than that. We had become a civilized and sophisticated nation, which meant that we had no time for GOD at all and that with each waking moment our minds and hearts were constantly on sin and the love of money. We were telling the world how to live when we ourselves did not know, or want to know, the first thing about real Christianity in Biblical form, and even our Bibles were revised to mock GOD Himself and we ignored that too and felt politics was the all important way to get things for ourselves in life. We were obsessed with power in any form, and even amongst our own family, friends, co-workers, and relatives. We had become worse than the animal kingdom because anyone, and there were a few, who had GODLY morals would be looked upon as oddballs and the abnormal was the "norm" in our heathen society, which was not just anti-Christian, but dabbled in the occult right out in the open and yet if one was caught carrying a Bible, they had to feel ashamed or at least we in America thought so.

Children were not allowed to be children and held to be the smartest of the smartest and were taught more about education than about a holy GOD, and we wondered why they were ruining themselves! We had given them Hollywood and the asinine athletes who cared more about ego and self than about their fellow man. Our athletes were slaves themselves to the people who bought them and controlled them with materialism and wanted them to emulate themselves in order to make more money and get more power. How much money was enough, since some had enough to last probably 1 or 2 thousand years? Children also were abusing parents and not just parents abusing children, and the numbers continued to grow and grow. There was no rhyme or reason to our madness, but since GOD had been removed, the insanity had come in full swing and we felt most fulfilled because we could "eat, drink and be merry" with no questions asked.

Gluttony was one problem we never discussed, but only being overweight, since being over weight meant that it was more a physical thing and not a spiritual thing. Fast foods and restaurants were making out so well that it showed in the way even our own religious leaders were built and that was obese. It also told us not only about our loose tongues, but how much we put into our mouths without stopping.

We were existing with no purpose in life and we continued to complain about nothing in particular, but just for the sake of what mood we happened to be in. We disciplined our children also to the mood we were in and our worst enemies were amongst our own loved ones. We forgot about agape love and forgiveness that our own consciences were becoming seared so that anything the Holy Spirit was saying was being blocked by our very own sin. Everything was in excess and in access so much so that anything one wanted to get one could get even if they were poor, and that included drugs and free sex. Our bodies were not the temple of GOD, and even our old ways before we had become believers were coming back to us with no problem or effort at all. Everything had a price tag on it, and that is what we lived for. Even things made in Red China by Christian slaves we bought and devoured up, which meant that as long as we purchase these things slavery in Red China would grow and grow and our capitalism would also continue to grow into socialism because after all capitalisms comes socialisms.

Things were multiplying, but love was dying within the soul of our nation and charity meant we could give to others what we no longer wanted or needed and it was not our last pence but only our excess. We had an abundant supply of evils from Pandora's

Box that things in our very own homes were occurring there and they were too horrible to talk about. My own mentor had warned me about this time and again many years ago and at that time he was not a believer, but seemed to have an Eastern mindset of Christianity, and not the West's mindset of John Locke. We had been warned, but to tell any of us was like we all had gone deaf and dumb and become oblivious to all around us and what we ate, slept and worked for was nothingness. It all would mean nothing and would never be remembered by anybody ever again, just like in ages past with empires that had come and gone. We were all going for the golden ring that was nothing more than more of this world, and we worshipped GOD with our mouths and not with our hearts or our actions. We had to be told by man what we should do, but if GOD said, through His Word what we should want to do we totally ignored it, and this was a very scary thing since this had fallen on believers too. Our churches looked more like warehouse supermarkets with their strange architecture.

Our children were given organizations of all kinds for exploitation, such as the youth organizations that competed to place young children and not adolescents into the Olympics, the sodomite organization of the Girls' Scouts of America; the Boys' Scouts of America that was to be like Hitler's Youth Organization with sodomites was to make waves in our Nazi court systems and many in congress, Big Brothers and Big Sisters should have said deviants wanted for child molestation; Little League of Williamsport and any other little league baseball organization that used coaches, and I use that word liberally since there was only a criteria to win at any costs, the YMCA and the YWCA where there were closed doors, PAL where there was racism, the Children's Miracle Network, the Jerry Lewis Telethon that had drug carnivals all over the country, et cetera. We were giving our own children to exploiters and exploitation so that we could make money or seek fame for ourselves. Even many churches, especially in Roman Catholicism, were using homosexuality against the child's will and molesting children for many years. Private little sports programs that involved the high schools, junior high schools, and even elementary were also involved. Drug dealing also could be included and the children that were taken in were recruiting other children to come along as well as Jehovah Witnesses, the Mormon Church, the Seventh Day Adventists, etc. all were getting to them when they were young, as a Pied Piper would. There was hardly anywhere one could place their child that did not have Sodomites or child exploitation involved with it, and the worst of it all is that we all knew about it and most continued to go along with the winner!

The hospitals were non-profit just like about 1,000 other organizations like the United Way, the March of Dimes, Easter Seals, the Shriners, etc. who all promoted the Nazi mentality of infanticide, homosexuality, euthanasia, anti-Semitism. Even Reformed Judaism could take its place along with Roman Catholicism and the Episcopalian church for homosexuality and pedophilia because wherever one was, the other was certain . . . The churches would not get involved because they were too busy with self-esteem, or too busy with self-preservation and the rights and wrongs of their "Christianity" instead of spreading the gospel one by one to others to protect the orphaned, the widowed, the poor, etc. As long as one had for oneself the luxuries of life and the accolades that followed, then all would be right.

We had failed as parents, as priests, as providers, as fathers, as husbands, as uncles, as grandfathers, etc. to do what GOD wanted to do, and we knew it, and it was not because of ignorance, but more because of a lackadaisical attitude and apathy amongst the biological and non-biological fathers in society. The authority figure, whether in the home or outside the home, was no longer respected since the sodomites, as few as there were, were pushing their brand of socialism where equality meant equivalency between the sexes and women were treated such as in the military and in sports as butches. The sport itself had nothing to do with it, nor the fighting. It was to neutralize the young males into "womanhood" so that they would become like full fledged Nazis had become during World War II in Nazi Germany, and that was homosexual pedophiles. The enemy was working overtime through these people because they believed in the ideology that said there is not GOD and also for the destruction of all mankind. Principalities were definitely at work. The more we brought in foreign religions, the more the enemy took a stronghold in America. Even Christians in this nation could not really see through this facade that the enemy was using to get at all our future generations no matter what he had to do. Yet we as adults would be accountable not to anyone here because the laws made it that way, but to a holy and righteous GOD in the end. We were too busy worrying about materialism whether it was in paying our bills or buying things that we just did not need, including food for gluttony.

Civil rights' socialism, as with affirmative action, was being used again as it was in Nazi Germany when the Jews were not allowed to hold any public or government offices because it was the Jews' fault that homosexuality in Nazi Germany was brought to the public's eye, and that was a no no for the Nazi Party since they ruled the country and were going for the rest of Europe. This same ideology was being sold now in America by the relatives of the same groups or families that had it then in Nazi Germany, such as the Krupps, Thuns, Janssens, Thyssens who made the ovens for Auschwitz. This was the ideology of this New Age Government that was setting up the Antichrist's system, another German idea, in the world.

Our own socialist judges in America had learned quickly from the 60s generation that crime does pay, so their rendered decisions were equivalent to those at the Nuremburg trials in the sense that the judges there themselves, at least some of them, were Soviet Gulag judges who were trying their fellow brother criminals in court who believed in the same ideology that promoted the lie called socialism, even though in Nazi Germany it was homosexual racist Nazi socialism, and in Russia it was class warfare lead by Karl Marx and Engels ideology to despise man and to destroy man in whatever way they could and their followers were in love with one another as well as with this ideology that promoted the lie. That is why in Nazi Germany, when the ally Forces came to the concentration camps they were so sickened that they wanted to execute the Nazis there on the spot, since what they were really looking at was homosexuality gone wild without any kind of control or criminalization for it since it was covered up. But the Jewish Holocaust victims knew well enough about it, if they could relive it by telling it to others, but then someone had to ask and someone had to find these victims before they all died off since they were all very elderly. Would now the entire world, along with the Arabs who also subscribed to this sodomy, fall into this New Age Nazism that would use laboratories to do experimentation on human beings, when the sperm met the egg called conception, or embryonic stem cell research, or actually with people who did not know what kind of guinea pigs they would be used for since now all governments were falling in line with this New Age Nazism, including the Israelis. That is where it got really scary, because in Israel is where the Antichrist would sit on the throne and take control by force once he had deceived his "allies". The scenario that appeared on the horizon was one that was catastrophic in nature, not to mention the red ideology of Red China and Moscow. These ideologies had nothing to do with the peasants or all of the people in these nations, but the leaders who would incite and control billions, since the evil power laid in their hands and now America, through capitalism was helping them. This was nothing new since Armand Hammer had done it in Russia for Occidental Petroleum, and even our own churches such as Reverend Shuler on television was going along with his New Age crystal rainbow cathedral.

Our own banks in America had become our "houses of worship" since we had the love of money as our own god. Everything revolved around money and what it could buy, sell, extort, deceive, bargain, etc. Our worship of money was this love of it and brought with many kinds of evils. We were content to have it that way, even though GOD Himself gave us warning after warning and still we would not listen to what He was saying to us even after the tragic 9/11 event when GOD had taken down His hand of protection and allowed, but did not cause, what had happened there. Many of our own lawyer politicians were homosexuals and not just the clergy in the major denominations as well as in most all youth organizations. This was their main reason for being involved always around children and youth so that they could exploit them and in some cases like Jeffrey Dahmer and John Wayne Gacy, who both were homosexual pedophiles, murdered and cannibalized. The media and Hollywood and government and churches were just some of the areas in our own society that promoted this sick and deviant obsession with Sodom and Gomorrah. Abraham, in his time, had picked the other side of land that was not as attractive as Sodom and Gomorrah in which Lot and his family did. The media was constantly paying tribute to those involved in evil, whatever it was, and had sold out America for money, fame and fortune. This cancer, though, would spread to eliminate them just like the Bolsheviks had in Russia eliminated all its opponents and even its own, and also like Stalin who eliminated people in his own party. The same would happen in America where different ideologies and not different denominations would accrue and metastasize into a great leviathan known as the second "Babylon". Some actually thought that this was the right thing to do since that was all they were brought up on and GOD had been removed and forgotten all about in our very own society. What could never happen here happened, and it happened in not the way most thought it would, but amongst ones own loved ones and family, what was left of that, and it continued to grow and grow until . . . .

In my own life I had once been attacked by a Greek man when I was 14 years old, but fortunately got away and so I knew the deviousness and hellishness of this abnormality.

We were spending billions of dollars for AIDS, but yet we were promoting homosexuality, the origins for AIDS and HIV. This was this Dr. Jekyll and Mr. Hyde syndrome that constantly was bombarding government and the people into accepting and promoting the abomination that GOD said was an abomination. We continued to inject society with this AIDS that was cancer-causing and inflicted upon others and ourselves this insanity that all would be well in utopia as long as we continued with this type of insanity. Who was there really to speak out for all the innocent children, not so much for when they got older but for now when they would be molested and they would be molested? The so called conservatives continued to go to the very same churches that promoted this deviancy yet even churches in Africa said "we repudiate all this and shall have no part in this evil" and so immediately separated themselves from them and from it. We were throwing good money after bad money to find, as they said, a cure when the origin itself was being promoted and in poor neighboring Africa a second strain was moving across their continent that would find its way to America in Sodom and Gomorrah land. The Nazis and the communists, as well as Islam, with all 3 being anti-Semite were growing more and more in America. They had a stronghold here for good and wishful thinking, or democracy, which was Greek oriented and mob rule, would not work. The oriental mindset of Greek mythology would also do no good since one blink and it would all be done. The American Biblical and the Messianic Jews were the only ones, plus some other Jews of the Orthodox persuasion also fought to have no part in it. It was the Jews again that would have to most likely lead the way to the deviant and sick and psychiatric abomination.

What would happen to my grandchildren? It probably had already happened with me not knowing where they were at all times and being suspect that at least two fathers were part of the Sodomite community who both had extremely good jobs. One was around youth and sometimes children many times. This was indeed an insane and uncaring and ungrateful society, since GOD had given us many good things to work with and we used to destroy not necessarily ourselves, but our innocent loved ones such as small children.

One employer in fact, that I had was such a gold digger that some of the men that worked for him had lost their homes because he refused to feel any compassion for the low wages he was paying, and he continued on in his pursuit of roman Catholicism's happiness in slavery. All that mattered was avarice, and he did not show the slightest remorse about anything or anyone. He also might have been a homosexual well disguised because many men that he had hired were just that, homosexuals. This was indeed a man with a seared conscience. People who were politically correct were being promoted even faster than the Masons. The Jesuits hated them, but nonetheless were like them in so many ways. America was for whatever profit that could be made and then some, and the then some was the major problem. There was no thought given to humanity and no compassion to the ignoramuses who were leading America to destruction so quickly. Many had already died horrible deaths in car crashes that caught on fire or sudden heart attacks with no warning, but still others pursued the same course, of course, until it happened to them and then it was too late. There was no charity at all from the Roman Catholics, but only the guilt trip of "I helped you" and that did nothing for the poor who actually did not really ask for their help, just like they did not ask for their religion to be shoved down their throats, that was anything but what Scripture had said it to be.

Some of the guys that I worked with would, at rare times, do certain things together just to stay in touch, but most of it was mundane and had hardly anything to do with GOD. There were about 7 of us who would, for instance, bowl or play pool together and, at least in any group no matter what, they were in the closet homosexuals. I knew who they were but did not say anything to them or anybody else but kept it to myself. This group consisted of Earl, who was a supervisor and of German extraction. He was ready to retire and had a blasé attitude about life. Next came Charles who was Jewish, but one would never have known it, and he was kind but so very liberal in all that he did. Then there were two brothers, Sam and Mark, with Sam being the older and brighter of the two. Both were involved with construction and both were Catholics with large families and had little time except for work and money. Then there was Jack, who was a loner and kind of a strange sort of fellow who I took for a homosexual. The last one was Dave, who was an easygoing English guy who was so liberal with his private life that he used to think of sex as if it was like drinking a glass of water. These were the guys I had met in the workplace and who I knew were not Christians, but who I did, at least one time, witness to before I called it quits with them too.

"I am the captain now on this team and you need to understand that we need to win these 3 games in order to qualify for the championship at the end of this year, so bowl all good games," said Earl.

"Just because you are a thick-headed German does not mean we all are the same," said Charles. The guys all started to laugh.

"Dave, I guess you can bowl before me since you are a better bowler than I am. Okay?" said Jack.

"Okay, but be careful no women are around because it might distract me."

Earl said, "Sam and Mark, you both can pick me up by bowling 2nd and 3rd after me so that it looks pretty impressive. Okay?

"Whatever you say, just so long as we can place a bet on the highest average for the night amongst all of us. Okay?" said Sam and Mark.

I said, "I guess then I shall bowl last to make it look like I am the weakest bowler and in order to pick up wherever I can for the team."

As we began to bowl the other team, which were a lively group of rednecks from another company, I said to all that I would be official scorekeeper for both sides since I was last, and all agreed to that. As we continued to bowl through the night Earl had such consistency that he amazed even the other team, since Earl practiced time and again to get it right and this night it was paying off. Earl had 7 strikes in a row, so the score card looked something like this: XXX=30, X=90, X=120, and another strike X = 150, and that was only in the fifth frame of bowling. It looked like he could possibly bowl a 300, but we all kept quiet about it which was the usual thing to do whenever someone was bowling this hot. The rest of our team as well as theirs pretty much were bowling their averages except, again, for Earl. As the night continued and we finished the first game, Earl had a 270 score in the 9th game.

Everybody was amazed and was totally in shock. Earl was good, but not this good and Earl himself knew it too! He only needed to throw 3 more strikes for a perfect game of 300 in the final and 10th frame. This first ball was a strike and there was no doubt about it as he released the ball the same he had done 9 times earlier. The second ball in the 10th frame went exactly the same way with the same result, and now he needed only one more strike to have a perfect game and be put down in the record book for all time in our league and at the bowling alley. Earl this time took a little more time and concentration before he released the ball just to make sure his steps and the ball were dry and the alley was perfect according to him and how he felt mentally. I could exactly see him trying to picture in his own mind how he had up to now thrown 11 straight strikes in a row and with never a spare to even have to make. As he approached the dots on the wooden floor and took his position, I felt an uncannyness about what was going to happen, but was not certain about it to say the least. Earl was ready to release the ball and then for some reason he stopped and did not foul, but went back again into his stand and concentrated harder. I had always felt one should just continue what one does and not think too much about it because when they did, then doubt would come into play in one's mind. But Earl was a tough-minded and persistent battler no matter his personality. He was a consistent bowler, but as I said before, he did not bowl this hot since I had been bowling with him. He looked around, then at me and I just stared at him and then he asked me, "Is this my final ball?"

I then said, "Yes!" I did not say maybe, or it could be or anything else, but yes. He then stared for a short time at the alley and the pins and then started moving forward and then released the ball with the same precision he had so far done tonight. The ball slid a little to the right and then hooked in from the right side into the head pin and was spinning so much it tipped the head pin, which gave the front pins such movement that all of the pins in the front were going down, but too quickly. Would the pins fly around the back pins and would the ball itself slide so much that it would not carry the 10 pin? As the ball kept sliding, the pins meanwhile kept spinning like tops and had a domino effect on the back pins, numbers 7, 8, 9 and 10 except that it looked, for a split second, like the 7 and 10 split would open and then somehow a rear pin in the back hit the 7 pin and the 10 pin was wobbling but would it go down was the question. Just as it looked like it might not go down, the 7 pin somehow from behind came sliding across the alley and just tipped the 10 pin. The 10 pin wobbled a little more, which seemed like forever and had to go down before the pin rack arm came down or it would be considered a standing pin or could even possibly knock it down, and that would be disastrous for Earl's perfect game. The pin for some unknown reason, edged to the gutter and fell on its own accord. The strike was made official and the 300 perfect game was Earl's and what a yell Earl and the rest of us let out as that all occurred at the very last moment. We all got up, including the other team and in fact others in the bowling alley had been watching from the electronic board posted above where I kept the score. They all started to cheer for Earl and his perfect 300 game. Yes, this might just be the night to witness to Earl and friends since this was sort of on the miraculous and Earl had never before bowled a 300, but had a high average of about 239. Would it be possible to have at least another person come into GOD'S kingdom since the Holy Spirit was moving tonight no matter how much the enemy was trying to discourage me from doing what I was commanded in Scripture to do at least one time to an unbeliever so that I would never regret having never tried to share the Gospel with all these guys, but especially Earl.

After we won our three games by a large margin, my mind and heart were still on the first game and what I believe GOD had given to me to work with, since this meant someone's eternal resting place or separation from GOD forever. I had to speak to these guys before they had the first round of beer, but how would I do that since we always at least started with one after we rolled the final game, win or lose? All I knew was that this now was my part in tonight's game and this would be not just for life but for all eternity! The spirit was always willing, but our flesh was weak, so I had to depend not on my self but on the Holy Spirit to interpret to someone who could not understand what it meant to be saved, unless they had become saved themselves. I prayed as never before and approached Earl as a true friend.

"Earl, what a game you bowled tonight, a perfect 300 game and just like GOD, your game was perfect too."

"Well thanks, Luke, I really appreciate that and I have been wanting to say something to you after the game immediately, but everything got so out of hand and excited I could not."

"Earl what was it that you wanted to say to me?"

"Well, do you remember when I had one more strike to go and I turned around and asked you if this is my final ball?"

"Yes Earl, I remember that very much because it took me by surprise that you, of all people would ask me when I know how conscientious you are about your game."

"Well, something or someone said to me 'turn around and acknowledge Luke before you roll this final ball!' All I could do was what I did not even think to do but to acknowledge just what I had heard. So I turned around and did that and then it all happened so quickly the perfect game. Does that make any sense to you at all?"

"Earl, it makes a lot of sense, and now that you have said that, what I have to say to you may even sound stranger when you hear this. Earl, did you ever know Jesus personally and accept Him as your Savior?"

"No, but I am ready to listen to whatever it is you have to say, especially since I heard some kind of voice and Luke, by the way, do not tell any of the other guys what I heard or they might think me to be a little strange, and if you would not have just mentioned about Jesus I most likely would never have mentioned the fact about that voice that said to acknowledge you before I threw that last strike. Does that make sense to you?"

"Earl, it makes all the sense in the world now that I understand that your perfect game was some kind of omen or sign that you were open to the Holy Spirit and the grace that GOD was ready to share with you. Earl, I am so glad that you did mention that voice to me, and I shall not say anything to anyone, but are you ready to accept Jesus into your heart this very moment?"

"Yes, Luke, I am and thank you again for your friendship that you always showed to me."

Right then and there I shared with Earl the prayer of salvation and he accepted the Lord into His heart with me privately. I then got up and went to the men's room. When I had returned, there was another commotion near where Earl and I had been sitting. As I made my way to that area I could see that this commotion was not one of joy, but of tears and hysterical crying by mostly the women around. There as I looked where Earl and I were sitting, I saw Earl lying on the floor with his eyes closed. He was not breathing, and one of the guys was doing CPR on Earl, but to no avail. Earl had expired. Some of our guys asked me if I was not just talking to Earl a few minutes ago and I said yes, but that I excused myself and had to go to the men's room and when I had left Earl was in the best of moods. What had happened so quickly while I had gone to the men's room no more than probably 3 minutes and within that time Earl was dead and gone. But then I thought back. He had accepted Jesus into His heart and just in time so there was no time for me to wait, since Earl had only a few minutes left to his mortal life on this earth. All I could do is thank GOD for guiding me and thank Him for giving me the courage to do what maybe I might not have done. That indeed was a scary thought since this involved minutes. Earl now was with the Lord in Heaven and was not in the other place where there is a burning lake of fire. Tonight's evening was sad though, since I had made a real good friendship with Earl and the way he spoke to me so earnestly and the way he held our team together and for making my night so wonderful earlier when he bowled that perfect game and I had the opportunity to tell him how much I really cared about him. I shall miss my good friend, Earl, but I now know that he is where Jesus is.

Later that night I said to my wife that I was thankful that I did go to the bowling match tonight because what had happened was a miracle, even though I did feel sad not to have Earl as my friend and my captain. I really loved this man with all of my heart, and our real friendship did not even begin to happen, but I know the Lord had His reasons for taking Earl with Him at that very moment. I did not have to cry, but I could rejoice like the Japanese do when someone dies in the family but they do cry when someone is born into this world. Can I ever doubt the reality of Jesus and the Holy spirit and how powerful and real they are?

I thought to myself the game of bowling had a sort of hidden message in itself in that there were 10 frames like 10 months on the Jewish calendar, and for a perfect game like Earl had rolled, there were 12 strikes with every third strike to be called a turkey and counted as 30 points, plus the fact that Earl was the lead off bowler and I was the last bowler that night. "Those who are first shall be last and those who are last shall be first" I know had referred to something else, but in this case it applied to Earl and myself and how we came into GOD'S kingdom. Even a perfect game meant to me that night just as GOD is perfect in all his ways, Earl had thrown a perfect game as a sort of sign or omen that something special was to occur, something that had to do with a perfect GOD. Earl did not now need to retire, for in heaven there would be much to do from now on. Thee had been much made about retirement in America, as if one would retire from life itself in order just to die, or live the life of Riley with nothing to do for anybody but self. Much of this Padré mentality had infected the elderly especially, and many younger folks resented this, since they still had to work for a living and the elderly seemed not to really care about what was going on in the world but only in their own lives or immediate circle. Social Security had ruined the elderly, which was FDR's ideology of socialism. More welfare to collect and then to pass along to ones who never even put a dime into the system, and now this President wanted to change the law that said one had to be in America and work for 10 years in order to collect—notice already they are waiting for a handout—to 5 years just of citizenship if one could call it that. This culture could never assimilate into an American culture because it was a foreign conquistador society. That is why when they came here they were so arrogant that they naturally felt it was all theirs to take over here in America, and our government told them as such. The Ugly American would work because it had worked in the 60s rebellion with the blacks, when the suburbanites felt guilty for whatever reason they had to play the go along role that the Great Society and the New Deal had set up just for them and that would make all things better. But it did not; it only created more resentment because it showed an admission of guilt for something they had no control over or, for that matter, were not even born at that time. America had gone too far to declare "freedom" without telling the other side what freedom really involved, and not just misappropriated government welfare as had occurred in Russia when the peasants were asked to give up their land for their freedom and then told to barter with cash, which they had no concept of, and then what would occur to them was even a worse case scenario of no land and no agricultural background which lead to alcoholism and other vices that were created by the monarch and the socialists who promoted this "solution' without giving thought to the fact that the peasants were not educated enough to understand that all could be taken from them so easily and, of course, the upper elites meaning the rich and well educated, would mostly benefit from all of this until, of course, someone like Lenin would come along with a little help from his friends, the Judaizers and, of course, the Germans who had a scandal to hide and had all to gain from this to leave Russia in a butcher's hand and, in fact, more than one butcher's hand, but one after the other who all were just this like in our own Mafioso, but even worse, since about over 110,000,000 would be involved in deaths when all was said and done. We in America relied too much on our reputation of the past until Vietnam when the country had such a weak moral fiber that that war itself, if one could call it that, would just about destroy America and not the Communists in Hollywood and the media. America had become that immoral during the 60s and since then has spiraled downward year after year, but we thought ground was being made, which was only self-delusion.

Well, back to the bowling incident that I was telling about and the one fact that I later found out was that Jack, the one guy I thought a homosexual was just an effeminate man who was raised by his mother, but who was a Christian and that is what happens when one judges quickly without even praying on it. Jack, in fact, led the other guys or at least some of them, into a prayer group after he had witnessed that very night after I had left, so seeds were planted not just by me, but mostly by Jack because he too had the Holy Spirit working within him. There are men who are effeminate, but who are not homosexuals and one must be careful to distinguish them, especially since another's reputation was on the line.

The prayer group that Jack had really started with the other bowlers were made up of Charles, Dave and Jack himself, but not Sam and Mark the twins who were both Catholics. The Catholics were the hardest to witness to, even harder than the Jewish people and even some KGB agents. The enemy had his claws into that religion because prosperity was it's main forte and materialism is very hard to give up when it repays you for your loyalty by way of affluence and in Latin America it was the Padre' mentality. One had to search high and low to find an ex-Catholic who wanted to really hear the Gospel of Jesus Christ since He Himself was a Jew and many knew how the Vatican felt about the Jews for centuries which were as bad as the Masons except from the opposite side. So Dave the Englishman, Charles the Jewish fellow and Jack himself attended faithfully. I am told this small group, or Bible study. Earl had passed away and I had one to my own Bible study do that accounted for all 7 of us who had once bowled

The many jobs I had consisted of many different things from factory labor work, which was probably the least inspiring because it was all noise and no brains, from a one time government job that dealt with adolescents and children, which was also horrible because there a Catholic was also the President of this non-profit children's home and while they ate filet mignon the youth got hamburgers and fries and also the president was able to build a brand new home, how unique. Yes Roman Catholicism from all of my years of experience was least tolerant of Judeo-Christianity most of all and of course the Jews as with Pope Pius XII during World War II.

My present job had a Roman Catholic president also and this time almost for sure I knew he was a homosexual since when I was hired almost 40% of them worked in the offices. If I did not already say, but we also had a monsignor in the Roman Catholic tradition who was a homosexual pedophile and also a state senator who helped campaign for JFK years ago and who also was a Roman Catholic, but a state senator and lawyer what else and who was a lifer in politics for many years and neither one was touched for child molestation ever which was hard to believe. Our entire area was predominantly German and also many Arabs lived in the area and now many Roman Catholics were getting promoted, that is the ones that subscribed to the Sodom and Gomorrah agenda. Many Greeks, some English and also the minorities were getting positions they never ever got before even with civil rights. This disorder was bringing with it the statute that said all homosexuals had even more special rights in America and since my area where I lived *was* heavily populated with Germans from World War II that meant that Sodom and Gomorrah would also be a huge part so the pieces of the puzzle were coming together. Many ex-Nazis for example took on Islamic names shortly after World War II and many Nazis also were pulled out of their German factories by the FBI during that time. There were only about 11,000 Jewish people in the area and the ones that were like Samaritans were mostly Catholics who knew nothing at all about their rich heritage and traded it in for a cult. Yes my area had many Sodomites around at high positions and were promoted often just because of their political correctness. More and more were also corning from India where the swastika came from and where the Nazis also "extradited" to America this area. Nonetheless I was not going to move, or give up my country, or residence ones who thought America was a politically correct nation. I would not, as they used to say, go where you like it". This was my nation and I was in for the long haul and was not about to relinquish it to Sodomites, or Nazis, just because they controlled the companies and the people, or had been bought out by certain individual ones who had billions of dollars that they controlled. Most Americans here went along with this type of "Islamic Jihad" because many Moslems controlled businesses with oil money that England and Germany was bringing to America. Along with France, Americans had lost their will to defend what they believed in, since money is what they loved most of all. Roman Catholicism certainly did not help, since as I said before it was all about opportunists, or affluence that kept them working for whomever just so they got to drive the new big expensive car, a new home, sex at anytime, but most of all the "go along with the winner" mentality that the Germans had always been known for, plus their virulent anti-Semitism. All the large groups here were anti-Semitic: The Roman Catholics, the Masons, the Germans, the English, the Arabs, which was a growing population, the Hispanics, which also was a growing population since the last two presidential administrations, were easy on immigration, or let us just say have no immigration for certain types of people from certain cultures since they had relatives of the same persuasion. Also a number of Polish Catholics and Italian Catholics that could only use the word "Jew" in a derogatory sense and never used the words "Jewish people" or "Jewish person". There were also many envious Greeks who were like Orientals in the clannishness, but the Hispanics appeared to be that way, except they would force themselves onto one and many American girls were getting pregnant and some even married to them to be chic. The whole entire culture was dumbing down to multiculturalism. One of my own relatives had told me years go, and I thought at that time it was absurd, but now no longer did I think as such, that the government and the rich and well educated waned to dumb d own the average American in society so that the wool could easily be pulled over their eyes and they could made as so called "slaves" from other cultures that were at least two centuries behind in education and in science and technology not to mention a lack of the Judeo-Christian culture. Also, there were, as always, the Judaizers who would go along with anything that would destroy the moral soul of any nation, like Trotsky had done in Russia. We now were a nation of misfits that would attack each other, since there was a total different type of belief system or systems now in America and not the Judeo-Christian culture that we had from the beg inning. When men wore earrings and women had tattoos on them and served in the military as fighting soldiers and other young men would not (because they were sodomites), it told one with enough common sense that what our soldiers were fighting for was not what the government told them they were fighting for, or the rich and well educated. All these lies were producing violence here and around the world. Soon all of this would catch up to us. There were some Americans that still believed in the old faith system, but they were far and few in between.

There was an other group of guys I knew, but this group was made up of athletes only.

Amongst the athletes there were some wrestlers, baseball players, tennis players, basketball players and football players not to mention a few pool players. In order to bring into perspective about 15 of these athletes I will first start with one at a time and give a kind of personal account of their background in brief, plus the sport that they played not always in organized sports' settings, but from a neighborhood setting that would play anybody in our city, or in the surrounding areas.

The first 2 athletes were twins and were wrestlers and their names were Tim and Tyrone, who both came from a fatherless family with only a mother and did not know anything about GOD but were truly dedicated to their sport and were even competitive amongst themselves. Tim was one of the strongest and best all around athletes in wrestling and in baseball and his brother was good in wrestling and somewhat good in baseball, but was more of the sportsman for hiking and camping and served a hitch in Vietnam with the United States Marine Corps while Tim never served. They both would do each morning while in high school about 150 sit-ups and push-ups every morning. They had tremendous stamina and would lift weights for that and not for bulk which meant absolutely nothing, unless one was going competition for body building which was an oddity. Tim was a good baseball pitcher, but had problems in his sex life because he thought shacking up was okay, even when he had gotten married and later had 5 sons who all were some kind of athletes. Tyrone was more loyal to one wife but had gotten a divorce and was married twice with about 4 children. Tyrone got a purple heart in Vietnam for being wounded while there and always liked to be outdoors and got a teaching degree-but never used it ever. Tim was an all around handyman with machinery and mechanics.

The next guy was Robert who as a youth was a redneck and later matured after military service in the Navy to a decent family man and had 4 children, 3 boys and I girl and was a wrestler, baseball player, football player and basketball player. His best sport though 1 felt was wrestling. The 3 above guys all were short but were built low to the ground and had good balance. Robert, or Bob, sometimes had a very explosive temper.

The next two guys were brothers, but had completely different personalities. Mike, the oldest brother, spoke 4 languages and wrote and read them as well, and they were Greek, English, German and Thai. John, his youngest brother, was not very coordinated, but Mike was even though Mike was 6' 2" tall and about 250 pounds. He had quick hands and a quick mind in football, and John was just fair in football and was the more vociferous of the two. Both were raised by a grandmother who was Greek. Mike served 30 years later in the military and John got involved in politics.

Bill was the next athlete who really was an excellent gymnast and used to like to go hunting, and his brother-in-law was only so good at football but was an excellent sharp shooter as Bill was. Bill had part Indian in him and was usually very calm about things. He also, along with his brother-in-law Hank, was in Vietnam. Bill was okay in football, but always tried hard. Neither of these guys either went to church or ever talked about GOD.

Next came Fred and his military mindset even when he played football, but was very strong like a peasant and worked very hard even when he was young—He was in the army as an MP, but was too wild about guns and was like a redneck even though he grew up in the city itself. He had been stationed in Korea for a while and gotten married to a Korean woman and had one son.

Then came Dave who was soft spoken and was better at pool than at the physical sports. He was not an academic, and in fact none of the above were, but they were fun to play sports with, since they did it with all they had and we had good times. Dave's daughter had died of a drug overdose.

Marvin was the next athlete and was about 6' 7" tall and was a Negro who played basketball the best and was a distant relative of an old NFL football player who had a bad heart, but nonetheless would sneak out on his mother to play basketball and some football.

Next came Roger who was a very good pitcher and basketball player with excellent jumping ability and could touch the rim which was 10 feet high, and he was about 5; 10" tall. He was a DI at Fort Dix and told me some horrible stories about how young and how inexperienced the trainees were at Fort Dix and even described to me in full detail some of the weapons we had in Vietnam and how the Vietcong fought. Dave had about 4 rolls of ribbons when he wore his uniform. He had been stationed in. Germany and had 2 hitches in Nam. He was in heavy artillery and had gone deaf in one ear. He believed Vietnam was a poor man's conflict so people like Bill Clinton never had to fight for their country and there was a lottery that one could get drafted from. At this time Mohammed Ali refused to serve as Moslem in the Vietnam conflict Roger was also an easy going guy, but also was loose with his morals in regard to sex and drinking. The military would either make, or break a man or youth. One of the guys described it as being under "Communism" because someone always was telling you what to do all the time. Roger many times had to write letters to parents back in the states about how their son died or got killed in action. Roger used to at times wake up in a cold sweat after he left the military for good.

The next 3 guys were all mediocre players in any of the physical sports, but played nonetheless because they knew all of us and we had a camaraderie amongst all of us. All these 3 guys were from better income families.

Scott, Brian and Carl all were fairly good at pool and bowling. There was nothing in particular about them that stood out because they kind of followed the crowd. Nonetheless they played mostly football and some baseball with us in the city. Again there were no coaches that coached us. We did all our own coaching and would play anybody that wanted to scrimmage us, including high schools, colleges, yes colleges, and other sports programs. Much to others' surprise, we had an excellent record of wins and losses. These were the 15 guys, or most of them, that played sports and I played sports with when growing up and hardly any of us played for any school because most of us worked after high school. There were no free rides. We took care of our own without government help and the accolades of ego coaches who were in it for the glory, whether they were good or bad coaches, and most were bad, as far as fundamentals. Too many were teachers and were already college soaked with socialism and the ego mentality of the 60's.

Some of our most exciting games came in different sports such as one game in football on a very chilly autumn afternoon on the weekend we played another group of guys with no equipment on for either side. It was scoreless and I was quarterbacking, but we were getting nowhere at all and the ground was somewhat damp and slippery. Well one time when we went on defense and I was playing defensive back with their wide receiver, but staying back, their quarterback threw across his body and across the entire field from one side to the other to his tall end as the football was on target and he was about to catch it high with both hands I somehow timed the ball and stepped in front of him to intercept the ball and run almost the total length of the field in the opposite direction for a touchdown which won the game for us and was the only score of the game. Very rarely did anybody ever kick field goals, or even extra points. I was so excited that I finally contributed to our team cause in a positive way.

At another athletic event that we had we were playing basketball and there were only a few more points to be scored to win the name since we played by points and not by time and small Bob stole the ball and made the winning layup in our own basket to win an outdoor full court game against a pretty good team. There were other times when Tim, one of the twins, would pitch no hit, or one hit ball and who threw hard, but was always very accurate and did not tire. I was a catcher and liked when he pitched because of his consistent accuracy.

Yes, there were many good times we had for sporting events: instead of us hanging on the streets and guess what, nobody had to tell us to stay out of trouble, because we were all too busy with school, work, home and good leisure time in sports that had no drinking, or drugs, or women while we played our games. This was a unique group of guys who probably did more to help their community than even the local churches did in regards to setting a good example and not prima donnas to the younger ones, or ones, that also had younger brothers and sisters and cousins. This was a fun group of guys who loved to play the sport for the sake of the sport and not for hero media worship.

On a heavier note I also remember talking to older men myself about politics. I remember that one man used to say that the National Democratic Party was pro-Communist and the National Republican Party was pro-Nazi and that is why most Jewish people voted the Democratic ticket and also because they thought that Roosevelt was their friend, but little did they know that he helped socialism worldwide which is what Nazi Germany was. It was the form of socialism that was racial nationalism, but they fell for the lie that it was strictly fascism which is when something is privately owned, but run by the government. It gave them a false sense of security, but they did not know that. The Republican Party had dealt with Big Business most of the time, but later came to be anti-Semitic even though the GOP, or the Grand. Old Party was started by Abraham Lincoln and many Jews at that time supported Abraham Lincoln. All political parties have some kind of ideology and capitalism was just an economic system gone completely wild so that eventually it always fell under the reign of socialism. When socialism was in America well and alive, I was not surprised because of what I had learned years ago listening to older men, much older than myself, speak about where the country was going and also speaking about the White House and most politicians in Washington D.C.

Now a Jewish man as a Catholic was running for President and this would mean; if anything negative would occur in America with Islam involved, Islam would not be blamed, but the Jews would be blamed and more anti-Semitism would spread in America very quickly and the scapegoat mentality like in Nazi Germany when they revealed the German elites secret vice would spread like wildfire. Gentiles in general had a misconception about Jewish people and thought they all were money hungry and Hollywooders, but it was the fact that they were liberal and not in the sense that they were to the left, or even socialists, but that they would be so benevolent that it always with each new generation in America go a step or two further than it was ever meant to go and so with all human nature, if not restrained it comes to the end of itself, or self-destruction, This is where materialism came in since the Jews were always brighter then the average Gentile and would stay with something to perfect it until completed and often would read into things too much which also got them into trouble, because then they would perceive that equality would be fair and would protect them from anti-Semitism since in centuries past they were left vulnerable when they had trusted the religions of the Gentiles, such as in the Spanish Inquisition or the German Reformation that both sounded good in doctrine for Gentiles and Jews, but later turned out to be a tool for worse anti-Semitism.

Maybe when Tribulation came, GOD was not just saving a remnant for His own, but also judging the world for how they treated the Jewish people as a whole or as a nation, and that would mean that Jesus could be no part of their real world no matter how much they talked about it. It was their preconceived intentions that got the Gentiles into trouble with GOD. We cannot presume to know GOD'S mind even though we all do it sometimes by human nature. Where could the Jewish people turn if both Roman Catholicism and the German Reformation, not to mention Russian Orthodox fall would not try and love the hard to love Jewish person since the enemy did not want the Gentiles in any nation to love GOD'S people?

Yes, a good education I had gotten from elderly folks and not senior citizens who were dead before they hit the grave already. The elderly then were listened too until the 60's generation scared the heck out of them and the government starting with FDR poisoning their mind with socialism in the form of-when to quit in life like they did the rich and well educated for after all was it not for them to retire early once they made their first million or maybe 10 million, or more with no end in sight? The elderly got senior and in turned failed to lead and were ready to give up and give in since they were intimidated by the young who were glorified for whatever reason, but not one good reason. They stagnated and fell behind and no longer lead with experience and helped the young, find their way in a world fallen in sin and why would the rich want it any other way? It was hard to deceive the elderly then, but as time went by the senior citizen lost all perspective about life and their own nation and their own people as well as a government that ruined them and embarrassed them into submission again because of the 60's generation that was a complete failure since the older generation did not want to see them go through another depression, which is what should have happened if all the extra money was not given to deadbeat relatives.

People who never had money had money, and it was ruining them and our economy as well as moral environment. Socialism had no moral really to it, and so with it came this deluge of evil. Most people had given up on believing GOD and were into believing what they could see. There was only one way of thinking and that was in opposition to the Bible and insanity was occurring in all forms such as people wearing earrings even in their months. and women wearing tattoos on the bodies and athletes such as black ones were doing all the abnormal things that was rendering their lives useless and short, and the Hispanic culture, a cross of this was emulating too whatever it saw, plus some of their own idiosyncratic tendencies.

As time went on, the above athletes went all their separate ways, especially after the Vietnam conflict. Tim moved to a camping park with his wife and all his sons were grown up, but one son never visited them at all. They were not as close knit family. Tim's brother had gotten a. government job and had about 4 children and was doing fine. Bob had gotten married to a Catholic girl and they moved to another state and their children were very wild, but all out of the house and in fact the oldest son was divorced with two children which was a shame since he was the nicest of them all. Mike had gotten a divorce and gained 400 pounds of weight and rarely anybody saw him, since he also moved out of state. His brother was around, but was involved in politics with the fire companies. Hank got married later in life and built his own home in the country, and he and his wife had no children. Fred, as I said before, had one son who married an Italian girl. He too got a divorce. Dave was still married and that was all 1 knew about him. Marvin had died of heart failure due to rheumatic fever which he had as a baby and that is why he used to sneak out of the house to play sports which he was not allowed to do. Roger had married and had 2 children and had a small roofing business. Carl, Brian and Scott all also left the area, and I did not really know what their lives involved. Only I was left in the city where I was born and all the others had given because of multiculturalism that invaded this area due to slave labor by certain companies and judges as well as other professionals while the elderly who lived in the suburbs either died or had moved to Europe. The rich always seemed to know ahead of time what was coming way ahead of time and so they would get up and emigrate to another country or to another state, lock, stock and barrel. The city looked like a third world country with rodents, garbage all over, children running the streets all times of the day and night, illegals living here and there, illegitimacy that government still promoted, drugs and prostitution, murder and mayhem, slums and more slums where at one time use to be family homes and doctors' offices as well as other professions. Nobody now wanted to come in town because of the violence and crime that kept escalating left and right. The politicians were in the major bank's hands and would do anything for a buck. Nobody voted hardly anymore, and criminals were allowed to run for office because civil rights' socialism that benefited the rich and well educated who lived in heavily patrolled areas with exclusive streets that were far from the city. The poor got poorer and the rich got richer, but these rich were foreign Islamic rich who wanted to take over at least here and possibly America with their arrogant culture and civil rights' socialism was helping them do just that and the ones now who benefited from this were all part of the problem. Anyone who went along with this no matter if they were professionals or laborers, white or blue-collared workers were contributing to the demise of the American Judeo-Christian faith and one could see how these people lived and acted with nothing worthwhile to a normal person. Highway after useless highway and plazas and malls kept going up because the rich could make money on this and did not care what it would do to our environment, and the building of dams was also creating flooding conditions when there were heavy rains. The whole natural environment was being ruined because of capitalism which had served its short-lived purpose and now government and the people had to turn to something else called socialism since the deterioration was so great. Diseases and other illnesses were filling our hospitals quickly, and the doctors were now business men known as god in their own eyes and were investing, yes investing, not in their patients' time, but in stocks from pharmaceutical companies. We had come full swing from a healthy, clean and spiritual moral society to a dirty and unspiritual society in about one generation, or a period of just 40 years. Our own relatives lived like the illegals who had come here with the help of the federal government and all the lawyers who were paid liars. It was strange to see that these foreign religions were growing more and more amongst our very own people because they believed this would be a new life for them (the 60's generation) in their ending years.

As each year passed it got worse and worse in America and it became so surreal that even the land at many places did not look the same and the styles from clothes to cars started to look either all the same or so ludicrous that the work environment condoned this idiocy and nobody really cared what was going on because their lives were coming to an end. There was nothing original in society and in fact it was the old evils from other parts of the worlds such as the caste system and our own money looked more like play money and was useless. Every thing was done in plastic and in paper work so anything could happen since, to me, it was all based on the theory of "this is what I own, but . . . " Everything became relative, that is everything was subjective to not being any kind of absolute authority and so objectivity was lost in moral relativism.

As long as America had their cardboard houses and tin cars worth thousands of dollars and of course their stomachs full, it did not matter what the rest of society did for a living if they even worked at all, since even drug dealing and prostitution was considered an occupation. If one wanted to get married, they had to be sure to check another's background before saying "I do".

The things that GOD had given us, though, were still somehow there, and they were free and man eventually too would try to sell that to the highest bidder in the world and in turn sell out

America for the good of the cause. We were no longer a nation of one people but a conglomeration of heathenism, and if people wanted to sin, one was not supposed to oppose that since the laws that were made had all become legal, including murder. That is why people from other counties were coming to America to take advantage of not only the system, but of the people. Government loved it that **way** since our government was a global one based on world factors as never before. We were an unguided ship at sea without a rudder. The captain had abandoned ship and each was for their own, and that meant that even family was an obsolete term. Why would the American Jews work for Moslems who were killing part of the worldwide family, but not support Messianic Jewry, who had done nothing to them at all? The Jew was sort of between a paradox and a dichotomy in that they wanted their cake and eat it too, but in this case they had eaten too much of the same kind of cake that made them sick before. If they wanted to leave America and they did not, then why stand in the way of what could be their greatest revival at any one time ever on the earth? Were they not coherent as to what this involved as far as their eternal salvation which had nothing to do with the Gentiles and everything to do with the Messiah? Who could make them at least listen to reason as to why they should want to help their own and not the enemy's? They were indeed stiff-necked to say the least and had this too proud of an I mage about themselves and yet showed that they had a terrible insecurity about who GOD was and what He would do for them if they came as they were! How can one tend to another when one won't even render the fact that they are sick to begin with? One must not treat the symptoms as if that was the cause for to do that would, indeed only cover over what it was that was causing them this spiritual illness. All the medicine in the world would not help if it was not the right kind, or the right diagnosis. It is a dangerous thing to fall into the hands of a powerful GOD when one refuses to believe that He had a Son and that this Son was GOD. The hospital was already full enough with Jewish patients and more were coming in, but there would be no cure for any of them if they did not listen to the Great Physician. Who could now heal the sick if He was not who He said He was? Where did any of the Jews get their prayers answered if not from Messiah? It was not in reasoning, but in faith like Abraham that GOD always had worked. Who was obedient enough to listen all the time to GOD? No one had ever done that, even in the Old Testament, and even Enoch and Elijah both saw God and did not see death, but both know who Messiah now is and He is here! How is that even when one is taken and does not return, they refuse to believe that he has not seen God, the one in the flesh with the nail prints and the scars forever, and who said, "He was King of?" Was it the church or was it the Gentiles who set this faith in motion? Where in the Bible does it say that the Gentiles were the first believers and first spread the Gospel in the Old, or the New Testaments and why was the Old Testament there at all? Was it just for a history lesson to show the Gentile world what kind of GOD a Jewish GOD was? And if that be the case, how is it that now Israel is a state which was in the waiting for almost 2,000 years and yet some, or most, Jews see it just as a secular state and nothing more? How bewitched can one's own misgivings be that would lead them to believe that the earth was flat? Why were Gentiles all over the world and of different races and classes reading this Book called the Bible which had no errors in it? Did they want to study the history of the Jews? Could it be that the Truth was contained here and nowhere else?

After the ages and still there is no Messiah is that is what we have been waiting for if we are foolish, or if we might just be right? Who can tell us the Truth if not GOD Himself? Must we look to ourselves and other men for the Truth when no man has it in him? How is it that GOD continues His plan to help the Jews no matter how many Gentiles oppose Him? What is it that one must listen with, their heart, or their head, and if their heart, was not that the way that Abraham listened and trusted in GOD? How could Moses even in Genesis write US when it says, Let US make man in OUR image."?

The Jews are special because they were chosen, and not chosen because they were special. That means that GOD Himself has done all this and man has had nothing to say, but only to repeat what He has told them to say whether they be Gentile, or Jew. The hypothetical word of man is no match for the living Word of GOD for it breathes and moves and has its being. Who would give anyone unconditional love and listen time and again to a people who even have rejected what His own Jewish relative had to say and is still saying to all who would listen? Do we all imagine that everybody is right and good, or is it that only GOD is righteous and good? GOD is never too busy to listen to anyone who sees that His relative in Jewish flesh has done that there has to be done and nothing else can he when it comes to grace, This is this unconditional love from the Father that He is sharing to the world when He calls them into His kingdom for eternal, and the ones that listen.

It would be okay for homosexuality to run wild and even for children to be molested, and yet the American New York City Jew would still prefer that over GOD, when the writing was on the wall, institutions of Jewish extraction were even defending homosexuality when six mil'ion, yes six million Jews were tortured, deceived, raped, experimented on, shot, poisoned, etc., but all that would be okay, or would it? The Jews were too smart not to know that that had occurred. in Nazi Germany, if even some Gentiles knew that and were willing to oppose Nazism again for that is the virulent nature of Nazism, or its origins of homosexuality which had started in the 19th century and kept getting worse and worse. What was the real reason the American Jews could not see what the Holocaust had done to their own people and why they were murdered? There were still some Holocaust survivors to tell them that that was what World War 1 and even \World War II inside Germany was all about and this was this master race breeding, meaning that when one breeds they take men of "special caliber" and chose certain women for them and not for marriage, but for this superman the same kind one would see on television years ago. The Soviets called theirs the New Man, but was a different type of prerequisite. When one breeds one must experiment on something or someone in order to prove their theory of a master race that needed no women for marriage but only for procreation with the right or Reich man. This pick and choose method was Aryan pure, so pure that sexual intercourse would not be needed in the embryonic stage now in America. Who but the Nazis would think of such a possessed plan for the world, or at least part of the world, except the Jews who the enemy knew was Messiah a Jewish man! The occult had much to do with this with their 2 lightning bolts on the SS uniforms that signified they were bonafide occult Nazis who did everything in opposition to GOD'S will and that is why the Jew had to be eliminated because He was a Jewish man and the enemy wanted the entire world to forget this. Also that is why the Nazis talked about this 1,000-year reign, because Satan liked to emulate what GOD always had in mind for the world for good while he wanted to use his for evil. He was a liar from the beginning. Who could tell the Jews, at least in America, that two women in bed or two men in bed had absolutely nothing to do with family or procreation at all?

Civil liberties, or civil rights, were anything but civil and made no sense at all when one saw that what this meant was superior rights. Is that not what the Nazis had said that all the Aryans had and the Semite people did not, as well as the Poles. etc.? The right to total freedom to do as was done in the Book of Judges which was that. all things were legal so they had to be right, right? An Anglo-Saxon government had something about it that was inclusive and exclusive, and that was what the trait of each culture brought to the table of liberty. Why could some be free and some were not? Now it was being said that George Washington was an anti-Semite and that for sure would rally the popular notion that since he had slaves he had to be an anti-Semite, yet the very same people today who pronounced that also pronounced that they had discovered a new America where all cultures were equal and all people would be equal according to THEIR indoctrination of socialism. This utopia would have to put somebody else on top and it did not matter if it was raced based, or whatever, but just so that it opposed GOD and appealed always to human nature which always had to be right? This had to he part of the thinking that went with this type of philosophy because the secular Jews certainly were not doing it for the Old Testament people, nor the New Testament people! The American Jew, no matter how sincere, had once again fallen on the wrong side. No, this time they did, but back before World War I they had fallen on the right side, and so it was that reason they had to be eliminated from the scene as quickly as possible. Even Stalin liked Hitler's plan of the Holocaust, or should I say Hitler liked Stalin's plan of the concentration camps that he emulated them right in the center of Europe for all the world to see, yet Roosevelt said he did not know, yet he knew enough to appoint Joseph Kennedy, a Nazi, as ambassador to England! How coincidental that was and the fact that Chamberlain saw more than would meet the eye, but then again we were dealing with superiority weren't we? Now in America we had become so smart and educated that we now knew the secret of how to "create" this New Man, or Superman without sex. That was very similar to something else once before for all the world to see, wasn't it? Or at least world Jewry? Who was deceiving whom? The Jew had left the Eastern mindset and developed this John Locke metamorphosis that would transform man from working the land with his mind to a mindless machinery technology that had no spirituality to it and this new Enlightenment would solve the world's physical labor problem since it would bring utopia, but ever since that had occurred things had only gotten worse and worse. The West thought it was the best since it had the least physical and mental amount of work to do. There now were computers to do our thinking for us and there were machines from cars to plants that produced in mass quantities nothingness that would last for only a short time (more planned obsolescence). What a joy it would be to do nothing meaningful and. to have all the free time in the world to worry who was going to take from you which was yours forever, or at least that is the way it appeared on the outside. We now could worry more about mundane things and nothing eternal since this was the one life to live, but really was it? "The brave die but once, but the coward dies a thousand deaths." So if one could live on earth forever without any physical death than that would mean the one with the most toys wins, right? But what if that was not the ease at all and but by a. slim margin it would be the other way that is we could die right now and go to Hell, or know for sure that this life was only a second in time which meant that eternity had no time so that seconds, minutes, hours, days, weeks, years, decades, scores, centuries, ages, millennia all meant what? Nothing? If compared to eternity they could not mean anything, but what they were to be used for according to GOD. "Race relations" were more important than race relations. "We are all one race the human race." Communism, or it's predecessor socialism, meant anti-humanity, or no human race! It was the self-destruction of man from the world, himself and the enemy. GOD was the only one being that could do anything right and the 3 persons of one GOD meant that like a good egg it was whole and all one. "If you have seen Me, you have seen the Father, I and the Father are One."

As we got older in life we all, or most of us, must have thought at times "Is that all there is?" No, there was much more for all in one of two eternal places, but meanwhile here we were to do for others first and not through groups, or government, but through a Body and ministries that became organizations were not living organisms, but just that reasoned out.

At our next national election it would decide what way our nation would go, but that had already been decided some years ago by the socialists in both major parties. The nation was under the impression that what they thought was important, when it was what GOD thought or what He wanted us to do many years ago, stating with obeying His Word and not some parchment paper that grew old with time. Man's words always grow old wit h time, but His Word remains the same always. This election would decide, if anything, just how quickly we were going to fall in the abyss and had nothing to do with a level playing field. We, as a nation would have to hit bottom to now know what GOD was really like when His discipline would be used to control our disobedience to Him. This was not for some election in democracy that meant little if anything to a GOD of the universe. There was, of course, an entire world that we had abandoned by the way we set our example for the world and it did not look so good for any of us to say that we were free, since we were in bondage to sin from head to toe. We believed we had what it took to overcome this illness and we would soon see. America had English foundings, and that in and of itself could prove most disastrous since the English always wanted to do it their way, or according to the way England lived, The transplant could not work for America since we were a much larger geographical nation and since we had many backgrounds that had assimilated for ones who wanted to and for ones who did not and for ones who wanted to just take over regardless of whatever. Whoever would win this election would get much more than, they ever bargained for and would be much more than just a popularity contest and heaven help that individual for all the pressures that would attack with such force that one person might even want to forfeit the reign as President. This no longer was a position for the rich and well educated but for one who would be able to hold a power so strong that it could take one's very life. The principalities would be at work more now than ever and doctrines and demons would come into play since we chose as a nation to regard other gods more important in our very lives than Messiah. These gods we thought would serve our every need such as self-preservation, gluttony, affluence, avarice, gambling, sexual promiscuity, addictions of all kinds, homosexuality.

The rich always needed a lot for a little more and the poor needed only a little more for a lot. While one side struggled with the enemy the other side made deals with him and had the time of their life. The poor would have to look to Jesus and the rich would look to themselves and this dying world. The riches found in this world though would not last even though it appeared in mortal time that they would when one was especially young and foolish. As one had gotten older and had an easy life they then realized that they did not want to get old for now the real truth in age would tell them that all they had lived for was a brief moment in time and no matter how much they wanted to slow this clock of time down it could not be done. Reality was they did not want to get old gracefully. Their youth was gone, but now they had much more money and wealth, but less time to spend it since time was running out on them. So, reality was so much harder to face and their hearts had been hardened by the fact that they had heard about two roads and they chose to take the easy road in life which would bring death and this death would be an eternal death. When life came it would come and the best that any human being could do was not be surprised at the good luck so much, or distraught at the mishaps of life itself These were the ups and downs of life itself that would be the field to test one when nobody except GOD was looking and some of the saints unheard of would be in line first with a holy GOD. The crowns would be given only to those who knew who He really was personally and not like a famous celebrity, or athlete or politician that would come and go, He would never go and leave us, nor forsake us. "I shall be with you till the end of the age."

Yes, this election was different only in the fact that now how far would we as a nation fall into the abyss since it looked like for sure that we were not in the least interested in what: today, or the future would bring for even our own children in the spiritual realm. We thought we could plan it all out even ones who had the wealth. The wealth in this world was only temporary, but the spiritual wealth that Messiah gave would last forever if only we could now see again it, but then again faith says "not seeing is believing" Abraham did! The senses can be and should be used to enjoy the good that GOD has given us, but not for faith!

We had the actor Jimmy Stewart who was a cheerleader at Princeton, and men who at home would cook instead of their wives, who were too busy with materialism and not their own families and children. The men of the house were just that, of the house and would do the cleaning, cooking, washing of clothes while the women would be too busy at big business, serving capitalism's goal that would always lead to socialism and give women a fair and equal balanced share in life as far as it takes two to do things, of course in opposite rolls. The men themselves had an identity crisis. Who were these stay-at-home men who let go of the authority that GOD had given them? It was bad enough that deadbeat dads were not there and were setting their own trend as far as how to procreate in our very own society, and the lawyers in government, where they always settle to and of which many were homosexuals is where man found his niche in the life of Riley and not ever knowing what fatherhood and at the age of 40 was about. This was more of this equality, or equivalence, that the rich and super rich liked because it fit their own agenda to a tee. More individualism from mothers and fathers and less family orientation as one unit and not as separate units, would do no good if things were to be sold lock, stock and barrel. The wealth,, or the materialism of a nation was now more important so that our children could learn what their unisex role would be and that with motherhood and fatherhood dead one only needed to be a partner in crime to this wonderful world of make believe. This utopia would only last for so long for in a good foundation such as the family the institution of mother and father and children and grandparents could never get old, but only now things that were popular would be welcomed with open arm so that man knew his place and women could excel in all the things that she was not supposed to. We also had men who were doing sewing and who were fashion designers and who made the front pages and would show women in society just where they belonged as well as their own husbands. These were the icons that would make the news if one could call it that. Man had a dilemma and that was he gave up to Eve what Adam had given up and that was his GODLY authority for the easy way out. So women said, "I shall take over from here and from now on." The Jean Factor meant that she now wore the pants in the house, and the boys in the family learned not to use what GOD have given to them by nature. The society was setting up a new type of man for the future where women would rule the roost and since there were times of the month that had many changes, they would make vital decisions based on mood swings. This is where also we got women judges, women politicians and women in business to take control of whatever came along and who would play the role of leader as if we were in a Third World country, of a Latin type culture, or now an even black culture where the breadwinner was the female most of the time. So that is why LBJ AND FDR liked to play the role of leader only when in the public eye, but at home well . . .

There also were men who loved so much to cook that it took them away from being the father that they were suppose to be at home with their very own sons. Many were volunteers outside the home, but inside the home the authority was relegated to the female partner and whether or not he liked it, it would be that way in this society. The Saxon mindset was dominate for America so that man was free to do all the things that he was not supposed to do. He stayed at his job, or occupation, or profession so that he could be away from home and have less to do with his family and more to do with materialism and the nonsense of capitalism which was nothing more than economics. When the real change would come is when the woman would equal and then supersede the male image of the father in the home. So now many men who were raised as such turned out to be just what every mother wanted every daughter to be and that was effeminate and feminine, but of course that would mean a unisex, or no role for the separate sexes and so homosexuality would be apropos' for this to take place and to have less children since procreation would be a bother, but partnership in the home along with self-esteem would be the goal of most, People followed this like sheep going to the slaughter. There would be no roles for anyone, so why have a family unit as a major institution? All we needed was to live the life that gave each one a group mindset of individualism and the "me, myself and I" mentality.

The Western man just could not understand why things were not working out in marriage and as for now he seemed not to care in the least. The Western women also enjoyed this!

The best athletes in the world were not necessarily in the Olympics, and that was not because they were not professionals, but because there is always someone faster, stronger, quicker, smarter, more skilled etc. Yes, there is always someone who is always better somewhere in the world. The Olympics were ruined first because politics played a very important part and as well as money for some of the athletes. Some, as I said before, were professionals and some were real bona fide athletes who really worked hard and was not that what the Olympics were about free play_ or non-professionalism which was capitalism's way of saying we were the best and socialism's way which was all paid even at home of also saying our way is the best. Sports meant good citizenship, but how would people who were just experiencing freedom for the first time respond to this challenge of amateurism? Now there were he/man sports which meant more socialism. There were spores that were not really y sports in the sense that they represented a team concept, but socialism could always show them that.

The advantage to socialism was that there were virtually no worries about life since health care, pensions, meals, living quarters, etc. were all paid by the state and, as in the Soviet Union,

Community Development monies would provide all that would be needed and then some. Medical expenses were all paid, but the kind of care one got was another thing except for the rich and well-educated, or the Royalty of government and big business. The HMO's of Bill and Hillary proved to be the way of the future and like it or not they were the ones told to do what they got in office for and that was To promote socialism at all costs and to spare nothing. Even the metric system of Europe was not only meant to confuse people here in America, but have a world unit` in this one world government. How wonderful it would be to have a government take care of all of one's needs with no questions asked except one, "Do you believe in the GOD" and this was the GOD of Abraham, Isaac, and Jacob and not of Islam or of materialism which is of this world. Many signs and bumper stickers would say GOD bless America, but what GOD, or god, were they referring to?

Early on Saturday mornings New Age occult cartoons were already indoctrinating the mass "peasants" who could only watch what the world had to offer, and that was death.

The children had no choice since everything became electronic and they wanted to be up to date with the rich and well educated who got the same education via college except at a higher level of evil. This was the Pied Piper of America that had infiltrated our schools, homes, churches, etc. There was this god of the age. Just push a button and one's human nature could be fed all it wanted and then some. The internet was even worse because it meant worldwide connecting with anything and anybody at anytime. How exciting all this was and not always in English, but in the language of your choice! People were not human anymore because technology was the way of the future and would solve all of one's problems, or so they thought, and in fact was the problem. Even the senior citizens were getting in on the act and it was chic to be informed with nobodies. Just read and believe and all would be well!

The state certainly had a vested interest, but not in family, but in the universal one world government. It would set all criteria for all things including food, clothing, shelter, etc. One had to know the right medium in order to be on line. WWW.COM.THE OCCULT. It was innocent enough to delve into, but then all of a sudden something would happen that would "transform" one into something totally different that the Bible ever had in mind and in fact the new bible would even have new pronouns in it. This was more of that one world government of utopia that man for ages had been looking for. Now he had found it, but at the wrong time with the wrong leader and at the wrong place. America was just a name of a geographical place and had become a network that with in unison with this one world government. People had become like robots. Oh yes, they could think, but of what and who had been the teacher? Since nobody would get anymore than anybody else, it would be okay.

Even now in hospitals they had patient tags that electronically kept tags on all patients while in the hospitals no matter where they went and this was good for tracking, but this was only the beginning. Wait till one would be tracked into one's own home all the time and upon leaving that home and wherever else that person went in their entire life. Nothing like a New Age "guardian angel"! In Israel already they had chips in food boxes so when you ran low on a certain food product it would tell you by giving off a light high-pitched sound. It would send a signal to the origins of where the produce was made, shipped, boxed, etc. This was an excellent system to keep track of all food supplies, but convenience more than caution was the most important thing.

Many Americans in the spare time took trips to places south of the border where they were actually hated and where armed troops, not ours, were located. The American had no where to go to relax. They should have gone to Israel. At least they would have known that terrorists are there and could kill one easily, but to the islands and small coupe countries they appeared on the outside to be benevolent, but . . .

Americans were complaining about the south of the border padres' coming north with the free help of the federal government, but yet would waste their money going to these same places when all they had to do was go to any large inner city and they could see the same things for free! They had to get away, but from what? This was the dumbing down of America for sure. Spending money to support regimes that killed and murdered people and from their own background! Young people would buy homes and not pay their mortgages and just move out when they got behind. Did they know something us older folks did not know? Even the hospitals and their non-profit status could now only admit patients on a criteria basis and not an individual basis!

People who were ignorant did not know and people who were educated loved it. The majority rules, or rules by the mob, to get what they want and sometimes what they do not want. Our nation had fallen prey to all kinds of lies and the lie was believed time and again. The, young were glorified and made to lead and the elderly followed along as robots afraid to challenge the young on any kind of debate, or topic at all for fear of intimidation, or lack of popularity. How insane was that? We would walk before we would crawl.

America and it's people had no real purpose in life except for the believers because theirs was eternal yet strove to do right here what GOD wanted them to do for others first. Capitalism always stressed me first. "Hurray for me and the hell with you." This was ego.

Some of my Jewish friends and I got together to discuss the Passover meal that was so very important to them and to me and how that was the true "Easter" and not the Easter that all the Gentile religions worshipped on. This was the one that GOD had talked about in the Bible when Pharaoh would not let the Israelites or Hebrews s go and wanted to keep them as slaves.

Abraham said, "How do the Gentiles hope to witness to the Jewish people if they did not even get the holidays right?"

I said "It did not matter to most Gentiles if the Jews were saved or not, just so they could. make a. good impression on their fellow parishioners and friends and family."

Jerome said, "That would seem pretty shortsighted for them to think along those same lines wouldn't you say?"

I said, "Yes. I totally agree that it was absurd for the Gentile religions to make up holidays of their own even though they meant no real harm to the Jewish people, but would do more harm to themselves than they could ever possibly know. If one would look at Christmas time how the Messiah was ignored and only His birth was stressed and not even His resurrection which to you is neither here nor there but is so very important to the whole Christian way of life for without that it would have no meaning at all. The resurrection of the body and the soul to everlasting. One could contend that for me to say this to you, Jerome, Abraham and Joshua would be out of line, but the only thing out of line is if I do not tell the truth and at the right time and that I know what all the Jewish holidays are so I can come from where you are and not come from where I am."

Joshua said, "Do you wish so soon to make me a believer in Messiah who once came and is coming back again?"

I said. "If i would not try, then you could call me worse than an unbeliever, and I could not really face you at all since it is I who have to live with a clear conscience."

"You understand that much persecution has been made in the name of religion?" Abraham said.

I said. "I would contend that if I was to be blamed for that in the past that I would not have to acknowledge what I am not a part of. Since the Roman Catholic Church had much to do with anti-Semitism and heresy within Christianity for many centuries and was the only church around, then since I do not subscribe to that same religion and I believe that to this very day it is a cult, I shall pass on your question of persecution just like I would on Liberation Theology."

"So you are passing the buck to someone else to make it appear that the Gentile with religion or no religion is not to blame and it was the enemy, right?" asked Jeannie.

"No I shall take blame if it applies to me or my faith, but again Roman Catholicism's very idea starts with bread and only that and cannot even interpret Scripture because it finds church religion more important than GOD the very same way you find your tradition. Mine is not through tradition, but through a now immediate faith given to me personally by a loving GOD and that is why the Jew is Christian in nature because through nature GOD came in the flesh to live as man lived and to come to die for the saints in the world whether they be Gentile or Jew, or should I say, Jew or Gentile."

Joshua said, "So since you have all the right answers, please answer this one for me. How come bad things happen to good people?"

"Joshua, first there are no good people according to GOD. Only GOD is good and that is another reason that Messiah came to this earth for without this man could never know what good is. He could know right from wrong, but as far as being good, he never could, and the fact that bad things happen is to say that there is no human nature or an enemy in the world. Nothing that happens passes GOD, but GOD does have an absolute and a permissive will that He uses, but one must know which will is being applied before they can say anything for certainty, and even then the speculation of a good man can. never be, since Adam's fall from the Garden of Eden. Adam was innocent and not perfect like GOD. So no bad things do not happen to good people. Good things, though, can happen to bad people, meaning that since we are all sinners GOD does do for us many things that are good for again bad people."

"Luke, since you are the 'great physician' in the way you speak, can you also tell me why GOD would allow His people plus 7 million Gentiles to be murdered in the Holocaust?" asked Joshua.

"Joshua, I cannot tell you why that occurred in relation to what GOD was thinking because no one knows the mind of GOD, so if you say GOD was at fault, then you are doing what I would be doing if I would give an answer for GOD, which I am not about to do. But I do know this, that in Nazi Germany even the German Orthodox Jews tried to stop the Holocaust by reporting what was happening with the elites in Nazi Germany even before World War I and not too many Gentiles would listen, or Germans that is, and being the fact that the rich see their god in the different kind of flesh such as materialism and sin, this abomination that occurred there possibly could have been averted if the rich and well educated in Germany before World War I would have spoken out and told the German populace what was really going on since it was the Jews who, as I said before, are Christian in nature and who were forewarning Germany not to lead the people in that nation astray. So it was homosexuality, this horrible abomination which is also a psychiatric disorder and now has brought us AIDS, HIV, a strain of TB, and many other horrible things such as an increase in pedophilia straight from the pits of Hell that we now are in some way experiencing the mild wrath of GOD. One cannot ignore the real truth in history to answer this question of why you think bad things happen to good people. If people were that good would they and not GOD have allowed what had occurred even after being warned about it?"

"Well since your dissertation has explained your supposition I think we shall call it quits," said Abraham.

"Abraham, all I can say is that this is not my supposition about GOD or about the question of the Holocaust, or why bad things happen to good people for it is the truth and one must be able to deal in the truth first by knowing who Messiah is and realizing that arguments do not win with reasoning, but it is the heart, the spiritual heart that must change, or be transformed into the likeness of GOD, and since Messiah has come in the likeness of man, would not one say that we must trust not man but GOD in the flesh?" I said.

"I think for now the matter has been explained at least for the hope of one in this room and if for more than so be it, but remember it is hard to love the stiff-necked Jew and all his flamboyant and extravagant ways, especially in the West, but now so much more in the East, that Israel looks like a Western state and not an Eastern state that it was set up to be and that with no constitution it is not bound by history in the context of man, but in accordance with the GOD of Abraham, Isaac and Jacob," said Abraham.

After that we all dispersed for that evening discussion. I went home to my wife and discussed with her the proper approach to the unbelieving Jew who has for centuries and ages refused to hear or even believe in the truth when the real truth is being spoken, but if another should come in His name they seem ready to believe in whatever may come. This to me was very upsetting since their assurance was based on hearsay and not the word of GOD.

My wife Rebecca said. "Remember how hard it was for you to come to faith? Well now suppose that you were a Jew and had been brought up all your life to watch out for the Gentile religions that preached one thing and did another, such as in the Spanish inquisition or the Pale of Settlement. This takes fasting and much prayer and sometimes it takes many years, with others, of course, praying earnestly about the salvation of one let alone the Jewish person. We are our brother's keeper also means that we must lift him up in prayer and not become antagonistic for any type of reason we feel that we have a right (which we don't) to feel. This can only strengthen the enemy's hold on someone, especially the Jew no matter where in the world, but especially here in America where GOD has not been needed for a long time since, one would suppose, all of our needs are supplied. Bu t then again, this type of a "need" is not of this world so it comes in an opaque form in the sense that the one who can see through must understand that the other cannot because they have been blinded by the enemy and it is not as transparent as one would suppose, or maybe instead of opaque (which means no vision) I stand to be corrected because it is translucent for them since they cannot see, but we can.

"Rebecca, I think I understand now what. it means to witness in love at all times and not hit the Jewish person with the Gentile religion that has almost no understanding with the heart about the most peculiar person, the Jew. I believe, though, that also It is not free will alone that brings one to their Messiah, or for that matter, any Gentile to Jesus. If one would suppose that that was the case, man might forever be lost in his own sins. Man always needs a Guide in life and the blueprint, the Bible must be there at all times to help with all the decisions that we make moment by moment. Judaism solves none of the problems that only Messiah has already dealt with so you too must understand that with so few Jews in the world at any one time we often, I believe, do not get the opportunity to witness because the Jewish people are a closed people in this world and were meant to be the kind of light in the world as a people and as a nation. With all that said, I also realize that in future time GOD shall show what all of man's history has been all about and that shall be in the Millennial reign of Messiah."

"It is hard for me to argue with that, not that I would want to argue at all, but again this is the Commandment we are given to do and in love and no matter how impossible it may appear, it is not impossible with GOD."

My wife again had explained it so beautifully in those few words that I understood more than if one would have made a sermon on it 3 or more hours long. I guess the believing Jew is better equipped to witness, not that they should be the only ones to do so, to the unbelieving Jew. Some say that the Jewish person is the hardest person to love, but then again Jesus nonetheless came for His own and even though a few believed now through all the ages, few Jews have come to believe, so one could contend until it is His time nothing major involving the Jews shall occur until they say, "Blessed is he who comes in the name of the Lord." A few who had believed for eternal life and a few, or a remnant, shall also be as Scripture says, but just which ones we do not know. It is vital to witness with Jewish love in a Jewish way to the secular Jew, or their religious Jew, Orthodox. or Hasidim in the flesh even though I always feel a certain kind of affinity with all the Jewish people because, again of their Christian nature that is very rare among even believing Gentiles!

As my time on earth was going by I could see earth that this age was coming to an end. American citizens had all become 2nd and 3rd class citizens, and was that not what the Russian believer under Lenin and Stalin had become? In America one was looked at with disgust and much animosity if one would contend for the faith or even speak out on moral issues, so few Christians ever did and felt that was the best way in this life to go about it since the Bible said not to argue, or do not let the sun go down with anger on your heart, to paraphrase. But what had been the real reason that Christians in America refused to stand up and be counted? There was much verbalizing, but little action on the part of most Christians in America, and only the money issue kept coming up and to see the way that most Christians lived in luxury no not moderation, one could see what the problem was.

How many times had I myself refused to do what GOD wanted me to do, or in fact, not to do all of these years? I could not regret the past in the sense that I would live, or want to live, it all over again, but only the fact that now and from now on I should strive to do what He wants me to do, because we cannot go back in time, but only forward. To use history as a tool for discouragement was what the enemy had planned so many different times before in many different nations and in many different ages. Was the Word. always silent through man? No, I believe each day on earth from the time of Jesus someone somewhere was doing what GOD had asked the Disciples to do, and that was to deliver the message of who Jesus said He really was and why He came to a sin fallen world which He did not have to do but so chose to do. He was about His Father's way and till this day and in the future until time itself would stop for good, that would be what He would keep doing, and that is interceding for us saints continuously and be with us to the end of the age. In time there are always numbers, but in eternity there are no numbers. The clocks on the wall shall have no hands. We shall not be late, nor shall we be early, but always in unison with GOD. Was that not what Jesus was when He too came to earth for sinful man? He was One with the Father. This Triune GOD was forever and ever, and when is it when He was not? Never! This is truly the wonderful mystery of GOD the Father, GOD the Son and GOD the Holy Spirit. Too much is placed on "seeing is believing", and in John Locke's world that is what happened!

Lenin had said that he wanted to get rid of all the bright people in society because they were the debris that has always caused the trouble, and one now could see that in America that very thing was happening. No one had to be qualified to hold any position in America, and the more GODLY moral, the less they were needed in America. The home of the brave and the free had gone completely backwards as that, so in America all the deadbeats were running the streets while the brave were giving up their lives like they did in Vietnam. All these nobodies on American streets with nothing to offer but just what Lenin and Hitler, along with Stalin, had planned to do: get rid of the truly bright ones with high morals and angelic souls who could help a nation grow without deformity. Our own government had not one man that could lead the nation who was even close to the top in his particular field. The executive branch of government was a conglomerate of well educated socialists who knew absolutely nothing, and Lenin would have been proud of them since he himself was a shortsighted man who never knew the war had started in his very own country. His esteem in the west from all the loggerheads was just what the master ordered. Have the slaves in the system, like Hitler had the criminals in Germany, run a nation to the ground completely. They did not even know how to lose let alone win a war. They would not even surrender in Berlin when the time was up, like the Italians had done to Mussolini. These were not the brightest of the bright no matter how much money and power they had obtained. Money and power only meant not how intelligent they were, but just how vicious and cruel and inhumane they were. This is what socialism is all about and nothing about equality where it would say that the best in society are the ones that strive by a Biblical moral code. Utopia could only really mean according to some thug who would take by force or coerce something that was not his. Had not Satan done that, in part, to this earth through Adam and to Eve?

Yes, where could we find a ruler, not a leader, since ruling requires more than elections and mob rule and right by might, but bona fide authority that GOD can only give to a ruler and not a leader as in the leader of a gang. What is there to lead if a nation has no GOD of its own and relies on the lies that produce violence?

With no authority in government whatsoever, America now had to rely on the few in the nation who could call out to GOD and who would answer according to His will and not to any type of government that supposed itself to be Caesar and above GOD Himself. We had given up what GOD had given to us and gave it to the enemy and now we wanted GOD to say it would be okay to do what we wanted to and have Him bless us. This is what the Christian religion had come to in this nation, and all it mostly involved was money, power and celebrity status which stressed the I and the ego in man and was diametrically opposed to what the Bible taught because when ego is first then man himself becomes his own god.

People, even professionals, no longer worked and were dedicated to their own professions and in fact so in life just another reason to take a vacation or retire forever from life itself.

Pensions and Social Security kept the senior citizens in peace, but such a peace I would not wish on my worst enemy. We had failed to discern that what we thought were blessings were actually curses, because it served the flesh and not the spiritual. "The spirit is willing but the flesh is weak."

Islam in America was growing because we invited the unwanted guest into our very nation by not opposing it and always saying "some of my best friends are . . . " But this had totally nothing to do with good vs. evil because it was this ideology of religion that was bringing with it death and destruction to all in America. As we kept ourselves in self-delusion, the self-esteem of ego, we continually hoped that this would be what GOD would follow us with and notice not that we would follow what GOD wanted or said in His Holy Word, the Bible. This is the arrogance that comes when we feel we are invincible as a people with really no one god any longer that we worshipped. In fact we had become somewhat like Hinduism with its many thousands of gods which were nothing but demons. India was growing so fast in America and all the evils that could be came from there that even some Christian missionaries who had been there found it the worst of all nations to witness to. There were rat temples, the swastika, crippled children who were made crippled by their parents so they could go out and beg, Nazism as in Aryanism, Bill Gates and his pro-infanticide, socialism with Indira Gandhi. India was somehow a major part of this New Age Nazism and also was a great part of the occult with their reincarnation and of course the sacred cow while millions starved, and prostitution, no Bible preaching, but when Roman Catholicism was there it was clearly all right. This was a nation that the Nazis in America took a liking to because it was the same anti-Semitism that Nazi Germany had, and the people, because of the caste system were very arrogant. New Delhi is where most of all the money lay, and for some mysterious reason America was latching onto this evil in chains. This was not a nation of believers. We also were involved in a nation that never had even one time Christianity of any form in it and yet we would make them into a democracy, but heaven forbid if the Gospel should be preached.

Iraq was the old Babylon and was America the new one? What a horrible thought to have thought, I thought to myself. But who could not see that that culture over there was now over here and was growing like a cancer just like Islam was and all the American churches could do was fight over who had the largest congregation or who had the hugest building in the nation. What the church was supposed to do it did not do in America, and what the government was supposed to do it also did not do. Abnormality had become the "norm" and America, it could be seen by some, was at its end and quite soon according possibly to GOD's time.

The two I's, Israel or Islam, were battling still for the heart and soul of America, and America looked more like a Moslem nation than it ever did look like a Christian nation. We had become the spectacle of the entire world for ones that knew about us and our materialism. What was important to us was what had been important to all civilizations that eventually die and go away. They forget about GOD. Drunken with the wine of sin and evil, we could no longer walk a straight and narrow line and broad was the road to destruction. Our children were being lost to us daily by all kinds of heresies and lies. The family, or the American family, was long gone and now tribal mentality and group mentality was ruling the roost. Multiculturalism, Marxist/Leninism was our ideology. Who could now say America was healthy and at liberty except ones who believed the lie. Free will could never make man or a nation see the light of day, and darkness had set in here.

The physicians had become like the HMOs. They were good with all healthy patients. Since Bill and Hillary found it in their heart to install real socialistic medicine in America, many had died unnecessarily because of their love for their ideology and the National Democratic party totally agreed with them being it was pro-communist. If one really needed a medicine for a severe illness it was not only the pharmaceutical companies capitalism, but also the HMOs bureaucrats who loved to make socialistic decisions without even being an MD. This is what just the start looked like. How would it look like in one, five, or even ten years from now in America?

Rizzo had said that the blacks only vote for blacks running for office, and since most were in the socialistic Democratic party, they voted for them knowing full well that to do that would bring America down with socialism and would not equate infanticide with slavery even though both said the people were objects and not human beings! Since Rizzo had said that he could by their non-discretion, be called a "racist" for telling the truth and that is how socialism works with the lie. If the lights went out and a valuable woman's necklace was taken when they came back on and the first person said, "Do not look at me!" then check that person out first. The "squeaky wheel" was getting the oil through civil rights' socialism that deemed some superior than others according to socialism's rights and responsibilities. No one could call a spade and spade for fear of being labeled a bigot when in fact the bigot was the one who had done the labeling. One Negro friend of mine years ago had told me that some Negro people were much more prejudiced than whites, but many people did not know that. Why would anyone think that people of another race would be less prejudiced than people who were of European descent? Were not all people from all different cultures guilty of being sinners? So why were some treated by the rich and well educated like they were superior, including themselves even when they hated their very own country?

The reason, or the lack thereof, just went to show that Americans were being dumbed down to do what the elites wanted them to do so they could make America into a slave mentality with the use of materialism that all good socialists believe in! Europeans were guilty.

On a Sabbath we got a phone call that was doing a survey by tape as to whom we would vote for, giving us 3 options and they were candidate #l, candidate #2, or undecided. The problem with this first question is it did not address another possible answer in all its shortsighted arrogance, and that answer was what if I was decided and I felt that neither candidate was according to my faith? One candidate said that Islam worshipped the same god that we as Christians and Messianic Jews did, and the second candidate was an outright lying socialist who only thought what his ideology told him to think and nothing more, plus the fact that he represented the billionaires in all of this. There was no respect for GOD by doing surveys on a Sabbath. My life did not consist totally of who would win the Presidential election already when we had almost 3 more months to go and this had continued for the last 4 years. The war in Iraq was a quagmire because anyone with enough common sense knew that the Islamic world could and would not accept nor understand the meaning of freedom with liberty for all. The other side opposed the war, but not for that reason, but because they were anti-Semitic even though their candidate was of Jewish extraction, but hardly knew what that meant since he had become a Roman Catholic. Hollywood was scared to death of what Osama had said he would do to Hollywood because of the sleaze that came out of it to all parts of the world. There were socialists of two main kinds, and there were the Communists and the Nazis in Hollywood and secular Jews who could care less about Israel since these were worse than even the Pharisees who at least knew the law!

In Hispanic Latin America, Roman Catholicism had not brought much truth to those people since it had been there because a majority of them of Portuguese and Spanish background mixed with Indians and Europeans in Brazil and Argentina knew mostly only of the padre mentality that said all would be taken care of for them and nothing about responsibilities, since many of them were on the welfare roles in Social Security and State Welfare in all 50 states. The rich and well educated wanted it that way in order to bring America to its knees and, as I said before, create a slave mentality and bring wages and benefits down so serfdom would occur in America and many foreign heathen cultures would bring about animosity and hatred.

The Jewish people, by their very nature, were not warlike except possibly from the Tribe of Benjamin. In Israel America along with Islamic Arabs and other Islamic peoples, plus of course, the Anglo-Saxons all were anti-Semitic and had been for centuries. The Jewish people were antagonistic to say the least, but when it came to hunting and guns, they had rarely ever showed any interest like the Saxons had. The Jewish people were book learners and sometimes too good at that since what they read they tended to always believe except the Bible, which in a strange kind of way, was a sort of paradox, but then again it was the spirit of the age. Israel had won a war in 1967 and in 1973, and all the land they got back was already theirs plus more, including all of Jordan, but the Gentiles in the world, including the Western church had no good knowledge of this at all since they were into materialism and self esteem, which had absolutely nothing to do with the Bible.

In seminary schools they too were going the wrong way and saw things in a different light. Sometimes one thought that this light was a form in which Satan himself can come. The most obvious thing was through the church and our schools, the children so that they would never get to know who Jesus was. The enemy was working overtime because he knew his time, in mortal time, was running short, so he had to stage his last hurrah!

If a Jewish person was very liberal and my neighbor, I did not have to worry about if they would attack my family or friends. They were too bright for that. Other groups, though, thought completely different and thought the fist was the only way to handle others who disagreed with them. The Jewish Defense League one time, though, did challenge a Jesse out of a building for making anti-Semitic remarks and he never came out. But yet large corporations complained that they were deathly afraid of Jesse because of his people, which made up only 12% of the entire American population! One had to wonder where, if so, they ever got that kind of fear when in fact they had joined, many of them, the Socialist Party or Progressive Party and the Communist Party, including Jesse himself who was supposed to wear a collar. This is how far and how bad things in America had gotten that anybody with no authority could do and say anything like the rappers in so-called musical lyrics and also Jesse making trips to countries that were enemies of the United States government, and he was not even a public servant who would have to swear to uphold the U.S. Constitution. But then again, this is what civil rights' socialism was all about as had occurred, as I once mentioned before in Nazi Germany with affirmative action which outlawed the Jews from holding any government positions there. Maybe that is why the American Jew had many government jobs in America, so that would not happen again, but to their chagrin even their own this time around would turn them in if push came to shove. There were spokespersons from everywhere in America who said anything to anybody anywhere in the entire world, and they were not prosecuted and jailed for breach of our own U.S. Constitution, so who was it that the federal government was trying to fool, or to please for much bigger reasons than could meet the average eye?

Americans had lost their sharpness, and all socialisms have a tendency to do just that. They were non-caring homo sapiens who would "eat, drink, and be merry". There were so many colleges, but whenever it came to major positions in government, the word ivy always came out in the end and one had to wonder why since there had been a book called, "HOW HARVARD HATES AMERICA."

Where were the elderly to lead and instruct in the how to do's of life? Why had they hibernated for such a long time? Why were the lawyers or politicians always appealing to the socialist doctrine? Even doctors now no longer had to take the Hippocratic Oath and were being taught in colleges and universities and hospitals about death and dying like the Hemlock Society would.

Technology was thinking for most Americans and this take-for-granted attitude and ungratefulness was running rampant amongst especially the young and now even the old, who both could care less what would happen to the other guy let alone other free countries such as Taiwan and Israel and parts of South Africa. Heaven forbid if one was not always for the underdog in all situations and circumstances! One had to be politically correct, a term that Lenin or Uliayov discovered years ago and not some weird 60s hippie.

When soldiers would come home from Nam in San Francisco—where else—they were mocked. The ROTC officers and the generals as usual had botched up many wars and conflicts over the years and the sergeants and the privates had to carry the weight of those generals on their backs for most of their careers. Who would acknowledge the soldiers in the trenches for the job that they had done and would be doing in Iraq and elsewhere. The interviews were always with some kind of officer who knew much less about fighting than the drafted or enlisted NCO. If the military could recognize homosexuality with the top brass, then what could one expect from all of its officers who tended more to get drunk and fall under friendly fire too many times in too many situations. And now women were going to improve this situation?

Some failed or refused to become an ROTC candidate even did much worse by going to the Kremlin in 1973 under invitation by the Kremlin itself. The pictures of Stalin and Lenin must have smiled at that sight when it had occurred. Now in America if one said law and order it meant that they had to be against America, or at least what some thought was America in defense of the terrorists time and again such as after 9/11 and on the streets of San Francisco, New York City, Detroit, Los Angeles, Chicago, Miami, Philadelphia, and many other cancerous tumors that one could possibly think of.

America had contracted, as a nation, some form of cancer in its spiritual body. Many were now blaming America not so much for the war in Iraq, but for not following the ideology of Lenin and Hitler and Marx and Engels! The young did not know too much, even though they were widely educated, more so than ever before, but it was in what they had been educated that said that their professors and not even the parents or even the GOD of the Bible could possibly be right! The young would be ready to die for ideology, but not for their own nation when it stood up for the Judeo-Christian faith.

Most teachers could not spell nor add properly, but yet knew the idiosyncrasies of socialism backwards and forwards, and just think it all began in the 60s with the college professors. These were not the absent-minded professors, but ones who knew exactly what they were doing to America and this nation's soul, and tenure or not, they used every excuse to say that they cared. To intentionally lie and also to coerce in a classroom to betray one's country when others died!

Both my parents were bilingual so why was it that I spoke only one language and there were no signs to help me understand in a foreign language or learn a foreign language on government forms, government buildings, government tapes, government phones as well as in business for job applications, for Social Security, for welfare, etc.? Whose money was being used to pay for all of this second language? My mother spoke English and her second language, and my father spoke English and his second language, but never was it used to insult others or to abuse others, and yet our government found it to be just the right way to handle the American citizen. Of course both of my parents' languages were not 3rd World languages or Hispanic, a broken down and slang usage of Spanish, or in other words, street slang like Ebonics. The assimilation factor into America by being good American legal citizens through Ellis Island had its normal criteria and not what the rich and well educated wanted to coerce on all Americans to melt down our culture to meet the needs, no meet the demands that one particular culture was calling for. This could not be for assimilation at all!

We came here to work as legal citizens and not by political decree with someone in the White House dictating what he believed was right for all concerned when he knew himself he had a conflict of interest at hand. If second languages were to be used, it was always understood without question that it was to educate and not confuse the American people and not for vagabonds and carpetbaggers that the federal government felt they could give out "freely" with our taxpayer monies to pay for things for people who were not even citizens! Socialism from Hispanic Latin America now too was here through the Vatican so more could be coerced into their one world religion of materialism. These newcomers had so much money they were buying new cars, new homes, etc. and were buying anything else money could buy since it had been given to them from our own taxpayer treasury and the resentment grew no not on our part so much, but on their part. We owed it to them for all that big business had done to their homeland! Who, though, had taken their valuable resources?

Money that should have been given to those who were American citizens for disabilities was now being given to ones who could not even speak English! Thanks to our wonderful federal government, there had been Vietnamese interpreters for Vietnamese people in California who wanted to go on welfare but mostly Social Security, and guess where they got the interpreters to be translators for those applying for these funds that they never worked for. Vietnamese from the streets! Also, other 3rd World people were getting on the rolls because David Rockefeller, the Eatons of Ohio, the Stoshberries of Philadelphia, the Fords, etc. all were promoting this one-world government because many of them would themselves soon die, so what did they care about how they had left the world except that it would stay in the family if one could call it that. One could also not forget Robert McNamara and the Hearsts of Knight Ridder publishing. These were only the few in the world that were controlling not only our president, but also any U. S. president that would run, and especially the one who would supposedly win.

There was one young man who had made a woman from a complete dysfunctional family pregnant and they had a son and were not married in holy matrimony, but this woman had now 5 children from 4 men with 2 of the children being taken from her and the 3 youngest sons all in daycare under her care while she worked and collected welfare and support money from the 3 fathers. This young man, because of a corrupt state law made up by politicians who were all lawyers, had a law now that stated any man who wanted rights to see his child, or in this case his son, had to get an attorney. Some years ago a man could get a domestic relations officer to arbitrate the case without any lawyer, but of course the trial lawyers, as I said before, made sure, through friends and other politicians that the man and only the man had to go through this process even if he could not afford to pay for the attorney. The attorneys were all heart, that is made of "gold" so that they could live the so-called good life of materialism. It was not to be concerned over the poor innocent child, but if payment would be made in the hundreds of dollars. This is one major reason America went south in whatever it did. One needed a lawyer to blow their own nose. Lawyers, politicians and lawyers helping their fellow political lawyers who, after serving would go right back to their own legal practice to pimp off of society and the poor even more. The National Lawyers Guild had strong affiliations with the communist party. The one, two, three or more party system never did work because every party has an ideology, as Lenin and Trotsky or Mr. Bronstein realized.

Roger and I got into a very interesting conversation about the Vietnam War in which he had 2 hitches there.

"Don't you think, Roger, that we should have won the war in Vietnam?"

"Luke, all I know is that we were kept from winning the war by Hollywood Communists, the Pentagon, World Bank with David Rockefeller and Robert McNamara."

"What could we have done to win the war at all if that was the case?"

"The best that could be expected would be to disobey orders in the lower ranks, because for sure the officers were not going to give up the good life, at least most of them."

"How many men did you have under command when you were first there, and were you not only about 20 years of age?"

"Yes, I was about 20 years of age, and I had about 20-25 young men, all mostly from the heart and soul of America and none from the rich and well educated at all like the Bill Clintons. If one would die, I had to write their parents or loved ones and sometimes some of them even would wet in bed and get Dear John letters so I had to be almost like a father to them, and some could hardly read."

"I can now see why you had called it a poor man's conflict and not a war at all. Our government officials never even considered helping our lower ranked soldiers at all. Is that right?"

"Congress was made up of lawyers and controlled by the National Democratic Socialist Party and so what could one expect from socialists in our very own government, but what we got a defeat at the hands of tiny Hanoi, which pleased the rich and well educated in America and in Europe. They made out like robbers on the deaths of our soldiers and still today they are alive, these rich and well educated and have lived to a ripe old age."

"Does that make you angry about this when you now talk about it?"

"Not as much as it used to, because I now know no matter who leads this nation they shall always be controlled by the Ivy Leaguers in this nation and the Cambridge and Oxforders in England just to mention two countries in the world who just both so happen to speak the English language."

"If there was another war or conflict to fight for America, would you fight for it, that is your nation?"

"Luke, I would first rephrase the question to be 'Would you fight for America knowing for sure that the enemy here at home was not involved in hating their own country?' then of course my answer would be yes. But that again is a utopian vision and nothing else, so no, I would never ever again put on a uniform to fight for the rich and well educated here or anywhere else knowing that people like McCain are now heroes. His father and grandfather were both admirals, and he is now a U. S Senator and a millionaire. Do not think that the Vietcong in Hanoi did not know that at the time to promote their communist ideology. The soldiers who they tortured and never came back are the real only true heroes since they either killed them or took them to the Gulag in the Soviet Union at that time."

"Would you then, Roger, consider yourself a hero?"

"No, I would not, like McCain has for his own ego. I did what I felt I h ad to do to defeat the spread of Communism in that part of the world when I was at such a young age. Seeing us today trading with Red China because of the U. S. Senate tells me how right I am about now what I believe in and that America has been sold out for materialism, or socialism, and in fact even Roman Catholicism preaches the very same thing about Liberation Theology in South and Central America. Nelson Rockefeller when he went there, almost started a revolution by the Indians there and not by the Hispanics alone. That is how bad that name is in Latin America, and with Mr. Hesburgh, ex-President of Notre Dame University, a good friend of none other than Daniel Ortega and the Sandinistas of Nicaragua. So much for love of one's country amongst these elites who only meet secretly and plot to promote their own socialism all over the world because they hate their very own country."

"Roger, do you really believe all that you just said to me?

"Luke, I would not have said it if I did not mean it!"

After this conversation I thought long and hard if I myself would let any of our relative male men now serve in a military that was being used to promote this one world system no matter how sincere the soldiers themselves were. No one could argue with the soldiers though so brave!

On another conversation with Roger some time later in the year we had another discussion that was quite interesting.

"Luke, did you know that LBJ had construction firms in Vietnam and that there was oil wells there as well? Our own politicians were involved in corruption up to their necks in this conflict too. That is why Congress had never declared it a war since they were not really interested in fighting Communism in southeast Asia. It was a good show, but nonetheless over 58,000 soldiers who were still part of the 60s generation had a weak moral fiber in regard to their private lives as well as their public lives.

The Vietnamese ate dogs and cats for food, and little children used to put bombs in lighters, and on postage stickers when licked LSD was on the surface. The prostitutes there had blades in their vaginas to slice a man's private parts and Vietcong used to come on motor bikes at night across from the DMZ to infiltrate our lines and also during the day would ride right by us as spies. One could not always tell the enemy from the South Vietnamese. Also, we fought against the South Vietnamese without knowing about it since the Vietcong flushed them out of their farmland, which was rice paddy fields, and all along the Pentagon and the State Department knew about it! Also, many Vietcong came to America for $10,000 a head in gold to escape, and guess who got out first? It was the rich businessmen and some of their family members. The Communists knew quite well also how to deal as capitalism did but for a Communist cause. This was nothing new, Luke, since most people now coming to America had some kind of money to pay their way here and it had nothing to do with religious freedom."

"Roger, you mean to say that there are some Vietcong now living here in America and in our own city?"

"That is right, Luke. They are living free as a bird and our government knows all about it! Our nation had been sold out by the super rich and super well educated from the Ivy League Schools. Where do you suppose Bill Clinton came from after he left Oxford? By the way, he did not graduate; he was one of four students not to and left immediately for the Kremlin by invitation with a beard and was not a conscientious objector but a true blue, or should I say Red Communist! England knew all about this and the London Tribune wondered why it was not brought out when he was President of the United States. Luke, you know he was impeached from office, but the socialist U.S. Senate did not remove him from office because they themselves were up to their own necks in socialism since all were millionaires, which meant materialism and which meant pure socialism. Even later U.S. Senator Santorum, a Roman Catholic, could not resist the temptation when he supported Specter instead of the other candidate for U. S. Senate on the Republican ticket. The U. S. Senate, the millionaire's suite, and the U.S. Supreme Court were both now socialist branches of the U.S. government, and so whenever anything would come up they voted according to ideology and not according to conscience if they had one at all. The churches in America only addressed how purely white a Christian could be so they too silenced up unless it was for more money and to blow their own horn. Television had distorted everything including the Vietnam conflict, and anything would sell on television except a morning cereal by the name of Maypo. If one ate it one could see why that was the case.

Also, drugs and food products were first brought onto the market to experiment on the American public before the FDA even tested them. In a book called "THE POLITICS OF CANCER" written by Dr. Epstein, he goes on to explain how this works. Also another book called "MEDIA, THE CULTURE OF LYING" showed just how corrupt the media and the newspapers were, such as Hearst Publications. Those books showed that one did not have to have a degree in journalism, but a good writing skill to write for any magazine or newspaper. But the degree politicized it more so that the new journalist would write the way the media told them to as well as the socialist professors, etc. A real good journalist writes for the truth and as I said, does not need a degree to write for a newspaper but a loyalty to their own nation and of course good citizenship.

But again, colleges and universities would take care of that and that is also why jobs that once required only high school diplomas now needed degrees to get the job because that too was to politicize it. Politics had to be involved in all things, even the main line churches like had occurred in Russia years ago when the Patriarch sold out to the Communist Party and Lenin replaced the Russian Orthodox Church with a new religion of Marxism. We were traveling the very same path about 100 years behind them and it looked like man and not history would repeat the same thing even though we had been warned time and again about this. America had chosen and that included we the people that what we now needed was more self-preservation and materialism and more so-called freedom from all moral laws and freedom to do whatever we so chose to do and not to do such as speaking out against evil and also spreading the lie. Christians were too scared to speak out, not because they now would lose their lives, but because they would lose all their worldly possessions that they had, including their good paying jobs."

"Roger, that is an awful lot for me to swallow at one time. I must digest it again in my private thoughts since you gave me so much now to think about, whether I believe in a democratic/republic with its roots in avarice capitalism and with the people themselves sold on the idea that might makes right and that the so–called "good life' was 'eat, drink and be merry.' I am always amazed to find out from you, Roger, what even other military people and soldiers will not talk about and wonder why they never do. This has always remained a paradox for me since it was them who put their lives on the line!"

"Luke, you must remember most of them want to put the past behind them and get on with their lives and families. This is not too much to ask for them to do, is it?"

"Roger, what I meant is that as long as they are silent, then this evil shall be perpetuated even more so to the next generation and the one after that and that would mean what kind of world or nation would we leave to our very own grandchildren?"

"Luke, there is no accountability anymore, and these veteran soldiers know just that so why bring up the past?"

"Roger, the people responsible I know shall never be put on trial, but I do know that if one remains silent too long then evil can plant its stronghold in America and America will have wasted all those valuable lives that fought for what they believe in even though I myself never served in the military."

"Well, Luke, you are at least honest about yourself and are concerned about your fellow man, not just here in America but in other countries as well. But you are in the minority. Even nice mothers and wives have been brainwashed into believing a Phil Donahue rather than someone who served there or even gave up their very own life for their freedom with liberty, but not for freedom alone in the physical sense but in the spiritual sense, which means if one was not physically free they still would live a moral and GODLY life. Sometimes or many times I have to remind myself of that too! We must have faith in what we cannot see but just know that what we do must not go against GOD'S Word and never ever collaborate with evil or the enemy even though we may pray for them. There is that fine line that we must be able to distinguish from where we know when to speak and when to keep silent, when to act and when to not act, and when to speak the truth and when to wait, etc. Does that make sense to you, Luke?"

"Roger, everything so far you have said has made sense to me. It is just scary now to know that our own people here in America feel that way about life in general and are apathetic except when it comes to money and what it can buy. Now I see why all democracies are mob rule because the people themselves, by human nature, always want more for themselves and do not care in the least about universal freedom such as when there is a plane crash the media always plays up the fact of how many Americans died, but totally disregard people from other lands and cultures as if they were not there or even important to other people in the world!"

"Luke, you will find out lot more than this if you seek the truth in GOD'S eternal justice, which means one must search for it for it will not fall into your lap like mammon from heaven."

"Roger, that was so well put. Yes, I know I must seek the truth no matter how long and difficult it may be and must not be so much concerned with mundane things in this world because all of that shall pass away. Sometimes, though, the truth is hard to find in the sense that one keeps on hearing lie after lie till one starts to believe that very lie as the truth. This is where I believe I must do better to search for the truth in the right places and at the right time and not for myself alone but for loved ones and others who share my belief system and even sometimes those who do not since we still have time to s peak out freely before we are silenced totally by our very own government which is now a popularity contest of how one looks and how one acts in front of a television camera."

"Luke, I remember when the Prime Minister of Israel Menachem Begin was old-looking and not attractive looking and was looked down upon by even the Jews in America, but when Golda Meir, who was born in Milwaukee and a woman and who was fascinated by Henry Kissinger because she was a woman and the mystique of the man everyone thought that to be good for the State of Israel. I also remember the time when a mayor in our own city who was a woman was looked upon as a savior for the city and was re-elected to a second term, something that had not occurred in almost a century, all because they said a woman would make a difference. This in itself should tell any normal person that there was no sound reasoning to this, and in fact to have a woman would mean anything could occur since women are made different than men and for good reason. This may sound chauvinistic, but nonetheless it is the truth."

"Roger, so you feel that women should not serve in public office of any kind, right?"

"Luke, if you read the beginning of Isaiah it is very clear about that, and also in the New Testament Paul speaks about it in a similar manner. Even the head of every household should be a man as with Adam and Eve, even though they both went outside the boundaries that GOD had set up for them as a man and then a woman. Who are we to change what GOD has made to be with the first man, Adam, and the first woman, Eve?"

"Roger, how do you feel about women in the infantry and as fighter pilots?"

"Luke, I am surprised that you would ask that question to me after what I just said to you. No woman should serve in the military as far as in the infantry or any other fighting capacity or as a fighter pilot or go to any military school that is not co-ed even though they have broken with tradition on this. The reason they broke with tradition was because of socialism that now only promotes women where they should not be, but demeans man and also shows women to be even superior, which is another lie. Adam was created first and then Eve and in that order, and nothing man does shall change that truth no matter how many mistakes this government makes or our own military makes just to prove their own ideology which is all based on the lie!"

"Well Roger, all I know, and I am far from being a Communist, is that the communists do not give official positions to women in any capacity that leads. This is that tribal mentality or group mentality from their point of view but nonetheless it is more importantly a fact of nature. One cannot argue with nature itself, even though now lately we have tried to do so from a socialistic world view, which just goes to show how far we have fallen that we now have nothing to compare with since the truth is relegated to the refuge dump of human nature. Our seared consciences have done this as well as the influence of the world and the enemy whether one believes it or not. One's opinion is important when it falls in line with the truth, but if of no opinion other than what comes along, we shall accept anything which is very dangerous indeed."

"Well Luke, it was good to talk to you once again since you are a very good listener and can discern truth from life, fact from fiction, etc. We will have to do this again sometime soon. Okay?"

"Okay Roger, I agree, but let us make it more sooner than later."

"Well until next time, Luke, keep searching out the truth for it is always there!"

After that long conversation with Roger, I for some reason, thought of my mother and how she used to keep us well and would treat us when we were sick or ill in bed without going to a doctor all the time for pills and needles. Mom always had this green medical journal that she would refer to and also had this uncanny knack for knowing just what to do for us children if we got sick, which was not too very often. For example, if we got a fever and an URI infection, mom would give us a teaspoon of Nitre and a little sugar and then wrap us up and rub Vicks on our chests and then put a heated towel on top, and we would stay bundled up under the covers and by morning it was gone, the fever, and we felt so much better. Or when we got an upset stomach she would give me saltine crackers and some ice cold ginger ale to eat slowly and drink slowly and that would settle my stomach. The child diseases will all go, but that was normal and in fact mom would say it was good at times to get a common cold since she believed it reduced our risk of cancer later in life. My mother would use a vaporizer for my younger brother when he got sick with an URI and had trouble breathing. No animals were allowed in the kitchen or in our beds, and rabbits we did not keep because they could spread some sort of fever if they would breathe on you. Many doctors today think this type of talk is for the middle ages, but you know what? It worked for us, and I had a grandmother who lived almost 102 years and had no ailments such as high blood pressure, diabetes, etc. because she always ate in moderation and not in between meals or junk food and would fast privately many times. She was, of course, a very devout and quiet woman. Her meals were 3 times a day and small portions of all the important vitamins and minerals, and she always kept her weight down.

My mother also would teach us how to take care of ourselves many times to prevent illnesses and sicknesses so preventive medicine was even better than the so-called cure. She told us how we should eat and what to eat and to eat in moderation. Mom had this unique ability to discern also who was a friend and who was not. She was very open or broadminded while dad was the opposite. Yes, I can still remember these remedies and other things she taught us at home that not even some doctors even knew about. That is another reason I believe people got sick, because they put too much faith in doctors and not enough faith in GOD. The doctors then would even barter if one could not afford to pay them. These were true family doctors who did not make various trips to Europe and elsewhere and have an over caseload of patients, too many to treat properly, at least I felt. The general practitioner was the all around doctor that came to the house with his little black bag and would come at most all times of the day and the night. Then the specialists came and things got much worse, even though medical science had gotten better. The older order of doctors had their hearts in what they did to try and heal the sick while the new doctors had a "god complex" and were worried about things they should not be worried about. But of course the trial lawyers, those scoundrels again, made life difficult to live, not only financially, but also health-wise. They were the so-called "pimps" or "parasites" of society and the more people became greedy, the more popular they became even though most people felt they were corrupt as a used car salesman or a politician. But then again were not most of our very own politicians lawyers?

The courts, meaning judges and trial lawyers, would release criminals as well as the laws that the other lawyers in all levels of government were now passing to the colleagues on the other side of the bench or bar. One good deed deserves another, right? This is why America had become a country of litigation with no end in sight, and when Dan Quayle said that loser should pay all the socialist in Congress, in Hollywood, the Bar Association and many others attacked him unmercifully because it meant a stop to their avarice and not profit for they had no interest in profit but pure unadulterated greed! They attacked him the way they attacked Anita Bryant when she spoke out against homosexuality and attacked Clarence Thomas when he spoke out against civil rights' socialism, though at that time he did not even realize that and only thought it had to do with natural law and affirmative action. The only one they dared not attack was Barry Goldwater, a conservative Jew from Arizona who carried much weight in the area of politics and knew a lot of scoundrel things about the biggies in DC and in Hollywood and the Media. No one dare call him a McCarthyite because he was part Polish and part Jewish!

George McGovern, as Alexander Solzhenitsyn had so well described him, was all that he said he was and that was a true blue communist. Others such as Walter Cronkite (by the way Barry Goldwater called him that too) kept silent about what Goldwater had said. Even Henry Ford apologized for anti-Semitic remarks made and a Supreme Court Justice and I think it was Goldberg made Henry Ford apologize!

Yes the Germans knew their place in America was not stable as long as the Jews kept them under control and they did until the 21st century came into being and then the Jews themselves were self-destructing and betraying and inter-marrying amongst the Gentiles when such a thing for a Jewish woman was so unheard of. The Jews were falling apart from each other and never even realized it till it was too late. Then they chose, at least in America, the wrong side to defend and protect. This would do them in. Sometimes radio announcers like Michael Savage pretended to be for the Republicans, but when he spoke on radio he always somehow defended the Roman Catholic Church and that itself was a dead giveaway to his contradictory tirades that he performed on the radio. He was very good at it, so good at it that the public believed him. Since the one candidate for president was a Catholic Jew, just the fact he was Jewish was enough for Michael to defend him. He did this by condemning him on air every night, but when one read between the lines, one could see that it was a charade to say the least, and he was collecting more votes for Kerry.

In other words Savage who was Jewish himself and sounded like a New York City Jew knew to promote Kerry he had to make it known that Kerry who was Jewish let it not be known and let it be known only that Kerry was a strong and firm Catholic since most voters were Catholic and Roman Catholicism had much anti-Semitism so to keep silent about Kerry's real name Kohn which was Jewish would be the best thing for Savage's candidate Kerry even though Savage sounded as though he was against Kerry knowing the listening public would do the opposite of what a Jewish broadcaster would say for the majority of people who would listen to him and give Kerry a better chance of winning in the Presidential election. It was reverse psychology that he was using to deceive the public into believing he, that is Savage-was against Kerry. Kerry was Jewish so Savage too who was Jewish meant that silently Savage was Kerry's Fan! He knew not to mention what Kerry really was, for to do that would mean anti

Semitism for Kerry and to do that would be disastrous for Kerry since the word" Jew" has always brought a negative response in a Gentile majority world.

These were some of the angles that the media promoted to get their candidate in office because some Jews felt to do this would be beneficial to the Jewish people in America, but would only in the end bring along even more anti-Semitism and blame the Jews here and in Israel for the world's problems and economic downfall that was almost sure to come to the Western world for a while. With a Jewish President it would be the beginning of the end for most Jewish people here and in the world, but the American Jew could not see that at all. Their false sense of security was in a Jewish President which always showed in the past that whenever a Jewish person was at the head that meant for sure more trouble for the average Jewish person wherever they happened to be and in this case it was in America. Then Islam for sure would grow and grow into a leviathan and devour Judaism and the Jews even more and the escape goat mentality would again be used against the Old Testament people until the Antichrist would appear directly on the scene as the great deceiver and most likely be a Jewish male.

It would go from one extreme to another extreme as far as the Jewish people were concerned and the way Israel was developing in computer technology would control worldwide markets! The Jews in America always felt that democracy in America was the main thing to be had, but in future years that probably all would change since a new king was coming on the scene to reveal his peace plan to the entire world and sit on the throne in Israel. Since the Jews were sincere but usually hard to make listen even to sound reasoning, again their concept and GOD'S concept would be totally different from each other. Democracy in no way would form to rule the world because if America itself was too big for it what would the Western part of the world and beyond be like, but chaos and everyone knew that one would almost certainly choose totalitarianism over chaos!

Other things had come back to my memory through no effort on my own and so I contemplated on them time and again. I recalled when I was small and we had a nice home, but how my parents could not keep it, and the time I was in an oxygen tank and almost died of triple pneumonia, or the time I was hit by a car which a doctor was driving, and other things such as being almost a simpleton because I could not speak clearly at all and had to go to speech class for 3-4 years and all of a sudden unknowingly it left me. There were many places we lived from above a car garage to a trailer at the edge of a steep hill. Life though was adventurous to say the least and there was always something new coming up, unplanned of course, but nonetheless we continued on in life and did not complain as children and did the best that we could and my parents were really "peasants" with very limited education for both of them even though they could read but at a lower level of proficiency. My dad would often tell me, when I became discouraged about some school work, to get up for 20 minutes and come back to it later and I found out that that had worked time and again. There was much common sense to my parents that the rich and well educated did not have, but in other ways too my parents had educational shortcomings just because they did lack such a higher education and in those days it meant quality education to say the least.

I must have lived in a total of about 35 places and had about 30 different jobs and most of the jobs were mindless mechanical industrial plant jobs and offered no real challenge to both the mind and the body, except that the body did many times become tired because repetition for me was so awful. There was no connection between myself and the land of my own nation and this is where that John Locke socialism came in which had drowned out almost all the humanity in Western civilization. The agricultural farmer was different because they were one with the land and one with their own nation having to work the land with their bodies and having to know much in farming, hence so using their mind. It was not this plant mentality that seemed to fit for some people such as the Germans who had no problem settling into motorcycles, trucks, power mowers, chain saws, etc. Theirs was almost from birth this kind of acceptance that this must be my thing in life with no questions asked. I for one could not relate to that, and in fact my maternal grandfather had been a dairy farmer for many years before he died. This took an individual man and made him one with the land and his nation and gave him a purpose that no Industrial Revolution could ever do! There could be no place for socialism, Marxism, Leninism, fascism, etc when one lived this kind of life on a farm in a quaint type like little village with hardly any stores anywhere except a local general store for dry goods and farm equipment This is what man, such as Adam was to do after he sinned, work the land with his hands and toil at this. Cain had been the one who developed the urban lifestyle which turned out to be anti-national for any nation let alone America and also brought with it the cancerous tumor of squashed in living conditions and crime and corruption, because man could not breathe the fresh air that GOD had given to him. As a good American one had almost to be a farming person and not one in technology, or the industrial convolution that machinery and mayhem brought to the Western world which had helped to destroy the sanity with the brutality of such loud machinery that it showed how callous we had become. Everything seemed to be based on automation, or the computation of not being able to make a healthy decision without the assistance of a mindless and soulless computer and the extra extravagance of modern machinery to the point of insane absurdity with cars and more cars that were only status symbols and big toys for small minds and so childish in thought and design. We only lived for the moment so our touch with GOD could not have come before or after for the instantaneous was what we all wanted which proved to be a failure to the humanity of man.

This American President thought that Islam yes Islam was the same as Messiah, GOD in the flesh! About 75% though of American Jewish voters would vote socialistic and for the

Democratic Party and the blacks would be even worse. There was something that excited both these groups and they were groups because they voted by ideology alone and blindly no matter what. Would there be a black Jihad in America since 30% of blacks in America were Moslems and could we trust them since they had shown their true colors about socialism too?

Why would Negroes want to integrate when they were one with the land years back and the slave owners certainly were not? A Jihad in Detroit which had for so many years been a hotbed for the rich's socialism was now installing more of the same kind of hatred for authority that they had in 1946. This President had a Christian calling but would only go half way and did not know of this special calling or he would have gone all the way Biblically. The same had happened to Khruschev being a peasant, but persecuting the Christians even more, not that Bush was doing this, but was backing down to evil and the other candidate was totally a socialist and so was his billionaire wife of instability.

Terrorists, or all of Islam, were at it again in Russia, but our government would not call it Islamic Jihad but kept playing up on what Moslem countries we were making into "democracies". How foolish we were to believe such lies. Russians would not fight for Putin. They had done that once before for Communism during the Revolution and Putin was a Communist.

It was said that in Nazi Germany another socialist country that German women married to Jewish men would protest vehemently against the Nazis and one must remember that the Nazis were homosexuals so they had no appeal for their own German women? Could anyone ever trust the homosexual Nazi Germany that murdered 13 million people with Nazi allies such as Chamberlain, Sunoco, Ford, Krupps, Rockefeller, etc. The English were up to their old tricks once again and this President being English was the only President to acknowledge that there should be a Palestinian State. No other President ever made such a statement and that is why again the Jewish vote would go to the Democratic Socialist Party. The Scottish Presbyterian Church in America said that Israel should take down all its walls. More of the British Isles' anti-Semitism. Who could trust the English for anything or the rest of the Isles for that matter? They had lived like kings and queens for so many centuries that is the rich and well educated there while their colonies were made slaves and all we kept hearing was what our own Founding Forefathers had done! One must take the bad with the good and quintessential efforts to camouflage would not work. The English knew a lot about Parliamentarian government, but were poor with the monarch type of government to say the least and was the only authority government that the Bible recognized. All one heard was this democracy will do this and do that as if it was a utopia. We in the West could only think one way and that was this mob rule and popularity contest that always appeared in elections and some of our worse citizens were public servants and in fact criminals!

Even the American people thought that Islam worshipped the same GOD and not doctrine of demons! No wonder nobody needed to vote; they were too ignorant to know even what religion the Bible was of! We as Americans had fallen a long way from GOD and it was not GOD who removed Himself from us, but us from Him. Would the incumbent win and have us go to socialism a little slower, or would the socialist take us much quicker by winning the election? The blacks were hoping to be slaves for good this time and the Jews wanted more of the same anti-Semitism that was in the Middle East. What a strange way democracy worked and that is why it was called mob rule. Who could argue with the point of view? The English thought it **was** quintessential to all of life and there could be no other and capitalism was their breadwinner and we from an opposite direction were doing what the Russians had done exactly almost a century and now we would have to stand alone even against GOD. GOD could not bless evil or sin that we as a nation had built up so bad. We kept avoiding the sin of our nation and as a people, and infanticide was only talked about as far as stopping it and no state of emergency was used by the Commander In Chief. We had moved so far toward socialism that now we thought if someone said right that it was right, but it was actually left, not extreme left, but nonetheless left so the true left had to be Communists. Socialism was around since man and there were many kinds and the doctrine and the state and especially the state was the first form of government as the Incas and Mesopotamia both had many centuries ago. The individual was not to be and equality meant that the state would see to it that no one would marry for love, own land, or raise their own children. This was the ideology and not the economic system that we put so much trust in known as capitalism. This is what the West only knew. The Jesuits knew how to run a state socialist country if one could call it that. Plato loved his socialism and that is where we got democracy from. The Hellenists Greeks were a bad influence to copy no matter what.

We can only see through the eyes of capitalism which is not even an ideology but a way of avarice for human nature which needs no coaching. In Russia the peasant villages were more prosperous than the towns and the cities but the Communists promised the peasants land and fair labor and they got extinction and America too was doing the same thing full speed ahead. Where were our rulers who knew what statesman was all about and not diversity which was a tearing apart and the collaboration or covert collusion of some for the millions who knew no better and thought that physical freedom was always first?

The West was shortsighted in all of it's moral decisions and socialism had nothing about it that was in the least moral about it! We thought that democracy meant freedom to do whatever one wanted to do with no moral restraints. We also thought that this was how our world lived and so that for the moment was all that mattered. Universal brotherhood and freedom with morality was not set by any democracy, but only the mob mentality. What criteria could one use for officials in government if mob rule had gotten them in office? It was this leader of the gang mentality that we road to the end. The nation would live but would it be moral? As of now all we had was materialism and this utopia of eternal happiness that was just an illusion filled with sadness and confusion.

The young would rule by extinct and emotion and pretty soon revolution could possibly be in the air since diversity was to break apart, no tear apart the moral fabric of America. Just as we had inherited goats for children since even the educated said we had these kids everybody else starting repeating this and the definition to many words made no distinction of good and evil.

This instinct in man was socialistic in nature and hence it drew the young people in because it stirred up all kinds of negative emotions that worked on the subconscious such as with the Bolsheviks and now in America with no helmet laws that said one could ride a motorcycle.

A safety helmet death wish when at first it was because there were so many Nazi helmets being worn that the American Jew wanted to get rid of all helmets then without so called censorship by making it mandatory and with human nature it would always choose the most dangerous path of no helmet at all. The national standing of that America was to blame for all the ills in the world would be that foreigners, even Islam and Latin America, could bring their death wish mentality for one and their conquistador mentality for the other and the fact that NAFTA had to have natural resources from Latin America and the trade off was that for the importation through government for their people to come here to disrupt and turnover our national heritage from the English and the English language and create more socialistic hostilities and who would know that some of these Latin Americans could even be Sandinistas in disguise sent here to socialize America downward since that culture had nothing in common with the European culture? The rich and well educated loved this because that meant that their form of capitalism could continue to thrive and had done so also in Communist Red China not in order to promote freedom, but to make a profit and more for the sake of avarice by the elites. Capitalism, not socialism could show any promise for the future since the media in the one was commercial and in the other it was propaganda. Pulitzer started this in the West and Lenin in the East and the socialist state in the 19'" Century came into being with Marxism turning over to Fournier who saw the world differently such as pink lemonade for the seas and oceans and the whales for transport for one continent to another and the ending of the world into destruction with no moral purpose in mind as with the religionists that had a moral purpose in mind. Natural resources such as water, oil, air, soil and some others could not be replenished nor could one substitute for the other. Once they were gone that would be it and that time was coming quickly. The New Ager wanted to hoard all this for the Antichrist and his false kingdom here on earth. All socialistic societies had short lived lives. The Communists in Russia took the Russian language in order to destroy the Russian nationality which could never totally be destroyed, but would even make most Russians believe that it was their nation and not the ideology imposed, or embraced by them that almost destroyed the Russian nationality. In America that too was occurring with the elites who would do anything for natural resources in light or heavy industry. The large scale industry was prevalent in both capitalistic and socialistic societies because of their appetite for more production even though the control of production was done differently one from another. The one under capitalism had competition and planned obsolescence and fashion as such was light industry and had to now constantly change in order to sell Madison Avenue's products to create a demand and in a free society when the demand went up the prices went down, but in an unfree society prices would rise when the demand increased and in an unfree society the quality of products were much worse because the state party ideology which only meant no matter how incompetent one was they could still be promoted, but in a free society they would be fired. Also the military machinery in an unfree society meant that the state there had a vested interest and oversaw that all would go well or else and this was because under socialism they needed to expand internationally with violence in order to run their state of totalitarianism. Planned obsolescence was being used in the West to create a "market" to keep buying and Madison Avenue had a vested interest to do that no matter who they had to deal with as far as totalitarian or dictatorships. Now the world was running into a major problem because natural resources were running out all over the globe which meant a catastrophic incident could occur, but the Western businessmen appealed to these dictators because they did not want a revolution here due to lack of products to buy and there due to a sort of coupe, or revolution.

The car industry was a prime example of why cars would stay here and why oil would be what was needed for to change all this then the workers would have to be retrained, new million dollar technological changes put into place and other things that would totally destroy their profits/ A status symbol *was* done by advertising this time and again and even pornography would benefit since there could be no censorship in a democracy which was one of democracy's downfalls unless they had an elected committee without any party affiliation to offset things such as pornography that greatly offended religious people. Socialism would not last long and never had, so with democracy too the same could be said. Neither had the answer to solve the future world's problems because they themselves were part of the problem.

There were about 2,000 nations with only about 150 states in the world and now even the village a plebiscite wanted in some parts to be an individual entity bringing even more hostility and confusion onto the scene, hence multiculturalism or socialism. If nations could not get along, how would nations and villages even be able to or even individuals get along? The United Nations was mob rule of the nations! It was a businessman's organization to get what they could for either socialism, or capitalism. Big business had a vested interest in Moscow and in Red China and now Latin America and in Asia and in Africa such as South Africa being the fact that South Africa was the richest nation in Africa for natural resources and whatever it took they the businessman would do to procure these natural resources to create and supply their financial needs regardless of whom they had to deal with.

So it bad absolutely nothing to do with democracy, or freedom, but everything to do with big business and their open supply to any country or nation just so they got what they needed to supply their peoples with the so called" necessities "of Western life which was now influencing the **East** but not for the good, but for the good of the cause. By using smaller businesses and computer technology the West and the East could maintain a proper amount of production even so minute' as one per item and much smaller amounts than capitalism, or socialism ever could. No mass production for waste in capitalism and ego, or for waste in socialist countries that were mismanaged because of party politics as well as party ideology!

Human nature would always appeal to the flesh no matter what and once any democracy lost it's self-discipline than all would be gone quickly. Limits or self limitations had to come from individual to individual (and not like herrings that had no separate, if you will, personalities like say geese that mated for life) and private property, the family, etc. all played important roles in a moral and tree society. Relationships were null under all socialisms and hence Karl Marx who loathed mankind along with Fournier. Engels, etc. promoted this death wish of mankind to destroy himself which had prehuman origins as I just mentioned above. It was in essence good vs. evil. Constant bombardment from the media that held no allegiance in this nation to America, but just for the internationalists was destroying the concept of America as it had done in Russia about 100 years ahead of us.

Under socialism though one did not have to worry about crimes or crimes that involved the rich and well educated and the over exposed stories in the Western Media and also one's job was provided for, but of course then one had to toll the line of the straight and narrow and so though most people living under socialism were actually afraid of the free society with all it's worries and problems and so chose to stay where they had "security". The Western free society put all lands of pressures such as what if I lose my job what will happen to my family and my home, or the a fact that crimes and criminals were increasing and the fact that the world situation of gloom and doom was a constant worriment but not in a closed society. Again of course the disadvantages were quite severe in a socialist society, but the West had proven how fast they had fallen under the democratic mentality of all free will to do what one wanted to do and the constant bombardment by the media of all the negative happenings in the entire world and then some that could only depress the citizen of that society.

It had been thought that the Europeans had killed the other cultures and their people and also their infringement on their cultures, but more than that to their mortality rate was the fact that people from the West tried in good conscience to change their lifestyle for the better by improving sanitary conditions and medicines, but yet their own native people were now dying even earlier then before and were getting diseases that they never got before. So this change from one of the tribal to the Western style was proving more fatal then any other factor.

A Russian couple had years ago taken in a child who was conceived by a girl of the village and a soviet Moslem chief and raised her as a Russian and still sat as a Moslem with no training!

Now the Iranians who are not Arabs, but were Moslems were involved in destroying Israel. This Islam was a menace wherever it went, but in the Soviet Union it was left alone because it was innately socialistic. This too had a death wish for mankind. America would have to find out for itself this inviting Islam into America was the worship of another god and the First Commandment was explicit about that. Christians were more worded about catering to a foreign religion that had absolutely nothing to do with Judeo-Christianity and everything to do with principalities such as demons and doctrines of demons and the worship of Did not the Bible say that all foreign worship of idols was actually the worship of demons and nothing else, so why did America think that Islam was some kind of part of America when it was the worship of idols?

Anywhere Islam and its Moslems went it was bad news for Christianity and the Jewish people. From Iran to Russia to the Arabs into the heart of America such as in Michigan where Allah speakers 6 times a day were on to worship demons. This was like the Old Testament when the Israelites wanted to have a king like the Gentiles and Samuel told GOD they had refused him (Samuel) and GOD said, "No, they have refused Me." The Jews were not to even mingle, so why did Gentile America think it could otherwise with an Almighty and powerful GOD? Who had deceived us into believing having Islam in America as just another religion was okay, when in Scripture it was plain enough to see what Islam really came under and in the Koran where it spoke of murder of human beings?

Why would America share its heritage with Satan so quickly with Islam and the Moslems when all should have known that

Satan came to deceive and to destroy? But the English knew better than GOD Himself, right? What foolishness led them to believe that mixing oil and water would be all right with GOD? If socialism liked Islam why would a Christian nation like it?

The hatred stemmed from the religion itself as with an ideology such as socialism. Do not believe the lie. We refused to believe the truth! One nation under GOD. What could that mean even though Moslems would say Allah for "GOD" which meant not the GOD of Abraham, Isaac and Jacob? Was there 2 different gods in the universe? Why did we believe so? Why were the races separated by different continents since the races never did or probably ever would really get along cohesively for the majority's sake? Why had the English always made it their business to rule the other peoples in the world and then come to America with different races and on not such an auspicious note and till this day it was still turmoil even with civil rights and possibly worse? What was their purpose why they could not work the land with their own hands instead of "hired help" which in turn meant that resentment would always be there from the novels that dealt with history more actually than did any history book that was non-fiction?

The races had separated because of different interests and by their own human nature probably since Noah's time and so that was to be that. But then certain people so called opportunity to take advantage of other people, not to influence them for good but to be used as machinery for the things that the English did not want to do, since they were to lazy to work the land with their own hands and not "borrowed hands"! They could not let well enough alone, and whenever the rich and well educated got together they did it for ego.

Since America had the European history or background what made them think that even after 300 years that things would be still all right, when nothing really was but was only getting worse and worse and now with civil rights' socialism what had Europeanism done to these minorities that held them in bondage and when released it would mean the so called right to take it out on the surrounding communities and not the elites and rich and well educated?

This was the crux of the entire matter of capitalism vs. socialism besides being atheistic and that was physical labor vs. mental labor! One would work and get tired and the other would get tired without work, or physical work and would show that in their appearance. When has a businessman looked like a farmer in our own country since one worked the land and was closer to its soul and the other did nothing but rape the land and was far from the land's soul?

Agricultural America later became industrial America and hence America, so money for less or no work while in the beginning it was work as a family for a nation of one people.

With the murder of over 55,000,000 unborn children, or infanticide, by judicial decree our federal government has now allowed more Hispanic Americans to take their place so that would "make up for the tax base" which meant that all could be forgotten, but of course not for these children that were murdered in cold blood! Who would speak for them since we had a First Lady that was pro-infanticide and yet hugged the children from Hispanic America as if our own children had some kind of plague of some sort and her husband the President loved to replace these 55,000,000 children with ones of his own such as from Mexico for then the tax base would stay solvent if it ever has and no one would need to go off of welfare for years to come including social security. His convention speech appealed to the Hispanic since he spoke Spanish. It appealed to the Moslem Arabs since he did not refute his statement about a Palestinian State the first President ever to do so and I had said this once before. He appealed to the religion that Dostoyevsky called socialism with mysticism that replaced the truth with materialism and in America it readily showed and also the fact the 25% of the votes were Catholic and out of the percentage 55% voted Democratic and 45% voted Republican. He appealed to liberal Jews because he supported Specter and his pro-Iranian and pro-infanticide stand and did not support the candidate Pat Toomey who was pro-life. He supported open borders to the south and north did not want to come here for good reasons but the south needed free handouts for their natural resources that he was instrumental in obtaining through NAFTA. This first couple talked a lot of good but failed to show any of it when it came down to action and in fact this President was moderate and to the left and had taken no stand because as Commander in Chief he did nothing to remove women from battle or to remove all homosexuals from the military. He was emulating the Nazi mentality that had mostly homosexuality in it's higher ranks, but should one be surprised at that since he too was an Anglophile and his Vice President was pro-homosexual another Anglophile who were cousins to the Germans? They had lied through their teeth and even when a hurricane went through Florida he was campaigning with no remorse for what had happened there. His previous term was one big campaigning mess. He could care less about the American poor, but only about the Hispanic poor because he needed their votes to get re-elected as President and that was all that mattered! The other candidate was a total imbecile and thug because he was nothing but a pure socialist and he wanted us to come to our end quicker then did the incumbent President who would rather drag it out.

Both candidates did not represent the Judeo-Christian faith even though one was a Catholic with his materialism and billionaire wife and the other with his father and his New Age mentality. The incumbent was the lesser of two evils-but was not one to vote for unless one wanted more multiculturalism in America whose roots were from Marxism/Leninism. Again one was a Catholic Jew and anyone who thought the secular Jews were bad had to see a Catholic Jew because all a Catholic would talk about was money and more of it and of course homosexuality and how far it had progressed in their church, yet they still attended and sent their children there for the so called "faith and only Church"!

Again the media could not be controlled and were for the Catholic Jew only because he served their immediate goal of socialism right now. They had waited long enough the 60's generation for this next revolution that would be unspiritual the way it now was going. Now was the time to act and Hillary in 2008 might be far away to get that spirit of socialism back again as it had been under Bill Clinton and Hillary Clinton! Time was of the essence and the socialist party in America had its candidate in office and the other party then would follow along.

Who would win the election? The one who wanted us to go full steam ahead with socialism or the one who thought Islam was the same as Christianity? What a wonderful choice one had to pick from! One pretending to be a Jew, because the only Jews were Messianic and one pretending he was holier than thou but had really nothing to show for because when push came to shove forget it. Many television ministries wanted the incumbent in for they knew the other candidate would close them down and quick while the incumbent wanted to make the church part of the government and not the government part of the church. He had it totally backwards. This meant the same as what Lenin had done when he usurped the Russian Orthodox Church with Marxism at that time. America had moved even more to the so called left or what I liked to call socialism which was more accurate and defining. The comparison with the incumbent had always been with Clinton, but never with Reagan when push came to shove. He was strong against Communism because he thought it was another economic system, or at least that is the way he treated it. He also could care less about what had happened under his bureaucratic administration and all administrations were bureaucratic to the Christians in Red China for he had not even one time mentioned them that I could remember at all! All he talked about was his friends the Arabs in Moslem countries where they murdered Christians and Jews or Islam itself like it was the second coming.

Yes, Yale had done a number on this guy for sure as it had done with all the rest of those who attended the socialist think tank. Even when they started out as seminaries did they approve of slavery because for sure in the New Testament it mentions all those who deal in the slave trade as evil doers. Since the English were bright and intelligent but their private lives were to be desired, they would get away with it once again because the world for centuries had been fascinated with their culture as well as their language and monarch.

America always had to do what England had done whether it was good or bad and it usually was bad such as socialized medicine, homosexuality approved by the House of Commons, the recognition of oil money for Islamic Jihad. No matter how much they talked about Al Qaeda, or Hamas, or Hezballah, they never wanted to say all of Islam for that would mean to give up all the wealth and power, since oil was their idol and self preservation the ultimate goal. They wanted their cake and to eat it too! "A wolf sheds its fur, but not its habits."

All of the British Isles including Ireland where a revolution was occurring between the "Hatfields and the McCoys", the Welsh with their English aristocracy, the Scottish with their Presbyterian church in America that was totally anti-Semitic because it wanted Israel to take down their walls. The people here thought they would once again rule the world, but there was something now that could not protect them even though they had an excellent geographical location.

"Godly repentance is what America now needs don't you think so Luke?"

"Yes, Abraham I think that is just one thing America needs to do but also to have self-limitations, or self-restraint with self-discipline."

"Well Abe how do you suppose that we should go about that when America doesn't even in our own majority believe in GOD let alone the majority of Gentiles," said Andy?

"I believe we all must repent as a national body for our nation has a soul too and if we do not then so be it and also the so called church has nothing but ant-Semitism, or guilt and that is not really true repentance when all it does is call to mind the things that our nation America has done that were sinful whether we were here, or not "said Abe.

"So you believe we are accountable for our entire history even though we were not here at the time such as slavery and the anti-

Semitism after and during World War II because we were truly anti-Semitic since we fought only because of Pearl Harbor being bombed and not because of the Holocaust?" I said.

"Well as for me and my household we shall serve the Lord," said Joshua.

"Don't you think, Joshua, that you are being facetious since you are quoting a passage of Scripture in the Old Testament that was spoken by a person you know very well who had the same name as you and followed Moses?" said Jerome.

"Well, what I meant to say was how can a nation repent when we are individuals to begin with and a nation is a people with many different types of individuals?" asked Joshua.

"I think you are missing the whole point of what I mean by repentance of a nation and why it is so important to repent as such since we as a free people must do what is GODLY right and without coercion or either go into oblivion or into the unknown of history because we do not have much more time to do what is right as a nation anymore," said Abraham.

"I agree totally with what you have said Abraham as I said before because the church itself in America has been sold on the idea of socialism, or materialism because their begging is beyond belief and their guilt trips for ones who don't give is heresy," I said.

"Okay so a Gentile such as Luke agrees with Abraham, an Orthodox Jew about our nation's lack of repentance. How shall that make a difference now?" asked Andy.

Abe said, "Listen, we are Jews except for Luke, our great physician who has one thing in common with us and that is the Old Testament, and so we should at least acknowledge that it was I who first introduced this national repentance where we forgive all injustices that our very own nation has committed here and abroad since its inception, and who better than the Jews should do this since they were the most persecuted people in all of mankind's history?"

"So you are saying, Abe, that we as Jews should also include ourselves in this repentance even though the Holocaust could have possibly been avoided and let bygones be bygones. Right?" said Andy.

"Andy, yes we too need to repent as in the Day of Atonement and as you well know of in Yom Kippur once a year where we pray for our own forgiveness and the forgiveness of others so that the day of Yom Kippur is not done away with but includes our whole nation of America and that we as Jews must once again let it start with us no matter what other Jews may think or what the Gentiles may think since no nation like no person has ever gone on without any kind of sin. Is that easier to understand, Andy?" asked Abe.

I then said, "What if it starts with the Jews but does not end there and then the Jew might be blamed for this so called repentance of America? What will the rest of America say? Will there be more anti-Semitism if it comes right now when Israel is being blamed silently for the terrorist attack of 9/11 even though they do not say this out loud too much, but are for sure thinking it since I am a Gentile and since the Jew has so many other times been the escape goat for what the Gentiles have done so many more times?"

"Again I repeat, it does not matter what the nation thinks of us, but just so that all of us truly repent including for the sins of our own fathers for they did have sin just like us since day one in America and before and must not someone forgive first to start our way to self-healing with this GODLY repentance that GOD is calling us to do if one reads the Old Testament properly," said Abe?

"We must acknowledge then all the sins of the church and all the sins of the people including Founding Forefathers since they knew right from wrong and good vs. evil. We can now find no more excuses nor do we have the time to. We must start now and not look back to see how bad it was, but more importantly to look forward to what could be in store for us now and for our children and grandchildren, since they will have to live in this world after we are long gone," I said.

"Why must the Jews do it first?" asked Joshua.

"It doesn't matter who does it first, but just that someone somewhere go through this repentance and self-limitation now," I said.

"That is easy for you to say for you are a Gentile," Jerome said.

"No, Jerome, it is for now us believers must take the brunt of the blow that is about to come into this entire world and shall even be opposed by some of your people and in fact most of your people. Remember when Russia tried to repent for the Pale of Settlement and for the Middle Ages when the Jews and the Old Believers were both persecuted and murdered for their own faiths? This is not a time to be different in the sense that we are not to blame any of us, for to do that would be to then believe in the lie that has perpetuated this now for 3 or more centuries here in America, and remember also that some Jews in America took away land after the Civil War that belonged or was given to them by the government. No Jerome this is not a time to repeat what man has done before and not what history has done because common man is the one who really makes history," I said.

"Either we listen to what each of us is saying, or we do what our own human nature says we should do which is always sin in the flesh," said Abe.

"Abe how can you defend a Gentile when you know that us Jews must stick together?" asked Joshua.

"Joshua, sticking together as you so called it is nothing more than group mentality that is being used to the fullest by socialists in high positions so that they can gather us up into one group, or as a minority called the "Jews". Do not let the enemy blind you by his tactics that have been repeatedly used time and again and remember here as in Russia why would GOD have placed so many of our people in both countries if it was not for His goodwill?" asked Abe.

"Well maybe you do have a point in that since America has been good to us in many ways and even George Washington had said that the Jews in his time could worship in their own synagogue," said Joshua.

I said, "Now with self-limitation in which the politician will have none of that for himself but wants it for all others since his is a road to ideology and ego and nothing more and has no loyalty to nation, or GOD, or his own people no matter how many speeches he preaches since one rarely if ever sees any positive action being taken that says he will fill in the gap as the leader of this nation and first be accountable to GOD and not to a party. We must understand that if a person does run for political office they must run on no party ticket but run on what they truly believe in and that this must first be done at the local level and then if elected he can pursue to a higher position with real true credentials and not what the commercialized media that even government can no longer control He must be able to prove it by his record when he served in a lower position and do not think that the people in the Eastern part of the world think like us about many things let alone democracy's panacea of quintessential happenings! We have too believed too many lies about ourselves and too refuse to try a good alternative to democracy which there is as there is an alternative also to capitalism and socialism and that is small and free enterprise where no mass, or large scale industry is in control of our nation whether it be democratic or socialistic. Both systems do not work and are out dated. We must be original in the sense that government must only provide for the common defense and make laws, that is Congress and then enforce those laws that should all be moral or GOD given. This is real agape' love and not a utopia of lies that socialism no matter what kind race, or class that is promoted for the group of rich internationalists now who would rather see a kind of slavery by all the nations and countries so that they could control all that they do at the top and use the politicians who they know shall have no self-limitations since party ideology shall never allow that even one time ever!"

"Can we agree to disagree in this a so called democracy?" asked Andy.

"If we continue to procrastinate the way Russia did about its own moral mistakes intentional or not we too may find that it is too late to do anything but wait for the judgment of GOD on our entire nation and remember this is our nation whether we want to admit that or not and from beginning to end. We can no longer blame the so called other guy for what we should have done long ago and that is to act in accordance with Scripture to pray and to do what GOD wants us to do as well as not to do what He does not want us to do any longer," I said.

"Well we are still free to choose what we want to do are we not?" asked Jerome.

"Jerome we really never have been free to do what we want since there is always consequences for sin and its contagious affect upon man. Free will alone does not make it right nor does it improve anything, but in fact it always does what is wrong since GOD is left out of it if one states it that way," I said.

"So you shall be our judge and jury alone, right?" asked Joshua?

"No I shall not be your judge and jury but GOD shall be that and is already judging each one of us as well as our nation since it has more freedom to do the right thing but refuses to do it," I said.

"Luke I can agree that we must obey GOD in all things, but how can we as Jews and Gentiles ever come to agree on anything since yours is to believe in His second coming and we in His first coming," asked Abe?

"Remember Abe, to whom much is given much is required and America that includes all of us too. has not met those requirements that GOD has set down for us for if we would have met them we would not have enslaved people and brought them here and we would not have murdered our own children by the millions and we would not have approved and sanctioned or even thought about sanctioning homosexuality which is an abomination to GOD in the Old and the New Testament, plus the fact we have become the derelict of at least the Western World and now produce and give service to anything and anybody just so we can live in peace for this very moment with no regards for the future generations here or elsewhere and you ask me that we have no common bond if I am right between what you believe in and what I believe in and all

I can say is that is what Messiah had said, "If you have seen Me you have seen the Father I and the Father are One," I said.

"So since we do not agree as of now we still have a common bond but shall be left out of the rewards in heaven and we shall not be there at all no matter how much we strive in this life to labor here for our own place with GOD is that right Luke?" Abe asked.

"Since you have understood this so well and have already heard the truth then now it is upon you to decide for yourself if you shall believe by faith with grace and not in what the flesh can do, for it can do nothing for salvation as you just quoted and the only way is through Messiah and for the Jew first and then the Gentile," I said.

"It that all you are going to say Luke?" asked Joshua.

"I shall not show pearls in front of swine any longer," I said.

"So now we are swine or dogs that do not believe nor understand what GOD wants in our own lives and you do?" asked Jerome.

"No, Jerome. All I am saying is that either you accept through faith in Messiah and hear the Father's voice like Abraham or you don't period there is nothing more to discuss on this," I said.

"Then why again have you tried to pressure us into what the Gentiles believe?" asked Andy.

"No Andy, it is not what the Gentiles set out to believe but it was because the nation or the people such as yourself refused Messiah's love in your heart that is your people, when Messiah was here and up and including now you continue not to believe as a nation of chosen people to see what He had come for so on the part of the Jews. In not believing, the Gentiles have come in as a branch and your people as the roots and yet only a remnant shall be saved that is of your very own people in the future during Tribulation and thereafter which means very few Jews shall be saved and GOD is always accurate when it comes to the Jews since He always uses numbers in the Bible which means that it is always referring to the Jews and not the Gentiles such as He fed the 5,000 or in the end there shall be in Petra 12,000 from each of the Tribes or 12 tribes of Israel. Since all the Old Testament saints believed in what I just said but had not seen Him but were waiting for Him they too shall see the Kingdom of GOD," I said.

Then Abe interrupted and said, "This is even too hard for me to believe that we shall not be part of His Kingdom since we are Orthodox believers."

"Abe I shall wipe the dust off of my feet now for I have to go to others to preach this Gospel and not be detained any longer, unless of course the Jews shall say, "Blessed is he who comes in the name of the Lord." After I had said this I then got up and left Abraham, Jerome, Joshua and Andy and went home. There was much mumbling about what I had said, but I did not pay any attention and just left as I have just stated. There was nothing more to discuss they have heard the Gospel with love and still refused to believe, but chose to believe in tradition that would get them absolutely no where and it never has and never will and even many Gentiles had and now do believe in tradition for salvation which amounts to nothing also with GOD for when one does not believe what GOD has said about His own Son and continues to believe a lie and call GOD a liar one can no longer have anything to discuss with that person, or persons. As with the rich man in the New Testament who had gone to Hades when he died and the poor man who laid at the rich man's gate for water and bread he went with GOD and it was too late for the rich man now to come over or even get a drop of water or even to warn his brothers what was in store for them once they died and did not believe in grace and grace alone by the shed blood of Calvary through the death, bury and resurrection of Messiah. It all had been done there was nothing else to do but believe when the Father and the Son call and to answer as His sheep as Paul had done on the road to Damascus.

This was again another group this time Jewish who had refused the saving grace as a free gift and not something to be attained or to strive for, but nonetheless GOD would know who would be saved without interfering with freewill but would call His sheep and they would hear His voice.

Our nation too was at this very point since it too had a personality all of these years and it, or should I say we as

Americans, had to now decide who we would follow. The judging of the nations was for sure very real, and we in America all of us had to understand that this was a very serious thing that had to occur and that was repent, GODLY repentance and self limitation, meaning that we do not or should not live for this world where all things are passing away and that now was that time for repentance for all the sinful things we as a nation had done so that we could meet GOD with a clear as a conscience as could be, or let all of our consciences be seared so that no truth could no longer be heard and that only individuals few in number would be able to see the Kingdom of GOD.

We kept getting bad weather and catastrophes of all kinds and still thought little about it as a nation. We were not getting the message from GOD that it was soon over if we did not change our ways as a nation and get right with GOD. How much longer would GOD hold back His anger from a nation He had blessed and not really anything we had done to deserve it since we all had deserved Hell as sinners, and now our nation was at stake even though it was so young compared say to Russia which had 1,000 years of Christianity. Even Abraham Lincoln in the last 2 years of his life came to know the Lord, and not before. This was a spiritual heartfelt thing.

With little or no reasoning we were acting like the animal world, but even worse we would murder our own which the animal world also was capable of but rarely did! We seemed to rely on instinct which only animals have since they cannot reason, hence they have no soul. But we as human beings do and we as human beings were taking out the human and just being. We were just existing for what would come next in our many sinful urges and passions and felt fulfilled in pleasing the flesh. "The spirit is wining but the flesh is weak." Messiah came in the flesh, but did not even once sin since He was GOD in the flesh and so chose to always do what His Father wanted Him to do.

Democracy could not really help anyone in making the right decision about GOD. Each individual was given a soul and a mind to reason, but more importantly a spiritual heart with which to discern things that could not be seen, and is it not faith in things that cannot be seen?

And how much repentance did we have to do as a nation? If we went too far we would indeed not have a nation or a nationality called the American, and anything or anyone could continue to blame America for all the sins in the world. There also had to be a limit to our national repentance or we would no longer be a nation at all of Americans. There had to be some important thought as to the good that our nation had done and not just the sins of our nations. We had to, so to speak, start anew so that we could become an even better nation known as the land of the free and the home of the brave, but we had to know also that with repentance came suffering which is never pleasant but nonetheless it had to be that way. We could change our course and not go too far for our accusers (who, too, should have been tried and convicted) would now never be and their goal was to destroy this nation known as America which always had to start as an idea as Dostoyevsky had said in the 19th Century. All nations must have an idea for that always precedes a nation. The state is something different from the nation. The nation is a body of people of one nationality which meant coming under one nation such as in Russia which also had all races, colors and creeds. Not until socialism came in and chose to blame the nation, as was occurring in America now, had Russia really lost its identity. No, this did not mean Russia had no sins from the past, but what it did mean was that the Russian people were a living organism and not just a state. We in America now had to decide if we were a body of people and uphold our own belief in the only GOD in the Triune head as Father, Son and Holy Spirit and not just any nation or any other nation but a nation called America and we as Americans!

A nation had also to revive or come back from repentance with suffering to a new kind of feeling about itself that was wholesome and healthy so as not to take repentance too far that it totally would do away with nationhood. We were one people as Americans who should speak one language and come under GOD'S laws, and also the self-judgment no matter how hard it would be, must come and not so called what others had done against us or better known as civil rights' socialism!

We were our brothers' keepers so that meant all of us (no one excluded) would first do for others.

Socialism had no reasoning and there was no right from wrong, good vs. evil, hard working vs. lackadaisical, etc. This was the insanity of socialism, but yet it drew in many people especially the young because it did not care if it lied or contradicted itself. Socialism would come right out and tell just what it exactly stood for and made the young especially on fire with a passion to die for even though nothing about the hereafter. It was this that so attracted its followers and others who would eventually come into its group. This was this instinct without reasoning, as I said before, that would kill and be killed with no remorse whatsoever. This was the danger of the lie of socialism in the sense that the ones involved felt it their calling to be involved in it.

Also this anti-humanity would come when Communism would be reached and that is the way it is with all socialisms whether they occurred in Russia or in Nazi Germany, and that is why Stalin trusted only one other person who was like himself and that was Adolf Hitler.

Millions upon millions of human beings, good and bad, involved or not involved would be annihilated since a majority, yes a majority, would be caught up in this passion for this socialism that was here since the origins of mankind and before, as I had said about the herrings and the geese. This was the instinct and emotion without any reasoning but this death wish or this urge to be fulfilled. That is why it was so dangerous because it was appealing to the human nature in man and we all had to deal with that, like it or not.

Even Mao had said that, "Even if half of the world's population would be destroyed that would be a very good thing for socialism!" This is how far it could go and even farther if man did not use what GOD had given him: a mind to reason and a heart to be transformed. We were not the animal world, but we had become worse because we were the only species to kill our very own time and again and mostly ones who really had nothing to do with this ideology called socialism in the fact that they were not members. It catches up and sweeps along all those in its path regardless who they are and the ones who are a major part of it are even sometimes the first to go and fight not to be right but to still be a member of this party in which ideology and not faith is supreme. "Let us reason together." This would not concern the socialists in the least. It was an embodiment of evil.

In the ex-Soviet Union. and not Russia in order to get published there one had to promote socialism or disguise it as not the cause of most of all of Russia's problems in the 20th Century and had to emigrate somewhere else and be "bold" since they had been out of the Soviet's jurisdiction and probably somewhere such as England to blame the Russians for all the ills in the world. Books published there were published for propaganda and lies and nothing else. In America books mostly were published for avarice and capitalism's excessive extreme of for the first million and then the second million and that was not necessarily in sales at all.

Capitalism, more than anything else in the world, had contributed to the spread of socialism in the world and was continuing on more and more. The West needed to get, in whatever way they could, those valuable resources, and human resources or not, they would get those natural resources or the human resources in all cases. The governments in the West were not to be trusted for anything, no matter what they said they would try to do, for it would be for more of the same, avarice and ego.

Socialism on its own would die, but the Western businessmen such as Armand Hammer and now David Rockefeller and Henry Kissinger and Alexander Haig would all sell out their own countries no matter what, and be that as it may when they died (and that would be soon) they did not care how they left this world, let alone their own country. Their collaboration (and here the word is being used in it's right context) with others from wherever did not matter, but their shortsightedness was for sure a disease of the rich and well educated no matter where one went in the world.

The auction block of so called free trade was nothing more than to obtain what they could no longer get in America through natural resources, so they had to obtain it in whatever way but most in the form of slavery to one people for natural resources here, so that capitalism could still be called capitalism and democracy could still be called democracy instead of the uneuphemistic names and their real name, such as socialism! Most Americans neither understood nor cared about this because they were having it all too good and thought this panacea would last forever or at least until they died. They did not even care what would happen to their very own relatives. This was what the rich and well educated were made of! This would be their epitaph that we could remember them for if we had the time ever to do such a thing, which we did not because these very same people had made it dog-eat-dog just like the Communists had done in the Revolution. The peasants there were murdered and their uprisings were put down by the Bolsheviks very quickly without a peep from any of their writers or their media. Nothing but silence for at least 50 years until the truth finally came out about them and the Western Internationalists who also played a big role in all of this bloodshed for the sake of avarice, power and ego!

Yes, I could remember when America as a nation had nothing to do with Communism except the rich and well educated who continually sold out one nation of people after another for their so called capitalism. It was a no win situation for our military and they knew it, but somebody had to fight the rich man's war, right? It of course would never be any of their "wonderful" children who only knew how to riot, take drugs, do violence by lying, and all the other 60 things that went along with what their well-to-do parents had instilled in them from the very beginning. Their parents did not really want to raise them, but just send them off with money so someone else could put up with their rebellion of America and the GOD of America! That is why day care, Soviet style, had become so familiar to them because they too had done the very same things but behind closed doors.

The lives of the super rich business world was always the most private one that could ever possibly be, and they wanted to keep it that way, but now with the Internet and computers it would be even harder, but no matter they had sold their idea that the state rules above the church because they in turn ruled the state from behind the scenes just the same way the owners of a newspaper rule the editors from behind the scenes as well as the journalists.

The so called news that was fit to print meant whatever lie they could promote here (such as infanticide) and abroad. Or the cliche "well that is the way it is" and by a Communist himself who Goldwater said he was, but of course would not retaliate because of Goldwater's strength and power in the Republican Party at that time. One sometimes must meet force with force.

The only thing the elites were worried about was that they would lose their wealth, which meant their holdings onto different geographical locations in the world which could include even certain whole nations or countries as well as the people in those nations and countries. They had to worry about giving too much pay for a decent amount of work; they had to be careful not to let there be too much freedom of the press, or free speech, and had to keep the people down as much as they could without anybody the wiser for it. This was their biggest task, at least in the West where public opinion was important and in countries where there was totalitarianism then it was brute force to silence those who meant to do well to their fellow man.

All they needed was for someone, or anyone, to open up too much and give the people what they really needed and not what they wanted, and that was the filth from Hollywood worldwide and the violence that was being committed even in democracies such as America with 55,000,000 murders of the unborn children. To do violence and then speak of freedom was a contradiction in terms, for violence meant one always had to use lies and more lies so that it would appear that freedom and liberty were on the rise when in fact these too were lies in and of themselves.

Democracy did not make one free or more free in the spiritual realm of things. Even though it did give one physical freedom, it did not transform one into what GOD would have them become, so whenever democracy was used it was used to deceive the people into believing that our way of life had to always be superior to all others even though we had done much worse with all our knowledge and money making that was enough to make one sick and nauseated. Only the ones of a lesser type of mind and heart were all for this and because it appealed to the flesh we all were guilty of this at one time or another.

One always had to include oneself when they spoke about the evil done by their own nation and could never use "them", but had to be inclusive to mean us also. We were all part of the problem and could all be part of the solution if we had a change of heart. The poor could be set up to be envious, and the rich could be set up to always be for the underdog.

One evening I had stayed home when my wife had invited her women's group to converse on the things of the day, and decided to be a part of their discussion. This was a very different kind of dialogue for me since I usually had most discussion with men only.

"Well Alice, Martha, Elizabeth and Jessica, this is my husband Luke who shall be sitting in on our conversations tonight and participate if he feels the urge to do so," said Rebecca.

"I am pleased to make all of your acquaintances," I said.

Alice was a tall woman with blonde hair and was a lawyer for estates. She was married and had no children. Her face was angular and her nose was kind of long, but her skin was almost perfect in complexion, with green eyes. Her husband had a PhD and was a professor. Martha was a mother of 4 children and was married. She stayed home to raise her children. Her husband was a real estate agent. She had brown hair and was on the short side with brown eyes, beautiful white teeth, and a most pleasant face when she smiled. Elizabeth was tall and had black hair and dark black like eyes. She was very attractive but was single and had her own beauty salon. Jessica was married and had 2 children and also was a stay at home mom. Her husband was a police officer. She had auburn hair and green eyes and looked much younger than her years would say. As the women stopped talking and started to get together for the meeting I sat next to my wife and kept silent at the start of the conversation.

"Rebecca do you think that some foods are harmful for you even though the government has said they are all right?" said Alice

"Alice I believe there are some foods that are very dangerous to eat every day and can cause cancer in most all people, so an individual must watch for themselves what they eat no matter what the government says about them," Rebecca said.

"Well do you know which foods are the most harmful if eaten daily?" asked Martha.

"Martha, the ones I read about are the following 5 foods that if eaten everyday shall give anyone cancer, and they are: soda pop, hot dogs, potato chips, sugary cereals, and bacon. If one would continue to eat these 5 foods daily they would eventually contract cancer or carcinogenic tumors somewhere in their bodies," Jessica said

"Rebecca, if I may ask, where did you get that important information from?" asked Elizabeth.

"Elizabeth, I got that information from a book called THE POLITICS OF CANCER by Dr. Epstein who did much study on foods as well as chemicals and medicines that were either harmful or were not even tested to see how good they were to use or whether they were even safe to take or not," Rebecca said.

"You mean our own government does not screen out all the products on the market in America?" asked Jessica.

"Jessica I am afraid that is so and that it is also very scary to say the least," said Rebecca.

"Today now they have this ionization for homes that send out negative electrical charges in the air to disintegrate harmful things in one's own home. Has anyone ever heard about that?" asked Alice.

I said, "Yes, I had heard about that not to long ago, but some of the systems are very expensive and require a lot of maintenance in the sense one must keep the filters clean. Then there are others that are more expensive that require little home maintenance and are very affective for household air mites as well as other germs that might be in the air, or even some kind of pollutant."

"In our own home we had gotten rid of all our rugs and had gone with hard wood floors just to eliminate rug mites and other kinds of possible infestations that might come in, and we believe we are healthier for it," said Jessica.

"I know the business that I am in that all the sprays and aerosols cannot be good for one's health, but that is the profession I so chose to go into and I really like the business a lot even though one must constantly listen to everybody's story day in and day out," said Elizabeth.

"I know when my husband sells homes he has told me that some people in new homes want the hard wood floors to be covered with rugs right away just for the aesthetic value," said Martha.

"Some of the homes I go into are beyond belief, especially when the elderly die and there is no one to take care of them or wants to and the older homes have many different odors and are sometimes even infested with all kinds of bugs. Nonetheless, I always try to do my best to accommodate the client I am serving and always have the place looking nice and clean and any repairs done that really need to be done. Estates are sometimes a difficult thing to work out, especially if there is no will, and the state can almost claim the property because of back taxes or the fact that there is no will or no executors on the will, sometimes even if there is a will. It can be a very messy business when it comes to money and estates and wills," said Alice.

"I do not think I would like to have to deal with all that," said Rebecca.

"Well Rebecca, my profession pays very lucrative and with my husband's income we can do many things such as have a child now since I have been in the practice for about 10 years and my husband has been teaching for about 15 years. We both wanted to be financially set before we had even 1 child. I will be 34 years old soon and I have no more time to wait to have a child," said Alice.

"Well I kind of feel sorry for anybody who does not have more than 1 child since an only child is a lonely child and to have children too late means by the time you have grandchildren you shall be almost too old to enjoy them as a grandparent," said Martha.

"Well each to their own, and by the way there are too many children now who are abused and should have never been brought into the world at all," said Alice.

"Alice how can you say such a horrible thing as that when you know already children we have murdered through infanticide?" said Rebecca.

"I will have to agree with Alice since my husband sees a lot of child abuse in the field of work he is in and he says many times they should never have had children at all in the first place," said Jessica.

"Jessica, don't you think your husband meant that they should take better care of their own children instead of abusing and neglecting them, and not to destroy them? The way you worded that it sounds possible that he felt sympathy and compassion for the children and not so much that they should have had an abortion."

"Well Martha, I guess you and me are what they call old fashioned since we believe in big families and the sanctity of life for all children except in the case of the woman's life which, by the way, is very rare and is less than 1/4 of 1% of all aborted babies. We want everything to be convenient for us so that we can have the life we want regardless of the affect on the rest of society. We have become too self-centered to see what we are doing to our very own nation," said Rebecca.

"Well we can disagree with you and Martha and still have a strong belief in our own nation, which means that we believe in America," said Jessica.

"I am afraid not. You cannot, Jessica, have it both ways. Either you love your country and the children that are in it, including the children in the womb, or you hate your country. That's all there is to it. I am very much offended by your statements about children since I have children of my own who I love very much indeed and would not trade them in for all the money in the world," said Martha.

"1 guess I must really be a bad person since I do not have any children of my own, right?" said Elizabeth.

"No, Elizabeth you have time to make the decision if you want to get married and have children of your very own," said Rebecca.

"Oh now one has to be married to have a child. Is that right?" asked Elizabeth.

"Do you know how many single mothers there are in America and how many children are destroyed in America or have been destroyed in America since 1973, Elizabeth?" asked Rebecca.

"All I know is what I can do with my body and my life since it is mine and I have the law on my side in regards to all of this!" said Alice.

"You very well may have man's law, but you certainly do not have GOD'S law and that is the only one that counts. Murder is murder and that is all there is to it Alice!" said Martha.

"Well my husband is a police officer and he enforces the law. Does that mean all man's laws are now bad because I disagree with you and Rebecca?" asked Jessica.

"The laws that your husband upholds are nearly all good laws set up by the 10 Commandments," said Rebecca.

"Rebecca most of those old laws are right now being outdated and the police will have to obey what the court says and the Congress," said Alice.

"Whether they obey the court or not Alice the point is it is still morally wrong no matter what our United States Supreme Court deems as law because it is not in their place to make law but just to interpret it and that is all," said Martha.

"Well all I know is that I am a law abiding citizen and whatever is "legislated" from above I shall follow no matter what," said Elizabeth.

"So in other words Elizabeth you feel that since the U.S. Supreme Court legalized infanticide that that is the law of the land and should be followed to a tee? Let me tell you now what I think, I think all the laws that the Supreme Court or for that matter any other court made should be ignored and in fact a state of emergency should be applied to all abortion clinics in America and the National Guard should be sent in to close them down just like we closed down the camps in Nazi Germany when the Allies came in to free those Holocaust survivors," said Rebecca.

"Well just because you are Jewish you do not have to be so offended by what we said," said Elizabeth.

"Elizabeth if it was only that I would not be so vehement about it but since it involves many lives in the future to come into this world I believe some of us must now stand up and be willing to fight a moral fight for what we believe in and no matter what happens at least we know with a clear and not a seared conscience we fought the good fight," said Rebecca,

I intervened because I could see that this was really heating up to be something that all these emotional women might be sorry for and not only because my wife was right, but because they had to keep their hats on, so to speak. So I then said to all the ladies if they wanted to go to the local restaurant for some good dessert and they all agreed. Later that night I told my wife Rebecca how proud of her I was since she spoke up for what she believed in no matter who was for her or not. She kissed me and said thank you and then just started to cry.

A few months later I decided to pay one last visit to my three friends Adam, Jake and Tom and this time to see how they stood on GOD'S Word the Bible.

"Well you guys you might as well know up front that I have come for the last time to be able to share with you the Gospel of Jesus Christ which shall determine your final eternal destination as to where you go after you die."

"Okay preacher," said Adam, "pretend I am the first man and I have sinned by having sex in the garden with Eve now what will happen to me?"

"First of all Adam sex was not what Adam in the garden had done to commit sin. It was he took a bite of fruit from the one tree that GOD told him not to do out of all the trees in the garden along with Eve even though Eve was deceived and Adam blamed it on Eve," I said.

"Well Luke let's say that I murder someone like Jeffrey Dahmer did and then would come to the Lord could I still be saved?" asked Jake.

"Yes, Jake you could be saved and in fact that is exactly what had happened to Dahmer when he last went to prison where he was murdered, but had accepted Jesus as His personal Lord and Savior first before being killed," I said.

"Are you trying to tell me that I who have killed no one at all shall go to Hell and Jeffrey Dahmer shall be in heaven or is now in heaven and he killed many people especially many minorities and then even cannibalized them and is now I repeat in heaven?" asked Tom.

"Yes Tom that is the truth, because he came to the Lord before he was murdered and because of that the shed blood at Calvary covered all of his sins no matter how heinous they were for that is why Jesus came to save sinners and we all are sinners and to be transformed by Him into a new person in our spiritual heart," I said.

"I don't know about the rest of you guys but I think that Luke has taken this religion thing one step much too far and is ready for the men in white coats," said Adam.

Jake and Tom both agreed with what Adam had said and I then got up and did not say a word and left their presence and till this day I have not seen, nor heard from any of them since. They had not heard the Father's voice for they did not receive the gift of salvation.

1 had thought about what I had read in today's paper about what the Moslems had done to those Russian children in Russia and thought to myself that Putin a Communist could care less about the Russian people just like Stalin, Trotsky, Lenin and Khruschev had. Now that Islam was attacking Russia would they retaliate for if Putin did not he could possibly be removed from office? He was not fooling the Russian people about his class hatred and his ideology of Communism. They had been through that for almost 75 years and knew how the Communists felt about the Russian people in general. If it would happen to anyone in the

Communist Party well then that might be another thing. Would Magog and Gog, Moscow and Tubal now be ready to blame Israel for this since the Communists had done this many times before when they held power in Russia in the 20th century? Would the Russian people now have repentance which would open the path to self-limitation. This would be an inner transformation that would take place. I also thought to myself why had not Hollywood not taken one of Alexander Solzhenitsyn's novels or plays, or stories and made it into a movie, not that he would let them, but why did they not? Could it be that since they mostly were socialists out in Hollywood that that would reveal to the American public just what socialism and Communism was like and that whether it was Nazism or Communism they both were to the left and were socialistic and both pointed toward Communism even though one was racism and the other was class warfare and in fact in America the blacks now had some race warfare going since about 30% were Moslems and mostly always voted for the pro-Communist Democratic Party no matter how devious the candidates were like Bill Clinton. Angela Davis, Jesse Jackson, Ron Dellums, Martin Luther King, Jr., Ted Abernathy, the Reverend Leon Sullivan from Philadelphia, Congressman Fattah from Philadelphia, Jesse Jackson, Jr, etc. were all members of the Communist Party. No body could say anything for feared to be called a bigot and a racist, but it was just the opposite way around and in fact it was even worse since they all hated their very own country and wanted to see it's downfall as soon as possible and most of them were pure materialists since most of them were millionaires and had said many anti-Semitic remarks as well as non-Biblical speech such as hate speeches with Louis Farrakhan and his brotherhood of Islam

And the now famous Moslem attorney with his Moslem black body guards Johnny Cochran.

Along with civil rights came homosexual rights and none of the civil rights' leaders said a word about it which told me even more about their love for their own country of America and the way they always wanted to be referred to as African-

Americans which in and of itself said enough to me to mean I no longer love my country tis of thee sweet land of liberty and yet the Jews who had been persecuted more than anyone else loved America even though they too were far to the left. Why had there not been any quarantining for AIDS' patients like they did for TB and for leprosy? This was a deadly disease that was being spread intentionally by homosexuals and also one could not forget pedophilia which a major portion of them were also homosexual pedophiles! There had to be a quarantine for this virus that came from really a perverse and psychiatric mental disorder and was also dangerous to all school children. The thing was that there was a cure for homosexuality, but most homosexuals did not want to opt for that at all and in fact they preferred to stay the way they were because the government especially the courts had given them their perverse lifestyle and make it legal by judicial fiat. The homosexual was playing Russian roulette and so much that they wanted to share what they had with the general public and the civil righters kept saying that AIDS was from the CIA because they themselves were very promiscuous with sex as well as the Hispanics in America and no one could stop one if they wanted to "inject" themselves with a cancer causing virus. This civil rights' socialism had gone too far and soon I believed that it would eventually back fire because all one court had to do was to decree that affirmative action be reversed which started in Nazi Germany and that would be it, but then again they did not know or want to know the truth since they too refused to live GODLY and moral lives!

Some time later the President put into affect a law that said that people making less than about $23,000 a year would be entitled to overtime by law and the laws would be clearer to understand, but there was one catch and that was he was doing this to make up for the illegals who were taking jobs away from Americans here and overseas by big business and so if he could please the lower income working man with overtime when in the first place he should not be part of the proletariat at all like the unions who were mob run and were supporting socialist functions through their Democratic Party. He also should have known and he did that making it up to these low wage earners was not what they needed but a fair pay for a job well done and not government socialism just to win an election. The minimum wage law was such a shame that to offer a man $5.15 an hour was an insult to Americans who lived here all their lives and the rich were getting richer and the poor were really getting poorer and the other side was even worse because they would want to take all the meat and then when the government threw them back the bones they would say, GOD save our government, or as in England, GOD SAVE THE KING! This was this cat and mouse game of all political. parties. Their ideology could not be changed and had nothing moral about it at all.

The standard of living would go down meaning it would become unsanitary for Americans to now live in America plus the wages would stand still, but not the taxes meaning the dollar was worth absolutely nothing so when one went to work they really went to work for nothing at all since government was bankrupt and socialism would have to buy out everything piece by piece until everything would be taken care of by government including who would live and who would die and that was just around the corner.

The American people bought into the lie that what they had was theirs for good, but in reality it belonged to the state because everyone had to pay taxes and property taxes would go so high to support government that people would rather live under socialism knowing that they would always have a job and not to have to worry about shelter for that too would be taken care of by government. It was just a matter or a slight of hand, that would do it and prestidigitation all would belong in common or collectively to all the cogs in the machinery, except of course the socialists and the Communists and the rich and well educated who really never cared what had happened to them below but only that they would be taken care of for life.

America. had never gone through this before so the wool could be pulled over their eyes very easily by giving them now all that they wanted and needed and then more. There would have to be a price to pay for all of this and that would be one's physical and spiritual freedom!

Who could now bring us back to free enterprise since our own corrupt government and it's officials had brought socialism into just about all parts of our society except with the possible exception of physical residence which would be inveritably next. Monopolies and non-enforcement of anti-trust laws was wreaking havoc in our free or once free enterprise system. Prices were going up while demand was high and that was anomalous to what should have happened! We had lost our own bearings and Islamic oil would be needed for years thanks to David Rockefeller and Henry Kissinger who culminated through World Bank to decide which nation or nations would get loans and since now most had to be multicultural to exist those were the ones getting the loans, of course just so they could pay back the loan with interest no matter if they dealt such as in Latin America with drugs and the drugs cartel. The money would be available to them to promote capitalism yes capitalism and then socialism which it now was because of some of these internationalists. When they would die then it would even get much worse since their very offspring and followers would even be worse than they were!

We had polluted our own air, rivers, lakes and streams as well as oceans and began to build artificial dams which would only do more harm than good to our natural environment and this is what real protection of the environment was all about and not the ones who wanted to confiscate private property. Land should be sold to all at a premium meaning that no big corporation could buy land whether they were American or foreign owned. We had enough land that is for everyone not including illegals or others who were never citizens, but for Americans so possibly they could once again work the soil and provide for their own families and our government and big business and the rich and well educated had to be removed from the scene in regards to this so that America first could get healthy physically and most of all morally or spiritually. After that then we could look to fair trade with the world and have other countries pay the world prices that others were paying and not to give away like we did to the Soviets wheat for example in exchange for their appeasement. We had done what the Soviets had done to Russia but from capitalism's side and we were now up a blind alley and had no way to turn around. All capitalisms do eventually run to socialism. The banks should not be a panacea!

Islam was doing all it could to destroy capitalism and big business by using terrorism all around the world except for Red China and I knew why that was. It was quite evident as to why Red China the dragon was left alone at least for now. Pakistan and India would soon go at it alone with Iran and Israel or Iran and the Western businessman. That is why Osama Ben Laden had attacked the two World Trade Center buildings because he knew what was making the Western World's monetary system work and he also knew that oil was just one of its components. Remember he too was from the rich and well educated. Islam though was like socialism in that now most of it came to it's real roots of violence and the same death wish that all socialisms have, but on the outside look different just like in America when we had murdered 1 and a half million unborn children and nobody went to "war" against those involved in that because it did not represent wealth to them but for Christians it did represent a different kind of human wealth much more valuable than any one could put a price on. All the wealth in the world was so close and so tied together that one more major thing and a catastrophic occurrence would occur world wide and the West would fall quickly. Red China could still wait a little longer to test our resolve which we lacked so for them it was just a matter of first getting Taiwan and Japan and Korea plus all of Southeast Asia and Asia itself with no one to match the lethal arsenal that they had and that they would use and not like the Soviets who used it to impress. The Red Chinese would use it soon if things continued on the present course and nothing surprising would occur in Red China, but in the West much would change in only one day and that would be all that would be needed.

When we had won at Grenada we thought that was a big to do, but what would we do if we now had to defend the oil wells from the Red Chinese who could care less whether they took them or whether they blew them up just to wreck the Western economic system that was so interlocked together with hard assets and of course the stock market with it's paper tiger facade that was not really worth anything except in theory. The Communists understood about financial ends to support a major war for Lenin had taught them that.

Our actual population was about 200,000,000 of English Americans who were loyal to GOD.

I could see many white American children who were poor being neglected by our own government for in order to qualify for something one had to be politically correct and non-European as far as ancestry or why ask if one was anything but white on job applications, but everything else? These humble poor white children one could see had to struggle in life since their parents had to really work for all they could get. These were not run of the mill minorities who were so pampered by the educational elite and by the rich and well educated probably because they had a fascination for either their men or their women and hence controlled things in—our society for their own hangups.

These children wore clothes that were old and ragged and nobody even noticed them because again it was not a politically correct issue to be dealt with since they were plain and ordinary white children who did not complain but continued on with school and tried their best to read write and do their arithmetic if that was ever taught any longer besides tribalism, racism, multiculturalism, and socialism of the group mentality and if there was a YMCA or a PAL it was strictly for the minorities who earned their right to cry and whine about everything and anything they could since this government was not only for the underdog, but because it appealed to the rich and well educated since most of their children were intermarrying with these foreigners or malcontents as such. One had to belong to a group to get any benefit from America's multiculturalism which meant repeat the lie enough and even these poor children would start to believe that they themselves had something to do with all this and were to blame and were also in fear since the authorities would always go after them since they too were trained that way. The unnoticed white American child who got no attention and not the suburbanite emulator that imitated everything that they saw and their parents who made good money and were prima donnas in our society because they too went along with the winner mentality. It was not like the Jewish children who were innately smart whether rich or poor, but children whose parents just struggled to survive and there was this culture shock of "I really do care for my children and love them so very much" but government and the educational realm could care less because it had become a popularity contest to see who could get the most trophies."

I took notice that many white European girls who cross dated with minorities had usually some kind of emotional instability in one way or another and were not very moral about their own lives and seemed to want any kind of attention. Again there appeared to be a mental illness amongst most of these girls if one studied them very carefully along with a rebellious attitude towards their own family. In some families all of the children intermarried without even thinking about the great differential between cultures and the animosity and the fact that most minorities were more prejudice than their white counterparts for if America was truly racist it would not have allowed 12% of the population to do just about anything they wanted to do, and then the Hispanics and then the Orientals, the Romanians, the Jamaicans, the Cubans, the Puerto Ricans, the Indians from India, etc. all developed an attitude that they did not have years ago and that was to resent the things of America, of course with government's liberal help and the fact that sex was the predominant thing about all of this. So that is why also I believe that homosexuality was included by the civil rights leaders with civil rights as well as most blacks and Hispanics who were intimidated by the blacks but nonetheless followed their footsteps because they too wanted to achieve special favors from government at all levels. Nobody dare say a word about this for if they did they would be labeled a racist and Lenin in the beginning of the 20th century had kept his eye on the American black to set diversity and hatred in and today all the ones who were benefiting from this knew all along what corruption and racism was involved, but nonetheless took it in stride and if they were found out they could always cry prejudice!

The mulatto children were wanted by nobody. The blacks thought that they were too light and the whites thought that they were too dark. This is what our culture had come to. Having sex because of lust and physical attraction and to prove that certain men were really men by having children out of wedlock from all kinds of women, which would give them the status by the rich and well educated in sports, television, radio, education, politics, etc. It would take years to mingle the right and proper way without using race as a tool to obtain what one wanted.

The disrespect that the black male showed for the Negro women was shameful since most of them found marriage to be a white man's thing, but yet the Bible set it to be GOD'S thing! The Negro women would have to work and provide for their children and the biological fathers were being rewarded by the rich and well educated with the most lucrative sports professions, acting roles, government jobs, etc. which mostly went on political correctness. If there was to be this so called equality in America then why was it that 85% of the basketball players in the NBA were black? Yes a double standard was set here, but who would ever have the audacity to say anything since the 60's had set a precedent for this and this was about one generation or 40 years later and I myself had grown tired of the rich and well-educated's game of political correctness. If the others in society could be made to follow the dead beat dads then that would mean all the cogs in the machinery would be equal a quote from Stalin! Young people were easy to impress if it was constant ly shown on television and promoted in Hollywood and the news media and colleges and universities tuitions were paying for the dead beat athletes who could not even read and write but who the millionaires would take in so that they could make them millions of dollars plus make the people come to more of a slave mentality.

If the rich children did it then it was good enough for everybody else. No one would discern, separate and differentiate at all but would just follow along like a herd of cattle would with no one to guide them. It was chic to be this way rebellious and wild and disrespectful to ones in authorities, because the iconoclasts had done the same in society like 0. J. and others who even had gotten away with cold blooded murder. Not all were fooled by the liberalism of not to let man be truly free, but this blind eyed instinct of impulse that said, "Do your thing".

The European family unit was being destroyed from within by the rich who by the way never wanted to raise their children and by the dead beat dads who thought exactly alike and both also thought infanticide was good since sex was free and easy and the taxpayer would be forced to pay for their promiscuity that had become prevalent and so prevalent that even the average population thought that good was evil and evil was good. The wild youth of today especially from the middle to upper classes to the minority poor and now the not so minority poor who were getting jobs and positions, that is the ones who would do what the rich and well educated told them to do by affirmative action, quotas, set asides, etc and no one that I ever knew clever refused to take this hand me down! The churches too became a part of this because most of them were from middle to upper white class neighborhoods and felt this underdog mentality was a thing to go along with and this sort of false guilt about what they did not truly always earn but had taken from someone else, "beg, borrow, or steal. "Yes, the poor average white child was neglected since the 60's and became lost as to their cultural European background which had always been part of the Founding Forefathers culture. Now it was taboo to even mention that one was a white European that wanted to contribute to America too and not through hand me downs. They wanted to earn it if they could just get the chance to do it. Remember this was the poor and not middle and upper class whites in America who would go along with anything as long as it meant the status quo. They had to work twice as hard to get a position or a job as had occurred years ago-when a Negro had to do the same. Was this poetic justice? I think not since these children had nothing to do with what their fathers had done and if relations were to be even keel then we had to make sure the best qualified got the job and not one that another one could pull the wool over the other one's eye! This had to be an even and balanced playing field for all concerned.

In major league baseball we seemed not to have enough white American baseball players from college or from the Negro community to make the majors, but yet players that usually stood out were from an average to poor neighborhood, but yet Rockefeller's pull had Hispanics in the Major Leagues like there was no tomorrow and most hardly even could speak English and had a bad attitude in regards to discipline that they had gotten from the blacks and some of the Moslems in sports and Roman Catholicism would not help that would be for sure since that meant get all that you can and even more from America and be indifferent to Americans no matter what, and the government played it up as well as the lawyers and the courts and again the rich and well educated.

All these elites never lived where most or some of these athletes came from so what did they know about that lower part of life and did they really care at all? They too were good actors and played their roles very well. Yes, some athletes were good, but most were really minor league players.

The Jewish people sometimes reminded one of King Saul in their unruliness and then at times like King David with honor and kindness and respect. They were a most difficult people to understand at times and many times their actions proved opposite than their speech. They were the most charitable people in America and made up 2% of the entire population in America and yet gave more than all the Gentiles combined. This was their Christian nature as a people world wide and it showed, but they did not reveal this at all so they were silent about their charity while the Gentiles would put up stain glass windows with their names on it to advertise what they had given.

Many American ministries tried to get on the good side of the Jewish people knowing that they were very charitable and did not really care if they witnessed about Messiah to them. The America church was money and consumer oriented even when disaster struck and still continued to beg for more and more money on television and radio as well as in the mail and elsewhere.

There was no stopping the Protestant pastors from living like a king and one could see it in where they chose to live with lawyers and judges. In Roman Catholicism there was no doubt that money over the Bible rated first with them, because they hardly ever even read it at all and did not care and thought that they could take their riches to Hell with them, since they believed in works and not the grace of Jesus Christ alone. Tradition just like Judaism was it for them and praying to the saints in Scripture when the Bible was explicit about who to pray to.

In fact the Jewish people were more charitable then Roman Catholics and would donate to the poor, but rarely would a Catholic give to the poor in need in the form of monetary funds and usually when they gave it was in the surplus that they had. No one in Judaism was pushing Judaism on the Gentiles and that was probably for a good reason and they really never even knew it, since GOD wanted a remnant to be saved that is the Jews all over the world which meant most likely a very small number.

The more the blacks became anti-Semitic in America the more unusual things were happening to them just as had occurred in Russia. Any nation or group of people such as the Nazis who murdered the Jews found themselves given over to reprobate minds to the third and the fourth generations.

We in America had to possibly go through the coming judgment of GOD, since we in America had allowed the murder of over 55,000,000 babies better known as infanticide. We also allowed our own government to promote homosexuality, pedophilia, multiculturalism, socialism, Nazism, Communism, all kinds of racisms, lust, gluttony, avarice, drugs and not medicine, child abuse, disrespect for parents, etc. America was noted for two things all around the world and they were stealing and taking drugs because Americans had no real purpose in life since affluence had not fulfilled anything even though Americans went full speed ahead into oblivion. We had no kind of leadership anywhere in government. Our children were becoming strangers to us more and more.

We started with slavery which was racism and now we would be ending with slavery, but reverse slavery because the 3rd World people were now coming here and demanding everything because they thought we owed them a living, when we all owed the world a living. Our natural resources were almost depleted from big business and big government and most land was owned either by foreigners or by the government and little people in America knew this nor did they really care because they were anxious to do things by impulse without even thinking about what they were doing.

Relationships were fragmented beyond repair and Islam could do anything it wanted just like it had occurred in Russia before the Revolution and in the Soviet Union after the Revolution and in fact it was left alone. We were in a war that should have never been fought but had only sent aid to help the people, but others such as some internationalists had other ideas and other internationalists were for the war. This was causing more cataclysmic occurrences in the world. Red China as of yet had not been attacked, because 1) it had closed borders and 2) they would wait till we gave them all they needed to defeat us by checkmate, or do a conventional type war or a nuclear war. They had all the time in the world since the West was so impetuous to give anything for capitalism and materialism.

We had lost the will to live a moral and upright life and so we were on the road of no return, The West had nothing to share except its money and technology for socialism's natural resources as well as human resources. People and peoples were expendable for avarice and power.

We were being poisoned to death by eating the foods that just about had all preservatives in them and also pesticides and other chemicals. People in America were actually, through government, eating foods that should not have been on the market. Fast foods were also poison to one's body, and obesity and diabetes and other illnesses were afflicting millions of Americans. Also people even from other lands were being afflicted with these same disorders. One other thing I noticed was that no matter where one had come from in the world most all people coming here had gotten worse in their lifestyle plus their attitude. That is why many wanted to come to America because one could be as wild as one could be with no laws for punishment. It was as if America was possessed with some kind of demonic spirits.

Probably the two worse inventions ever devised were the telephone and the television because it made one have no will of their own and influenced one's mind to emulate what one saw and was seen instantaneously around the world, which would produce shock to different cultures. To other cultures it was already there and the telephone was also bad because it showed nothing from nothing leaves nothing, meaning the airwaves of voices would transmit, but could never supplant as one being there and if they were not there then progress had gone too far! This airwave technology was nothing but waves of sound and even light that transmitted images at an instant and was meant not to teach, but to restrict the use of one's brain.

This "Babylon" known as the West was so to burn out because it had no self-discipline to restrict itself with nature and was consuming for the entire world and then some with no regard for the others in the world. In fact a Communist Sultan wanted to form a group of nations in the third world to take control of the West. What could the West do but adapt to their way of life which really was not a way of life, and then again neither was ours. One day when our enemies got what they needed, which would be soon, then the West would have to concede all freedoms that they felt were not really important since we placed no value on them at all. The West was out of supplies so to speak and now could deal with nothing more since the most important natural resources were just about used up and the socialistic countries would now make their move to entertain the West with either a takeover or a war in certain areas or the threat of a war for that nation's sovereignty, but then again GOD could just pull the roots out since only weeds were now growing there and there was no wheat for the harvest any longer. Now the powerful and rich in the East had what they needed to destroy a good part of the world that had been a bother to them and had no more use, plus the fact they needed more land for their billions of people who they could care less about but only continue to tell them lies about imperialism and how it made them suffer, which would be their arsenal since we did never show any compassion for the peoples of these lands and they knew it.

We were or had been our own worse enemy and we had to love our enemies, but we could not do that since we did not even love our own country enough. Thugs could now take over just so we could be provided for with shelter, a job, medical care, etc. Everything we needed would be there or so we thought. We lived like there was no tomorrow.

The purpose in our own lives had become useless, since we did not do anything to stop this cancer in the body of America. It was spreading rapidly through America's body and was soon terminal and malignant. Then there would be no cure when all of this or most of this could have been prevented. Our own town looked like a 3rd world pigsty and we just went about our lives just like it was not there because it was out of sight, out of mind.

Urban plight was like emigration from one's very own nation with no love for it, but just apathy. Who had taught us to behave like this over night and what would happen to our children and grandchildren? We had been hypnotized by our 5 senses of the flesh. We had to have everything now and immediately. We were anxious for all things. Stress had now become anxiety. Our national body had become old when it should have been young and vivid with about only 3 centuries in the being.

What we saw we wanted and wanted it now with no foresight for the future. All we had to do was to curtail our appetite for this world and forget about self and look to help others in need and be also concerned for people we had never seen nor would ever meet. This was universal freedom and socialism was just the opposite universal destruction.

People could become like animals in that they would follow or even stampede into oblivion. And still there was no deportation of any Moslems en masse from America and we were in the 3rd year after 9/11 and neither major democratic parties' ideologies would venture even to do that when terrorists attacks here and abroad were being committed. One had also been committed in Los Angeles International Airport at an EL AL waiting line when a Moslem terrorist was going to gun down 40-80 passengers in a line with an automatic weapon, but an alert EL AL security guard spotted it, attacked the terrorist and killed him with a gun and saved the lives of many people in line. Yet this President had said that after 9/11 there were no terrorist attacks on American soil. He was still believing his own lies and Jewish people did not count as people according to his tabulation.

This administration or bureaucracy and all administrations are bureaucracies kept playing politics as usual and really got nothing done except catch Saddam Hussein who had gotten

Klaus Barbey's attorney to defend him and should that surprise anybody that the Arabs and Nazis had been in bed before, during and after World War II and were at it again. Israel was blocking what these internationalists wanted to do and Bush, as I said before was the only President to have ever made the statement that he wanted a Palestinian State.

A good Anglophile really never gave some in America a President to vote for since the other "same party" candidate who was a Catholic Jew would be even worse because socialism or materialism would be his criteria with no defense of America and this socialism would eat him and America up so quickly and Islamic Jihad would for sure have it their way. The President or incumbent wanted to bring socialism much slower to America and the other candidate wanted to bring it to America right now! Also this President wanted to change the federal law that said Hispanics had to be here for 10 years and have a job to 5 years with only being a resident, and he said he was for protecting our own borders?

Both major parties were the same and the Republicans were starting to catch up with the National Socialist Democratic Party. One ideology to serve both parties, socialism. Everyone would have health care, have a job, because it would be illegal not to have a job, resident permits, less crime, and the state would raise the children like they were doing now with homosexual pedophiles.

I knew that in one place that I had subcontracted work with was like Sodom and Gomorrah and supported the Moslems and the Nazis were funding this corporation with money to continue on with their anti-Semitism and the drunken Irish were also contributing to the cause. Most of the employees were bisexuals, homosexuals, homosexual pedophiles, etc. There were also Moslems that were there and all this under the boards' auspices of them. They also supported Nazism in a covert way and even had some secular Jews working for them who did not even know about all of this. They supported infanticide and black racism and multiculturalism to the fullest. The normal white average European heterosexual male was indeed very rare to find, and ones who said they were Christians were only social Christians. They were too afraid of losing their good paying positions even for Christ and regarded money first.

This entire community was pro-Nazi German, and if one did not have money or was not an Anglo-Saxon, or a homosexual of any kind it would be hard to make the ranks and the media in this area was controlled by the English. Many Jewish people who lived here were professionals but did have people such as on the police force one police officer who was Jewish and one in the one major hospital on the board who also was Jewish because of this area's virulent anti-Semitism. They had to be watched now more than ever after 9/11 because the Germans in this area had it in their blood to be anti-Semitic. They were not friendly to outsiders and were as cold as ice and lived in their . . .

The blacks in this area were also highly anti-Semitic and so were the Hispanics, which had come as no surprise since both these groups resented the fact that the Jewish people were so bright and affluent and also extravagant. There were also many Catholics in this area, which also meant more anti-Semitism. The urban area was strictly of the Democratic Socialist Party because it gave free handouts for ones who worked or did not work. There was no criteria for achievement or non-achievement whatsoever. Even the charities favored the Hispanics, especially Roman Catholicism because most Hispanics only knew this type of religion and not the religion of the Bible or of the Jews. In fact the Hispanics would always call the Jewish people, "The Christ killers". One always knew where that had come from.

Once the American Jews were no longer needed in America it would become like a "Pale of Settlement" but even much worse because there would indeed be a restriction on where Jews and Christians could go. The American Jew was much too informed about our own State Department in regards to Israel and about what part Islam and the Nazis played in all of this in America. They had to be restricted and that is why I believed they had brought out affirmative action just the same as the Nazis in Germany had and that is to keep all Jews out of government jobs so they would be ignorant to what was happening and also to be eventually an enemy to Israel since the West would always need the oil from the Moslem terrorists.

The reason our own government kept using euphemistic names for these Islamic terrorists was because they wanted oil and this one world government to come even quicker then it was. Names such as Al Qaeda, the PLO, Hamas, Hezbollah, etc. were all excuses for Islam to ease up on their sanctions on the West in regards to oil and its supply as well as prices. We were dealing with Red China because we in the West were begging the Red Chinese Communist government to give us more natural resources for our missile technology and the space race was really about who could control this earth from outer space from space stations and satellites.

Europe wanted to place first as far as doing it through materialism and Red China could care less if it was by technology or by human resources because they already had too many people and needed to get rid of them, but not like the Soviets had done to the Russian people in Gulags alone but more for a conventional standing army. Even Reagan had sold the AWACS air plane to the Saudis to spy on Israel when the Saudis did not even have a standing army! Who was kidding whom? One way or another the Gentile powers wanted to dispose of Israel and its few allies, but as of yet they had not been successful and in Israel the Chief Justice of the Supreme Court was the one calling the shots even more so then in our own U.S. Supreme Court.

The enemy knew his time was short so he was trying to accelerate his hold on the Gentiles since there was one more Week for the Hebrews and of course the name of Messiah that had all to do with GOD. "If only the human race could forget Messiah and His followers of Jew and Gentile and even Ishmael's relatives, would this be the kind of world he could more take control of?"

The English were quite bright and had a good sense of humor, but in their private lives it was totally derelict and liberal as one could have it be. Their research in medicine was good and in banking they were excellent and they were versatile people but hated the Russians with such a passion. The German were not too bright and would do something over and over again until they would get it right. They would play follow the leader no matter who it was and were very sneaky and were ice cold. The Polish were good at usually one thing and were not a versatile people. They were in love with money and Roman Catholicism because of the prestige it gave them, they thought, all over the world. They were an obstinate people and usually were good at only one thing and would excel at it. The French knew everything there was to know and were Jesuits who opposed the Masons but stood for the same thing: socialism. They were anti-Semitic and did many things on impulse. Etiquette and cuisine was their thing, but their sanitary manners were terrible. In fact in France they had no doors on the ladies' and the men's rest rooms and ate live monkey as delicacy. They usually had a mistress and a wife.

The Italians were nuts about clothing and food and were also money hungry because of Roman Catholicism. They were quite smart and very versatile, but too hot headed and emotional and were bad politicians, but good law enforcement officers and pretty good judges. They were womanizers too many times. The Sicilians were a mixture mostly of Turkish background. That is why the murders in the Mafia or La Cosa Nostra were done so brutally and viciously. They were good barbers and pimps. They had few manners and were very crude and had made it bad for most Italians in America. One had to be a total Sicilian in order to be in the Mafia. This feud had gone on for centuries and centuries. The Irish were bright and versatile, but had a tremendous drinking problem and to be around a drunken Irish person one then had probably encountered the worse kind of person. All one had to do was look at America's Kennedy clan and their pro-Nazi leanings and their wild escapades. That is part of the reason they were killing each other in Ireland even more so then because of religion. The American Negro was now Black and were very cheap but did support their local pastors quite well. They were not versatile but were good athletes in only certain sports, especially the ones that one had to use their feet on the ground and quick movements. They were cold like the Germans. Even though they appeared emotional it was more of a wildness on their part. They could have been hard workers like the Poles and Germans, but they resented slavery in the past that much that they felt the white American government owed it to them. This was a matriarchal culture. They were gradually achieving, but the Europeans and the Hispanics did not like that too much since it meant that they would soon catch up with Anglo Americans in education and would no longer need affirmative action or quotas, so the elites invented these two plus others for now the Hispanics and now they would be the poster boy for the federal government that was taking its orders from the internationalists, and now the American people were satisfied with this since they were doing pretty well even though they whined about things they did not need to whine about and since they were doing what the government and others wanted them to do and that is be apathetic. In that way it would be much easier to take control. The Hispanics were also a matriarchal society and very clannish and prejudice to ones outside their group even though they played up to the American black. They were not good in politics and their men were not good authority figures since they had lived under the Spanish and Portuguese cultures who were gold diggers. A few centuries of this and that is what one could expect: "conquistador" mentality along with our government's help. They spoke a slang form of Spanish and did not want to assimilate but wanted to take over, like the word conquistador indicates. They were highly excitable and very impatient and lacked a lot of self-discipline in life. Machismo meant that when they were married, the husband could cheat on his wife and even the children were told this was all right, almost like the French. The wife, though could not do the same and their daughters were taught this, so when they came to America the women rarely married because of this. They just would instead have sex and have children and the mothers would do almost anything for their own children, including stealing if it came to that. Their mind set was not European because of this conquistador mentality and because of the Hispanic culture. Big Business had robbed and raped their lands and was continuing to do more and more since they had more natural resources in Central and South America than even the United States ever had! Our government was only following orders to their census here. The Orientals in America had assimilated considering how much prejudice was held against them. The Chinese were very smart in business and medicine, but were isolationists. The Japanese had been scared to death and became Westernized because of the atomic bombs dropped on Nagasaki and Hiroshima. They were diligent workers and family oriented even to the fourth generation just like America had once been. The Vietnamese were almost like lost vagabonds and were more humble and were not liked by the other two. The Vietcong here were like true blue Communists. In all these languages it was "look say", but in English it was phonetics. Some schools in America taught both look say and phonics which made the children develop dyslexia on purpose.

The Russians were a humble and kind people who did have tempers but were very smart and extremely good in literature and science and medicine. They were a friendly people and very easy going to get along with. They were not liked, though, by the Anglo-Saxons because the Anglo-Saxons feared them immensely because of the wars they had lost even with superior odds.

The Jewish in America were very extravagant and knew nothing at all about even the Old Testament, but donated millions and millions of dollars to Israel, but also wanted to tell the Israelis what to do with this money and the Israelis would have no part in this at all. The Israelis in fact were rough and ready and the American Jewish male was anything but rough and ready, but was versatile and smart in all fields. The Russian Jews I believe were the smartest group of people barring none in the entire world. The American Jews were very spoiled and secular. They could always get ahead and were very good providing husbands for their wives and their children.

The Indians from India were smart but very arrogant and were highly anti-Semitic, but then again in India the Roman Catholic Church had been there! They were very money hungry and had volatile tempers and would not conform to customs here in America. They did not assimilate and their culture was insane to say the least from rat temples to crippling their own children so they could go and beg for them. The swastika was from India and the New Age originated from there and Bill Gates of Microsoft was pro-India along with all of their other idiosyncrasies. And I could go on and on with this wonderful" diversity" which would include Nazi Germany's homosexuality agenda and also the English with theirs. This was that "people with disabilities Act!"

This diversity meant there was no good vs. evil, the worker and the lackadaisical, etc. It meant nothing about GODLY rights, but everything to do with anti-American sentiment and the Germans who would always follow a leader and the English who would stoop to the lowest level would be all for this. The blacks liked it too because it meant that they could do more than before and that would mean that all things would become legal just for them! They were striving to be "perfect", but not like GOD was because only GOD could be perfect. This diversity was in essence multiculturalism which had its roots in Maxist/Leninism and many did not even know that. All they saw was a way to get even with the European who they thought should not have what he had, even if he had worked for it fair and square and that is why they took these special jobs with affirmative action and quotas knowing themselves it was wrong but their own human nature told them it was owed to them right now Our government even supported this ideology with full knowledge This diversity so the politician could not say that he did not know what it meant when it would eventually come back to them in a different way than they had ever realized!

The word diversity, even if one said it slowly, one could hear the tearing apart of something and in this case America and as far as the East is from the West. It was to destroy America into Americanism, something even the average American was now doing and that was blame all of America for all of the world's woes! This would surely entertain all the socialists and Communists and Nazis in America and including the secular Jews and the blacks that had become so arrogant since the 50's that one would never had known that they were from the very same country called America! Was it America that did this to them, or was it their own freewill, because many people foreign born appeared to have this hatred for America and the GOD of Abraham, Isaac and Jacob and Messiah? Blame America for everything since we had achieved what these other cultures never achieved in medicine, electronics, physics, aerodynamics, etc Where else could they have gotten their free ride to America thanks to our own very government and the rich and well educated who too either hated America or were always for the underdog no matter even if that underdog was a foreign ideology!

Our children were being told lies and lies and that could only produce violence in America itself. This was the time to pickup the money and run. Even reparations were said to be in effect, but that was from the American taxpayers and not the rich and elite who, in the first place, were the knaves in all of this! But nobody cared about that just so they had their eye for an eye and a tooth for a tooth mentality in the sense that one would get even someday and today was that someday, but then again why would the poor have to pay for what the rich had been doing since almost time began? The rich always ruled and that is the way it was and the way it would be in the future that is in this world, because this was not really GOD'S world in the sense that there was sin!

I am my brother's keeper had no meaning and did not mean that what one could do for themselves others should do for then such as redistribution of wealth. It meant responsibilities for one's own actions and rights for others which were not always written down, but came from the heart and not from guilt Roman Catholicism worked well with self-criticism just like Stalin had taught.

Money was being taken out of the country also besides technology and with the government's knowledge and of course the rich and well educated who instigated it all for themselves for now. The nationality problem became more intensive because of the socialists in Hollywood and in the media. If one was a true American that had to mean that they had to be a scoundrel! They would be the one to blame just like the Jews were to blame in Nazi Germany, except it had nothing to do with the economy but everything to do with morality!

We had surrendered to what we thought we had done and that was false guilt and nothing could be done about false guilt. No one country can be blamed for this for nations just like individuals have all sinned and have had their good and bad times. America now was though having it's bad time because it had gone along now with the lie that was being perpetrated on the nation's soul and who could do that?

We were Americans and not multiculturalists like had happened in Yugoslavia; when Tito died and all the different nations within that country went after each other because there was no common bond like there had been in America It was diversity, yes there is that word again this time used in the right context. See how diverse that Yugoslavia is! Now that is what this same diversity was meant to do for America and since the 60's it was progressing towards that goat, English was lost!

As Lenin had robbed all the banks in Russia before and during the Revolution, the banks in America too were getting too much power and were left to themselves until it was found out that Moslems or terrorists were channeling terrorists' monies through banks again and again and still our government was sleeping on the job in this regard. Everything was centered around our banks here and worldwide who were actually creating many problems and if one could usurp their power then one would most surely control all the financial conditions here and abroad. With computers and the Internet there was a good possibility that the banks could be taken with one fell swoop. It was a matter of time I believed, before this would eventually happen, because if one had all the money in the world and no food or water, then it would be worthless to the mass public and the theory of the dollar would vanish. America's stock market would be liquidated for sure and the rich and well educated in America would have just that paper money like monopoly money. It would have no value because the American people would no longer believe in this theory or even trust the banks and so a barter system would have to exist if one wanted to trade and do business amongst the common person.

Too much had always been placed on money with big business and Communism and the Communists knew that eventually that in order for the capitalists to make money one had to have the natural resources to deal with and if they did not then their money would be worthless since we were giving, not selling anything. The natural resources would be stopped and the West now would have to face the music of just how to survive and to protect what they thought they had: No legal tender, but only a symbol to buy and sell, and the rest would all be waste if the symbol was not there; no matter how much stock one had, or how much money one had to buy and sell, it would do no good now that this symbol was what was needed.

Governments would go bankrupt and would not be able to feed their own people. Only a few nations would have control of the world economy and those would be the ones with the one world government and one world religion, and who better than the Jew would be best for this to occur? Even England would have to bow and Germany and America to this new power on the world scene and how did it get all its strength so quick and so fast and all at once?

Rebecca and myself took a short trip to New York City, the cancerous tumor of all cancerous tumors of cities in America to see just how bad it was in regard to heathenism and multiculturalism not to mention socialism. Now a billionaire was mayor and was trying to do what he thought he could do to protect his turf. The billionaires in the world all did not see eye to eye and were ready to let all hell break loose. The south side belonged to one and the north side belonged to another and this was nothing new as far as turf and as to who owned whom. These were internationalists that had to come to a meeting of the minds no matter what culture they came from just so that there was an agreement not to interfere with their flow of money and power for if that would occur then somebody somewhere would have to then put their life on the line. It would not be the billionaires but ones below them that owned businesses and were in government ideology. Big business would even have to concede to these internationalists if they wanted to be where they were and of course the smaller millionaires would also do or not do what they were and of course they still wanted to live the life of Riley.

Networking was being used for this so that this world government system could not be knocked out by hitting one network for they were interlocked, but yet would not affect the outcome of the other networks. These were now all over the world and were growing and growing and no one really knew where the ultimate power would stop and with whom. It had roots going all over the world by different names such as fascism, socialism, Communism, multiculturalism and all the millions of people who would follow their book said, "They had to do or not to do in order to stay in the system." The one in control had been around for thousands and possibly more years and knew where to take this Babylon of the world. The lady of the world that was also a false religion had also, as I said before, a false government so government and religion of one kind in this New Age was what this was all about. Either one played along or else!

Well as I was saying, my wife and I did our very short visit to New York City and saw a glimpse of what hell on earth was really like. There were no morals or absolutes and the sights that one saw one could not believe and this was only one part of America, a hub sort of that transmitted its filth worldwide by media control. This is where the United Nations of the world was at and acted in best regards to the world business system and most of all world socialism or this New World Order!

Yes, the enemy could play havoc with the weather, but also was GOD maybe allowing this to occur? In the Florida peninsula hurricane after hurricane was coming through where such things as Sodom and Gomorrah's Disney World was, Rush Limbaugh lived, Jean Biese who had been selling occult things on QVC a television sales program channel, plus the retired citizens or senior citizens that had said, "I've lived my life and you live yours", but then again there were other poor people who lived there. The rain does fail on the just and the unjust! As in the Old Testament though it appeared that GOD was allowing this to occur and in fact His permissive will was telling us to be obedient right now and no longer procrastinate with our own immoral lives! We had to be about our Father's business and right now do what He now wanted to do and give up our affluence and freedom to abuse our own free will the way we thought we should which could possibly . . .

It had already hit places where Satan had a stronghold and was continuing on by rioting and looting even when people from the same culture were suffering severely. This was like the Old Testament Israelites that would many times refuse GOD'S immediate warning to stop sinning and come to their senses. The culture in Florida had changed to a heathen one as well as an affluent one that said, "Do what you want anytime you want to whomever you want!"

All of our 50 separate entities, and that is what they had become were like 50 separate cultures and much more and this multiculturalism was running rampant all across America and was getting worse and the two candidates really thought that they wanted to rule a no man's land! They would have more grief than one could imagine, but their egos were leading them astray with,

"I must at any cost to this nation called America, because I know better than GOD and I know for sure what he wants me to do" and the other candidate said, "I am a god!"

These were not chance occurrences that were taking place in America there's no such thing as chance or so called circumstantial events for everything has a reason, but it is just that we do not know what the reason is. GOD is in control and His thoughts are not our thoughts and thank goodness for that or we all would be done for. Man's human nature was insane and getting worse by each day. We had to hit bottom, but what then would occur after all this havoc and chaos if we would be turned over to the enemy's territory? One could only wonder how worse this would get.

It had been exactly one full generation, or 40 years that this had all started and now retribution instead of a respite (for that was now over) was beginning to set in. Our 60's generation was now living out their last days, and we had created such a disturbance that had no real meaning and never really stood up for anything that had any decent value or purpose in life and now some of the remnants were appearing on the horizon and with alarming rapidity. People continued to work on the Sabbath while Islam prayed to their god, or so called god, but then again the enemy had control of them so we had no excuse to act like heathens even though we did time and again and how long would this continue to go on as I said before until we reached the point of no return?

We invited heathen cultures, that is the people, because in a democracy the one fault is that the majority of people are the government and so we are responsible for what our government does. It is not like a monarch where one individual takes the blame for all since they are ruling. In our case we got the government we deserved because mob rule is democracy and by and for the people. Even Benjamin Franklin had said, "It is a republic, now try and keep it!" Not to good of an omen to look forward to and from one of the Founding Forefathers at that.

We had acted like we all had just one main brain thinking for all of us and so we were like a lost herd of sheep with no shepherd and the only Shepherd that would do would be Jesus, the Good

Shepherd. We had fallen down and lost our way and now the wolves were coming in to devour us with no protection because we were just that way, wanderers. We had many "nations" in one country and our government officials were sold on socialism which meant there was no GOD! If GOD was not needed what were we getting all so excited about, but then again while some in Florida were suffering the rest of the country continued to watch sports and more sports and get drunk and take drugs and Hollywood was the same, no had gotten worse.

The churches had nothing to preach except wealth and affluence and self-esteem. I had never seen so many rich and well-to-do social Christians in all of my life and they were enjoying the life of Riley. There was no repentance as a nation for we had forgotten what that was and had thought that it was only Islam at 9/11 and had nothing to do with our way or new way of life which meant ego and selfishness and not selflessness. This all for sure was coming to an end, for if GOD did not protect we were doomed.

Why was America taking drugs and not medicine when we had not really gone through anything nearly like the Gulag or even the concentration camps and remember the first camps were invented by Stalin and not Hitler and had killed about 66,000,000 people in all with at one time 15,000,000 peasants? What had America really gone through that was so dramatic? Was it our own affluence that made life seem more and more useless? What had America achieved at least in the last 40 years that was nothing but evil and sin? What had worn us out so quickly? Had been too much of this and too much of that but not enough of Him? People could hardly walk, and that was the young. Obesity was prevalent eating had become all that we chose to do day after day to fulfill our own depression. Affluence has a way of making us grow sideways and also the other extreme was malnutrition. Even our eating had become sinful by not eating in moderation instead of dieting and by eating anything that was unfit to eat even for animals! What had happened to sanity and reason instead of instinct, passion and impulse?

With each next generation came more deformities and sicknesses and illnesses and diseases. We were giving our own children anything but GOD' S true love and would not sacrifice our time, but made no conservative effort to stop the insanity of buying anything and everything. People would rather gamble then eat and take drugs rather then live and have sex and possibly die, but not get married first and have a family in the normal way of things and then we wondered what had happened?

America had no excuse to be the way it was for it had fallen on each one of us to do something for GOD that would not be seen or benefit us such as a tax return for charitable donations. Those type of donations were meant to do the work of GOD and not for restitution, after all it was all His!

Our doctors were only in on office hours 9-5 weekdays and the hospitals were giving second hand help to emergency needs some too late and much too little. The churches were going either to picnics or swimming parties or were driving the luxurious cars on Sundays to get away, but from what? We were weak from what? The moral fiber of America was so weak that just one major incident and all would be gone that is our excessive materialism but would that not be a good thing, maybe then we would come back to our real senses and start to see the light and come to know that materialism meant little in our lives and that GOD wants our love and not our love for money or even His creation?

My own wife who had many physical ailments never even complained about them and yet always had time to help ones in need and not just within our immediate family circle like most Catholics did. Going outside the realm of family is where real Christianity started, because what one did for one's family was what was normally expected. To go beyond this is where real Christianity and not to get rich and live in luxury, but to accept one's plight in life with no complaints for who were we to complain when we had so much materialism that our own poor people were rich compared to the rest of the world? My wife had a herniated disc in her cervical column in the back of the neck with severe pain, and the neurosurgeons said "live with the pain"!

She also had ulcers from a man who had no feelings whatsoever for anybody or anything besides himself. He had grown up with no father and was sent to a private school by his mother who, by the way, was a teacher herself! My wife had two bad knees, but because her insurance was government insurance, they would not do surgery and wanted to use her as a guinea pig. Even one of their best doctors retired so he could go into business in the Philippines Islands with his brother. What dedication! There was one Jewish doctor, though he was near 80 years old, who was still in practice and did make house calls. Yes house calls! My wife also had high blood pressure, osteoporosis along with pain in her back, neck, legs and some migraine headaches, but no complaints. She also had trouble losing weight because of her arthritis in her body which reduced her movement much, but only ate a small amount of food a day such as some crackers and half a sandwich and a glass or two of milk. She was not gluttony, but ever so kind to ones when she had the money or when she was broke. GOD always honored her loyalty to HIS charity, and she needed no one to tell her to do this. In fact at times I thought I had to restrain her, but how can one restrain such a loving and compassionate woman in this day and age, so I had to treat my wife as Christ had treated the church! She had total sclerosis of the spine and curvature of the spine to also deal with and could not get down on her knees and get back up and could not lift anything really over 5-10 pounds, but helped others whenever she could and was a most wonderful mother and grandmother that one could ever have had. That was thanks to GOD, and I, her husband, was mated with a most beautiful and wonderful wife. Her kind deeds were never ostentatious for she never even thought about that, but only to help ones in need, first the believer and then the poor.

Who had turned our very own children and youth to the enemy, but the 60's generation that made the filth and garbage that came out of Hollywood and the media in New York City! It certainly was not the children who had made these films that were mass produced one by one by derelicts and knaves who had no conscience about whom they were hurting physically, mentally, emotionally and spiritually.

It was all for money and the love of it with no end in sight, and our own government never even tried to close them down because they too had become as devious as the producers themselves and enjoyed it also. This was what they called their freedom of speech and freedom of expression, whatever that meant to them. They pursued this filth and garbage with liquid manure and movies, if one could call them that that glorified murder, drug dealing, blood shedding, abuse to children, homosexuality, and made evil prevail in the end. The Christian church was silent too about this like all religions in the past and only the real body of Christ could now pray for GOD to take any Christians involved in this so that their bodies would be turned over to Satan and the souls would be saved.

The Western Church was even investing in stocks that produced this filth and garbage and never even took the time to find out about it! This is how much consumerism had taken over the religions who professed Christ Jehovah Witnesses, the Mormons, the Seventh Day Adventists, were just a few cults and even some thought that the Roman Catholic Church was also a cult because it promoted many things that were non-Biblical, but did believe in the Trinity. It was a time of little Christian discernment and few Christians even thought about discernment let alone to boycott this filth on television and in the movies. We also should have boycotted use of much gas in all of our cars so that Islam would suffer a slump, but pleasure was the number one priority and so even more gas was being used because the American people refused to give up anything that inconvenienced them. They would have no part in this at all.

The elderly had given up and the other part of the elderly were enjoying life too much to care about anybody else so the young and the wild savage beasts were taking over since the rich and well educated were dying off from the 60's. No one wanted to sacrifice anything, but they would sacrifice our own children to just about anything that was put in front of them from pornography to liquid manure.

Legal guardians was a better term instead of mother and father in our nation of Soviet day care. Families in America were having fewer children, and especially the Europeans because convenience and luxury which they got from the 60's parents was rubbing off on them even more so now that they had children of their own. Houses were being built so that people could have only 1 or 2 children at most and that is how selfish this nation had become. Luxury and convenience and work that really was not physical work since all the equipment was power driven including screwdrivers and drills and saws and whatever else the younger generation used. This was a lazy generation due to technology, which also was bringing in a new form of non-work such as computers and other devices. People were now getting more sick because of overweight, and the elderly though were living longer so now the population would boom when the baby boomers would retire when that generation alone made up 2 to 3 generations in and of itself. More would be living off welfare and less would be working, and with the illegals the numbers would go up even more and more! Government loved this because then they got more to spend that was not really there at all to spend and were dealing just in theory hoping for more of the same trade as in Red China!

"We will bury you" was not a play of words by a peasant, and in fact if a minority in America got into the White House one would see how far they too would go as far as this peasant from Russia had gone. The lowest income people sometimes were worse then the upper echelon especially if they had gotten into power since there was that envy always present to encourage them to get more for themselves and to also be even more brutal since they had given up on their old way of life and found ideology to be to their very liking. This is what was appearing on the horizon right now.

Anything to promote capitalism more than anything else except socialism since capitalism had contributed to socialism more than anything in the world. This was this utopia they had always talked about these civil rights' leaders and other minorities, but where were they getting the money to do all these power moves and who was allowing it to occur since we were talking billions and billions of ready made dollars?

Yes America's families were almost extinct and the tribal mentality of the Germans as well as many minorities was in vogue. The African tribal chieftain usually understood more about Communism because when a leader of a tribe got old they got rid of him and it was not like a democratic republic!

The "imports" from Third World countries met the demand for the supplies that were being made in Red China a Communist country and the internationalists loved this to no end! It meant more people any kind of people from anywhere would now buy foolishly more of these slave products because most of them were simple in life and did not even understand what democracy was so how would they even know how Communism worked, or was it the other way around? This was the so called supply and demand theory of today's world market in America or this so called globalism was nothing more than greed and to promote socialism through capitalism at an even faster rate. It was an artificial system that would make it look like America's economy was growing no matter who was in the White House. We could pay them now or pay them later for to them it did not matter in Red Communist China and not just China like our government used to like to call it over and over again.

Supply and demand and the prices were so low or they appeared that way that one could buy the very same item in a well known store but at a Wal Mart for example the very same product label could be bought for as little as sometimes 75% less than at a well known store and it all said made in China and never said Red China because our Congress was in bed with the Communists there and hated the peasants there with a passion as well as the about 100,000,000 Christians in Red China as well as in the rest of the entire world where people believed in the GOD of Abraham, Isaac and Jacob, but the Communists would play off of this too by saying it was the imperialists' pigs in the West that were to blame meaning the American people and not the Rockefellers, Kissingers, Haigs, Clintons, the United States Senate, the President, the State Department, no we would certainly take the blame since no truth would ever get to them and they were doing what the Soviets had done in Russia and that was to use the English language as the Soviets used the Russian language and that certainly was no compliment to them. The Russians at that time and certainly was no compliment to all English speaking people in the West since it made the people themselves look like the knave and not the ideologues in big business and in government. How would the different peoples ever get to know the real truth about this, until it was too late and then people would be killing people for the ideology of socialism and the economic system of capitalism that brought all this socialism to the world more than anything else good ever possibly have!

The resentment of the 3rd World peoples who had come to America was done by the rich and well educated on purpose because now all the colleges and universities in America taught was socialism, which made it look like we were going all along with the Communists in other countries and that many foreigners coming here were also Communists and socialists ready to change our country here from one of GOD to one of anything goes and guess what, our own government was involved with this up to their pretty neck as only a scoundrel could, and they knew it. Take it out on the American citizen for he was to blame for the plight in life, and look now how well the socialists in higher education treated them so good and decent since they made special provisions for them according to multiculturalism which had its basis in Marxist/Leninism.

This is what was making our government so strong and not just the special interest groups that had no brains and thought that only brawn would be needed to handle anything that they always wanted to take it outside! We were being undermined by a corrupt and illegal government that did not care and did not have even the backbone to defend its own sovereign nation known as America. When could any politician now be trusted to do any good? If he was elected in whatever way, then he had to be part of the problem itself and had to be in it up to his neck in this. There could be no two ways about it, but one who benefited from this had to be a scoundrel of huge proportions or else he never would have gotten that far where only now the very rich could get elected and once elected then so be it. They were owned and controlled by others and their love for money to the fullest. They would do anything and everything to stay in office as long as they could and knew they would get a reprieve if they did something so corrupt and evil that it no longer matter what they did! This was now their very mindset since all the rest in Washington D.C. and in the other 4 levels of government were also getting away with even murder!

Did democracy work at all and if not why not and what had it to do with the truth at all since democracies are never a search for the truth at anytime in history no matter what. The people in America had been dumbed down even more since public education was OBE and the higher levels of education was nothing as I had said before, pure and straight socialism and nothing else and the professors did nothing to hide this since the NEA and other unions made it perfectly clear that they were for man's end.

"Rebecca don't you think that most Americans have become down right lazy in general and always need to participate in some strenuous exercise because their bodies do know real physical labor and they continue to diet and diet to no avail and it would be better if they had jobs that were both mental and physical like a farmer and the fact that most laborers used mechanized machinery such as electric saws, power lawn mowers, electric screwdrivers, electric hammers, cars, etc.?" I asked.

"Luke I do agree with you that most men in America fit that exact description that you just mentioned, but as for women, that is the ones who stay at home and raise their children and do a woman's work that is never done, then I would have to disagree with you completely," Rebecca said.

"Well I never considered that, but you are right. Now Rebecca, how do you feel about the Presidential candidates that are running, at least the two major ones?" I asked.

"Luke, I do know something about the one candidate, John Kerry. I know he only served 3 months in Vietnam and everyone there served at least 1 year unless they got a medical or mental discharge. He should have gotten a dishonorable discharge and if he would have, he would not have been able ever to own property in America!"

"I know that he was in the Navy and tried to get a purple heart but was thrown out of the commanding officers' room. He also said he was in Cambodia on a secret mission but when they talked to 3 high military officials, one of which was an Admiral, none of them ever heard of such a mission. He was hated by all his follow officers. He was later a full fledged Communist who went to Paris with Hanoi Jane Fonda to talk with the Vietcong and denigrated all our soldiers in Vietnam just like Senator Edward Kennedy did. Kennedy said that our soldiers in Iraq were mercenaries, and should have been impeached as a United States Senator, and John Kerry should be disqualified for Presidency for being a Communist like Bill Clinton is," I said.

"Luke those are very strong words to use for someone who has risen that high, don't you think?"

"Rebecca the whole National Democratic Party and especially the Black Caucus are all socialists and use their race to hide behind their ideology and no one takes them to task about their nefarious dealings with the Communist Party that is even in the Congressional Record when we used to have in the House of Representatives the Committee of UnAmerican House Activities that investigated all Communists in the United States, but was done away with by a liberal socialist U.S. Senator in the south by the name of Sam Ervin, who helped prosecute Nixon in the Watergate affair."

"Luke this whole thing has gone too far that now even Communists are in our very government at all levels and nothing is being done about it. I also know this about John Kerry, that he never filled out the proper forms in the Navy for a purple heart all three times that he got one. Even though he is Jewish, he is a disgrace to my people just like Mr. Bronstein, Senator Jacob Javitz, Mo Annenberg, Allan King, Shimon Peres, Henry Kissinger, and Senator Ribicoff who, along with Javitz, increased the amount of immigration by Arabs coming into this country, which could only bring the Islamic problem here, plus the oil problem here eventually since the Moslems knew that many Jews in America held prestigious positions in just about all the professions."

"Rebecca, continuing on with John Kerry, the only sailors who liked him were the ones that only spent 2-6 days at the most with him. The self-inflicted wound in the gluteus maximus was done by a hand grenade. I also know he missed 76% of all Senate sessions since he has been a Senator. I wonder where he was at all those times? He did vote for the war in Iraq though! Rebecca, remember you just said how hard stay-at-home mothers work and I agreed?"

"Yes Luke, I do, but what about it?"

"Well did you know now that many women make more money than their husbands so that they can promote socialism and not because of any so called equality issue?"

"I did not know that Luke!"

"Rebecca, also in today's economy I make less money than my dad did because of all the illegals here and the over taxation from the government and the socialism in government that is being coerced from the American public to redistribute wealth and not just income. Also the dollar is only worth about 2-3 cents because we are some 15-17 trillion dollars in debt right now!"

"Luke, that is a very worrisome indicator!"

"Rebecca, what do you think about France's law that says all cleric scarves on girls who go to school there are illegal, that is of the Moslem religion, and that now in Iraq they are taking hostages since that law was passed?"

"Luke that does not surprise me a bit about Islam whether they are Shiites, Sunnis, Sikhs or any other form of Islam such as Hamas, Hezbollab, Al Qaeda, etc. This is a demonic type of religion and for this President to say Islam and Judeo-Christianity worship the same god is horrible. He should retract that statement immediately, but this election is more important to him than GOD on this issue even though he is a Christian. He also opens the door for demonic activity when a Christian such as him or anybody else sins and does not repent immediately. I know they say that if I do not vote for this incumbent that John Kerry shall win. To tell you the truth Luke, I am tired of playing socialistic politics, because with John Kerry we shall get there immediately, and with the incumbent much more gradually, so I'd rather take my medicine now and not vote at all since for me to vote for either one would be a sin."

"Rebecca I totally agree with you on that because the very First Commandment in the Ten Commandments says that we shall "have no other god before Thee ". It could not be any clearer than that for me also. The incumbent is missing his opportunity as to why GOD put him in, but probably only when he meets GOD face to face shall he know how important it was to never say that about Christianity and Islam. GOD must always be first in one's life and nothing else. Being a politician is not excuse for what he said. He reminds me a little of another leader who, though, came from peasant stock and did not know why GOD had called him to be a leader in the Soviet Union and that was Nikita Khruschev."

"Luke let me ask you this question about Germany. Do you feel that since some Germans felt so much remorse that they went over to Roman Catholicism from Protestantism because of the Holocaust and because Martin Luther was a virulent anti-Semite?"

"Rebecca, I really never gave that much thought until now. I do feel, though, that you make a good point in asking that because the Jesuits who hate the German Masons, but who both uphold both anti-Semitism and socialism but come at it from different ends. I also feel that since Germany was in bed with the Arabs during and after and up to now, that France might have just imposed that new scarf law because of this difference. It is something like what is happening in America in a way. Whenever anybody talks about anything important besides sports, the weather, Hollywood and especially non-racial things or socialism itself, then it is not to be discussed because anything other than those things would be politically incorrect, a term that Lenin started years ago."

"Why do the English and the Germans fear so much the Russians, Luke? I know why the Jewish people dislike the Russians, but why do those two nationalities fear Russia?"

"I think they fear the Russians because, for one, it is the biggest country in the world and, second, they both had been beaten even with extremely good odds and equipment years back and know how good their fighters were (that is the peasants) when it came to fighting for their Christian nation. The Germans because of homosexuality and their demeanor love the uniform, and the English just like to swagger with a uniform on to make themselves appear superior to all others. That is why I think these nationalities fear the Russians, and also the fact that the English and Germans had a lot to do with the spread of Communism at the Yalta Conference and when Germany put Lenin and his entourage in a sealed train from Germany to Moscow which started world Communism! I would also fear a nation that did something so horrible as that!"

After our discussion I thought about how words and their meanings had changed, such as good and evil, "kid" and not children or child, "laterally challenged" and not overweight or fat, "vertically challenged" instead of short (which most of the leading Nazis were), "administration" instead of a bureauracy, "gay" instead of homosexual, "lesbian" instead of Sodomite, "server" instead of waiter or waitress, "senior citizen" instead of elderly, etc.

I was very glad I had that discussion with my wife so that we knew what each other exactly thought, not that we could not change our minds, but then again to do that would be to give up our very faith, and that I could not see from Rebecca or myself now or at anytime in the future. She was a loyal and trusting wife, and I was a loyal and trusting husband. We were both one in Christ Jesus that made us one and not two, like most marriages are who are either both unbelievers or one is a believer and one is not. We were like the Old Testament Israelites and even though Rebecca was a Messianic Jew and I a Christian Gentile, it was somewhat like Ruth in the Old Testament.

It appeared that the Jewish people were inventing computer bites that would do many things thought impossible except by George Orwell in his book 1984. They now had bites that could be used in forest that were about the size of a baseball and were even getting smaller and in England. There were cameras at traffic lights and other corners to keep terrorism out or at least they thought so, but were actually inviting the enemy to increase his one world government. The Israelis had already invented in Israel mites that would give off a signal to say when you were low in a certain type of cereal for instance, but would also transmit it back to the manufacturer and that would eventually be big brother or the State. This computerized generation thought all this to be wonderful and protective instead of deportation of all Moslems that were in Christian nations, but then that would of course ruin the enemy's plan as an excuse to make man a slave to the one world government and this thing called globalism.

Even now we were on record as to where we lived and where we went and who our relatives were and were being marked as just a beginning that would surely get worse. We all just seemed to go about our own lives nonchalantly as if this was no big thing since it would protect us, or do the very opposite and in totalitarian countries where one's private and public life are one they knew the consequences of all this, but in the West they just took all this for granted. Soon the internationalists would be first to get hold of this and already had it with them. They would open Pandora's Box and out would come something that not even they could have ever imagined. If one ever read the Communist Manifesto in full they would see just how brutal and vicious man could really be, but few ever really read it including the Communists themselves.

The false trinity was seeming more and more everyday to becoming on the scene and the entire world was coming under or at least the West was for sure to start it with all it's modem technology. But we were giving it to the Red Chinese which meant that it would even be much more worse than one could ever have imagined.

Computer bites so small that they would be just like dust particles and no one could be able to see them with the human eye and this would most surely set up this system of the Antichrist.

England, America, Germany, Israel were the 4 major countries contributing to this technology.

When GOD told Satan, "You can do anything to Job but take his life", it appeared that that was almost occurring in America since we were getting hurricanes and tornadoes and other kinds of violent weather across the entire nation of America. America too had a national soul and Russia had too experienced it, but only a few Christians remained and for them to do that they were tried time and again by the enemy such as Solzhenitsyn was until Dr. Kornfeld witnessed to Solzhenitsyn before he was later murdered that very night in a concentration camp. Solzhenitsyn had taken GOD seriously. We in America seemed to be more worried about money and how much damage it would cause in dollars and cents and not that we should thank GOD. It was not worse that Satan was doing to us since I believed that GOD was allowing this to occur because HE LOVED us with an undying love and was trying to get us to repent and sin no more! There were pagan tattoo shops, gambling casinos, pornography houses, the Mardi Gras, Disney World, and the very rich and well to do that lived in this area and all this sin that was now bring us our own retribution and for Christians it meant demonic influence if we Christians continued to sin.

We had to come to our senses about sin and not wait like Adam waited to see his own death physically and spiritually when he too was warned about his sin as well as his wife Eve's sin! Nobody was quoted as saying, "We must repent from our sinful ways as a nation or else allow maybe Satan more into our nation by disobeying GOD who is a fair and just GOD. How long would it take and if we did repent would it be too late as far as our own generation to see a healing process?

America had fallen so far and illnesses that were strange and different were afflicting all of us which were quite different than ones when I was a young boy. We as Christians just might get to heaven quicker than we ever thought and did we really want that? Were we accelerating GOD'S judgment on ourselves and our nation that started over 300 years ago and built up to this not overnight but through all years and continued up to the present day. Did we have to see the beginning of the end or the handwriting on the wall to now know that we were turned over to

Satan by GOD since we refused His love and His protection and served Him with only our mouths. "The rain falls on the just and the unjust."

"Who would save us from this wretched body?" that is the body of America, which did not mean the Body of Christ. They were totally two different things even though they both had a personality, one that was full of agapé love and one full of filial love. Christianity had to still be in America or we would have most certainly been gone long ago as a national entity, or one people. We had not been the Tower of Babel, but a one language that meant unity and not chaos which is not of GOD. Chaos could only bring about totalitarianism and nothing else since survival of the fittest would come into play. People could run away from the storms, but not from GOD EVER. We all had to face some sort of music that we did not want to face no matter what.

With Jesus it was not, "You can pay me now or pay me later" but it has all been paid in full! We at this moment would not get a so called second chance to remedy the situation because we were all different human beings with each a different soul since the beginning of man on earth. This would be our one time to do and be obedient to GOD now and not later since our life this time in the mortal realm was in the here and now for us and it had been for others and it would be for others to come. We had to do what GOD wanted us to do or not to do! No less no more. We made sin complicated because we had forgotten about GOD. Without sin it would not be complicated since that is what GOD had wanted Adam . . .

The secular Jews in America made it even scarier since that got worse and worse the majority of them. Thanks to my Messianic Jewish wife I could see Jesus in her many times and when even she did not know that what she ate which was little, or how she prepared things in the house she had done it just like in the Old Testament. This was an uncanny thing for all the Jews I had ever been around but now with a wife who was a believer it was even more incredible this love of GOD in her life by the power of the Holy Spirit. It was wonderful to watch her do things that she was not even aware of and yet did them in such a Biblical way and sometimes I would mention this to her and she would sometimes cry and say, "I love you Luke."

I knew I wanted to see my wife again after this mortal short life here on earth and said so to her many times. She felt the same way even though we both knew one did not marry there! One in Christ Jesus that did things in such a mysterious way that was wonderful to know that GOD cared.

Capitalism came to mean almost the same thing that socialism and Communism came to mean in the now defunct Soviet Union who by the way still was run by the Communist Party since most all the peasants had been killed and the people now also lived in dire poverty. In America no one would do anything without money or one could not do it just for free there was always a catch. Avarice had gotten into the people somewhat like socialism had gotten in to the people in Russia except that the peasants were lied to and the Americans were not. Americans knew exactly what they wanted and it was more of the same. Even the younger people had been destroyed as far as being kind and that was saying pretty much since children and young people are usually kinder then most adults.

The more the rich and well educated got the more they wanted no matter who they had to hurt or destroy in the process. They had become as cold as ice. The blacks were the same just plain stingy and the Catholics were even worse. The English and Germans also could share in their own greed along with the Polish and Italians two groups of Catholics. Now with Islam the greed would even get worse and worse. America did not know what hope, faith and charity, yes charity, which meant love was all about and did not care to.

Like the Soviet Union also government was buying out big business one after the other and would not let the business just fail. The airlines were regulated as well as utilities and the insurance companies and everyone called this capitalism, but it had long ago had not been capitalism but just good old socialism. The people would surely be taken care of! The elderly could care less what happened to anybody else and that started with the socialist FDR. Then LBJ came along with his bleeding heart for more socialism in his Great Society so between that and the New Deal we got socialism plain and simple.

Prudential owned so much in other things then property and the banks were involved up to their necks with government handouts that the stockholders would never see. American Express also got involved and donated to infanticide as well as Prudential and they both thought nothing about it. If one looked at what America really produced that did not involve infanticide, pesticides, smog pollution, noise pollution, pornography, filth and sleaze, drugs and stealing, homosexuality, and pedophilia, euthanasia, dishonest taxes and dishonest labor, drunkenness, over prescribed medications because of medicine being invested in that field which was a contradiction according to the Hippocratic Oath which by the way they never had to take or say, foster care, day care, cars that were built as planned obsolescence, amusement parks galore for adults, gambling for the politicians, prostitution, tattooing, cosmetics, jewelry at extravagant prices, etc. it would be pretty hard to find. So America itself was actually a type of "Babylon". Our profits involved the most corrupt and vile type of commodities that one could ever think of ever!

We were selling the world the worse of the worse with the natural resources we got from all socialists nations for their expendable human resources that were being killed or dying at an early age because of many nefarious activities on the part of their so called governments. America was now not manufacturing to help others but was just a service country that had nothing to offer since farming was almost gone and even the farmers at least some of them started to get greedy.

No one in America ever owned their own land because there was always taxes to pay which meant that the land would revert back to the state many times since the elderly in particular could not pay their taxes for the illegal criminals that our government kept bringing here each day. It made the politicians' pockets fat. Just go and vote and that would be all one would have to do, but the question now was "Who do I vote for?"

There was one ideology that one could vote for so since there were many parties there was many candidates, but it was just the same as voting for only one candidate who was running for office. One could not distinguish one from the other and they all appeared to be like clones. Where could one get a constant pay raise plus all the perks and special privileges without doing any work whatsoever?

The paid liars or the lawyers were behind just about all of this and they had absolutely no morals to speak about and many secular Jews who were innate with law because the Law had been given to them were now making unGODLY laws to benefit themselves each and every time. This was promoting socialism more than anything else besides capitalism. The politicians were all lawyers. One good turn deserved another.

It appeared just about every other business had become non-profit like the hospitals and the United Way just to mention a few. They took in millions and millions of taxpayers' dollars from government and also charge usurious amounts for care and treatment as well as one's stay in their facilities. For a hospital to call itself non-profit was beyond belief since the administrators, or bureaucrats, were getting huge salaries and the United Way funded homosexuality, infanticide, black racism through your local YMCA who would pump weights and then go out in the streets at night and mug and rob people. This was what just some of the non-profit organizations were so called doing for us. Also the bureaucrats in the United Way made up to half of a million dollars a year as a salary and the IRS did make them pay taxes! Also Big Brothers and Big Sisters and the Girls' Scouts of America were both Sodomite organizations who molested children and this too was to provide for us a better society well maybe in Nazi Germany!

Non-profit was just another word for socialization of our culture by our own government to promote for them That is the government what was bad and vile in society and making money off of the sick was indeed bad and taking money as the unions and United Way had done out of one's paycheck reminded one somewhat of the young organization of the Komsomol in the Soviet Union. I remember one time that my employer took out some money for the United Way and I told them never again to do that since I was not asked. The unions still did it to intimidate the workers so that the Socialist Democratic Party could use the money for a Communist like John Kerry who should have served time in San Quentin, as well as Bill Clinton for many years! But here he was like Clinton running for President because the lawyers or the politicians all too had some kind of criminal immoral record so they had to go along with a cover-up or else they too would be under investigation.

Non-profit meant, in a way, a sort of mutual fund with no stockholders so that the cream would always go to the top the way it did in corporations and the illegal so called funds of profits that never incarcerated their own, that is the CEO's like at Enron, but did incarcerate Martha Stewart to prove that women were equal to men. Ehyrlichmann and Haldemann both went to a country club atmosphere since they both were just like Nazis in the Watergate scandal which too was a cover-up for something much more important since Nixon took it sitting down and he was one not to take things sitting down even though he was a Quaker. The Martha Stewart fiasco also meant that Communists and Nazis and even Moslem radicals could run corporations in America and that would be all right because that meant that America had been sold out already.

It was just like the time when the present incumbent in the White House was a governor in his state and sentenced a woman, and a Christian at that, to the death penalty but could not sentence now terrorists to the death penalty by a military tribunal because it was a military affair and not a domestic affair like the trial lawyers and the buddies, the better-red-than-dead group made Saddam Hussein's trial and his Nazi lawyer. The facts were all out there for all to see, but since it did not hit home with them it did not matter, just like when Art Linkletter became involved in the anti-drug campaign when his son died of an overdose of drugs. No, in America people use to get involved in things that were good and opposed openly things such as the murder of infants, homosexuality, etc. In fact I knew one doctor who had gone to prison for performing an abortion on a young girl many years ago.

The Martha Stewart was, yes, a fiasco to anyone who looked at it for what it really was and not because she perjured herself in court, because if that would have been true then Bill Clinton first of all would have gone to prison long before he ever became President of the United States since he was indicted no less the 12 times and was exonerated all 12 times and that was before he was impeached as a President, but the socialists in the Democratic Party had to keep a party member in good standing to promote their standing towards more of Communism in our very own government.

The teachers in our own country such as Bill O'Reilly were flakes to begin with and would support always the underdog like Mr. O'Reilly supported homosexuality and said that military medals meant nothing at all in the military. The reason John Kerry said that was because he was a Communist and a Lenin Prize would have meant much more to him than 3 Purple Hearts, a Bronze Star, and a Silver Star, which were all illegitimate by the way. This is what Communism worked on, lies.

We were definitely under socialism and liberalism would not just do in describing the truth. These people meant to destroy America and the party ideology infected them like it did Al Gore and his wife when they used to be pro-life. It is this anti-humanity ideology and not anti-Communism because Communism had no moral authority to rule, but only to destroy human life even though it was a type of an oligarchy which was totalitarianism run by a group of thugs just like the Mafia but much much worse than one could ever imagine unless one had lived under such a regime like the Khmer Rouge who, by the way, were Oriental so that meant that if a yellow man murdered another yellow man of the Christian faith that would be all right since the real religion was Marxism just like Lenin had replaced the Russian Orthodox Church with after the Revolution in Russia!

Yes, America was taking the same road that Russia took but by not killing all of it's own, one by not using the word socialism or Communism ever, and by not ever mentioning that government was funding corporations and businesses it kept this ideology undercover. So much so that the American people had bought into it since this was a transformation from a democracy without a violent revolution like in Russia and we were not a monarch like Russia was and which Russia had only 8 months of democracy from February to August of that same year. This would be the same ideology, but by a so called different method and a different approach since most Americans knew hardly anything about Communism, but they knew everything about us.

They had sold the American people a bad bill of goods and also the American people were apathetic which is probably the worse thing that could happen to any people and that is accept anything in place of something!

The lawyers of the world had the same ideology no matter where they practiced law and this is why and how the World Court in Europe came to be since Communism must continue to expand internationally with no end in sight. In the Nuremburg trials there were Soviet judges there that should have been on trial since they were trying socialists like themselves and this "social justice" was nothing more than a direct goal towards Communism. I knew what justice was, but Social justice—what could that possibly have meant but the promotion of socialism like social security, etc. But since the American people were getting their pockets full that was all that mattered now and there was more of that to come and of course a new way of life and for unbelievers it would not matter, For every action there is inevitably an opposite reaction and this was from liberty to chains! A slavery that would be much worse than any slavery that America had ever known ever!

The rich and well educated—did they really want a revolution, or was it the magnetic draw of socialism's outwardness that drew them to it? And yet the Communists, though, like Kerry and Clinton appeared that had been their entire lives of waiting again since the 60's a revolution a physical one at that to come to America. Many did not know that these "Bolsheviks" would obliterate them that is the socialists, just as quickly and even more so then the ones for democracy since they did not go all the way. The teachers in our society could not even spell and read properly and were supposed to be educating our children, but since when did we really have qualified teachers in that profession since almost anyone could go to a state teachers' college and get a socialist degree from the pockets of the taxpayers!

It appeared the talent was going to the banks and social services and not into engineering because the money was also in government where one could easily become a millionaire in a short amount of time. They were leaving their positions and others were being educated in the different fields of laws so the cream went to the top that is they were taking only the good paying jobs and that was just what they were jobs with good pay in a socialist society. The government kept increasing and that meant more government workers and that also meant more and more socialism so that the rich and well educated's children would follow the same path that their parents had gone and that was into government business which also meant that our private lives now became our public lives just like in good old Kremlin and England had started this move in America and we of course followed like blind sheep!

There were also artistic people who were being buried because their morals were true morals and the state was trying to snuff out the last of the artists in all the fields including the field of literature which is where America now was so very weak and always had been for many years. Mark Twain was an agnostic while Solzhenitsyn and Dostoyevsky were both Christian artists in the field of writing and literature and yes the novel could be more accurate than most of our historians could ever have been! To write when things were occurring was the time to write and not transcribe solely from other sources that could possibly be false and distorted especially since today's higher learning and before had socialism's lies in it most of the time.

My athletic friends were having a class reunion and I was invited to go so I decided to go just to see if anyone had gotten real older looking or had changed the ways about certain things or if they were almost just the same as they had been. There would be much discussion, I was quite sure and that was the main reason I was going, to see how they felt about our political society that was stressed now more than ever than the spiritual part of life which made for an increase in socialism even though most of these guys probably would never understand what it meant to be a socialist, but subscribed to it.

We were holding it in a local bar where the clientele were from our age group in the 60's. We had all agreed on this and I would not be a legalist as to where we met since this would be where the guys would speak out more openly and so I too agreed to where we were going to meet. "Luke it is good to see that you could make it for once," said Hank.

"Well Hank I did not want to miss your drinking binge that you use to put on," I said.

"Well Luke, I can still hold my booze like I always could. You know that," said Hank.

"Like the night that you wrecked your Corvette?" said Tim.

"You know it was not my fault that that dump truck cut me off and totaled my car completely," Hank again said.

"We'll forgive you on that one," said Dave.

"I'll match you anytime, Dave, at how many beers you can drink," said Hank.

"Okay Hank, but let us first get something to eat, okay?" said Dave.

"Wait till Fred comes in. Then you'll see whose the boss at the bar," Tim said teasingly. "Like the time he got stone drunk on beer and wine at the same time which was such a fool thing to do," said Hank.

"Hey, BROTHER, how are you doing Hank?" asked Roger, an old Army pal from Nam. "Hey, BROTHER how are you doing Roger, you old DI?" said Hank.

"Let's say we go to the bar to drink for starters," said Roger.

"Okay Roger," responded Hank.

After some good humorous teasing and a few drinks, we were ready to sit down and shoot the bull. Of course my own drinks were soda and no alcoholic beverages which I really took a beating on. I could now be myself by not drinking at all and could be bold when I had to be and not like when I was much younger I needed the alcohol to build me up to defend my issues! Then Tyrone, Tim's twin brother and a vet from the Vietnam War, got up to see if all the guys were there and they were, which was good to say the least since we all had gone our own ways. Tyrone was a Marine in Vietnam and got wounded badly in the abdomen and had to take morphine for quite a while until that no longer helped. He struggled with severe pain for a few years after that, but nonetheless did not give up and was now a teacher.

"We present and accounted for," said the slightly already inebriated Fred in a satirical and funny way just to upset Tyrone's old Marine mentality!

Fred had been an MP how he did that I never knew and was raised by a mother and was always gun nuts and use to fire a .357 Magnum many times and many times spent a fortune on the ammunition on it. Fred though had always been a hard worker but was what one might call a sort of "peasant" type with a major lack in academics to say the least, but really was an all right guy once you got to know him and just how much he could eat at one sitting alone. Fred was big boned with black hair and had the face of a German, but much broader and a sort of raspy throat and would often talk loudly without even knowing he was doing it at all. He had married a Korean girl and used to call them "slope heads" for some strange reason, because as I said before he was not the brightest guy and was in Vietnam. He had told us that if a Korean girl had a baby from a black American GI the relatives would try to dispose of it as soon as possible! What a horror story that was, plus other things Fred use to say, but then again one could not always c know in what Fred always had to say since he liked to brag most of the time and most of us were so use to that that we would just ignore him or tease him even more about it.

After we all had a good meal, we moved to a back room so we would not bother any of the other customers who were coming in for that night. Our stomachs were full and most of the guys had had a little too much except Tim, Tyrone and myself since we three did not drink and Tim and Tyrone even when we were young did not drink. They both were excellent wrestlers in high school.

"Well Tyrone what do you think about the war in Iraq as opposed to the conflict in Vietnam?" I asked.

"Well Luke, first of all you are right to say that Iraq is a war and Vietnam was a conflict, but nonetheless the first one we should not be in and not because of Michael Moore or Oliver Stone who are both Communists and in the Vietnam conflict we should have won easily if World Bank and Robert McNamara then once president of World Bank who was Secretary of Defense would not have listened to his boss David Rockefeller. It was to stop all Communism in Southeast Asia. My reason is as such and here it is. Again. Rockefeller for many years had major control of Exxon which has now merged with Mobil and controlled what was pumped as long as they were willing to oppose Israel, but when that happened they had to initiate a war through Britain and hence today years later we see what has happened when the internationalists control the media and big business in the West. How much worse was Osama Bin Laden than David Rockefeller who got millions and millions of people killed through their loans to dictators and totalitarian nations such as the Soviets? The Soviets even waited for one whole hour when David Rockefeller was late coming to Moscow and since they owed him $50 billion, but did not even wait for heads of state like the President of the United States, because he was just elected, but Rockefeller would be there for life," said Tyrone.

"So you don't believe that it was just the Arabic Moslems involved in all of this?" I asked.

"Oh they were involved in this all right because they too wanted to see Israel liquidated and were using petroleum to get what they wanted and that was more money and power that is the sheiks. who were not really a monarch, but more lake dictators ever since Islam which is innately socialistic," said Tyrone.

"Listen you guys I also was in Vietnam and I know that we could not trust the Vietnamese at all and that too was a major problem for us guys over there," said Hank.

"I will say this as for myself, our politicians over here were involved also into all of this and up to their neck in treason since they felt they could sacrifice our soldiers for their own power and Nixon was good friends with Moscow and Peking who adored him. LBJ had construction firms 23% in Vietnam and also Nixon took Watergate sitting down pretty much because this was his way of getting out of this Vietnam debacle' once and for all and to save face for the Republican Party, but the Democratic Party was just as bad or even worse since it was true blue red. They were sending young poor boys from America who had no experience while the people like Clinton were commit ting treason against them. Now they are dead and this Clinton guy is a hero to some here in America and is writing a lot of bull about his libelous life along with his wife another Commie baby," said Roger!

"Roger I know you had two hitches in Vietnam, but why then did you go back again?" I said.

"Damn it to win the damn war. What else?" Roger said! "Well better you than me there Roger," said Robert. "Robert just shut up. You are so drunk to not see straight as it is," said Roger and Bill!

"I know most of the guys in this room-served in Vietnam and anybody who didn't I do not believe is some kind of scoundrel," said Tyrone.

"I totally agree with that," said Hank.

"Well all in favor of that motion say aye," said Roger.

We all then said aye and started to laugh and had more drinks served of course Tim and I kept drinking soda while the other guys were getting stoned, but they had a reason too since they were called baby killers and we all knew where that term came from out on the West Coast.

I later found out that all the guys there were married and had at least one child and were doing okay in life and were providing for their own families with no assistance from government. It got to be about 3:00 AM in the morning and Tim and I and Tyrone had to help drive home everybody else there and we did no matter what they said and only 1 or 2 guys lived close enough to walk home so we let them do that. It was a good night for me since I knew all these guys would go on with their lives, but could I, since I always felt I had to write about this war in detail and knew that the real criminals besides in Moscow and Peking lived in America and especially worked in DC. I also knew that the Red Chinese, we never call them that anymore, had sent in millions of workers to repair bridges that our own Air Force was bombing but all these bridges were made out of wood and in a few days these bridges would be built again, but that was not the main issue. It was the fact that our Air Force officers were not allowed to bomb military installations, gas depots, etc. but only these wooden bridges which meant nothing and was risking the lives of good officers who wanted to bomb where it really hurt. That was our Pentagon that one could not be trusted for any thing. I had to go back in time to find out the real truth why we lost this war and I know the guys wanted to get on along with their own lives, but mine was to tell history the way in happened and not how I thought it happened, or wanted, or hoped it would happen, but how it actually happened!

The responsibility of an artist is to write it as if one had painted a picture but in words so that people could see it come off the pages just as it had occurred and this was no easy task. One had to always be truthful and shed the light of beauty about what one wrote and one had to write not for money or fame, but for the truth alone and if anything came with that good or bad then so be it.

Could I live up to this in what I needed to write and write it so that the truth would be finally written and not to line one's pockets with money. America was starving to hear the truth, at least people back here were and since most of the guys over there already knew the truth and wanted to forget about the past. Again I could not let that happen, the truth had to be told because that is what lead us to the debacle' we now were in at the present time.

Most all the so called heroes in sports and in Hollywood during the 60's were true blue red doper diaper babies and that was the way it was and that is now the way they still are to this very day except they are not much older and have done nothing in life whatsoever that anyone shall remember them for that was good and wholesome.

They had believed their own lies and this poisoning ideology that they worshipped as a religion that is why they fought so hard against us, because this was their god. These were the bleeding heart liberals that wanted nothing but to disrupt and rebel in society and if it would not have been Vietnam it would have been something else, but since It was Vietnam we were talking about many millions of lives the world over that would be affected by this lost not only in Southeast Asia, but also in other parts of the world where freedom was crying out while my generation never as a whole ever stood up for anything wholesome as a whole or for the majority of them.

Now that crime was so common place in America plea bargaining came into being to mean that since drugs were so prevalent that other crimes too could fall under the heading of" misdemeanor" which was something that could now possibly mean treason against one's own country since the U.S. Constitution said, "high crimes and misdemeanors" and the sentence of capital punishment. How could our Founding Forefathers been so harsh! Was it not to strict to say that even treason was not serious enough to sentence ones to a capital offense even when murder was involved just like this President had sentenced a Christian to death in Texas even though she was a woman and they could have kept her in prison for life and the fact that she did not beg for them to spare her life so she was convinced that she had to be such a "terrible person" while the rich and well educated would get compassion because the professionals knew that they had done even worse and so wanted to rescind the laws because they could all possibly be next in line for felonious crimes hiding behind the legal system with robes and degree after degree and of course "prestige "? Did they really believe that we believed that they were purely idly white innocent? How many hard core criminals did they repeatedly let out to go and kill again and again and for real misdemeanors they too would be put in with homosexuals, rapists, murderers, drug dealers, racists from all sides, psychopaths, etc?

Was it their consciences that really bothered them or was it something much more scary to them? One would with good common sense have to conclude after some serious thought that maybe they themselves feared for their own lives and the lives of their children and relatives who might already be involved in crime so what was good for the goose was good for the gander? Plea bargaining was nothing more than not serving time for a serious offense so that chaos could be promoted and so that fear mongering could run the streets laughing at true justice in the sense that the law applied.

Just how rich or how poor and that only when one was to differentiate was when one knew that it was not felonious, but then again if the President could commit treason then why could not the rest of society do also likewise or in some line with another felony?

No, the American prison system was corrupt and bad because restitution and rehabilitation was not included that would build character once remorse and sincere remorse for the crime could be seen or heard for the defendant. It was the O.J.'s of society and the Koby Bryants in America who got away with civil rights' socialism type of justice! They were innocent until they were proven innocent! Yes, law abiding citizens had to be fearful because the trial lawyers and judges and the politicians more lawyers, and of course good old television and Hollywood would do their part to see that they would promote crime in every way possible. This would be their contribution to society and it had nothing whatsoever to do with the rule of law. The poor would envy and the rich, well they would continue to make the laws to benefit their type of crimes which meant that millions of people and not necessarily dollars was what real justice involved and not democracy's mob rule and the court of no justice was what would be for sure what they would continue to institute time and again, but the victims could always wait to rise from the dead!

No-the American way was not the only way to enforce the law and the only way for justice to prevail since in. a democracy a search for the truth never comes to mind when one is running for office and running away from the real law the Ten Commandments and was it that our own prisons were crowded and bad? The maternal part of society was never meant to discipline in a home setting, but the paternal part was and that would mean political incorrectness would prevail! One could never have that, since one always had to look out for the underdog no matter how bad crime, because they were the ones that kept the revolving door open for the courts and the trial lawyers and corrupt judges and of course the ever "effervescent" politicians!

If Martha Stewart who was rich and well educated had to serve time how much should she serve because all it really involved was America's lifeline money and capitalism, but just murder someone and see how quick they are to cry insanity or plead the 5th under the grounds that they might incriminate themselves, or in essence be forced to perjure themselves in court which would mean less time. The other scenario was do the time and still tell the truth and the 5th one could throw out of the window since it was mostly used to protect the hard core criminal from ever serving because the technicalities of the so called law could always be sure to see the guilty go free because of turning state's evidence Which meant if they could do that they could do it with felonious cases! So all the laws would be legal and anyone could blame their environment and socialism would always prevail, right? This was the group mentality not to take one case at a time and forget what the individual would be responsible for and that was himself? This is why the court jury was not working and because democracy was not what people said it was all it was cracked up to be. Repeat offenders had to be understood, but the victims they could dolt on their very own and English law had an English mindset of we the people meaning not the individual and not individualism which were diametrically opposed to each other.

The panacea or utopia of the jury itself was nothing even close to fail safe since now the courts had to get behind crime in the sense that crime would lead the way and the jury could be anybody that they so fit or unfit which ever happened to fit and in these days it was the unfit came to the jury for approval and the worse the crime the more the delay and the less the crime such as financial matters the much shorter the delay. Do not ever believe one could steal and get away with it but murder the unborn and that would be okay and in fact it was "legal"!

As each felony came up the US Supreme Court continued to meet the challenge of the innocent by saying you are too late, or that does not matter because you cannot speak for yourself. Well of course not! Can the dead resurrect themselves to testify? This was the insanity of the West judicial system that was not, as I said before, even close to what Scripture said should happen when one sheds another's life New or Old Testament.

We of course would never see the real criminals like had occurred in the Soviet Union never be brought to trial like Molotov who died in 1967 at a good ripe old age, or even Khruschev's son who we took quickly in the state of Rhode Island before the peasants in Russia gave him real justice and it appeared the same for Clinton, Kerry, O.J., Bryant, Angela Davis, etc. for they all were alive and well and if anyone spoke evil about them, heaven forbid# and that is what Solzhenitsyn called "in defense of the terrorists "just like Yassir Arafat. One must not distinguish between good vs. evil: but always compare one case from the left that was a little worse and so as is the monetary case which always had to be worse superseded the murder trial since circumstantial evidence would always come into place! This would setup the socialism of the socialist state which meant," Do your own thing to anyone at anytime just so you meet the political correctness theory and the capitalism of the West that said money was god!

In America husbands and wives used separate checking and savings' accounts so that a woman could be independent from her husband and could provide for herself saying in essence that she did not need a man, but only to procreate. For example an account like Jacqueline Kennedy would say-when she married twice would be Jacqueline Kennedy Onassis, or Hillary Rodham Clinton. This was taking the maiden name in the second case and taking the first marriage name and adding the second manage name to their full name which meant they were never fully attached to their now husband and had to be left alone. Children of their own would see this and come to realize this had to be the right way!

Many times also the word legal guardian or even the word parent took the place of mother and father and also when a husband could not review his own wife's record such as with the socialistic government's own Social Security started by FDR America even in nice household had accepted without question, either because they were so busy because of government interference or because of television or because they just did not care and it was a bother to find out as to the why! This is what America had come to within the marriage realm.

Marriage had become a legal and not a sacred rite to last for life and divorce was even more easy to obtain then a driver's license and Social Security numbers were used for identification purposes. Big brother was in everyone's business except for it's very own such as protecting it's own citizens which meant provide for the common defense and became the "solution" to all of our problems but was the reason for most of all of our problems! Government was with a big G and GOD was with a small g which was why America was dissipating into an amoeba mass.

Children were not raised by mothers and fathers, because motherhood and fatherhood was dead and without that there would be no families and the socialists allowed homosexuals to marry and even adopt children! There was no end to this madness. On and on we went down into the abyss of nothingness and our children would indeed suffer for this and Hollywood was the one to look for as the solution also to all of our problems but turned out to be the cancer in society!

Sex was now a dirty word and marriage was made fun of as if it was an oddity. People shacked up instead of getting married. Children would become bastards and would become confused as which mother and father was their real biological one and in the Hispanic culture it was even worse since the biological mother's children each had a different name for as many as the children she gave birth to. There were step brothers and step sisters and half brothers and half sisters and almost 2 million Christian families wanted to adopt any child from any background with any kind of physical or mental impairment, but the trial lawyers did not want them to since they made this process of adoption usurious so that what would usually cost $1,000 now cost $10,000. What could have been used for the child was now used for the starving lawyers who would see to it that the money went to good use!

Local car accidents got more attention than did major catastrophes in the world even if it involved thousands of deaths. The media was hell bent on disguising everything it could so the truth could not be seen and if it was ever seen it was far, few and in between! Children were no longer a precious commodity, but a human resource like a natural resource which meant a value on life itself was made even cheaper. All ages, all sexes, all peoples were affected by this, since money was preferred over fact in all that we said and done.

The hero was the dead beat sports' dad who was not really a dad at all and had to be told to share his fame and his fortune with the less fortunate in life! One could go through many names for the heroes of the media and of Hollywood and the mass majority followed along like a herd of cattle and that too was getting much worse. Anybody and anyone could watch these small innocent children without anyone else questioning why the mother and father were either not married or why the mother and the father could not properly raise and provide proper love and guidance to their very own flesh and blood?

Children's clothing except for sneakers and jeans became so high in price no matter the demand that people dressed their children with no thought for the child in mind. There were no dress codes in the public schools at all since boys were allowed to wear anything but the proper attire and girls' looked like Hollywood starlets which of course the Communists in the ACLU loved to see. The ACLU also loved to see the demise of America since it upheld this worse of the worse and could be compared to the

Red Chinese government as well as Moscow's government and Havana's government.

Our government provided and invited every other culture heathen and atheistic that anyone could imagine here with all expenses paid for by the average American and just mention the Judeo-Christian faith no matter what age and one would be in trouble for loving GOD out loud! So now our private lives were are public lives and we had to watch what we said-because it might offend someone who had no regard for human life and liberty or their children were raised in the manner of such. This had come to be the average way of life in America and we were wondering why our very own children were living like heathen or why they lacked moral authority in their very own consciences. The 60's generation had done the best of the worse in all possible ways and we were very proud of that to say the least!

No one was held accountable to any authority and manners were' Just to be polite and not as to the why and not from the heart. Reason, pure reason, was the excuse for our society as to how one should act or conduct themselves as human beings but then that could possibly mean anything goes as the saying went! We collected trophies and awards like there was no tomorrow and saw glory in ourselves. We had become our very own gods. Even toys on the market spoke about the New Age rainbow to get into our children's minds at an early age and bilingualism was being used not to educate, but to separate!

The public schools did also like our very own government did and involved themselves where they should have been teaching the 3 R's instead of sex and OBE education. The poison was in the pudding Our children were being abused by our own professionals and by our very own government as I just said. Hollywood was setting the very trend to hell itself. They were the ones that were now in charge also of "guiding" our children as well as the so-called athletes who could not even read or write in English properly or be able to speak in public and were born here for the most part.

Democracy proved to be short and mob rule such as a majority and that proved to be ever fatal. It was in this type and form of government that we had to cope with and survive in day by day and could one imagine what a small child had to endure on a daily basis with such retrograde parenting by the government or better known as for the peoples and by the peoples! Did I make the word people plural? Well was that not what multiculturalism was all about this tearing apart from the family also known as diversity*? This was all well and good for the ones who did want to have sex, but not the responsibility of raising even their own children and play acting was performed on a daily basis to impress others just like the kind of cars we drove were status symbols and no more and no less. It said nothing about character and the development of the mind and heart into a complete and whole person, but since people were not considered to even have a spiritual heart the "doctors" of the mind only treated the aesthetic value of man and that was what one inlay see on the outside and in the West if one wore an expensive suit, for instance, then it was for certain he had to be an honorable man!

The simpletons of success thought this to be in the best interest of all concerned since it meant that happiness was the pinnacle in life all the time and not a state of mind It was sought out and was found wanting. What was one's purpose in life now? Who would lead the people now? Who would now think for us as a people? Would we understand let alone communicate with each other at all?

None of the above mattered, but just so we had what we wanted not even what we needed which could be a lot less than could meet only the eye! We were sold a bad bill of goods. The government was producing, but what they produced could be produced in Communist countries!

We had removed ourselves from the land and the land was no longer our attachment to our very own nation, since money and the love of it would see us through!

We had become our very own worse enemy and the enemy within was destroying each one of us unless we came to GOD sincerely and completely and repented one by one wholeheartedly. We used our own children like one used disposable diapers. We threw them out! They had gotten in the way of our sexuality and convenience of mind! We had more important things to do in life! Such as infidelity, homosexuality, thievery, adultery, drugs, drinking, sports, amusement parks, Hollywood, liquid manure, materialism, ego, etc.

We had found our stay in life and with most Germans they already knew it from birth! That was incredible to say the least. The Anglo-Saxons and especially England was setting our pace here.

My athletic friends would meet exactly one year from this year and again get together to discuss how our lives now were doing and I was looking forward to that, but when that year came there was some major changes. My plan was to share the Gospel of Jesus Christ with them then at that time, which I should have done a long time ago. Now with Roger dead from Agent Orange I had missed my chance and with Roger not wanting to hear anything about religion and with only Robert who already had become a Christian through grace alone and Tim just smiling and grinning and womanizing as he always did that too had become a lost cause and his twin 'Iron too busy to hear anything that did not involve his own family and one must remember both these good friends had no father ever at home and their mother was an alcoholic so that had contributed much to their own demise of salvation, because they could not relate to the Father, because they had no father early in life or any other time in life. With Scott and Brian who were both now homosexuals and both said," Are you serious we are born what we are and shall stay that way because this is what we believe in." So only Carl, Fred, Dave and myself could get together at a table and talk about GOD and His grace. Of course Robert would be there to help, if he decided to do so.

That one year came and the following short scenario occurred: With all the guys there except for Roger who as I said had died, only Robert stayed sober and Carl, Fred and Dave and these three of the most unlikely ones were what I had to say as the Holy Spirit directed me.

"So now Luke you want to save us from our own sins and by the way where is Roger now," asked Carl?

"First of all Carl, I am only the instrument that the Lord uses to spread His Word to the lost in the world and I do not do any saving for Jesus had done that on the Cross at Calvary that is He shed His blood to the fullest and died and then rose on the 3rd day in fulfillment of the Scriptures. If one accepts Him into their heart then they are saved and nothing more, nothing less and works has nothing to do with this nor your religion, or even your status, race, creed, or anything else. With Roger if he did not know Jesus then he would be in Hell and I feel bad now never having shared this Gospel and now not really knowing if he ever came to the Lord since last year's meeting and before he died," I said.

"So if we accept a simple prayer into our hearts we are saved?" asked Fred.

"No Fred it is not the prayer that is important, but that you accept Jesus into your own heart as an individual person and really mean it and it is a gift something that cannot be earned do you understand?" I asked/

"Well no thanks Luke I am going back to the bar," said Fred.

"Before I start does anyone else want to voluntarily leave this table and go back to their old way of life?" I asked.

Carl and Dave now were the only 2 left at the table to hear what I had to say in short summation with out saying it again or without coercion which of course is what the enemy always worked on. I started saying to both Carl and Dave as Robert prayed along the following prayer and asked those 2 to follow along.

"Dear Jesus I believe you died for me and all of my sins, past, present and future sins and I turn away, I repent from all of those sins, and I accept You as my personal Lord and Saviour. Come into my heart and wash and cleanse me from all of my sins. I know if I would have been the only one you still would have died for me. Thank you, Jesus for coming into my heart. In Your name Jesus I pray. Amen."

As Robert and I said this prayer and with me leading and Robert following softly, Carl and Dave repeated after us in almost a hard to hear voice, but nonetheless said this prayer of salvation to know now that they had become Christians by grace and grace alone and now works would come into their lives and not as a prerequisite to salvation, but afterwards for as James had said in his epistle, or letter, "Faith without works is dead" and this was faith right here the kind that the Bible spoke about time and again in Romans 10: 9-10 and John 3: 3-7, as well as Psalm 119 and Isaiah 53. So both Old and New Testaments said the very same thing and there was no contradiction at all. I then gave Dave and Carl both a New International Version of the Bible and told them to start reading with the Gospel of John first and find a church not a religion that preached the Gospel of Salvation even though they were saved and a church that spoke out for the poor and defenseless in our society and did not compromise on sexual sin for our bodies now were the very temple of GOD. We belonged to Him and Him alone!

I later found out from Robert who usually kept in touch with most all of the guys that Scott and Brian had already also died of the AIDS' virus and Tim and Tyrone were both killed in a horrible car accident and John was Greek Orthodox which meant almost more Catholicism who were probably the most hard to witness to ever here now in America barring none. So for next year only Carl, Dave, Robert and myself would be there, because with all the deaths and with Fred not invited and John not invited that would leave only us 4 to see how far we had grown in the Lord in all of our lives and this time we would meet at a nice and quiet restaurant. I thought time is certainly short and we never know. When GOD shall call on us and some did die and not as they used to say, "Your time is up", because many times we ourselves preceded as to when GOD really was calling us even though He had allowed those deaths permissively, but not absolutely. That was a scheme from the enemy that old lying cliché!

Our generation was dying off very quickly because it had been an accumulative affect that carried over from the 60's and made all of our lives less and less healthy and wise. The law of averages was catching up to most all of us because we did not really take care of ourselves like we should have years ago. It was like my mother use to say, "One cannot really become athletic when they get older, because our bodies are now different and not young like they use to be to take the rigorous format that sports played on the body at an older age and chances are if you were not athletic then to try and act childish now would be to no avail and one could not make up for lost time."

How true all of that turned out to be. There was no denying that we had older and unhealthy bodies because what we believed in then affected how our bodies now were. And also we had a total reckless disregard for our bodies then and preventive medicine would only put off the inevitable and probably in a pre-mature state and that would be death itself.

Also later in the year I found out that Carl who had been a heavy drinker most all of his life had died also of liver cancer and so that left only 3 of us Robert, Dave and myself and Robert moved far away, because his job took him there and as for Dave after losing his daughter he more or less stayed to himself. This is what the 60's generation had brought to still a once young group of guys who mostly met a premature death because their lives at that time amounted only to oneself and this world alone. They would never be remembered ever for even having been here on earth itself since they died in their sins. I now was the only one left in my own home town where all of our roots started from and one by one they left this area for the so called "greener pastures". It was uncanny in the sense that it appeared like when Abraham took the lesser land and that was now where us guys had grown up and now had become mostly like a 3rd World country and Lot who chose the better land and that was actually Sodom and Gomorrah which eventually was destroyed by GOD, but had spared Lot and his family except for Lot's wife who turned around to look and turned into a pillar of salt.

Where had all of these flowers gone that I grew up with as a small boy and now they would be gone forever and only a handful if that would be going to heaven and so we would see each other there. was indeed sad for me since this would mean that our friendship had ended because they had no time for the GOD of Abraham, Isaac, and of Jacob and of course the Messiah, or Jesus Christ!

There were no immediate friends to be found and my life with my wonderful wife was ever so busy with now grandchildren of our own that we hardly had any time for many other things except of course to help the poor and witness to them as GOD would send them along one by one. Life would be lived one day at a time.

Things were moving too fast in the world and something had to happen since Israel was always in the news and was being blamed for what Islam had done all over the world. Satan had indeed planted evil ideas in the Gentile peoples all over the world.

The only mention of how many to be saved was again in the Jewish people and that was not so much a number as it was a word and that word was a remnant which referred only to the Jewish people at the end of the age of grace through to Armageddon and into the Tribulation of 7 years and then on into the Millennial reign of Christ from Jerusalem.

The time appeared short for the end of this age, when political and spiritual ramifications were both changing and of course the political side changed so fast with the spiritual at a much slower pace. It always takes much longer for the spiritual since this evolves at a much slower pace in mankind. The politics of the world were ever so rapid as I just said and even took up most all of many people's time since the spiritual would move much slower and man could not wait for that.

Once in a while I would stop through town where part of my childhood had been and was startled to find it looking like Mexico itself with strange loud colors painted on buildings that never matched and street after dirty street with young people of Hispanic and black origin roaming the streets and having nothing constructive to do at all and young girls with babies, or babies having babies with no fathers along with them and people in brand new cars driving all around. The neighborhood was so surreal that it was hard to go back in one's memory as to just how it use to be during the 60's and the 70's and many young American girls were having children out of wedlock from this part of the county.

Hispanic Jihad though was because mushroom farms to the north of our town had brought in years ago Puerto Ricans for slave labor and now were bringing in Mexicans across the border with the very knowledge of the local and federal authorities. They seemed to have been paralyzed by some one or something that kept them from enforcing the naturalization and immigration laws and the quotas that had always been there but this President and the one previous had removed that through executive orders and one wondered why they could not do the same to deport and remove them as well as use executive orders or privileges to do the same against killing our own children in the womb and on the streets for drugs?

The courts kept releasing these criminals more and more and the death penalty in our own state had not been used since 1963! They were murdering anybody and anyone that got in their way and there was no remorse about it at all. They kept having children who they did not really care about, but collected tax funded benefits from the county and the federal government which included Community Development monies the same kind that the Soviet Union used when they were in power in the USSR.

It had come full circle this socialism and now Hispanics were doing just what they wanted to do and this incumbent wanted us to vote for him for a second term! This was the incredible part about the arrogant and coldness on the English's part. Now that they brought them here they wanted us to be coerced to like them for better or worse and hopefully worse so that they could continue with their oil enterprising business in Mexico too! They always had a way to put the blame on someone else besides themselves and refused to protect any of our borders and in his speeches all he kept saying was that we were winning the war in Iraq and thought us to be just as English as he was and the other candidate, or comrade which was a better term to be used wanted us to vote for Communism right off of the bat! Make no mistake about it this candidate was another Bill Clinton" better red than dead" one.

He and his were billionaires and would do anything to destroy America and the rich and the poor minorities would vote him in for sure because first of more illegal ways to get money in the first case and in the second case more ways also to get money "legally" from the state and to have the wealth of the nation redistributed and here is where envy came in on their own part.

One could take the poison right now with the second candidate or take it in small doses in the incumbent. Which one would it be? You can pay me now or pay me later was the slogan for the second and then the incumbent in consecutive order. It was a no win situation for America and we were told to vote for the lesser of two evils? Which way did we want to destroy the nation? Through time lapse photocopy sped up or through the old silent movies where one could read their lips only but knew almost what they were saying with all their contortions and gestures.

This had become a 3 ring circus between the judicial, the executive and the legislative all three blind as 3 blind mice and thinking they were leading the nation along when what they were really doing was destroying the nation even faster and faster and conservative and liberal just meant what type of socialists one would be! It had absolutely nothing to do with morality or the Ten Commandments even though our own Bill of Rights was set up after the Ten Commandments but then again in law school all they really learned about was socialism and all laws are legal. The medical profession was not very far behind them with no Hippocratic Oath as I had mentioned before and were being taught death instead of saving lives something else I had also mentioned before.

Yes, the professors in college were good Komsomol technicians and nothing more and hardly knew about the classics or about real science or the languages and history of our own nation or that of other hostile nations or they would not have let them in on purpose would they?

The teaching profession had fallen so far that even people with GED'S were accepted as well as people who Could not speak proper English and knew absolutely nothing about the Judeo-Christian faith. The social Christians in government were the most dangerous of all!

All the way from birth in day care till they got out of college did the young people learn socialism.

Whenever there was an increase of fatherless families moving into a neighborhood and they were non-European, the Germans were the first, along with the English in America, to move out as soon as possible because both cultures' males were—how would one say it?—wimpish to say the least, and the Italians stayed in their neighborhoods to the last. They quickly fled the area and went to suburbia or the country yet were the first to want to use socialism such as in the Great Society since most of them had government jobs because they had the right last names and the right street addresses and were just like Masons!

It was hard for even some Jewish people to obtain employment because they were afraid that the Jews might take over the company, and with the Germans in charge that was not saying too much. They were braggadocios about how much of a soldier they were, but when it came to protecting the neighborhood and without a uniform, they fled. The English who always wanted to make colonies did not now want these same peoples to live with them even though these Third World people now were indifferent when they came to England and so England felt that America should share in the charitable immigration policy that backfired on them in England. We always had to do what England did, as I have said so many times before. But were the English a people or a nation that anybody really wanted to follow to the end?

They once ruled the oceans with their navy, but now could hardly blow their own nose when it came to liberty and just plain saying no! They wanted to rule America from across the Atlantic time and again. Who would defend England's interests now in the world since they were a 4th rate power? Good old America with its own blood would shed it for the Anglophiles!

Just like the English people in London had to support the royal family that owned about 1/3 of London itself they now wanted us to provide for them the task that they had started and could not now finish. What was good for the goose was good for the gander. There were no more colonies in the world really under British rule and one could see what had happened afterwards. In South Africa apartheid was put in place there, in China the Communists, etc. and in many other places they made a demise of nation after nation with their better-than-thou attitude.

Churchill gave up Israel to the Arabs in 1928 and also dabbled in the occult. Chamberlain went along with Hitler. FDR and Churchill the dynamic duo both sat down with the butcher Stalin one of the most cruel men ever to be a dictator who had murdered millions and millions of Russians as well as other peoples.

Our own American farmers were told what to plant and what not to plant and that lead to more socialism or the collectivization of our farms so that farmers could not make a go of their farms and the inheritance tax was also killing them since the taxes on the property were already paid! They had machinery, but still that was so expensive that they had to take out second mortgages, and the banks loved that because they were also in cahoots with the government such as the IRS, FDIC, OCS, etc., which all played the tune to "more in it for me". One then would think that with all the farm technology that the farmers had it made, but that was far from the truth and so this incumbent got a brainstorm of an idea and said "Let us bring illegals from Mexico to work here in America for cheaper wages" bringing down America to a Third World status as a nation. Someone had to pick up the ball so that America would be dumbed downed even more than it was! They would be entitled to government handouts that meant real Americans got less of what they had put in, but this was all for diversity and multiculturalism and to keep the middle class from existing and having then only to contend with the rich and the poor, and since also English would not be learned people would be even more ignorant in America than ever before.

The rich could then rule without any kind of interference from the "peasants" below. They could pretty well promote socialism which gave them such a thrill! Yes, replace the farms or privately owned farms with migrant illegal people and then appropriate from tax dollars what they saw fit to appropriate with other people's money such as the American taxpayers. This meant that more renegades could come to America no matter what the law said or did not say. Laws were meant to be broken and government most of all broke the law more times than anyone else ever had and continued to add other so called laws to amend the Constitution, no destroy the Constitution as Scalia had said time and again.

What was this incumbent waiting for also on the U.S. Supreme Court since a majority was held by his party in the Senate, including the Vice President? Did he really think that all of us were really that stupid about judge placement as well as judge impeachment? What had he really done in his four-year term but to negotiate with terrorists and allow them a haven in America continuing on where Clinton left off? The parties were synonymous with each other.

We had invited happy the clown into our very large city so that when one went back after so many years only their memories could remember what it use to be like since now there were hardly any Americans left there and they could never relate to this city like one who had grown up in it years ago. People were speaking all different languages, and it sounded like an auction house. Maoism for the minority masses with Hispanol growing and growing. Mass exit from the inner city blacks occurred because now the blacks were outnumbered. Would either of these ever assimilate since the one group had not since this country was founded and the second group wanted to take over as soon as possible? The rich and well educated saw that as an advantage, of course, for themselves. Would it take a millennium for the blacks to assimilate since they hadn't done so in about 300 plus years now? And as to the other group, why did they come here if they did not like America, and they did not? They did not want to work but sell drugs and make women pregnant out of wedlock and have the taxpayers fork the bill. They also did not want to speak English on purpose and the government and big business encouraged it because now they were in positions of authority to make change, or radical change!

All I could think of was Liberation Theology and coups and revolutions from where they had come from plus this diversity that stressed anti-American sentiment for even American-born workers or employees, and they had to be indoctrinated if they wanted to keep their jobs.

These people rarely had benevolent smiles on their faces, but faces of revenge and anger all the time. Was it the nature of the beast, or was it that a wolf sheds its fur but not its habits, since now they had been transplanted to America from foreign very foreign soil with no concern for liberty or freedom because they never would understand what it was all about since they had lived in dire filth and poverty and yet wanted others to think because they now had materialism that they knew how to appreciate the finer and gentler things in life and without benevolence which they took for weakness because their cultures taught them that they were a fish out of water to the ones of us who know better no matter what government tried to pull?

Even the lower classes somehow seemed to agree since envy had also gotten a hold on them too! The middle class would have no real job and hence socialism would have as it always had a poor group and a rich group which controlled everybody under them and the state became the ultimate and destroyed religion in America. The anarchy that would occur had to bring on totalitarianism and the rich and well educated told the people that if they wanted a government it would have to be an oligarchy,

Some years had passed and some fatal news I found out about my once Jewish friends who were not really Jews at all but nonetheless I called them that just to keep the peace. Well anyway, Abraham, Joshua, Jerome and Andy had taken a trip to Israel and were killed in a terrorists' attack in Jerusalem while on a bus. This was a sad affair to say the least. Now 4 friends that I had known were, too, dead from Islamic Jihad and this time in Israel. I did believe that it would happen here very soon. since Islam had more than a foothold in America's government and big business, and the American Jew could care less just so that they had what they wanted (more extravagance) and felt safe, which was a false kind of safety. It would have to happen to them on a much larger scale for it to affect the American Jew and for them to Aliyha to Israel also. But even then, would they want to? They could "eat, drink and be merry" and had trusted even America when they should have learned from the Holocaust, which they almost totally had forgotten about.

I guess human nature worked that funny way in regards to self-preservation. People would talk about the horrors but when it really came down to it, they would do nothing until it hit home. This was the gullibility of the Jew, especially in America since to them America had almost always been good to the Jew like no other country, including Israel as of now. Land in Israel was being given up to the squatters and Sharon and Netanyahu disagreed within their own Likud Party as to what and what not settlements should be given up. Remember Sharon had to answer to the American Jews plus the Israelis' Supreme Court Chief Justice who ruled Israel, and Israel never even knew it because it thought it was being ruled by a parliamentarian type of government, which was not the case at all.

Yes, it appeared more and more that a proxy of a ruler was settling up this throne before the end of this age was up and no one knew exactly for sure when that would be, but it could possibly be very soon and much sooner than any of us ever thought it to be! Yes, now with these 4 Jewish males now dead, they had lost their souls just like that and refused to accept Messiah in their hearts and so now eternity would be spent where, I was quite sure, none of them thought they would go to. But pride can do that to people and especially the Jew in particular because the enemy spent overtime on them since Messiah was a Jewish man and was the only one who had power over Satan.

My generation was going quickly to the grave and continued on in their heathen ways of rock and roll. They did not want to give up their adolescent ways which they had in the 60's and continued on and on with whatever they wanted to do. No matter how bad it got in America they were wrapped up in their own little world with little minds and had felt that they had no more to offer to society besides religion and the religion that would not talk about the immoral evils then, and now in our very own nation.

Why go back in the past, but dwell only on race and more race and watch as spectators as our very own parents had done and go from one church to another seeking GOD Himself in the pulpit or so it would appear. This kind of religion was nothing more than self-preservation since it stressed over and over again self-esteem. If they could not have their way again (a trait of the 60's generation), then the hell with it all!

It had to appeal to them and speak just to them or else it was no good, and all that amounted to was ego. Yes, the major denominations had long ago given up on the entire Scripture where Jesus Himself is constantly correcting the ones He came for and then to the Gentiles, not selling anybody a bill of goods, but giving them a free gift of salvation, but also telling them to speak out when they saw evil in their presence when guided by the Holy Spirit. Religion was just that religion and not faith in Jesus alone and each denomination thought that their way and not Jesus' way had to be correct! What did Jesus say? Who did He get angry with in society at that time and were we as a people as Americans the same as them? He had done and now wanted us to do not what others, this world system, or even our very own denomination wanted us to do. Somehow in the West the churches did not want to bring morality into government since they were misquoting Scripture many times as to remain silent when evil was getting worse and worse. The Christians here wanted to live a life of peace and quiet at least for now, and would not dare to involve morality with government or the laws themselves and sat on the shelf of a spectator sport, which faith was anything but! One had to make a decision for life and that meant to give up the materialism they had and the easy times in America and get to the core of the evil and express it as such and not subterfuge it with rhetoric and donations so that they could clear their own consciences. Even the good ministries would not touch infanticide, homosexuality, euthanasia with a 10 foot pole. How could one taste the salt if the salt went bad?

There was too much free time to gossip and socialize and not enough time given to the real poor instead of to what party politics and ideology was infecting the church with. The elderly wanted to retire in peace, but not the kind of peace that I would recommend to anybody.

The young adolescent wanted to emulate Hollywood, and their liberal 60's parents and grandparents and the middle agers wanted the 60's never to end at all. They always had taken things too far and always had to be for the underdog no matter how bad it got.

One could easily see that there was no discipline especially in public places and profanity was used by both male and female. Not many families were together at all. The ones that were were struggling to make ends meet and also raise their children at home and not by the state, which was raw power that would corrupt without religion and the type of religion that the Bible talked about, not what was taught in seminaries who showed little courage to speak out even when evil was right in their very face. The men in society opted out of fatherhood so that they could watch sports and more idiotic sports. They did not spend time with the family and their own children, especially their own children. The military people thought that fighting for one's country was the only thing one had to do in order to keep America's liberty, but it took fatherhood first at home and then later in the community. If one was a renegade like the Hispanics and the 3rd World men, then there would be nothing left to America as far as the family was concerned, and bigot or no bigot this was the truth. The word bigot was just an excuse to subdue fatherhood and motherhood because ones who were true Americans made sure first that it started in the home, but then the schools and the universities started to sell propaganda about mother and father and that the professors were like gods but from hell. That would direct now these pliable minds that had no experience in life, for if they did they would not have done some of the insane things that just a professor would tell them to do! They would have investigated and checked it out, but then again the 60's generation never were in for reading good healthy books, but just Hollywood, sports, gambling, television, movies, sexual pornography, liquid manure, drugs, tobacco, pills, profanity and most of all a lack of responsibility as mothers and fathers. They were very easily swayed since it appeared now that the majority, a democracy which had to be right, went along with all of this mumble jumble.

No fathers to tell their sons about bonding and how much they loved them. No mothers to say how much they loved their daughters, but only materialism such as cars, stereos, liquid manure, Hollywood, drugs, profanity, sex of all kinds. This is where bonding between mothers and daughters was lacking and between fathers and sons was lacking, so what occurred first of all was this confusion about one's sexuality without the sex, confusion as to what role they would play when they too would have children. The sons and daughters weren't learning that marriage was a vital institution, not just a group of people together biologically and nothing else, but was a spiritual realm that GOD had given to man to use for the procreation of loved ones and to show man that fatherhood and motherhood were so very important even though man appeared to know more than GOD, or at least he thought so!

There was one incredible man, and he was not an American, but who was born into Communism and never really knew about freedom the way that Americans had some years ago. He was taught everywhere he went that Marxism was the religion of the people in Russia, and yet with all this concrete he came through it and was not smothered by it. He now knew what GOD meant to him and knew about the liberty that only GOD could give to man since man was lost in his own sins no matter how hard he tried to correct the situation and also knew that anything he did was with the power of the Lord as long as he was listening to the Lord. This man could not go to a church and read a Bible like we in America, yet turned out to be one of the most powerful Christians in the world through literature that the Word of GOD ran through his very pen and had said to never believe or promote the lie. This was quite a remarkable thing, but nothing was impossible for GOD OR WITH GOD!

He had come from the very pit of hell on earth set up by men mostly in the West who we worshipped as heroes, but wore costumes all the time when out in the public and who thought that they were the ones that made history, but it was the common man who did! From torture to near death with the Lord's help always this Satanic force called Communism could never quite devour him into it's belly and he came to America to tell them that that monstrosity was now here and that we should take heed from one who had been swallowed, but could not be digested because GOD does not allow his own to be taken out of his kingdom and money played no role, nor power and he held no important position except the power of the Truth that Jesus had given to him time and again and GOD had defeated them and their web of deceit, lies and murder into the millions upon millions and who rode on the red horse!

He was still now living but in Russia, the land he was born in and loved his country but not their sins along with his sins. He was a true artist who described exactly what it was like before, during and after the Russian revolution or civil war which was the worst kind of war ever. This was a man who always included himself in what had been done before he was transformed by the Lord and real Christianity and not playing church was what came through loud and clear. Self-preservation would have never gotten him through if that was another reason to stop and also to run away from the problem in the country he loved. This he did not do like so many Americans were doing who called themselves Christians and could only see the poor in other countries and the sick and uncared for there, but could not see what America was dying from spiritually because again religion and not faith and that is what the Bible talks about. To do something about the evil in the world and not just for self-preservation and leisure and pleasure or to ease a guilty conscience which did nothing for the heart but only for the mind!

A spiritual transformation that occurs like this that through one man GOD used His power to bring to it's knees the vast Soviet empire and the fact that the West still had a remnant of faith left in it's own spiritual heart to bring down a regime that had lasted for about 70 years and had done much harm to our fellow human beings. We had been more interested and our own parents too in what Hollywood had to say that never really made any kind of normal sense! One man against about 18,000,000 members of the Communist Party that were bent on his very destruction, but when that did not occur they then headed for the West and we gave them refuges of haven since they would have been taken care of or would see what their justice would have been with the common person over there, but we chose to be again part of the devil's plan to continue on until we ourselves would too have to face this menacing ideology called Communism.

We had been warned so very clearly but still even the Christians in America took it all in with a grain of salt and it went away like a fad with them and took no root in how to protect America the land we loved, but only this religiosity of going to church to once again clear our guilty consciences and to enjoy, yes enjoy, the singing lessons that we all had week after week. But who would put their very life on the line or even give up all they had to go and serve the Lord, Jesus Christ?

Even the Christian network made one wonder where their minds were, since all of television was run by Satan and the computer network was being taken over just like Hollywood was and banks and big business and most Christian denominations. It was not denomination that one had to follow but GOD.

My wife and I one day had a good discussion about some local politics as well as national issues.

"Rebecca, for some reason in this area that we live in the Germans have control and with their coldness it is not hard for them to step on the poor, and the English also are quite cold, but are at least smart, but both nationalities have major private problems in their lives involving morality and decency and honor. They do not feel for anything but what they can get it out for themselves and after all the Anglo-Saxons are cousins."

"Is that the reason that a lot of Jewish people have trouble just getting jobs unless they have degrees?"

"Yes, Rebecca that is one of the reasons and in fact they are behind a lot of the magazines, newspapers, and are always on the Internet with pornography and do not read the classics for that is above their heads. They are noted for their systems in the world otherwise they probably could not learn that much. They and the English are mainly responsible for our government becoming just a state, which means sure socialism and they are, that is the

Germans, the biggest collaborators one could ever find. They are also big promoters of women's athletics, which is making them masculine."

"Luke I had heard that the German people per se are in bed with the Moslems here and over there and had even helped, that is the Arabs the Nazis to take on Islamic names to hide them after World War II. Is that true?"

"Yes, that is true and now they are turning over the gambling casinos to them for ownership, as well as the local hospitals, restaurants, gas stations, banks, and churches. They are set up like the Sicilians had done with pizza parlors as fronts!"

"Luke I also had heard that capitalism and democracy was not all that it turned out to be and that we in the West brought Communism to China itself, especially England and also the fact that here in America as a woman it appears that the European male is afraid to death to protect his own culture?"

"Rebecca, first of all this is not Israel, but the European male could be more fatherly and protective of his family and not fear for his life when he sees any kind of minority who is not even hostile to him. Yes, we in the West taught Ho Chi Minh about Communism and took it to China and taught them Communism and then afterwards Jane Fonda, Tom Hayden and John Kerry (Kohn) all made deals with the Vietcong and sold out our soldiers, just like Hollywood now is and the National Democratic Socialist Party is. Why would any normal person think that we went to Iraq to establish democracy when we or this incumbent wants a Palestinian State which would be a dictatorship, and since the Moslems have had mob rule for centuries, giving them democracy would not be anything new to them. That is how Saddam Hussein came to power, through mob rule and murder, and Islam is innately socialistic. If I say I am not for capitalism or democracy or both that means that I am not for materialism which means socialism and I am not for mob rule!"

"Luke why is the Jew all over the world hated so very much?"

"Rebecca, this is not an easy question, but just please bear with me. I believe the reasons to be: The historical Jew is hated because they would not assimilate with others and the fact that they are the brightest group and use to have high morals such as in Nazi Germany when they opposed homosexuality. The now Jewish person probably is the hardest person to love, and the fact that Satan likes to play a number on them since the Saviour was from them in the flesh. There are some that want to weaken America very much by promoting anti-Semitism and also to weaken and destroy Israel if possible, but destroy America only if it is willing to deceive Israel now. These are 2 sovereign nations. Also from the fact that I believe that all the Gentile religions fall very short and do not understand the "discipleship of the Jews" in Scripture. Now this of course only has to do with the Christian denominations and Islam, multiculturalism, Nazism, Communism, Jehovah Witnesses, the Mormons, the Seventh Day Adventists, the Amish (who stay to themselves so far), the Sung Yung Moon church, etc. Please just stay with me a little longer, Rebecca. There was Marx, Freud, Trotsky (Mr. Bronstein), Javitz, Ribicoff, Einstein, but then again there were the Rothchilds, Senator Jackson, Senator Goldwater, Jonah Salk, David Ben-Gurion, Moshe' Dayan, Menachem Begin, Ezer Weismann, Jabotinsky, all posthumously speaking, but then again there is Alan King, Justice Blackmun, Caspar Weinberger, Kirk Douglas, Joan Rivers, Rodney (Cohen) Dangerfield, Mo Annenberg, Ms. Streisand, Mr. Spielberg who just paid a visit to Castro, Larry King, Ruth Bader Ginsburg, Ira Glasser, Barry Manilow, John Kerry, Henry Kissinger, and the late Bob Hope and Jack Benny who, though, were very decent individuals as far as loyalty and honor to their own country of America and to Israel. Most Jewish people do not have to go to Ivy League schools where socialism is taught and the ones that go there might have a high

IQ, but that alone does not make for a highly moral person, since most well educated people are rich people and do not have high Christian morals at all. Moral intelligence, as I like to call it, stems from the spiritual heart and not the mind alone and is only sustained through the spiritual heart. Does that all make sense Rebecca?"

"Luke I shall contemplate, if you don't mind, all that you just said, okay?"

"Yes Rebecca, by all means please do that now so you do not forget what I have just said!'

Our conversation ended and then I thought about a variety of other things, such as the Kennedy family and their father Joseph Kennedy, who was a Nazi and was made an ambassador to England by FDR. And also the fact that Joseph planned all of his sons' futures for them, but his favorite son was Joseph who had died earlier. The Kennedys, I believed opposed Communism so much because of their own like for Nazism and did not want Moscow to rule the world of the National socialism of Germany even though they were Irish Catholic, which in and of itself spoke of another type of anti-Semitism. This was a legacy of some evil in America! When Bobby Kennedy insulted and made fun of the Mafioso it was his doom because with some people you just cannot do that, no matter what or how high of a position you hold in government and is a very dangerous thing to do! John Kennedy was not a kind man to Jackie and was married twice and a great womanizer like most of the other Kennedys, another story in and of itself!

The environmentalists always seem to get upset, and this time they were upset about our nuclear submarines, that was the only thing that kept Moscow, Red China, North Korea and any of the rogue Moslem states who had nuclear weapons from attacking America. These environmentalists were really after private property and wanted to disarm us, and when Ronald Reagan came with SDI the socialists in America, such as Hollywood, mocked it since it was a good defensive missile plan.

I also called to mind the many teams that I had coached such as the fatherless sports programs where only a relative or a mother came and never a father most of the time. They were too busy themselves growing up!

I remember when my mother used to buy apples, for instance, by the basket and now they were charging by the pound. Many other products were similar to this as well.

The 60's generation from the years of birth 1946-1964 were the ones that created a revolution and more of a degeneracy or lack of morals in most all things from birth to selling drugs to also homosexuality, which at that time was not that well known because they did not have the authority that they now had.

The blacks and the whites got together all right, but for all the wrong reasons such as rioting, liquid manure, profanity, promiscuity, fornication, adultery, pedophilia, abominations, which in essence meant that blacks as well as whites could have sex without being married. Nobody would condemn them for it since it involved race, and anyone who did would look like a bigot for correcting the situation of couples of different races shacking up and then either committing infanticide or having mulatto children which would become part of government's problem such as the Great Society or the New Deal even. The previous generation had now to get used to this master race plan that the rich and well educated came up with and could not be reversed. It was just for pleasure, this sexual promiscuity, and not for procreation even though the blacks thought they were producing another generation of blacks with the whites this time no matter how it would be done!

Civil rights' socialism was behind some of this, but the Communist Party had already done this in Russia or the Soviet Union! So what had really been accomplished was nothing more then heathenism with the help of our own government and as one black man said, First I raped my own women and then I raped white women. This was this so called "discrimination" which, as I said before, was nothing more than sex without any restraint or concern for the children, but as "trophies" to say "this is what I have accomplished for the brotherhood of man this immorality, but now involving all the races and not just the one. Now, whatever the blacks would do the whites and the Hispanics would look up to and call it being "in" or to do your own thing was the exact terminology.

The womanizing cultures or nationalities and races were the following because of the insane revolution of rebellion: The Greeks, the Italians, the Sicilians, the American black male, the American Hispanic male, the French, and then the subcultures would be such as Little Richard and Liberace' were the Greeks, the Germans, the English, the Moslems (the Arabs) and now Roman Catholicism's own clergy as well as the Episcopalian church and other Protestant denominations. This again was this front for civil rights' socialism which meant superior rights now and also for all homosexuals and had nothing to do whatsoever with the so called "hate crimes" which was nothing more than New Age Nazism, because children were being murdered, raped, and molested, and none of that was called into a special legislation. Also, NAMBLA was honored by the UN and John Wayne Gacy and Jeffrey Dahmer both were homosexual pedophiles along with 6 others out of a total of 10 of the worst serial killers ever in America! This is what the 60's generation had brought to America with a little bit of help from their friends on foreign soil. What was more hateful than to molest innocent babies just like the Nazis did in World War II and just like them were going after the Jewish people through Reformed Judaism which itself was founded on German soil. The Anglo-Saxons had done many things, but this was the worse that they had ever done and that was to harm innocent babies now out of the womb as well as small children, and also pre-adolescent and adolescent youth who now had become like wild savages because the mental disorder of homosexuality was now being induced into our own schools and churches as well as organizations wherever children were just like Hitler's Youth Organization!

Americans were selling out to homosexuality because they did not know that they could still retain their jobs if someone approached them as a homosexual no matter how bad that corporation would try to make it on them. This mostly involved the ACLU, big business such as World Bank and the IMF as well as big government and of course the Ivy League schools especially Harvard which had a book written about them called HOW HARVARD HATES AMERICA! There was a "brotherhood" amongst these homosexuals, but did not uphold a nation's sovereignty just like had occurred in Nazi Germany when the Nazi socialist Party took over! They were just like the Communists in that one had to really belong in body and soul and heart in order to comply with this disorder or ideology of hate that always included the abduction and abuse and murder of children, as I have said so many times before. Now we as Americans did not get the message when catastrophes occurred in America and we wondered why GOD was not answering real prayer for the safety always of our children here in America and elsewhere! Sodom and Gomorrah was what America was involved in. Places such as San Francisco and Harvey Milk, New York City and the UN (which approved of the North American Man Boy Love Association), Orlando where Disney World almost injured a mother and some small children in their parking lot when a group of vicious homosexuals came after them and the authorities such as Mr. Eisner was President, Bill Clinton, when he got elected and sworn in and the first thing he did was promote homosexuality, the State of Vermont who legalized it and the State of Massachusetts where that state, along with Cape Cod, was loaded with Nazis and the civil rights leaders and organizations as well as the Girls' Scouts of America, Big Brother and Big Sisters of America, Providence Town where in New England what one ever saw was homosexuals and Hollywood and the media and all the pornography magazines with Hugh Heffner and others! If Islam was serious about what they said was deviancy then because of the above groups no matter who or what they represented meant that because of them we in America would be in serious trouble and open for Islamic Jihad even more so than ever before and that is one of the main reasons that Michael Moore and Bill O'Reilly were both pro homosexual and were not for our veterans at all, but were so scared because they knew that they had created this haven for Sodom and Gomorrah and the Moslems in America knew where and who they were, but would not discriminate because a small few rich and powerful people such as even some billionaires were for this and not the majority of Americans yet they were making it look like the American people were for it and so wanted to keep peace with the warriors of the East, Islam for their own self preservation, but it was too late for that because Hollywood had been an original target and then was canceled and the Moslems also knew that our government and our US Supreme Court could stop it if they wanted to, but they did not since this mental disorder was also an addiction that could be treated! Osama Ben Laden was also a billionaire and so was Saddam Hussein and so the war or open war amongst billionaires was now in the open and all of the rich and super rich had to be very careful because now they too could be in harm's way!

I did know that Saudi Arabia, even before 9/11, did not want any American blacks on their soil and yet the American blacks here were daily becoming Moslems and the percentage was about 30% of the entire black population of America and was growing and they made up only 12% of the population and yet the media and Hollywood made it sound like if a socialist won that it would be the blacks fault. This was more of that Anglo-Saxon mentality that always passed the buck when it came to instigating trouble with their own Masonry and of course the Vatican with it's celibacy and cover up of homosexuality The Vatican also was worried not about the world of Catholicism, but because they too now were under the gun from Islam and were taking over in Europe and the Jesuits in France had to do something to stop it.

Even though the Masons and the Jesuits hated each other, they both came out on the same end when it came to homosexuality. Both had tried to cover it up under the premise of either not knowing or not being the reason for it! Islam, though, knew better more than the American people themselves but did not want to say this because they too had it in their own Islamic culture. The motorcycle gangs in America had a leader from guess where? None other than Hollywood itself? So now this insanity would still involve so many millions and millions of innocent people who had absolutely nothing to do with religions or with politics, but the rich and well educated knew better and also knew that they them selves had started this ball of deviancy rolling toward a sort of type of Armageddon all around the world and even in Red China in Peking there was homosexuality, but Islam would really have to think that one over because the Red Chinese would not blink an eye if they were attacked and Islam would be nuked if that is what it took with the Red Chinese government!

They would not hesitate to use nuclear armaments because theirs was not an industrial nation and the West kept portraying them as such and even with all the technology they still would not be for decades to come and so they had nothing to lose also because of too many people, just like Indira Ghandi sold out her own people to the Soviets in Moscow, but later herself was done away with!

Which of these two were worse? Red China with its do not blink an eye, or Islam with anything goes anywhere at anytime to almost anyone? They both only understood that one had to meet them with a firm hand or either go under and the way it looked Red China had the advantage because they would trust no one to fight their war like the Moslems did! They would annihilate immediately anyone who would threaten them now with the armaments to retaliate and had so threatened to do so even to America especially when Clinton was in.

The Chinese could also do a conventional type of war since they were almost near the 200,000,000 military men that would fight for them and this would be the Sino racial war and not just a Soviet class warfare would be no room to share with capitalism because now their oriental mindset would say go and that would be it! They would only wait so much longer before Islam would try again, but then again maybe Islam had already made a deal with the Red Chinese Government because of its hatred also for the West and the fact that it resented the West even more now that it had wimped under to their demand.

Too much of what Americans believed was good old hearsay or gossip or just plain lies and Americans would repeat what they heard without checking out if it was true or not and they talk about being childish! For example most Americans thought that most Moslems were Arabs, but the truth was that most Arabs were Moslems, but most Moslems were not Arabs! Also the fact that they thought that one could pray for a group which was not a living entity, but could only pray for individuals and individual nations or countries. Groups of people were what socialism spoke mostly to and about such as class and racial warfare which had occurred in Nazi Germany and the USSR. An example for this would be when Jonah the prophet and that is when one is never wrong because it is from GOD was told by GOD to warn and to witness to the people in Nineveh and that they should all repent knowing that the people there were enemies of the Israelites at that time did repent and were spared, but only after Jonah was in the stomach of a big fish for 3 days and 3 nights which was a precursory to Messiah rising for the dead after 3 days and 3 nights.

Another contradiction more than a lie was that in our very own town the blacks all moved out of it when many Hispanics came and in fact when the blacks were outnumbered and then realized what it was to live around people who had a real prejudice against them. When people become so ignorant and just plain dumb nobody wants to associate with them especially if that person is foreign and the other person is an American.

After 9/11 we all came to know how important it was to have good security guards, but the only problem was that those very same security guards were paid poverty wages and so the government and business got what they paid for about 98% of the time which was terrorists coming into America so easily! Security companies usually hired anybody they could get and still do just so they do not have a criminal record. They could be as old as 85 years old, or as unclean as one could be, or not be able to read, to write, or even to speak proper English! For instance in Israel they were the ones even more than the military that put their lives on the line since most of them were located right where the bombs went off in the cities and neighborhoods! Many were injured severely, maimed, or even killed in all those Islamic terrorists bombings and yet back in America the security companies still would not pay above the poverty level knowing that innocent people's lives were on the line! They continued to accept that is the security companies, a much lesser amount because they were too greedy to lose the contract so the security companies could care less about how much they paid and that in turn put many lives in jeopardy time and again, but again the love of money was the root of all kinds of evil. The people who ran these security companies were not the brightest of the bright and so that also had to do with a lack of intelligence on their part, because most of them never so the light of day when it really came to sincerity and honor and fair play. The airports also were filled with security guards that were even from Moslem backgrounds. The only ones that were really qualified were the Israelis, but like I said before they got little pay. The military which had also become incompetent because of lack of experience and because the only reason one became an officer was for a higher promotion and to make general or admiral if possible because then the retirement pay would be fantastic as well as the uniform and the world wide traveling and escapading here and there with all those unearned medals for most of these career people. Somewhat like a paid career politician that stayed also in for life so that they too could make life a bowl full of cherries. It was the NCO'S and the enlisted men that held the military together and not the so called officers' corps! Even Douglas MacArthur in Korea made a mess of things when he was there which was not too often and that was in his later years!

As I looked around more in our society I could see the filth and sleaze of pornography, gambling, the occult, and even the cars were designed to look like something the Nazis had come up with such as the motorcycle and the PT Cruiser! The VW Bug was especially made for Hitler which had no gaskets or no water radiator plus it had self tightening lug nuts on the wheels. The more one drove the tighter they would get. Cars were basically status symbols to make one feel how important they were when really inside they were so insecure and the pick up truck mentality was usually driven by short and round men with an insecurity problem and served no useful purpose for them except to help build up their own ego! Most new cars looked like clones and were made, one could say. of tin like material with nothing but plastic trimming no matter how much one paid for them. The much older cars all seemed to have a menacing grin on them where their grill was. This all came from an infantile disorder.

I had recalled to mind also when I thought about 9/11 that somewhere at the end of the 18th century till about 1806 America once before had problems with Islam, that is why in the Marine hymn we hear the words "From the Halls of Montezuma to the shores of Tripoli" which was exactly in reference to what I just said.

I noticed that the rich and well-educated donated a lot of time to their favorite "social" organization in society while at the same time supporting the party that was out to destroy the spirit of America and their cliques were as such that that only they could get these most prestigious positions since they were the elites no matter how unqualified or ignorant they were! The upper echelon was not what most people took it to be because when they were around them they would be in awe when they saw the cars they drove and the houses, or mansions they lived in. They would always forget what they wanted to say and also wanted to remain in their good graces and some would even as we use to call it "brown nose" their way to the top no matter what it took just so they could act and live like they did.

Americans, for the most part, had lost their own self respect and did not even care how they spoke in front of innocent children and when older women were around or in fact when any age of a woman was around. They had taken on the heathen cultures that the rich and well educated coerced upon them and picked up right off where these foreigners left off if they ever left off at all! America no longer had much to be proud of and it was noted all over the world for two things and they were stealing and taking drugs, not medicine since most of the time the well educated would constantly refer to medicine as a drug. The constant barrage of the war on tobacco became so ludicrous that no attention was paid to alcohol on television because they were in with the internationalists and the private tobacco companies as of yet were not. Not that tobacco was any good, but was drugs, or pornography, or homosexuality, or infanticide, or drunkenness? When had anyone here in America ever killed for a cigarette yet the drug dealers get a lesser sentence than did the ones who sold cigarettes to minors!

Yes, we were on the edge of a precipice and were ready to fall into an abyss once and for all and most people almost seemed oblivious to all this and would only talk about monetary things or the weather which got to be almost like talking to an idiot in a conversation and it was a repeated experience that one could hear and participate in time and again. And if it was not that then it was for sure food and the sports and celebrity worlds which really were the dumbest of the dumb! They had nothing whatsoever to offer a young child or a young youth and were really nothing to look up to. These were our politicians!

If one would listen to music, if one could call it that, from the 1940's, 1950's, 1960's, 1970's, 1980's, 1990's and past the new millennium, one could see how liquid manure developed from bad to worse and never was liquid manure ever good even after World War II and on. It was all body gyrations that were vulgar and crude to say the least and did nothing at all to express any type of art whatsoever. It kept getting more and more crude and violent and the words to all the songs were about how one could have some form of sex without marriage and fornicate and now abominate and most, people listened to it including some Christians! The lyrics were horrible and said much about what kind of lives we were living and now even the elderly who had gotten old were dancing to it and looked as ridiculous as they had when they were young, but even now more so since they were much older. They would never grow up into adults and would die with this on their very souls this liquid manure and in fact one woman had suggested that we take this music and make hymns into them. This would certainly make our churches even more liberal than what they now were.

There were songs that glorified shacking up between the different races as well as with one's own race and went against all rhyme and reason as to why one would have sex with anyone outside of the marriage realm. The country and western scene would only sing about a woman, a truck, and a beer, it appeared, and we all were supposed to like what the majority of people called music. The young never really understood what real music was, such as the classics and what talent and genius it took to write and play this kind of real music. Any idiot could perform on a stage and act possessed and idiotic and yet the American people spent a lot of money on all this liquid manure. The atheistic Beatles and Monkees were just 2 groups that people spent millions upon millions on just to excite the inner passion of lust and had no healthful purpose to serve one's heart or soul!

The English were sure vulgar and profane in whatever they tried to do especially in music and in fact it was hard to name even one famous composer such as Mozart, Bach, Beethoven, List, the Strausses, etc. that wrote beautiful and timeless pieces of music. Only real genius ability could do this then too the blacks came up with their own liquid manure and then the whites really started to like them then and not when the Negroes had such beautiful spiritual hymns that they use to sing in their churches, and in fact many of their people left the church to sing this kind of black liquid manure just for the money and fame and thought that this was what their American image should be or at least the liberal Jews in Hollywood thought that that was what the real American Negro was all about. The white man's world of capitalism was not what the American Negro was noted for, but for the spiritual and GODLY music they would sing that would warm one's heart and not the heathenism the Hollywooders had done to almost destroy entirely, the American Negro who had much to offer besides this liquid manure because a Hollywood freak or millionaire thought it was good for them (that is, the millionaire) so that they could excite their very own passions with a forbidden fruit!

Comedians also were so vulgar that it made one sick just to hear one of their crude and filthy jokes again that the socialists and Communists both thought was in good taste according to their half witted mentality in Hollywood! Then came the authors or writers in America such as Mark Twain who was an agnostic and why would I want to read something by an agnostic or something by Ernest Hemmingway who was an alcoholic? This is what most of our own literature came down to. We had no Tolstoy, Solzhenitsyn, or Dostoyevsky at all, or Dickens, but an Edgar

Allan Poe, though, who was morbid and depressing in what he wrote about most of the time and was also involved with incest!

America really was a major part of Europe in the past but could not be original because of England and its promiscuous mentality and the lack of artists—of originality. They lacked the real creativity to produce masterpieces even though it appeared that the upper English elite had an ear for good music, good literature, or a good culture. They tended to be legalists most of all and would dwell on their own rights in England but none for their colonies!

Abraham Lincoln was probably one of the most prolific writers we ever had in America, but he was self-educated which meant he was not ruined by the rich and well-educated English! His Gettysburg Address is something to read as well as understand plus other documents that did not constantly dwell on one thing while he lived another way and it was though only in his last two years that Mr. Lincoln became a Christian!

One would have to search high and low for really honorable artists in the field of literature to find real genius that was put into words and that the artist themselves were always dedicated to telling the truth. Keats and Kipling even glorified piracy, but did not have to spend time in the Soviet Gulag.

In America, at least it was common to say one was anti-Semitic when it would have been most proper and less euphemistic to say one was prejudice against Jewish people just because they were Jewish, but the Jewish people unlike the blacks and other minorities did not want to be called a minority but an American and not Jewish American. Also, the word Jew was a derogatory use of the word for Jewish, which was a word that could be used and was not like the word Greek which had no other word for that nationality. If one was prejudiced, did it only mean against ones who wanted to be called minorities when the Jewish people, as I just said, did not want to be? It was exemplary that the Jewish people did not want to be included with the word minority, but did strive to help them achieve an equality but went about it the wrong way with civil rights' socialism because one could now see what the ACLU has done to help destroy America when they believe in ideology and not in the faith in GOD!

As I would go outside to food shop I would many times see girls and women with tattoos on their bodies and earrings in their mouths and tongues and many earrings in their ears just to mention a few absurdities that the taxpaying public school officials did not want but the excuses were that they did not want to be sued by the Communist Party's ACLU! How could a majority of Americans allow a Marxist/Leninist organization run America into the ground on the basis of lies and more lies that would only produce violence such as infanticide and euthanasia as well as Nazism's homosexuality?

If one knew how far the other would go they would have realized that confiscating their property and counter suing them would be the best way to defeat them because without money they had no power and without the corrupt lawyers such as the ones on the 9th Circuit Court Of Appeals which was loaded with socialist judges whom Bill Clinton had put on just for that very reason his socialistic ideology and the insanity they would perpetrate!

Just know that if one sues another and the other has much property, then they are usually hesitant to really get involved in a court law suit if the suit was made against the individual and not the organization since our U.S. Constitution prohibited Communism of any kind in the U.S. Take what they love most, their property, as the narcotics officers did even though it did jeopardize private property and make it all around a little easier to confiscate anyone's private property. Also go for the leader of this gang. Once one knew who to attack it would be quite easier then to defeat them and take them to the fullest extent of the law and then some over and over again no matter where they appeared with no regard for one's own property, because when someone has little or next to nothing then they know that you do not fear the money problem, but they would fear their money problem once they started to lose and they would lose.

The gun control politicians and socialists wanted only the state that they were seeking to take over to be able to have guns as had occurred in England and Australia when the people there were foolish enough to turn over their guns by agreeing with the lie that they would be safer with this new kind of legislation! In Switzerland everyone, that is every family, was given a rifle by the government and the state was held back and the immigration policy was as tough as nails. In some places years ago if one could not shoot properly and own a weapon they could not vote! The ones against the right to bear arms would do surveys which by the way usually always lie about real numbers when the question asked was phrased in such a way that the word in "self defense" was hardly if ever used, and in the press also it was hardly used so that people would always think that only criminals now had guns so guns had to go for sure. This was the way all surveys were conducted that is with a lopsided question. Rarely did the media tell the American people that sometimes in one whole year over 1 million people had used a gun, not always firing it to protect themselves, which saved many lives until the police got there and also helped law enforcement while it hurt the liberal judicial system. The judicial system, by the way, wanted women as judges or politicians when they were a totally different type of species when it came to these two professions. Biblical concepts always had a man in charge of authority and there was a good reason for that and that was because it was Eve who was deceived and not Adam, the first man, even though Adam blamed the sin on Eve, but he and GOD also knew what the real truth was!

This hodgepodge of nonsense was started by women feminists who lacked the femininity, and many times one could see how many times they either came down constantly on the wrong side or they went back and forth on major important issues time and again.

It gave the men in America, and I use the word men lightly because of their squeamishness in approaching a political or religious issue head on and allowed what most women shall do and that is usurp a man's authority as did Eve! This was her way to say, "Well if he is not going to do it, then I am."

Since the media does not take an oath to uphold the U.S. Constitution, which they should, they could care less about the average American citizen and are only interested in the Pulitzer type of journalism which is really commercialism and not meant for the average buying consumer that might read the news paper so the owners of the newspapers such as a William Randolph Hearst or their heirs publish what they feel is appropriate and I use that word very cautiously in their newspaper syndications such as the Knight-Ridder news publications which is owned by the Hearsts. In fact in San Diego they have a museum with mostly gold objects in it The New York Times is another socialist outlet that plays to the tune of the National Democratic Socialist Party which also has ill regard for what it prints in regards to the truth. It is like democracy itself which is not in search of the truth, but just about party ideology and each group or party has its best regards only for party ideology and hence only the individual has a particular point of view.

In England and in Australia both those nation's peoples allowed their government to let the state take control of the right not to bear arms so now they too live in a more closed society with the use of many cameras everywhere so that now George Orwell's 1984 has become more than just a novel but a true living reality and since in America we use the excuse for the Patriot Act which does do some good when we should be deporting many Moslems here in America and use Internment Camps just like we did for the Japanese and Chinese who by the way did not attack our own civilians on our own sovereignty which is an act of war we pander to the oil rich sheiks who too are involved with terrorism up to their necks!

In Switzerland each family must have a rifle, which the government provides and in some places it use to be that if one did not own a firearm they could not vote at all! This was to keep the government where it was, out of our private law abiding lives that were GODLY and our public lives separate, but now big brother has tried through the socialists in this country and make no mistake about it they are socialists and much much more! As you heard described the right question is stated or asked in the wrong context as to the use and ownership of guns and if one does explicitly say that it would be used in self-defense then the question itself becomes totally irrelevant The media has a way of lying constantly also so if one keeps hearing a lie they really start to believe it if no one reputes it as such and the truth is not told at all. Lies upon lies produce violence which means even in a free society the truth must emerge so that a true public opinion must be formed which would be an informed public and not an uninformed one as they have in Red China or had in Moscow or in Cuba or North Korea for the people there only here one side of the story just like our very own news media in America! This is how far we as the American public have allowed this to go since we appear to be saying that this is irrelevant! We must not allow ourselves ever to trust another to hold our liberty and freedom in totally in another's hand since in today's world the one in office always forgets why they are there and serve only the party interest as I mentioned before which always is party ideology which has no particular point of view.

When crimes are committed the percentages still rise even more again since the number that are reported or that should have been reported are never reported and so again the media in total disregard for freedom and liberty take the liberty to want to choose totalitarianism since all good journalists if one can find one must first be a good citizen in their own sovereign nation and not affiliated in the sense that they would uphold the UN or any other world organization that is a socialistic organization that appears on the outside to be a businessmen's organization! It allows anyone at anytime from any nation to spout whatever they feel they should and upholds totalitarian regimes and coupes all for the sake of power and so called prestige.

In America since we already had one civil war which is the worse kind of war, we have now again forgotten that eternal vigilance must always be present in the general public's eye so that ones who would usurp our freedom for their personal ideology do not run our own country amuck with propaganda such as a gun ban on all weapons. I do not personally have a vested interest in guns, but I do know that if we allow any government to let the state take over we shall find ourselves like England and Austral is and since we always appear to do what England does could too be on the very precipice that could take us into an abyss for this issue shall not go away. In the USSR the two things in this order they did not allow in their closed society were first the Bible and second guns of any kind. Remove the freedom to defend oneself and the state shall end up defending what the criminal would want in all cases and that would be that all laws are legal and that the state would dictate as to who would live and who would die!

It is not hard to assimilate the facts as has been done, but this information needs to be published in larger amounts such as through samizdat in our own nation so more public opinion can take place that has a true perception of the gun issue and not a distorted one. We as Americans should have a vested interest in our very own liberty and freedom. If we do not, then freedom and liberty shall be lost for no one person or even group can hope to survive the onslaught of the socialists in our very own country. Make no mistake about it, they would take us to the very end and as always all socialisms point only in one direction and that is total Communism or what we like to euphemistically call "social justice", not justice, but social justice.

There are about 163 words that have the word social in front of them which does indicate that socialism is here and is growing like a cancer. That is why one rarely hears the word social such as socialism or socialistic and we only hear the word or words, "to the left" or "the liberal left" which does nothing since it is fairly new on the scene since the 60's which call good evil and evil good! We also change the meaning of words so that there is no longer a moral base such as pro choice instead of infanticide which is defined as such in the 1898 Webster's Dictionary that was to be used so that America had its own, if you will, English jargon to speak, write, and read and in a more orderly and proper fashion since too many people at that time were illiterate as to a one kind of one English language with one land of vernacular and not a multicultural one such as Ebonics or the slang version of Spanish we now hear coming to America more and more and which creates animosity and resentment for all those involved and stresses this "diversity" or tearing apart of society into factions and schisms and is what Lenin the very shortsighted Lenin thought would bring a revolution to Switzerland because of their many different nationalities.

Lenin liked to play on the diversity or the differences in people, culture, language, etc. and in this way create a multi-cultural society where everyone would be at each other's throat which would enhance Communism even more so since Communists who are even born in a certain country hate that very country so much that they would do anything to destroy it and mankind if given the opportunity and that is why also John Kerry or Kohn a Catholic Jew who speaks French fluently and is not Irish and was born amongst the rich and well educated and proposes to do what the Russian elites had proposed there before the Russian Revolution and that was totalitarianism where nobody really votes but the state takes over to dictate from birth to premature death what is what. Therefore there is no moral foundation upon which to build a normal society but only a total absence of not only the physical, but the spiritual freedom to worship, to bear arms, to assemble and so forth and so on, and that is why also the ACLU upholds at random for anyone almost like a libertarian would which would mean even children could sue their own parents such as in Hillary's Children Defense Fund which is anything but that, but which promotes this "village" concept that the state again is first and family and GOD, or GOD and family is not important, and the institution of family would be superseded by gang or tribal like warfare against the very people that they wish to own and control all the time. The gun issue, yes, is quite important to all even to ones such as myself who do not own a gun, but who know that to be "gunless" in any free society is to invite the very same kind of thugs that we call criminals into our very own mist and our very own government which have already appeared too numerous to count! This is my generation the 60's generation that had no moral authority to do anything moral in our lives and hence now we are starting to see the beginning of the end of

America as we once knew it only a few years ago and remember we only have each one of us a few years of mortality and so to us it may at times appear short because we were once young and had the opportunity to live in a free society and not a society where the state is all and that is also why the rich and well educated never want to get old gracefully! All of our blessings came from GOD and the common people or person that GOD worked through and not the elites like we always like to believe and that is why I state again that an entire generation of immoral individuals started to think like a group and would have rebelled at anything no matter what and also because we as a generation were so large that we did not assimilate into the main stream of American society and came along with what we thought was good regardless of the outcome or of other generations who had tried and tested the "process" and of course had the experience of life!

The very moral fiber in America was what really brought down the loss in Vietnam besides our very own State Department and World Bank with people such as David Rockefeller and Robert McNamara who then was Secretary of Defense and also President of World Bank! Again the rich and well educated took it upon themselves to promote their capitalism which always brings on socialism because one is an economic system and the other, socialism, is an ideology which is a total way of life. Nothing more than capitalism has promoted what now you see in most parts of the world and that is socialism and not, as we are constantly told, democracy.

We must now retain, and yes retain, the right to bear arms for if we do otherwise then the real criminals in society in high places shall continue to do more vicious and devious things to all regardless of who they are and even if they are the "Mensheviks" in America and shall use the so called legal law that our own courts have passed without referendum or Congress but by the great tribunal that sits in D.C. and also the 9th Circuit Court of Appeals that Bill Clinton appointed most of these socialist judges into their positions! They are for the very destruction of mankind and have this urge for this death wish which so fascinates many of the young all the time and which is spoken about just as it would occur and they do not rescind the evil they propose no matter what!

We are at the controls in our own society, but shall we have the moral resolve to do what is right and not just speak with rhetoric just for another so called election? This very Presidential election is so scary because most Christians shall not vote for either one since both candidates also have this urge but one is ready to take us immediately to socialism and the other in a more gradual process. One upholds his right to do what he sees fit like an anarchist and the other is too soft on Islam and on illegal immigration and is of course the incumbent who also believes at times that he is right! He has stated that Islam and Christianity worship the same GOD and that is a horrible thing to say and needs to apologize publicly if first he wants to win the election and second, if he wants almost 5 million Christians to vote for him. To most it is not important, but to Christians it is vitally important because they would have to sin to vote for him now. The First Commandment is quite clear enough and so there is absolutely no reason for him not to apologize and one can also forget the polls and surveys and—so proves that case in a very excellent way! (The next is the inner self.)

You yourself have said what is what I am trying to say and that is the truth must sustain us and not the lie and do not believe the lie even though you have not used those exact words it comes out to mean just that. It is vitally important for America to forget about the love of money and start remembering who really to love as He loves us. There were 4 democracies in the 20th century that fell all to totalitarianism, and they were the Weimar Republic, the Italian Republic, Russia and CIA's Republic in China. Not an auspicious showing for the 21st century. Democracy can only work in a small geographical area such as Greece and not like America, and that is why, after a little over 300 years we already see the end in sight.

In a final summation in this issue one must always remember that in a democracy or a democratic republic that one has to be always swayed by elections when one is running for office but in a monarch the only one above him is GOD. There is no other one to please and the majority never has the truth endowed to them in a democratic republic. Terms and words can be changed and often are to the delusion that might makes right. The only Biblical form of government is a monarchy out of only 3 forms of government that there are. The monarch is brought up with the way they must rule a country and does not have to concern one with elections and a short term at the helm of government for he is in it for the long haul meaning a full lifetime. The people can be easily swayed and so a monarch can do what he must do and does not have to play party politics which is just ideology and the fact that the politician must go to and fro as to what today he is for and what he is not for. The stabilization process is one that alternates like a pendulum so in essence even with guns in a democratic republic it is not by far a fail safe system and so hence we are left with more rhetoric.

The monarch is law, and of course with GOD at top of that that would mean always a moral society since the monarch has a vested lifetime interest in the country of his birth. Some monarchs would be worse then others but nonetheless totalitarianism has yet to overtake a monarch, but has in many instances overtaken a democracy or democracies time and again. Russia remember had 8 months of democracy before it went over to totalitarianism and the extreme change from a monarchy to a democracy with a constitution proved to be fatal for a 1,000 year nation of Christianity and we are only approximately 300 years old as of now. Republics have a way of being swayed by that very same public opinion that I just mentioned earlier and can take a nation to the very end. A constitution cannot hold because it is not a living entity like a monarch is who can pray to GOD and do GOD'S will!

No constitution can keep any of it's promises while a monarch does not have to make any promise since as I said before he is in it for a lifetime and so has a much more vested interest in his nation as a ruler and not just a leader or even an administrator, or bureaucrat, that always leads to mediocrity. The monarch is a form of government that coincides with the will of a moral people, but a democratic republic never actually confirms this in due time and now as it shows in America we can see the ill affects of what a democratic republic fails to do. Israel too wanted another form of government, another "king"!

To have freedom as an ultimate goal like civil rights' socialism is indeed a dangerous foregone conclusion since nothing stands above that or this so called equality that is nothing more than equivalence. Free means to man's human nature whatever man wants it to mean, and that could mean anything from anarchy to totalitarianism. There must be a higher voice to answer to. The spiritual realm without physical freedom can prove to be better morally even though one is restricted as to one's movements as to where they go or where they can even live. It does not usurp one's conscience this almost restricted way of life and does not call for a total kind of physical revolution where the only thing is freedom and again this freedom could mean revolution. The American War of Independence was not a revolution but a spiritual revival and was fought as such.

The Russian Revolution was a civil war that pitted one against another and caused the workers or proletariat to side with the military while the police were at least they thought upholding justice by the government by their leaders or officers in charge believing in something that had not even occurred and hence started to fight and kill both proletariat and their instigators which were few and the veterans who kept hearing about all the wrongs that the monarch was doing by rebel rousing Communists in the crowd. Today now in America we hear it from our very own courts as well as certain parts of government not to mention the better red than dead Hollywood elites who have always supported socialism whenever it made a strong showing in the mass media or by ones in the celebrity world of the rich and the famous.

This played exactly into the hands of Lenin in that he said he wanted to get rid of all the brains in society which to him meant the monarch and to the people meant the government that was then ruling! This was Maoism exciting the masses so that no one could oppose the majority and here it is, the people and who are the people would want to change the government without having ever studied what the covert side was doing amongst their own nation and with foreign elements from the Internationale involved with this up to their necks from Europe such as the Finns and Germans as well as the English and the French and even good old America with it's pure form of capitalism which upheld socialism.

Now that we have said that this freedom is the most important of all things we have fallen into an abyss that we may never get back out. In order for the peasants in Russia to understand freedom no one ever told them how to spend real money since they always bartered and did not understand the system.

It had gotten so bad in America that it appeared that wherever there was homosexuality, infanticide, euthanasia, pedophilia, socialism voters for the National Democratic Socialist Party that many lands of disasters were occurring and even so called social Christians were attacking people like Dr. Dobson and were calling them radicals because they themselves two parts in their public and private lives meaning that in public they appeared as Christians and behind the scenes they were anything but! Many kept saying live it up to the fullest while the nation was crumbling right before our very eyes with such debauchery that all this was looked at with desensitized eyes and civil rights' socialism which also destroyed the peasants in Russia before and after the revolution when it was too late then to go back under a monarch. They too had been lied to, and the only ones or few ones would be the Lenins, Stalins, Hitlers, because even Trotsky, Beria, and others all got theirs from their very own comrades in the Communist Party. The only thing Stalin did different than Lenin was kill members of his very own party for he trusted absolutely no one except Adolph Hitler!

The cult of a personality meant that only one figurehead could stand tall even though Stalin was only 5' 2" tall! It appeared also then that most of the Nazis were also very short in stature and in brains. After all Lenin himself had said he wanted to get rid of all the brains in society and he did just that and so did Hitler because he chose sexual deviants like himself to, hold high positions even though Ludendorff and Hindenburg were not themselves homosexuals. The criminals and thugs that were involved in

World War I and World War II were in charge of millions of people and murders that amounted to hundreds of millions when all was said and done and when America would win a war they then would allow this evil to prevail even amongst our own high officials who had degrees but were not that highly moral or had no morals at all. In Japan almost 2,000 years of a monarchy ruled there and we chose to use 2 nuclear bombs on Hiroshima and Nagasaki and one maybe could see as to the why, but when none were dropped on Berlin or Munich where the homosexuals were in charge, then one had to wonder as to why! Of course Sunoco Oil and Ford Motor Company both were involved and both were anti-Semitic, no, Jew haters! Yet they along with the Krupps, and the Rockefellers plus other billionaires at that time were also involved in trying to liquidate all Christians and all Jews and make no mistake about it they wanted to get rid of all the Jews in the world and that included England and Germany. The Vatican along with the German Reformation with Martin Luther's virulent anti-Semitism! The Italian underground or peasants had got rid of Mussolini and nobody seemed to pay attention to that too much and the fact that Mussolini's wife was a stay-at-home wife and cooked and cleaned for her so called husband. The Italians could in no way stomach what the Nazi Gennans saw as okay and later what the Vatican and Bill Clinton also promoted and saw as okay. America now especially after Bill Clinton had accepted the molestation of children in broad daylight and glorified it and no one in government ever executed them because both England and Germany and Poland had legalized homosexuality before America did but nobody was saying much about that either.

The Roman Catholic Church should have closed its doors in America until they could weed out the multitude of homosexual pedophiles, but then again people who were heterosexual continued to support and donate money for the purpose of the Vatican who owned so much land and so much gold! The only important thing to them in America was the fact that money was the dominant factor and no matter how devious it got they were going to support their "Church"! Yes, what had murdered the Jews during the Holocaust, as I have mentioned many times, and was not in accordance to any Biblical Scripture New or Old Testament (Paul in the Book of Romans—reprobate minds) and there was treatment for this non-birth mental disorder so one was not born one but became one for whatever reason and continued through in life many with guilt because who would believe a child over a dignified priest and a celibate church when GOD had said, "Be fruitful and multiply", but then again most Catholics never ever in their entire life had read the Bible so how would they know, but they did know because GOD shall not allow ignorance as any kind of factor for not knowing His Word the Bible. We all have freewill to choose and to decide though sometimes those decisions are harder depending on where one was born and raised, but in America we hardly had any reason to fall under that category since we were a free nation, but then again children innocent children no matter what would not understand for that is why this crime is so horrible and yet the government blames the courts which was true, but then again they themselves and the public did not pursue these sexual deviants, but only continued to hire and promote them as if it was Nazi Germany and also because most of them at the top were of this so called "brotherhood" and now the Moslems and the Arabs had much of this in their own culture too and that is another reason why they were allowed to come and stay here so that England and Germany for some strange reason had a proclivity for this mental disorder and abomination that GOD had called it The Moslem women wore their garb not because so much of narrow mindedness but because it was in the very socialistic religion as it was in Nazism! Who had sheltered the Nazis after World War II and had given them Moslem names and who had taken land away from the Jewish people in Israel? Was it not Germany which the Jewish people ought not ever to trust and the English who the Russians should have never trusted and also of course Arabic Islam?

Socialisms all have a way of coming together from different methods but none the same coming to fruition if left to "blossom "into full blown Communism or this so called" social "justice or multiculturalism was just another front for socialism that sounded good and plenty good to most Americans! Was this prejudice against these different cultures and nationalities or was it just the truth about a part of history that few knew about and most did not care to hear since maybe in America many were of that background but could not come to face the truth about their very own relatives and families? What could one say to refute what Stalin did along with Lenin in the Gulags or the concentration camps long before the Nazis even thought one up or the fact of Hitler also along with the Communists who hated the Jews so much that they disguised whatever they could to make it look like Nazi Germany and Soviet Moscow and Red China were not all involved up to their very necks in this deviancy? Whatever happened to public opinion the paradox or quintessential of all democracies or democratic republics? Had the cat swallowed their tongues not to even speak out and that included the average American who now had almost become like the Nazis as well as the 18,000,000 Communists in the Communist Party, covert?

If the Jewish people had done what was done to them especially in Nazi Germany what would the Germans and the English along with America and the rest of the world have done and said about them? The Roman Catholic Church especially in Hispanic America had for many times and many years called the Jewish people "the Christ killers "and nobody seemed to get upset at that at all, but why? Who was Jesus, or Y'eshua who came in the flesh as a Jewish, not a Gentile, man? He was half man/ half GOD and came onto take on all the sins of the world and to die as He so did so by choice for nobody could have really taken His life, He gave it willingly and this cross was a symbol of pure love until forever and one could now see or would see the nail prints that were there from the crucifixion of which proved that the Romans did it, because that is the way they killed all believers, Jewish or Gentile!

In America it appeared almost like most Americans were under some sort of delusion that it did not matter how bad it got they were not going to oppose this all encompassing evil that was getting more and more prevalent First the men had gotten into this homosexual pedophilia and now the women too were doing it plus the fact that crime for women was going up and up because of feminism and Sodomy that was like opening Pandora's Box! It appeared nobody in the public eye really cared about these immoral and evil things occurring right before our very eyes and maybe that is why now in Europe Islam now was taking over because of what it had done to the Jewish people and was now trying to do to Israel and plus the fact this is what Jesus said would occur in the ends times! The clergy in most churches would not touch these evil things even including anti-Semitism or hatred of all the Jewish people, because now the enemy was allowed to do in America what he had done there, but all peoples had been told by GOD to repent as a nation for their sins and they refused and that is why the story of Jonah was so very important for all to read and know because of how Nineveh was told to repent and were real enemies against the Israelites!

"Blessed are those who bless my people and cursed are those who curse my people" and now with Nazism New Age homosexuality one could really begin to understand what just might be going on and why now the door was closing on all Gentiles because of the 70th Week of Daniel that was for the Hebrews. How many Christian ministries were really witnessing to the Jewish people that did not have an ulterior motive? Could they be counted on one's finger? Why was there this virulent anti-Semitism against a small nation such as Israel even though we knew about the enemy, but what about all of us who had freewill? Did that mean that the Jewish people were always right even in sin? Heaven forbid! But to hate the very flesh that Messiah had come in certainly made no Christian sense at all, at least to some of us and in fact after reading Scripture and being warned time and again and seeing the results in history one had to question the sanity of man over all and now in our very own country that refused to tell the Jewish people they had to repent and not allow them to continue as usual as we all do for this indeed was important to a Christian nation that once stood for GOD and the Words of the Bible that our Founding Forefathers had followed!

Why would we choose slavery or socialism over Christianity and why would we not be thankful?

If John Kerry would become President the even worse fear that most people and mostly the American Jews failed to realize that if something went wrong in America doing his term then almost for sure would the travel out of America by any Jewish person would be stopped and anybody trying to come into America would also most likely be stopped also. So Aliyah would in essence be impossible where over 6,000,000 Jewish people lived most of them being in New York City! How could the Jewish people not see the facade that the Democratic Socialist Party again was perpetrating against the Jewish people just as they had in Russia before and during and after the Russian Revolution? The blame then was on the Russians and not the Communists and here it would put the blame on the Jewish people and Israel and not the Communists working behind the scenes of the National Democratic Socialist Party. They would continue to dupe the Jewish person because they did want to eliminate the Jewish people totally from the face of the earth. Would they succeed? No, not entirely but most of the Jewish people would be eliminated before Armageddon at least that is what I felt would almost surely happen and America would not be the land of the free and most of all the home of the brave since the Red Horse of the Apocalypse was Communism in symbolic terms. One of the 4 Horsemen that the Book of Revealation spoke about.

The 7 hills of Rome designated what the Vatican was all about, but did not indicate that the Antichrist would come from there and in fact it most likely would come from Israel sitting on the throne in Jerusalem to emulate what Jesus would do during the 1,000 year Millennial Reign of Christ. Satan then would be put away for those 1,000 years. Yes things were now moving so fast that it was indeed hard to keep up with things even if one was trying to do so day by day and prophecy was coming very fast since all these things that Jesus spoke about in the Bible were now upon us so very quickly.

Yes, if Kerry became President they would not look at him as a Catholic for the CIA would bring that out about his real background, and it would not be like a John F. Kennedy who also was a Catholic of Irish descent, but Kerry's mother was English and French and his father was Austrian Jewish. There was enough alone in the nationalities and faiths to indicate that somewhere the scapegoat mentality would come to light as Kerry would be Commander-In-Chief who would have no resolve, as President, to deal with the military since he too was another one who loathed not only the U.S. military, but also his very own nation. That is why he had married Teresa because without money he knew, like Lenin was also told, that he could not take control first of all without money. Teresa also knew that marrying a Catholic Jewish man he would have a good chance of winning the election because of the Jewish and black votes and the fact that she too wanted more than just money. She wanted power and a world famous name like Hillary Clinton worldwide! The collusion behind the scenes meant that the blacks could vote for Kerry and Kerry could win and because the Anglo-Saxons wanted it that way the blacks in America would not be blamed, only the Jewish people would be, and guess what, it was working so far even before the election since most all Presidential elections were fixed in one way or another! There was no honor amongst thieves!

The blacks in America could then be used as brownshirts to go after anyone in America the intemationalists felt they should go after, and of course it would be the real Christians and the Jewish people, believers or not! Someone had to do their dirty work for them and so once again as the Communists used the Russian language (which was no compliment for the Russians), they would this time use the Jewish people as the cause of all the problems when it was the socialists whether in Islam or from the Communist Party. Man appeared once again to repeat doing the very same thing and it was not history that repeats history but man himself and that is the man who knows not the meaning of GOD'S love since most people in the world or America by were not believers in GOD'S grace and grace alone.

This was too the bottom of the barrel the Communists wanted in office to deflect once again the blame from Hollywood which always had Communists in it and in the majority of times and again would promote the most socialistic candidate they too could promote while the incumbent had to be sure he was doing what GOD wanted him to do and not what party politics wanted him to do or ideology or else after these 4 next years no one man would want to be President at all whether they were a socialist

Jew on the Democratic Party or a Christian from the Republican Party for either way only socialism could win unless, as I just said the incumbent would do what GOD only wanted him to do and not what even he wanted to do or his so called advisers who were not believers so the enemy had them already. There was much anti-Semitism in both parties but the Republican Party got more of the blame because of the Anglo-Saxon background, but now the Democratic Party had the million man march and Farrakhan, etc.

Who would appear one night late on C-SPAN but the foreign minister to the Islamic Jihad Sudanese government in the North and decimated the Christian tubes in the South by crucifying them and raping their women and murdering others and selling their children into slavery and yet the UN was allowing this butcher of a government to be represented by a terrorist of thugs for a government! But where was the representative for the Southern Sudanese people who were the victims of mass murder? This appeared once again as another rendition of Nelson Mandela of Marxist/Leninism when he too spoke at the UN. Then this same minister along with the socialist media in America called the Southern Sudanese rebels because they took the slaughtering lying down and also the media in America was also condoning the mass murder of millions ever since Bill Clinton was in and he refused to take Osama Bin Laden off of their hands and not because he did not know or care, but because he was promoting knowingly the murder of millions of Christians as he had done also in Red China!

Now this incumbent was appearing to do something about it after he had served 4 whole years as President and was claiming to be a Christian? What kind of a Christian would ignore what the enemy was doing to fellow Christians elsewhere in the world? This publicity charade had one the incumbent as a Christian and the other as a Catholic Jew for whatever that was worth since most Catholics voted for socialist candidates and that meant money, or materialism. The incumbent appeared to want to listen to what he wanted to hear and that was his downfall. Both sides though were controlled by the Internationalists and their ideology was the same, except as I said before one would be gradual and one would be immediate. Nothing but freedom and democracy or mob rule and physical mishaps that had hardly any spiritual realm to it which was completely ignored by either candidate though they both spoke a lot about things all in generalities. This incumbent felt he could deviate from the Bible when he felt like it and the other was a new man "Pharisee" from the robes of the Vatican! This democracy was the panacea for all the world's ills to be resolved in.

Most Americans lived in their own private little worlds and kept doing what they had been doing with no regard to how bad America had really gotten. Even though, yes, the rest of the world was much worse off. The world had revolved around them like in all Eastern religions. The American Negro also needed real help some years ago and only the Jewish people would hire them before 1964. Now that the black people had so-called progressed in America many "social" organizations coerced by our socialist government in the bleeding liberal hearts to help to destroy a people that were once close to the land and farming now would be better if government would interfere forever in their daily lives and they accepted it since their education was not there and so were tied to by the government and big business and the rich and well educated to believe that big brother would always be there to comfort and guide. One then started to notice that the Negro humbleness became black racial arrogance and would serve the socialists in this country just find! There had been collusion and collaboration on many parts of this.

It appeared to me that I myself was becoming an island when it said that no man is an island unto himself. I felt as though most people only followed their noses or somebody as to what was right and what was wrong, or what was good and what was evil. For instance if one opposed a black man in office, or running for office, who was for infanticide or homosexuality they had to be prejudiced, but was not this kind of "prejudice" the very kind that America needed right now? Civil rights' socialism was just that racial superiority rights like in Nazi Germany when the Jews were not allowed in government which occurred over a period of a few centuries for it to come to full fruition and now here in America the same thing was happening but to Christians of European stock and it was called by the very same name as they had once over there and that was affirmative action. Now to get most government jobs one had to speak the language of David Rockefeller and that was Spanish or German with lesser English! One could not call a Puerto Rican a Puerto Rican and one could not call a black an American Negro!

Some strange oddity that I myself picked up was that the blacks and the Germans in America had some similarities between these 2 people. They both were austere and quite cold, but so were the English, and second the total disregard for others not of the same background or origin and even then they lacked the compassion for their "fellow man" amongst their very own! This "race" issue was a constant from the KKK to the NAACP.

The American peasant in America wanted nothing whatsoever to do with the government and did not play up to or vote for government that is big government because they were smart enough to know what that would mean in the end always. The Hispanics were brought here for the Padre' mentality and the part of American Islam was already here but would be called the brownshirts.

Young teenagers and adolescents would constantly use profanity and vulgar language and not through a fit of anger but as common place language and none of the older adults from the 60's or the generation before that would say or want to do anything about it even when wives and small children were in listening distance. This was emulated from Hollywood itself.

They also hung in groups as if they were tribes of some sort or gangs of guys and girls that had no families even though they did because these were the white suburbanites that could do anything since their parents were from the 60's generation the most misfit generation ever in America! As just one example a father said after his son got caught stealing and was questioned by a principal about what his son had done wrong he said, "He got caught!" This same generation also thought that smoking marijuana was nothing important and they usually gave their children huge sums of money to leave them alone but to go out on the streets and raise a living hell! If any type of authority would report that their son or daughter had gotten into trouble without even knowing the facts they would instantly say not my son, not my daughter!

The 60's generation had never grown up to accept the realities of life and always did at random whatever they wanted to and so they were bringing up their children the way they were brought up in affluence. This generation by generation debauchery was getting worse and worse all the time, but most of society took it all in stride and did not even consider for a moment that all of this would eventually come to an end and that their very own grandchildren would suffer severely for all the sins of the fathers.

Many people I grew up with had no morals then and still had no morals now and they just laughed when their very own children did crude things and said outlandish remarks at anytime to anyone. We had fallen as a race of people known as Americans and we had no self respect whatsoever in our own lives. We only saw what we ourselves could get out of this which would be little or next to nothing normal. Who had allowed this to occur? Was it not the previous generation, the one Tom Brokaw called the greatest generation when he too knew all along it was what he favored and had absolutely nothing to do with morality and GOD?

The lies kept building up and up and no one in the public eye could really bring to attention any kind of rhyme or reason, but only the fact as they so thought, "Well what can I do?" This here was the beginning of the end and it did not start over night but had started in Hollywood with vaudeville.

This one world god first seemed to appear in America with Roman Catholicism and then later came the ECT Document and then the Mormons, the Jehovah Witnesses, the Seventh Day Adventists and then now Islam along with other Eastern mysticism and heathen religions coming to form this one world religion where the Antichrist will eventually sit on the throne in Jerusalem. Many did not worship GOD but Satan's "son"!

Halloween was like a major holiday now and the occult items would go on sale at the beginning of September and the occult itself was growing and growing starting in the states of Vermont and Tennessee. America was on a downward spiral and our money or our love for it would not save us, not that it ever could save us. We had gone over to the other side. The young especially, knew nothing about GOD and the average American housewife was too busy tied up with daytime television's feminism. America, the "Babylon "was fighting in Babylon where no Christianity had ever been before! We were a bankrupt society, but the American people and government did not even realize that we were bankrupt spiritually nor did they really care! We love money over GOD in the entire Western church. A spiritual vacuum had occurred since our own negligence was the order of the day.

We as a nation said we loved GOD but our very actions and thoughts did not show it. The Western church was influenced by many different types of socialisms such as class and racial warfare and the race that Jesus talked about had become anything but human and caring!

Samson, King Saul, Annanias and Sappbira all died a physical death plus one in the church that St Paul said they had to pray for Satan to take their body so that their soul would be saved and the Bible said not to pray for ones who had committed such a sin because physical death had to occur because they had lied to the Holy Spirit as St. Peter had said so the healing was not to be but immediate death in the physical realm.

Astrology was more well known than the 10 Commandments or 12 Disciples of Jesus. This was devil worship too. There was much prophecy or had it been more hyperbole' since money always seemed to be the underlying factor on most all television ministries and self-preservation and also these ministries would rarely if ever address the immoral issues that were occurring in America to our very own children. They also promoted liquid manure and called it Christian music. Many young people as I said before knew little about classical music.

Another high official was caught being a pedophile in fact it was a Bishop in the Roman Catholic Church but he would be exonerated because of the statute of limitations and never mind about the victims. This would now set a precedent for another like him to do more of what?

Islam and other false religions would find out soon who the real GOD was. Jesus was a part of a Trinity in the flesh and not a god without no Triune god head! Judaism was also out of touch without no Triune GOD head. Israel is blocking the road to the West's capitalism so now what for America? More elections for a facade affect of nothingness? Nero fiddle while Rome burned but now Kerry set "Rome" on fire.

Would an incumbent allow himself to equate the GOD of the Bible with a god of the Koran? Would an incumbent also encourage and allow illegals into America and reward them with welfare, voting rights, for his election and drivers' licenses, etc.? Would he really continue to deny that oil interests are not involved in the Iraqi so called war when in Israel he was supporting a Moslem state? He could not have it both ways could he? This democracy in Iraq was like saying fish could fly and was only another form of mob rule which they have had for many centuries under a different name called Islam! What was this election really about and all its insane mania that would prove to be useless no matter who got in office because both candidates did not have the resolve to deal with the enemy which was in our very own nation and not in the Middle East? In the USSR they too had elections with one candidate and one ideology we had a set of "twins" with the same ideology but one was gradual and the other immediate!

Islam was buying out America through our own federal government and big business and mostly through the banks, and transportation means which included a lot of different things in America.

The "social" organizations were like the Komsomol and Hitler's Youth Corps combined. Atheism with homosexuality and then some. Anti-American "social" training into young minds for future reference. Who needed a degree but just the party ideology and of course Islam had its own ideology! Well then let the Party pay for all the pensions of government workers, all the pork barrel from either party that promoted it, and all the election expenses and none at all from the taxpayers' pockets!

Hollywood movies always had an insinuation as to some kind of promoted evil or to make it "legal"! Elia Kazan, Ronald Reagan, Charlton Heston were all enough proof that Hollywood had been and still was associated with the Communist Party for many many years and was trying once again to pull off a revolution within the United States or a civil war but still had to get control of the White House because than a weak Congress with a weak Constitution would then be nothing to take over through the power of an executive or a democratic dictator!

Was this incumbent really wanting to lose since he was doing everything that it looked like so to do? The war in Iraq was not really any war, but just a international oil deal and the illegal problem he kept endorsing it knowing that most Americans were not for this! As it now appeared and not by totem poll surveys, but by his very actions that he was throwing the election to Kerry or he wanted it to be or appeared to be closer than it ever really was and who could now ever have a clean election since a Communist had once served in the White House?

I had thought about the Old Testament and King Saul and King David and Jonathan who was the son of King Saul but was for King David even though he himself would have been king but not by the will of GOD! In this instance Jonathan was very sincere and with this election neither candidate was sincere be cause first of all Kerry was too a Communist like Bill Clinton and the incumbent was not doing what he knew GOD wanted him to do since he made it so very obvious as to his intentions day after day. If he kept sinning then demons would from now on influence him and even if he won he would probably be like King Saul who also knew better but kept on lying to himself and others and to the Holy Spirit!

This was not a game as these politicians thought because GOD had put this incumbent in to do His will and this probably would be it for America if he did not. In a small kind of way this incumbent was like a monarch because as a Christian he was first accountable to GOD and not to his party or ideology of which all parties have no matter how conservative they may appear. Maybe after he had won, if he won, he would not ever want to be a President because it could cost him and this nation so much misery that he had allowed sin in his life and was deceived in some way by the enemy!

I thought strangely about St. Peter and when he healed people with his very shadow but that was just for that time since the Jewish nation was still being given a chance to repent and come to Messiah and so start GOD'S 1,000 year reign back then almost 2,000 years ago. There was still about 1 month left . . .

The "almost" normal Christian family mindset by the Judeo-Christian faith, not that hardly anyone could totally live up to it, a husband and a wife married for life as believers with no pre-marital sex ever or shacking up ever with anybody, and if children then the children from these 2 biological parents and if willing and "lead", adopted children not fostered children bringing them up from infancy if possible to know about Jesus and the Bible. At the age of accountability share Jesus with them and have a stay at home mother and only the father would work. Have good and close grandparents or ones that are living in and the children attend a real Christian school no Roman Catholicism (cult) or maybe home school them. "Spare not the rod to spoil the child", meaning corporal punishment. Own no television set and buy no Internet at all and allow no heathen liquid manure or any other Hollywood objects into the house such as movies. All subjects in school should be taught from a Biblical perspective and context. Teach them to love all people and pray for their very enemies, but do not pressure or allow them to be pressured by group thought to give a guilt complex. They are too young for that already and it should never be indoctrinated because of the parents' sins.

Groups such as an African or Hispanic or Italian-American are all political indoctrination. See people here in America who are here legally here and who love their own country as Americans. And teach them to also love other foreigners in other lands where they live, but most of all treat all like human beings, and if you have pets treat them humanely. If of age, baptize the child or youth if they are willing and they should be by Christian encouragement which shall mean their free will. Have them read wholesome books and the Bible especially or read to them the Bible every day. Tell them to pick their friends and not to let their friends to pick them.

Teach them especially to not hate the Jewish people or be in anyway anti-Semitic, and if in a house of worship or elsewhere that is, get out no matter what they preach. Teach them to respect all their elders and of course the 10 Commandments. GOD or Jesus must be first in their lives always. Their diet should be three meals a day that is wholesome and no in between snacks such as soda, chips, too much candy, etc which does spoil the appetite for healthy foods. Stay away from processed foods and fast foods if at all possible. "All food is blessed by GOD." Do not coerce, but discipline with love as GOD does. If they really need to go to college make sure it is a Christian one and go there and visit many times and know the professors and make it be a local college where they do not live on campus.

Show them from small age that Passover not Easter is the resurrection of Jesus and tell them as to the why. Have patience with importance and tell and show them that once you start something that they should finish with care and pray constantly to their friend Jesus and this should be the idol! Teach them to pray to Jesus as if they were talking to a close friend that they loved or an uncle or close relative. The Holy Spirit shall most of the times lead even if they feel distracted or discouraged. To keep a close relationship with GOD if they sin tell them to ask Jesus immediately to forgive them and repent from that sin so that their relationship with GOD is restored. Be specific even though GOD does know your thoughts because to worship GOD is a wonderful and loving thing that He always loves. Pray alone many times and pray in the Body of Christ with other believers and also be careful who you pray with.

Motherhood and fatherhood are not easy, and neither is the Christian life, not lifestyle! Teach to them to honor you as mother and father which comes with a promise from GOD and teach them parents should not anger their children and set the example by not putting anything such as caffeine, nicotine, alcohol, drugs (not medicine) into one's body since their body is the temple of GOD just like Jesus told the Pharisees He would rebuild the temple in 3 days when they said in took 46 years to do, but Jesus was talking about His body which would resurrect after 3 days and 3 nights as will ours when we die and or when the twinkling of an eye shall occur. Each child is different and teach them when old enough the 4 major personalities which no one is exclusively of one and they are phlegmatic, sanguine, melancholy, and of course choleric, which are the fewest in the world. Teach them also about the geese and the herrings and why human beings are more like the geese then the herrings.

When disciplining them never do it in anger or when you do not feel good, but do it as soon as possible and explain why you are disciplining them. Explain the Biblical concepts of following the rules and also why parents must correct their loved ones as GOD corrects adults. Speak to them as equals and never down to them. Don't be a legalist. Remember each child is an individual even in the same family. Tell them they too are made in the eyes of GOD. Tell them Jesus loves them with unconditional love and you too and hug and kiss them and touch them so they know they are loved and know what it is.

As a father bond to your son, and as a mother bond to your daughter for sexual identity. When going on a vacation, take your children along. Do not spoil your children with materialism. Do it in moderation as all things should be. Keep them away, if possible, from negative or destructive influences as well as amusement parks. Occupy their minds with wholesomeness. If they can read the classics at the age of 9 or 10 then let them.

Teach them that animals do not have souls, but that we must love them and take good care of them as pets, but not before human beings. Remember GOD is everywhere, all powerful and all knowing and only He is. His love is unconditional and salvation is always 100% through grace and grace alone.

Teach them that one must learn how to love (agapé love) and when married which is a lifetime commitment with vows made between husband and wife but before GOD also. Teach them that dad is the head of the household and mom is a help mate. Marriage is for a lifetime and for only one time. Before they marry as believers they must stay with believers like in the Old Testament with the Israelites and do not mingle with unbelievers. Witness once to a person and do not coerce or show your pearls before swine. Associate with believers and date only believers. Christianity really starts outside the home for we are expected to provide for and help our own family first.

Explain to them the Trinity is like the egg with 3 separate but whole parts but from one. "Let US make man in OUR image." Also Romans 10:9-10, "If you confess with thy mouth and believeth in thy heart thou shall be saved." (Heart to mind back to heart).

GOD always hears the prayers of believers and to unbelievers only according to His will. No one can murder an animal, but they can kill one. Whenever one hates his brother than he is a murderer. Teach them that if one thinks about sinning but does not sin such as stealing then thinking of it is a sin, but not doing it is not the same as if you did sin even though the enemy may tell you "You thought of it you might as well sin." Sports are about good citizenship and the spirit of the game means when one goes beyond the rules such as helping your opponent up which is not in the rules. This is your opponent and not your enemy. Respect people in authority as long as they do not make you sin by coercion, and in that case remove yourself from them and do not argue.

Teach them that very few educated people have high morals so if you meet one listen carefully to what they say. Teach them the true history of their own nation. Teach them the 3 R's and the value of money. Do not buy the Internet. Teach them to look at the spiritual heart of people. Beauty is often misdefined as outside, but real beauty or harmony with GOD is on the inside. Teach them to write with tears in their eyes and from the heart. Do not donate to unchristian organizations and make sure they follow and open the real Bible and believe in the Trinity. Teach them there is a heaven and a Hell. Teach them that we are all equal members in Christ as believers but not in life itself. Remember Charles Spurgeon said that most Christians were from the infant mortality rate at that time which says little for seminaries since Spurgeon did not go to one.

Teach them to love the Lord with all their heart, mind and soul and to love their neighbor as thyself. Free will must have obedience to GOD and it is here that we must choose to what GOD wants but then on His strength not ours. Once into the family of GOD you are always a family member just like in your own family. Teach Jesus was a Jewish man and half man/half GOD. Teach them about real and false guilt and that real guilt was covered and false guilt needs no covering since it is not sin. If one continues to hear the Gospel and continues to refuse it their conscience becomes seared.

The Bible is inerrant Word of GOD written by men under the power of the Holy Spirit. If one has a GODLY father then GOD the Father will be much easier to relate to. Teach them the story of Jonah and was i n 3 days and 3 nights in the stomach of a big fish means in the New Testament. Teach them about Job and how GOD allowed Satan to do anything to Job except take his life. Teach them about the Book of Romans and St. Paul. Teach them about Daniel and the Book of Revelation that go hand and hand. Teach them about Abraham and Isaac and what that means in regards to the only Son. Teach them about conception and where and when life begins according to Scripture. Never believe in hearsay but check it out in the 'Bible and in fact know the Bible before hand.

Do not lie to your children about Santa Claus or the Easter Bunny because they did not die and resurrect on the cross or were born without sexual intercourse. The opposite of peace is not war but violence. Lies and lies produce violence. Do not be anxious for anything. Patience, longsuffering, perseverance and dependence on GOD'S guidance. GOD shall not do what you can do. Sometimes one needs fasting and prayer and to be used time and again in words that speak with GOD and not to Him as if He was a statue. GOD shall not tell someone else what He wants to tell you personally. Remember one's personality is made up from the ages of 1-3 and 85% of it is the amount.

Teach them how to put on the Coat of Armor of GOD: The helmet of salvation to protect the mind from the enemy, the breastplate of righteousness to protect the spiritual heart, the shield of faith to protect one from the fiery darts of doubts and unbelief from the enemy, the belt of truth to hold the armor on, one's feet are shod in the salvation of GOD in order to preach the Gospel and the sword of the spirit one's defensive and offensive weapon against Satan and his temptations.

Personal prayers: Search me oh GOD and know my heart and try me and know my thoughts and see if there be any wicked way in me for you did not give me a spirit of fear, but a spirit of love, power and discipline and a sound mind", or "We destroy arguments and every proud obstacle to the knowledge of GOD and take all thoughts to the obedience of Christ".

Let them read with you Isaiah 53 and Psalm 119, John chapter 1, Romans chapter 1, Philippians the entire book, read Daniel and the Book of Revelation side by side, read Ruth, read about Joseph one of the sons of Jacob and about Daniel and how both are not condemned in any way in Scripture. Noah had 3 sons: Shem= the Semite people, Ham= the homosexual people, Japhreth = the European people and the rest of the people on the earth. The Messianic Jews are the only Jewish believers. Iranians are not Arabs but they are Moslems and most Arabs are Moslems, but most Moslems are not Arabs. GOD looks over Israel and an angel looks over each nation.

All of this came out so quick that I had to retain it on paper so that I could refer to it myself and share it with other Christians.

As my mind kept wandering I thought about some strange things in regards to the war against Islam, such as Afghanistan which exports drugs all over the world and the fact that our generals in Iraq were looking for promotions. And what about our very pullout from Vietnam but our staying in Iraq which I thought was over oil? Was civil rights' socialism that important in 1964? Had the Yalta Conference been approved so that Russia would be intentionally swallowed up by Stalin.

Our farmers were being forced to sell out to the government of socialism in America and were given credit in the form of money that was worth nothing and the land that was worth everything. In essence they were getting nothing for very valuable land that was something tangible and workable but IOU'S would not in the end amount to anything that our bankrupt government could do since the farmers were feeding the cities and the rich and well educated who did not have to give up any thing, but the farmers had to give everything because socialism was eating out the mainstream of America and the prices the farmer paid for equipment, etc. were out of this world, but the prices farmers were getting for their crops and produce was next to nothing and hence the farmers were again feeding our government just like when we gave the USSR wheat for nothing and loans at less than one percent and less then American home mortgages! Yes our government and the rich and well educated were again selling out to the highest bidder to Red China and elsewhere just so the gentry themselves did not have to pay for it and the administration which was in essence bureaucrats was reaping in the profits and were being paid for jobs that were not needed and the farmers lost their so called "right to vote" because the inner cities had the most populous areas and electoral college or not they would reap the benefit of the farmers hard labor and the farmer would eventually go bankrupt plus their sons would be the ones to fight in the wars all around the world and for what?

These Presidential candidates both had daughters and could care less about the ones who had sons to send to the war zone and would this incumbent have been as ready to send our sons to war if he himself had sons of his own? I think not. America had no real leaders, just lawyers at the top with nothing for brains so they themselves had others to think for them! One could see that the farmers' sons and not farmers' daughters would be the ones to pay the price since they probably would not be coming home too soon or even want to come back and the daughters would leave the countryside for the cities so that they could get better paying jobs with no kind of American traditions like the farmers had for many generations. What would the rich and well educated know about tradition and hard work and the use of the body and of the mind when all they did was lie for a living as paid lawyers whether they were defense or prosecuting attorneys? They certainly had nothing to lose from all of this and gain what they already had and this was more socialism from the courts and distant and not local government that grandfathered everything to centralized government for to the victor belongs the spoils and so that is what the agricultural products and produce did and that was spoil! It was better than having lower or stable prices and the rich and well educated knew it from the start that is why they represent their own from the top and were allowed to be there as long as he did strictly according to what the internationalists wanted from here in America to all over the world and this incumbent . . . Then he had better get off his tuft and do what he was elected to do and that was protect the sovereignty of America and not Islam which was nothing more then a radical form of socialism that was innately in all of Islam!

The Ivy League was just that to American sovereignty and that was poison like in poison ivy! All they saw was multiculturalism because they had nothing to do with the Judeo-Christian GOD that was setup in America about 300 years ago and were whatever the wind from the left would blow in time and again. Our own borders had no protection physically and from the air. The only thing that kept us from nuclear attack was the Polaris submarines circling the globe continuously day and night and being able to stay under water for at least half a year without coming up to refuel or get refreshed. That is why the socialists wanted homosexuals in the military because they tended to go to the Navy all the time where out on a vessel they could do many things and the fact that now women had become so to speak equal to men meaning they could easily get pregnant while on ship!

Who would strike if they knew that missiles were coming back on them that is even Red China's Communist government because we knew where they were at all times? This was the key that could not as of yet be broken and even Bill Clinton had failed to give them this kind of information because he did not have security clearance even with the entire Pentagon. The internationalists would never allow just one man or the military people to have the last say in any of this!

Kerry, though being Jewish, would have access to certain information that even Bill Clinton did not have since he himself was an internationalists being a billionaire when they always said it was just his wife so that they could confuse and deflect the real reason he had been picked to run for the presidency. For anyone from the Democratic Socialist Party to get picked he had to be part of the Trilateral Commission, The Council on Foreign Affairs, etc. These were the lowest of the low who were selling out other countries that opposed their plan for a one world government and that also included Israel, but here it was posing such a problem that the internationalists had to be careful not to step on world Jewry's feet unless they wanted it all to fall heavily down and then what would they do except possibly give arms to rogue states for the sake of taking out Israel and America! Kerry would do what it takes to get rid of America and Israel and one could forget that he had Jewish roots and the Mossad must have known that since Mayor Koch himself would favor Bush and not Kerry and the fact that a Jewish President would also make a good scapegoat and the socialists in our own government knew that, and the Ed Asners or the Communists in Hollywood would be for all that plus much much more. The American Jew would be none the wiser since they were blinded by many things and were having a ball of their lives, but were not ready for what was about to come upon them and having no homeland America would turn out to be worse than they could ever imagine it to be so without Israel as a homeland they would not be able to escape even in America as I just said the elimination of the Jew worldwide except possibly, but then again I think they really must have known or do know that America was only temporary since they donated millions and millions of dollars for the Israelis' state which in essence was the end of the road for world Jewry and not America where it was not the promised land, but Israel! Would they see and if they did how many would see this and would it be in time?

The events were continuously leading up to this and the American Jew for the most part did not even see what was staring them in the eye and this had nothing whatsoever to do with America in the sense that it was the Jews themselves believers or not-that would be the ultimate target worldwide! Christians knew because of the Holy Spirit and some Messianic Jews would also know because in Scripture it speaks of "even the very elect shall almost be fooled", which meant to me the Jewish flock and not the Gentile believers who were going along with what was good for America or at least they felt! This is how much the enemy was working overtime to deceive GOD'S people worldwide and possibly even the church and the Body of Christ which was the believers in the world since the 1040 Window was closing quickly and the Eastern church was being persecuted.

The middle class in America was being totally ignored in America and that is why the minorities and the rich and well educated would vote so that they one could get more free healthcare and two the rich and well educated could make out like real bandits. These so called immigrants could get funds that not even real Americans could get no matter how much they tried so the American public was at the mercy of government to bring on universal healthcare which meant full and total socialism. Everybody then would be covered day and night and when one was sleeping, which meant all the time, no matter where you went. This is what Bush had done with Hispanic America as well as India and other Islamic countries that were buying out our own corporations and the middle class were losing their health care first then later would come their jobs to illegals and other unqualified people from the multicultural world where the most extreme and not the most qualified always got the government jobs and bilingualism was in since they already spoke a broken down language of Spanish and had the advantage of getting those jobs plus learning how to speak English already which left the average middle class American out in the cold intentionally. None of these two candidates had any regard for America as a real sovereignty since none knew what a basic American ever lived or worked like. They were confiscating our tax dollars and it was truly taxation without representation. Only foreigners need apply since they had already received from the American taxpayers over $540,000,000 for such things as a college education for a Vietnamese woman to go to medical school in California, a lady from Iran who wanted a beauty shop got cash also for the building as well as the business from this $540,000,000 given out by our own federal government, and last but not least a new van for a couple from Mexico in cash also. Who had ever heard of such socialism in the history of America?

Even the Social Security Administration, meaning a bureaucracy was giving away our tax dollars to illegals so that they got Social Security checks because they too were politically correct or in other words they did not speak English, read or write it either. Even Judeo-Christians and the ones here in America who wanted to get what they needed would have to go along with this present day corruption that was destroying America and it's world businessmen organization of the UN which also had no sovereignty, but was usurping our sovereignty day by day and these 2 candidates did absolutely nothing to stop it nor did they talk about it at all.

If one did not have a socialist government job such as a mail carrier, or a professor or in local, county, state, school district or federal government then they were pretty much out of luck as far as benefits and wages. Many young couples had to drop their insurances because they could not pay for them no matter what and if they or their children got sick then heaven help them and more on the poverty rolls would occur and this meant that the socialist parties in government loved this even more so big brother could implement who would get and who would not and the parties became in essence the Party the one that stood for everything that was truly anti-American and ones with no conscience and ones with no GOD could care less since to them if one stole it, took it from others or whatever way they could get it was all that mattered and that kind of was the way that the rich and well educated made their millions and billions of dollars, illegally and immorally!

Even our food was being imported to America and flowers and things mostly from Red China, and who could undersell real Christian slave labor in China where no wages were paid at all?

In America where a peso would buy the pot and two pesos well at least for the rich to do' or at least they thought so. Should not the Hispanics set the lifestyle and the income from their so very rich culture that coupes and revolutions were sprouting time and again! This is really what America needed what Lenin had hoped for in Switzerland this diversity this speaking in foreign tongues and this multiculturalism that would work like cancer to eat out the very body of America and its religious code. The American could no longer exist; he had to go along with socialism from the top or else his children would go hungry and also would become sick and die, because soon the non profit hospitals would say no more free patients without payment and now that government was the biggest customer the hospitals would have to cooperate after all they were getting funds from the government at the taxpayers' expense and again they were non-profit!

The more one worked the worse it got because the government said and told us it had to take care of all, but to them all meant the lazy, the arrogant, the illegal, the corrupt, the liars, etc. If one did not believe the lie and did not promote the lie than for sure they could look to nothing in the near future besides grief and misery for the rest of their lives. That is why America was set up in the first place, right? To take care of all the people in other lands that were not even wanted there because of their criminal activities there and so with that in mind they would be drawn by another illegal government here which said 'come even if you break our law since your laws are like our laws, all legal!' This is how far and farther all this would go to get to what they call equality which was nothing more then the redistribution of wealth and not just wages and the unions were taking money out for dues and giving it to the socialist parties, but still the payees or the ones who "contributed" their dues were for some strange reason not voting for or with the unions! Corruption or those involved with were in all professions and since it paid rather good why not continue this play of socialism, and if one could not beat them then they could surely join them! This collaboration sounded more and more like all the other isms and lions that I had heard about so many times. Just let us show you how it works, no matter the fact that it never had worked ever in the history of man, but there was always this first time, right? This was what this utopia was all about! Trust us to take good care of you and yours and all would go well well at least for now anyways. And families well who now believed in that archaic institution when government by group mentality would always be better since you too could collect" free "health care and live any kind of life that you so chose without any accountability to anyone unless you told the truth and then you would lose it all. So it was the lie that they wanted to promote time and again so that they that is the rich and well educated and the derelicts in society could say now you too are a very part of this so have no complaining to do as it is! This would be the ultimatum that was being heard everywhere. Well everybody else is doing it so why not I? But with over 300,000,000 people in America how could all the people get health care? Well of course some would have to be ignored and would have to die and of course government would determine that since nobody ever asked what the catch to all of this anyways?

No there would be shortages of money and more importantly shortages of people of all ages and if the criteria was for you to be gone than so be it. This is what we had signed on, for better or for worse, and the worse was yet to come. Health insurance like they liked to call it was really socialism's way of saying okay this is the way it shall be from now on. We will get you your job and we will tell you where to live since land was scarce, owned by foreigners and government. There was not enough of it to go around and anyways not all the land had good water and good soil, so that meant the rich and well educated and foreigners and government would own all that there would be to own but others could borrow the land and build on it as through a government lease. Yes, the derelicts of society natural or foreign born would surely be catered to because the lie was what they had believed in. The lie would be the thing that would make them a great success in this country as well as the world and this was the real passport to America to break the GODLY moral code of do not lie and promote the lie and believe in the lie, but then again government too had lied time and again that is it's lawyers who all they knew was how to lie and were so good at it that meant it had to be beneficial to all concerned that is with not the truth but with the spoken and written lie again and again until others would be eliminated, For how could America provide medical coverage for all even under socialism even if the doctors were being taught about death and dying and not about saving lives at all and did not have to take the Hippocratic Oath at all? Yes diversity was a great panacea for the not too bright socialists and racists who had gotten their jobs not through qualifications, but through connivery and deceit and more lies just so that it fed their own ego and had nothing to do whatsoever with brains just like Lenin had said, "Get rid of all the brains in society."

Well we not only did that but we went one step even further and that was to make it look like they had brains because they had this so called higher education which was nothing more than more and more socialism. Socialism meant put nobody who did not think like you in any position where they could do damage to the government's utopia of lies! Who would believe government? Well some already knew and still kind of believed and so were in it for themselves and not anything in the past and this was indeed hard to pass up anyways. It was always easier to lie because it was our very own human nature to do that, but to tell the truth well that was totally a different thing.

Yes, government jobs had one criteria and that was how well you could lie at all times. Society would take care of the rest and the ones who believed otherwise that is the truth well they could wait till hell froze over! There was no room for the truth to be told and so that left just what Lenin wanted people with no brains or creative ideas of their very own. They needed robots that is why computers were so important because the person behind the computer would be able to follow their directions very well without any remorse!

As each day in America went by, most all were oblivious to what was going on in their own nation as well as in the rest of the world and they continued on as if nothing cataclysmic seemed almost certain to occur. People kept taking expensive trips to Europe, the Caribbean, and elsewhere in the world, except to the State of Israel where people might have thought GOD was punishing the Jewish people. Anti-Semitism, or hatred for the Jewish people as a nation, was worldwide but especially from Hispanic America, Europe, America and many other western nations. Even though some nations were in the Western hemisphere, such as Mexico, which was a thorn in America's side. They were anything but successful as far as how a real true nation should be run. So, as in all of Hispanic America, the countries' businesses, especially the oil ones, were owned by the state, which meant more world socialism and the big businesses were growing like cancerous tumors on the backs of the poor all over the world and were now having to sell out or so it appeared to the socialists all over the world just so they could keep their wealth and power and money in the world.

America had fewer and fewer resources here to barter with, so what we sold was our nation's very own soul to the highest and sometimes the lowest bidder because it was again supplying not the peoples in foreign countries, but their so called governments with more powerful forms of socialism. We had become the leader in the world in materialism and so all we had left was paper money, technology, and services to offer. When the technology would take over us, then the money and the services would be nothing with which to barter our freedom and liberty away, even though freedom was not the most important thing to any nation. We continued on along since at least the 60s with corruption and pollution, not of the environmental kind but of the moral kind that had dissipated us to a Fourth World level of nothingness, and we soon would know it if we did not by now know!

America had become an amusement park of fun, play, leisure and no consideration was ever given to what we would do when the end would come, and it would come to what we had once known America to be, a moral and upright nation with decency and morality, with not the kind of freedom the Hispanic America or even the African nations thought was freedom. We did have a few left here in our nation who loved their nation and were few in numbers for even the churches were dead in the spirit because they too traded in the truth for materialism.

Eating was another thing, or should I say gluttony, which was showing even on children just how obese they too were becoming, but had malnutrition, which meant what they ate had no healthy content to it. So America, too, was dying a physical death in regards to individual health and most women did not even know how to cook a plain simple meal and television dinners and other fast foods were all also carcinogenic chemicals that were inducing cancer into millions of millions of Americans and of course eventually death at an early age and if one looked at the obituary column daily one could see the deaths of the baby boomers or the 60's generation daily off even before their own parents which made for a confusing type of scenario in America since now their children were being raised by the grand parents and not the parents.

America was such a depressing sight to behold in regards to many things such as young people who hang in gangs and girls with the foulest of mouths let alone their boyfriends' mouths. The English language was dying more and more and the slang of many other languages that were blending into American English was taking over. The education system had very few qualified teachers because they were leaving the field because, of course, money was calling them to higher fields as had occurred with nursing. The medical health field also took a beating on good health care professionals or nurses as well as qualified doctors who were mostly foreign born and of a foreign religion and not doctors one could put their life on!

People only so for today and the money that they could accrue in theory such as stocks, bonds, etc. as well as playhouses built out of inferior products and the toys they bought for themselves and the many people who were not use at all to having money were ruining themselves as well as the rest of society and one could see wherever one went. Environmental pollution was bad, but moral pollution was much worse and since we had gotten use to heathenism in our very own nation we did not know the real difference between good vs, evil nor did we even care!

Our products, if we produce any, all had warranties which told one that the products were inferior or why have a warranty? The old neighborhoods had new neighbors not the kind though that one would want to live around for any period of time since they were almost from another planet. America had given up not its freedom, for that was only physical, but more importantly its memory of its very own history as a nation, which meant we had no future since we could not reference where we had come from, not that we would go back to that but would and could only go forward but as to what now nobody could really know.

Hollywood was making films that followed all the plots of Dostoyevsky's novels, but used it for evil while when he wrote them he was showing just what was really occurring in Russia in the 19th century. Movies first would glorify women superior to men; second the endings of most of them made evil win over good; third, if lawyers were bad, well according to Hollywood, doctors were 10 times as bad. So another lie was being promoted plus the fact that lawyers were almost always looked at with glorious type professionals when in reality they were promoting the lies. Fourth, some movies made marriage bad and shacking up looked honorable and the thing to do since everybody else was doing it, which of course was another lie from Jack Valenti himself, the Sicilian pimp with a Southern accent who worked closely with the Great Society President which told anybody with enough common sense just what he stood for!

Law enforcement officials were looked down upon while the lily white courts were paragons of vice though disguised as "virtues" at least for the Communists and Nazis in the heart of Holly wood and still these 2 candidates were more worried about Islam then their very own American people and that was because they both were afraid to face the enemy head on and they both had lived easy lives so they could never relate really to the average American and not in New York City or San Francisco or in our think tanks of socialism.

They placed everything on education, but never said just what kind of education they were talking about, just that it would get more money to waste on socialistic ideas. The ones who were not too bright would approve of that, but the ones who wanted classic music and classic studies, there were still some left because they could never comprehend what it was to write real music or real literature nor would they be able to even begin to understand what it was saying. This was the promotion of the simpletons of success who knew nothing about anything except force, ego, avarice, corruption, etc.

No one could get to this top if they were poor and moral or middle class and moral!

When the promoted advertisement of "paper" money and the theory that it was all that it said it was was eventually removed, then America and its citizens would see what they had been duped into. What could paper buy if the paper they were using was only confederate paper and the new world system was bartering with hard assets and not soft assets such as stocks and bonds and securities? At anytime one could hold out or flood the market because that is how much the world had grown smaller which told certain people just how much they controlled in the entire world and who would be able to buy what, when, where, how and for how much! if one did not have the right chip implanted then they would be out of luck and all would be for naught. That is why real estate and water, soil, air, minerals, etc. were so very valuable to governments now in existence. If one could not grow their own food or even get food and water, what would they do to survive or even be able to live? It could possibly go from an obese society to one of starvation unless of course you had the right chip and spoke the New Age lingo that meant you had sold your very soul to the devil for a piece of bread and for others for 30 pieces of silver!

With many people I once knew who now were dead and with no more new friends for friends (real friends were so very hard to find), I began to feel this isolation of being possibly one of the few who might have to choose between here and Israel in the very near future. That was not because I did not love my country, but because the chip invariably was just about being used for all things here and I wanted no part of that whatsoever. In Israel at least I thought my wife and I would have a better chance to still spread the Gospel since she was Jewish and over there they were in desperate need of heads to help their people there where children were going hungry and the Jewish population on earth for all Jewry was getting smaller and smaller, which meant for sure that the 70th Week of Daniel was soon imminent. America had become so surreal that I no longer recognized it at all!

Everything had changed so very much in America that anything that upheld human life was opposed to, and since it was a democracy the people themselves had been corrupted for the most part and did not want to change in the least bit. This was truly the scary part now in America when the average person had become like its corrupt leaders and would not even listen to common sense reasoning. Nothing appeared normal in America no matter what one looked at.

Why had Parvus, the German Jew, helped Lenin while in Switzerland to obtain financial help from none other than Germany and the National Socialist Democratic Party before World War I? And who said Germany ever was fascists and only in the sense that they had this subculture of homosexual brotherhood except for Hindenburg and Ludendorff? Parvus would supply the money from German finances and explained that to Lenin, but Lenin nonetheless never trusted him or, for that matter, anybody but himself to lead in this revolution. Germany had to win this war but not make a peace with the Russian monarch no matter what if this revolution and then civil war in Russia was going to be pulled off in such a crummy country as Russia!

While Trotsky and Parvus, both socialist Jews, were only talking about socialism, Lenin wanted in Russia to see acid thrown from the roofs of buildings, the proletariat to keep their weapons and agitators even from Siberia to come to Petersburg and Moscow to create havoc and also, to infiltrate the banks and the offices of government as if the monarch was the greatest of monsters while really Lenin was back in Switzerland hoping for the best. Parvus was guaranteeing to Lenin from Germany first 1 million then 5 million and was saying that he needed money to take power for without it one could and would not. So to side with Germany would be the wise thing to do since Germany the socialist state would be the one always or for now to support!

Parvus had already introduced the 8 hour day and the strike against the management and the unions could be thrown away like the rest of the other idiotic socialists who were too many to go as far as Lenin himself wanted to go, and that was all the way. One couldn't really trust in Parvus with his obese-like liberal Jew body that had a hard time getting up even from a chair. There had to be torchings in Russia, Molotov cocktails, shooting of police officers, shooting at random also of military men, and to incite the masses against the monarch always. Yes, Germany had to win this war if the revolution and the civil war was to amount to anything at all in Russia.

Lenin had not gotten involved that much in 1905, but now it would appear through Parvus' monetary resources from Western countries and borders could be overthrown and that national borders could be dissected. Parvus even was tying to persuade the Turks to go with Germany against Russia. While in Germany not only was socialism growing and strong but also homosexuality with the Kaiser Wilhelm.

The Germans as usual could not be trusted for anything when it came to honor, but just to their own form of socialism, even the anti-Russian nation since Germany and Russia were both Christian nations, but Germany wanted to ally themselves with the Turks in order to prevent a defeat against the monarch. They had approached the Romanov monarch, but it was no and so Germany had to find a way out of the impasse that threatened their own socialism in their government and Parvus and Lenin would eventually take that road not that Lenin ever trusted Parvus at all since he was a German Jew and Lenin hated the Jews, but if it would help the cause then he was all for it as long as he had thought of it and was the leader in control and not Parvus, because Parvus was too much of a bourgeoisie and Lenin hated even the word that did not spell socialism in word and to take and grab anyone at anytime just so that terror was always present!

Nadya, his wife, he could share some of this with since she always thought like him and supported him in whatever endeavor he got involved into and now that his mother was dead he had no one to rely on for financial support any longer. Parvus never aligned himself with the Bolsheviks or Mensheviks but was where the money always was and the media was to spread the right kind of propaganda all over the world for the fight for socialism but from behind the scenes well at least most of the time and Lenin well Lenin had never really spoken in public to more than 1,000 people. Switzerland was where it would most likely happen, but Parvus felt otherwise but could Lenin trust him yet Lenin knew that without money he was doomed and so he had to reconsider the issue of money in the millions to start a revolution and a civil war in Russia and bring democracy to the fore in Russia which the media was already saying in the socialists circles, Down with the monarch now with no time to waste any longer!

Lenin himself was getting bilious and could hardly walk, and Parvus with his elephant body was leaning more and more on Lenin, not just physically but mentally. So Parvus was someone that Lenin had to fear and only Parvus, but none of the others at all ever. Parvus could not be aligned really with anyone else, and since he came in person, which he should not have, he had broken protocol with the secret letters that were to be sent! Who had seen him come?

Why Angela Davis the lie and still in 2004 you expound on C-SPAN your lying on the Communist ideology and your part in the murder of a Los Angeles judge? Thanks, Brian Lamb for being able only to find such an author to fill your air time and, by the way, was there really nobody else that you could possibly find?

After all this and she had become old, she still hung to this deadening ideology. I wonder if she too wants to be buried in England like Karl Marx. The continuance of the lie on and on which shall continue now even more than ever before more and more violence.

When one begins to debate a liberal Jew such as Ira Glasser or a John Kerry (they are austere and have no conscience who would not even blink or think twice to tell a lie) and also to speak within such a dialogue and be attacked publicly, one can only do harm to oneself very much since the questions have been prepared by another socialist who also believes in the lie and expounds on it also. Also if one is brought up with non-confrontation then one usually cannot fair well since they have lived a sheltered life and come from a matriarchal home and the incumbent in this case shall be at a loss for words and continue to repeat themselves over and over even though the socialist is talking in circles and at the same time lying and lying over and over again. It is never good to try to express one's opinions or beliefs if one is sincere and the other is lying for it means nothing to the one who is lying so hence he shall not be concerned and feels he has absolutely nothing to lose in the process. What also comes into play is the fact that it is being done in person in front of an audience and not on a tape or newsreel. There shall be no remorse from a compulsive liar.

In our society today where the President is seen everyday which was not always the case this in itself diminishes the affect of the incumbent since people who have become ignorant and do not understand the workings of socialism and hence shall always tend to blame the one highest up on the totem poll for all that goes wrong in a nation when in fact it is the courts and trial lawyers, or politicians that have created these catastrophic failings!

The least one sees of a high official in a democratic republic the better it is in such a large nation as America in geography. The media also is so very intrusive that no one any longer has a private life, and the one in the public eye tends to believe the lie. The more the public sees him the more sympathetic they shall be is just not so. This delusion is also part of socialism that shall reveal what they intend to do even though as before they shall still be doubting about what it is they believe shall so be in the future plan of things!

The commercialization or the working of big business with government makes for very strange bedfellows, but so much pleases the socialists behind the scenes as well as in the front such as the UN which is just that, a world businessmen's organization but with no real power, only the power that the governments give to it as is such the case also with the IRS in America, which would also have no power would it not be for the U.S. Congress and the fact also that you are guilty until proven innocent!

Non—profit in America came to mean profit with no taxes to be paid whatsoever and to be funded by the taxpayers in such a way as if the unions themselves had made them pay their dues individually. Even little league has leagues that do not pay a sales tax since they had never filed with the state and the ones that did they would be on the list forever yet the ones who did not would never be!

Does capitalism itself attach to socialism, or does socialism attach itself to capitalism? Which one is the parasite that lives off of the other and continues as such to head for the destruction of mankind? Yet in essence does not freewill play a most important part in an economic system as opposed to an ideology which is a whole new way of life and encompasses in its totality of evil with atheism and lies yet capitalism also tends to make one believe that there are no limits to what can be done and still remain free and without restriction which in part adds to the lies and also feeds the stomach of the dragon even more so since the West knows very little what it is like to live under totalitarianism.

Referring again to this commercialization through government it does remind one of when Parvus the liberal German Jew who had helped Lenin through the millions that he gave to him through the German government through an import and export business and made Russia at that time buy more then it ever sold and in essence today in America we too are selling so very much and as much as what we get in return from slave labor in Red China, but more importantly the fact that we are doing what Parvus had done for Lenin except the names have changed to Kissinger and Haig!

Finally I thought about a preacher on television by the name of Dr. Ed Young that expounded very intelligently why infanticide is always murder and even provided a screen on which one could watch what happens doing an ultrasound to a baby that is only 9-10 weeks old. One could see the head, the hands, the body of an innocent human being wanting to live. It was conclusive and unequivocally a child and followed according to Scripture why GOD knew us before we were formed in our mother's womb. No other famous minister by any name had ever done this to my knowledge as far as I know and so it was a breath of fresh air to see the truth on television and know that when one expounds the Gospel that one must also reveal the evil in one's own society in order for the people to understand the real difference between good vs. evil and not just in a dialogue.

For the human being involved it is a matter of life and death and also shows how we ourselves had come into the world the very same way that this child was coming into the very same world. Often we hear the term that one is pro-life, which is a misnomer in the sense it does not fully comprehend what GOD has done in the formation or creation of each individual human being while in the womb and the fact that only when the sperm penetrates the egg is that conception and not before, no matter what one may believe, but also the fact that, as I said before and by Scripture, that GOD knew of us before we were in the womb of our mother and before the very foundation of this world known as the earth. This is the incredible wonder of a loving and wholesome GOD and the power which we are confronting when we refuse to believe the truth about the human experience, that we enter into this world with no real assistance from man except the fact that a husband and a wife procreate and repeat with GOD'S infinite love another person in the image of GOD and also extends in us a sort of immortality that goes on to another generation, one after the other. This is why the Bible says "Be fruitful and multiply."

The term pro-life, as I was about to say, is not strong enough to describe what it is we are talking about and it should be said that we are pro-humanity, or pro-humane to all human life and also in regards to the animal world, which we are not a part of but which we must take care of. Animals cannot reason and never shall be able to, and that we should all make a concerted effort to be kind to animals in the proper perspective, meaning that human life always prevails above the animal world since we were made in the image of GOD Himself, Jesus Christ!

Now that the Austrian Jew socialist, John Kerry, was a candidate in the National Socialist Democratic Party, the blacks (yes, the blacks and not Negroes) in America were supporting him and everyone knew that relations with the American Jews and the blacks was to be desired and yet why would the blacks in Philadelphia vote for Mr. Kohn knowing that he was Jewish and they were anti-Jew? This again went to show just how much this tribal mentality of the American black was steeped in ideology of the socialistic type that would eventually too be brought upon their own heads as would also the American Jew. The American Jew had to differentiate and separate and that they were appearing to do in this election since they knew they could not put all their marbles in one bag, and so like in Israel needed what appeared to be an opposition party to contend with. It was like I had said once before about a Jewish trial that had a young man on trial for murder and his sister sat across the courtroom yelling obscenities and calling him "a murderer". Finally when the long trial was over and the jury came out of deliberation they rendered a unanimous decision and found the defendant not guilty, the sister then ran across the courtroom and hugged her brother to death! This was the strategy that was being played out I felt with the Jewish community here and in Israel that kept at bay the Gentile powers from totally devouring the Jew from the face of the earth!

The blacks again would vote for race but this time it was race and ideology for all knew what John Kerry had done in Vietnam during that conflict with Jane Fonda while in Paris when they both denounced our own soldiers who were putting their life on the line for what they believed in while John Kerry only pretended to be a real veteran when in essence he went on to commit treason and got 3 purple hearts which would qualify him to leave Vietnam and go home so he could campaign for the Communist here and in Paris as a true blue red, or better red than dead Marxist/Leninist. He too was born of the rich and well educated and who spoke French fluently and was not Irish, but whose father was an Austrian Jew and whose mother was English and French. He also was hated by the other officers he served with in Vietnam except the ones that spent 2-6 days with him only and did not really know him, but as for all the other officers they hated him to say the least. He continually tried for a purple heart when one time the commander threw him literally out of his office and the self-inflicted wound by a hand grenade he planted to injure his gluteus maximus.

Yes, another liberal Jew was running for President and even worse than what Bill Clinton would be since Teresa Heinz would not be like Hillary who ran the show. He knew exactly what he wanted to do and that was put the final nail in the coffin for America and with his win that is just what would happen and Israel would indeed be affected by this most severely. No, not all American Jews were for him as I said before and they knew that with the word Jew for President that more hatred for the Jew in general would grow and grow and with the blacks also would they be categorized and since the incumbent was more for the Hispanic than the black in America the poster boy image for the American black was being removed by the Hispanics in America and this bothered the African-American since they now were in second place to government's socialistic handout program that really started with LBJ and his Great Society and JFK who also was a

Catholic but was raised also with a great deal of anti-Semitism because Joseph Kennedy was pro-Nazi! So again another so called Catholic but with Jewish roots would be running but with the mind of a Karl Marx or Parvus who helped Lenin as I also said before and the African-Americans would be voting more than any other group for him, but yet they made up only 12% of the entire population in America! This was not a real decisive vote but the media played on it for the lie that they wanted others maybe to believe that Kerry would win so why go out and vote plus the fact that the other parties would take votes away not from Kerry but from the incumbent and that the incumbent should not be voted for by attending the voting polls which meant that less would vote for the incumbent and change the percentages because percentages in numbers was a big factor and not in the polls that most people believed were the gospel truth! The slave issue would not go away until America went away.

Mount St. Helen was again acting up and no wonder, we had defied a living GOD and His Word as to murder in the first degree by whatever means it took just so that socialism and its lies could spread like cancer on the main body of America. And guess what, the American people (not the smartest now since they were melted down by other cultures and did not even know their own true history here in America) were more and more becoming a most dumb race of people no matter how one looked at it. The fact that the majority in voting was never in search of the truth nor knew the truth in voting, so it became a popularity contest like the Miss America pageant with judges.

What the Jew had done to Russia to help destroy that nation they were now attempting to do now in America with the ACLU and the National Democratic Socialist Party and their finances would help try to do America in especially from Hollywood as Parvus, Trotsky and Marx all had contributed whether before, during or after the revolution and then civil war. One must remember the revolution would overthrow the monarch and the civil war would take control and make sure that the peasants would fight against the monarch as well as the gentry and other middle and upper classes. The same had happened in America with a civil war, but now a revolution with a civil war was being initiated by the Jews of the left who wanted to destroy America for what it had done to the Jew! They wanted to destroy as quickly as possible since they could not do as they wanted to do, such as make every political issue be based upon the Jew the one who would seek to destroy the country that they were born in and could even care much less for Israel since it represented something so reprehensible that they wanted it to be destroyed so they could live without being in the limelight and would no longer be called the chosen people. But where could they hide but behind socialism and its instant spark for revenge. This was part of the Jew that was anti-GOD meaning Old Testament too since they felt that they too had every reason to make the final decision about America and how it would end up as they had in Russia where there had been pogroms and the Pale of Settlement! In America, though, what was to be compared to that, one could only speculate. They wanted to have their cake and eat it too! The blacks and the Germans would always follow the leader and not a ruler because they never really understood or ever had a real king as a monarch that they could relate to. It had been chieftains for one and Kaisers for the other and both had this cold austere feeling for their fellow man when it was them who always complained about the others who they said were heartless and uncaring. It was reverse psychology that they used time and again.

Whether it was good vs. evil or right vs. wrong it did not matter just so the end would always justify the means, or was it vice versa? This was how they now thought and were getting worse and worse as each election came along until even the ones they hated they voted along with since socialism was the very thing that had bonded them close together as well as the thrill for it to the end. One could let bygones bygones and that would be all right since the same mind set meant . . .

Celeste Zappala on C-SPAN, a grieving mother but perhaps more than just that, was making an appeal to stop the Iraqi war but seemed to be including the Moslems there also who were like the

Vietcong in Vietnam. In fact Vietnam was being included in the war and that meant that if one opposed it, it was for a good reason! Every mother loves her son, but to include anti-American hysteria was wrong. It was like a Michael Moore who was anti-American for the Communist left in Hollywood, Could one oppose the war and be patriotic? Yes, as long as they differentiated military honor from political ideology and the Islamic religion would have to be looked at in its totality. One size does not fit all. Much though was group socialism and most Americans in general were new to how it worked but were learning too slow that a Communist might just be put into the White House in anyway they could! Anything or anyone not for socialism meant one had to be wrong and had to be out shouted!

Incite the American mass into hysteria but Kerry or Kohn would have a better idea, right? I opposed the war because first in the Sudan where Christians were we never intervened there until it was almost too late but when Islamic oil was there our commercialization of government was with outstretched arms. To blame the incumbent alone was wrong since he had made a commitment and a quagmire had formed unintentionally by him. Soldiers' blood and lives had been shed and to come home might now prove fatal against socialistic Islam. Yet maybe by the troops being over there and not here there would be no disturbance yet! Hostility amongst them would grow! Would they as soldiers understand it all or would we understand it all back in the states? The ruination of the military by socialists in America was intentional such as Michael Moore, Bill O'Reilly, Dan Rather, Walter Cronkite, Ed Asner, Jesse Jackson, Jesse Jackson, Jr., Angela Davis, Ron Dellums, Congressman Fattah, John Kerry, John Edwards, Senator Edward Kennedy, etc. Theirs had no reason but just to destroy America. The lack of moral fiber in America was creating a stagnation and paralysis amongst the Congressmen and we were headed for disaster with the wall about to fall upon all of us.

They were not so much against Bush, but his Christianity that they opposed and until he "repented" and saw their light no matter if the troops came home or not he would not fair any better nor would America. One had to join the Party. This was the revitalized 60's radicals trying one more time for them to destroy America as we know of it as a free nation and once again as Lenin had noted about the blacks, the Jews and others would be involved and had to be involved. It had nothing to do with oil for them as some of us thought and were right to think that, but for them it was their love of socialism plain and simple and simple minded they surely were.

Since the soldiers enlisted and swore to uphold the sovereignty of America then they were obligated to do their duty as told by the Commander In Chief and not as rebels would do which was what the socialists wanted here and elsewhere. This was a freewill choice decision not that this needed to be said, but nonetheless I have. My personal opinion was mine and was not important enough to discuss just to say that I was not trying to coerce, or intimidate anyone who disagreed with me. Many senators and other politicians should have been impeached and journalists and Hollywooders be brought to justice for treason and this had nothing whatsoever to do with free speech.

To degrade and condemn not only the Commander In Chief but our own soldiers was nothing less than treason punishable by the U.S. Constitution and should have been prosecuted to the fullest extent of the law?

Now in regards to the Messianic Jew who was poor and devout, one had to realize that here lay the real Jewish person who was devout to GOD and not to Islam's kind of god or Judaism's god. There had to be a remission for man's sin without watering down the Gospel and the gift of grace from GOD the Father provided for by His only Son Messiah Y'eshua. This could not be any kind of "ism" or "tion" of any form but a GOD in the flesh whose work at Calvary paid it all. As far as Catholicism was concerned and John Kerry, it was like adding an additional avarice to an already secular Jew who was already a materialist Pharisee except he did not even acknowledge the fact that there was even a holy and just GOD or GOD head. "UNFIT TO COMMAND" was an excellent book to read about two individuals who were never

ever fit to command past or in the future. The Germans and the English again were up to their old tricks as well as the not so real Jews even though they thought so in this world. One was not a Jew unless by birth and most importantly if they had come to know personally their Messiah! There was no other way it could be done. GOD'S way or not at all!

Feminism or the Sodomite Nazis were one group and then there was the Communist party, then the socialists not yet graduated higher, then the civil rights' socialists was anything but civil, then the black racism and of course the Pharisaical Jew. These were the main rebel rousers of our day and all had no moral absolutes at all and were intent in taking America to Hell with them, but there was one flaw, all would not go along quietly!

This devisiveness was their everything in life and of which they would live for and only the Communists would die for revolution and real civil war and nothing else! Remember as the peasants in Russia understood little or nothing about legal tender or democracy at all so it was with most Americans. They understood little or nothing about racial socialism, class socialism and the more virulent of all Communism which they like to call "social" justice along with the New Age Nazis. One had to almost go through it to understand what it meant and now it would be voted on in this very Presidential election! Was this hyperbole? No, just the plain truth because no form of socialism is humane and the further along it goes, the more it meets its goal (this is communism). That is why America could have defeated Hitler easily because his phase was not where Lenin and Stalin had taken it, and that was to the inhumanity ideology of full blown unadulterated Communism which was not of any kind of authority but just plain insanity, and was run by thugs just as the Mafia was run but on a much longer scale and larger scale that one could compare as one would compare our own moon with the sun, and that included the 6 million Jews and 7 million Gentiles were a fraction of who were murdered by Lenin and Stalin and the others to follow in Russia or Moscow and in Red China, Cambodia, Vietnam, North Korea, etc.

The young did not want to work because they had learned what was good for the goose was good for the gander and in this case it was reversed since dead beat dads could procreate like the animal world and receive government compensation for all their efforts! It was not hard for them to understand that one cannot legislate date morality (another lie) but one could orchestrate immorality as such to meet their want or desire to do anything to anyone at anytime with no accountability to anyone! The 60's generation had taught their children coercion, drugs, promiscuity, intimidation, threats but to the other guy always and fast, and to be first and the fist to the face if need be and that is who taught the art of pugilism to the inner city peoples so that violence and not peace would prevail and intimidate others such as the elderly, the crippled, the very young, etc.

The male was the stronger sex, but with most American blacks they had become the "weaker" sex. Bill Cosby had expounded on that enough and so should have many whites in society who were in the public eye and really cared if they cared at all! All talk and no action. Can one be forgiven for committing treason if they repented and had a change of heart and showed it in their actions everyday? But of course along with free will one other thing is needed and that is to be meted out by the justice system, which would include incarceration and even capital punishment since felony, according to the U.S. Constitution, was "for high crimes and misdemeanors."

So in essence the criminal must serve time, but justice alone could not be served if it was never executed but if it was then they would have been most likely to have been found guilty and not only tried but also sentenced to serve the just punishment and not like Bill Clinton who got away with murder and treason even while serving in the White House! Only in this way would their repentance be sincere and not just on hearsay, since treason is a very serious crime that speaks to the very soul and heart of a nation which is in part its sovereignty of which we all are a part. No, just saying one is sorry in this case is not enough. It must be shown with action from the courts or judicial system and such as under the real rule of law which is founded in Scripture. Lying is worse than stealing because materialism could be replaced but a lie cannot be removed so easily and continues on almost forever so how does one make restitution when only the truth itself can do that and that is by it's own justice. Yes, that particular person or persons must be prosecuted to the fullest extent of the law. This puts undoubtedly on our very nation's soul a black mark which our nation also has a personality as opposed to an inhumane ideology! Millions upon millions have already died because of this lie which has destroyed and murdered life and soul in most cases. The truth was kept from them and hence an unspeakable crime had occurred while the criminals continue on especially in the West with so—called "honor" an almost "honor amongst liars" if you will. Even today more than ever before this lie is promoted time and again but the rule of law is ignored by our government and there is the public opinion and even if there was an end it would be the same decision as being exonerated by the majority rule. This is indeed a hard statement to make since we here in America live in the midst of all the ones who lie and continue to do so and reap the benefits from the blood that they help shed from innocent lives even though to some it would appear from a distance that their lives were somewhat sinful. Remember though we must take the log that is in our own eye for the splinter that was in theirs. Yes, we are going to be held accountable more than Russia and probably Israel too, for what we as a nation failed to do to help save these souls from the lies we either perpetuated or allowed to be even up until this very day and till the last day of our spiritual nation. We see these criminals or the ones in charge still walking our very streets and our own government (we) have said, "It is all right!" But is it all right and is it right that it was not you or me but them over there that could only accept their apology since it was done to then and not us and since we too are a Christian nation like Russia was? Does Christianity's forgiveness end after just one generation or is it not the entire history of a nation involved also up to our necks in this? We are, to repeat, a "collective" personality where all nations shall be judged by GOD! Our physical judgment may indicate at first the end is over or we have been judged, but GOD judges all the nations at one time outside of history and in His own "time" and then and only then shall we too be truly judged. Let us not take it too lightly especially us Christians that the end is ever over until GOD'S final summation if you will is made by Him and Him alone! If we believe our own lies then we too have spread the lie, not always with malice but nonetheless we have lied by not doing what were are supposed to do or not to do when faced with the lie.

The lie corrupts the individual, and being that our human nature appears as such to this we condone the lie not all the time but many times when we again refuse to hear and believe what the Truth has to say to us! How can one ignore what a whole ideology is based on, the lie!

Did GOD lie to Adam? Forget what Satan having rephrased the question to Adam and Eve. No! The Truth vs. the lie which has since that time and before that with Lucifer himself the lie had come to be formed by the enemy himself. "From the beginning" so he did have a beginning and was created no not to lie and had not always been around, "but was a liar from the beginning". So there was no truth in him even though he had free will and was an angelic being who cannot procreate and has no gender, but who also can and did lie. Through the unforbidden fruit came the lie in the sense first that GOD (Truth) said not to lie (eat that forbidden fruit) and Adam who was not deceived so, but blamed Eve and Eve who was deceived did usurp Adam's role or man's role. Two wrongs cannot make one right and the lie cannot be made into the truth since one is not eternal in the sense it was not always here in the universe but yes the other always has been forever and ever and that is Truth!

Is GOD that distant that we fail to see or know He is right here with us for ones who have individually accepted His Son Messiah into their hearts by free will and by GOD first calling them unto Himself?

This government is tempting the inexperienced in life to come on board with universal socialistic health care in one day which now shall look like a panacea, and if it looks too good to be true . . . But in due time shall be so grotesque that one could ever wonder how on earth one could have ever approved or voted for this candidate for this communist shall use the bully pulpit as a dictator! Do not believe that it shall ever come to a vote for it shall not! This Hillary and Bill Clinton escapade of HMO's was just a foreplay of what is really next to come and that is why she did not want to run for President at this time because she was told not to! Just as social security looked like a panacea to our parents' generation, so does this next socialistic move that shall be so much more extreme than FDR could ever have imagined since he too was sheltered all of his life as a blueblood! Yet he was elected to 4 terms because he gave the majority what they wanted, more socialism! He also did nothing to oppose Communism and in fact helped Old Joe promote Communism worldwide until this very day and planted the seed of it rig ht here in America, the same that Woodrow Wilson had done wit h the New Age mentality!

Does anyone really think that these socialists are for a free state of Israel? This is as far as the East is from the West. Americans bought it because it appealed to the flesh and meant an income for life no matter how short that might be and usually with retirement it was short. Also, there was a morbid fear: what would one do without social security? The question should be, what would one have done without this tax and other usurious taxes such as the income tax of 1913 which took most of the people's earnings and would have allowed them to save their own money and not have the redistribution of wealth. It would have kept government at bay and would not have been as centralized as it is today and so extensive into areas of one's private life that the law abiding citizen would be confined to the immorality of not just government and the form it was, but to the state which is ever so powerful in the hands of a few derelicts as we have in the National Democratic Socialist Party!

Create this constant phobia of apathy and fear mongering by socialists who thrive on other's misery, This is their idea of freedom and liberty for all! A lie cannot be repeated twice if one has the truth on their side. This Democratic Party would go so far, I believe, that they would not even tell if they knew where Osama Bin Laden was hidden!

The "peasants "in America from ancestry that did not come of their own free will shall experience just exactly what happened to the peasants in Russia after the revolution and a people shall be led like sheep to the slaughter never again to be seen!

Already their arrogance before this election means they shall try to do anything short of starting a war and even that is possibly here for this is their last hurrah for the 60's radicals before they die!

They attack just as all communists do, and one must respond not with fear of loss of materialism but with a strong character for good shall always prevail over evil if the people have the will to do what it is that they must do and that is not believe the lie and be any part of the lie no matter how enticing it might appear and no matter what mundane things you maybe promised for in the end not only them, but all of us also shall almost for certain be swallowed by the leviathan that has been devouring millions upon millions of people in the East and in the West which includes Russia and the other republics that the Soviets and not the Russians for Communism is an ideology and not a race of people who are made up of many nationalities.

We now must be ever vigilant and speak out against the evil that these evil men would now perpetrate on us as they had in the Soviet Union and now are doing in Red China and not just

China as so many of our own products have stamped on them to make it look like capitalism is hard at work to uphold democracy, but in essence is helping strangle the peasants in Red China.

In a world famous magazine there was a picture of John Kerry on the left and a picture of the incumbent on the right and as a friend laid it down I said out loud as I first pointed to John Kerry and then to the incumbent, "A Communist and a Christian." What can one expect from a liberal Jew like Trotsky and Parvus and Marx but a love for the unnatural. This unnatural is that ideology that Kerry has promoted for many years now. He is a senior fellow in the Communist Party and now with his wife's money he can hope to at least buy, if not actually steal, an election that has no rules for him. So Christianity vs. the devil himself in regard to Communism the red horseman in the Book of Revelation.

This also occurred in Russia under Lenin and the Saxons and their loyalty to socialism and homosexuality, and now again the Jew takes the lead to promote for himself the finer things in life such as absolute power to be used by him, not as a President but as he has learned many years ago and that is this Communist ideology!

In today's newspaper I saw a most horrible thing and that was soliciting young girls from 10-14 years of age and had not the common decency to know that girls at such an innocent age do not need to be exploited in that manner. MasterCard and capitalism has now gone so far as to say that there is no such thing as innocence in children and they would too allow their own little girls to be solicited like this since they too are from the socialists' mentality. This is pure materialism that will promote anything at anytime that is so repulsive that it makes one cringe as to how such evil men and women can devise such business deals and appear as a pimp would in front of all the world and then say it is to make a living!

We have allowed this to go so far as a nation and are even afraid of our very own shadows that can do no harm and the fact that not even blood is thicker than water because we again have allowed this disease of the heart to penetrate the vital organs of our nation known as America!

Yes, one could see what amounts to evil at just the beginning of their entourage of people with the worst moral violations that one can ever remember in the history of this nation and yet they say have a debate, but what for when one is a well known Communist and his running mate is a paid liar or a lawyer for hire in government to promote socialism?

How would capitalism thrive if no one would borrow with interest or if they did borrow it would be very minimal to say the least? Most borrowing is indeed unnecessary. Why make the rich super rich? Stay away from all kinds of interest. Yes, some small credit is needed and is helpful, but in small amounts. Do without, yes, do without and do not even make a budget, but for the third time, since this is so very important, do without! The obsession with Western materialism so much so that fools, all of us, pay usurious rates to loan money and the interest is more than profit to the banks and any other financial institution. If people also helped other people like the Jewish people do when they go into business for the very first time and give them 3 chances to make it a success with no interest and in some cases no payment back at all! . . . When has anyone, even in the Christian community, heard of such a wonderful plan in helping one's neighbor and in turn breaking down big business by avoiding loans as well as a lot of insurance, which many believed was the cause of the Great Depression. I notice for example, that many Polish men like to dress like royalty and wear white shirts that cost about $60 a shirt and then in their own business they overcharge for their own stupidity because they bought a shirt that cost so much. Also, the the shirt might say Arrow on it when in reality the shirt was either made in Mexico or Red China, but the label shall not say that. In our very own town we had a company owned by Mexicans who would only hire Mexicans and who would transport products made in Mexico to our own town and then put labels on them saying they were made in the USA! This is how very much government is not minding its own business when things like this occur. They are everywhere but where they should really be and that is to provide for the common defense and promote the general welfare. Beyond that there is not much use for them, according to our Founding Forefathers, and that is why they always went back to what they originally did before they held office.

The government is holding up the banks, public transportation, the car industry, etc. by giving our money to big business so that they do not go under. But let them fail and let another one try their turn at the business. That is what free enterprise is really all about and not giving a warranty to businesses that fail and now become a sort of fascist type of society when the business is privately owned but run by the government, which means more socialism and more restrictions on just what is government owned since anytime government gives anything outside of itself, it is then owned and controlled by government and is no longer called free enterprise. We also do not need any more wasteful spending for Pell Grants (Senator Pell) or Stafford Loans, which are taxpayers' dollars so that the big business of colleges and universities can make millions of dollars on selling more socialism to their students and anti-Americanism also, and support the real dummies that play sports. Since when has higher education meant sports first and education second. This too runs into how professional sports and the media make their living, as well as Madison Avenue and the advertisements they put on television. One thing leads to another, and all for money and the love of it. It is not about education or a GODLY education or even sports since the athletes today are anything but good examples of how one should live as a good citizen in their own country. The media has already been spoken for by Pulitzer and the vicious circle entertains the less than bright American that has no common sense or decency to know the difference between athletes and prima donnas who never worked a day in their entire lives. But the millionaires need to eat, right?

Also farm subsidies should stop as they destroy the incentive and practicality of how to run a farm without any government interference such as price control and regulations that destroy the land and the farm's ability to make a decent living while at the same time supplying this nation with the food it really needs and not from foreign sources. The government imports, yes imports, from Mexico, a socialist state, and Red China a Communist state, and that is why all these treaties have been signed and that is to involve government in every facet of one's private and public life.

Then, along with these products and deals comes the people from those very lands who hate America and what it stands for and know that they have a free ride while here, and the lawyers in government, the politicians, make ludicrous laws they have no business being involved in. An example right now is Bill Gates who is pro infanticide and lives mostly in India where the two go hand in hand since there is an overpopulation problem as in Red China. So this whippersnapper shall do as Armand Hammer had done in Moscow and Kissinger and Haig had done in Red China and that is exploit the poor masses for all they are worth and serve the rich and well educated in New Delhi where all the money is.

This is the commercialization of government in the biggest way and that is to take our money out of America and through these super rich, make themselves billionaires, not because they are smart or bright but are ruthless and vicious and shall do anything such as Ross Perot had done when he too made his billions from the taxpayers' money. Also, there is Mo Annenberg, another government billionaire through Medicaid and Medicare, and David Rockefeller who also made his money in much the same easy way. Even contributions to PBS helps pay the taxes for the above individuals. This is what the United Nations is for!

The redistribution of wealth and valuable resources goes where it is least needed and that is to the rich and well educated, because anyone in today's world who is a financial success is living off of the miseries of someone else's poverty. This is in the millions and millions of people, or how else would one ever get to have so much money and wealth and not go to jail or be prosecuted for corruption? Everybody is doing it; even the poor are. This redistribution of wealth shall eventually create havoc and chaos, death and famines all over the world and is meant to do just that since in order to make that much money and wealth, somebody has to really do without and that again means in the millions and millions of people around the world or even in this nation. Also it is when liberty is held up and harnessed because of capitalism's avarice with no limitations that socialism, like a parasite, clings to it and it also serves the best interest of the United Nations, the World Bank and the IMF. In actuality, no matter how much wealth or money one has, without food, medicine, soil, water, air, forests, etc. they cannot live let alone just survive and the foundation for liberty is gone and for totalitarianism becomes even greater since all is limited to a certain few all over the world who control through whatever means it takes to keep that wealth where they believe it can best serve them or their ideology.

To be poor is not poverty, and poverty is not to be destitute though all strive to survive through induced famines and yet continue to contribute to socialism knowing that it does not work and never shall work. This means only what the earth or the ground has in it can it grow, and that is next to nothing since even the soil has been made useless by socialism's collectivization. America has too much that is not needed, but then again that is the very purpose of the billionaire, to always keep the American people in a sort of want for each and everything that is humanly possible for without this false production of need then there would be no need to continue this insanity of affluence!

Physical freedom in excess is an infringement upon the soul of a nation since there is no praying (real praying), but all playing of all ages continuously without stoppage. And affluence is the disease when one nation has too much of a good thing, but there is never enough of a good thing is there and is there really ever enough to share with others?

Yes the love of money is the root of all kinds of evil and not the necessity that appears always to demand what is never really needed, but just wanted or desired. To prove this point look at the peasants in Russia. Did they use money to buy and sell things? No. This is where the John Locke of the Enlightenment period of the Renaissance had created this materialism without any regard for the spiritual world of man. It is now an obsession like drugs are an addiction with anything material or tangible that makes one wonder just how sane or normal any one man is. This collection of antiques and other paraphernalia is beyond normal reasoning and to value them above another one's life and limb is where the barbarism of man lies so many times.

We waste our entire lives in the West and in America with immoral leisure such as television, movies, car racing, sports, drugs, alcohol, cars themselves for us, anxiety, worry, never enough, avarice, etc. and the list goes on and on and while we could be enjoying a real life blessed by GOD we always seem to choose for the less. So much time to do and yet we sin continually by passively doing things that offend GOD. We were created for His pleasure and our joy should be what He has given us to enjoy and not any of the above. Even hunting gets beyond reason since we are overweight enough and food is not sparse. Think of our countless hours doing nothing because our purpose by GOD is not even thought about let alone done at all. We are creatures of habit who pollute and the habit most of the time is sin itself. Yes, as I was saying, we pollute the earth (we will not walk), and we eat till we are sick and ready to vomit with all kinds of carcinogenic foods or debris that passes by our very mouths and eyes. There is nothing really in our jobs that is conducive to mental as well as physical labor and so computers think for us and machines, with all their noise (power tools), do our lazy work for us and our children do not know how to play or pray. We do not know how we should raise a Christian child any longer, and now this spirit of Narcissism envelopes all of us daily and we see just how spiritually impoverished we have become. This has become the symbol for America it is called the American Ego and not the eagle that used to soar and fly so high and free!

We have become our very own enemy because we allowed what the flesh wanted us to do and so now we are seeing just the beginning of what happens when a nation forgets about GOD. We are no longer what we now think we use to be, and we keep deceiving ourselves all the time with, again, the lie in regard to who is really first in our lives. We say it verbally and even wear the right face to along with it, but deep down inside something is dearly missing.

We only hear what we want to hear and see what we want to see, so our senses have taken over where faith should have always been since GOD supplies that to all of us in some form and to us believers we are probably the worse in the entire world since we have too much and we give very little of ourselves and feel that money is the answer to everything or every problem in the world and it is surely not!

We will do anything to make money and that means abuse children and animals, both of which we should be protecting, so I say to myself Where is the authority invested in us that comes from GOD to speak, to do and to never continue on as if this self-preservation or "born again" issue is all that matters in life. Forget what James had said when he said, "Faith without works is dead." Was he espousing that there is a prerequisite for salvation in the thing known as works, which it is not? This is why Roman Catholicism thinks of materialism because they believe and wrongly that one needs money and hard work to get into heaven and so they miss what the Bible says that one must do and that is to believe!

This constant working for money and only money with no relaxation is destroying the institution of family since no one is home to be a mother or a father but a work machine that never needs a rest except the kind the one never wakes up from and all because we have this insatiable appetite for money and what it can buy and the security and ego building it gives to us.

We are just like the Hollywood actors on a screen who contribute zero to society.

So they would continue to molest the altar boys and now the altar girls, but what would the Vatican or the head do? Monsignor, or "my lord"—how Anglophile, yet also so arrogant with Pharisaical roles to dazzle the money bags and please their every whim. "Oh he knew I was at mass, etc." When would they close their doors and what more would it take? They were in many government positions and yet again with the Anglo-Saxons the three could promote . . . Some people I already knew had experienced some of their Hugh Heffner stuff, but not one to prosecute? Some had been women who also were too embarrassed to say anything, as well as small children. Who would believe them over the Pharisee? The Poles were now more proud then ever and had their "royalty" where they wanted it. In fact, as I said before, Poland had legalized homosexuality! This was their "church", but of course no one read the Jewish Bible. Some homosexuals got to enjoy molestation and molested others' children as well as their own, and promotion like the Masons was in line. We had in our own area one state senator who was not effeminate on the outside, but a Catholic not married who attended all male youth sporting events. He loved these! His eyes were not opaque but almost transparent. Then there was also a monsignor or my lord who was like as sly as a cat like Felix the cat. His family were millionaires. This made for more compensation on the part of their church. "Socialism in mysticism", or "happiness in slavery", both phrases coined by Dostoyevsky and meaning materialism in ritualism and giving up the truth for money and this world. He never knew this third one, homosexual pedophilia.

The Poles were just like the Finns and the English. Anything to destroy Russia, even if it meant selling out to Islam and the Pope shaking hands with Arafat! How much more anti-Semitic could one possibly get? This was anything but Christianity and look who brought it to America, the Irish and look at the debacle that is over there right now! Money vs. what? How come the Soviets never crushed the Vatican church when they had control of Poland for so many years? Was it anything like the Moslems and the Komsomol?

Again in our area there had been Nazis who were well to do since our area was predominantly German and now Hispanic. There was an unusually high amount of blacks also in the area for a small community. I had heard a story that in Germany after WW II the German women went wild over black GI'S that were stationed in a small town in Germany.

Yes, in this area homosexuality was prevalent because of German ancestry which came from Nazi Germany many years ago. From one generation to another in a matriarchal society meaning the sons had no bonding with their fathers and both German and black cultures were analogous in this.

Now election time was coming up and the media said that illegals could vote because the government had no way of checking to see who they really were. This too was another lie. With all the surveillance and computer technology they could not detect and track and set up a system that worked to prevent voter fraud? This was just to have the numbers so more people would vote and now that we had alone 11 million Mexicans here that would mean

Hispanic Jihad at the polls and would counter, they thought, the Democratic Party's illustrious record of cheating by voting 3 and 4 times by the same one person in one election and that is how Bill Clinton got into the White House.

It was first the driver's license voter registration which did no good, then the punch the hole or pencil # 2 to mark with, like in the state of Massachusetts, then of course anybody, or just about anybody, could vote also! This government was condoning more lies just for an election that would not make a bit of difference but only until we would hit bottom. Socialism would rule no matter who won but again with one candidate it would be expedited so quickly that the surgery would have to wait for months to be done and medicines would run out early with of course universal health care as they had in England and Canada who both had much fewer people in both their nations. Add about 10 million and not 47 million to the addition number of extra people without healthcare and that would doom the medical profession from one of compassion to one of death and that was just what the doctors were being taught to do with no Hippocratic Oath at all any longer! These 10 million people were people mostly in transition meaning going from one job to another or changing occupations from one to another. The illegals, minorities, and also foreigners of none Christian origins would get the first and best health care. Remember John Edwards had more high profile malpractice law suits against OBGYN's then almost any other lawyer in the nation and helped bring down the amount of doctors and nurses that were now going into other fields such as Senator Frist. Also the neuro-surgeons would be next on that list. Dan Quayle had the right idea when he said that loser should pay all and in that way there would be a lot less law suits in America and the trial lawyers would back off with the idiotic law suits since they always got a percentage out of the millions they made, the way a pimp collects off of his women! These law suits are what brought socialism even more to the fore since it would convince most Americans that this was the way to go by universal health care where many or most physicians would be unqualified to practice medicine and the good ones would get out of the profession or take on another line of medicine and then fewer babies would be born and infanticide would grow and grow and Planned Parenthood would make millions of dollars from the American taxpayers even though the majority were against this genocide!

Also there was in government a way to try to break the small businesses and private enterprises for good by the courts that were as corrupt as the Soviet ones were or the ones that sat on the benches at the Nuremburg trials. This is what made this whole election a fiasco because one candidate wanted more illegals and the other wanted more than the 12% of blacks to vote and more than the small percentage of Jews to vote because till they were done there would be about 50% blacks who, by their count, would make up 50% of the entire American population, so each candidate had to count the numbers much higher since fraud would once again take place now on both sides when before it was only the Democratic Party!

Our government would change and not the state, and that would mean a democratic/republic, if one could call it that, and would dissolve overnight while an oligarchy would be installed. That is why this was their last chance to once again try to rob, steal, or any other way win this so called election and most of the American people believed just what they were being told by the media and still did not get it right about how socialistic it was as well as all the branches of our government.

Now I thought to myself which candidate could I really vote for when one the incumbent was for no borders or the moving of the borders like Lenin and also his love for Islam even though he was a Christian and the other a Communist was for infanticide, homosexuality to destroy us, etc.

Ellis Island was it just mostly for ones from Europe who were influential or of well to do means from themselves or their relatives or ancestry? Many who were poor and destitute had not been able to get to America. Why was that? Did it once again show how real history was re-written by not telling this side of the story? I know my parents were first generation parents here, but had been told that their family relatives held important positions in Europe itself even though my own parents were the black sheep out of a large family from both sides. Did this really mean that once again money provided a way to America? How could one enter our borders in any other way? It had occurred in Vietnam when the business persons there were the very first to get out of Vietnam when they left by paying $10,000 a head in gold to the Communists!

Now today the same was still occurring here but much more. Ones who were non-Christian made up the vast majority of immigrants while Christian asylum and they were only in the thousands. The illegals were also another story. They would break any law to get here, but why? There was no love lost for America with Hispanics? They would not assimilate just like the American Negro never quite really did without coerced affirmative action, quotas, day care, shacking up, matriarchal African tribalism which pleased the feminists, socialisms, etc.

In the 60's, the blacks started segregating from the Whites although not because they thought that it would mean better equality, because they had become in fact more prejudiced than the white people in America. And the government said and put it into law that they could take over if only they became aggressive in society and would use the fist more often, but it yet was still to happen! What was there to take over or get even with and who planted such an insane idea with an entire race of people anyway? One Negro friend had told me that his people were more prejudiced than whites and that no one could tell him about his own people better than he could. He mentioned that the mulattos were usually worse than the darker skinned Negro persons, and this man himself was very dark and had large huge features. If one looked at him they would think he was mean and vicious, but he had a heart of gold and would help many people, but was not stable since he never got married and later died of brain cancer.

I noticed as time went on the black people became more and more arrogant and unfriendly and the rich and well educated promoted even more of the same, such as the Kennedys! They were going backwards in regard to getting along with others and even began to do harm to their own in major proportions. Prostitution and pimping now turned into drug using and drug dealing, and white suburbia of course had to emulate it. In the 50's, though, there were white gangs and some were grown men who talked slang, and some years later the blacks picked it up and carried it up to this day! This vernacular, jargon, or ebonics was not what the Southern Negroes spoke like. It was meant to put fear in anyone who could be intimidated, and that was most white males. I do not mention children, women and the elderly because no one expects them to hold the front line. There were some, though, who held their place in society as males, but not too many! Some knew that one usually had to attack not physically, the ring or gang leader to disperse the government which upheld what exactly Lenin wanted when he viewed the Negro from Switzerland since Lenin was really a Westerner at the beginning of the 20th century. Create diversity and schisms and animosity and out right hatred amongst the different races, nationalities, religions, etc. Lenin was truly a man possessed, and even before the Revolution comrades would slap each others' palms, something we now see even in today's American sports world. Habits never die, it would appear, and wolves shed their fur, but not their habits. This was a form of symbolism that meant just follow me and there shall be no trouble. Funny how semantics and body motion sways the subconscious even more so today.

People today have more affluence but even more inner fear of what they could lose if they stood up for what was truly right. It would prove that silence was golden and why rock the boat since one person could not do anything! But they could and some did and it held back for quite some time, this onslaught of Communism in America that was coming to full fruition. Americans were noted for "verbalizing" even their good inactions! Who has made our streets unsafe? Government lawyers or politicians and especially the judges and defense attorneys like Allan Derschowitz, Johnny Cochran, F. Lee Bailey, Mr. Spence, and the breck girl Edwards! These are the ones running our country into the ground.

One night I saw with my wife 3 children and one of the children was a beautiful little girl of 9 months old. When my wife struck up a conversation, she found out that all 3 children were foster children, and it broke our hearts to know that these parents, but especially the children would have to be given up to another family because the trial lawyers, the parasites that they were, were charging at least $10,000 to adopt a child when it should have cost only $1,000!

We are electing criminals to protect and to serve, but whom? Insanity? Now athletic criminals could serve their prison time after the sport season for them was over, and how convenient that was to know that! This goes beyond the idiocy of plea bargaining, wouldn't one say? One notices, of course. it is starting with the minorities and shall be emulated by all, I am sure, just for equality or equivalence!

Why would Jewish Israelis, for the life of me, ever want to visit a resort in an Arab country and be murdered on top of it by well known terrorists? Of course they did not know they would be murdered, but didn't they realize there was an Islamic Arab war going on against them and the Christians? It is the faith above all, just as it was and is with the Communists. Socialisms breed contempt and hatred, and civil righters' socialism allows only certain ones this "privilege" which included, of course, the minorities and the homosexuals and children known as hate crimes!

Group hiring had become popular in America. If one was qualified forget it. It had to be based on pure socialism where the criteria was by group such as race, age, gender, religion (not faith), etc. Some people such as one young college girl who was a black (1) homosexual (2) woman (3) of a certain age, and (4) could qualify for more free handouts or entitlements. This was socialism's educational network of nonsense that only taught theories about life and fairy tales. There was no foundation to build upon because this was built on sand and not solid ground.

Colleges and universities gave nothing to behold as far as a GODLY and real and only kind of education. It was about feelings, television, emotions, get even, separate, division, diversity, multi—culturalism, racism, discrimination, and so much much more! This would indeed benefit America!

That is why crime was not all reported because over 75% of our population would have been incarcerated for some felony of some kind and since there were more serious crimes to pursue such as money these ones that involved murder were irrelevant! This was now what America had in store for itself since criminals were trying criminals in front of and behind the bench.

I thought about something that was too hard to even comprehend and that was that we as a nation, America, had up to now become the most brutal and vicious nation that had ever existed on the face of the earth, and we still did not recognize or repent of it. There had been many nations and countries that had done some horrible things in the past, but as I said right now or up to now we had become the most horrible nation besides Red China and that just told anyone how horrible that nation or should I say regime and not government had become? Ours did not involve slavery; no, it was not even slavery and it did not involve people who were in the Holocaust or in the Gulag which was saying so very much or even in the Dark and Middle Ages, but it involved up to and including today and tomorrow and the day after and our churches were worried about self-esteem and self preservation since our very own government and big business or commercialization had first given up free countries in all of Europe and then now were selling us out to the same ideology that was as old as man except it was more sophisticated in its technology. We as Americans had found a so called scientific way of how to do something so horrible that we as a people were very closed mouthed about it and would only say, "So what" or "What can one do?" or "It doesn't matter", or "it will go away someday" and that was the hideous and gruesome elimination of people who would not harm any one and who were so innocent that it bottled the imagination that one had to wonder why GOD had not set in motion a destruction for this nation and who knows maybe GOD already had since His time is not our time and with Him a thousand years is like a day, but even with this even that day might be shortened to one "hour"!

We kept going about our business and that is the only word that can also describe this horrible money making machine and it had been very lucrative for the so called "survival" of these United States because it produced our most or should I say reduced our most important human resources to torture and pain and unending horror that not even the most grotesque movie in Hollywood could be this extreme in murder and in blood and in destruction, and that was what many liked to call pro-choice, or even abortion, but nothing but one word could really describe it like Webster's Old Dictionary which called it by it's true name: genocide and no less and perhaps even more. Yes even more and that was first degree pre-meditated, cold blooded murder and was called INFANTICIDE! I know many shall say that is the wrong word, but it is not. It is the very word for murdering all children in the womb and now out of the womb, which in itself was called partial birth abortion which also was a euphemism for the total murder and destruction of human life for the planned reasons of avarice, socialism, and insanity!

Our nation had become insane, yes insane to the point that now almost 60,000,000 infants, infanticide, had been murdered and now outside the womb such as partial birth abortion which I just mentioned and had been working on children less than perfect or toddlers and little children. Even in California they tried to pass a law that eliminated children up to the age of 6 years old, but it did not pass. Then there were people in comas, disabled, retarded, crippled, of a different kind, the elderly, the Christian, the Jew, the Negro, the Hispanic, the Chinese, the Indian (India) and this list was growing and growing. I could think of no time ever in the history of man where that many children were murdered in any civilization and so many in such a short period of time. Now the children that did survive were being either molested, given drugs in due time, murdered in another way, starved to death, sold in slavery and foster care, and yes even in adoption for the wrong reasons. But guess who promulgated all of this horror? That was none other than the entire legal profession from top to bottom as well as the entire medical profession because not one of them ever put their life on the line to stand up against this horror and never even risked the chance of even losing their wealth and money and worldly possessions! No one was standing in the gap out of all the millions of infants and others that had been murdered! No one in government, no one in the church, no one in the medical profession, and on and on because why should we bring up the past and lose so much that is our mundane possessions that this nation could never take to wherever took the nations that He would eventually judge to have been wrong and evil!

It started in 1973 as an official proclamation by none other than an atheistic Jew, and now one could see why I had always believed that Messiah would always be attacked through the Jewish people because He came as a Jewish man, and that is who Satan had always attacked, the same blood line or chosen people in the sense that Jesus came in that flesh as a Jewish man!

We all were accomplices because we did not give up our own lives for these infants let alone give up all our possessions as Jesus told the rich young man who walked away sadly even though he had said he kept the law, but it was the heart and not the law that Jesus was interested in and the fact that one should follow Him immediately! There was no time to be lost, but he did not because his heart had not been transformed by his decision, reasoning, and turning over his heart to the King of kings. Yes, one had to think about this decision because Jesus did ask a question that was for all time and beyond. It dealt with the conversion of the spiritual heart from the one that Adam had to the one that Jesus always had, and that would mean to follow Jesus in whatever He said and whatever He wanted done because He was doing the Father's will always! This was a gift of grace, but yet this young man did not even want this gift that would last forever but just what he thought he owned now and in the present which gave him an easy way in life but only in minutes as compared to eternity! We as Americans were asked or at least I felt we were asked to put our very lives on the line by not being violent or which means not going along with this lie or any other lie. We had to stand for the truth and not behind closed doors. We had to go public about it and continue to speak again and again not only what we had done but what we had failed to do and still were failing to do each and everyday. Would we ever do just that to begin with because one could not know for sure what GOD would have us do besides that even though prayer many times was said more as an excuse than as a real reason because with or after prayer things happen and we as Christians are not spectators in the literal sense of the Word. Each individual had to do something as a believer and there would be no getting around it since GOD had said, "Be fruitful and multiply."

The American race's mortality rate had to exceed our own birth rate right now and with others already here how many of them too would be eliminated through socialized medicine called HMO'S that only provided for ones who were healthy and would stay healthy or were rich enough to buy their health or otherwise we all come to the part to our own mortality. But now it had been accelerated to mean you could be next since one who gets sick (and we all mostly do sometime in all our lives) shall be under rationed care meaning we would have to even wait in a life and death situation in America even for surgery and medicine no matter how serious it was, live or die or be murdered through wantonly wanting to destroy man the full knowledge that his body would break down and when it did most people did not know; hence it meant that when it did, well you had to draw high on the lottery draw, no doubt about it and the odds were slim and none!

This is why human resources or the words became so popular because it meant that we were no better than the stars or the ground on earth or the animals which in fact got better care since infanticide came always first, second to infants or human beings with a soul and that universal health care would even promote this even more because then it could say they did not have even to take care of all and so only the ones they felt should remain alive and themselves should get the decent and correct kind of medicines and surgery that was required to give when and how it was given and not to be procrastinated to the bin of the forgotten and the lost. The television ministers also did not have to worry about health care because they could afford it and again the Hollywooders, the

CEO's, the rich and the super rich had to stay there so they too could get not only proper care but care that would extend their life with plastic hearts and cures for cancers, new blood vessels, preventive medicine which did not mean the same thing that the HMO's had proclaimed for the victims or so called "patients". Don't get sick or else! With the rich it's 'what can I do to extend my life from ones murdered' and that would be donors as the Communists Chinese did so well there to young Christian men and women who were healthy. But these Western businessmen needed that organ now and not later and not always because they were extremely ill but because they knew the death wish would also apply to them if they lost their clout or carte blanche with the one world government. Yes, this was world wide in a computer system. In fact the U.S. Air Force also had something that was called anti-matter that kind of dissolved any kind of matter but most likely it would be human being matter!!!

We had come this far in medicine and in law that there really was no law and there was really no kind of medicine to speak of. The doctors and lawyers were attacking each other, but eventually the lawyers had to win and hence then the witch doctors could be brought on the scene such as Joseph Mengele and the Margaret Sanger of the world who believed, "Don't do as I personally do, but only do as I say," and this was even in the Holocaust!

Be healthy and physically fit or else, or be rich and powerful or else so they too, for the most part, had to walk the straight and narrower for themselves and could care less what happened to others, but did know that this chip would do the trick because no one wanted the ultimate treat and that would be death or murder, no hesitation at all, regardless of what good one had done in society and in fact they would be the first targets!

They had to keep all Christians and all Jews locked out of the entire world system because, in the first case Christians (Christ) and in the second case Jewish (Messiah). These two had to be excluded from this world and quickly since Satan already had most all others in the world under his very control. Yes, some Jews were not believers, but just the word Jew implied in the mind that

Messiah would be remembered and that could not possibly be, so the chosen wanted to hide and belong for as long as possible on this earth and the sad part was that most Jews now felt that way and wanted nothing to do with being Jewish in any way, no matter what. But the enemy knew who they were, all of them, and collaboration or not, he was out to eliminate them all very soon. Again, that Jesus was a Jewish man must always be kept in mind and that is why most Jewish people were more hostile to Messianic Jews than perhaps even Christians were, and that was, it gave them away and told others who Messiah was and how they were related and how the enemy told them in his own dialogue to get rid of those Messianic Jews and do not spare any. But he did not tell them that then they too would be next to go. There could not be one Jew left, and that is why Hitler also wanted them all dead because he too was controlled by Satan. Hitler held such a high position in the world and had much power to use against anyone that Satan wanted him to, even though he had free will but not the kind of freewill GOD had given to man but the kind that said, "Do it or else, or see how bad they are making it for your life" of course without telling them that they would also be doomed for eternity, but just do the very job at hand and do it very quickly!

There would eventually be no place at all on earth for the believer or the Jewish person. Notice again that's not all Gentiles, but in the second scenario it was all the Jews anywhere in the entire world! Many believers did not know the venom that Satan had for the Jewish people since it was GOD the Father who chose His only Jewish Son to come to this earth to redeem man, and it was Satan that knew he had to act fast because time for him was running out and his so called "kingdom" would not be here as a final place but in the burning lake of fire for ever and ever!

Good vs. evil no less and no more except with evil now the insanity would include most people on the face of this earth and the good was in what Jesus or Messiah had done on Calvary and not anything that we could have possibly done, because we could never have done what a perfect GOD had asked His only Son who was also perfect and in a diseased and sinful world! The human race had to be destroyed!

When Kennedy and Nixon were debating in 1960, Nixon was for higher taxes (the rich again) and surprisingly Kennedy was for lower taxes. Kennedy admired the socialist FDR, but of course FDR appointed his dad, Joseph Kennedy as ambassador to England. Kennedy was also for Medicare to be an option (following what FDR had done in 1935), and Nixon said he was not, so there was a contradiction for both of these candidates. Kennedy won the Presidential election. Nixon later would, but was friends later with Peking and Moscow and was a Quaker. Kennedy was a friend of Germany where he told them in a speech that he himself was just like a Berliner.

Kennedy, though, had been strong against Khruschev's vessels bringing missiles into Cuba and made them turn around. Later Khruschev was called back to the Kremlin and never heard of again. At this time Solzhenitsyn had been in the process of getting his book ONE DAY IN THE LIFE OF IVAN DENISO—VICH and later too won a Nobel Peace Prize for Peace.

These were the Cold War years when the Soviets were making their move under the very liberal administration until Reagan got in. Kennedy did mess up the Bay of Pigs in Guantanamo Bay, Cuba by not following through with what he was supposed to do and hence lost much appeal with conservatives. The Republican Party at that brief time was for higher taxes, but less government control.

At that time even in schools we were being indoctrinated by politics and our spiritual realm was already falling apart. Too much was being made of by the media and government about the Cuba missile crisis and Castro to this day has outlived both opponents and friends from Peking and Moscow and from the United States. He himself was also one of them, a lawyer. These lawyers always knew how to revolutionize things in the most violent way and even John Roselli was brought in.

Civil rights had not quite come in and the radicals the liberal Jews and the Jane Fondas were almost ready to get their revolution started here in the United States. These superior rights were all a part of Lenin's plan for diversity` and his political correctness that was to be carried out even before World War I when some of his agents such as Shlyapnikov, the founder of the Communist Party, had come but with little or no luck since there was no support or enough money while Lenin just stayed in Switzerland hiding like a cockroach here and there and constantly on the move as an emigre'.

He had thought that Europe and America would first have socialism before Russia ever would! He was so shortsighted that he did not even know that the revolution had started in Russia. He was such an idiot that his close comrades were also criminals like him who all should have been kept in Siberia for years on end to serve out their terms for subversion to the monarch, but of course the monarch had seen otherwise and it proved Russia's fate as well as the monarch's fate with much help from Finland, Latvia, Germany. Even England and Turkey got involved in the act to destroy a European nation and not an Asiatic one.

As years went by others came along and carried out Lenin's plan and only Stalin strayed the line one time, when he did not trust even members of his own Communist Party. That is how paranoid they all were and were scared for their lives to serve prison time but had no hesitancy to make millions of others serve in the Gulags along with Germany and England and France mainly. This was the Europe that could not defend itself from outside forces and yet it was the West's own creation, this communism that spread all over the world.

When in 1949 China was overthrown by Communists they eliminated the drug users and drug dealers by gathering them in a public square and shooting them in the back of the neck. The English had brought this drug problem to China as they had brought apartheid to South Africa years ago. It was these colonial•ists that owned and made slaves of so many other peoples that they continually escaped the evil they had caused repetitiously. Now, though, it appeared that their turn as well as all of Europe this time would come under the gun including America for turning a blind eye to all the problems we all had caused in the world because we always did whatever England did.

The West was a hollow shell of nothingness and now could not even defeat a small enemy in Iraq that had no sophisticated weaponry and no real army but only terrorists. Israel itself had done more to hold back the whole Islamic world by destroying the nuclear reactor in Iraq some years ago. Their raid on Entebbe in Uganda we ourselves could have never pulled off because we had gotten used to the lie of no vigilance and the luxury and leisure we had been living for so many years and thought with the Yalta Conference that all was over, but that with the conference it would just begin and eventually spread into the Orient and oppress those people. The rich and well educated in the West got what they wanted and now had nearly died off or were ready to die off and their children would take over.

The incumbent also was another generation of the rich and well educated as well as Kerry and the Rockefellers, Kennedys, etc. This would be worse than their predecessors. We would have to at least struggle with them like the previous generation had not and that was my own 60's generation who had not changed one iota. They still wanted to listen to rock and roll, take drugs, and shack up, and of course wanted leisure and luxury to the ultimate which now gave them over weight and obese offspring who already were getting diabetes very young due to this and a very poor diet and little or no work that required any labor. In fact the less labor one did, the more it looked like that was an achievement, but in actuality it was only a form of the status quo that continued not to work for an honest living and so they too would be worse for it and so would their children be!

The Greeks in our area were starting to take over businesses, especially restaurants and all would be lost because they, like the Orientals, were not at all very friendly or at all sincere like the Jewish proprietors were years ago who had delicatessens that served kosher food and were very clean. But as for the Greeks, they were anything but clean like the Orientals also. This was this new form of immigrants who would be rude to the American home grown people and added also to the demise of America since the Greeks were so envious that the famous tennis player Sampros had neither his mother or his father ever come to any of his matches, not because they did not like the sport, but because they were envious of him and this was their own very son! Incredible? Not really when one would talk to them and find out that all they talked about, like the Catholics, was money and how much more they would need when in fact they did not need a penny more. They in fact were keeping it all for themselves of course until the end and then it would be used for what they probably never wanted it to be used for!

The Romanians were also here in a huge mass and for some reason they too were part of the same mentality that thought that they could come here and just get rich and did not understand in the slightest nor did they want to that America was not formed for them or anybody else to get rich in and that included even up to today. These foreigners would always remain foreigners because their GOD was not America's GOD and hence the more that came here the more America began to look like a 3rd World nation with no manufacturing or craftsmanship of any kind. Even their children were going to college and did not even work in the labor force, but how could that be since they were new immigrants unless, again, only the rich and well educated came here or the government was giving them a free ride on the backs of the middle class and the poor! This would be nothing knew, but why did it seem that all these foreigners were so damn arrogant when they came here? Did the government tell them something or were they here to only get rich and then take our American dollars back to their countries to fight against America whenever they wanted to? This was so prevalent over and over again that one could become nauseated about it.

The elections kept going and had the audacity to ask us if we would vote them in again and the other non-incumbents were so dumb they could not speak right when asked questions on a television debate. No one had to be qualified in the government to win and hold an official position since so many socialists were in it already and mediocrity would now rule supreme in America like it had for so many other years even before the 20th century came along.

The radicals in America used to say many times "Love America or leave it", which meant even if government and our own society was corrupt and evil, one was to still love America's evils and not America alone for what it had done years ago. There was to be no separation between now and then in the past so it would become like Germany's follow the leader no matter what it may lead to. In our own area the Germans and the minorities did just that because it was a sweet song to sing for them and they did not have to rock the boat. Let us forget about America and how it used to be and now accept anything that came along and grab hold to it for dear life and never let go, but not all the people thought the same, and thank heaven for that We were not all Anglo-Saxons or minorities that had to have it their way, which meant any old way but the moral and decent and honorable way! It was called "do your own thing" and the blacks especially used to like to use that term time and again for it gave them the superiority at least they felt that they never had and never would have but would be used just as pawns once again, this time for socialism and its extreme slavery. But no blacks were complaining about that kind of slavery at all, only the one that refused the "me first" syndrome. One could murder and rob and steal and still they would not be considered a harm to society! This is how far it had gone with the blacks in America, and it scared the heck out of the average American European, but not the Indians, the Orientals, the Africans, the Hispanics who all came here with that same attitude "I shall do as I please." This was the arrogance of big government and big business that had rubbed off on them so quickly that one wondered how could one learn it that quickly and not learn the English language except for the Russian Jewish children who had learned it the fastest of any of other people in the world? The Russian culture was different because it had its own GOD and not one of Europe the continent's GOD and so all these European nations had one or the other GOD and it should have extended to as many GODS that each nationality on their own could find. The conglomerate of two world religions for so many different nations in Europe brought nothing but grief and misery to all those nations and for Russia it was even worse since they had found their own GOD by St. Cyril and St. Methodius! This was what was upsetting to Europe. The fact that the German Reformation took on a German personality, that meant that the Russians were not anything like the Germans and were not anything like the Vatican that somehow even the Poles felt so close to for whatever reason!

America had its own GOD and we did not need Catholicism or the Reformation or Islam or any other foreign religion including the Anglican church in England. Is that not why the people that came here left England and not only against the King who confused GOD with himself?

The Hispanics were okay with Roman Catholicism so let them keep it in their own separate countries if they could not find their own national GOD. And now Islam was trying to say that it too worshipped the same GOD and also our incumbent said that they did too and I guess the Roman Empire of Nero also did? This is how lies perpetuate themselves over and over again down through the centuries, and most people just took it for granted that this had to be right, but it was not!

People did not learn to think for themselves but were use to thinking like a group or groups of people and faith was not about groups like socialism was, but about the Body of Christ in its believers and even though all over the world they would worship their GOD a little different nonetheless it was still in the Body of Christ and GOD would not be boxed in because one religion or denomination from a certain country felt superior, which they should not have because it was not them that had found anything but only what GOD Himself had revealed to them, that it was His Son and not their own religion or denomination that was the ultimate truth since only GOD was perfect and knew all there was to know and no church ever got it right 100% or near to that at any time ever, but did many times want to coerce others, but did GOD ever coerce others?

The vicissitudes of life are as such that one man who was being successful with a lovely and loyal wife found not only himself incarcerated but also his wife while a famous black football player for the New York Giants a linebacker went scot—free in a most serious embezzlement case. Yes, this athlete never served a day in jail. This was all part of the political correctness.

There was another man who had a different experience. He was a sailor on the Pueblo and was held in a North Korean prison camp for 11 months and was tortured and beaten, but what kept him going was his faith. I had felt, though, that both these stories should have made front page headlines. Both men now had known that faith is the thing unseen but that can keep one on the straight and narrow and can keep one going even when it looks like the end is near. Mr. Ginther and the other fellow, an Italian fellow in the first scenario, both now understood what it was that they did not have, their freedom which was a once taken for granted thing, but now no longer would it be.

Too many people in America were so busy on who to vote for as far as financial matters that they totally forgot what the important issues were of the day and none could be no more important than the moral issues between life and death and murder and compassion. Compassion is something that America had lost a lone time ago. We now knew less than we knew before even though we had gotten much older but none the wiser as this 60's generation continued down the slippery slope.

The end of what we knew as a so-called democratic republic was just about gone and the people kept thinking that they were free and had liberty on their side since they could do just about anything they wanted to. But the problem was that we were next to chaos, which meant that man would always settle for totalitarianism before chaos. Once there was no real liberty then this freedom would be so wild that it would destroy us all because freedom is not what it is all about even though'. many politicians would render this to be the paragon of all societies when in essence it was the death of a nation because self-discipline was not anywhere to be found and hence the people confused this freedom with the random attempt to do what the emotions dictated to do with no regard for the other fellow and to some this is what civil rights' socialism had come to in America but now the wolf would shed it's fur but not it's habit. This was the very nature of man and that was to be free from all restraints like Adam was in the Garden of Eden. This was this total free will that was not what anyone really wanted.

Our own U.S. Congress was doing exactly what the Duma had done before the Revolution in Russia and that was to interfere with the monarch and spoke like windbags that made no sense at all and had paralysis because they did not have the courage to take control of the form of government that they constantly talked about and the generals' staff like a Colin Powell or a Sanchez or a Franks did not already know about how to serve without accolades They had the bench jobs on the sidelines and directing things from a distance. We now were faced with a change in government if the incumbent did not change his attitude and say he was wrong. Would he sacrifice an entire nation like the monarch did over there years ago with Nikolai? Was he too indecisive about making decisions about his own country and would he take the country down with him because he was too ambivalent about what one had to do and what one should not do?

He appeared to be following the `read my lips' President, which was his dad who knew nothing about any winning strategy but only how to placate something with a foundation for something with sand. He was not presidential material and his son was too young and inexperienced but in a way as President he reminded one of the monarchs in Russia, and one had to feel sorry for his inability to make sound and pertinent decisions when our country now needed it most. He had to be told by people of lesser authority and administrators what he wanted to hear and had to campaign so he could get away from it all and convince himself that all would be all right!

He had become a pathetic figure even though sincerity was for real but he was wrong, dead wrong, to continue and ever have invaded Iraq just because his father was asked by Margaret

Thatcher to invade Iraq because of a loss of money to England because of the oil wells, and so his son now had to finish the job and was under the authority of his father who had also gotten us into the mess and was nothing more (both of them) than a Vice President as Ronald Reagan had made him. Both of them were not presidential material because one, the son, lived a sheltered life and the father had the mind of a general who was in it for the glory plus the fact they were English and we always had to do what

England had done or what England had asked us to do!

Kerry was 100% pure Communist and would prove that if he got into office and also would make a great target for the Moslems since he was Jewish. Even Moslems in front of the White House were bowing to Mecca in Saudi Arabia and someone in government had to tell them to get the hell out of America as soon as possible before we had another vicious attack on America and then all hell would break lose and that is why I had thought this President did not want to return our troops back home all at once since they would be ticking time bombs waiting to go off after their horrible experiences in Iraq and elsewhere in Allah land. They had to be very careful about the militia in America which could start a revolution back here because that would be all Hollywood would need to subterfuge their own guilt to the nation itself and our sovereignty. No one could ever trust the Communists in Hollywood such as Ed Asner and others too numerous to mention.

Our Founding Forefathers would roll over in their graves if they knew that this was happening under any President since he was the Commander In Chief, but did not know how to use his power in America. Islam was never meant to be embraced here no matter how much the blacks wanted to be a part of it and this tribalism! This country was setup for Judeo-Christianity and just like Scalia had said about homosexuals that we did not want them in our homes, our businesses or our government we also felt the same with Islam since one would do that they would be bringing in demons and the occult with them all the time. This was not some kind of variance with Christian denominations that our

Founding Forefathers kept referring to. This was a whole different ballgame! WE did not want Islam to be recognized no matter what and the mosques could also be removed before a right and just GOD would say enough is enough!

Islam was never ever free and could never ever be free. Our nation was set up for a religious and free people, and Islam was neither free or religious but fanatic with its innate socialism. That is why I felt many blacks liked it so very much because it was almost innate with them this Islam!

It preached violence and destruction and that had to go or America would go and if it offended so what? This was our nation and it was for the people and not the rich and well educated and the government to decide what we would allow to occur in America that especially involved hatred and violence. This whole ideology, and that is what it was like Lenin had made Marxist/Leninism to replace the Russian Orthodox. They too that is the socialists in America wanted to replace the Judeo-Christian faith with Islam.

The American Jew in this country had thought that the Judeo-Christian faith in America was anti-Semitic and also the Bible but the truth was the Bible was just the opposite and that is why Messiah was a Jewish man and that the European religions that came from Europe now they were anti-Semitic! Roman Catholicism and the German Reformation both had severe anti-Semitism in them and it was very unusual for the Jews not to be able to differentiate and separate as to the two that is the Bible and European religions and where else did the Jews make such a success and not necessarily in money but in academics of all fields but in America?

Yes, they had confused the two with one and so the lie of Europeanism prejudice would have them think that America did not have its own GOD! Where had they done so much in so short a time even though America had its anti-Semitics? Every country does. They had confused apples with oranges and that is why these Communists and Nazis in America wanted to get rid of the Sovereignty of America because once it did that they felt that then they could exterminate all Jews everywhere since America would have been defeated and it would also weaken Israel. They were not really thinking so straight as to what was going on because they could not see the forest for the trees!

The American Jew did know much of this but just could not decipher the most important part that in America we neither held up the German Reformation or Roman Catholicism, but the Founding Forefathers faith of Scripture and none of them came either from Italy or Germany at that time! The American Biblical was different in the sense that we had a completely and totally different society then Europe ever had which had always been anti-Semitic when it came to their religions. They had 2 religions for all the nations in Europe and we had one faith for our one nation yet others who were peace loving and kind could also worship, but not Islam especially after 9/11! The Soviets too did not bother the Moslems while they lived under their rule because they cooperated with the Communists. One way they did that was by sending their own children to the Komsomol while Christian parents refused to, knowing what atheism it taught about! Now how religious was this Islam which the rich and well educated were selling to the American people in the form of a bold faced-lie?

When somebody harms and murders another nation's people through a form of an ideology and is covered under "religion" called Islam, then that so called "religion" must not be free to preach hate.

One does not need to wear a uniform to stand up for justice if a national and being that he could be wrong and then his service to his own nation is or could be a detriment to it and fighting for an unjust cause would in essence be to no avail. No matter how sincere one is it would be upholding evil and not justice and the rule of law. What once made our nation moral (not great because greatness has to do with mundane things of this world) was GOD. It is like treating the symptom and not the cause which would mean that the illness that our nation has shall only succumb to its own death premature most likely. One does not treat an illness by the symptoms, and that is what we have done in America with socialism and multiculturalism. This could hinder the nation since money in an affluent society would always lean toward the ego part of man and the growth for money that grows very easily on the human nature. Instead of having agapé love one would have sentimentality which is a mind set and not of the spiritual heart.

The uniform shows a sign of authority but only in so much as that man who is wearing it always has character. The Bible describes events as they actually occurred and is not anti-Semitic and hence European religions have taken it to mean just that anti-Semitism and so they have often brought death and misery to themselves and others because the Bible is pro-Israel and Jesus came as a Jewish man!

If Kerry was that intelligent, he would not be a Communist because Communists have no moral and intellectual character and being also that he is Jewish only goes to show that Marx and Trotsky have once again risen, at least in theory for now, and most of the National Democratic Party and their entourage of other Communists in that Party, which is indeed subversive to our own national way of life and is atheistic all the way. Lenin was always for this kind of diversity this wedge that separated people as to race, nationality, religion, power, avarice vs. benevolence, violence vs. peace, etc. He was for what one now sees in the Democratic Party since it adheres also to multiculturalism and has everyone at each other's throats so that the ones behind the scenes can take control and use the power that they usurp from the people with even their own knowledge because paralysis has occurred both in society and in government as to good vs. evil and hence they say there is no difference!

"What good would it do a man if he gained the entire world and lose his very soul?" In today's world or at least in America for some insane reason people think that this excitement with socialism shall fill them for all their mortal time and it just might be so but then again their life might be somewhat shortened and then the eternal spotlight would come on . . .

No matter if one had so much it still would not last him for an eternity even if he could take it along for that is forever and ever and who can say how long their own supply shall last and if one could which they cannot so hence all is lost for them in such a very short period of time called life. This or their life shall never ever be remembered by anybody no matter how famous they were here on earth if they did not know Messiah in their spiritual heart. The ones we know of now and are remembered is because GOD has not finished what is known as time or the mortality of man.

I also began to notice the great deception in America even amongst candidates that ran for political office and one thing that really caught my eye was the fact that political signs that denigrated a politician were actually bought and paid for by that same politician or candidate running for office. I also noticed that a certain news commentator continued to condemn Kerry too much and I began to doubt this man's sincerity as to what he said over the air. I felt that he was in fact for Kerry since he was Jewish and from San Francisco and really drew people to the point where they would get so frustrated with him that they would in turn vote for Kerry! He was a real con artist on the air and had everybody buffaloed with what he was saying about Kerry and how bad he was but I knew much better since I had heard of such stories from my mentor years ago and how it could affect the outcome. This Michael Savage was one of the best, though, I had ever seen and his ire was really perfected so that one would believe he was really against a fellow liberal Jew like himself, but did not want anyone to know since that would ruin the election for Kerry. A sucker is born every minute and in this election even Kerry would lie even when he looked one in the eye, which meant he was a sociopath and could lie and lie and would, just like Michael Savage did on the radio. What a way to try to win an election but such an old method that was used for many different Things years ago. They would do anything to win this so-called election because the socialists and Communists needed someone even worse then Bill Clinton and that was John Kerry a Marxist/Leninist Jew that would do anything and I mean anything to anyone just to gain the power or executive power one got with as President and Commander In Chief and would he be for Israel? Not on your life for he was against Messiah and His Kingdom that was to come.

Now the renegades that represented John Kerry were actually stealing the signs of the incumbent off of people's own lawns so that no one would look like they were supporting George W. Bush and this was even before this Communist had gotten into the White House which of course he still did not. This was the bottom of the barrel for both President and Vice President in order to destroy America's foundation with a trial lawyer and a Communist Jew billionaire and who knows he could always get another wife!

In our own neighborhood they were carrying signs and blocking a road with Kerry on them and no police escort. If we thought it was now bad with this Communist it would get much worse because the minorities were not that smart to know the difference between socialism and a democratic republic or why bother voting for a Communist unless one believed in that ideology and some said they did but did not really know what they were talking about because if they did they would know that they themselves would be the very first to go.

If Kerry won we would only have a state and not a spiritual nation and this would mean literally the end of America with a Communist billionaire and yes of course socialists were just that pure materialists. This is what they wanted to occur in America and the rich and well educated and Hollywood wanted it too because they too hated their own country even though they had made millions in it. This too was a dilemma to understand that someone who was successful, not for any real talent but because of capitalism's unrestrained usage with money and power and no anti-trust laws in effect. One could see, as my mentor had told me, when you see many blacks and other minorities then know for sure we have been sold out and qualifications did not count and that is why affirmative action and quotas were being used to instill people who were not too bright and not too moral but would take orders well or else!

People in positions of authority were not use to making decisions for themselves but did know their ideology is what they wanted to follow to the very end no matter what. They had convinced themselves to believe a lie over and over again and it showed by how they lived and what they believed and did not believe in, such as GOD and the GOD of Abraham, Isaac and Jacob and our Lord and Saviour Jesus Christ, Y'eshua Messiah. Our nation had one more chance to get rid of the Communist Party!

When I was much younger and in my twenties I thought about GOD but not in the sense that I needed Him in my heart, that is my spiritual heart which is not the physical heart but the one that GOD looks at to see if you are a child of His and the condition of it not that He does not know that. As I was saying, in younger days I did drink beer and wine and mixed drinks with a very few cigarettes, but it never really did anything for me except that it gave me nerve to talk to the girls since I myself was very shy and somewhat backward concerning the birds and the bees, as they like to say.

Each day I think I thought about GOD in some way but could not comprehend what GOD was all about since I had never read the Bible. Later I came to the Lord and gradually and ever so gradually I started to learn about Scripture and even today I am surprised to see how much I do not know about the Bible. In the Old Testament, for example, there were kings and there were judges where everybody did what they wanted to do just like today in America. Even our election had so many people voting for a Communist as President of the United States not once but now twice so there had to be some kind of spiritual deception since these folks were being deceived by the enemy.

How much more proof would it take to believe that this John Kerry was a Communist when he went to Paris with Jane Fonda to meet the Vietcong and condemned our soldiers in Vietnam for which he should have gotten a dishonorable discharge so he could not own any property. He got instead, because he was rich and well educated, the red carpet as in better red than dead treatment. He was another one that Hollywood and the media and the rich and well educated glamorized and this too was in defense of the terrorists One after the other in America and the American people still did not get it since they were either retired-or part of the 60's generation or the young who acted like savages. No one spent any time to follow at least how much America had fallen away from GOD and so they now would vote for a Communist, and what did that mean to them except that that was very bad but for what reason they did not know.

It kept getting worse and worse and the American people took on other cultures without even knowing it. It was like my mentor had said who was Russian Jewish that the American people were not that very bright and that was at least 25 years ago. Many people thought that he did not know what he was talking about but it was them who were behind the times as for the truth. Their spiritual eyes had been blinded by the enemy and they could not really see what it was or who it was they were voting for and thought that universal health care meant less visits to pay for in medicine and medical expenses but what it really meant was rationed health care so much so that if one needed surgery they would have to wait for months and if one needed important medicine they might not even be able to get it even if they had the money and this is where socialism came in because it had it's own priority as to who was to live and who was to die and euthanasia would be used on the senior citizens to get rid of them since they could not carry their weight and were getting government checks. The government was trying every way it could to get more revenue even if it meant selling drugs and by the way what was in Fort Knox?

People's property was being confiscated by the government when the elderly could not pay their taxes or heating bill or medical bills and so government was claiming or usurping what really was private property. With all this occurring the American people still did not get it and would not get it until it was too late and they had been warned plenty of times by people who lived under the totalitarianism role. One can lead a horse to water but they cannot make him drink it People kept hoarding money the ones that had it but that also would do no good if one was not into the one world government and its system.

People were buying condominiums which actually was a form of socialism in that a group of people owned one property and had to pay a percentage and also the fact that they owned no real land such as in acreage and that was the real estate that the government was trying to get their hands on more and more and the United States Supreme Court was socialism at it's best as an oligarchy which was when all would be ruled by a few and one could forget about the Congress because their hands were tied.

The President was the last position to get a hold of in order to control the military and once that occurred then all would be over for America's liberty. If a draft would be installed it would be by the one world government and guess who would be for that? None other than John Kerry, the world socialist in America but who did not represent our nation as a sovereign nation but only to be used as a tool to help the United Nations establish control over the entire Western Hemisphere.

Materialism made people even blinder to what was right before their very eyes and still they refused to listen to reason no matter who said it and no matter how truthful it was All they saw was that they were against the incumbent and for the underdog who was not really one but a part of the Internationale.

One could see now daily the Clinton Presidency homosexuals holding hands even of the high school age and so Clinton had done what they told him to do and did it quite well and also too sold out our nation to the highest bidder and that was Red China! America was sick indeed and nobody seemed to care and the male specie kept buying his pick-up trucks and the Hispanics their macho and insane lust for women all the time plus their arrogance when they could not have their way and that was all the time. They did not know how to compromise or even know what the word meant and the blacks were being made into living legends in Hollywood and in sports since they had come full circle in socialism and were worse off then when they were slaves because at least then they were close to GOD and did not have preachers lie in church about the Bible and which socialist to vote for time and again and the civil rights' socialists kept getting the oil from government for their continuous squeaky wheel!

Men did not really know what it meant to be a husband and a father and women did not know what it meant to be a wife and a mother and hence the entire scene in America was totally insane. Motherhood and fatherhood was dead and now the heads of government were already dead but did not know it and neither did the American people. They kept putting them back in time and again. The American people were emulating what they saw in Hollywood and in the foreigners who came here who were like fish out of water!

Our children and grandchildren we would not know since they were constantly bombarded by filth and garbage at home, at school and in the stores and on television and radio as well as magazines. Every where they went demons were attacking more and more and that was a sure indication of the end of the age just like when Jesus walked the earth and there were many people who were possessed and others who were schizophrenic from many evils and sins and hereditary sins I believe that went to the 3rd and 4th generation.

Hardly anyone really preached the Bible the way that Charles Spurgeon did and they only ignored the basic moral facts that were hitting them in the eye day after day and still would not preach on it. The attack by Satan was vicious indeed and still money was constantly being preached about and self esteem in the churches and now homosexuality which was a psychiatric disorder was being promoted like Sodom and Gomorrah and still people went to those very same churches and that denomination.

So one could now vote for either a Christian or a Commun-ist as President of these United States The incumbent was a Christian but his track record was proving to be not that good because he had not taken heed to follow the Word of GOD so we as fellow Christians now had to be on our knees praying for this Commander In Chief unless we wanted to see real disaster because people who were not Christians would surely be voting for the Communist and most not knowing and the rest well . . .

This incumbent had gotten into a war with the Moslems and had allowed our sovereignty to be jeopardized by the fact that he refused to protect our borders especially in the south but still had time to change his mind and do what was right for our nation and not worry about what others thought or whether or not he got re-elected. He had to do it now and if he delayed or waited too long then the American people would lose trust in him and he had to forget for whatever reason again what others wanted him to do including his advisors because who could tell if they were not socialists themselves. He had appointed individuals I felt because of their race and gender and not because of their qualifications and this in part also was his major problem. He had allowed women to rule over him and did not use his authority as President in the way that would have been more constructive. He allowed family and friends to interfere with his decisions which can never happen and he could not be decisive enough when the time proved to be important. There were things that he upheld that were very good but the main issues or the ones that the public saw were the things that were hurting him right now and, as I said, he needed to conform, not so much to public opinion for whatever that is worth, but to the fact that he had made a mistake and had to change or help change America's course before election day or he would make this race a lot closer then it should have ever been since the American people voted for the one that they kept hearing about from Hollywood the corrupt media that would sell out America and did not take an oath to uphold the United States Constitution. The American people were believing the lie that was daily spoken about over and over again and there was no free press and the wimpy conservatives had swallowed their tongues including Pat Buchanan who always had a lot to say but this time said nothing because he too did not want to become unpopular or lose his millions or forget about himself and for once serve his nation! This was the trouble that this President had. No one wanted to really serve their nation and had forgotten why they were there.

Why did the socialists in Hollywood and the rich and well educated and the media want embryonic stem cell research which meant that a human life had been formed already and to do this was to kill this unborn life? There was stem cell research without conception that could be used and was just as viable to help people with different diseases and illnesses as well as disabilities. Was there something even more devious than that these socialists had in mind such as Joseph Mengele, the Nazi physician had done so? One could say that the German mentality was again involved in this.

Would the Nazis ever give up on their idiocy about This superman mentality which was nothing more than the homosexual not being able to procreate so that test tube babies could be tested for and to see which would be the superior race and we all knew who that would be didn't we? With homosexuality anything was possible and nothing would stop these insane people from doing whatever they wanted to do since they were in control of what we called human birth and they called just a blob!

Who could have done what these homosexual Nazis had done in Nazi Germany that made one turn and look away and be able never to get use to what they saw at Auschwitz? Although to the Nazis all with this mental disorder it meant nothing and that is why they were so strange and so cold and also because the Germans per se were not that bright to begin with. They would continue until maybe even the Antichrist would come in some molecular form as such or even worse!

Planned Parenthood in America should have been done away with long ago, but there was capitalism, yes capitalism, that fed socialism and that is why to this day infanticide was not done away with at all! Avarice and convenience to have sex time and again and for others in government and doctors and hospitals to make money no matter what and no matter who they had to murder to do it like they had in Nazi. Germany.

The United States Supreme Court had done the most evil thing that man had ever thought of since it always involved little children who all wanted to live life just like we did but never were given the chance because America had turned its back on them and only thought about themselves! We went along with whatever our government did including murder and first degree murder with premeditation and no concern at all for the human being inside the womb no matter how much one showed them that this was a human being, but then again homosexuals in Nazi Germany also did the same.

James Garfield was a preacher as well as a president and 24 of 56 of the signers were preachers also. There are 60 million Evangelicals in America but only 15 million vote, which means 75% do not vote at all because most have been told that it is not Biblical. One should vote for the individual and not the party since all parties have an ideology and an individual has a particular point of view. Today in America many evangelicals who are born again and ones who read their Bible daily and go to church weekly. Roman Catholicism is not under any of this at all.

One can see that in many homes the husband or the son or sons in the family like to cook for their wives or families instead of the mothers and grandmothers and aunts! This in itself indicates that there is a spiritual vacuum. The German Reformation loves to sing and sing and do nothing as far as speaking out on the moral issues which Dostoyevsky mentioned in the 19th century. The Christian Russians have been telling us not to make the same mistake but it goes on deaf ears and the Russians are laughed at, but now a Catholic Jew and remember alone about Roman Catholicism let alone a Trotsky or Marx is now running who is a billionaire because the American Evangelicals refuse to participate at work, in their own homes with the own children, teenagers, adolescents, etc. and also are silent when it comes to who one should vote for and why.

Poland has had about 9 constitutions already and we have had only one even though a constitutional form of government tends to be mob rule. Only a monarch is a Biblical form of govern-ment! America I am afraid must also like Russia go through it to the very end before we all realize all we had was from GOD'S blessings and not because we were good because we never are. It is more important to be a good nation then a great nation because one is from GOD and one is of this world.

Rarely do we hear of sergeants and privates who have served in the Iraqi war but of the generals who actually are there to make a name for themselves the same as Russia had and that was incompetents. We have often heard that politics and religion do not mix, but see where now our country has gone because of this lie said over and over again just to avoid the truth of the matter time and again.

Do not let foreigners rule over you means that our own President has to be born here. The Bible is 4 times above any other source that our own country was founded on! The Bible never gets old and so called separation of church and state is another lie by the socialists in government. People vote $!

The underdog mentality kept on going and going and thought that this was all there was to go by. It did not matter because if one was poor they had to be decent and honest, right? This was our society and again, as in the 60's, this generation too was following that same line of thought. Be for the underdog each and every time no matter what. If it was in sports, politics, religion, government, education, etc. one had to be for the underdog! This incumbent too was for the underdog that is why his whole cabinet was so diversified because he thought that would too buy him votes, but guess what? John Kerry was for the underdog but for a different kind of underdog that wanted to destroy what America stood for and being a Roman Catholic Jew even sounded like an absurdity since materialism started and ended with both religion and ethnicity.

A Jew that even the blacks would vote for and also a Catholic which most blacks were not! That too was a hard one to figure out, but maybe not so hard if one thought about this underdog mentality being the fact that there had only been one Catholic President and no Jewish President at all and guess what neither religion was representative of our Founding Forefathers.

Who had invited Islam to America besides the oil people and the rich and well educated when America was only for one GOD and none other? As in the Old Testament the Israelites were not to mingle with the heathen cultures. The same was of America too! But now with this Islam we too had mingled with another false god that GOD had said to the Israelites not to do and for any other Christian nation to for it meant sharing GOD with another god which meant idol worship. "Thou shall have no other gods be fore Me." It could be no plainer than that. Yet we accepted this

Islam not necessarily as our faith but as part of our own nation/ What had Columbus tried to do? Was it not to find the variable winds that only the Moslems had known at that time since they did much piracy in the open ocean?

Our Founding Forefathers for sure made no mention of Islam let alone Roman Catholicism which never did any preaching on salvation or Bible reading for all those centuries and yet here we were being ruled almost entirely by these two foreign religions that knew nothing about Scripture at all and only sought to impose their will coercively upon other nations and did not want other nations to find their own GOD! This too was the underdog mentality because it meant that a minority would rule the majority even though we had no plebiscite in our nation as in Yugoslavia but the socialists were certainly trying hard to accomplish that since the Vatican took its money out of America and into not even Italy but the Vatican center in Rome and Islam of course to Mecca and Medina which was in Saudi Arabia. They were world religions that had nothing whatsoever to do with a personal GOD since they roamed all over the world and did not stay in one nation alone. GOD was a personal GOD even to a nation and that is why Russian Orthodoxy stayed in Russia for the most part and did not invade other nations to convert them to a national religion like Roman Catholicism!

America had gone too far with GOD and His patience and we had to wait not for the election but for His judgment since He was a just and fair GOD. We had done some of the most horrible things ever to be done in the world especially since the beginning of the 20th century. What we had done before that was negated, and now we had to face the music and yet not collaborate with the enemy in any way still not look for blessings but for judgment and discipline and yet respond as a discipline child would respond to a loving father. It was not that we were to repent and all would be well even though we had to repent as individuals and as a nation but the fact that judgment had to be meted out to our nation since we chose money over GOD time and again and were warned time and again. It was like the Old Testament king who thought that since GOD gave him more time to live that that had been a blessing but it was anything but. We had to be ready to accept whatever it was that GOD so chose to do and still be faithful as His children.

He was our Father and our Creator and His Son the head of the Church and this was the worldwide body of believers that were all over the world and not into religion but into Jesus. Religion could not save anyone, but only Jesus could. We had gotten religion mixed up with real faith which GOD gives to all His children and the, amount also is up to Him. We forgot to make Him first and not our nation and in affect created this sin problem since we felt like other nations had that we could do no wrong and if we did, so what? This was this underdog mentality again that posed as the minor thing in our own lives. It was not minor to GOD since it involved GOD Himself! We had to be American Biblicals and not of foreign religions because GOD would present Himself different to us as He had to all nations that He called to His side. We did not choose GOD, but He chose us.

Even though the American Jewish people were mostly non-believers we still had to love them as GOD'S chosen people and that did not mean we had to let them sin, but we had to remember that GOD sent His only Son to this earth as a Jewish man and not a Gentile man. The Jewish people were Christian in nature. To be anti-Semitic was a sin and every major religion Christian and non-Christian in the world was anti-Semitic and in no small part! This was where Satan went to work on the Gentiles time and again and when the church said it was Gentile there was something wrong since its roots were Jewish. Even though the Jewish people as a nation rejected Him, that did not mean that man could do what he wanted to do. What it did mean was GOD would do what He said He would do and the two, GOD and us, were not the same in this area because this was for GOD to decide when where, how, and why. We though had to remain true to His Son and yet not be anti-Semitic at all. We of course could correct the Jewish people if any Gentiles ever really had done that! They were here because GOD I believe wanted us never to forget what His Son had done for us at Calvary and through the Resurrection.

No one thing could ever replace Israel in GOD's eye but the Gentile world for the most part thought that GOD was done with the Jewish people, but there still was much more to go! They too as a people were His first sons and we had to always remember that no matter how bad things got to look.

The Jewish people were sometimes a very hard people to love, but nonetheless we had to do it through Messiah so that some would be saved even though GOD Himself knew who would be saved. This was the mystery of GOD. We were also blessed in America because we had taken the Jewish people into our land as strangers but treated for the most part like brothers even though most did not know of Messiah in their spiritual hearts, but that was why they were dispersed because of their disobedience to GOD and it was for GOD to choose what He wanted to do with them since there were only 17,000,000 usually in the world! Whenever the number got that high and that again showed that the enemy liked to do to the Jewish people since there would always be some kind of reminder for us that Jesus came as a Jewish Saviour and a Jewish man in the flesh.

Israel always had to remain our ally no matter what, or we too would be doomed for GOD would want us to help them as they through Christ helped the flesh, meaning a Jewish GOD in the flesh, but for all men for whom GOD so chose to be with Him when He called them! We were to be sincere with them and not play up to them because we felt we had something to gain financially. We had to protect them.

Hebrew has no swear or curse words in it. It is a GODLY language because Messiah was a Jewish GOD. There are 22 consonants in the Hebrew language, and it never really died out, meaning that GOD had not forgotten about His chosen people with His chosen language. Shem, a son of Noah is where the Semite people come from. The 5 Semitic languages are: Hebrew, Arabic, Aramaic, Akkadian and Ethiopic. The Greeks and Romans and European peoples got their languages from the Canaanites. The close identity to Hebrew can be seen in the Hebrew alef or "a", which is alpha in Greek; the Hebrew bet or "b" which is beta; the gimmel which is "g", the Greek gamma; dalet "d" for the Greek delta; and zayin "z" for the Greek zeta.

Hebrew was a living language until GOD exiled them to Babylon in 586 B.C. and it was replaced by Aramaic. This is the time of Daniel. Even Antiochus Epiphanes the Hanukkah story was when a pig was brought into the holy temple to desecrate it But Hebrew still survived. Alef is the first letter and bet is the second letter and tav is the final letter. The Hebrew alphabet is as follows: alef, bet, gimmel, dalet, hay, vav, zayin, chef, tet, yood, chaf/kaf, lamed, mem, nun, samech, ayin, fay/pay, tzadik, koof, reysh, sin/shin and tay. There are no vowels in the Hebrew alphabet. Each letter also has a numerical value, such as alef, bet=2, gimmel=3, etc.

The ancient symbol of the cross is not Gentile but Jewish. When the Puritans came to America in 1639 they saw their exodus from England as that of the Israelites leaving Egypt, the king of England as Pharaoh, the Atlantic Ocean as the Red Sea, and the New World as the Promised Land. The Indians they saw as the ancient Canaanites. The Puritans used the Biblical Law as the basis for all their legal codes.

The Hebrew Bible also played an important role in our own higher educational system which included Harvard, Yale, William and Mary, Princeton, Rutgers and Brown. The seal at Yale has an open book with the Hebrew Unim V'Timum on it. This was the breastplate of the high priest in Temple times. Dartmouth has El Shaddai or GOD Almighty in a triangle on its seal. Even some students gave their commencement speeches in Hebrew in the 16th and 17th centuries, and courses such as the Bible and Hebrew in college were required. The most fantastic thing was that even Hebrew was to be the official language of America at one time brought about by the Puritans and English was to be prohibited!

So one can now see how very important it is to treat the Hebrew with love and benevolence so that a people and a nation can be blessed with the goodness of GOD. We have a nation that had emulated the Old Testament and the New Testament and made the GOD of Abraham, Isaac and Jacob their GOD too because they knew that that was the only GOD except that the Irish brought Roman Catholicism here and the Germans brought the Reformation which both had anti-Semitism in them from the start!

Here is where I believe America went sour since Europe had always been anti-Semitic and America had not been at all. The English of England were always a problem for many nations, not just Israel, and of course Germany always had this homosexual and anti-Semitic belief somewhere in the warrior-like culture that sometimes appeared Asiatic as in India and its swastika and its New Age Nazism.

The Masons were first thought to be the Protoccols of the Elders of Zion which were false and then later the Masons were a furtive organization that chanted to Satan above the 33rd level and had cliques all through the American society and were too anti-Semitic. Again, the English of England and the Germans of Germany were up to no good as usual when it came to the Jewish people. They always wanted to usurp something or somebody like they did with Lenin when they sent him in a sealed train to Moscow so that the Russian peasant would suffer.

Remember the Hebrew language had no curse or swear words in it at all! What a wonderful revelation that is to know that Hebrew the language of Messiah was the only GODLY language. We are blessed to have the Jewish people in our land and must show them the way and not through Protestantism or Catholicism but through the Bible as to how rich their heritage really is and forget about the Gentile Christian religions that always got it wrong like the Crusades, the Spanish Inquisition, Constantine's Christian state, etc. GOD does not coerce one to believe in Him. It is free will, but GOD does call all His children unto Himself. His sheep hear His voice and they respond to Him. Many are called but few are chosen.

America was good because it was GODLY, and when it became great it became mundane! A nation does not have to be great, but it always has to be GODLY if it wants GOD'S best for itself all the time. That is why I believe many nations in Latin America have coupes and revolutions because of their anti-Semitism in Roman Catholicism and their language of "Christ killers" and not "salvation is of the Jews".

We have about 6,000,000 Jewish people in America and they make up only 2% of the population.

America had now married a violent man by the name of Islam, and he was a deadbeat dad! He would abuse others plus his own and hence we started a new family or tribe that subscribed to violence always first and was demonic in nature. We had left the GOD of our Founding Fathers and decided that this god would be better because it had oil money and much to give to an avarice and spoiled people that were so affluent that even a minor change in their life affected them to no end and that any kind of inconvenience such as having a baby was too much to handle so we decided to murder the child for profit and hence we embraced also another religion called Marxist/Leninism and its entourage of multiculturalism which was this diversity that the possessed Lenin preached time and again. Always find fault and never agree or trust anyone at any time no matter who they are for one must be one's own god in this world that is Satan's world even though they would deny that there was a Satan nonetheless there was and that was the truth of the entire situation.

If we love this world, then the love of GOD is not in us means if we choose this world's god, which is Satan then the truth is not in us. We are to enjoy what GOD has made for us and to be able to pray first for the ones in authority and then our own family and then ourselves and in that order. As I was saying before, the Jewish people of only 2% gave more than 98% of all the Gentiles in America, and no one even knew that because with the Jewish people it was not an advertisement.

If one had to win Kerry over, it might just be through a love that only GOD could give and that meant agapé love. Yet we still would not know for sure but only GOD would if he would respond to that. If he won the election and as President we had to pray, he did not abandon us or Israel as an ally, which the incumbent seemed to do when he called for a false and unBiblical Palestinian

State, which meant that a state was to be built on land that GOD had given to Abraham forever and ever, and this was no easy or short matter. This incumbent had to reverse his policies quickly in accordance with Israel and if he did not, then what would possibly occur for us here in America would be the very worst of the worse.

We had truly gotten the government we deserved and that was mob rule by a majority whether they voted or not because one election could never change America as to the way it use to be and we could only go forward and repent as a nation for our own horrible sins against man and humanity and now against Israel, which was GOD'S absolute will.

Now Sharon was in deep trouble because not only was he going against GOD but against his own people the Jews in Israel and needed bodyguards to protect him and was listening too much to what our own corrupt government was saying by pressuring him into doing what he should not be doing and that was to remove Jewish people from their promised land!

Our elections were a sad affair in most cases. Some of the candidates that were running were pro-life but wanted at the same time to give up our sovereignty because they were pro Hispanic and liked their women, so the flesh was stronger then the spirit even though the spirit was willing but the flesh was weak. So they voted for things that hurt the average American, such as English and how to make a living when Americans now were struggling to find a good paying job when they were exporting jobs to Mexico and other places in the world through the Republican Party's globalism of internationalism and the Democratic Party's black racism that put that above even the infantization of the unborn because nothing could ever outdo the racism within the Black Caucus and not even murder in the first degree and cold blooded at that and of course dead beat dads and their star athletes which was the pimpism that Stokely Carmichael and Malcolm X had believed in and now again the rich and well educated supported no not the female Negro mother but the black racism of the civil rights' socialists who had done absolutely nothing to support the Negro family, like Bill Cosby even said they should. But government had too much to lose in the election and money making process and it anyone disagreed they had to be prejudiced and no European could oppose this civil rights' socialism and the promotion of infanticide, euthanasia and homosexuality now that they were supporting through a Michael Jackson, a Dennis Rodman, a Little Richard, or any of the other NBA black athletes that were having sex, like Magic Johnson who had contracted the HIV virus because of infidelity, adultery, or abomination! They had to be protected right? All this was political correctness disguised in a black coat of civil rights' socialism and no politician would oppose it and come and call it for what it truly was and that was black racism with pimpism because that meant less money to be made off of collegiate and professional sports as well as the entertainment industry as well as the government program of black Angela Davis' communism that said all roads lead to the same end and that would be social justice and multiculturalism and so-called "equality" or better yet "equivalency" or all the cogs in the machinery are equal as Stalin so quoted himself many years ago. This was this class or race mentality from the left of the all encompassing group mentality that socialism, whether from Hitler or from Stalin's class warfare was still being pushed from government so that more socialism could be brought into our very daily lives all to please for the present time a small minority who had lost their moral conscience to vote Biblical for at one time in their lives and not the way that their race at the top told them to vote no matter how immoral those elites of the same race voted time and again and were themselves multi-millionaires who could care less if another minority child would be abused and in this case the worse child abuse called infanticide!

The underdog mentality was again being promoted by the rich and well educated to suck in the ones who had a white guilt trip of having too much but never really relinquishing any of what they owned in materialism themselves that is the rich and well educated minority elite! They would again continue to deceive and to lie to their very own and their very own because of race that blinded them would once again do what they had done so many times before done and that was become richer and richer while they murdered or helped murder their very own race of people in the womb and outside the womb by socialists' politicians. Socialism did not stop at the door of race, color or creed and outside was taking along many innocent children because the 60's generation did not want to own up to the fact that they were still in the wrong and still promoting evil to an uneducated class of people while they themselves were highly educated but all the more dangerous for it!

I had seen this abbreviation of words and organizations and many other things that also showed to one that socialism was growing amongst even the words we used time and again. Some of the abbreviations were as follows: the ACLU, the NBA, the CIA, the IRS, PBS, ABC, NBC, CNN, CBS, the WWF, the UN, the IRA, the NHL, the NFL, the FBI, the CIO and AFL, the NEA, the states of the United States (PA, MASS, etc.), etc. This was this socialization of words!

We had candidates that were homosexuals and supposedly pro-life. Ones that were racists, but for lower taxes. Ones that were divorced and deadbeat dads but were for non-profit charitable organizations, and the list went on and on as well as the diversity and contradictions as to the way they lived their lives daily.

America had lawyers in a corrupt government with the people themselves only concerned about.

Why was it that the American Jew could not, for the life of them, be able to pick their true allies and continuously picked what or who were out to destroy them? They even supported the same ideology that these Nazi Socialists supported and being that was so, the murders did not stop with 10 or 12 but continued into the millions and millions. That is how one knew for sure that this was an ideology because of its longevity. Take for example the Spanish Inquisition which was really the Roman Catholic church that murdered the Jews and here in the present with nothing having been changed the Jews apparently vote for another Catholic and a Jewish one at that for president of the United States. It totally made no sense that this was occurring, but nonetheless the Jews in America lost their smarts when it came to good vs. evil and Israel and Nazism. They just could not see the light and continued to support Nazi people as well as Nazi candidates because they believed that Nazis were only in the Republican Party and not one was ever in the Democratic Socialist Party because they also believed that the Nazis were to the right of center, whatever that meant, and the Communists were the to left of center. They had gotten the equation only half right and this was now into the new millennium. But when would they get educated and informed as to the truth about what Stalin and Hitler both were? Both were friends of each other and even signed a pact. One would suppose since the Republican Party to them represented Nazi Germany and the Democrat FDR represented the Democratic Party which meant Stalin, a Georgian, that meant that what was worse was the 6 million Jews that were murdered and the 7 million Gentiles also. The only thing, though, was that Stalin murdered 66,000,000 people that were not his own but were mainly Russians, and since the Russians had pogroms and the Pale of Settlement that meant it would be okay with them if the Russians, all of them, got just what they deserved! One could then say to those Jews today the very same thing since they too felt that Christians least the Evangelical got what they deserved but what had they done to the Jewish people in America that was bad?

The Jews started to think like the blacks in America where they voted by race and race alone no matter if the candidate was a Communist, a Nazi, for infanticide, for euthanasia, for homosexuality, etc., just so that their Jewish group mentality would be voted for no matter how evil it was and no matter how much it appeared to resemble, no emulate, the New Age Nazism that the homosexual Nazis promoted in Nazi Germany. They could not tell their friends from their enemies and hence they chose their enemies over their friends time and again. Talk about stiff necked!

The Biblically ignorant Catholics would be voting for another Catholic, but who was Jewish, but that would be a plus to their pocket book. That was the important thing about being a Catholic one had to have money and more of it or else they were a "poor" Catholic! I personally could not understand what the Jewish people had in common with the Catholics, but then again it was all about money! This is what drew the Jews to Catholicism and also the fact that one burned candles for the dead and one lighted lights for the dead and the ritualism was so much alike also because neither group ever read the entire Bible from Genesis to the Book of Revelation.

Where there was money there were Catholics more so with them then the Jewish people since they were much more charitable then the Catholics had ever been. They gave of their surplus both of them. Money also would marry into money to keep it all in the family. I had known pretty many" Samaritans that turned to Roman Catholicism because mainly I believe of materialism and ritualism. The real Jews though never mentioned anything about Roman Catholicism but did know that one had to be saved by grace and not good works and that too was a commonality between these groups and one which was very large and powerful and the other one that was small and very powerful.

The American Jew per se could not even mention any of the Old Testament Books in the Bible as well as the Roman Catholic who both felt this close affinity to materialism. It had absolutely nothing to do with GOD or the GOD of Abraham, Isaac and Jacob or the Messiah even though they kept Him hanging and the Jews kept Him away for now!

If this was not part of this one world system then I did not know what was! Who had launched the Crusades? Who promoted Libertarian theology in Latin America? Who had a Pope and not a high priest or King like in the Messiah? There were so many good qualities! It does speak of an antichrist with a small "a" that is already in the world that is the Bible does. This is not referring to the Antichrist that shall reign in the Tribulation period or the 70th Week of Daniel. Yes, the Jews certainly knew how to pick strange bedfellows when it was those same ideas that had caused so much anti-Semitism, but in America anti-Semitism was not as important as money and the flesh. The American Jew and the Roman Catholic were like the Book of Judges in the Old Testament.

Now that the arrogant civil right socialists did the same way as the Anglo-Saxons, it would be all right to promote not the Negro cause, but the Nazi racial purity but in the form of the black. Athletes of all kinds were appearing all over and many were criminals and their antics on the field emulated those very same routines one could see in Hollywood and elsewhere in the large inner cities and the language was brown shirt mentality to scare the hell out of anyone that did not belong to that race or was not coerced into that race even if they were white. A leopard cannot change its spots. The Nazis were at it again because both the blacks and the Germans had a coldness about them and a mean streak of vengeance and yet proclaimed as social Christians to be in the know and not at all bigoted as long as one did what they were told either by body language or forced integration however one looked at it. But one could now say the equal and superior rights had come to both the Nazis and the blacks that so chose to go that way and that was most of them. The Germans were noted for collusion and collaboration as well as going along with the winner time and again and that is why they did not surrender Hitler and went along with him to the end. And I thought the 2,000-year—old dynasty in Japan was bad meaning their emperor, but the Germans and the blacks in America had much commonality.

The Germans now wanted to belong because they were scared straight to do otherwise and their children likewise wanted to follow the leader no matter who that leader was. Why even some Catholics did not follow the Pope's rulings all the time!

Now we had another group of mixed people who had intermingled with the blacks for many centuries. They were the Hispanic group, and now it would be hard to tell which was which. If one made a mistake, feelings would be deeply hurt! Yet these two groups did not really get along that well, but only when it came to extracurricular activities! That was always beneficial to all participants. Our government from all sides endorsed it because it would be more political correctness for only some people can ever sin and well for the others . . . .

America looked now like a Third World nation with all the different languages and lack of communications between even close neighbors and the European foundation was crumbling day by day, but then again. Hispanic America and multiculturalism and diversity which meant that anyone anywhere who was from who knows where was indeed welcome, except of course the foreign Christian and the European.

Yes, who had invited Islam here to America a Christian nation? Was it Javitz and Ribicoff, or David Rockefeller of Exxon, or the Anglo-Saxons such as the Bushes, or World Bank and the IMF and their NAFTA? Or was it the government and our own United States Senators who had investments in oil in the millions of dollars? Someone or some organization had to have invited them here as well as abroad such as the Bechtel Corporation in Sandi Arabia where most of the terrorists that attacked America were from and now our own government was going there with our sons and daughters to protect what belonged to the rich and well educated at the expense of our soldiers' blood and death!

Also how had, like England, so many Moslems reached important positions like in major corporations, major colleges and now in major positions in government? Someone had to have wanted to sell out America to the highest bidder for avarice and lack of Christian faith since Islam was an ideology and, as I mentioned before, all ideologies never stop with their killings and went way beyond what even Dickens wrote about when an evil man stops and repents. With ideology such as Islam it continues and that is why in America the blacks were at 30% Moslems and still growing and were being rewarded for their treason against the Judeo-Christian faith and one could always count on the ancestry of the Jesuits and especially the Saxons who would do anything for anti-Semitism and own wellbeing no matter if it meant serving a false god. They did not hesitate to do what they had to do with no remorse even after 9/11 and made every kind of excuse for not opposing the religion of Islam and its followers who continued also to grow. They were leaving what kind of nation for our own children and grandchildren and could care less about them but just about self preservation as we had in Europe with the Soviets? We let them take country after country and did nothing to stop them as we had at the Yalta Conference. This time though we had gone too far and now our own liberty was at stake as well as the national soul of America, but our own motto became "eat, drink and be merry".

We had become a nation of ungratefulness since GOD had given us so much to be thankful for. We passed this onto our own children and they too were being afflicted with the same kind of disease known as socialism which was atheistic and materialistic. We wanted our cake and eat it too.

This ungratefulness had become a way of life and we felt that it was old to us and felt also that it was a blessing from GOD, heaven forbid. We had let the enemy deceive us into believing our own lies.

This is where this poisonous ideology had come into all of our own lives. We nurtured it from young till the present day and only when we would all experience something catastrophic would we then possibly know what it was that we had failed to do or had wrongly done and that was to lie and lie even more so. Islam, since it was invited, was such a huge sin for our own nation, and we meandered about like it was nothing to worry about and put bumper stickers on our own cars and said slogans that meant really nothing at all. We would not wake up to the fact that we had to now sacrifice probably our own lives in order to restore GOD into our own nation since we had failed to be vigilant. We had let bad go to the worse end of the spectrum and only thought about sports, materialism, sex, leisure, gluttony, etc.

Now we, like the Jews, had become our own enemies. The more we got the more we wanted and that for sure was not a very good thing! We ignored things or the reality of life and pretended only to know about the weather and our cruises and trips to get away from America, but where would we then go once that all would eventually stop? We had to constantly hear some kind of noise always to keep us from being alone and lonely. We would listen to the most horrible music if one could call it that and continued into the abyss that went down and down until we would eventually hit bottom. No one or nothing would let us not enjoy our sins and we could care less what was really happening in other parts of the world and now was here and ready to reap its havoc of destruction upon our entire nation. Our leaders who all were millionaires and billionaires were taking more and more on the road to socialism and its mass destruction of a society whether or not we had another 9/11 or not. We were destroying our very selves.

We had been warned time and again years ago and still refused to believe the truth but instead wanted to believe the lie and retire into oblivion as good blooded Americans! We had lacked the resolve and will to live and live an honorable life. We had also refused to obey with freewill a loving and patient GOD.

Everywhere that one went one could see this evil metastasize itself into a larger and larger monstrosity. We only shrugged our shoulders and this included the church and really did nothing to stop this evil but talk about prosperity and self esteem which had absolutely nothing to do with the Bible. On and on this went even into elementary schools and Hollywood never stopped and our government officials refused to do anything legally about it! The ones who had it too good wanted never to get old.

The paid liar was coming to our own town to speak about his candidacy for Vice President and would go on and on about the lies he just had to spread so that it would most likely corrupt even more people then they ever knew. Just as Fastenko had known Lenin personally he had quoted what Descartes had said and that was, "Question everything!" Now he did not really mean everything?

This ideology was spreading more and more. Some of these candidates would even cry even though they had so much cruelty in them. Susi had said, and especially with the German national trait, that cruelty was inexplicably linked to sentimentality!" This could only then mean that what was good for only one's family was what mattered, no matter how cruel they treated others, and they did treat others very cruelly no matter how hard they sobbed, almost like a cleansing of one's spirit if that could be possible with socialists of this kind!

This ideology was conforming or America was conforming more to its own type of socialism one that was somewhat different in method but nonetheless with the same end. It was also known that businessmen were not too bright for it did not take much brains to be a thief or scoundrel and have others such as Americans do the dirty work for yet even a Moslem at the top and that of course was this Germanic mentality and Catholic mentality of follow the leader no matter who he was just so that we knew which way to go and what to do at all times and so that we could live a life of ease and comfort.

The lie as I have said many times before was the whole so called foundation of socialism which in essence lead to its fruition if helped and allowed to spread lice cancer through the spiritual body of any one nation. It would create the underlying violence at first and then would come public violence since no longer could the lie do anything good or worthwhile and camouflage itself into chameleon not that socialism had ever had anything good about it, but yet the American people with all their so called education could not pick out truth from lie and not fiction because the lie was a sort of "truth" in that it was dead serious about death and murder itself It would never go back on its word that this death wish was what it wanted and the destruction of mankind which was diametrically opposed to what GOD had wanted for His people when he created Adam and Eve.

I had also thought about the Biblical numbers such as the number 3, 7, 12, 40 and so forth and so on. The Trinity had 3 personalities and there were the 12 tribes of Israel and Noah had 3 sons. It rained for 40 days and 40 nights, Jesus rose on the third day, a Biblical generation was 40 years, etc. Yes, numbers were important to GOD and the number 6 always meant incomplete! We even had 12 months in the year and our clocks were divided into twelves.

As this election got closer and closer Kerry was losing but just how desperate the rich and well educated had become with their lies in the newspapers and on televisions and in their make believe polls. They would do anything to win this election including murder if it came to that since we were dealing with Communist ideology that had enveloped the black people for at least the last 40 years!

On and on they too kept believing in the lie, and of course the Germans with their own not-too-bright mentality would go alone or in fact would create this atmosphere because they had someone else they could control and who was not educated into a democratic/republic but almost innately knew about tribal mentalities. This was one reason Lenin had kept his eye on them because race alone would prove to be so diverse since it could be readily seen and not one word had to be said to explain that some of us or all of us did look different from each other and our own human nature along with Leninism would make us have doubts and distrust for someone else who appeared to be different when in essence they were not, but just the appearance of this lie would make all the difference in the world if one came to believe it was what they thought to be the truth!

This was true diversity that worked hard to separate and instigate that human nature amongst men that said if one was this they had to be that! Here again was the lie that was promoted by these socialists because like Clinton. Kerry too would always be seen with people of a different color and this could only mean, since he was a billionaire and had no relations with these people, that if he looked the part then it would be what they wanted to see and then would lead one to the false conclusion that he was for this so-called "equality of all things" or this utopia which kept getting confused with individual effort and that all the cogs in the machinery would be equal, which meant that down below where the peons were they could fight it out amongst themselves while the billionaires had the easy road to revolution by staying outside this perimeter, but in the meantime the very ones who had created this animosity because it meant the more the merrier for them and their comrades here and elsewhere wherever Communism had a stronghold and it did have a stronghold especially in Moscow, Peking, Havana and in European lands as well as in America. The blacks were now playing their row as the Germans had wanted the brownshirts in Nazi Germany to do, and the Jews again would lead like Marx, Trotsky and Parvus had done to get the finances in order. This sort of was the line of protocol that was being followed, plus the fact that Islam would be used for all it was worth to achieve this one world government when the violence got so bad in the world that any normal person even would have to say, "We need someone to help us out of this quagmire in the world or else we shall not be here at all left on the face of the earth that long!" Oh, Satan was very good at emulating through ideologies and religions that preached violence through lies since he was the father of all lies and would want to be head of this one world government through one of his emissaries known as the Antichrist and the False Prophet which too would count to the number 3!

Nation against nation and tribe against tribe was now occurring in the world, plus the fact that now races were all getting involved in all of this to deflect from the fact that the enemy would use what he had to deceive all if he could and he could not since there were some believers on earth still. But to most, that is the unbelievers, they were already deceived. It was the believers he had to go after time and again as it says in the Bible as he had even done with Jesus though his own pride had deceived himself into believing that he could even get rid of Jesus if he died on the cross, but that was what had really doomed the enemy's fate once and for all. He had been judged but not as of now sentenced but he would be along with anyone else who refused the love of Jesus into their hearts by grace and grace alone and not by what one said or what one did. This gift could not be earned for all the money and power in the world.

Man's human nature wanted to believe this was a trick, of course with some help from the world and from the enemy himself! This gift was too good to be true to man since man did not think like GOD who gave up His only Son so that we might be able to spend eternity with Him and on this earth to not only spread the Gospel but help through the power of the Holy Spirit the way GOD wanted us to. This was not a game to be played as I had once mentioned to my wife and it was just as important to tell friends that if they were voting for Kerry they had to know that he was for the murdering of the unborn and whether or not she lost a friend did not really matter if she told the truth in love and if it was a friend chances are she would not lose them anyway since a friend is one you confide in most all the time.

The American people thought or may be they never thought, that the party was the solution to the problem but the party like all parties was the problem since all parties have an ideology and with that need one say more than that for with ideology came always the ends does justify the means. When had a majority ever known what the truth was and when had any election ever voted for the truth alone and not for ideology? If a politician was ever asked if he knew he was right and not right by might but knew that the majority of people were wrong in wanting him to support something would he still vote the way they wanted him to vote or would he vote according to his own conscience if it was moral and chances are no better yet he would vote what the majority wanted since a group is what gets one elected and the truth is not important just so the popularity contest is later won at the polls!

America had deceived itself into thinking like the English who thought that parliamentarianism had to represent what was good for the people no matter how wrong or evil it was! The Reichstag voted Hitler in from the Weimar Republic and the Italian Republic too came or had fallen from democracy and Chek's China into Mao's Communism eventually and of course Russia from a monarch to a democracy to totalitarianism and notice that it was not from a monarch to totalitarianism and of course the so-called monarchs amongst the Arabs and the Moslems was just a euphemism for dictatorship for whenever has Islam known about liberty and freedom from death and destruction and only about death to the infidels? If one goes back in history and looks at the Roman Catholic church which was always a pyramid then one would certainly know that this had nothing whatsoever to do with the Judeo-Christian faith because the Bible to a Catholic was an unheard of thing and was obsolete in the sense that it was never read and now with homosexuality they still kept their doors open to all when they should have been closed the same as the Mormons and the Jehovah Witnesses which also did not represent anything resembling the Biblical Christianity because that is why they tried so hard to parallel themselves so close to the Bible that it would deceive others that much easier, but with Communism there would be no deception because once they got control and had the religion of Marxist/Leninism then the rest would be child's play for them since one could fool so many than one could also continue to do as communism always did and that was destroy as it had already done and with socialism already in America millions upon millions of innocent lives. This was where the average criminal would differ from the one who had this religion of ideology that would not stop and did not stop in America since 1973 and where now we were going on into the root of evil itself and that was Communism where even Islam would have to bow or else! Islam though would have no problem with Communism since in Russia they had cooperated so much so that they even sent their children to the Komsomol but here in America would not send their children to the public school education system! Yes, for Islam it would be a blessing to live under the regime of Communism since Islam was innately socialistic.

All the politicians in America were either millionaires or billionaires or from the rich and well educated and that told one for sure that materialism or socialism was alive and well in America and that now with Communists running for office in so many different places that the American people had been dumbed down because they did not even recognize it when they saw it because they had really never lived under it themselves and so that is why this form of socialism took it out on the most innocent part of human society and that was the unborn for they could not speak nor remember!

Either destroy the young or brainwash them to believe that if one could get away with murder than all things had become legal and they too could do whatever they wanted to do with their own lives as well as others' lives. This is why Islam did what it did because no one ever questioned the fact that just maybe all the murdering in their own societies was evil, but since it had been done for centuries than the innate qualities of that very people would accept it as just another day in the life of a Moslem and would never assimilate or want to assimilate with the infidels since as I just said it was ingrained in them for centuries and centuries. This is also what made democracy so ludicrous a reason as to why we were even in Iraq but to the rich and well educated no matter how sincere they just did not get it at all!

Hollywood in America was more respected than even the Bible was and that meant that our own icons would be from the very pit of hell itself for whatever did Hollywood ever contribute to our own society that was ever wholesome besides its vaude-villian nonsense and its lackadaisical attitude towards work itself in the true sense of the word and the fact that these were not the brightest and hence is that not what Lenin himself had wanted all along?

Since they were rich and famous they had to be good, right? No one questioned though how they stole, or as some liked to think made their money or their so called living! This was the dilemma that the American people could not get over. Why was it so bad if what they were doing was almost the same thing that most Americans had done and believed in and that was this nothingness of Hollywood's materialistic socialism that really had no truth but all lies to it on and off the screen and yet was still making money since our own government had no morals or should I say the vast majority of Americans had no morals since it was the people who were our own government and if they did not care then who would care? This was more of that Anglo-Saxon mentality that did not even fit in with what true Americans actually felt and believed in and hence those in the minority now were what once were a majority even amongst unbelievers and that was crime and ideology does not pay because Thugs are thugs but the worse thug was one with an ideology which kept them from stopping their own evil and perpetuated it time and again. This is why millions and millions of people in the East had been murdered and were being murdered and now America itself had become an accomplice to that since it felt no kind of remorse for the Christians that were being murdered right now or when Lenin or Stalin had ruled!

The West was on a short road to destruction and our own nation had read the sign that said dead end but continued to travel on with no regard whatsoever for the future or for themselves. This was the thrill that socialism had given to the blacks this sort of high that went along with this at random or if you will do your own thing mentality! The pinnacle in American life had been reached and now we were descending down fast and faster and we as Americans were in this for the thrill of it but also for the end of what we knew as America whether or not we wanted to face up to that fact now or wait until it would be soon over.

Socialists on television were interviewing other socialists with nonsense questions that meant little or nothing to a Christian nation but had all to do with socialism and capitalism the biggest contributor to socialism that one could ever think of America was eating itself out of house and home and did not even know or care where the next item that they purchased was even coming from but just so that it would meet their needs, no, that it met their wants and desires at the price of other peoples' lives no matter how many. It was again the Yalta Conference but this time a democracy or a whole nation would and could be indicted and not just the English bluebloods!

Not one of the politicians would say deport the illegals en masse because they were too afraid of what might happen to the easy lifestyle and their lifetime job as a politician without ever having to work at all for a living. They also refused like scoundrels to say deport all the Moslems since they knew that special interest would not support them for re-election the next time and so the rich and well educated continued as before to control from the top and not from the bottom and the majority by the way did not know themselves where to find the truth so they left it in the hands of the ones they thought would give them a return plus interest on their money and morality had nothing to do with it and the churches were also silent for so long that they too did not know or did not want to know what the truth was and if they did they were not saying. "Is it not the rich who take you to court?"

Most of the people one would see either on television, in the newspapers, or on the sports' scene never ever had worked for an honest living or they would not have been chosen the spokes person for the rich and well educated. They always went so far and no further because life had been very good to them and why mess up a good thing. They too were following this ideology that was deadening. The asinine athletes, the Hollywood freaks, the scoundrel lawyer politicians, the media, and all the rest of the television interviews along with so many know nothing writers and journalists ever knew what it was really like to work for a real living with the hands and their backs and never ever knew what hard work in the field meant. They had all come by the easy road of so called education that taught one how to most evade of working for a living. These were the ones now supposedly leading our country but as to where they themselves did not know or could care less. Some of the pro-Hispanic American leaders had liked the women from that part of the world so their decision was based on sound reasoning, right?

Politicians always wanted to limit everyone else but themselves because of party ideology and this election was nothing more than a popularity contest to see who looked the best on television and not who the most moral candidate would bet That is why democracies never worked for the long haul and our own nation of America was once again proving just that. Lifetime politicians with law degrees and party ideology along with wealth and a good education would always get one elected. It had absolutely nothing to do with qualifications of the individual or the morals of that individual. Some candidates could never tell the truth about what they were really like, but one could usually tell if they really took the time to listen, but then again our very lives seemed to be consumed with nothing but politics so much, that the spiritual part of our lives became null and void! This is what a democracy had done to a people who were spoiled by never having a foreign enemy on their soil until now and by ignoring all there was about morality just so they could be left alone to live in peace and quiet!

The peace though that was coming would be anything but real peace and we as Americans played our little game of utopia and pretended that we had it so difficult and complained and moaned and groaned about everything including the weather since there was really nothing to complain about. None of our complaints involved the real issues of the day such as homosexuality, infanticide, euthanasia, illegals, corruption, pornography, drugs, avarice, gluttony, etc. It was always something that would not step on another person's foot. Keep the peace while 60,000,000 infants were already murdered in the womb and also say nothing or next to nothing that had any spiritual value but constantly talk about race and more race which meant the bogey man was coming! This indeed was chicken little since it took precedence even over children in the womb, but still they cried and cried like the Germans did and yet were so cruel that one had to suppose were they from the very same tribal mentality?

This cruelty with sentimentality was a Germanic trait but others soon learned to pick it up and so they became the spokesmen for this but could care less about the innocent since they too kept voting in the ones who were murdering the innocent. It was a little like being for slavery and yet not. If one was a slave then so be it, but if they happened not to be, then okay. They would defend the unborn but yet they would defend the dead. If one was against slavery as owned property, then one would think that one would be against slavery that prevailed and said she can do what she wants with her own body, but she already had done that when she had sexual intercourse, did she not? This was certainly a contradiction because it had nothing to do with morality but everything to do with revenge and self interest!

The Jews also were more concerned about the dead then the living because they too were for infanticide just like the Nazis but continued to vote just like they too had come from the same tribe as the Saxons! In memory of, but did that include the whole human race and ones that were not murdered but were going to be murdered? This was the insanity of it all! Do not help the living but help the dead? This kept the flame of hatred alive and gave them a reason to do what they wanted to do at random with no moral restraints to hold them back.

So, if I had gotten the politicians statement correct, it said that "it did not matter how many illegal people came into America because the American people could fund the bill, mind you, and not the politician, heaven forbid and that only certain people with an axe to grind against the rich and well educated were being given their opportunity to take it out on the American people themselves and take back what was rightly theirs through government decree?"

The upper echelon also said which included these politicians that Islam now would be recognized since the super rich could not make a deal with the Arabs over oil and wealth so that now they too could take over America financially and religiously since these politicians knew nothing about the GOD of the Bible? Also the fact that now that we no longer had a republic a full blown democracy would do the trick in the sense that the majority would always rule but in reality the minority of the rich and well educated would now rule. This is the type of people who were seeking political office and more and more of them were getting elected because America was sold out by their own perniciousness of evil and avarice and what is in it for me!

We had fallen so far that the horse and the pig could not be disguised as well as the different and diverse cultures that said all cultures were equal and just and so this equivalence known as equality was what was being promoted to the end and soon that might just appear not for the state but for the American spiritual end. We would have a new god to worship at the foot of Baal. Now the liberal Jews could have nothing to say about this since it did not contain the real holy GOD of Abraham, Isaac and Jacob and our Lord and Saviour Jesus Christ, Y'eshua Messiah!

Ideology would replace faith as it had done in Russia at the beginning of the 20th century and thanks to the Anglo-Saxons who wanted to win anyway they could this would satisfy them since they had accepted defeat at the hands of heathen cultures. What was good enough for them had to be good enough for us but little did most Americans care and know that they too would have to pay a dear price for such insane thoughts that lead only to pure reason and nothing from the spiritual heart.

GOD now would almost have to make His judgment no not on these foreign nations but first on America because He had given so much He expected then for us to do all we could do to spread His love.

The next major holiday on the American calendar was Halloween and many homes even a month earlier had begun in Christmas style fashion putting on their occult tapestry on the outside of their homes as well as on the inside of their homes. This was the day of Satan and Americans and most were ignorant to this, displayed their sort of Satanic tide that would offer up their own children to Satan himself along with other children just so they could be like the others and wanted it more for themselves than for their own children but nonetheless were introducing their own children to Satan on Satan's day when worship of him whether or not it was intentional meant that this was what had taken over now in America and especially with Islam and other heathen religions and cultures that brought doctrines of demons to the fore.

There was no harm to this at least that is what most of the American children were told and very young ones had already learned it was okay to worship Satan but not go to church to worship Jesus. Americans had been dumbed down and were like the peons that never learned how to read even though they did know how to read It was another celebration in the year that would bring more sinfulness at this time of the year and would mean a step farther away from GOD. It was more important to them to follow the crowd and this included the rich and well educated as well as some churches such as Roman Catholicism.

Many were following the spirit of the season and no one said what spirit that would exactly be? On and on went this type of insanity to offer up their own children to Baal. All that mattered was that they have a good time of it but then so would Satan and cohorts also have a good time of it in deceiving the majority of adults into believing this was all for fun and games and meant no harm, but whether or not they believed this was wrong and sinful and most all evil to participate in such an evil day . . .

The property taxes would never be rescinded because that meant that the confiscation of private property could never continue to occur when the government so chose to do this for whatever reasons or reason. To eliminate these taxes would mean it would be harder for our own government to make the land their own that is the state would make all the land their own just like socialism preached for centuries. With taxes in place the government could get revenues whenever it felt it had to and that meant watch out for the scoundrels who would do this for the sake of their own ideology.

After all they could not please all of the people but only a few such as the rich and well educated.

Real criminals today are living legends and can go scot-free without serving time whatsoever even if DNA convicts them as such. The non-criminal can only be released with DNA proving him innocent but as for the criminal he needs no DNA for he is almost always pardoned after his crime or he can serve his time when his sports' season is over! This is in defense of the terrorists such as the Moslems of 9/11 who have a friend in the National Democratic Socialist Party who wants them free so that socialism, either through Islam or Communism, can take over like it did in both Moscow and in Berlin. The Germanic tribe in both cases had something to . . . Paranoid? Hardly. We have O.J., Kobe, Jeffrey, and Ted just to name a few, and in fact the last two admitted to those crimes. One was murdered, one was executed, and the first two are still scot-free, or as some of us like to say. "free on bail ".

Hollywood is scared to death to incarcerate any Moslems now that they know that Osama had wanted to do away with them because of their filth and garbage that they spread all over the world! In America for the most part with people with the best paying jobs outside of government had this paranoid fear of losing their jobs so they never rocked the boat no matter what, but under socialism everybody must have a job or be employed so what was the worry? Socialism had saddled upon the back of capitalism so what was the worry?

Women, foreigners, homosexuals and affirmative action candidates all attain or are given high positions to attain the best jobs on the market just like the Masons are and the honest and bright male Europeans who must support their wives and children usually do not fair as well even though they are in the majority! Others in the work force at this level and some who were Christians could care less because they had been also taught to keep silent or else and to always be for the underdog no matter what!

How easy it is to persuade the American to be for the underdog. For some it is to go along with the winner for others it is false guilt! Also the more Americans show in helping or with a helping hand the more the underdogs resent them and that much more!

The billionaires today seemed most of all to be young, but then again maybe they were not billionaires in the true sense like J. Paul Getty since the price of a dollar was about 3 cents. This could be an ominous sign.

The super rich have already left their American home! Some have only a vacation spot here as of right now. The treasonous spirit of the college educated now in America was to serve other gods such as through Islam, infanticide, homosexuality, pedophilia, pornography, drugs, socialism or even Nazism! The work that was being done in America amounted to not very much conducive to an atmosphere of love and non-violence since most of it especially at the higher levels made them recipients of avarice and self preservation for without GOD as a determining factor nothing was at all worthwhile even though we in America thought so.

Children's clothing have no demand in the market so the price of children's clothing goes up and stays up. There are though some other reasons for this. Over 60,000,000 infanticides and still counting! The slave labor mentality from Red China where most of our clothing comes from. Most people either can not afford or are too self centered to spend that money for their very own children and plus the fact that the clothing line is multicultural or is of the 60's. This final factor was of course capitalism's constant feeding of socialism where in if the demand is great and the supply is somehow met the prices still go up and up!

I thought about the war in Iraq and knew that we ourselves were brutalizing not only our children but also our very own women by making and enticing them to go in the infantry and the Marines and also encouraging them into the masculine endeavors such as driving trucks, digging ditches, climbing poles, because most of the males were either at war, retired, were foreigners, or did women's jobs! The strange thing was that most butches did not do these jobs but held the higher paid jobs in society. We also were brutalizing our young men in the Marines, the Navy Seals, the Green Berets, the Rangers, etc. They teach them or brutalize them so much that they want to tear anything apart from the hostility and anger that is injected in them when they are done with their training and in some cultures the trait is already thereto begin with! They lose their compassion as human, beings, the above group, and become also so over ambitious that all their energy is given to one thing! Cruelty with sentimentality also occurs!

Another source of anger that was building up was in our very own Soviet style daycare where the children would become angry since they were deprived of the mother and being put in a group setting almost like the military and at such a vital young age. They then resent that and one can see that with deadbeat dads this already has occurred in the inner cities. It is a kibbutzim type of effect.

Now they are in our own backyard propagating whatever way they can lie and more lies about their new utopia of universal health care plus the Great Society and the New Deal, etc. when all around one can see moral decay and decadence. They would give us that is the people what they thought we must have just as someone would give or would inject into us a needle with cancer! This would rectify things quite quickly and a new dawn would begin where Clinton left off. "Free" handouts for all would participate or vote for their ideology and not them. One could forget about names and only party ideology would remain but most Americans could not decipher what this meant since the name Democrat was attached to it. The incumbent was more decent, but quite weak and did not have the chutzpah to be at this vital time one with much more assertiveness and hence took a back seat to an atheistic Jew who would spew out his venom upon a democratic/ republic. Natenson and Company were again up to their old tricks!

Our government had dementia and was senile and getting old at such a young age. The bag of goods was spoiled but no one on the outside could see that readily. This was the bottom of the barrel as only the true blue, no red, socialists knew how to pick as they had done with the homosexualist Clinton. Who was this "Jew" in disguise and why was he pretending to be one when he was really not? Even the criminal unincarcerated element was waiting to elect him so that they along with other thugs could dictate with an iron fist against the Judeo-Christian faith?

Possession was 9/10's of the law but Kerry wanted it all for his ideology that opposed liberty, but upheld totalitarianism as in Moscow and Peking. Paid liars or lawyers would work It all out in the end and for America spiritually this would be the end and suffering would incur not only now to the innocent and defenseless but to others who chose faith over fiction.

What thou now had would belong to thine. Confiscation of property, no more private, would occur almost overnight! How did this ideology appear to have that many followers though never near a majority but then again who needs a majority?

The blacks and not the Negroes were promised like the peasants in Russia many things but riots would occur and the judicial system would come to the fore as it had in the Dred Scott case years ago. Though with a Kerry lost this New Age of Nazism would have to wait another whole 4 years if GOD allowed it so to "validate "their entry!

Hillary/Kerry or vice versa would be the new ticket for the `new man". Create havoc and dissension for the next 4 years and anything could happen and would if the "red" necks had anything to say about it! A calm and peaceful society just would not do and already infanticide was doing violence! One needed violence and not necessarily war, unless it was a civil war! That would mean revolution but who would fight and control since Kerry and Clinton could not? Their uncalloused hands were not made for this, but the "brownshirts", now there was somebody you could count on.

Would some retain the traditional jobs and roles in society? Well the new worker would do what be could do best: nothing! The unions had taught them very well. The American worker had become anything but productive. A barren soil grows what?

One could almost tell who and what and why and how these "candidates" were supported by behind the scenes. One, money had to be gotten. Two, homosexuality had to be prevalent and made legal. Three, diplomacy would be double dealing as with the English as it always had been. Four, the Teutonics wanted a piece of the rock. Five, the military one had to control and the union and workers.

In our society the foreign bred ideology of racial socialism had its imprint from only one country that one could possibly think of, plus the fact that sexual perversion was prevalent. Ones who had nice quiet neighborhoods always needed a few more individuals or groups from the affirmative action crowd so that most American males were scared straight! They were seeking this quest for the uniform whether it was in law enforcement or the military but especially in the Navy. This was their so called brothel or harem haven with the quota agenda! It had the sterile atmosphere of Boston's school bussing. It was imposed by government decree and said all are of the same equality but meant to say equivalence and all the cogs in the machinery in slavery.

It would not be right not for Americans to assimilate although the others want to take over as soon as possible and start given their marching orders. This was the tail wagging the dog. Government Gestapos would be summoned to handle things quickly with affirmative action as in Nazi. Germany by outlawing any Judeo-Christians first from government jobs then later higher education. So many of one kind for another and you could all just get along! Your children would "blend" in! This was truly Hillary's "village". The rich and well educated would administrate as a bureaucracy from a distance at first and would be "qualified" by their position by the elites so much so that night flight would occur even during the day!

This was the Boston Tea Party once again with Kennedy-ism. It could not be by European nationality but only by race, foreign religions, or foreign ideologies not so foreign to all anymore. If one had roots they had to be pulled out first to make room for the weeds that would grow! What counted was that again all the cogs in the machinery would be equal in slavery. Most people were lead to believe that it was good always to help the underdog no matter if they smote the one cheek then turn to the other cheek and the other one . . .

Yes, government had plenty to offer through very persuasive means. Do strike back if you were hit though on the head first with a crow bar, but keep your arms down! Walk around any trouble that others might think that you were up to or were the cause of. Allow strangers into your home welcomed and unwelcomed or otherwise! Even if they stone you and attack your family, turn the other cheek! The police are there to serve and protect that is the politically correct! Oh, how uniforms draw a crowd, especially just to wear for show. It was like the neighborhood that always had an Irish cop on the beat or the Teutonic tribe with a uniform ready to brutalize but not defend his own neighborhood unless led to do so!

The time had come to come clean fully and admit yout total guilt by out qualifying and out working your underdog! It had nothing to do with "Where overseas were you born and raised?" This was the multicultural question!

So if one did not go along wit h the "law", however made but mostly instituted by ones in robes, then they could be tried for obstruction of justice and not telling on another soon enough! So there was both a time limit and impeding the authority thereof.

"But I had not known."

"Well, you should have made it your business to know!"

Guilty until proven innocent, but without reasonable doubt, and one knew what that meant if one knew anything about the l-a-w!

I remember one day my mentor, who had a store for a short time, had a robber come in and steal something. My good friend chased after him, and simultaneously an undercover detective comes walking up the outside steps to the store. My friend, seeing a badge on him and knowing his face, yelled "Stop him! He just stole from me!"

Detective: "What is your name?"

Friend: "Officer please, again stop him."

Detective: "If you don't give me your name right now I am going to arrest YOU!"

This was political correctness at its fullest and now today my mentor is dead after 5 muggings, and this detective is a warden in a prison! Just reward, right?

Much booty during and after the Russian Revolution went to not gay Paree', but to gay Berlin! Gold, foodstuffs, oil, etc. all went there sent by Lenin while the Russian peasants starved with famine because of socialism. "A deal is a deal after all, right?" Take one step forward and two steps backward.

Russians were eating their own children, and there was absolutely nothing to eat, but Vladimir promised the Teutonics would not strike a bargain of peace with the monarch but would strike a death blow to the Russian peasants! And all to the father of Communism! After all to deal with the devil himself was much better than to deal with a king. Those Russians were certainly barbaric especially those peasants! More Anglo-Saxon diplomacy. Harbingers as scalawags!

As my mentor use to say, "They were not smart enough to think this all up by themselves; somebody else had to be behind it!" I thought to myself that meant it had one head and many arms like an octopus. Only though 1 or 2 arms were strong the rest had nothing! But which 1 or 2 were they?

I remember when my own grandfather, who was a gang member had said, "Without the leader the gang is nothing, so always go after the leader." That then made me think again. That is what should have happened to Lenin and Clinton right from the start! Take the head off!

In the 50's there were adult male gangs whose turf consisted of certain areas and who after sometime either died, got arrested, killed, or just grew old and wiser, but then guess what happened in 1964 and a little before?

The mindset in America came from John Locke and Thomas More which was basically Anglo-Saxon. The Saxons always seemed to know what they want to do almost always in life from birth and well the English were versatile and quite smart with a sense of humor but were scoundrels when it came to a promise or the real sincere diplomacy or in their private lives! They had this veneer of genteel persuasion. Our educational system was basically for the non-creative and the legalistic Pharasaical Jew also. The creative mind was not prevalent in America and was given little room to flourish with the possible exception of Edgar Allan Poe. We had no creative writer as attested to by the greatest novelist of all time and that was Fyodor Dostoyevsky! Children who had pure creative GOD given talent were ignored for the most part and others with a different mindset such as the industrial revolution and brutality of modern machinery and technology were accentuated by education that did nothing to soothe the human being! America was very short on real music created by geniuses as well as in art and literature and not be cause like Russia where they had socialism yet Russia still had more talent in literature then any other single nation! Oh, we needed the educated and the rich to sell their over rehearsed and overused academics without any creativity. One can go over and over some things and get it right, but artists do not have a preconceived idea of what their finished "product" shall be. Hence certain nationalities fair well as op posed to others who have to master what is already done or set down before them!

With technology now this robotic mind tends to go to the Germanic tribe as well as the Jews, the Orientals, the blacks, and the British Isles and also the Indian tribe from India. Rote and repetition work quite affectively for some and for others it discourages. Creativity uses more of the spiritual heart than does the logical mindset. It has compassion not passion alone, care and not fear and love and not shove as to one's fellow human being. Ones who lack this usually appear sterile and stereotype and too efficient and use reason alone to decide issues of morality or what they appear morality is! This mundaneness in some cases is necessary but we loaded with too much of this type of mindset here in America and it tends to separate and not relate people. Mass production a German invention is robotics to the fullest as well as piece rate. Only the artist can portray whether in music, literature, or painting as to how GOD most likely Himself would have wanted us to experience it. If one goes further with this even our

English language is phonetic but not Chinese, which is look say, yet neither of those languages portrays the poetic beauty say of Italian not Sicilian. Beauty, though, cannot be destroyed ever in any way. Italian is almost sung out that is why I believe that opera is so conducive in that very language itself Spanish almost conveys as much too and not the Hispanic vernacular or jargon or slang that one often hears in America!

The language as such as to be smooth and almost rhythmic and not guttural when spoken. Of course the Jewish background lacks a lot here, especially in art since they were not allowed to draw, paint, carve, sculpt or even write with the intent of a graven image! Sometimes if one separates and differentiates as most Jews do then one can tend to become almost cynical and with that the mind pushes aside creativity for logistical thinking and reasoning.

America is logistical in our thinking since one can always see that our technology is in demand but shall not save us. And now more then ever it shows it and relationships play little if no part and loneliness even in a crowd. It is called to be alone. Many things in our own culture are divisive such as phones, computers, cars, televisions, radios, planes, etc. They take away from one any spirituality. Even infants should hear real classical music which soothes and comforts which all real music should do and not alarm and shock!

Also bi-national or tri-national, etc. people tend to be more receptive not to foreign ideas, but to the similarities that another nation may have if it is home based such as the Judeo-Christian faith. Some nationalities are very poor at choosing candidates in elections for example and the pure bred shows that almost always all the time! With this faith Judeo-Christianity there are hidden guidelines that originate from it such as compassion which means passion is separated or should be since they are not from the same root. One stems from the Adam in man more and the other from GOD that is in man's makeup since creation. "Let US make man. in OUR image. "There again is that relationship of One GOD in 3 persons as with an egg. The Father, the Son and the Holy Spirit. Also as father, mother and Holy Child!

Many times one can hear said, "We are what we eat" which in essence means what we put in our mouths is more important than what comes out and nothing could be further from the truth. The tongue is an uncontrollable weapon and it stems from the spiritual heart and whether or not it has been cleansed.

In America we had many non-profit organizations such as hospitals and some television ministries that called themselves that but too were really all businessmen organizations to make money or a profit which was never revealed and now this incumbent wanted to involve like Lenin the church with government but with government having all the say as a state so there would surely be a separation of church and state with the state controlling! One ministry that was truly a GODLY ministry was the Mercy Crisis Pregnancy Center that helped with young girls who became victims through deadbeat dads, our own government and even some of our own churches! This ministry never took any corrupt dollars from the so called non-profit United Way or any government funds so they were a Body of Christ ministry as opposed to an extension of the state! Kenneth Copeland and James Robeson both had businessmen enterprises and one could tell by the way they lived just like Dostoyevsky said they had like kings and queens while the poor lived in dire poverty as in London at Haymarket Square. This was this sales pitch over the air to make it look kosher to ones who were looking always for something for GOD to do for them and not them to do for GOD. We were so used to being spoon fed that we even got use to the churches spoon feeding us as if we could not think or do for others as well as our own families and always needed government to arbitrate family problems no matter how little they were.

The IRS which got its power from the Congress almost always agreed with whatever the present administration or bureaucracy went along with since their rules were so many that even their agents contradicted themselves as far as advice as how to fill out one's own income tax form, but then again that is the way that the lawyers wanted it so they could get more business on the side and the state could confiscate more private property and non-profit came to really mean actually more socialism to be spread around such as in health care with Medicare and Medicaid and other millions of dollars that each hospital got each year from the federal government budget that had to be spent before year's end or the funds would not be replenished. It was not to encourage any non profit agency to ever save any money and be in the black but to always be in the red and there again is that word!

It is like having an overdrawn checking and savings account and still be able to spend as much as you liked and the more you would spend the more that our socialistic government would give to you and to the efficient ones they would be penalized for having some left over after the fiscal year now that was being very liberal with of course other people's hard earned money called the federal income tax as well as property taxes. Who gave more to the underdog than the middle class who also now were getting a piece of the government action since 80% of all the American people got some form of government assistance. We were at full saturation as far as government being involved in everybody's life 24 hours a day, 7 days a week and 365 days a year!

Always in our back pocket so that they could usurp as all good lawyers do usurious amounts from us so that we thought it was a good buy by our own government. Yet we seemed more and more to have less moral freedom and more of a one kind of life which meant no private life, but just a public life! We nonetheless liked big brother to be able to take care of us too like it did the dead beat dads for years on end and now people who could not even speak English and were not Americans at all but only through the generosity of our own federal government handout program that the rich and well educated who made up all the politicians at that level had given so graciously to them without our even knowing about it let alone approving it by referendum on a ballot! This would be a secret ballot that no one knew about and never even remembered voting for at all no matter how many times we thought about it and a sort of public amnesia took over our very minds because to tell the truth there could be no memory if it never occurred now could it?

Everyday all one heard about was our government but nothing at all about GOD and so we had become idol worshippers because we loved Caesar before we loved GOD who had given us all our blessings and government was taking them all away yet were we not the democratic we the people of government? We only understood that as long as we could get along with whatever help there was then that was all that really mattered. We did not care whose mouth it came out of and it did come out of someone's mouth all the time.

Many black preachers opened the Bible but preached ideology since they encouraged their own congregations to vote always pro infanticide since most blacks voted the National Democratic Socialist Party way! One could not really say this publicly and not even the conservatives for the little that they were worth would mention it because most of them were Catholic! Yes money does talk but the talk is cheap because it has no honorable speech to it at all.

Lydia's house was the first Christian private home in Europe to meet as a church and she was well to do and sold fine linens and purple garments. Mostly women attended. Today again we see women more serious about their faith then men because most men are not good fathers and husbands.

Campaign contributions and votes are another object of concern since provisional ballots shall be accepted and military absentee ballots were almost considered not to be and one would contend that military of all people should have every say as to who should be President since with a Communist running their very lives would be in mortal danger. Votes from Iraq and Afghanistan should make it here; if not then wait till they do!

Rick Santorum defended our veterans but he also defended Specter's pro infanticide who was one for many years because of party ideology and Roman Catholicism, money! This is so much like Kerry, a Catholic with Jewish ancestry. Along with this campaign Mr. John McCain helped pass his bill to stop contribu-tions, but not for the super rich. Well what could be expected from one whose father and grandfather were both admirals? Another money-qualified U.S. Senator? This now has led to the Sandler family and Mr. Lewis, both billionaires, to support Kerry! It is heart warming to know they have what it takes to get elected and that is lots of money!

Americans in general have become dependent on government for the free lunch program but when moral issues arise they want privacy and heaven forbid if even one Congressman should propose GODLY morality! Never is murder a private issue. It is always a public issue unless socialism exists and in that society, then one's public and private life is the same! Ideology blends both as one and is atheistic.

One who continues to plea poverty and racism usually themselves are the main culprits through their own frustration or by discouragement from the enemy. They shed crocodile tears for lack of want or de sire but none ever for the need of an unborn child's life.

The incumbent does not have an opponent, but an enemy and if Bush turned around I believe Kerry if unseen would viciously attack him with a rock or a large stone. Remember a Communist believes in murder as a "moral "issue! This is good vs. evil and faith vs. ideology. One is to destroy the other no matter how weak to also destroy life and liberty. If the incumbent wins the next 4 years he shall see so many horrendous occurrences from Kerry and company. We have a Parvus and a Lenin who, by the way, was a terrible lawyer that is Lenin was! Edwards had attacked OB GYN's and one does not wonder as to the why since he hates babies in the womb and promotes infanticide and loves money the root of all evil and Pharasaical power!

Now that Arafat has been warned by GOD it is time for him to repent and come to Messiah before it is too late! Yes, he can know Messiah in his heart and be saved, but his end appears near now and GOD'S chosen shall not be harmed. Jerusalem GOD shall not render to anyone but Messiah a once Jewish man, but now even much much more!

I thought maybe we could get all the American Nazis into New England where Kennedyism and the Ivy League piranhas swim constantly.

In regard to Hollywood's home for American Communists we could even pay for them to leave America and enjoy more fun in the sun in Havana or if they like skiing in Moscow or better yet Chinese Red food in Peking for a one way ticket. After all, Alec Baldwin promised to leave America if Bush won the election for President, and it makes no sense for a whole government to move when just one man and his friends could do that much easier. Why even Steven Spielberg paid a visit to Castro's sunny Cuba! Maybe Havana will have another Tito who is independent!

The Achilles Heel to Islam is to be without and to also remove oneself from within. In other words deport all Moslems including American blacks and bring our soldiers back now and help support only Israel and deport the Moslems on the West Bank and the Gaza Strip to Jordan where they always belonged. We shall as American taxpayers even pay for them to relocate and give money to build houses for them as well as an infrastructure. Now that is allied support to Israel and charity to ones in dire need. Let us also work with the Mossad and our CIA and no longer recognize Havana, Moscow or Peking any longer since they are Communist regimes and do not represent their people at all! Though China has already allowed 3 million Bibles in their schools, but one must know what kind of Bible? Where is a Reagan now again when we need him and no panda dolls or ping pong teams from the U.S.?

Let us also drill for oil in Alaska and the Arabs can kill each other like before and eventually lose the status quo in the industrialized world as well as the World Bank and the IMF which is the culprit in this affair!

Years ago there were blackouts in New York City and now in some of the Eastern states but really were tests to see how orderly or disorderly or chaotic or calm Americans would respond or react.

Again Communist Clinton is interfering, and now since he is out of office he should be tried for treason, not for his administration but for his nice visit to the Politburo in the Kremlin in 1973 and Kerry and his visit in the same year, what a coincidence to Paris with Hanoi Jane to agree with the Vietcong and degrade and name call our own soldiers sent there and in some cases by force by our own government who was in bed with the Communists themselves! Both should be tried and given the death penalty if found guilty and I am quite certain they would be for treason to their own country in the right tribunal or even the U.S. Supreme Court and just the publicity would help stem the tide of Communism in America! They both now are civilians now what is the wait? Of course I forgot the Supreme Court has to pass that law, right? Then too we would also have to indict Blackmun if he was here and others who help orchestrate murder of unborn children and to euthanize the elderly and the disabled!

Should pensions for government employees be paid for by taxpayers or the party? The party should pay all fringe benefits since it is not free enterprise and consist all of party ideology! No more free hand outs or free lunches here and pork barreling also. Use the Internet now for mail delivery since there is no real privacy in one's own life even though one does sign many facade type forms against an invasion of one's privacy. It is coming anyway, so why not save time and a waste of more money!

Will the Gentiles, which include the Pope, the Arabs, the Moslems, America, Europe, etc. ever get Jerusalem? I really doubt it since Jerusalem is where GOD'S SON, THE MESSIAH, was crowned with a crown of thorns! This is GOD'S absolute will!

Now that the NEA has destroyed our educational system, we should close down many public schools since most of them teach socialism and lies to our students everyday and that is why so many now would vote for a real Communist in America and it is worse now than when Clinton came in office since he got only 22% of the popular vote that voted.

We have allowed ourselves the liberty of being too naive' and so with that comes the lie that we are still a free nation when not all the people in this nation are not allowed to live or even see the light of day. Who shall say that America shall not be judged by GOD since GOD is righteous and just?

This probable first new lady was born in Mozambique and calls herself an African American, and should one be surprised as with Kerry himself? The most liberal male Jewish mindset but then again his first lady? Was he born here, since he is of a foreign ideology? He appears as one does as if his surroundings were surreal and as if he was voting in the Politburo. Then again, maybe he thinks . . .

Maybe in a few years America would just have the state. The growth life was dead and GOD needed repentance more than revival from the silent Christians and not the ones that were murdered. Even our own leader lacked the courage to withstand the barrage of unGODLY and GOD forsaken heathenism. Americans had become a people of groups with the worse group being NAMBLA. No embarrassment at least for the Anglo-Saxons or the civil rights' socialists as well as the main stream Jews.

This candidate lacked the intestinal fortitude and this was the only one of 2 candidates that a normal person could possibly vote for. Unless, yes, unless one did not compromise himself and did . . .

Voting for the other one was like not voting at all for America. It was another Mr. Bronstein! Should one really vote? Was utopia possible?

Nothing could reverse America's role as it was already part of Tarshish. We were part of the European Market which meant the Antichrist would control us for sure while the rest of the world for the most part would do battle since famines and starvation were manmade prevalent. Our own perniciousness of reprobate minds was already producing its by product of degeneracy. (Romans 1).

America had no language our money was changing and most of all our god had changed. Our churches if one could call them that, thought that GOD was concerned about what we always wanted and needed to the point of obsession and avarice, but we had already gotten things like Pharaoh had gotten and more was coming. We even had a plague of a special kind and it was spreading. It had the constant abomination of sin involved in it.

Was it "give me liberty or give me death" or was it just now death and a silence on liberty for all who GOD had chosen to live? Families were enemies within their own household and had become cold and only the love of money as an issue to help soothe things over. The ulterior motive was wealth and power, fame and fortune to the tune of total insanity!

But who would plead insanity when it would be insane not to love more and more money and what it could buy? The ones that were abnormal were the poor. They had to be eliminated or ignored by the millions and probably become non-existent. Only the strong would survive and survive they would but only more and more would be demanded from them until they became blasphemous criminals against Messiah though their numbers too were decreasing and mortality exceeded birth by far. This earth did not have enough room for so many billions!

Another holocaust would occur and was now occurring in non-Western industrialized nations who had to eat their own. Human flesh was their next meal!

Americans had totally become oblivious to the "angelic" dangers around them and only saw in the flesh that is only saw materialism that always appeared brand new. The extremes were occurring now and "so what" was the mental response and others felt good about their Christianity and that was all. Lethargic as to real prayer, sacrifice, doing without, sharing, caring, giving the last of and most of all pence to help the destitute where one already was.

These demons were multiplying daily more and more until nothing appeared normal or safe. People were getting strange sicknesses of all ages and medications just about everyone was taken and consciences were seared, minds were reprobate yet new buildings and cars and strange clothing as well as other waste or store merchandise was being sold for no real good reason or purpose. People ate any kind of edible processed food and obesity was from gluttony and previous generations like the 60's.

America's hope was in America and not Almighty GOD Himself Our children we leased out to any one at anytime and mothers and fathers were foster care guardians! Children went from one so called "village" to another so they never really got to know their parents at all. The state was the authority figure and if the law said "Do this and not that" then they followed the law. Right and wrong were perceived since infancy so the personality could not change and their lives were not really their own but group thought yet they thought they were an individual, but were all ideology.

Hospitals became as supermarkets with customers in and out constantly for the most unusual reasons one could ever imagine and some were for major surgery and were out the next shopping day! People had no relationships and it was more like gangs and tribes and comradeship but never like a family the institution that GOD created with Adam and Eve.

There was so much talent in America that one had to work in the woods to get away from it! Music was hardly ever heard anywhere. Also art and literature could only usually be seen in old museums and then one had to watch out for pornography! Our writers or journalists and reporters who wrote all our books were good stenographers for the ideology. They would write as quickly as they could for tomorrow's edition, but it was always harder to remember when something never came out sounding the same, or in other words it was a bold faced lie! They would conform these journalists and media would teach through the owners of the newspapers and publishing houses. There was so many hellish works of art that their appearance would spell profanity in one's mind with automatically a four letter word or worse! Picasso they would put to shame with his one eyed wife!

Sex was doing, being, having, wanting, showing, destroying, anywhere at anytime with anyone or any thing. The mind was normal considering no thoughts resonated any kind of decent and wholesomeness. It was abnormal though if one thought about higher things. The ones who were criminals were the strange ones who would not work on a Sabbath, or use profanity nor steal words in the sense of lying! These were the ones who had to be constantly watched if they ever got into the public eye so hence they rarely did!

The criminals in the courtroom were the ones at the far end of the room who sat much higher than anyone else. Bibles were not sworn upon, but a New Age Testament that replicated a god was used instead. If one would only just keep quiet and die peacefully and also very quietly then politically correct justice could be justly served fast and swiftly. The churches were harems of Sodomy and entertainment halls for gambling and other perverse things. The schools were hatcheries for cracked eggs! What were the courts for if not to prosecute those who could not speak, walk, talk or sometimes would even scream if they got the chance which did indicate something that was hardly intelligible, such as a . . . Yes, many voices were drowned or even strangled or left to be alone until the noise would eventually stop. Sometimes even covers and towels would be used to silence this awful noise that one could hear! Why would this thing not just die quietly? Sometimes hospital linen was the best to use. After all one should go quietly and quickly and without a sound if possible by all means! The noise that some will make just to annoy and bother others and even sometimes for only a minute or two!

There were a cast of millions of ants, but not a majority by far who had this wonderful ideology that had instructed man how to murder more efficiently and by the millions only and not the thousands alone. A few of these head red ants were at the very top of the bill with no brains whatsoever, just the way Lenin had said he wanted it but then again he was referring to himself because he was a failure for a lawyer! And as far as trust, one could completely forget about that! But then again if one cannot trust a comrade in arms then who could they trust besides ideology itself but perhaps the devil himself? Could I trust even myself knowing that later in life I too could come up on charges for failing the party ideology and that was only the one party and no more than one! Maybe this party would retain me as one of their true and loyal ones for all of eternity or at least for this life? No one ever really dies but they get transported . . .

If one did not go along with the crowd or even old friends, then one was considered an outcast since one did not conform to what Hollywood felt was just and right! They were the tribal trend—setters and most all Americans wanted to be in with this in crowd. It took no brains again Lenin to become a member and no responsibility to hold any type of position just the willingness to be told what one was told and do it without any questions asked!

There was no one generation now as a majority that even had the faintest idea of what life was all about and one could see the old imitating the young no matter how it looked or how vulgar it was. This was the cart before the horse. A follow the leader type mentality that would be just fine for most Americans even though they said they believed there was a GOD, but so did Satan believe that!

There had to be more to life then just what one could see, but for now that was not so important since one had to live for all the gusto no matter what another one would say when giving good advice.

Vanity too was a disease with all men since most men saw only beauty on the outside and this was a pretty package with nothing in it! Inner beauty is what GOD looked for in man, so why did we do otherwise? Solomon did say, "Vanity of all vanities" which to me meant everything to man's senses was vanity and sin since Solomon had left his faith to go with strange and foreign women.

Why does America have this Western mindset that says it is always just the leader or dictator that has committed all this evil whether it be Hitler, Osama, Stalin, Clinton, Kerry, Mussolini, etc? There had to be followers that also must take the full responsibility no matter how enticing the evil was and their ideology that they chose to follow no matter how it attracted them. There must always be accountability for those evil actions! We like to take short cuts or short circuited thoughts, as Dostoyevsky used to like to call it, by being prejudiced against any people, and prejudice's connotation does not mean that it has to be, for example, the white race against. the black race. In fact today the opposite is true that the darker raced people have an arrogant attitude because our own government and the rich and well educated have taught that your enemy is one who looks different than you when really it is usually the ones behind the scenes that control a society by wealth and power and very few know their name or names!

We must, though in a democracy, even though it is mob rule to be accountable as well as in a totalitarian society also since in each society it is made up of individuals one by one. We cannot forget that sin is contagious and some have more trials and tribulations but nonetheless someone always has it harder than we do and we must keep reminding ourselves of this since we all tend to see another fall. We enjoy other people's misery; hence this is our human nature and it is wrong, and that is why everyone needs grace. Who can say they did it all alone even if no one else was there in the physical sense? No man is an island which also means that GOD is there always everywhere.

We must indict ourselves for example in America for all the infanticides even though we might have opposed them. We did not shed blood like Jesus did and with no sin so we shall not be able to blame one in our society over another, but we can repent and turn around and come to Jesus' grace. Many would say Hitler was a monster and in doing such a thing they once again set up for another person or persons to commit evil since others will follow always. Hitler must be made accountable for what he did as chancellor even though he was elected by the Reichstag a democracy, but we cannot exonerate him by saying he was a monster because he was a person who had what we had, sin! In war sometimes we do not see who we kill but nonetheless we do take a life which is no pleasure but in war we must oppose the lie that is violence by some of us fighting as soldiers to uphold the truth and to always protect the innocent. Yes Hitler was not a monster since he was a man like we are and must be held accountable for what he did for if we do otherwise we allow him and others like him to become excused for what they did by claiming monsterhood as a way almost of a legend which also is very dangerous. He was an evil man yes, but he was nonetheless a man who again must be held accountable as such and not as some only one who could have ever committed such a heinous crime since anyone of us could in essence commit sins as such and for most people this also is hard to believe but that is why there is grace for those who do repent such as Jeffrey Dahmer who became a Christian before he was murdered in prison. Yes, he was forgiven by a loving GOD for what Jesus had done on the cross at Calvary and it was by grace alone or undeserved or unmerited favor.

Now if we prejudice ourselves in such a way that we protect our own or our own background or nationality or even race or creed than we too tail to see the harm that we too can possibly fall into since we refuse in essence to forgive in the sense that a people or a group of people who did evil things must be made legally accountable, but with jurisprudence according to Scripture and not to our whim and any other way we find to our liking or even misinterpretation which is many times done. For example Justice Blackmun a Jew only by birth had written the majority of Roe vs. Wade and now about 60,000,000 unborn beautiful and breathing babies have been murdered like happened in Nazi Germany but on a much larger scale here and yet this Jew by birth did exactly what the Nazis did to Jewish women and had been even done by Martin Luther himself. See how far any one of us can take sin when we without always realizing it want to hate the way we want to hate and then in essence invariably do the same that was done and hence are as much a criminal or even more since this ideology makes one kill or murder in the millions and we can talk in the nation about millions. Also take Ira Glasser or Nadine Strossen both of the ACLU which is a Communist organization founded by a Communist and yet they say they are libertarian which in and of itself is also meant to say there should be no restrictions on man's freedoms which means that anarchy and chaos shall form and of course the people shall always choose totalitarianism over anarchy and chaos since some group shall be spared and at random murder could strike and man would eventually eat man as a cannibal so again we have the law or the 10 Commandments and not 10 suggestions to follow and who but these 3 Jews now supplant their own will and evil ideology and the same kind that Hitler had for them because of homosexuality and for them the issue or retribution to our own nation no, matter how much we were involved or disagreed vehemently and with just cause since their ideology is the very same that they say they oppose and so hence they lie and lie and violence like Hitler and others again is allowed to now grow in America and has been growing and using the excuse because I am a Jew shall not do it! We do not hate them, but it is their ideology that must surely go. Also we cannot be silent and nothing should be personal, but only if they have contributed to murder and they have then must we seek prosecution against them and bring them to trial no matter how long ago it occurred since no one's life quite that long that everyone shall forget the horror and that accountability is there always. even though most people say, "Do not bring up the past", but we must bring up the past, especially if they are still alive and well and be brought to justice or what was all the Nuremberg trials about if not to get the criminal and not monster, to repent and say if possible I am sorry and have done evil and then pronounce the sentence. Yes, some of the judges were Soviet judges but does that mean that since we too have those Soviet judges here that we should not prosecute them and let them judge as they had done at the Nuremburg trials?

Today murder is relegated to the back room of if no one knows who should care and if they do then so what it does not affect you. But it does affect all of us since we also become more brutal and cold and accomplices in the sense that we do nothing at all! It is man who must bring his fellow man to trial and only then can one really talk about justice and liberty for all and since Mr. Glasser and Mr. Blackmun have mostly caused the murder of the poor and people of different colors then what can we call them but what we also called Hitler and his followers and that is Nazis!

One cannot excuse oneself from the arena of life by claiming the status quo of today or the political correctness of this hour for to do so would again be to do not what history would repeat but what man would repeat since history is created by man himself Something that cannot be proven is usually a theory but if it continues as such then it is relegated to be false, but even proven beyond a shadow of a doubt that it is no longer a theory than it is in fact the truth of the issue and like faith which is not seen it though works with a real and living GOD!

Yes, monsters are for the play world and not for men, so let us not excuse for one time ones who would dare almost glorify these ones into some sort of gods that either were superior or did not know better and again exonerate them from the evil deeds! We now see in our very own nation criminals and not monsters.

All were born unsaved and hence which means that all people without grace go to Hell and then the burning lake of fire there is no redemption for man to get into heaven at all. Bur the Father and only the FATHER has provided a way into His presence in heaven. Of course Adam did not have to die and Jesus GOD in the flesh was perfect)being GOD Himself and small children before the age of accountability are the only 3 exceptions. Adam sinned so he was then ruled out because he was born in innocence, but not perfect before sin. That would leave only 2 other ones that would not die and as I said before they are Messiah and children before the age of accountability where free will is not really understood in regards to salvation and the ability to know who Jesus was and why He did what He did! As Charles Spurgeon had said if it would not be for many infant mortalities there would be in his day not many people in heaven because man himself cannot accept or learn to accept a gift of love from GOD with no strings attached.

It is so very vital that a child know that salvation is theirs at an early age, but not too early since they shall only at this age of accountability that there is a heaven and a Hell and that one is going to one of 2 places and both are a choice if the Gospel is preached in a Biblical way and not by any type of denomination or religion that says otherwise! It is GOD'S Word that tells us how this is done with no exceptions and life is too short to debate if GOD tells that truth which He always does or if the world, the enemy, or man does which is never with GOD'S blessing. "Teach a child in . . . "

We are at about the end of the 6th millennium and/or millennia being in the plural Latin gender. We as man have come only 6,000 years and now the 7 millennium is soon to occur when the Father says it is to occur only. How many have missed heaven and the rewards on earth in doing GOD'S real will in whatever endeavors that He has given any of us here now and in this present state of mortality? They say talk is cheap, but that is not so if the spiritual heart is converted by GOD, but free will must occur which GOD has allowed us to have all of us and we must through His calling hear His voice and become His sheep knowing that "If one shall confess with thy mouth and believeth in one's heart you shall be saved", and this is from Romans 10:9-10. There is also another well used Scripture and that is John 3:3-7 which speaks about Nicodemus a Jewish Pharisee who is being told by Jesus Himself about being born again and Nicodemus does not understand because the Law or the Book of Leviticus is what he only knows and now at night hiding from the Jewish authorities he ask the very One who can only make it possible about this being born again of the spirit to GOD Himself in the flesh! Tradition had kept Nicodemus from before that from understanding what Jesus could possibly mean so Jesus the Teacher tells him that this is the only way to come into contact with the Father since the Father can not come into contact with sin. The bridge that connects man to Him is through Messiah or Jesus and there again is no other way to cross that bridge without Jesus because He carries us from mortal death into heaven for eternity because of what He did according to the Father's will and this yes is the same Father spoken about in the Old Testament time and again and who all the saints then bowed down to but had to wait for the Son or the Messiah to come!

"If you have seen Me you have seen the Father I and the Father are One ". The message is not meant to harm or even scare but to convey to man that he must have a remission for his sins and since man is born in sin from Adam's fall there is no way to absolve this sin except by the shed blood of Messiah at Calvary and His resurrection onto life and Jesus too chose for His life-was not taken to do what He did for those who would be in His family for eternity.

Now with the elections in this year of 2004 one can see a total disregard for GOD'S holy Word and one would have to now seriously ask oneself," How long now Jesus until the end or until America is no longer under your guidance or protection and we have in fact endorsed the lie time and again and since that is so Satan who is the father of all lies has taken us where we should not want to go as a nation.

Lois Murphy for instance in our Congressional District is for Sodom and Gomorrah and possibly worse since she believes that homosexuality has marriage in it and that homosexuality is actually a form of healthy and clean sex and assume that embryonic stem cell research shall bring the new man. The New Age organization the Sierra Club supports her and so does the governor that repealed the motorcycle helmet law, which it and of itself was just insane and also the media supports this woman who might even argue that point since somehow she must believe that two of the same sex can in a normal way procreate? This is the end of the road for America when a government official is allowed to reach that high a level and still be heard as well as supported by many who Satan owns to himself and he has blinded them. Even Adam and Eve had children and procreated or else where would man have gotten? This is one way that the enemy can work in our very lives when we have chosen to turn our lives over to him for whatever reason and whether it be intentional or unintentional. With her opponent Jim Gerlach too is not a Founding Forefather since he upholds multiculturalism but does uphold life by being pro-life and yet he too has sent jobs overseas and has hurt America as a nation not in the horrible way that Lois Murphy has who one might say follows Murphy's Law which says., Whatever can go wrong will go wrong, but in her case she herself is creating this by her belief in socialism! With Gerlach it is money also but his is a to a lesser degree not the imperial mindset of abnormality or perverse lifestyle of Sodom and Gomorrah but he too tends to treat the born American citizen to the role of second class and the ones from the Hispanic world as a welcomed sight even with about 11 million Mexicans coming here in whatever way they can and confuses discrimination with dislocation. These are not what our Founding Forefathers had in mind when they set up this nation and so he is the lesser of two evils such as is Barbara Cummings who is pro-life and a woman running for office but is pro-life with her opponent a lifer in politics plus he is a lawyer and most of all he is a homo-sexual within the Roman Catholic religion! Again one must vote for the lesser of two evils or not vote at all since with each new election the first choice becomes more like a second or third choice to ones who subscribe to the Bible and to what our Founding Forefathers set up and by the way there are no "Founding Foremothers" which now appears as some kind of oxymoron.

Since most of these candidates are not believers than we are not under any type of obligation to vote for anything or anyone that appears in front of us and just represents a party ideology and not a particular point of view! We must, though, search our own consciences and decide if either candidate breaks with sound Biblical teaching or in anyway breaks the 10 Commandments. That is something that especially each believer must do by himself if he is to really seek GOD's will in this election year and with each new election year it appears that one must almost now be voting for the one party system that the Soviets had years ago since all political parties do have an ideology but only an individual has a particular point of view.

We also, as we the people, must also understand that we are the government and we will be held account—able no matter what we say we knew or did not know at all It is left to us or mob rule in a democracy to decide about our own nation and it appears that we are severely failing in this manner thumbs or hands down. We have allowed the self or the I in us and the world and the enemy to tell us through many dialogues with the enemy himself which we do not recognize most of the time yet there is this doubting that goes on in our very own minds and hence Satan uses his dialogue to confuse and distort the truth just as he had done in the Garden of Eden. No nothing is really ever new or is it ever original when it comes to sin and the father of all lies. This now has continued on for or since Adam's time and before with the fallen angels who left their positions in heaven and rebelled when Lucifer wanted to be "GOD" HIMSELF! When the conscience is seared then one cannot hear what GOD has to really say either through His Word or through another saint when the Holy Spirit is working. Yes it does happen sometimes that a line is open so that the unbeliever if he is really in search of the one true GOD that GOD shall honor that and shall hear that prayer of grace or the asking of grace to accept what Jesus did on the cross, but more so to accept this GOD/man into one's spiritual heart once and for all. Now some people say it but do not really mean it and hence they are not really saved The spiritual heart must be receptive and that is by prayer the prayer to repent and turn away from sin itself and know that this is all for real and for an eternity and not just a catechism lesson from a religion or another prayer that man thought up, but this is original and is from GOD who only can be the ORIGINATOR!

The elderly in America want the wrong kind of security and not the security of life everlasting but only for this moment and others such as the 60's generation want once again to repeat their own rebellion into oblivion but in this process take along with them a nation that was founded on the Bible so Satan does have his eyes on our own nation right now since we had been followed by a loving GOD! Elections come and go but the Word of GOD lives forever and ever. We in a democracy have come to rely too much on government in a democracy which is never in the search for the truth and most do not know the truth themselves. We should direct our attention to GOD no matter how bad things get and they shall and continue what He wants us to do and not to do and not what we choose to do since our ways are not His ways.

Voting sometimes for the lesser of two evils is not the solution and voting in general affects others just as our own sin does, but with ourselves we do have a real choice as an individual to make a difference without the help always from government since all governments are a power and GOD'S love is just that love. Man works through power and GOD works through His infinite love and compassion and this is agape' love the only kind of love that is useful to man.

The Negro slave in America was never really freed in the true sense of the word, because its leaders themselves had already sold out to the socialist cause being the fact that most did not know or were educated about socialism itself and others like Angela Davis were quite well aware just as Paul Robeson in Hollywood was about what Communism itself was and both had a passion for it The Negro in the early 60's went from discrimination to socialism and never entered into what they thought was liberty and justice for all. LBJ had given them the Great Society was nothing more than subservience to the federal government by welfare handouts to enslave even more the Negroes to believe that they were getting compensated for what was taken from them when in actuality what they got was enslaved not by individual slave owners but by the state that now would give them benefits but would totally destroy the family which slavery already had done, but this would be even worse since this would be what the peasants in Russia experienced until it turned to bloodshed when the peasants in

Russia finally realized that they had been had. Many things too were taken from them and promised to them and then eventually their lives were taken and they too were taken to the Gulag under Lenin and Stalin and never would ever regain their freedom and would almost become extinct. The Negro has gone most of this road except for the final part where even more bloodshed shall be spilled and they too shall become extinct since their following is larger and now they with other foreigners make up a large proportion of these United States. With this election can come where this final road shall start. I though personally am afraid that it is already too late to turn around or even refuse what shall be now forced upon not only them but all of us. The Federal Reserve for example is a private corporation owned by private banks and the United States Post Office is anything but united since that too is owned by private individuals and also is run by the federal government to make people think it is a government entity. This is what is known as fascism where the individual has ownership but the government runs it and that is why nobody can be fired. This is what Nazi Germany had with its affirmative action programs that would not allow any Jew to hold any government position because these jobs were privately owned but run by the Reichstag which elected Hitler as chancellor and then eventually let the Nazi Party a socialist party control all things through force and through race meaning only blonde hair and blue eyes could hold positions and no one could be of an "inferior" race. It also meant which most people do not know that homosexuality was a major criterion and without the proper genes the Nazis could not test tube the right people and would have, again, an inferior race of people. This is why today in America again the Nazi New Age is prevalent and even many Indians from India are brought here since the swastika was brought to Germany from there. Now we see that the Nazis again are inviting into America not only these New Age Indians but also Arabs who help hide Nazi war criminals by giving them Moslem names after World War II and now even the liberal Jews such as Barney Frank of the good old Nazi state of Massachusetts has not only him but also this John Kerry who is a Communist and Ted Kennedy who was raised as.: a Nazi since his dad was one and planned each of his sons futures for them with the help of FDR and others in England and that is why Neville Chamberlain made his visit to Nazi Germany and Churchill. took Jordan away from the Jews and now in America the ignorant socialist Jews like Ira Glasser and Nadine Strossen and others have fallen for the trap again but this time they agree with the Nazi ideology when Samuel Igra and Mr. Harden, both German Orthodox Jews, exposed and fought against this sexual perversion that started at the top since before World War I and even back as far as Martin Luther, who also was a virulent anti-Semite himself.

Now how can one suppose that since the Jewish people worldwide know of this that they would have anything to do with Protestantism or Roman Catholicism which too had its share of anti-Semitism starting with the Spanish Inquisition and Pope Pius XII and now again with Pope Paul II who shook Yassir Arafat's hand knowing he was an Islamic terrorist but then again the Pope took fear since he himself was wounded by an Islamic Arab from that very part of the world!

Yes, capitalism again has promoted socialism more than anything else in the world and we in America have too experienced it now more than ever and now we even have full fledged socialist candidates running for office for President of the United States and he is also Jewish which shall make their cause even that much stronger since they have the ones who first opposed their homosexuality as I just mentioned a few lines above. Who would now oppose what both the Negroes and the Jews in America seemed now to be for and that was these new civil liberties that gave the Nazi New Agers all they needed in order to promote it in all of the Western world and hence take control of all the world finances in this one world government already on the scene and neither Germany nor England shall alone have control as they wished they could! We have come to this crossroads now of good vs. evil with almost no way out!

Back in the 50's in our city there were 2 gangs which were both made up of white European males. One of the gangs were called the River Rats and were all grown men and the other gang was called the 3rd Street gang. There were no other types of gangs in our city! at that time. The slang they used was then emulated by the blacks starting in the 60's and from there metastasized more and more until today most of the blacks spoke this slang including the Hispanics of which the Puerto Ricans were the first of the Hispanics to come here via a Commonwealth which was setup by the Rockefellers.

They both had their own turf and usually left others alone and were not like the minority gangs of years later who robbed and took drugs and vandalized everywhere. There was some graffiti out most of it was under bridges and at that time there were no bypasses only main arteries to go for example to a larger city such as Philadelphia and New York City. With these bypasses then came dams and other menaces that started to ruin the habitat and so it was our own government officials and the well-to-do that brought the environment down.

Today if one was a lawyer it was looked up at, and this made no sense at all since they were the ones who had become judges and politicians and helped bring in socialism. Like Lenin who also was a lawyer, they clung to their ideology that spread amongst the minorities first since they were not educated and were naive as to the plans these "technicians" had in mind. Also at that time there were many teachers who clung to the old ways, but there began to appear teachers of a new breed who were learning in colleges about socialism and so it spread first from there into other teaching institutions and public education. Then of course with business being so secretive they were at the top of it all, but many never knew that and these businesses were huge organizations made up of the Masons, the Knights of Columbus, the Jesuits, etc. One could see that avarice and wealth and then power was their goal.

The Anglo-Saxons at least the Saxons in our own area wanted to keep their rule over any other nationality or group that came here by keeping themselves at the very top and then in later years started to import Arabs and Indians from India since both groups had much anti-Semitism and then we were being told that these foreigners were hard working and smarter than most Americans but the truth was that they were just gold diggers or opportunists who had this same anti-Semitism most of all in the tradition.

Our lawyers grew and grew all over the nation, and then on television they were made the iconoclasts of America and were the finest of the finest which surely meant since it had to do with Hollywood that these were the scoundrels that were ruining America's values with only a few that understood what honor and decency meant. Most were not really that bright when it came to other things such as farming or creative things in society and the rest of higher education followed along this same path and pretty soon one did not need higher mathematics or even one foreign language to get enrolled into college and in fact one college that never gave athletic scholarships started doing so and went quickly down hill and the dorms for the athletes were like castles compared to the students who were academically high and so once again the not too bright Germans wanted no one to supersede them in smarts!

The tuition in one local college went from $3,000 a year to about $28,000 a year. Now they too would be paying for these not too bright athletes who could not spell or even read proper English, but only slang and more slang and pretty soon the liberal Jews started with the liberalism like they did in Russia but we had no Pale of Settlement and so they took over in the 60's and too started along with Hollywood started to destroy America by getting to the children first and as they grew up that generation did much worse.

The students that I went to Jr. high with were at least in my classes from the upper business and professional classes, but the students were very arrogant. Even though their grades were high, they lacked the kindness and also the honor of knowing how one should act if they were to be our future leaders or good citizens of tomorrow. At that time only one Negro was in our entire school so no one can say that minorities made it bad for them. This was a lime of great frivolity where again the students in our public school would use their money to gamble and as I said before were not kind in the least and the older teachers though did not pamper them as in later years when the rebellious ones would get out of hand and by now it was almost too late to do anything since they had become grown men and grown women. They could care less about what was happening in the world until their balloon was broken by Kennedy and the war in Vietnam and the drafts but then again the draft was a poor man's conflict that was being fought and LBJ was early in his life a teacher for Mexican students so one knew that he too would somehow get promoted since the Rockefellers were pro-Latin America until in the new millennium it was being forced down our very thoughts even their own language of slang that most Americans did not want to hear including Spaniards born in Spain itself who had pure white skin and coal black hair and spoke a different or higher dialect of real Spanish since they were from Spain and were more educated, but the rich and well educated liked it this way so that they could through wants and desires have these people with lesser educations buy their products of luxury such as cars and more cars and gamble and drink and also get involved into sports itself so much so that that was all they seemed to know. One of the very first families from Puerto Rico and one could tell from then that they too had a completely different culture and in fact our own landlord kept his buildings discriminated with whites in one building and blacks in another and with Puerto Ricans in another and this was before 1964 and things worked out find and in fact these 3 groups liked it that way since government interference had kept out of our own private lives. Not only till government became big brother did things that were negative begin to happen since more attention was then given to race and nationality intentionally so that the politicians could live off the diversity and conflicts they themselves would originate with laws that went too far in one direction or the other and were being backed by socialists who themselves were the most prejudiced since they always lived and till this day still do live in quite different types of neighborhoods that were well-to-do.

What was good for the goose was not good for the gander and hence racial tensions grew because the leaders of these groups were first of all socialists from well-to-do parents and who did not have to work to go to college so their idle minds thought up many devious things with a little bit of help from their foreign friends and that is why Khruschev, a peasant had said, "We shall bury you" since he knew what America really was like especially on the East and West coasts and how we educated our children and youth almost like they did but about some years behind them.

The Cuban missile crisis was a debacle for both Khruschev and Kennedy, but Kennedy did get to stop the Soviet ships, but only after some missiles showed up in Cuba and Adlai Stevenson was put in the UN to stagnate such a brilliant man while people like Eisenhower and LBJ got in! Khruschev was then called back to the Politburo and was later removed. He could never ever finish whatever he had started.

The Monroe Doctrine had said that no foreign power or ideology would be allowed in the Western Hemisphere until President Gerald Ford did away with that and also refused to meet Alexander Solzhenitsyn and to this day not one of Solzhenitsyn's novels ever made it to Hollywood not that he would have let them have it but neither did they want what he exposed Communism just for what it was so very plain and clear that it was for the destruction of mankind and its anti-humanity and held no real authority base such as our own Founding Forefathers had brought here with them that spoke of decency and honor for all. Why would the rich and well educated want others in America to know what they supported whole heartedly, but would not ever say that as of yet? In due lime though when the educational system from top to bottom would be controlled by these rich socialists and materialists and there was no turning back then they would use civil rights' socialism as a guilt trip for all Americans who really had nothing to do with discrimination the way Hollywood made it out to be! Most people understood that different races would live the way that they wanted to and so they stay separated, but the liberal Jew saw a way to make money on other people's misery and hence promoted their guilt onto others since they were at the top of the class as well as the good old English with their hodge podge society.

Even during the Civil War the Jews took the Negroes' land just like socialists in Russia took the peasants land by making them accept money, something they were not use to since they always bartered. When the peasants got this money, it ruined them but quick and they started to drink and carouse about all over instead of going back to their roots in farming but then again that was the whole idea of Communism, this equality or equivalence where all the cogs in the machinery of slavery would be equal. Only the ones on the very top would get away with murder and agitation and rebel rousing to keep Americans at each others throats in any way they could. They devised methods from a foreign ideology that they brought across the ocean and which was not what our own Founding Forefathers ever had in mind

The rich in all societies always run that particular nation or country, for better or worse, and usually for worse. They always made sure it was dog-eat-dog and nothing less. While the average American was working for a living they with others from abroad were working to bring down a democratic/republic because their ideology was crumbling and our society was not and so they had to accelerate our own downfall by selling from Hollywood to our children and youth the lies that help also bring down many other nations. This was their pied piper for the 60's and hence from then on day by day.

We could even see the young having sex in the streets since Hollywood said it would be okay, and then the people who were more physical well they would exploit them for all they were worth.

Many said after the 60's just educate the blacks but then the blacks started to become more and more arrogant and were being educated into socialism and the revenge and get even syndrome from the white rich colleges that promised them all the sports in the world but no real achievements for their people at the bottom so more infidelity and out of wedlock children were either conceived or were infanticized. The deadbeat dad syndrome basically started when the civil rights' socialists at the top sold out their own people for millions of dollars for themselves and could have cared less since they never really addressed the issue or occupations but more help from big brother and never ever dare address the reason why so many Negro women were abused by their very own men. But the rich and well educated had a big part to play in that because of sports; that was the utopia and hope for their future, but not really their future but the future of the millionaires who owned the teams. Most of those very athletes such as Mohammed Ali or O.J. or Magic Johnson, who did exactly what they were told to do or what their own egos wanted. None of the 3 did anything to contribute to higher good education but the pimp image of the rich and well to do! Bill Cosby had at least donated millions of dollars, even though his money was being used for socialism too at Temple University and for multiculturalism and racism from the socialist blacks who were black racists and anti-Semites which of course he had no real way of knowing, but Jesse Jackson, Sr. did!

The black person per se was no longer seen as an individual but as a group even if one spoke to one at a time and they knew it! They were blacks with no individual personalities and had to play the false role that the rich and well educated wanted them to play, which did nothing to enhance them as individuals but only led more to the black racism because the more they emulated what they were being told, the more it did not appear like they were who they really were and so their own creativity was smothered by Hollywood also, and there would always be a few blacks willing to do anything to become anything for tokenism and nothing at all for their own communities! Again this was ego in the black male especially, and the black sports males were iconoclasts not because they were talented but because they made millions of dollars on each black athlete that played professional sports because their following was again by their own who believed that someday that they could send men children to safe schools and have the opportunity and not from big brother but from free enterprise to compete for themselves in the world of academics just as individuals and never have to feel discouraged as they had for so many years since they too were lied to for many years. The government always had a catch to it and that was anything or anyone who had received handouts. No matter how desperate they were would owe the government and its own ideology their very soul if they ever wanted to get ahead in this world and in America. This was nothing like what was proposed at the beginning such as the equal opportunity to get decent paying jobs so that they could support their own families. It was not necessarily education that they always needed but the individual status as a human being that said I can do all things through Christ who strengthens me. The rich and well educated, including Hamilton Jordan represented only themselves and did absolutely nothing for the Negro individual. If one were a Negro they had to for some reason support these government organizations such as the NAACP, the PAL, the YMCA, the UNITED WAY, the BLACK PANTHERS, etc. Why was it that just one plain Negro male could not acquire a job without the coercive methods from government that said, "You must do it this way or else . . . "?

This was not what was meant by equal job opportunity, but do your thing, which meant leave all your upbringing in the church here at government's door and we shall provide everything for you, BUT this is what you had to give in return! There would be no more the image that the Negro was a hard working American and one that was just starting to get along and was making achievements into all fields and then the atheistic Jews and the rich and well educated pushed their socialist agenda and guess what many Negroes suffered for 2 or 3 generations because again of the lie that was repeated over and over again and by that time the next generation was already hooked onto this socialism but was beginning to realize that they had been lied to and that all that this represented was just another form of slavery that kept them down for good. Had the inner cities gotten any better since government and the Great Society took over?

Why was such a large population of Negroes now being located in the inner cities where crime was promoted, yes promoted, by the rich and well educated while they themselves lived in. the white ivory towers? Now the Negro could only hope to reject anything that government said or it again would be slavery via the state which would be the worse kind of slavery just like happened to the peasants in Russia when they too were deceived and their land was taken from them and the government there also lied to them till their end would come a few years later after Lenin and Natanson and Company got into power by the Germans and the atheistic Jews!

Tomorrow's election for President is between a Christian and a Communist! It is that simple. The incumbent is pro life and anti-homosexual and against also embryonic stem cell research! His enemy and he is his enemy but he does not know that really is for infanticide and homosexuality like a Nazi would be. The incumbent went to Yale and got a bachelor's degree and a master's degree from Harvard Business School. He was a pilot in the Air National Guard. He is a millionaire and his wife Laura is pro infanticide and was a elementary school librarian and they have a set of twin girls now. His running mate is pro homosexual and served under the Nixon White House staff and was chief of staff under the not too bright Gerald Ford who eliminated the Monroe Doctrine and that is why he would not meet Solzhenitsyn as an honored guest at that time when he came to America as an honored friend. He was Secretary of Defense during the Gulf War which may say why this incumbent picked him for VF! He and his wife had 2 daughters and one is a Sodomite!

The other side who are a Communist and a socialist are John Kerry who went to Yale and graduated and got his law degree from Boston University. His dad served under the Iron Fist Administration. He has 2 daughters from his first marriage and his second wife, Teresa Heinz Kerry, has 3 sons from her first husband who was a U.S. Senator John Heinz and she is the heiress to the Heinz fortune. His running mate is a law suit scoundrel who attacked OB GYN's in law suit after law suit because he is pro infanticide and he also loves money and power like his buddy Kerry and both are vicious and cold and would destroy America if elected. Edwards' wife Elizabeth also is a lawyer! They have 4 children, 2 girls and 2 boys, but the one son died in 1996. There is not much too choose from but there is only one way to choose and that is for the one who is a weak Christian and never one who subscribes to the Communist ideology!

An atheistic Jew like Trotsky vs. a weak Christian man who we must now pray for even more, since, as I said before, he thinks Islam and Christianity worship the same GOD and if he is lying heaven help us all because he is our link to Almighty GOD as President of these United States! For Christians if they vote and believe in democracy and capitalism then they must vote for the incumbent and if one is a socialist and an atheist then they should vote for . . .

Whoever gets to be President this time shall definitely have his hands full and does not really know what he is getting into because now Israel's time is soon here and so very very close one can almost feel it.

The Pilgrims should really be credited with the founding of a Christian nation because they were the humble and the poor that came here while the Puritans and others including the Quakers were well to do. The Pilgrims founded Plymouth Rock and made the Mayflower Compact and were the first to celebrate Thanksgiving day in 1621 and most of them were also farmers and not of the English or European nobility. The Puritans had their own little colony of Massachusetts Bay and started growing more and more and soon outnumbered the Pilgrims and soon took over. The Puritans still part of the Anglican church while the Pilgrims were not. Governor Bradford was head of the Pilgrims in 1621. When Columbus, who sailed for Spain and Roman Catholicism, came they were more in search of gold and other things even though they did develop some farming and settlements. All of New England became controlled by the Puritans and John Winthrop was a Puritan. In the middle states were the Quakers, such as William Penn. who himself was kind and allowed others to worship as they pleased within Christianity. Maryland also was good about religious freedom when they passed the Toleration Act that said even Catholics who at first had control and as well as others could also worship freely. The Puritans were not so broad minded.

There were 5 European nations involved into coming to the Western world all for just about the same reason except that Spain might have been the worse when Cortez eliminated the Aztecs and changed the name of their area to Mexico City, and Pizarro eliminated the Incas. England had its claim in America, Portugal had its mainly in Brazil and Holland and France both had theirs in America to some extent Spain took South America, Central America and even Mexico.

In Pennsylvania many Germans had settled because of William Penn's religious freedom. In New England they had public schools so that children could read the Bible. The Middle States were made up of Catholics, Quakers and others and both New England and the Middle States dealt mostly in trade while the Southern States dealt in farming of tobacco and cotton and wheat and traded with England for merchandise and belonged to the Anglican Church in England. In the South also was slavery to work their huge plantations plus indentured servants which were poor people from Europe who had to give so many years of service to the ones in America who brought them by ship to America and then they could be free and buy their own land in the South. The slaves could not do that because of the well to do nobility. The Indians in 1492 made up about 800,000 people, and in 1950 they made up 50,000 people. The South home schooled because they were separated much more than in the North or New England. In New Jersey and New York the Dutch had colonies. In later years John D. Rockefeller, Jr. rebuilt Williamsburg, Virginia since it gone almost to nothing.

In 1950 the United States had 3 million miles of land, not including Hawaii and Alaska. We also had about 1 billion acres of farm land with about 5 million farmers out of 170 million people. We then had 6% of the world's land mass and produced 1/2 of the world's corn, 1/3 of the world's cotton, and 1/7 of the world's wheat.

The 13 original colonies were Pennsylvania, New York, New Jersey, New Hampshire, Massachusetts, Connecticut, Maryland, Delaware, Virginia, North Carolina, South Carolina, Rhode Island, and Georgia which was taken because it separated Spanish Florida from England's 13 Colonies.

These are the states and their admission into the Union: Maine 1820, New Hampshire 1788, Vermont 1791, Massachusetts 1781. Connecticut 1788, Pennsylvania 1787, Maryland 1788, Virginia 1788, North Carolina 1789, South Carolina 1788, Georgia 1788, Alabama 1819, Mississippi 1817, Louisiana 1812, Florida 1845, West Virginia 1863, Kentucky 1792, Tennessee 1796, Arkansas 1836, Missouri 1821, Illinois 1818, Indiana 1816, Ohio 1803, Wisconsin 1848, Michigan 1837, Minnesota 1858, Iowa 1846, North Dakota 1889, South Dakota 1889, Nebraska 1867, Kansas 1861, Oklahoma 1907, Texas 1895, New Mexico 1912, Colorado 1876, Wyoming 1890, Arizona 1912, Montana 18891 Utah 1896, Idaho 1890, California 1850, Nevada 1864, Oregon 1859, Washington 1889, Rhode Island 1790, New Jersey 1787, and Delaware 1787. Alaska and Hawaii are not included in the above statistics because of the time. Again this was in 1950.

We can now see that there were many different people and counties competing for America at that time and not just England and the Pilgrims were probably as I said before, the most humble and true to life part Christians since they were poor and humble and made friends with the Indians and also had founded Thanksgiving Day which is probably one of the only Biblical holidays found in the entire Bible. Their appreciation of the New World was a joy to behold and they had many hardships as the others did also but their kind of denominational Christianity took on a form that was not like the religions in Europe at the time who were all well to do.

The Jesuit French Revolution in 1789 exported its revolution to other countries. The American Spiritual Revival did not. Washington, Hamilton and Jefferson wanted no part of Europe at that time. This was our main players that would set up our government here in the colonies.

In 1704 the Quebec Indians attacked at night a small settlement of colonists and murdered most of the settlers and the rest they took captive as half breeds. This occurred in Deerfield, Massachusetts which was near the Canadian border. France at that time had control of Canada and the Mississippi River area all the way down to the Gulf. The French came here only for exploring and for furs. Later on their settlements dissipated and the Jesuits tried to coerce the Indians to Roman Catholicism, but had many problems with that. With their French governors there was no freedom. The French soldiers many times were against the English colonists who had no army. The French King Loius XIV was vicious and ruled from 1661-1715. Then came the French and Indian War.

George Washington at the young age of 21 was sent by the English government to tell the French they had to get out of the Ohio territory. Later Washington fought the French at Fort Duquesne and lost. This in itself actually started the French and Indian War. General Braddock was the commander in chief of the English colonies and failed to listen to George Washington about how to fight the Indians and lost badly.

The Battle of Quebec was won by the English and was one of the greatest battles ever and decided which language would be spoken French or English when this battle was over and hence today we speak English on the North American continent except for Quebec Province.

In 1763 France and Spain surrendered to the English and the English got Florida from the Spaniards. From 1763-1775 the colonists fought England and the Indians at that time decided to kill all white men. This again was because of this Ohio area.

Grenville said that the colonists needed an Army and then proceeded with the next 3 acts that really upset the colonists and they were the Proclamation of 1763, the Navigation Act and the worse of all the Stamp Act Tax which brought about the phrase "taxation without representation." Patrick Henry also opposed this tax. King George III had started this tax which was a bad idea to do. Then Charles Townshend passed his Act which limited the freedoms for all the colonists and Samuel Adams opposed this act. Then in 1770 the Boston Massacre occurred when some youth angered the British soldiers and killed some colonists in the process and made the rest of the colonies very angry! After that the English brought tea from the East India Tea Company to the colonies without a tax and destroyed the colonists profit on tea.

Then the Boston Tea party occurred to oppose this and Samuel Adams was involved in this also.

Carpenter's Hall in Philadelphia on September 1774 with 50 men about and 12 colonies held the very First Continental Congress. It was later, on March 23, 1775 that Patrick Henry made his famous speech of "Give me liberty or give me death." John Hancock also was involved at this time and Paul Revere came to warn both Hancock and Adams that the British were coming! In that same year of April 19th the Minutemen fought at both Lexington and Concord and defeated the British in Massachusetts. Then came Bunker Hill and Breed's Hill and again the British were defeated and England had to leave the Boston area. After that came Dorchester Heights and then Ethan Allan at Moore's Creek in New York State and he won there. The King of England then hired Hessians which were German soldiers to fight the colonists.

Thomas Paine wrote Common Sense and this inspired the colonists even more to fight on. On July 4th, 1776 the Declaration of Independence was signed by Jefferson and others.

Meanwhile in Latin America while our nation was preparing for a democratic/republic there they were having wars, coupes' and revolutions. First with Father Hidalgo came this revolution of liberation theology from the Spaniards and the creoles (French Negroes) got involved. Then a Creole officer by the name of Agustin de Iturbide takes over in Mexico by deceiving the Indians there. Then in Venezuela with Francisco Miranda he too followed with the Creoles. In Colombia Simon Bolivar continues this kind of revolution and took also Colombia and Venezuela since he had met Francisco Miranda earlier. Bolivar went to Argentina with San Martin a native there and San Martin attacked Peru and Chile and the Spaniards there. Bolivar and San Martin meet and because Bolivar fought for ego he took over as complete ruler and Spain was finally defeated. And until this very day in Latin America or Hispanic America there are wars, coups and revolutions!

Brazil was the only country left and the Portuguese had settled there. Negro slaves were brought there to work on the sugar plantations. At that time then Dom Pedro ruled Brazil. While this was going on back in America met for the last time on March 1, 1787 and allied with France. The Articles of Confederation were established which provided for a Congress which included a upper house which was appointed and a lower house which was elected. The small states were not for this because they wanted all land beyond the mountains to become common property for all the states.

In Philadelphia on June 1787, 30 men met in the State House and Washington was made chairman at 55 years of age and most delegates were from the well to do such as James Madison age 35 and Ben Franklin at age 81 who at 17 started as a poor apprentice. Governor Morris wrote most of the U.S. Constitution and was crippled but nonetheless had done an outstanding job. The states and in this order adopted this Constitution: Delaware, Pennsylvania, New Jersey, Georgia, Connecticut, Massachusetts, Maryland, South Carolina, New Hampshire, Virginia, New York, then by 1789 North. Carolina and Rhode Island accepted too the U.S. Constitution while also the Jesuit French Revolution was occurring.

This is what this document provides for only:

To form a more perfect union, meaning America was still in the making and the union of states had to be under one form of government; to establish justice, which meant that all of these United States from then on would uphold the rule of law for all citizens based on Biblical foundations; domestic tranquility to protect and serve our citizens from criminals and to keep the peace according to the Judeo Christian faith in our homes, neighborhoods and communities; to provide for the common defense was to protect us from foreign invasion in our nation by providing for a military; and the blessings of liberty which meant not that all men were created equal but that all men according to their Maker had certain inalienable rights and they were life, liberty and private property. Since men had different talents, certain men would be on top such as in government and others would serve below and would be citizens. That is why this equality or equivalence became a nomenclature and did not in any way uphold slavery or now infanticide! We would have to keep a vigilant eye, as Ben Franklin said, for this liberty!

Famous men such as Jefferson and Mr. DuPont of Delaware met sometimes to discuss the state of affairs in our government. Alexander Hamilton was the one who created the party concept which meant that ideology would always be followed and not the individual particular point of view. He would tax the poor if he could. There were opponents and not enemies as in today's very election of Kerry vs. the incumbent and these opponents were Jefferson and the Republican Party. Hamilton belonged to the Federalist Party, which could lead to an oligarchy. John Adams who owned no slaves could be a tyrant at times, but approved the Sedition Act which said one could not talk against the government which was very dangerous When President Monroe ran there was and this was the only time in history until maybe now that there was only one party in that election!

The famous writer from England, Charles Dickens said after Washington, D.C. was horrible because of its mile long avenues with no endings and no homes or inhabitants, and he had a good point there. In 1789 there were about 4,000,000 people in the United States. At that same time Jefferson who was in France did not help write the US Constitution and maybe that is why to this day it is weak in content since for instance no mention of sex is in it whatsoever since Jefferson appeared to have foresight. Jefferson and Patrick Henry were for freeing the slaves and Jefferson wanted them to be returned to Africa!

Before 1793 the South opposed slavery for the most part and then Eli Whitney with this Industrial Revolution from John Locke's socialism promoted slavery even more! Then also Horace Mann another socialist proposed the public school education.

The Whig Party was made up of rich people and really was the Federalist Party. Martin Van Buren was the first President to be born an American rather than a British citizen! Sometimes in today's Democratic Party they accuse our Founding Forefathers of hating the Indians, but since the following states were named after Indian culture and Indian names, I find that hard to believe. Those state are: Alabama, Missouri, the Dakotas, Kentucky, Idaho, Michigan, Connecticut, Arkansas, Illinois, Texas, Utah, Wisconsin, Wyoming, Indiana, Iowa, Kansas, Massachusetts, Minnesota, Nebraska, Oklahoma, Tennessee and New Mexico where the word Mexico comes from the Aztec culture which means war god!

Other cultures or national ties were for example the D.C. in Washington came from Christopher Columbus; the French such as Florida, Colorado, Louisiana where the French Creoles lived, and California; the Spaniards such as Montana, Nevada and Arizona; the Dutch in New York, and the English such as Georgia where prisoners earlier were kept for England, Delaware, Maine, Maryland, New Jersey, New Hampshire and the Carolinas.

The French Jesuits in Louisiana, or at least their culture, celebrate the Lenten season with a pagan Mardi Gras in New Orleans, Louisiana. Also Mexico City had no freedom and today with 22,000,000 people one can still attest to that and the St. Lawrence Valley had no freedom because of the French and because of Roman Catholicism in both places.

At that time though the Massachusetts Bay Colony had freedom for their people in representative government where religion did not intertwine to take total control of the people as in Roman Catholicism! While the people in England always limited their kings, in France and in Spain they did not. The English first started with the Magna Carta of 1215, then the Petition of Right which was when or at the time that the Puritans came to America and had left England, and then of course the Bill of Rights. Each state or colony had a governor and a legislature, all 13. Rhode Island and Connecticut elected their governor, Maryland, Pennsylvania and Delaware the proprietors picked the governor such as with Pennsylvania and the Penns and with Delaware the DuPonts. The other 8 colonies' governors were picked by the King of England. Certain strict denominations, such as the Puritans in Massachusetts could only vote. In all colonies no women could vote. (" . . . And ye shall be ruled by women.") Mostly land owners and free men who were like indentured servants could vote and one had to be 21 years of age.

The New England states had town meetings which was very conducive to what our Founding Forefathers had in mind. The Middle States had county and town governments. The Southern States had a sheriff for each county plus a Lieutenant Colonel for the militia and justices of the peace. One could see a little redneck mentality here, but then again they were spread out that is their communities then up North. The colonists still were loyal to the King of England, but wanted self-government.

In New York a man from Germany named John Zenyer the owner started what was called the New York Weekly Journal something like Russia had at Dostoyevsky and Tolstoy's time had and that is how War And Peace was actually first published by a monthly journal and in fact Dostoyevsky and Tolstoy wrote for the same journal. This paper, though could have been a harbinger for a paper such as the New York Times that now is the largest newspaper in the world, but is a socialist newspaper like Pravda was! Pulitzer would see to that later in our own history. He sold for commercialism and not the private consumer.

Later on with technology and huge industries came avarice and slave labor for children and women who were being made to work the same long hours (between 12-14) like the strong men. This is when the unions were most affective and the AFL or the American Federation of Labor which was for skilled craftsmen was started and the CIO the Congress of Industrial Organization which was for unskilled or mass production labor or something like the proletariat in Russia before the Revolution there. The AFL and the CIO later both joined to form one organization and it has been said at least back in the 1970's that this organization did not make deals with the Soviets as did the English ones did in England itself. But what later happened for instance in other unions such as the Teamsters, or the railroad unions or the garment industry was that they started to support socialism at the beginning of the 1980's maybe before by making their unions members contribute to one party with their union dues that they took out and that was the National Democratic Socialist Party!

Around 1950 the 5 major nationalities at that time that had come to America were the following: They were first from the British Isles; then Germany, the first nation and then Italy, Ireland and then Great Britain. Today that has severely changed and it appears wherever the Germans settled such as in Pennsylvania in Berks County and in Milwaukee, Wisconsin that socialism appeared and since these were the only two cities with socialist governments, one would have to give second thought to that for sure indeed!

We then got, in 1867 Alaska from Russia with a phone call to Seward, and in 1898 we got Hawaii and annexed that too, but they did not become states until later in our own history. Today we also have imported through the executive branch many Hispania Americans (with no say from the American people) and that exceed by far any one group of people ever to come at one time into our nation in such a short period of time itself and with no referendum from the people or, as I said, from the Commander In Chief who has failed to provide what the U.S. Constitution says by, "domestic tranquility or to promote the general welfare" when most of these people cannot even speak English and come here illegally to our Founding Forefathers along with the Islamic world which has no mention of Christianity in its foreign religion or that of GOD in the flesh, and that is what our Founding Forefathers were all about and the Jewish people had to be included since Messiah was a Jewish man and for another not so good reason or viable reason should I say and that was because of finances in banking which they learned in Europe where that was only what they were allowed to do and the fact that all that brain power would be missed here in America. Our Founders were not dumb at all for including the Old Testament people in regards to the brilliant minds though at times one had to watch because of what GOD Himself called stiff-necked.

On this very day of today we dodge the proverbial bullet, but in reality we were spared I believe by GOD from an end to our spiritual nation which had occurred under Lenin and almost for the very same ideological reasons and in fact that ideology is socialism even though ours appeared somewhat different and hence at least Lord willing this same incumbent shall learn from the past and first establish a Palestinian State that in no way is on Abraham's land and that he expels all homosexuals from the military or be just like Nazi Germany did with homosexuals all at the top and elsewhere and also the fact that if John Kerry would have won more anti-Semitism would most assuredly happen with a Jewish President because the enemy would make sure to blame all the Jews in the world for their problems and because of Messiah who was and is and always shall be a Jewish GOD.

One can start to see now how at these times we are so much like Russia was before their imminent fall when they had a Revolution or a kind of civil war amongst themselves as to what was best for man with no regard whatsoever by the rich and well educated as to what did GOD want? The Finns in Russia were like our Hispanics and others here, that is they did not want to speak Russian, while these Hispanics do not want to speak English and both that government and our government encouraged it. Why else print in both Spanish and English like they print in Quebec, first French and then English? That is what we our coming to since there are no words in Spanish for compromise or dissent which means there can be no meeting of minds. It is either their way or no way at all, and the way the rich and well educated in this country are going; they want us dumbed down by a culture that has never shown the ability to know how to set up a government with liberty and justice for all since right now Mexico is a socialist state and the government of Vincenté Fox owns all the oil wells and our own government made a treaty called NAFTA just so capitalism could support socialism, which it always does with no regard for our national sovereignty at all!

The English showed us how to set it up and now they want to show us how to break it down but so much quicker with the latter! We have lost the right to rule as a people because the judiciary has gotten so strong that an oligarchy has formed and no one shall incarcerate the Communists in the ACLU because the House on UnAmerican Activities is no longer so and it was a Democrat Sam Ervin who removed it. By the way, he too was from the redneck south that seems to carry this sheriff mentality and guns.

Now the incumbent had won this Presidential election but why had John Kerry so graciously conceded with such a close election? Had someone amongst the Jewish people somewhere very important say something to Kerry to accept defeat as is and this someone or something such as a organization had to be pretty powerful and hence also said that only more anti-Semitism would occur and he could not do like the Gentile Gore had done when he lost too? This Jewish mindset could see being played here once again since the popular votes had been honest and the fact that Bush had killed many Islamic terrorists which allowed also Israel to go after the terrorists in Israel more like they should have done many years ago but then again there was no 9/11!

A radio Jewish announcer had to constantly even after the election severely oppose or had to make it appear that he severely opposed John Kerry because if he did not then more anti-Semitism would be created even though Kerry lost and with that lost too they could once again blame Kerry because he was a Jew for that also! This was the norm for the German, the black and the English votes let alone others who would always almost vote against a Jew but this time they could not lose in the sense if he had won then they would get their free handouts and follow the leader mentality as well as their liberal ways that would or could blame as I said before, Kerry!

The Jews had also dodged a bullet but Mayor Koch and Joseph Lieberman no conservatives by any means had to know that in Nazi Germany that homosexuality was their main proponent for the master race breeding that meant there had or was rarely any normal type of sex since many were queers and could not procreate and so the master race would be by test tube matches with homosexual persons coming to be in positions of authority which was normal for the average German mind since the male image as a father even to this day compared to the blacks in America as well as the Puerto Ricans and was again called deadbeat dads!

If one spoke to the uneducated then perhaps to them one would think with a Bush win that one had to be for discrimination because their very own lifestyle was no different then that of the blacks and the Puerto Ricans and to cover their own guilt they had to get angry at others who would not go along with the liberal lifestyles, but at the same time could not completely comprehend this because of a lack of white education.

As I was saying, this incumbent had won, but was not that very strong of a leader because of his moderate view on "don't ask, don't tell", which was following what England had done and that was to legalize homosexuality down to a certain teenage year and hence he being English could not astray from his own ancestry and hence once again America was following what England had done! Also the fact that he really did not push for any judges that were anyway like Bork or Scalia! It was a show and tell type of appointment and also because he knew he botched up what his own dad had forgot to finish and hence and made a serious mistake and should have supported Israel to have all their land and put the Palestinian state in Arab soil. Why else did the Islamic terrorists want it on Israelis' soil. and not their own soil and that was not because of Jerusalem, but because it would keep Jews and Christians out of Israel and hence appease the Islamic creed for greed and blood which is all it could show for all its history except when the Soviets under Stalin and others destroyed them too?

Again this President was a weak leader and could not carry through the same as Khruschev would do and that was never to complete what he had started and hence would always be a thorn in his side. His moral values were there but that was it for this incumbent and he was nothing like Ronald Reagan and even Reagan backed down with his nomination of Bork! The British Isle people were just not made of the granite that it took to run a nation that was strong in moral values because their mindset always went back to the mixing of races instead of the moral issues from the Bible!

One cannot coerce people to get along but they can first establish through government moral values that would be upheld and that said all would have to follow this rule of law no matter what and if one did not then they had to mete out the punishment and not worry about how many votes one would get in America. If that was the only real reason to run America then we would be in big trouble and it would not be the beginning but the beginning of the end! Strong leadership meant high moral and GODLY values no matter what happened and now no matter what others thought including your own ideological party! One had to now lead as with a particular point of view and that meant no group thought which looked good on television and in the newspapers and magazines when people saw the color of the skin and not the moral character of that particular person. Enough about race had been said and with the blacks voting for Kerry had gone to show that the moral issues amongst them did not matter at all!

So what would it prove if the United States Attorney General's Office did absolutely nothing about the terrorists since that was the job in the Justice Department to do? Now John Ashcroft, a conservative (whatever that meant), would be resigning because he too did not have what it would take to bring criminals to justice like Frank Rizzo had done in Philadelphia when Rizzo had to also deal with Communists, and who also was supposed to go after the judges that wrote their own laws. Was it not the justice system? Where was the law enforcement on the part of these wimpy officials who only wanted to be politicians and the President who also was derelict in his own duty by not going after criminals such as illegals and Moslems as terrorists? That fell under the name of Commander In Chief and the words were all capitalized for sure, but where were these filibustering politicians now that they had the authority but would not use it to enforce the rule of law even now in the lawless court rooms?

If it is too hot in the kitchen, then get the heck out! This was not for the weak at heart or the whip or will that would do nothing to insure American lives here since that is what the US Constitution said. One had to know what and how to do it and expedite it as such and not procrastinate with rhetoric which is what the rich and well educated usually did when, it usually came to the real action and was this the time to go run and hide? Either there was a rule of law and the talking had to stop and action had to take over now or all that one said and did if not to uphold the rule of law would all be for naught.

One could not appoint generals because most of them were just lifers and glory seekers and usually got where they were because it was not deserved and that is how the military worked. As far as who one could trust, it would have to be as Frank Rizzo had picked military people at an average rank that did not go to high and who were patriotic for their own country and would not be afraid because they knew that their own boss was also not afraid and would back them up 100% when the time came to incarcerate criminals and keep them there. It was a man's job and not a politician's job. All talk and no action meant to one's enemies and opponents that this man was an easy to be overcomed!

Where was the FBI and the CIA involved in all of this instead of hearing about the Peterson case day and night to ad nauseam? Why did not they go out and do their job like Mayor Giuliani had done in New York City when he took regular police officers and made them undercover people and went after and did not wait for them to act that is the gangs, the drug dealers and the pimps and prostitutes?

It was bad enough that we had criminals in the courts and they were neither always the defendant or the prosecutor, but the socialist thug that sat in his or her nice long dark colored robe like an honest monk would have! Where was the executive branch of government as well as the legislative branch of government that could pass laws to restrict such an oligarchial ruling by these great tribunal jurists that meant only that the crime or the criminal did not pay. The victim was the one that had to worry about if they would be seen as being in contempt of court if they posed their innocence too much to the jurist in the black robe for after all the one up high had done more than that by releasing felons so that they could go out and work on the average American citizen that obeyed the rule of law and had a decent respect for other people and no more of this phony "for one's brother" since all that meant was if you are not with me than you are against me" and that would mean then that their kind of justice could not prevail and that was to let the felons free!

This was more of the equality, or equal justice under the law but no one ever said just what law that was! Was it the law of the jungle or was it the law of the land such as the Great Tribunal with at least 6 pure socialists who said all things are equal even in crime and hence since one committed murder it was no different then if one stole a dollar from the state for that would mean that the state was much more important than the human being and the ones who would rule had left the human species long ago!

The juries too could not make up their minds if one was innocent or guilty and not based on the rule of law so much as the underdog mentality of he was poor and had no job and hence . . . But this only lead to more and more of the same outbreaks of justice that is it meant that there would be no justice for the victim since one's civil and they were anything but civil could not be broken no matter if the one was now in a cemetery! This is what this new judicial system was all about!

Should one now report a crime against them or should they not and that was the question? And if one did report such a crime would the judge release them in order to intimidate them, but the judge did or would not do this on purpose oh no because it was a matter of his bleeding heart liberalism that he had brought with him from his days back in the 60's which said always to one's left and never look right! This was like going through an intersection and a busy one at that with no regard for other on going traffic. One could not moony about looking both ways since this was a one way street now except that they . . .

With today came a very important discussion about OPEC and how it regulates prices and exportation of oil from the Arab oil producing nations and some others. Kuwait, though before the Gulf War made a deal with the United States to export more than their allotted amount to America set by OPEC. Saddam Hussein 3 times warned Kuwait to stop pumping this crude oil which was destroying his nation because he had run, or Iraq was an oil producing nation and that is how they made their money financially. After he warned Kuwait 3 times he then started to destroy their derricks and oil wells but George Bush, Sr. and congress decided to side with Kuwait and declared war on Iraq and Saddam Hussein but April Glass our United States Ambassador to Iraq okayed somehow Saddam's entry into Kuwait when he was approached by or he approached April Glass. Somehow then Margaret Thatcher appeals to Bush, Sr. to stop Hussein and he initiates this war with Congress' approval but then is told to pull back. So Hussein is untouched and his Republican Guard is hardly encountered. Of course there were bank accounts going through London bank accounts that handled this oil in the trillions of dollars and hence England was getting rich and the Bushes also and being English. favoritism for Bush, Jr. to finish what his father could not even though Hussein was a dictator and we compounded that by our own mistake by going again into Iraq because this dictator had weapons of mass destruction or we were told but yet we still deal in slave labor in Communist Red China which is 10 times worse than Hussein!

Did this English President and in more than one way lie to us about this war in Iraq or did he believe his own lie since his own father's pride was on the line? The Israelis' years before had already knocked out a nuclear reactor! The Islamic Arab world is always a powder keg ready to explode and the Bushes are friends with the Saudis who attacked us at 9/11. Why not attack the Saudi sheiks? One now has to wonder why Bush, Jr. went in again to Iraq? Hussein did not kill Christians before the war in Iraq because he knew I believe that they were no threat to him as far as violence. Today though now everybody is fair game and why was Baghdad not bombed completely all at once and Hussein would have been killed? Heaven forbid again if this was for a Rockefeller, a World Bank the IMF, etc. or because of England and a son wanted to protect his profits and his father's pride, but would he use a nation to do this and in the Middle East?

Now with this Palestinian State and why Abraham's land, if Bush is sincere as he says he is and why was he the only President to call for this Palestinian State? This next comment is conjecture but nonetheless has been said many times and that is Bush, Jr.'s grandfather funded the Nazis. Now that would make sense as to why this President would call a Palestinian State on Abraham's land! Was this anti-Semitism? Israel does block all roads to Arab financial oil!

Why did this President want a multicultural state in America as well as in Israel just like England had with 1-2 million Moslems? Again America was following England. The English have been mixing cultures and races but not on their sovereignty until now and have been doing this for centuries and our own borders are unprotected for the most part and we shall look like Yugoslavia after Tito or London with its cameras on virtually every street corner.

More of socialism's big brother and this one world government or New Age—Jeb Bush has married a Mexican woman and this again is their choice but do not coerce us by ignoring, as Commander In Chief, our borders to accept your "marriage" through NAFTA between Mexico and the United States for the past history between us two is not good at all!

The English have gone to China years ago for drugs, and to India for valuables and possibly the swastika and also the apartheid in South Africa and not the South Africans. The elderly who did this are now dead or are near death and could care less about our world. But now their heirs are doing the same "tradition".

I was never for the war in Iraq even though it protected Israel from Hussein's Scud missies and Quayle got the defensive systems for Israel through the Senate. As to making Israel stronger and at this election time I did not vote for either because I did not vote and do not believe in mob rule by a majority. There were no 2 viable candidates that I could trust. One was an anti-Semite Jew and a billionaire and was a divorcee and committed treason in 1973 and the other candidate did nothing at all to him or to Bill Clinton also who committed treason in 1973! So neither candidate inspired my trust as an American and one should be tried and incarcerated as well as the other. This was indeed a strange election with Bush Jr., who is pro life, anti-homosexual (don't ask, don't tell), but so far has done nothing to stop either, sodomy laws, etc. The English's private life as Dostoyevsky once described it is atrocious to say the least and they show their poor and 1/3 of London itself is owned by the royal family which has proved to be a disgrace because of the Prince's homosexual affair and the Queen's approval!

Now in due time and soon this second term shall tell us about the illegals, Palestine in Jordan, and getting all of the homosexuals out of the military as Commander In Chief, and deporting many Moslems, enforcing Sodomy laws (which I have already said), having Congress impeach judges on the Supreme Court or any other federal appellate court when they make law. Four more years is just a cliché. It is how we as a government, we the people shall make inroads to destroy this socialism within our own society and especially in government and not follow the Ivy Leaguers who would wish us for them to be financial businessmen while in turn serving in office and at the highest levels of government!

If Bush Jr. disobeys GOD we all shall suffer here and quicker judgment shall occur as we have already seen. One can legislate morality but one cannot legislate immorality if it is to remain a spiritual nation and not just a state. GOD'S Word is His will. This thing with Israel is not GOD'S permissive will but His absolute will and human being life and Abraham's land is not up for grabs by no man or nation no matter how strong they are.

Maybe then afterwards if ambivalence persists one could conclude that subterfuge was being used here back in the United States in regards to the illegal Hispanics in the millions now with only 4,000 French men allowed here a year and that asylum and immigration were two very different items and the former spoke to religious freedom and the latter spoke to multiculturalism! When has a crippled ever helped an athlete and that was what Mexico was to America!

With conjecture again for the present we can only assume :hat Biblical advice or an unheeded response as such to Biblical advice shall after these next 4 years tell us ah about 9/11, Hussein, the Hispanic “Jihad”, the oil problem which is really non existent with Alaska, the English and their Londontown, etc. We can probably wait we are use to it and the motivating reason shall shine through to some of us and not so much as the “intent” since that only masks what one intended to do which could be anything or nothing or “Well I wanted to but . . . ” The motivating popular vote was for Biblical reasons and not financial reasons or party ideology. This was a very slim margin of choice in what one as a people said and what now they expected to see in regards to their own nation and its national leaders no matter how much they might disagree with them!

This second term would leave in what kind of state say perhaps if Hillary ran, was nominated, and then won? Would it make her oblivious as to how effective she was as taking apart America? Would it enhance her socialistic agenda more? HMO’ S came from where in 1992 and behind closed doors and now look what they promote and that is only care for the young and healthy but nothing for ones who have preexisting conditions! Would her anti-Semitism prevail with power and would we lose our sacredness as a nation completely?

Red China is watching and has played innocent to all this now in the Middle East and nobody is attacking them? We now have limitations but not here in America itself yet the tide can be easily reversed to an English speaking Bible believing nation even with GOD’S judgment. What “obligations” would our own government unnecessarily take on and would totalitarianism be temporarily belated before chaos and anarchy?

Would our leader regret in later years with hindsight what he ref used and knew to do but did not or was ambivalent about? All politicians want to limit and restrict all others but not themselves. This is their short sightedness. It is called progressive thought ideology. With capitalism always comes socialism. Ideology or group thought or say as opposed to faith and an individual particular point of view with no special interests almost like a monarch and not a dictator! Now John Ashcroft is resigning as the top law enforcement officer in the nation and maybe because he has become discouraged because he could not be allowed to do his job but could not say so.

No not all religions are equal or are cultures and Christianity is not Islam, heaven forbid, but profit exceeds prophet with all ideologies as well as with capitalism. Now GOD and one would have to decide accordingly to GOD'S will meaning Messiah or Y'eshua or Jesus Christ come in the flesh and would the people believe a lie from Satan or the truth which is never sought in any election even though some do vote in that order but it is in the minority. Shall we too oppose Israel and be left on the rubbish heap of history like so many other nations have like Russia, France, Germany, Italy, etc.? If we have any anti-Semitism make no mistake about it if we take Abraham's land from the Jews and from GOD if that is possible which it is not then heaven help us all in America! Israel let alone America are not multicultural states. The Arabs are 1st sons but through sin, the Jews are also a first son but through GOD! Both are Semite people from Shem, one of Noah's 3 sons, but both are not Jews since it was Abraham and Sarah whose faith finally held and not Hagar's whose son was Ishmael and his religion became that of the Moslems or Mohammed who, by the way, never said he was GOD in the flesh and in fact only One ever had said that and that was GOD Himself who hung on the cross and then resurrected to defeat death. The Gentiles then are Arabs too and the Gentiles shall surround Jerusalem and let us all hope that it is not on this President's watch that this would occur since things in the entire world are moving at such a rapid pace and we as citizens and human beings on this earth must stay true to the faith which means that Israel should always be our ally and if we do that and still. GOD would seem to oppose us then the Father has made up His mind to do so and then we must follow along with faith as to where that would take us in the future in regards to a nation in which all nations have a soul just like an individual and not a group like in socialism which is not of His doing but has been allowed to occur because man in his own human nature wanted the creation more than the Creator.

We are our brothers' keepers and that would mean that we must uphold Israel as one would uphold a dear friend and allow them to make the decisions that is best for them or in the way that they would see it to be since it too is a sovereign nation and not pressure with things such as George Bush Sr. had done with the private banks here that wanted to help Israel with a loan but he refused and hence he lost the election and he also was for this one world government and the skull and cross bones which can only be symbolic to something that is unGODLY!

Let us again keep Israel our ally and not be swayed by our own flesh or Adam's fall in the Garden for since we have known GOD'S grace as believers we now must do according to His will and not to our own will, the world's will or even what the enemy would suggest to us in a private dialogue in our very own spiritual heart.

One nation under GOD indivisible with liberty and justice for all. We too should want that as a beacon unto this evil age which is soon at its end where political ramifications exceed the spiritual which is always the case and so we must guard with care our own hearts that have been cleansed by Calvary for all who would believe and who the Father has called to be His own for He has lost none of them.

It would more than appear that the asinine German Nazis and the atheistic Jews have embedded themselves into Hollywood more than ever. As I was going through the channels late one night I came across a movie which appeared newly made that showed a black male and a German male dressing up like women or cross dressing. For a few minutes I watched it to see how far this filth would go. It went as far as these Nazis (the same as in Nazi Germany) wanted it to go. Now the blacks had become the brownshirts in America including the homosexuality part that was once in Nazi Germany. This was the sin to the 3rd and the 4th generation, and no one could now compare the blacks any longer if they did at all to the peasants in Russia who had also been so cruelly treated for so many years, but never stooped to Sodom and Gomorrah! They were hard working people without forced labor and in fact wanted to be left alone by the rich and well educated as well as the soviets. The blacks in America had gone along with almost everything that they could get away with and appeared more in line with the Germans and the English who were as cold as ice. They did not have much compassion and sympathy even for their own women that is the black male nor for their very own children and now were emulating again what the NAACP, Bill Cosby, and others now were telling them what to do. They were appearing through reason to be good fathers, but the change had occurred so very fast and also the fact that the blacks wanted to force themselves on others mostly all the time and really not even the Hispanics could get along with them. These blacks had become the poster children for the Nazis and the Communists in Hollywood, in our own federal government and most all things that were promoted in the newspapers, television, radio and magazines. Since all of this was to the extreme left that is their terminology, but in actuality socialism; this appeared to be almost an innate thing with some of these groups of people who appeared in a great majority of them to want to go along with the prevailing wind and not like in Russia where the peasants were fooled and then forced, as I said before, to go along with the death wish of socialism. The peasants in Russia were doing well coming into the 20th century and they had had for centuries many more than the blacks in America been treated terrible by the rich, and well educated, but here in America the rich and well educated wanted more and more of their own degeneracy and since the blacks made a most convincing case for most ignorant Americans then it was indeed working.

Americans really knew nothing about socialism or Communism because they had never lived under it nor did they even try to educate themselves about either Nazism or Communism. They only knew how to make money and so the love of money was what they only really knew about which meant for sure that we as a nation were coming to self-destruction. These Nazis were not all by far Germans but included a variety of other groups such as the Greeks, the English, the blacks as I have already said, many

Catholics in the priesthood as well as many that had served as altar boys who now were grown up and now doing the same things that the predecessors had done to them and also Nazis were also at the highest levels of government, of church, of the corporate world, in sports, etc. These Nazis, and this word was thrown about like the word "the", but whenever I thought about it always reminded me of the homosexual pedophiles in Nazi Germany, such as Hitler, Goerring, Himmler, Hess, Roehm, List, and the list would go on and on and included the Hitler Youth Corps, but one group or nationality that basically could not stomach any of this were, of course, the Italians. The only Italians involved in pedophilia were the ones who were either priests or who were Catholics and had been molested as children serving the type of religion called Roman Catholicism. Dostoyevsky never knew how right he was when he called Roman Catholicism socialism in mysticism or happiness in slavery, because in actual fact it was socialism, just the kind that Hitler had in Nazi Germany. It had transplanted itself for sure here in America! Hitler used racial socialism which said that the Teutonics were the master race, which meant that interbreeding would be the thing such as men with other men which was nothing more then sexual deviancy. As I continued to study this psychiatric mental disorder I noticed that again certain nationalities and races were drawn to it more than others and one could see it especially in their males, but now the women and teenagers and adolescents were getting involved in it and the earth would spew us out and quite soon. That for sure was what the Old and New Testament had said about homosexuality plus the fact that it was an abomination and the people who would not listen to GOD would then be turned over by GOD Himself to reprobate minds! This indeed was a scary thing not the homosexuals, but the fact that GOD Himself hated this act and kind of thinking so much that He Himself would judge a nation very quickly in regards to this type of horrible sin that would destroy the family unit, our children like infanticide had, pedophilia amongst 60-70% of all homosexuals, AIDS and other VD diseases, murder, rape of children, pornography, and all other kinds of evil actions and thoughts. This was the very pollution that the United States Supreme Court as well as the rest of America who appeared not in the slightest what happened to their very own children because if they did they had to be now informed or at least take a bold outward stand and start to apprehend these Nazis no matter who or where they were in America or how much money and wealth they had or what position in our nation that they held or had held. There were already priests and bishops and now Cardinals in the Roman Catholic hierarchy that were being sought out but not being incarcerated and tried severely for their crimes because some of the defendants' attorneys were only concerned about financial retribution which would not stem this tide of evil within America and within many nice looking homes in the suburbs as well as in the countryside and in many youth and children's organizations!

They too along with the very ones who committed infanticide and treason were allowed to perpetuate their form of evil that not even GOD would allow too much longer and to GOD a day could be like a thousand years and because it involved children Jesus too, I believed was not interceding with the Father because children of all ages were being used in the most horrible manner and Jesus had said that if anyone hurt any of these little ones then they should have an albatross put around their necks and thrown into the sea. Jesus did not even address the Pharisees in this way! We were reaping ourselves into a most horrible type of judgment by GOD because GOD is everywhere and the quote above did not in anyway refer to baby Christians as many liked to say. It was being used in the literal sense of the word.

With America we had become obsessed with sexual deviancy of all kinds and one could include in that lust, adultery, sex outside of marriage, shacking up, rape, torture, etc and our own government pre tended that nothing was going on and the church worse of all was silent and was a very part of it such as the Episcopalian church here, but not in Africa and most of our own television ministries spoke little or nothing about it, but only spoke about financial matters and self-esteem or how to improve one's life for oneself but not how to search out and protect our own children in our own nation. Doctors too were involved in this as well as hospitals where they had access to many patients who could not defend them selves and the administrative boards too could be included with the homosexuality.

This was their so called pure race and one nationality more than any other had come to America through all our years and that was the Germans and this sin would go to the 3rd and 4th generation and Biblical generations were always 40 years another Biblical number. People were not watching and questioning in their own minds the many people who they trusted too much. Even if they knew for sure, they would not speak out and this was indeed wrong because we had to prosecute and bring to trial these vicious criminals the way one would bring to trial someone who sold drugs, or had murdered someone for money, etc. Little Richard, Liberace, Joseph Lieberman, Reformed Judaism, the Roman Catholic church, the Episcopalian church, John Wayne Gacy, Jeffrey Dahmer, Hillary Clinton, Bill Clinton, Madeleine Albright, George Stephanopoulos, Dick Morris, Paul Lynne, Charles Nelson Reilly, Truman Capote, many hard rock music groups, the Masons, many people who worked in children's agencies such as counselors and scouts which included the Girl Scouts of America, Big Brother & Big Sisters of America, the United Way, the YMCA, the Olympics, Billy Jean King, Martina Navratilova, Rock Hudson, the New Agers, etc.

I also had now wondered if, because of old man Krupps himself the Nazi billionaire, Henry Ford had not been one along with David Rockefeller with his very effeminate voice and mannerism. I knew that some men who were effeminate were not always homosexuals but were brought up around women or were from the upper class of society and just spoke that way. This yes was a serious sin problem that no one wanted to touch, but if we did not then for sure GOD would because GOD is a just and righteous GOD and would not let his children, all children, be tortured to death or be allowed to grow up and perpetrate this evil action to many many more children! It also went against His Holy Word!

Yes, this was the issue that no one except a very few people (and that included people who said they were born again) just did not want to talk about it for some strange reason let alone seek out or better yet keep an eye out for ones in the teaching profession no matter what they taught for money or for volunteer service, the medical profession, and the food service industry where it could really spread like poison. Dr. Lorraine Day, when she had spoken about it, was not even a Christian but was threatened with death by radical Nazi homosexuals in San Francisco just like it was Nazi Germany. For the most part, it appeared not to bother most Germans, and I had to conclude that that was why the Jewish people kept bringing up about the Holocaust because somehow they knew the Germans made their own evil actions irrelevant so much so that even today with this homosexuality I could see that same kind of blasé type of mentality now in regards to sexual perversion.

The English too were involved in this at the highest levels because as I once mentioned this before Prince Charles and the Queen both approved of this homosexuality and in public and maybe that is why Princess Diana had gone with an Islamic Arab because she herself could not cope with such deviancy and know that there were sons involved also who would or could be affected. The Arabs themselves were noted for this sexual deviancy for years and even in Peking it was happening and of course with the Communists anything evil would go!

I remember when a very fine lady by the name of Anita Bryant was the first to voice her truth about homosexuality and was attacked unmercifully in the press and television. She had won Miss America, which stood at that time for lady-like femininity. The butch type women the Germans seemed to produce in their culture did not have an ounce of femininity in them because first of all fatherhood was missing as it had with the blacks, and second this affected the women to go after other women since their very own men were cold-hearted perverts. Now in America, men as well as women who were married and heterosexual were leaving their mates once they found out that their mate was involved in this horrible mental disorder and who would not condone it if one had children. Yet the courts, or should I say the trial lawyers, judges and counselors were turning over children to homosexuals and the New York Times had even shown a young adolescent on its front magazine as being raised by Nazis, as I just spoke about. One now had to know that another Jewish Holocaust was going to occur and that this time help was coming from the Jews especially in America such as Barney Frank the Congressman from Massachusetts who was a homosexual pedophile which also had been proven and then had the nerve to appear on television debating his mental sickness!

There was a cure to this sexual deviancy, and it would take 3-5 years of real Christian counseling and most all homosexuals could be helped, so it was not like a death wish like AIDS was. So there was no excuse, yes excuse, for not wanting to get help. Who knew more about this Homosexual Anonymous more than the homosexual themselves! So what was the excuse for not prosecuting them now? It fit into the New Age system That Constance Gumbey, a lawyer, had written about but did not even herself know about this part of Nazism when she had done such a very fine job on her book called THIS NEW AGE or THIS NEW AGE BARBARISM. This is how well kept it was since the Germans and the English did not want this to get out because then the Holocaust would show how vicious the Nazis were, which we already knew but would show why they were so vicious and that was because of this same homosexuality that now even the United States Supreme Court was promoting and would continue to promote until our doom! Since Protestantism itself was very anti-Semitic and the Germans and the English never ever appear to want an Italian as head in any of their Synods nor that any Italian might want to who was not a Catholic it showed to one that they too wanted to be in control of their own destiny but also wanted to rule the roost, but were they that smart to do that?

Yes, there was much prejudice amongst the Anglo-Saxons in America too because could one name any President that was Italian, Polish, Jewish, etc.? There was not a one. Why had some of our ancestry here in America worn silk stockings and wigs and funny pants with a sword dangling at their side? These were not the knights of old that I myself had heard so much about, were they?

Yes, my own wife had said, after she asked me some questions about our own American History which she had forgotten, that indeed America was a very young nation, and if one thought about it, it was even less than 150 years the Civil War was over and not even then did the Negro have their freedom. All kinds of excuses could be made as to the why they brought another race of people here through coercion and why they themselves could not work the land like other farmers could. This did not include plantations because all that meant to me was that more land meant more money!

Again the rich and well educated wanted to take the easy road to success but on the backs of others who I am sure loved the "occupations" that they had picked out for them ahead of time! Then some will always say well he released them which meant absolutely nothing since coercion ruined their lives and the lives of others for years to come and this anger would never heal quite well or should I say this wound no matter how many facade like civil rights' socialists that they had installed that is the Anglo-Saxons in America!

When they released the slaves and said, "Well now here is your freedom", what did this mean to the slaves at that time? It was like the peasants like I said many tunes before and shall say again and that is when they gave the peasants land and then the rich and well educated bought back the very same land because the peasants were not used to dealing in money but always bartered was this not the very same kind of principle that applied right here in America too and being the fact the many Jews bought that land from our own Negro slaves just like the rich and well educated did in Russia and that was to swindle our slaves, yes our slaves, even though all my people had come here years later and my own parents were first generation but still were part of the very Europe who contrived both the slavery here and in Russia! Is that why the blacks now had been bought out by sports and Hollywood so that they could cover up, especially the Anglo-Saxons own guilt because of really what the direct line of ancestry had done? I too though had to take responsibility for this since I too was an American citizen raised and born here. Whatever affected America affected me as an artist and a writer and if I, for some strange reason saw things in a different or even a true light, then I too must include myself since I too live here!

Why had the Negro accepted their dirty money through the New Deal (FDR) and the Great Society (LBJ) and also the millionaires and billionaires such as Steinbrenner, Rupert Murdoch, the Rockefellers, the Roosevelts and their blueblood and a host of others that offered certain blacks so much money that they would step on the graves of the ones who died in slavery for these Anglo-Saxons who also wanted to rule the roost and now the ideologues that followed the Europeanism religions?

When the Negro appeared to be catching up from being held down, then they came along with ones in their "tribe" who could be bought out because they had accented as a down payment the dirty money that the 60's atheistic Jews and the Anglo-Saxons and also Hollywood, the media, television, radio, sports and had really in essence taken what they should have had such as land in all part of this land to work or farm in the way that they so fit and as long as it was used not to destroy the habitat which I am sure back then that the Negro would not have done, but now they have been all centered into the cancerous tumors that we call cities that take everything just like Moscow and St. Petersburg had taken from the peasants by force to feed their faces now in New York City, Los Angeles, Miami, Hollywood, San Francisco, Chicago, Philadelphia, etc.!

No, history does not repeat itself but man does and it is the common man who makes that very same history for if the common man would not venture out into the unknown then the rich and well-educated would have what to show for and would have done what to improve man's being? No, it is not the rich and famous that we constantly hear about that made America good it was the lower echelon meaning the ones who worked the land whether that was farmers or plantation slaves. It certainly was not the elites who could only think of how to make their own life a life of Reilly on the backs of ones who again worked the land with the hands and their backs and not their mouths so much. These rich and well educated from the beginning of time had always ruled on t op and that was nothing new, but now when we said that we believed in GOD that is the American people why did we do what we were explicitly told not to do and that was get involved in slavery which was evil?

No matter how I construct this in my own mind, I cannot condone what we did as Americans to another man and his family with no regard for them and even followed the course of Darwin who of course came from England and the fact that Karl Marx himself is buried in England when he was born in Germany goes to show that the English still too insist in having it their way all the time and one can look at even Ireland where the English agitate as they had done with the Arabs and their oil, but guess again who gets to fight another day? No, it is not us but the ones who worked the land. When agriculture is taken away from a people who are close to the land it takes away the spirit of a man like no other thing such as metal tin cars, bulldozers, metal railroads, metal planes, metal chain saws, metal race cars, etc. It forms a cold and brutal society which has grown accustomed to brutality and viciousness and infects all of us with this progressive mindset that says success in any shape or form is what it is all about!

The Biblical interpretation for this was, "And the love of money is the root to all kinds of evil and the way a man can get into heaven, no the way a rich man can get into heaven is through the very eye of a needle" and I know some are going to say that that was another kind of needle in regards to a city!

I guess, as I have said so many times before, that was what Alexander Solzhenitsyn had said it best when he said, "That lies upon lies produce violence". Taking as Satan had in the Garden the truth and twisting it into a lie! "Now GOD did not say . . . "

We are not what we eat but what we think, and also the words that come out of our mouths which also stem from the spiritual heart even though it is through the mind that sin originates! Not war and peace but peace and violence since one can now readily see that we fight a war overseas while we allow murder by infanticide to our most innocent and precious of all human beings and that is our or GOD'S children since we do not know how to be good stewards and no not in money but in parenthood such as fatherhood and motherhood!

Now in America, with the movie the GODFATHER, the Italians had become the worst enemy to the blacks in America, which was believed by most. Right? No, first of all the blacks were wrong in their assumption to confuse these two people as one since the Turkish Sicilians were not Italian even though they spoke a slang form of it just like the Hispanics spoke a slang form of Spanish. There were no blacks allowed anywhere on the island of Sicily. The Sicilians were good barbers and pimps and were what the Mafia was all about which was a feud just like the Arabs had had for centuries and had absolutely nothing to do with the Italians proper. The Italians were very bright and were versatile and could do many things.

Hollywood and others wanted many to think and also wanted to subterfuge the whole issue because the Italians were not at all for homosexuality and so if they could be alone made to look like the knave then the acceptance of homosexuality through civil rights' socialism would have a better chance of going through to all the blacks in America. The Anglo-Saxons were again up to their old tricks along with the atheistic Jews who by the way loved the American black women but would not marry them but had sex for them only. Now that many mulattos were appearing on the scene and some of these women were very beautiful women, the Jewish male in America wanted to have his cake and eat it too. But these mulattos were caught between a hard rock and a stone! What side would really want them for who they were and not how they performed in bed? Their outside beauty now all of a sudden appealed to the Anglo-Saxon too, but they were too cold and non physical for the mulatto woman.

Since beauty or worldly beauty is only skin deep (no pun intended here), but this beauty was seen as a way of undetermining these people since they would hardly ever—many of them unless it was follow-the-leader mentality—be ostracized like years before if the races mixed. Probably the only ones who had respect for these women, and this had in no regards anything to do with race and that was if two real Christians loved each other and would marry first before having sex and stay married then in this case one knew almost for sure that this was a marriage where both partners loved each other with an agapé love and not with a phileo or romantic type of worldly love that said, "Look at my trophy."

Yes, the Italians had much to be blamed for since they opposed homosexuality in major numbers with in the Italian community and did not think like the average German just like years ago the average Russian did not think like the German either! But who, by the way, did think like the average German? Yes, maybe the English perhaps since they were cousins but the English though were much smarter and did have a sense of humor! One could not certainly attribute that to the German in any kind of instance. The Poles, though, appeared to get along with the Germans for the most part. But that too maybe could be attributed to the fact that the Poles considered themselves royalty of some kind and always above others but really had not too much to show for it. Pulaski maybe was an exception to the rule in this case since he was both versatile and very bright. Would I be supposing where one should not suppose because at least in America the Poles had made great inroads into America by owning many things but than again they were more into Roman Catholicism than even perhaps the Italians were themselves?

The royalty of Europe or this illusion of grandeur was what had kept them down for so many years and also the reason they probably could bear the Soviets to rule over them for all those years. Yet when tiny Vietnam did not want them to, we said that the Vietnamese, who by now were being called (at least by our military) slopeheads, were said not to have the courage to oppose Communism. But yet America had faltered here and also Poland who both had more technology and knew how to defeat or at least give them a battle and no one said that we or Poland did not have the courage to defeat only Moscow and Peking!

The Poles were hard workers, but maybe for the entirely wrong reason and that was their being steeped into Roman Catholicism so very much and that now even the atheistic Jews were becoming Catholics! This is where this materialism surely came in for anyone who had a love for the businessmen's association. The Poles also knew that without money not faith, man could do nothing that is in America but it had to transcend from somewhere in Europe did it not? Yes many unbelieving Jews were turning over a new leaf on life and they too were going for the gusto or the gold rush!

If one could profit that much from the ideology then it too had to be related somehow to socialism and what better way to disguise it than through a religion of European origins even if it meant that this ideology was and had always been anti-Semitic, but that would not happen to the Jew in America, or would it? If one could be miserly it was the Pole. They could collect money along with the Germans like people collected stamps and baseball cards and yet appear poor as a church mouse in a cathedral!

A final summation on homosexuality and homosexuals would be that they loved the uniform, which most likely described the German to a T. The Israelis, in fact, mostly wore khakis and were not uniform nuts. Even in America the German heterosexuals loved to use the uniform and were gun nuts and always seemed to want to go hunting which they considered a sport but was nothing more than ego. The knife was a weapon of means more for the darker races since most every black had a knife cut on their body. Every people and race had some type of group sin that transcended generations. The Anglo-Saxons also like to appear with the attire they wore as to what they either were or wanted to be such as many cars that had the bubble gum top on them but were not on any police force or department. So the uniform was almost an addiction that the homosexual loved to wear time and again, another reason they wanted to stay in the military, and the uniform gave them a feeling of Eros!

Now police departments were hiring them in greater numbers. Anything with a uniform was what they wanted, because their own brotherhood of deviancy made them feel that they had power. They would sell out their own country just like the Nazis did in Nazi Germany for their homosexuality. Even Maxim Gorky made a comment about the homosexuality in Germany years ago. Some of the worst criminals in the 20th century even could not stomach this nor could the prison inmates. Yet we in society allowed it to be what it was and in fact the United States Supreme Court only ruled 5-4 in a case on homosexuality when the ruling should have been 9-0 against and not 5-4 against! Even John Kelly got about 60,000,000 votes and many had to know what he stood for as far as homosexuality was and that he was for it and if they did not then they had become ignoramuses to say the least. This was no small part on the media to subterfuge this entire issue and in some cases some nationalities took it with a grain of salt which to others could not be believed!

That is why democracy in such a large nation does not work because the candidates are not well known and since the National Democratic Party tends to pull these candidates out of a hat or the bottom of a barrel like Clinton or the Clintons then one would say it was just like the Nazis who chose Hitler an Austrian because two other Germans were too close to pick so they picked an Austrian and the same went with the Vatican in regards to picking a Pole such as Pope John Paul II and not that he himself was a homo sexual but that he had not been an Italian like Luciano was who preceded him and then died so suddenly!

Now the Vatican was turning its eye towards Latin America where they had held a stronghold since most of the population there was Roman Catholic and many were anti-Semitic. Now also would be the time to appoint Hispanics since most of them hated the Jews and were not educated enough to really know about the Bible; hence that was what the Vatican wanted, an ignorant people to rule over in the same way they had ruled for so many centuries before. This, though, was the padré mentality which would do all for them the same way that socialism promises but does not deliver at all.

This is where Christ killer had been said many times with ill regard to who Christ Himself was and that he was Jewish, in fact a Jewish Messiah! The meetings and appointments were now from Hispanic America even in Europe because Latin America still had many natural resources from which to draw from more so than even America did. All the Latin cultures subscribed to Roman Catholicism such as France and Italy and now in the very heart of Latin America. This was not a ministry of the Gospel, but a worldwide intrusion into other people's nations to promote their socialism in mysticism.

Where would all these funds go that this "church" was receiving from all over the world? Liberation Theology also played a huge part in this especially in Hispanic America who were very volatile people. They would often act before they had thought something through. The Mexicans were the most volatile of them all and the Puerto Ricans were probably the least educated or knowledgeable of them all. Cubans were the businessmen of Latin America and that is why the Communists both Soviets and Red Chinese took and helped the island and supplied Castro with all that he needed and in fact like Lenin, Castro too had been a lawyer before he became a vicious dictator!

How many lawyers had now become what these two men were? We in America alone had more lawyers here than in all the world and were producing more and more paid liars. Would this insanity ever stop that was growing in America in regards to lawyers and to our own judges and politicians who made all the laws that now all appeared to be immoral.

Just as Russia had the vaudevillian stage with the Soviets, we too years ago had vaudeville right here with W. C. Fields and Charlie Chaplin and others. Did not Lenin say use the theatre to promote the cause? Now just how asinine was this Lenin? One could readily see, since he lived like a scavenger himself for so many years in the West, when he served time in prison in Russia, it was the life of Riley for him since the monarch in Russia was too soft on these revolutionaries. In fact his older brother had tried to assassinate another monarch and was executed so this entire family was a crime family. The monarch allowed too much, except in this last case for these revolutionaries to work in Russia and did not really use the death penalty even when one monarch was shot at many times! This is what helped create this liberal mindset we in America now had too. We also did not want to execute these criminals that were now in our very own government, and for whatever foolish reason we all would be paying for it. There had to come a time when this all would back up like it had in Russia when they too had a sort of 60's revolution that at first failed, but later in 1917 came to fall fruition and from a democracy and not a monarch!

How many criminals in high places in our society were being allowed to roam our streets also? That is why our nation was being attacked because it had no intestinal fortitude but only would congratulate itself if it was a small election and the ballot box Democracy would not heat the problem but only metastasize the issue by ignoring what the majority of people did not even care to talk about let alone deal with in a legal sense of the word and with prosecution and incarceration for those who even committed treason. They now were running the government and the big corporations could care less since they too were involved in this up to their own necks. This too was their life of Riley that they liked to live.

It again was follow the leader and that surely meant that the Germans had something to do with this and that England who we always followed also had much to do with this type of liberal insane mindset! The men in our own society had come to wear skirts and our military at the highest levels were only con cerned about how they would retire and not at all about a future for our children, but especially our own grandchildren in this nation of ours!

There were no qualifications to hold any type of position, another thing I had mentioned many times before. Where were all the males in our society whole in appearance appeared to be men but really wore these skirts? Would they not defend this land here and forget about the Islamic Arabs over there? This appeared again to be following the leader and in Hollywood all they wanted was to get out of what Osama wanted to do with them and would do anything now to tell him that they were part of the same gang as him and had always wanted to destroy the moral fiber of America for many many years beginning with vaudeville!

Since most Americans are not patriotic they allow Communists and their ideology into our very own society, but don't be the one to say that or they might say that you are not quite well yourself. But we do allow, including Christians, Communists to run for the Presidency of the United States and do not ask or demand for indictments and prosecutions for Bill Clinton and John Kerry and their treasonous acts and we might as well not have a Constitutional form of government! It would appear that the United States Constitution is void and null for if it would be applied that is legally applied neither of the two above men would have served at all in any capacity in any public office! The fact being that neither one has ever been questioned or have been asked to give up their ideology is another reason as an American I can see that we no longer as a people know what Communism is nor do we care! They not only show the arrogance that all Communists show but they laugh at us with this same kind of arrogance and Hollywood and the media and the Ivy Leaguers go along with the accolades that praises them as if they were real war time heroes who fought for our sovereignty.

If we the people do not care about GOD and we do not for the most part then who shall care? We as believers must stand for righteousness and not atheism and by being silent and to pray for one's enemies does not mean we accept a foreign god and that is what we do everyday that we ignore what is going on in our very own nation at the very highest level and one could not get any higher and that is why the Communists not only attempt to shatter or subvert our nation outwardly but they even ridicule those who would oppose their atheistic ideology. That is why constitutional government in a democracy never works for very long. We complain about environmental issues and speeding tickets, but we remain totally silent when atheistic anti-humanity Communism is allowed to roam free in our nation when in our own very Constitution it says "for high crimes and misdemeanors" referring to ones who would do just that subvert or overthrow our way of life once and for all and think not twice about it!

We had lost our patriotic duty even before the 60's with the Woodrow Wilsons, the FDR's, the U.S. Supreme Court and organizations such as the Communistic ACLU and People For The American WAY just to mention a few. We do not have the concern or intestinal fortitude and patriotic duty to defend our way of life here in the states while we roam the world concerned about other so called democracies that are nothing more then facades of injustice.

Here is one incredible story about how foolish our own judicial system is when it condones and compliments the Gulags that were in the Soviet Union and use to torture the peasants by making them work on the outside at 75 degrees below 0 Fahrenheit and some of them froze against each other or had to be shot if they could not make it from the work sight and could only crawl back to the barracks which was about 3 miles away and then their bodies would eventually be covered by the snow! After knowing all of this a judge by the name of Leibowitz of the New York State Supreme Court had not only known but had visited the Gulags and said that they were setting a good example! This is how far we in America have come that we not only visit a sight but also agree with the above scenario and some would say that I never knew that about the Soviet Union and one would have to wonder where have they been for at least the last 80 years? We have only been concerned for the most part at least our Anglo-Saxon government since it was the Germans that allowed Lenin in a sealed tram to enter Moscow and the English at the Yalta Conference to intentionally allow millions upon millions of human beings to be destroyed. To wine and to dine with the fox trot in the West and know all the time what Stalin, the Georgian, was and still went along with murder. These are some of the West's heroes who should have been prosecuted for aiding and abetting the enemy!

Now in our very own nation we too murder 5,000 babies a day through infanticide! We also allow homosexuals to run rampant and harm and molest and murder our children yet give them the very right to do all of this by a law called the "hate crime"! What is the hate the Nazi homosexual pedophile or the innocent child? One would have to question also the sanity of our very nation's soul and as to why we do absolutely nothing because some small tribunal says it is okay to promote anything and anytime and we do not defend the children with our own lives if that is what it takes since it appears that just the theory of a criminal law seems to exist and that even NAMBLA the North American Man Boy Love Association is approved by the scoundrels at the United Nations which should sit in Berlin somewhere and not in the United States as it now does and we contribute our own tax dollars in the billions and yet no one really gets to the heart of the matter for if they did it would stop, such as incarcerating them for life or even the death penalty for all who would molest a child. Too strong you say! How about Turkey which uses the death penalty for drug dealing? But we are not like them, no we are much worse because our so called civilized nation now allows murder in the first degree daily and pre-meditated so we all in essence are accomplices in that and all the prayer in the world are not going to help if we do not intervene like human beings and not a species from a lower world! We do not even want to repent and turn away from this very sin, and in fact all we see is money as the bottom line and a convenient way to not only have sex no matter with whom but also to be paid for it in the process by we the people known as the American government!

We are so despised by the Communists because we do not defend and oppose them strong enough to prosecute and incarcerate anyone who is a member of or participates in any meeting that has anything to do with the Communist ideology! We ourselves, like our parents have not grown up enough to understand that Disney World and Hollywood nonsense used to be for children alone, but now not even one who is half normal would want to watch the filth and garbage they air.

As I thought about that issue another one came into my mind and that was of this terrorist Yassir Arafat, who is a murderer of thousands and thousands of people just as if he himself had pulled the trigger or ignited to blow up a building himself and in fact worse because he planned it himself and did it to women and innocent children who had nothing whatsoever to do with anything and the fact that they use their very own children just like the Nazis did who in fact the Arabs gave aid and assistance to for many years right after World War II to the present time and we sit down and recognize and deal with anybody no matter how many they have murdered and then scorn Israel when they defend but 9/11 all of a sudden was a different issue because to get re-elected was more important an issue then to say once and for all that Islam is an enemy to America's Judeo-Christianity and no matter how one tries to undercut this by using euphemistic words it shall never do or ever change the truth about this most vicious religion that has for centuries maimed and murdered time and again with no regret whatsoever!

Now that Arafat is dead, had he at anytime said he was sorry, not that that would bring back all those innocent lives, but would at least show a sense of remorse if sincere, but no the media entertains to these terrorists attacks and incriminates themselves as part of the same kind of ideology that is innately within Islam itself! Since 1967 Arafat has lead this terrorists' organization all over the world but mostly in Israel to destroy Israel as a state and every Jewish person no matter what and our very own State Department assisted him in this by allowing these roaming Arabs to squat on Abraham's land.

The Father calls to all who He has chosen, and no one comes to Him on their own! In this statement GOD is Sovereign in His will as the Creator as to whom shall be saved and when or is already saved meaning through GOD'S omnipotence and omniscience GOD already knows. Does that mean we then should not witness? Heaven forbid! None shall snatch them out of His hand". What GOD pre-ordained GOD already knew even before the very foundation of the earth and also knew of me before I was in my mother's womb!

Did Christ die for all or for all sins? If Christ died for all would not all be then saved? No, not necessarily, because freewill plays a part but if the Father does not call them hence they do not come. GOD'S very elect are His to know not for us to know, hence we are to spread the Gospel not as though we do or don't know this elect but that only He knows. One might ask then why witness if He already knows and they will be saved? That too is a mystery of GOD since we in our finite minds cannot even begin to comprehend. In essence He has already chosen so freewill is not the deciding factor. Is that unfair? No, GOD has to call, "For His children hear His voice." GOD does choose His elect. We as His elect are called by Him to witness and if we are listening we shall do that. We do not save anyone nor do we know who GOD Himself knows who is to be saved. We are just the instruments. It is the spiritual heart that must be cleansed and is not the mind's reasoning that saves us because we believe in a certain church doctrine or denomination or works, etc. It is by grace alone at Calvary that is this gift that the elect come to be saved, yes by choosing, but first by His calling them or the elect to Himself

With the Holy Spirit we then do His work through Him alone and not of ourselves or this world. "On earth as it is in heaven" does not mean either self preservation or self esteem but does mean to do as if we were already in heaven. His good deeds then through us as instruments now which here is free will and obedience. This does not mean we shall always get it right Or that this is a prerequisite for salvation but a life full of GOD'S grace means that that believer shall do and is doing everyday for His kingdom. "Thy kingdom come, Thy will be done on earth as it is in heaven."

This is not again self preservation or ego or the "I" in me. What it is, though as a child of GOD is that we call Him Abba Father or daddy and don't children call their earthly father daddy?" I and the Father are One."

GOD's sovereignty is the ultimate as to what piece of clay shall be used for what!

As well shall "OUR FATHER" who can call Him Abba Father? WHO ART IN HEAVEN". And where is GOD'S home? "HALLOWED BE THY NAME." How sacred and Holy is His name. "THY KINGDOM COME." The 1,000-year reign of Christ yet to COME. "Thy Will Be Done." His will will be done. "ON EARTH AS IT IS IN HEAVEN." Now and in heaven later. "GIVE US THIS DAY OUR DAILY BREAD." God shall provide in His way. "AND FORGIVE US OUR TRESPASSES." To bring to mind immediately the sin committed by a believer and to confess it and repent for it. "AS WE FORGIVE THOSE WHO TRESPASS AGAINST US." Since we have been forgiven should we not also pray for and forgive those who do harm or sin against us as a fellow human being created by GOD? "AND LEAD US NOT INTO TEMPTATION." GOD does not tempt anyone but the spirit is willing, but the flesh is weak. "BUT DELIVER US FROM EVIL." To keep and to protect us from the enemy and the world for we are in the world but not of the world. "FOR THINE IS THE KINGDOM AND THE POWER AND THE GLORY FOREVER AND EVER, AMEN." It is GOD'S kingdom His power and love and to His Glory the Father through the Son by the power of the Holy Spirit as this is for eternity end of prayer with an "AMEN". It is finished and it has been done or complete by GOD already at Calvary!

All babies born and unborn are saints and all children, until their own age of accountability that again only GOD knows are also saved! So through mortality rate and now infanticide we keep murdering the saints of GOD in His own family. Heaven help us GOD has not called babies to be murdered, but He has them now in His kingdom, but shall the abortionist or the child killer be there?

So this is what 50,000,000 Americans voted for and that is this very ideology from the pits of Hell that is believed as any "religion" to be followed. This inhumanity of frozen bodies outside without any food, any shelter, and kind of warmth, any covering, but to die but quickly or else be shot to death because it is taking to long the death process! So malnourished that anything shall be found to eat, if they could have found anything!

Even upon death they do not stop for if one does not work one does not eat or cannot surely eat! But what is there to eat? Nonetheless get up and work!

How many millions were murdered like this and yet we suppose a believer of this ideology and we voted one already in as President and another one came very close! They both share this insane anti-humanity of Communist ideology. This is their belief system! Make no mistake about it. It shall metastasize itself bigger and bigger, as any parasite does and already has devoured 60,000,000 infanticides and now is pursuing the sick, the infirmed, the disabled, the elderly, the defenseless, the demented, etc.

Till now we have only said, "So what?" Yes, so what, but you are next! Not me! I know my ideology short and quick and as a surprise! It has a way of vacuuming all the little dust particles that now are in its way!

Doing wasn't enough, but it was how fast one could croak that made it easier for them! Just dig a huge grave and bury hundreds in it and if fortunate it would be deep enough.

Now this was this utopia too that Clinton and Kerry both spoke about, but of course not in the same vernacular as such. It was sugar coated with arsenic. No gas chambers, no problem, we have plenty of bullets!

Everything to be gotten had to be stolen and resold, but one had to hush up about it! This was the way utopia in socialism was; it was a concentration camp! Americans let the world revolve around them just like the socialists in Russia did but the others well they revolved around the earth or should one say evolved into the ground eventually! The only charity that was to be found was in death. Maybe there they were not handing out torture and more pain? Oh, and equal rights for women well that was another thing in the camp! The socialists had that all worked out by the pound. The proposition was that one had to sell out one's soul to stay alive, or did they? Yes, they never make mistakes do they? That is why no one is left or can talk from the grave!

Sometimes camp inmates have sex and procreate a child into that world. The parents are then separated and the mother is still pregnant when this occurs. After birth, the child is taken from the hospital to a children's village. After breast feeding, the mothers never again see their child, and the fathers as long as they are in camp never to be let out, do ever see the child at all. This is Hillary's village by the way in case one wants to vote for her in 2008! Any deadbeat dads wanted? Some children cannot survive artificial feeding and so they die. The reason for the present tense is that we now have it right here and it is also elsewhere. You may ask where. Soviet style day care in America!

When the women are separated, they either do one of two things: they either have a platonic relationship or they become lesbians or Sodomites. For the women it is always harder to be separated from the opposite sex!

Back to the children and that is the survivors after a year are sent to an orphanage or to us the term is foster care which is even worse! This is now what Americans want to pursue head on. All rights with no wrongs but also no responsibilities. This is socialism utopia that the Clintons and the Kerrys hope to uphold for all Americans since they appear to know best. And as to abortions, then out in the free world there on the outside the camps they then prohibit them, but not in the camps or the concentration camps! But guess who did not want their child at all? Again it was the thieves like we have in our own society!

Just remember all the above was promoted in reality by two nationalities and they were the Anglo-Saxons with Lenin and the Yalta Conference who spoke for all of us in the West and then some! Why were (and they still are) the English such cutthroats to so many peace initiatives as well as the trustworthy Germans? How can one not see how evil they have done in the 20th Century and before to others that they hated and how far they took that evil that was to last for some generations?

We in America have never really known what a war is like that totally destroy a nation's best people and hence we take for granted everything that we have and do not realize that we too may go the very same road to destruction since for so long we have been doing all the evils that these other civilizations had done and had almost been rewarded for good behaviour and as for Russia well they were left to rot Shall America too be the same to this world now that seems to be looking at us as they then looked at

Russia at that time? We can ill afford to allow our own morals and belief system to be undermined by ones who have half a brain and not feel the slightest for their fellow man, no matter who that might be.

Where do all our children go who have been brought up in foster care after they leave that? Does any one really care? Or is it the money in what one is doing that matters the most? These are educated college idiots that care not about anything but the I in ego and that means only for themselves and no one else. Yet we give them full reign to handle our very own precious children like a piece of garbage to be thrown out!

What has happened to the American conscience that tells one right from wrong and guides us?

One has to notice two things about America which are unrelated to each other. The first is that like the Soviet novelist writer of true history for Russia which was almost virtually impossible to gather facts perhaps only from the dead and so it also was in America the same in a manner of speaking to be able to find out anything about the superrich or not until we too had been sold out by the elites and then only negative things about the heartland of America were being said to try and destroy America because their chain of command into another generation was the same status quo who too would be as bad, no worse; hence now one had to be careful how far this negativity would proceed. It was too good to be true, to say the least, and usually the elites thought and worked that way with the escape goat mentality of blame the American people like they blamed the Russian peasants in Russia! In fact in our very own White House for instance and in his second term one could already see a repeat performance even before it got started and the filibustering with fancy speeches which meant absolutely nothing to the sovereignty of America.

This Anglo had the role all played out as before and was not a bad guy to have as a neighbor but as for Presidential material he was in no way gratified. This would encompass a statesman such as Adlai Stevenson or an Alan Keyes, yes a Negro scholar. Heaven forbid that the ACLU'er man did not get in! This incum- bent would not commit treason, but would not in the instance promote and defend the U.S. Constitution in such a way that was explicit to anyone who was normal read at least the very beginning of it. He was a daddy's boy that never had gotten away from his mother's strings. He meant well but did not have the intestinal fortitude to deal at all with today's violent world and thought brotherhood meant multiculturalism. This was indeed not only sad but very scary since he was so sincere but sincerely wrong.

This was the Christian part in him which he probably never even realized and that was to win a second term to serve GOD first and not even his own parents or financial advisors, but Yale had done a number on him for sure.

He lived in a play world since he never experienced real hardship only the kind the rich create such as 9/11 but then again others feel it more than they ever could. If prayer would help that would be a wonderful thing not that prayer does not help, but with one who has reciprocity and an open mind to be able to think and feel like America's peasants. GOD does not coerce. He had never experienced this quite like Ronald Reagan had. Reagan never appeared to lose sight and could not ever relate to this in the slightest way.

He was a wonderful businessman and who had personal morals, but could not extend them to the nation and was easily influenced by what he wanted to hear himself. This was his primary downfall. He was not open to corrective criticism, and our own borders proved just that as well as the Saudis, Islam and the illegal issue. He would ask a question with an already preconceived notion or idea he already had made a decision about but did not say. The thing that was troubling was that there was nobody in the wings waiting after him to lead our nation from a moral perspective after he would leave, and his leaving one could see would not provide for that either. Who would really take charge and be an American leader who would not worry about special interests or ideology? Santorum? No, not with Roman Catholicism! Alan Keyes? Yes, but he would never even be mentioned because he was too radical! He too was a Catholic, but his "peasant" background would come through.

This incumbent did show some audacity but not the kind that was very complimentary at all and that was when he invited into the White House Islamic Arabs to celebrate Ramadan after 9/11! In fact I believe it was the Saudis themselves the very ones who had attacked America. It was just like good old FDR and Churchill with Stalin! One should never be surprised at an Englishman's diplomacy!

The second issue was the height or laterally challenged people to be m ore politically correct. They appeared all over whenever Nazis could be found. One can only contend that someone had this in mind years ago when they thought of the stature as far as in feet and inches. This was not at all a figurative type of comment. Joseph Stalin was only 5'2" and Mao was very short. Lenin was no Amazon.com. Hitler could also enjoy that entourage along with Mussolini and Nazi Germany. They too were both physically and mentally challenged.

Now Abraham Lincoln and George Washington could not belong to this elitest club to the left and the extreme of left itself, but then no one would be left. We realized, at least a few of us, that in order to form a more perfect union it had to come from our 60's

Leaders and what they had put in front of that word, and that was the word soviet. Th ese were the new founding fathers such as "Your father is Satan who was a liar from the very beginning." This was our new way of government and to govern like the Constituent Assembly had done in Russia in 1917 and a little before, and that was absolutely nothing! Partisan, or bi partisan was also nothing but rhetoric and was a wolf in sheep's clothing. Many die hard Americans would be offended if one called them Islam's non-infidels, but what other name could one apply to them besides the word collaborator? And some were even Semites just like them!

Yes, this government all parties included wanted to ruin my neighborhood, my friend's neighborhood, and so forth and so on. They also wanted us to not "discriminate" from citizens and felons! (Where had one supposed that one had come from?) No referendums at least that held up in court, but were they not ever meant to ever be in court? We now had "neighborhoods" that were enclosed with guards and were called developments, but weren't these the ones that were promoting these non discriminatory statutes?

Nothing was too good, no not for America but for their ideology of "eat, drink and be merry", which was what all capitalisms lead to on the other side of the quilt and that was socialism! We as Americans, though, could not even get our very subconscious mind to be able to think let alone say the word socialism or socialist or Communism or Communist. It was not allowed in our own vocabulary. Only to the left or a liberal were allowed to be used or else one would be in serious trouble since most Americans had lived cuddled lives all of their lives!

We had given up the battle without a struggle, and the war had not even begun on all the virtues. Their guns were not even loaded, in fact it was a water pistol that they were now using and yet we surrendered as if they were real weapons. Incredible? No. We were our own worse enemy from within as in we the people. Democracies did not work and never would but it was nice to dream. So on and on we slept through and nobody woke us up but then again there was no explosion outside except for 9/11!

Now that this President had won the election they would go after the Saudis and not because they were patriotic Americans but because he had a hole in his knight of armor. They could do this because they also had nothing whatsoever to lose because who would oppose them in any position of authority? The Saudis were well protected at least for the time being as all "royalty" should be!

Hollywood was not strange to this type of thought because they thought exactly alike. The pendulum swung back and forth each time over and over again and again, but for some strange unexplainable reason it never stopped day or night or ever lost time but was a few minutes ahead of time, which meant that before it was midnight it was to them already midnight. Yes, our own clocks either ran too fast or too slow, but mostly too slow and in fact so slow that we were really in the PM of our time! We had thought up new ideas that were not really new at all but just as old as man himself. It was like Adam and Eve in the garden, but we took a bite out of the fruit and then our eyes were surely opened. The nail would not bend, but neither would it go in, but somehow with persistent effort we finally nailed in the last one to seal the coffin, that is our own coffin! Practice does make perfect, but depending on how and with whom one practiced was very important!

I knew a family who had 3 sisters and who all were from a Jewish background, but had somehow taken on Roman Catholicism. The first sister, when she was young was quite a beautiful woman and one could always tell by her type A personality and effervescent ways, along with her auburn hair and green eyes, that she was sort of a high socialite of the highest kind

Although she came from a humble background, and had even dated one of the bluebloods named Elliott Roosevelt. She was a joy for me to talk to because she reminded me of my Jewish mentor and her discussions were not about the weather or sports like some ordinary Gentile, but were about real life with no ego on her part at all. She died a most sad and lonely death because the executor of her will had also turned to Roman Catholicism and it broke my heart to see her that way.

The second sister was also very beautiful, but she had gotten married twice and the first sister had not gotten married at all and had no children at all. This second sister was the most intellectually aware of all the 3 sisters and the most educated. She had 3 children from two different marriages. One child, a daughter, was from her first marriage, and from her second marriage was a precious and kind daughter and a kind son. This sister had died in life because of the struggle between the Roman Catholicism and her Jewishness which was squeezing the life out of her.

The third sister, who was still living to this very day, loved Roman Catholicism. She never had any children of her own, but had been a hard worker and helped to raise in part the second sister's two children from the second marriage. Her attachment, though to Roman Catholicism showed itself when at times she would argue about a penny in the supermarket and would embarrass even the store clerk.

All 3 sisters were really Polish Jewish. The first sister showed though all the Jewishness which I enjoyed very much. The second sister showed an ambivalent nature towards, as I said before, her own two religions, but her bright Jewish motherly mind would often stand out by the love she really showed for her family and, by the way, she would help people while they were still alive. In fact she would not think twice to help someone with money and one time she threw away an envelope with over $2,000 in it without knowing about it because she thought it was something else one of her sisters was giving to her so that she would side with her in a heated discussion some days earlier. After finding out she said to her one sister, "Why would you do such a thing, first of all by putting money in it, and second I would not agree with you no matter what amount of money you gave me. So here it is. I found it in the trash for you." Yes, she was quite a lady too!

The third sister, sort of like a chameleon with no harm intended, acted more like a cross between a New York City Jew and a Roman Catholic, but a little Jewish would show because she would not let any go hungry, almost like the Italian culture. But one would have still thought she was just Polish by the way she kept all her pennies.

Out of all the sisters I believe the second sister was the most innately Jewish because it came so natural to her to respond as such. She had an Eastern mindset of family and nation. She was knowledgeable and self educated and could have married any successful businessman in the local area, but she refused to. Again the first sister attracted many successful businessman as well as politicians, but she always refused her hand whenever they would propose marriage. The third sister had married, but her husband had died years ago and she remained a widow all those years and took good care of herself and did not like to be waited on. She did marry a Polish man and grew accustomed to that culture more than any other.

It was sad to see that only one sister had gotten married and had children since the Old Testament people believe what the Bible says when it says, "Be fruitful and multiply." The second sister's husband was a kind and compassionate French and German man, and with this combination there were no traits of one or the other strictly. This husband even invited the oldest daughter, always, from his wife's first marriage to all the holiday events and treated her like his own daughter.

The reason I bring this story up is because of the lack of knowledge of the Old Testament people which included these 3 sisters who also did not know about the rich Jewish culture from the Bible. Of course, like I said, the first sister never married, which was indeed rare amongst Jewish women at that time.

In the big corporate business world there was no honor amongst thieves. These thieves were living off of the murdered Americans of 9/11 because they were not accountable to any government. We had little or no government when it came no not to law enforcement, but to the corrupt judges and corrupt trial lawyers who made up the laws just like the Soviets lawyers had years ago. Yet television portrayed them as the glorious heroes always!

The status quo would remain under all administrations because an administration is nothing more than a bureaucracy. No amount of voting in a democracy with such a large country could ever decipher the truth or background about any one candidate.

No one individual alone could stem the tide at least in government, but a few unconnected individuals could penetrate with difficulty the juice crusher that sucked all the juice out of the fruit. It would be improbable but not impossible to do, but it would take perseverance and much intestinal fortitude to get through. This was even worse than that it was like a pressure cooker. One—by-one, though, it could be accomplished. That is, one could bring to light the truth about our nation and where we were heading with no regard to profit or fame, but just the truth and nothing but the truth and not the way one wanted it to be or wished it to be but the way it really was also. It was faith vs. ideology.

Many said, "Mind over matter", but what should have been was, "Faith over materialism". One could not for the life of one, at least for me, ever understand why one's views had to be like a blue blood in order to be considered a true American patriot? The gangs on the streets as well as the "gangs" in college were doing a number on our entire society. They both accumulated degrees and then Degrees!

This 60's educational system at the higher levels made it all just plain and simple just like most of them were plain but much more simple as in simple minded! It had always been about wealth, not wages and power and not authority. "A wolf sheds its fur but not its habits."

Everywhere one went something always was stressed with an accent on money. The love of money meant not money itself necessarily, but the wealth and power that no one man should have because of man's evil nature. Absolute power corrupts absolutely. The higher one goes, the less they have as far as being an intellectual. Accountability was for naught, but as I just said, everything was made to be money oriented so much so that people actually forgot to eat, sleep, bathe, drink or even live normally. This was the underlying deceit that made money just the means to obtain the ends, or was it the other way around? Well nonetheless it led to more wealth and power which in turn lead to more and more totalitarianism because fewer and fewer people were now on top at the international level. This was beyond the control of even one nation or many nations and was now at the level of continents.

Today in the West, if one wanted to know what happened in regard to, say, an automobile accident, in a personal way the one thing that would almost always be stressed would be, "Well how much damage was done to the car?" Yes, America had a value system on just about everything, and it was with a price tag, even if one was dying. "Please sign here first." "But I am bleeding to death." "No matter, please sign here now!"

What if the American people ever got real knowledgeable and ever found out that all that they owned and all they had invested was really just paper because the whole system in our nation was bankrupt including not only the moral but the financial as well? We were living on borrowed time as well as on borrowed money from other countries that were stealing us blind as Americans. The American dollar now only stood for what in theory it said on any one type of dollar bill, which meant absolutely $0!

Our very own President had to rely on Arabic oil to make his living. We indeed were in serious trouble to say the least, but Americans had never had it so good. Then again they had never lived before! All roads were leading to socialism either through capitalism or Islamic ideology, and along with that a need for more of the same kind of government only that it was no longer a democratic/republic. In fact this President just as much said so every time he spoke of only democracy in America!

Americans were not afraid of losing their jobs. That is, the ones who were in the upper middle class for they knew the economy would have to almost crumble for them to go bankrupt. What did scare them was the transition to conform to another way or thought process, but even more so the fact that would they be able to get a new job and do the least amount of physical work they now were doing with such a high pay rate, but not to ever work like a farmer did who did not even know if he would split even at the end of the year. This is what they never wanted to do since money was their real security, and that is why government was so important because 80% of all the American people got some kind of public welfare! This is where Marxism led into America. Would I really have to labor hard and use my back to make an honest or dishonest living? Even the doctors had become businessmen, and they had to since the trial lawyers who were international had always belonged to the Soviet group of lawyers there that were also international. The farmer had to be smart and physically fit like a well conditioned athlete except of course with brains. Maybe that is why the government allowed athletes to be able to make so much money that it was ludicrous, but not of course to the IRS which the U.S. Congress controlled. One never really heard of a hard working professional athlete possibly for a rare and few ones such as Carl Yatstremski who was a potato fanner and had nothing whatsoever to do with sports once he retired like most of the deadbeat dads. As long as the real estate taxes remained high and forever would, the 3rd world people coming here love to make a quick buck and take the money and yes even sometimes leave because the American dollar say as opposed to the Peso was worth so very much more in their own socialist country and they could become rich here and rich there in a matter of a few years since our own government also gave out last year to them $540,000,000 as grants never to be paid back but no American born here or in Europe would ever be eligible ever! This was more of this incumbent's multiculturalism that now extended far into the pockets of the middle class that made up the heart and soul of our nation which included our farmers too who were being taken under more and more each year.

Yes, we had become the ugly American in more ways than one, and this incumbent thought that we owed him and them a living but then again do not the rich and well educated always think like a group? The only thing most patriotic Americans wanted was for government to leave them alone as well as uphold the Constitution and the Bill of Rights and be much less concerned about free handouts to dead beat dads, socialists, prejudice newcomers, etc. Just stay out of our lives and we as Americans would find our own way to survive without any type of government obstacle that they always proposed no matter how good they said that it was!

To be able to live in peace and harmony with our real neighbors and not some illegal who would sooner or latter and perhaps sooner commit a crime that involved either drugs or prostitution or pagan religion!

In Holland itself there were church burnings going on from the Islamic extremists and all over Europe that was occurring.

The President continued with his multicultural appointments such as Mr. Gonzalez for United States Attorney General who was no where near John Ashcroft in faith, brains, courage and honor. In fact this judge had approved of an underage girl to have an abortion without parental consent! This incumbent was too weak to withstand this heat since he had it easy all of his life. He did not like any kind of confrontation and maybe had a proclivity for Hispanic Women himself?

If social services were to be taken away from these Hispanics then most of them would return to their own country. The incumbent wanted an amnesty for all the illegal Mexicans in the United States which meant that these United States would not be that united after all. He was his brother's keeper. He as I had said so many times before was bent on this Hispanic Jihad here in America while he fought the Islamic Jihad with our very own military over in Iraq. He had a sort of schizophrenic attitude about the sovereignty of America.

He did not know the difference between Hispanic Jihad and Islamic Jihad and in fact there were now in our very prisons about 30% inmates that made up the total population of all the prisons in the United States that were of Mexican descent but this was not good enough he now wanted to release them with out any oath or any English or any background check which meant that anyone who would even follow this order had to be even dumber than he was. If one man could unravel this nation then it would take others to ravel it back to normalcy and maybe since his drug and alcohol days it was now affecting his better judgment. Americans though for the most part would go along with this since most were intimidated without even having to put up any kind of fight.

Why had we fought the Alamo? Oh yes, just so this President could promote his one world order like his daddy was trying to do and now he would finish the job in America. The English were for sure a piece of art to say the least. It also appeared that the mob when it controlled the city did a better job then what the courts were doing now in most cities. What gang in their right mind would want to mess with the mob, as for the justice system they knew for them that it was nothing but a paper tiger and that is why John Ashcroft resigned as a gentleman and not for his gall bladder. He had become frustrated at not being able to do what the top law enforcement officer in the nation should have been doing.

Yassar Arafat is now a worldwide media hero along with the Communists and the Nazis who both help train him and his popular entourage since 1967 when he took over the reign or the regime of the terrorists' organization known as the Palestinian Liberation Organization which one can readily tell that by its own name that this is in no way a ministry but an organization of rebel and murderers that want to liberate themselves from the normal way of doing diplomacy and that is to murder, maim and torture the innocent and to also use the type of name that also has nothing to do with Israel since Palestine was a place when Israel was not a state, but now that it is they want it again to be a totally Arabic Islamic state just like good old Syria, Egypt, etc. and without religious freedom but only for the holier than thou murderers of Islam!

Who are these terrorists that represent the very same kind of anti-Semitism since only the Jews are the chosen people and not the Arabs or any other Gentile and since the Arabs are Semites in this case it cannot be applied since anti-Semitism always refers to the hatred of Jewish and never to any hatred of the Arabs and after all Jewishness is a faith. Arafat with his six guns coming into the United Nations just as Castro had brought his chickens in tells one what type of socialistic organization that is.

This is where the meeting of minds come to be that is the meeting of simpleton minds and that is why Adlai Stevenson and Alan Keyes were both put there because They were the ones with too much brain power then the rest of them such as the 2 Bushes who were both not Presidential material. One was a military man and the other a businessman What could they possibly know about Marxist/Leninism except what they had learned in the Ivy League,

Now Mr. El Presidenté wants to negotiate his Hispanic Jihad within the United States and Islamic Jihad in Iraq but heaven forbid if it should happen in Saudi Arabia where their kings are dear good friends with these Anglophiles. After the Yalta Conference I think I have had my full of any kind of English diplomacy. They can never for once be trusted to do what is moral and just.

Time after time either it has been the English in England and here, or the dumb-minded Germans in Germany or here that have continued to bring havoc and destruction to other nations except their own such as in England and in Germany for they must at all costs be protected from what they themselves have started time and again!

EL PRESIDENTE is now leading two countries here in America. Arafat's death is revealed on veteran's day just by coincidence and Islamic Jihad comes to the United States Senate over the very knowledgeable Alan Keyes who, though, is Roman Catholic, knows Scripture too well not to know how to lead a nation at this very pivotal time. His wife is from India so Roman Catholicism has something to do with his conversion to materialism but nonetheless he now is best qualified to run our country instead of another blueblood.

The first story is about this President who wants truckers from Mexico to just drive into America without any checkpoint and he also wants more deals with the Saudis. He is a wonderful businessman as I said once before!

He also wanted to change the 10 years of working in America to 5 years of just residency in order to become a citizen and in order to collect our tax dollars through social services. Too much alcohol on the brain or Yale's inebriated socialistic philosophy has penetrated his brain. We congratulate EL PRESIDENTE' on his second term, but much more is in the surprise for us as well as his whole new administration and the fact that John Kerry's side threw in the towel too soon! But why?

This is in the defense of the terrorists which has gotten the National Democratic Socialist Party all work ed up and the news media also sends its best wishes to one right out of Hell. Numerous lives were murdered in cold blood but this hero deserves with just reward since the elite anti-Semites think he should receive them and hold him to their highest standard like the Nobel Peace Prize and of one nation under Islam here and one continent under Islam there. Their concern is falling short because they cannot revive the dead and the victims that he so murdered just as if he had pulled the trigger himself!

Also a United States Senator who is a black Moslem has won over Alan Keyes, a Christian man in the state of Illinois and nobody challenged it and I wonder why? Either the American people's pocket book needs more ready cash or they entertain to another 9/11 but on a much wider scale plus the fact was the election kosher? Wait till they get full control, then all things shall be much more than equal that is for them and only them! It is not give me liberty or give me death since the American people want innately socialistic Islamic Jihad's death wish.

With a find intellectual such as Alan Keyes in the sense but then again there are no blacks in. the Senate but now for this first Moslem ever! Being the fact that Alan Keyes was not the right color and the right religion he was not nominated for President and also being the fact he is not as good as a businessman that the incumbent is! Of course being an Anglo had much to do with it and a little nepotism.

With Arafat now dead, the regime shall want not less, but now more than ever for their businessmen in Saudia Arabia to help them. Of the two candidates, one of which was a Communist and one a multiculturalist, one had little choice but to now vote at all! It was good. I used my vote properly because I—how would you say—abstained.

Being it was Veterans' Day, what more wonderful way for the English and the Moslem to celebrate their "Ramadan" to the tune of trillions of dollars in oil money through Londontown's bank accounts. Now between the French Jesuits and the Nazis, one is in doubt as to who to give more credit to for trying to destroy Israel proper but then the English have always had a. very good reason, right? This is indeed their finest hour!

One has to wonder why the Russian peasants and citizens do not like the Anglo diplomacy. After all, it is not often one gets such a chance to reduce the best of one's population explosion and in such a big country with all of Siberia and the wonderful Gulags and the Archipelago! Does it ever cease to amaze just a few that how much alike the Germans and the American blacks both love to wear their black leather coats just like the SS and the Brownshirts? Also, it reminds one of the famous KGB who also wore them too. Gorbachev and Putin were both head of the KGB and just happened to be now our very best friends, that is the Communist Party in Moscow!

We are what we eat and it shows. Since the FDA chooses to test by the guinea pig method such as Vioxx and Red Dye # 10, one would say we all have a pretty good chance of being poisoned by our very own negligent government. Government interferes into everyone's private life, where it should not be but never as to where they save human life and liberty plus morality in our own nation. We now know who is the real enemy and they are we the people. They have blown up buildings such as in 911 and have polluted the country with their Koran of no value whatsoever to the normal person except the media and the anti Semites that are very rich in this nation of ours. This is a free country but nothing is free about murdering the innocent for there is always a price to pay and that is about $400 a pop to Planned Parenthood which is always open to murder and Nazism like its founder Margaret Sanger and now her grandson. The only thing that is free is GOD'S love from heaven to us and through Messiah's resurrection which, once and for all defeated death and showed His unconditional love for us for those of us who would just believe and even the sin of conception meaning Adam's fall which is innate in all of us.

If one is a Communist, then they have no nationality, race or tribe. They have forsaken the human race. Man to them is just an animal as Darwin had said and has to walk on all fours if he is in fact a Communist and is about as smart as dear old Lenin was!

Yes, one could always take it with them, or in other words, give it to their "heirs", who would in turn really sought most since everything including favors and donations had a price tag and a somewhat price back guarantee from the good old IRS. But then again, that is what all social Christians look for, right? And this sentimentality which the Germans are well noted for is, too, an ideology. One would say or might say, "But how can that be?"

Why sure, when one starves the poor to give to the rich and their rich alone. This in no way speaks about what Messiah ever said in the Bible. This has much to do with Europeanism's religions. It is always much better to give than receive, but only when in giving the so-called law of reciprocity is in effect, which means GOD owes it to us!

According to big government/big corporations, they are our best soldiers in the field. Where does it show that our government is promoting the general welfare or providing for the common defense when this incumbent refuses to protect our own borders and is giving away the store? This is all the name of "liquid" assets. Now with Mexico to keep us so busy, we cannot and most do not want to, focus on the real issue and that is GOD HIMSELF! We constantly hear social Christians many times use the word GOD, but what does that really mean to them? We appear to have no fear of Him, but when it comes to doing without, we manage with panic! Not to fear GOD is foolishness as to fear GOD is the beginning of wisdom. This is not your RC type of fear which always means to place a guilt, false or real, on the individual if they do not abide not by the Bible but by church tradition. It is called one by exclusion and not inclusion no matter how wrong they are! It is healthy to be in this sense, one of exclusion. To be aware of GOD all the time, most of the day since He is the great

I AM and not any other kind of "great" such as in a nation. We the people challenge GOD, no we ourselves tempt GOD by our continued sin to ignore what His Word says repeatedly not to do and we cannot claim ignorance ever since the Bible tells us that also. We use our bodies not as temples but as refuse dumps but we, or at least some of us, understand that inside our spirit is Jesus' love with His grace, and since we do not deserve it He has still, chosen to share it with us in His family as His children and the

Father calls us to Him and we respond with freewill and in that order and no other! With all these trophies, awards, accolades, certificates, and degrees one would think that we were GOD Himself or better yet that we were gods ourselves! I had thought that this democracy would at least stop with the Greek philosophy, but now it also includes their own great gods such as Thor, etc.! We are our very own gods in the sinful flesh no matter how much we want to play god by ourselves and have it over all others just to say that we are more much more than they could ever hope to be or want to be! We also are our very own idols; we worship ourselves as Narcissus did, and it is called ego, or the I in man. What is one to do?

Yes, America has seen much better days in regards to morality and life for all to live. We the people have become we the group and for one to ever be an individual one must certainly renounce the humanist ideology but if one would do that then they might even determine that we are quite ready for the asylum.

We have gone too far in what a group can ever do since we are robotic with the now computerized world of today which is exactly like Orwell's 1984! We know what to do but we just can not seem to do that at all any longer. We fail terribly to do our best. That is, we fail in not doing what the government or Caesar now wants us to do!

We can no longer think for ourselves because of modern man's love of computers which is a system and with certain cultures this might be just fine but with some of us have become the horrible dinosaurs. This is our own version of man in the jungle.

Our civilization has come to an end, and so with that now we must relinquish our very own humanity for to do otherwise we mean we are not part of the whole or better yet not part of the group philosophy that has become so very popular since the 60's.

We are our very own worst enemy, as I have said before, and we do not acknowledge that we have failed. Besides that we always want to blame someone else all or most of the time.

Scott Peterson was found guilty and now could either get the death penalty or life imprisonment for the murder of his wife and his unborn but 3rd trimester child. This case was forced upon us to glamorize murder even more and to give Hollywood one more sick film to make for avarice and the death wish ideology. Going on Christmas Eve to go fishing was, right from the start, for me a blatant lie since I had friends who for years were avid fishermen themselves and had never ever gone fishing on a Christmas Eve, ever! This publicity stunt again by the media when one could see no sign whatsoever in his face but just a cold blooded killer and yet we heard over and over again how our own Pravda dramatized this Scott Peterson to make it look more like he might just be innocent. Maybe to them he was since they themselves believed in the murdering of the unborn!

With the O.J. case, the Hernandez case, Jon Benett Ramsey and so forth and so on, we have made these cases more than what they should have ever been. The media was now like the National Enquirer and would do anything to dramatize when already we knew if the person or persons were guilty, so why the long drawn out continuous story day after day? There had to be this constant yellow journalism, yellow in the sense that it took no courage for them to continue this debacle and play with a so-called innocent or guilty verdict just to commercialize murder for all to see when other stories that were much more important were occurring in our very own nation, such as the over 86,000 criminals that were here illegally and the fact the 30% of all our prisons also had 1/3 of the prison population made up of illegals!

This appeared again to be a part of vaudevillian tactics that had more to do with theatrical socialism than with whether he was innocent or guilty as I said before! It was like a star studded cast of players performing except the two victims were murdered and the main actor was as cold as ice and played no literally was the way he appeared guilty all along. He could not do what O.J. had done because that would have not been politically correct because O.J. at one time somewhere in the ions of space and time had slaves for relatives which had absolutely nothing to do with his murdering two individuals as well as never having the trial where he lived but in downtown Los Angeles where they knew he would get off including Marcia Clark the prosecuting attorney and with almost a hundred other attorneys as Joseph Pugliosi, the one who prosecuted Charles Manson, had said and also the fact that they allowed the black Moslem racist Johnny Cochran to play his socialistic race card as if we were in Nazi Germany! That was a three-ring circus, and judge Ito himself had absolutely no control of the case at anytime and had some kind of conflict of interest in regards to his own wife! With 9 blacks and 2 Hispanics and one white elderly lady—and why would the prosecuting attorneys allow that since O.J. himself was black? When the shrunken gloves were put on that was so atrocious to make any normal person to believe that because his hands could not fit into them and also the idiocy of putting a racist on the stand who was known or his remarks before would almost make one believe that they wanted their hero Mr. O.J. to be acquitted from the very beginning and the White Bronco car chase in Los Angeles with a friend of his driving and with a gun and a few thousand dollars and a visa passport went itself to prove that O. J. was running away from the law since it was so very obvious that he had murdered his wife and the waiter of Jewish extraction and then would have the children with him at times was indeed insane to say the least. This was our own form of Nazis who kept saying they were either innocent or would never in a million years because they had no consciences to admit and say that they had committed these murders and would waste valuable time on criminals who all should have gotten the death penalty right away cut and dry!

When one has color that means he still has a claim to slaves rights in the sense that it was because America still had this slave mentality that especially O.J. should be exonerated so that reparations through one man would be the beginning of the restitution but I thought more like the license to murder by the blade which is an MO in some cultures such as most blacks in America have knife and razor cuts some—where on their bodies. It also goes to show that is why the government would want to band guns because then the weapon of choice would be still legal such as a sharp knife or razor and that that could always be used and the gun was more of a white man's weapon of choice, but one would have to question the gangs that would use even automatic weapons amongst themselves as well as amongst innocent people.

Yes, the court system of trial by jury was not ever quite as good as it was made out to be because how could 12 individuals all with some kind of biases and prejudices one way or the other or in fact with 12 citizens that most people if they served would not know the first thing about a trial even when it was all explained to them said little for a trial by jury system!

Now even with DNA all we heard of was the ones who were wrongly accused but not about the many who were caught by this DNA! It did not go both ways with the media nor with the courts. For committing a vicious crime now what would be the excuse for acquittal like in the Simpson case? All that was right the civil rights' laws always gave the benefit of the doubt in this case to the one who only could apply to and hence a criminal or felon got away with bloody murder literally! And the murder weapon was not a gun but a knife! What could be more conclusive than the fact of what choice of weapon for some would be chosen for some criminals from again certain cultures! No one though was outlawing knifes and razors or swords of any kind were they?

The American public was indeed gullible to ever believe that the weapon always had to be a gun or something that had a firing mechanism. One could even use a blunt object such as a stone as a murder weapon so why not outlaw stones also? This is how ludicrous this all had become because might makes right which means 11-1 with the 1 being coerced to go along with the other 11 or else!

Trial by jury was in fact not the best way to use jurisprudence to bring to justice since it required now almost an eyewitness to the scene and even then one could still walk away feeling like a hero! Thank goodness not all nations always had this English type rule of law because also at Nuremburg there were even judges who should have been prosecuted yet they were deciding whether the Nazis themselves were guilty and they were, but no one ever brought them to trial. One would have to wonder why?

Yes, English law works well for England, but not for America, and if one innocent person got convicted, then it is worth it to let others and murderers go if there was honestly a shadow of a doubt. Not all nations or nationalities think alike nor is their government set up in this way such as in a monarchy. There the monarch can determine who is more qualified than 12 individuals who know absolutely nothing (the law or the courts) at all, but with a monarchy he is taught all this when he is quite young and is ready to present the reason one would be guilty or innocent and not a guess or one could call it an educated guess.

Even when the monarch in Russia was shot at more than one time, he did not use the death penalty, and the Queen Katherine kept her word as to never to use the death penalty on anyone for all of her reign! This in and of itself is quite a feat to say the least. Blood begets blood. If one should be sentenced, then the hardest penalty would be life with hard labor and not with air conditioning and color television. Now we have ones who do not murder one but possibly thousands, and as one can see none of them have been brought to justice because of the trial lawyers and the trial by jury which can not bring to justice an entourage of criminals and murderers who have no remorse or feeling for another's life yet they either go scot-free or in some way allowed to be lost in our very short memories. Saddam Hussein has Klaus Barbey's own attorney and that for sure should tell one just how anti-Semitic that this hoax about this butcher of a dictator is still alive and well but yet we had to fight and are still fighting but for what in Iraq when at first it was for Saddam Hussein and the weapons of mass destruction and now it is to bring democracy to Islam?

What nutty bedbug ever thought up this whole agenda about how to get around from prosecuting any of the terrorists since they died in the attack, but yet the leaders go scot-free and shall most likely be given another identity and made to make a trade off for hostages that Islamic Jihad wants now to always too since they now know that America is just a paper tiger.

The American justice system of trial by jury is not the best way to judge if a criminal did commit a crime. When placed in a democracy, then the decision lies in mob rule such as in O.J.'s case where a criminal went loose because democracy failed, which it always does when that is the only thing that our own government is made of and in today's world it is virtually impossible to convict a guilty man but too many innocent men have indeed been convicted because of the incompetence of the poor man's lawyer and the fact that the rich lawyer has sometimes more say than even the judge himself in the trial.

We can also see with our very own United States Supreme Court that the court is a joke since it wants always to be an oligarchy to rule over everybody by just a few and for life which now means that anyone can now be convicted for anything since there is no set rule of law any longer!

Right by might or democracy carries this trial by jury just the way that democracy is never a search for the truth and with a jury neither is the trial after the truth but only the technicalities or litigation that can delay or postpone or even execute with expeditiousness in the wrong direction! Why should the lawyers pick the juries when it is them that have to convince them one way or the other? This in and of itself shows a conflict of interest since the lawyers would pick who they felt would best help them. In the case of O.J. Marcia Clark had to know that with race problems from the other side why pick 11-1?

There were so many wage taxes that it almost took away the incentive for one to even work since all wage taxes were part of our own government's socialism. The only tax that should have been levied was a tax on consumer items purchased which would in essence only affect free enterprise if there ever had been such a thing. With all these wage taxes everyone went to uphold the welfare that was being paid out but yet we the people (government) was already bankrupt because we our very selves wanted more and more from the government as handouts but after all it was the government that was robbing us blind so that no one could want to or could possibly tithe or give offerings and donations and so hope, faith and charity was so much more limited since Caesar was taking even that part that belonged to GOD. Very little went to the orphans or widows from individuals themselves because we the people wanted more and more, but it was our leaders such as

FDR who installed their own plan for socialism but then again he was voted in for 4 terms so he had to be handing out money left and right to the citizens of America which would eventually eat itself out of house and home.

If we the people were just those very same people in government who were American citizens then who could we blame but ourselves by allowing capitalism to guide our every wish day after day. We never even gave it a second thought as to where all these finances and expenses were coming from since there was absolutely no money left in social security but was each year allocated by the House of Representatives in the federal budget automatically so that it went through without any yes or no votes.

These were all IOU'S that we the people were giving to ourselves so we felt we deserved it and now the whole process had more than backed up to about 15 trillion dollars which looked like this to be exact, $15,000,000,000,000.00! This is what we owed to ourselves, which in turn meant that we ourselves were definitely living on borrowed time as far as our whole nation's fiscal system was concerned. FDR who was taught by Lord Keynes, who also was a socialist, taught FDR this plan for disaster because Lord Keynes was a homosexual and so the very thought process had to be for not owning private property but sharing everything in common for the brotherhood. With this kind of advice we would surely in due time fall to the roulette table of the stock market which was nothing more than gambling what one had earned and it was not an investment at all. Just as in gambling so it was in the stock market that numbers had percentages and the more that one played them the more that one would eventually lose it all and then one would be just like a gambler who always was living financially on borrowed time. This incumbent in office was offering another so called solution which was nothing more than feeding that very monster that they had control of with now most of all the American people's money this time with the gimmick that this would be for their retirement since they could no longer take out any more from our very wages and the amount that they did reduce amounted to nothing more than the bones that the king of England had thrown back to his people after he had taken everything and the people said, "GOD save the king."

It was in this way to appeal to the American people instead of taking it from CD's and IRA's and other private forms of investment which were nothing more than what the private banks had invested into the Federal Reserve system that owned this private corporation so hence one was giving to other stockholders so that they could pay their stockholders the banks and Allan Greenspan was praised be cause he was really working for a private corporation that was being run by the federal government which was a euphemistic way of never having to mention the two words called economic fascism!

What one made in real wages or one's gross income was never to be touched by the government ever. What could or should have been done was that this consumer tax should have been the only tax to be paid since the rich and well educated spent much much more on materialism in essence and this was again one of their own loopholes to pay no taxes or little taxes on all the items, trips, educations, cars, boats, homes, etc without incurring any real taxation since it would be taking from the common purse known as wage taxes! Our wages were just one part of our wealth and the word wealth in this sense did not refer to being rich or anything near that but meant what we actually owned and since all real estate or for most people and not all was being taxed then that meant that that part of our "wealth" would never ever be owned by us. That is why the officials in government did not ever want to relinquish property taxes because then that meant that private property would be just that private and not government owned, because if one did not pay these taxes the state could claim the property once and for all. This is exactly now where we were all going! Confiscation and no less of private people's property so that the government would become purely socialistic and then the incentive to own some thing would be null and void and hence then the state would be the sole power over all of our very lives and this is how we would become solely only a state and not a nation any longer with no spiritual realm any more as one nationality and that is why this incumbent was also pushing so much for illegals to come in so that they too could contribute to their wealth and in this sense the word wealth meant rich from the elites such as the Bushes and others. In fact even PBS would collect donations as they liked to call them and these "donations" would be used to pay down the taxes on all the rich people's taxes and had absolutely nothing to do with supporting PBS which was socialistic television which meant in essence it had nothing to do with free enterprise but all to do with socialism!

These elections were nothing more than to make the rich get richer and the poor poorer and have no middle class which is what all oligarchies are after and that is not only money, wealth, but most of all power. That meant absolute power and that is why they got away with so many immoral things because these very lawyers who later became politicians made these immoral laws. So what could one prosecute them for if they were on the books no matter how immoral but nonetheless legal in the very same sense that abortion and homosexuality had been made legal by these socialists in government?

Whatever was promised were all fairy tales and there was something always in the background that we the people could not see. We would have to give up not necessarily our rights but the welfare that government was handing out and our own families of at least 4 generations would have to pull together if we ever wanted to get out of this debacle at all! It was hard enough now to get husband and wife to have one checking and savings account with just his last name on the account and with both their first names on the account because of what women's liberation which was nothing more than equivalence to make men and women think that they were getting some kind of deal and that this would more then uphold a woman's total freedom to do as she pleased no matter how immoral it was, which led also to Griswold vs. Connecticut, which then led in turn to Roe vs. Wade. The right or as they liked to be able to infanticize one's own child which was really not their child but GOD's and call it her "right" to do what she wanted to do since now that she had had the enjoyment of sex she now did not want to have the inconvenience of raising another crying baby again and again. This part was something she or he did not plan for nor did they want and hence along came the racists, that is the Nazis with one of their own "solutions"! Let us quickly get rid of the Ham's descendants now! This was their excuse to say that since your very own men did not want the child but wanted the sex, then it was conclusive to believe that you should not want what he too did not want or you did not want. It was only a matter of semantics that one could now alleviate the problem that is the life of an innocent child by the quickest method and that would be to abort and do it now and of course pay a little fee for our own services and that the taxpayers were paying for "willingly".

This was the type of insanity that these Nazis here in America were all around and plus the fact that they did not want America to become a darker raced society so the quickest way to eliminate that would be also to abort because look how many criminals came out of wedlock situations and were mostly from the darker races. This was, again, this Nazi mentality that said eliminate them so we do not have more of them than us and so that they do not melt down the pure Anglo-Saxon race of blonde hair and blue eyes!

Well we now know that the master race was nothing more than a brotherhood of homosexuality that could not procreate but only by the state's permission which would also mean that girl babies such as in China and babies less than perfect or not wanted could also be eliminated at a faster pace since most of the young girls involved could and only then collect these social services that I just mentioned about One could see that one thing always affected another thing always and one lie had to cover up for another lie and hence what we then had left was violence which as I said before was the opposite of peace and not war because now we had both war and violence. War across the ocean and violence here in America so we were lied to twice!

We were robbing Peter to pay Paul, which meant that the taxpayers would fork the entire bill and then also give those lives to these elites through the rich-made schemes which they did not ever want to talk about. Peter (that is us) was giving, or lending as they liked to say, to Paul (that is them) what they needed for the state with no regard at all for Peter's children but only Paul's. This was indeed a vicious cycle of lies upon lies. With the truth one did not have to lie and so each man carried his own weight and not the weight of another healthy young man whose libido which he did not want to control since he knew that the elites in government would make it easy for him to sell drugs, have prostitutes and also have a sort of family of his own called the gang!

We now had to educate the world by the Western standards that materialism which was still being called capitalism was still the best way to go but it spoke about nothing in regards to what form of government our children would inherit with such a John Locke mindset. It was hurray for me and the Hell with you! Everybody even in Latin America would want once they had saw what they were missing what everyone else in America had and that was cars, clothing, drugs, alcohol, gambling, sports, etc. This was why they really came to America because where did Mexico have any kind of life like that where one could just do what one pleased and in essence also get government handouts from the American people who now too had a resentment just like the Hispanics had had one for so many envious years. It too was their turn to collect for reparations that also the blacks were getting at least at one time but now it would be their turn to get the same kind of red carpet treatment which our government officials were so very good at since most all were trial lawyers and had written most of these laws that meant that it had to be right and if not by them then the man at the top who just started more and more to appear like a dictator something that George Washington himself was always afraid of and that is why when they wanted to make him king he refused because of the absolute power that the King of England had had over them and he had wanted nothing to do with that at all!

We also needed more slaves or should I say a tax force of workers since we already murdered about 50,000,000 of our very own, and now these new illegals could make up for that in more taxes being taken from their wages now, but first they needed a handout such as a new car, a new business, a college education to indoctrinate them properly, and many other material things to get a head start so that our government could make their NAFTA work! If someone did not pay that is these wage taxes then for sure someone would dearly pay! The rich and well educated were not about to give up any of the things that they had so honestly and so hard worked for!

We the people bit off more than we now could possibly chew and the fact was like it or not the American people were getting new neighbors! Whether or not they spoke English did not matter because all of that could be easily taken care of with a flip of a finger called another law! Learn to live with your" brother "no matter what crimes or what language that you could not understand and be sure that you go all out to learn his customs as well as his language so that no one can ever say that you were a bigot! Let the animosity be taken out on your own family and frustrate you so that then you would be at each other's throats all the time! This is the way that the English always thought when it did not involve them at all!

In England they had to give up their guns because if they did not then the elites could not control them since they had about 1-2 Moslems and now there would be no turning back to the English or British nationality. We all had to get along no matter how much the other one hated us and wanted to take over and the rich and well educated could always leave and get away and have guards and elaborate security systems, but if their plan was that good why would they ever entertain that thought?

Australia also did the very same thing and they too had no second amendment to protect them and hence now they too could be taken with little or no effort just like that as a nation with no shots fired. Europe was installing its own system not to protect its own citizens but to protect just the elites who were now running the richest world and immoral system in the world. Even Red China's leaders were taken a second look for only themselves and not their peasants as to how they could also enjoy the life of Reilly yet remain in totalitarian control!

The 4 world divisions were now forming very quickly and soon many things would be happening and were happening to forever change the way we lived at least here in America and there would be no going back. Learn to live with whatever came and accept anything if you do not want totalitarianism. And this was said as a kind gesture on the part of these internationalists who had never ever even been to America or ever knew our own way of life but nonetheless their way would be the only way and there was going to be no referendum or election on this just as we really had had no election meaning no real choice either even though most Americans thought that they had because it was the financial that they were looking at all the time with no foresight for the future.

We had now really become the ugly American since we the people were what made up our very own government and who could we blame if we wanted all the desires of our little hearts with no thought for the consequences of all this but indeed there would be consequences make no mistake about that! We were the Babylon and were now fighting in Babylon so we did have something in common and that was this Babylon which at both ends had no time for the one true GOD and it was definitely showing.

Since I had grown up under the all encompassing world of capitalism it was give me this and give me that with little or no regard for anybody else on the planet but still I wanted to help others which was not totally any credit to me. It was this ever consuming of more and more with no regard, as I just said, for the other person. What was in it for me? After all, I too wanted to live it up and fantasize about what it would be like to be rich with no job to report to and no work to really have to do; hence I was very uneducated as to the real world and what it encompassed in the form of what good work had done for many being that it gave man a purpose in life especially if he even had something as a small plot of land to work his hands on, even though I never did but my grandmother did on the maternal side.

As I grew older and stubbornly clung to what I was taught as far as morals and not to steal and to respect other people's belongings and property, I just could not vision myself working in factory work, which I dreaded so very much because to me it was very tiring and extremely boring. and I always felt like a dumb sized robot performing something that I really had no real knowledge as to what it would be used for let alone who owned the company itself because I had thought at that time that only one person owned the company and had a life of Riley driving the El Dorado Cadillac with nothing in the world to worry about. So I too envied what he had and resented the fact that what did he have that I did not have except that possibly he might be born into a very well to do non-working family.

As I grew older I started to see their lifestyle of drinking, women, gambling, cars and more cars, planes, summer and winter homes while I lived in a little apartment which I liked very much as long as it was quiet.

I eventually came to the realization after many many years that this was not what would be in store for me and I do believe that GOD had kept me away from certain things since he knew that I too would become like what I had saw and that was all ego. I was to learn and I am still learning to this day that I was to take one day at a time and rely on Him for all my needs, which meant I had to work for a living no matter what even my friends had done or where their lives led them too.

Most every job I had I hated with such a passion because either it was so robotic or the sound was so loud that I could not stand it, or the job itself was very dangerous, which did not at that time concern me too much. It was the scale of little to no wage with no incentive and no chance to live up to my own potential and I knew for sure that these proletarians were not who I had cared to be around with their little minds for only themselves and nobody else with few or little morals. I had no interest in just making my job my entire life, but these guys seemed to enjoy what they were doing since now I believe their interests and intelligence were quite different than mine. But I never acted the better part; I just did my job as best I could, but would get extremely bored, and these mostly Germans seemed to know what they wanted already in life. Somehow from their birth this is what it was! I, though, could never really find the thing that I loved until the day that President Kennedy was killed and then I wrote my very first poem on how sad and horrible it was to kill a President of our own nation! This writing along with a couple of teachers at that time, who had given us many poems in literature as well as things like Julius Caesar, seemed to stimulate something in me and the passion for writing which I never knew I had this love and passion for.

Not until many years later was I given a small opportunity by a Negro man to publish some of my poems in a tabloid within the city; hence I continued to read and write much poetry and then on Firing Line there was this most incredible Christian that I had never ever even heard of before with an interview from the BBC. From then on I continued to read all this man's material along with another man's material which, by the way Malcolm Muggeridge had suggested on this very same program, and so within due time I did just that and found that my so called hobby of reading and writing was more interesting than any of my jobs had ever been. I did not get bored to say the least. Then when I married, my wife suggested that I write a short story if I loved to write so much and since I was so inspired by these two Russian authors by the names of Alexander Solzhenitsyn and Fyodor Dostoyevsky. Even though their reading was too hard for me at first, I read and reread all their books and about 25 years later, after about the 8th reading, it all started to make sense at what they were talking about. As I said before, my wife encouraged me to write outside of poetry and try a short story. I felt also I really had nothing to lose since it would be short. Well what appeared to be short was not short at all, and before I knew it I was writing a novel size book and one after the other and did not now care if they got published or not even though I was hoping but with not too much hope. So I just continued what I felt must have been a talent that I had always had but really had never used and never had had the opportunity. Only one time was it when I had really gotten the opportunity as a professional writer and I had just mentioned that before. The job did not pay much and in fact it only literally paid a few dollars, but nonetheless I was so excited to see my own writings in a local newspaper for the very first time in my entire life.

Not until the present time did I ever enjoy writing so much for the truth in writing and not as journalist or a reporter but as an actual artist that would write the truth the way it really was and no other way nor distort the truth by my own biases or prejudices but write it just the way it appeared so that if one would read it they could actually see it occurring right before their very eyes and that, to say the least, was not a very easy thing to do. I was not interested in fame or fortune, but only in making a moderate living for my wife and myself and to do the one thing I always wanted to do deep down inside of me and that was to write. I could spend hours and hours on writing and reading their books and never get bored, plus I loved to read the Bible at night before bedtime to learn more and more about the Word of GOD and to come to understand more about GOD Himself

Now at this time I have written, thanks to my beautiful wife, about a total of 5 books, none of which are published. But just because I do love to write, I continue this almost daily while I work at a job in which I try to be as conscientious as one can be, but it is not my love in life or should I say my third love in life with the first one going to Jesus, then my beautiful and lovely wife and third then my writing.

GOD has been so very good to me even though it happened later in life, but he did answer my prayer, one in which I thought could never be answered but it was and that of being married to a Messianic Jewish woman. There were not too many of them in the entire world let alone America since about only 6,000,000 Jewish people lived in America. I really never felt that I would get to leave this nation but always now wanted to go to Israel where my wife's long lost ancestry had once come from many many centuries ago.

As I was earlier saying, before I went off the track about my own life, what was now occurring in America were things that as a small boy I could never ever have imagined would ever occur here ever! The normal became the abnormal and the abnormal became the so called normal. Now men and women were marrying the same sex and we were surrounded by people who refused to even speak a word of English no matter how much opportunity they had to speak it. My grandparents from Europe never had the chance, but nonetheless always respected the American people and the American English language even though it was hard to learn. They were just glad to be here to be able to work and live in peace and harmony but these new vagabonds just wanted what their very own cultures had taught them and that was take all that you can and because they were poor they learned quickly how to be envious of what other people had in America!

Maybe, too, it was that most of these immigrants and illegals had no clue whatsoever about the Judeo-Christian culture and one could surely tell because even with government intrusion they seemed to have an almost inmate appetite to take what did not belong to them and could not learn to assimilate as guests in a foreign country and thought that freedom meant to do just what you damn well pleased to do!

There was no meeting of the minds and in fact our own government wanted this dissension more and more because the special interest groups had a vested interest in their own one world government where all would come to worship this so called one god when in the Bible it said that the Father would only call His own children and the fact this one world government that would eventually take all of the sovereignties away from all the nations and none would have any personal nationality which would mean a world of one for all! Since each nation did have a personality then that would in total be eliminated and we as human beings would be robots in this devious plan of this New World Order!

In America it was that if one came here they would assimilate as Americans with all the same rights almost that the ones who were born here would have but that all could make a living and could worship as they pleased as long as that worship and their public and private lives did not break the 10 Command—ments.

Where else was it like that in the entire world including Israel who were the Old Testament people? This though did not mean that all cultures were equal and one could just do as they wanted with ill regards for their own nation here in America and some were lead to believe that by our own government Here is where that they were lied to time and again and the American people had this weakness to always want to help the underdog all the time which could get one into trouble as a nation very easily. we were to be a United people that is why it was called the United and not divided States. But then for many years in the 20th century we had abandoned that and so now we were living as the 60's had!

This EL PRESIDENTE wanted these Mexicans here now in America because he knew that they would work for peanuts like they did on his own ranch in Texas. This would create for the big corporations, his sponsors very cheap labor and would let them do the work that Americans would not do because they lacked the education and the language and could almost work for slave wages and hence this would bring up the profit margin for all the rich and well educated in America but would kill the middle class in America for sure. He was not concerned about that at all because he was very well to do himself and hence another rich man was in the White House who had never worked a day in his life and did not know what it was like to struggle for young families who had to make a living!

He was a rich man's President for sure and could care less who did what for how much but just so that his own investments were not touched and that of his millionaire friends and the big corporations that now could actually pay minimum wage (was not enough to live on) even for the impoverished of America. This is what his whole mentality was about since he had graduated from Yale business school and they put the fear of not enough money in his mind.

He still continued with this Palestinian State because his Anglo anti-Semitism was still as great as ever and so he would continue us down the road to destruction since Israel was not up for sale and Jerusalem GOD would not let to the Gentiles at all.

We had to wait and see, but I knew for sure that this cold hearted Anglophile would do what he wanted to do just to look good in the public's eye and many Americans who meant well but were ignorant to what was going on around them had bumper stickers that said support the troops which meant that this Commander In Chief was doing such a fine and honorable thing!

Yes, now I could see the light of day and what this President was all up to and the fact that he would not do anything for our own security but wanted for sure to destroy Israel's security too! This made no sense to most people but to me it made all the sense in the world because he was doing just what the Bible said would happen in this place and this time. He was in essence doing not necessarily what GOD wanted but what GOD had said would happen. There was a difference and most Christians could not see the difference. They were more interested in money and what it could buy.

This is now what this Mr. President had now for sure come to represent and that was big business. This was even bigger the big business. This was the internationalists who were being controlled by the enemy that was now working on his one world government and one world religion and all the major denominations plus all the other minor ones and all the religions of the world would come together as one big anti-GOD system described in the Bible as the harlot. There would come many wars and rumors of wars which meant they were not wars yet but were coming to be and also tribe would come against tribe all over the world and it would become so bad that the entire world would look for someone to put a stop to this anarchy and chaos and would be ready for anyone as I said before to put a total stop to these wars. There would appear on the scene this one that would appear to at first be a peacemaker and who would deceive the entire world except the very elect chosen by GOD Himself.

There would also be earthquakes and under the oceans earthquakes which would create tidal waves and create other earthly forms on the surface and even possibly some nuclear attacks here and there. Billions of people would be destroyed by pestilence, famines and some manmade and otherwise, and also many sicknesses and illnesses unknown to man before and also the hoarding of food stuffs and good drinking water and there would be no land on the surface of the earth to farm or raise crops and many processed foods would be stored just for this Antichrist's system! GOD would allow His angels to do many things because this was GOD'S own judgment in the world.

Death and destruction because many still refuse to obey GOD and would curse Him over and over and when the 7 years of Tribulation would come then the Age Of Grace would be taken out of the world and the Holy Spirit would also be gone so there would be no contact with GOD but GOD would protect the 144,000 Jewish people from the 12 different tribes that would probably hide in Petra! These would all be Messianic Jewish people the same kind that were in the Old and New Testament that knew and believed in Messiah and the ones in the Old Testament were waiting for His coming and after He came the ones in the New Testament like the Disciples themselves would also be Messianic Jews. This had absolutely nothing to do with Judaism because Judaism did not recognize the Messiah at all and no matter how many different sects in Judaism such as Reformed, Constructionists, Conservative, Orthodox and Ultra Orthodox none of them would be saved since they all refused to believe in Messiah and the fact that He had already come once before but had returned for the real Church of saints who the Father had called to Himself and their individual freewill to come to Him. America was part of Europe and would not play that big a part in all this in the sense it would come under the European Union. We here in the States thought that we were the promised land but with a President now who had no respect for Israel one could see that even he was working for the enemy against Israel since he wanted to claim

GOD'S land for the Arabs which did not belong to them nor to him to decide, but for GOD to decide and that was for sure that it was Abraham's land given to Him by GOD with the promise that no one would take it away when the right time set by GOD would come and establish from there the Millennial reign of Christ from Jerusalem.

Since it appeared that even the Gentile churches were now turning away from Israel it appeared that Satan was controlling them. GOD though was still in control of all that was going on even though our very own President thought he could beat GOD'S Word in the Bible which explained all this very clear. Ivy League or no Ivy League would interfere with what GOD had ordained with His very Word in the Scriptures and yet the church in the West continued to do what it wanted to do for more and more materialism and wealth and money but that still would not stop GOD'S timing. GOD'S plan would be according to the Father only.

Even Israel's government itself was being backed up into a corner as little by little they were being enclosed by the Gentiles more and more and as I said before this President now would not listen to what the Holy Spirit was saying or what even the Word of GOD had already said about "in these last days".

No man no matter how powerful and any angelic being would interfere with GOD'S sovereign will even though things look right now so very bad for Jerusalem and Israel. But GOD would keep His Word He always did. This was where we were getting into trouble now more than ever and the Christians in America were looking more for revival than to protect Jerusalem and Israel with no strings attached at all.

Messiah's reign would soon be here, but not before the very judgment of GOD on this whole earth would be dealt by Him. Then the world would see what all this was about and then it would be too late for those who would not listen at all and be an ally to Israel.

Now that we were living in a multicultural state and there would definitely be harm then any possible good from it one had to know not to play follow the leader with the English colonists mentality of the rich and well educated and in fact that was all who could run for office in the Federal Government that is the rich and well educated. Either they were some kind of lawyer, doctor, accountant, judge, investor, Ivy Leaguer, socialist, millionaire or billionaire or had rich relatives and relatives with high positions in the country whether it was social government services, or big business or even professionals that had made it big. This was no longer a country for the poor to make it to the top since that was water over the dam and the only criteria would be accepted and that was wealth and plenty of it.

Promotions were in big corporations to relatives, heirs, ones who were already rich and well to do, were socialists, were politically correct, had married into money and plenty of it, etc. This was not the nation that most people thought it was. Those days had gone long ago and passed us by. Now we would see the cream of the crop at the top in all levels of government in the Federal Government even ones that were so foreign but their wealth and power was what this incumbent was all about. He was not for the "peasant" at all and all he knew was what he learned from the Ivy League who he thought was the Gospel!

He did not represent me or my entire family or any good friends of mine. He was a social Christian and that was all that could be said and when he ran for re-election he looked better than what he ever was but that was because he was running against an atheistic Jew who also was a Communist. It did not bother him who he would appoint just so he would please the majority who by the way could care less about the future of our very nation because they would live for only today. Most Americans like my mentor had said, "We're not the brightest people in the world." That was 25 years ago when he made that proper claim. They were too involved in sports, Hollywood, drugs, sex, materialism, want, desire, education to a far extreme, etc.

The "peasants" did not want to be bothered by government but did want the government to leave us alone and did not want any of the civil rights' socialism because we would make it on our own with the help always from GOD and not from Caesar like most Americans were getting day after day and yet were taking more and more away from them without them realizing it at all but soon too, would see the handwriting on the wall. It was again this tune of Babylon in the Old Testament, but then that first Gentile too was a believer at the end after he suffered as an animal for 7 years and then the kingdom was returned to him and this first Gentile king came to the Lord. This had been when Daniel was taken captive as a young man in the Book of Daniel and the temple in Israel or Jerusalem was not there. This ended the reign of the kings of Israel Also the dying prophet Jeremiah was alive at this time also. This is where the synagogue got started since there was no temple in Jerusalem and GOD allowed the Israelites to be taken captive because they would not give back the Sabbath that they promised to do for many years and hence King Nebuchadnezzar conquered them because of GOD and were taken to Babylon because of the above sin.

Daniel, though, kept the faith all those years and had many visions and dreams that foretold what would happen in the future and this Book ran parallel to the Book of the Revelation in the New Testament where St. John the one that Jesus loved was placed on the island of Patmos. It was all prophecy. That is why the Tribulation was called the 70th of the Hebrews because all outer 69 Weeks had been fulfilled in the past and each one of these Weeks represented 7 years only for the Hebrews and not the Gentiles. One Week was now left to go.

Daniel was one of two men that nothing is spoken in the negative along with Jacob's youngest son Joseph. Elijah and Enoch also in the Old Testament had never even yet died so they were taken by GOD to heaven just like that. GOD can pick and choose who He wants to pick.

The only way to please GOD is through faith and not money or works or prestige or fame, etc. King David had done some bad things and when one leader yelled terrible things at him he told his soldiers to let the man go because maybe this was actually GOD'S way of telling off King David who was a man after GOD'S own heart!

King Saul had preceded King David but had wanted to kill King David and King David could have killed him but he did not because King Saul was the King and the authority even though King David had done absolutely nothing to deserve this kind of treatment from King Saul and even Jonathan King Saul's son was on King David's side and tried to stop his own father from killing King David but to no avail.

Now apologies from us are in order for Osama Bin Laden because he said now he never meant . . . so forth and so on! There is no place now for him to go especially since this incumbent has made a deal with Osama's homeland sheiks! At the highest levels of our own government one can find the most corruption. They would lie to save their own" ideology "better known as capitalism to them and are not in the slightest worried about the sovereignty of America! Never trust an Englishman's diplomacy for they have none.

Now also with death penalties down we can all relax and know for sure that our courts are hard at work . . . Many more unreported criminals shall end upon our own streets to once again entertain our lawyers: Yes, we can rest assure that government cares about our mainland as well as its citizens and military now with our soldiers in Iraq, Afghanistan, etc.! This incumbent shall make sure also that Israel has safe borders or better yet no borders at all! It shall be good news for the many illegals, Moslems, Arabs and other criminals in this nation. Now they knew exactly where to come so they can intimidate and threaten and carry out their murderous schemes that there shall always be for them plea bargaining like Scott Peterson almost got with the one foreman that they had on the jury! How convenient wouldn't you say? Our judges, politicians, both lawyers, are working hard to serve the "poor" and the "underdog" no matter how many people are murdered! The average American male has put on a skirt. Now all he needs to put on are a pair of earrings!

Now Presidents of big corporations, banks, positions high in government were metastasizing in groups known as the untouchables! What else could ones of success off of the murders of the unborn, the pedophiles, the aids of euthanasia, the spread of the AIDS virus, traitors, gold diggers, ones of the persuasion of Nazi homosexuality, etc. be called? There were all the rights to do all the wrongs! The entire legal profession and about 98% of the medical professionals were under moral indictment seared consciences as well as for pastors, priests, rabbis and many other clergy and not clerics because we all knew what they are all about! These indictments were not for malpractice law suits, the over litigated cases of suing, but for the murder of innocent human beings and the molestation of and also that these scoundrels by their very own mentality even opposed our very GOD!

Forget about the race issue and our corrupt union officials we all knew what they represented but maybe the average ignorant American knew much less then we could give him credit for!

When it came though to money then, oh yes, then we all had to stop, look and listen! As for murder what was that to get all excited about? One less mouth to feed perhaps or one less criminal to take care of as I had heard many Democrats say time and again! What about just cold hearted Anglo-Saxon white males who made up the largest pro-infanticide group in America? How much did they contribute to their own cause and all of our own moral poverty? Was it a little? Was it a lot? Was it what, insanity?

Yes, insanity could best describe and yet they were in the right frame of mind! Anything without GOD is insane and that is anything! There is nothing apart from Christ that is not evil. "No man is good no not one!" "We all have sinned and fallen short of the glory of GOD!"

We complain about our food that it is too hot or too cold out loud even. We complain about our weather. We complain and whine just about everything that is not really important, but over cold blooded murders so what! Now 50,000,000 infanticides or even 5,000 a day and what? We love to just complain for when one is truly vehemently opposed, now not complaining mind you, there is almost this total apathetic silence by the major majority, well then we find an excuse, not a reason, to ignore all the honorable and decent in a normal society, but who said our society was ever normal? One does not have to look hard to find a reason to proclaim, yes proclaim, in a very loud voice, "Stop the murder!" Should we be passive, assertive or aggressive and should that question ever be asked at all? The first one which is passive has more than many times been used, the second one which is assertive has been rarely used as to the proportion of our entire population, and the third one which is aggressive now that really has not been used to prosecute all these criminals at least as state witnesses! To flee or fight, but they cannot, but if they could they would and yet they are fighting by screaming their lungs out but we have become deaf and hard of hearing! We are only talking about first degree pre-meditated murder because Planned Parenthood there it is Planned has no intention or never has had ever any intention of doing anything but murder the unborn and the born! Either we prosecute all or we prosecute none and we have chosen to prosecute none! This is our own contribution to this New Age of Nazism which was done before but this time we have the "medical technology" to make it quieter not for the victim but for the murderer and his or her accomplices!

Who shall release us from our almost like real chains, but that are invisible to the naked eye? Not like the ones that do confine these innocent children to be murdered, right? We procreate and are not guilty I would suppose and the children who did not do the procreating are guilty, right? We are not the victim but we are the perpetrator to the crime before and after and it is our own indictment that we refuse to see! We do not have any chains that bind us or restrain us around our mouths or around our hands yet we refuse to believe that or we would have done something with them!

Self—preservation speaks up all the time and says, "I have lived my life so you live yours" and this is from the septuagenarian and the octogenarian also! But the problem is that they cannot live or begin to live their lives for that much is certain and there are no graves or crosses for those graves to mark where they are "buried". Yes, refuse disposal! Why even the undertakers have not been burying them any of them! We have no new burial plots and the coffins well where are they? There are no viewings, no music of sadness to play or remember them by, no eulogy and not even the history of that human being! Now that last one is peculiar! Doesn't everyone have some kind of private personal history about himself or herself? It was if they had never been born? Were they stillborn? One would then have to ask, "Was it death from within, or death from without?" In other words did the angel of death come WITHIN the womb to murder, or was the death, as we like to euphemistically call, it from WITHOUT? Too many have come WITHOUT the angel of death and have been murdered! Is 50 too many? Is 5,000 a day too many? How about 50,000 in 10 days? Or let us say 500,000 in 100 days? How about also 5,000,000 or 50,000,000 infanticides? Not enough you say?

Does anybody shed a tear? I have already heard for myself at least one infant or baby cry out loud and have cried horribly for their own brothers and sisters! But why so young an infant that is not even accountable? "From the mouths of babes!"

Why in heaven's sake should the guilty "perish" when it is so much easier to make the "unseen" perish as well as the silent minority of innocence? What rationale of insanity from the ovens that are still warm from Auschwitz? There are never ever enough and there is always room for many more! Only ideology murders like this into the millions and millions repeatedly!

Just for convenience sake or the so called wrong sex or the ignorant or yes even for the lie! Public school ideology indoctrinates such as school based clinics; that is why daycare can only take so many and so few! We are over the quota if one was to include also you in this very capacity! You say but I am not an unborn child. No, but there is where it first started in Nazi Germany with! Are you too old or are you a little disabled or do you believe in the Trinity, or are you too small in size or have the wrong color of eyes or hair? Is there an end in sight? How about the moral and mortal soul of a nation? How about the very death of a nation with its most precious commodity children being murdered? How about only now the state and its existence? How about totalitarianism?

I have lived my life, or at least I had the opportunity to do so, up until this time anyhow, but what about them that are not yet—how do they say—"born"? Then next in line comes the born and then others along the way and then others and so forth and so on until there is only what or who left? How human then does one suppose that that race of people shall be and here when we use the word race we are speaking of the human race which will look like or act like anything but the human race! If Darwin wants to crawl on all fours, then let him, and if Marx loathes man then let him and if Stalin makes funny monkey sounds then let him. If Freud or Lenin or Mao or the rest of the psychopaths and their theory of evolution want to mimic ones in the zoo, then by all means let them! If Margaret Sanger 's grandson wants to head this organization called Planned Parenthood, but there is nothing planned except murder and possibly the murder of the mother also in some instances if need be by intention or unintention for it does not matter!

The animal world cannot reason and hence does not have a soul, but man who can reason and does have a soul should not take for granted the fact that what the animal world does has no consequences. But what man's psychopathic world does indeed has grave consequences and not only for those who do and assists in this, but also for the silent majority who have no say as to good vs. evil!

This jungle of man is this fall from Adam but also stems from man's free will to be his own god and to have as many followers until too they become the very next victim in line to face their own premature death. One can never murder an animal! They can only kill an animal, but a human being from conception until natural death, well that totally is another matter indeed and it does not matter, as I said before, what man believes or does not believe because the truth shall always remain the same unchanged.

What was the criminal code in America since now we had illegals and terrorists within our own borders and this Commander In Chief was turning over to our own society the incompetent ones who did not know how to enforce the federal statutes at all? We now had juveniles as young as 10 and 11 committing crimes and would grow up like the deadbeat dad syndrome children had grown up since the 60's with the Great Society. These children then and now had learned from the criminals in college and on the streets what to do with the citizens of America and no one wanted to testify. That is why the death penalty rate was down because what witness would want to testify against a vicious criminal knowing for sure he would be released for good behaviour in a matter of a few years and be back on the streets again!

Our courts were doing a fine job of incarcerating ones for stealing or damaging government or state property but as for private property they did not care for after all these were socialists we were dealing with. There properties would be protected since they got most of their income and wealth from the state anyhow. That is how many politicians and judges got around the fact that their own homes belonged almost to the state. If one broke a post office window they would go to a federal penitentiary, but if killed or murdered, somehow, like O.J., they went scot-free! This was more of that civil rights socialism that I kept talking about. This was by the group and was called group thought!

The children of these deadbeat dads and these day care centers would most likely enter the same non-traditional role models that they themselves had been brought up with and that was this group mentality. There was no respect for one's elders and no respect even for the family since their own family was the day care which had instilled anger in them from a very young age and hence now they would take back what belonged and why work when their own biological fathers did not have to nor did any of their friends or relatives or neighbors.

Now we were into the 3 and 4 generation in regards to this social state of affairs where now gangs from the once day care center children had now been formed since there was no authority figure at home who was busy making others out of wedlock children so that he could say how much of a man he was! This is how sick it had gotten, but the government for many years had promoted this image of the macho man and the prisons were filled with them. We could also include in that group of educators Hollywood's fictitious heroes that were nothing more then the very same thing that these gangs were all about except that they had become now famous for their very own misdeeds. Who would have been head of a household was most likely now head of a gang or a group of juveniles that worked for him such as dealing drugs and children also thought this was so much fun for them until they started to sentence them to stiff terms with hard core criminals, but then enough of these youngsters and they would be taking over the prisons and soon released all at once and another crime spree would occur. These sprees would come and go just like that because who would want to testify when the lawyers and the judges said it was the environment and poverty that had caused them to commit these crimes and had absolutely nothing to do with the absolutes in morality and character and the wholesomeness of proper family values which were taken off of the books long ago. There were no ghettoes but just slums that were breeding these criminals at a very young age and government would rather increase this recidivism then deal with the real problem at hand and that was crime does not pay in the literal sense of the word and one could do just about anything that they wanted to do!

This was more of the public education's role model in how to become a thug and how to take control and also take advantage of others who could not defend themselves or when the numbers were in their favor. The rich and well educated liked this type of diversity because it meant much more for the United Way and other organizations to teach them even more about how to beat the system and how to get along in life without any sense of responsibility just like the federal government had for many years when it came to spending someone else's money and when it came to character and honesty. Those were words that were not in these educators' minds at all!

If one could beat the system then go ahead and do it for there was much profit to be made just like the American businessman was making and with the same immorality! They too could earn a lot without ever having to work hard for a living, and why not? It was not against the law to be a burden to society at the age of 30 plus! We were indeed educating them in the way of the prison society and the recidivism did not matter because it was okay to destroy private property that belonged to an individual but never must one destroy property that belonged to the state!

•

I remember that as a young boy I was not to even walk on someone's private lawn and to obey with self-discipline what our parents had taught us at home and even, at that time, in the public school system. Then along came the latter 60's! They said that they first of all would lead this society in how to rebel against everywhere what one was taught in the Judeo-Christian home because the ones who had a dad at home would not be affected so much at that time It was the deadbeat dads' children that at first would be attacked for not having any authority over them since their own fathers did not know what the word responsibility meant in the first place and did not want to face up to that very responsibility!

After sometime others would follow by being taught by higher education on how to get high on drugs and then how to not and rebel at even a much older age. This transcended to now the average family today and if one was not for this then one had to be against the government's so called rule of the jungle and not rule of law. They had learned how to act like wild animals and did not really mean any harm if they robbed and mugged and disabled an elderly person or even would beat on a woman for no real reason at all, but what did the rich and well educated know about this since they had only heard about it and had been told that in order to help these people one had to first feel for them that is the criminal mentality and the victim would take care of themselves and then these criminals later in life would be placed in positions of authority that they knew nothing about ever in their very own lives!

Why arrest the criminal when the courts were just going to release them for their own very use towards socialism in our new society that would be turned upside down and on end! This was more of that civil rights' socialism which was anything but civil. In fact, the Communists had gotten hold of it and they then indoctrinated many into their ideology that was the same as in the Soviet Union, and that was treason was good and traitors could only be rewarded with more awards from high on top so keep up the good work!

Everything or almost everything was now being owned and controlled by the government in some shape and some fashion and socialism was growing by leaps and bounds and was teaching now this younger generation that had never experienced the normal part of life that said "Thou shall not steal, thou shall not murder", etc This was something now that they had never been taught but only heard about in fairy tales!

The publisher of these fairy tales was none other than our very own government!

Today I had quite a learning experience in regards to just how far I could go by GOD Himself in a most unusual way and that was when I was discussing with a co-worker about politics and hammered on the English and the German people plus the fact that the Ivy League people were the cause of most of America's problems. Well this co-worker all of a sudden in a high pitched almost sympathetic voice raised his voice and said that he did not appreciate me getting on his parents since I did know that his father was part German and his mother part English and that his father had gone to Dartmouth with a PhD. He said for one and one half years he had been listening to my whining about America and that I should move to another country if I did not like it here or if I did not vote! I felt almost like what King David had said when one leader of another people yelled and screamed at him and one of his soldiers had asked if he should silence him and he said no because he had felt that through this leader GOD was disciplining him and hence I too had felt the same since I was totally guilty of what this co-worker had said and in fact the Holy Spirit had warned me repeatedly.

The next thing has nothing to do with the above and was said by Solzhenitsyn and it inspired me so much because to me and my wife it was profound. This is the following of what I had read in one of Solzhenitsyn's books.

There are 4 stratums or at least there always had been 4. These two were the upper and the lower stratums. There were within these two stratums four sections or parts that went as follows. The first strata was the upper strata writing about the upper strata which meant that ones who had never worked with their hands for a living and were well to do and had the best education where they were in essence writing about each other. In this strata there came no great literature from because contentment kills the spiritual drive. The only way for great literature to be composed is when any individual who came from this strata was unhappy with their personal life or was striving hard to find the spiritual realm, One author that I thought of who applied here was the Russian poet Pushkin. The one who also applied here but did not strive like Pushkin but just wrote about his own strata I would have to say was James A. Michener whose writing were good but not great literature.

The second strata was when the upper wrote about the lower with so many good ideas, but could not ever understand the lower strata and were always like spectators on the side.

The only way that this strata could ever possibly write great literature was when external violence such as happened to Cervantes as his slavery and Dostoyevsky who was in a Siberian labor camp! I also personally feel that St. Paul would have applied here along with Solzhenitsyn.

The third strata was when the lower strata wrote about the upper strata which meant all these authors suffered and hence this created envy and hatred and so no great literature ever came from this strata. Also it was like the revolutionaries who saw only evil in the upper class and could not recognize that very same evil in themselves and so no great literature here came through Angela Davis was one that came to my own mind.

The fourth strata was when the poor wrote about the poor and this was all folklore and legends and because of no or little education no great literature came out of here. All these authors had suffered in this strata. The farmer's almanac is what I thought of here.

In all men is this egocentricity that always pulls man down. and hence without some kind of spiritual yearning and with no pride then possibly could literature be written great. So all of man had this ego problem in all the above stratums but only when the rich wrote about the rich but did so through suffering as I like to call it would it ever be great literature or this yearning for spirituality. Also to repeat from external violence could one write great literature.

In America the only author I could think of was Edgar Allan Poe and his writings! In England it would be Shakespeare and Dickens that would come to mind. In Russia it would be Pushkin, Dostoyevsky and Alexander Solzhenitsyn. And the last would not be Angela Davis from America! It is very difficult as one can see to write the truth with beauty and which beauty cannot be destroyed, but the truth had to be exactly the, way it was and not as one wished it would or could have been or wanted it to be. Here is where great literature comes from and if one reads the Bible they see it here. Not all the writers in the Bible were poor such as St. Paul since he was a Roman citizen but gave up all that for this spiritual yearning and ended up being in prison along with other catastrophes. He also wrote most of the New Testament and the constitution of the New Testament the Book of Romans. Yes it is the educated but only when that individual has a spiritual yearning or an unhappy personal life. That is why we see very few great writers of literature throughout all of the ages I believe.

Television innuendoes and gas for blood and the price of gold goes up and the value of life goes down as far as the Vatican is concerned. These television innuendoes started with vaudeville, which in the Soviet Union was very popular and so as Lenin said, "Use the theatre". Today we see Communists coming out of Hollywood from everywhere and none are prosecuted or rarely have been prosecuted as long as old man Lenin has been around or took power. It also took on an innocence that television would play and now has turned to the occult and witchcraft with Stephen King and also Nazi New Age homosexuality and pedophilia and black liquid manure rap lyrics. Here socialism of different kinds are alive and well and now even the New Age cartoons have come out with all their enchantments and witchcraft and idiocy. Even adults now watch these infantile batman and Robin imbecile type of other monsters that, as I just said, the adults from the 60's like to watch!

This gas for blood and of course not the rich and well educated's blood but that of the average American citizen sent not only in harm's way but to homicidal bombers so that this incumbent looks so asinine in his multicultural mentality. To him one of everything is the way it should be such as one culture for all, one solution for all, one party for all, etc. He is so bad that with Baghdad and now

Fallujah he would rather see death and destruction by our soldiers to save face with his buddies in Saudi Arabia and his love of his money for himself He even believes that Islam is multicultural in the sense that it worships the same GOD that we here in America do who came in the flesh! This is incredibly an Anglophile all the way with their conniving about all his so called diplomacy. We are now going to take Abraham's land and build a hornet's nest right in the very middle of it and with the Vatican who loves the Moslems for what they can try to do for the Vatican so they can once again be the one and only so called "Church"! Little do they know that only GOD knows who is saved and who is not and who is a saint not canonized but by the very blood of GOD Himself!

This is all part of Roman Catholicism's anti-Semitism that has been going on for centuries and centuries and this Kerry fellow was as much a Roman Catholic as I was a . . . He only pretended to be that since his wife had all the money in the billions and an atheistic Jew travels farther then the 3rd and the 4th generation for this love of money as in the money exchangers in the temple during Jesus' time on this earth! Satan had work cut out for most Jews in America and it was the making of money.

Now one can almost for sure assume why the Vatican was silent during the Holocaust because most of the priests were homosexuals here as well as there and elsewhere and now we are finding out that even nuns were involved in deviant conduct in regards to this celibacy and abnormal as one can get and yet all these centuries no one seemed to question it at all! Pope Pius XII was an anti-Semite and most Catholics are anti-Semites and when one is around them one can constantly hear it come out of their mouths yet they themselves have not to claim except fame and fortune for this earth but no salvation or saving grace or even the knowledge of a Bible because they just don't read it at all and are very ignorant to things around them that is spiritual and hence even the Crusades, the Spanish Inquisition, the Holocaust and now the state of Israel is a thorn in their side that they want to eliminate the Jews once and for all and also the fact that many Arabs are homosexuals and as one digs deeper one can see that all these homosexual relationships start to form something that is so hidden and so powerful in this world one could possibly call it the antichrist and not Antichrist.

The Nazis, the Arabs who were their accomplices, the Vatican who also lost their tongue to speak out and defend the innocent and the English now and the Episcopalians, the UCC, and so forth and so on including the United Nations with its sick NAMBLA have this common denominator of reprobate minds which means that one is not born a homosexual and one can put away the fairy tale that one is and give it to the Germans who, to begin with, are not too bright and let them cling to their deviancy but leave us out of this. Enough of their lies, for centuries now, have been covered up and still the Germans get away with it year after year as well, as the Vatican which is a pyramid and nothing more. It has absolutely nothing to do with Christianity yet gets credit for it while the cults are fairly well known for what they are and who they are. But as for Roman Catholicism that does just about any thing by the world's book one now has to say without any reserve that this is not in the least Christianity and not one person I know has ever been saved by this type of religiosity that they proclaim with such arrogance when it was the Roman soldiers and the queer emperors who first crucified Christ because they had the authority to do it. The Jews did not, and because they choose their own saints that are not really saints according to the Bible when Paul says and to the saints in Rome. He is not speaking of the Roman Catholics Church and its fiasco of St. Peter was the first Pope when first Peter was a Jew and the fact that Jesus never worshipped as a Catholic ever! This lie has been perpetrated on end for almost 2,000 years and now the truth must be told because too many people have gone to Hell believing in a lie! On and on it goes and the West especially herein America worships this lie that Roman Catholicism is Christianity! Again money plays this evil part and evil lies that never goes away and this little antichrist in Rome with its 7 hills and is a state unto its own and does not even belong to Italy should tell one and plus the fact that even David Rockefeller mentions the fact that he visited the Vatican when he was President of World Bank!

In Latin America where there is much ignorance, this lie is growing even more so because, as I said, they believe this lie along with Liberation Theology which is actually revolutionaries as priests and nuns who become involved in the world of warfare and does not open the Gospel to teach how one becomes saved and not if one is a Catholic which means absolutely nothing to GOD Himself for if it did then there would be no Messianic Jews now would there?

With the virulent anti-Semitism there can be no Christianity and the same goes for Protestantism whom Martin Luther was another virulent anti-Semite and that country has had homosexuality for many centuries just like the Roman Catholic Church and both belong to this world and not to GOD'S up and coming reign of Messiah's! Let us tell the whole truth and stop saying that these European religions preached love and kindness when in fact they hated all the Jews!

Israel and not St. Peter's Basilica is where Jesus shall rule from and set up His kingdom and there shall be no setting up the kingdom until Jesus or Messiah does it and no Kingdom Dominion Theology which says that man and his so called church shall setup this Millennium! Repeat the lie enough times and most people shall believe it. Some of the worst types of people and the most dangerous to Christianity itself are social Christians who do not know who Jesus really is. They worship the creation and not the Creator, and they have many symbols in the form of women and men as statues who they bow down and pray to and through.

This includes the Russian Orthodox Church which has still some of those remnants of the Vatican in it and the same kind of anti-Semitism. What would happen say suppose that the Antichrist himself was a Jewish man now just suppose what does one think then that the world would do to the Jews or try to do to the Jews all over the world just because he was a Jewish man?

Charles Spurgeon had never gone to seminary school and he so far is the only one to have gotten it right as far as what the Bible says in regards to salvation and both major denominations of European founding have gone astray in not only that but also in anti-Semitism. Just because GOD'S Word says that the Jews are a stiff-necked people, it does not mean to imply anyone who calls themselves a Christian can allow themselves to be anti-Semitic because Jesus or Messiah was a Jewish man! How can one love GOD when in the flesh He came as a Jewish man, and be anti-Semitic? If GOD does not call there can be no salvation for free will can never find GOD alone!

In seminaries they have allowed heresy to come in and play havoc with GOD'S holy Word some thing that no one should ever do. Now we have a President who wants to please Islam and not just the Arabs and wants to doom us to the bind of destruction by GOD Himself for GOD shall not allow us to take Jerusalem from Him and that is what this Palestine Liberation Organization wants to do and re member it is an organization and not a ministry or a church yet this incumbent thinks it is and that they have the same holy and just and righteous GOD that the Christians worship according to Scripture and for some reason the Gentiles have gotten many things so wrong because they now hate the Jew and have been doing so for many many centuries with no remorse or concern about what even GOD thinks!

This transformation has not taken place and even Dostoyevsky had allowed the enemy in when he chose to be anti-Semitic. Too many famous or well known people in history who claim Christianity for their faith have had this anti-Semitism in them and in no small measure! Europe is where the Antichrist shall come from and hence since most all major religions that claim

Christianity had come from there one has to wonder about their authenticity? Even the non-believing Israelis have taken in the Falasha from Ethiopia who are Negro and did not make them slaves like many of our own Founding Forefathers did time and again. The Bible calls slave trading evil! There is no other way to describe it when one is slothful and lackadaisical about working with their hands and their minds just like a farmer would who tills the soil with his own hands and also has to use his mind. This is where Man (got his power of propaganda because everybody could see That in all men they had this thing about not doing much physical labor in order to make a living and the fact that all men want to have it easy so they do not have to really make a living with some sweat and some brains. This is also where the poor write about the rich and go about describing as I just said the rich and well educated but have the very same vices that they see in the rich and also are revolutionaries so hence they are blinded by their very own pride. When I mention the rich and well educated I do not exclude myself from that not that I belong to that group because I do not but I do belong to the human being group that has this sin or fall from Adam and is not restrict. ed to a class of any kind and this is where this group fails to see that if they would look in the mirror they would see themselves along with these rich and well educated even though they themselves are very poor and that is why this group the poor writing about the rich never have any great literature because they have this envy and hatred! Here is where we all must take the log that is in our own eye! America refuses or we refuse to do this since we believe there has never been such a society as ours when we only know about this time in which we were born and cannot say for sure that our nation is the best that ever was since this would have to include what GOD had set up in the Old Testament and which later were run by kings even though GOD Himself wanted to be their King and shall be again when the Messianic Millennium comes and the faster we as Gentiles realize that the better it shall be to see the truth for what it really is according to GOD. This is the Father of Abraham, Isaac and Jacob and our Saviour Messiah. Remember the laws were given to the-Jews and not to the Gentiles and we must never pretend or believe that we have to replace Israel or the Jewish people as His chosen people no matter what the world and its own religions may or may not preach in its seminary schools which now have fallen apart.

It is this New Heaven and this New Earth that is spoken about in the Bible, and Jerusalem is the place where Messiah shall set up and not in New York City, or Berlin, or Moscow. So let us see what now lies before us before we venture in our very own self destruction by the lies that Satan now more than ever is spreading because he knows that his time is very short indeed!

"If you have seen Me, you have seen the Father. I and the Father are One." That could only mean that at that time when it was spoken that when one looked at Messiah they literally saw a Jewish man in the flesh and not a Gentile who was half man/half GOD. So, He knew how we felt and could understand what man was all about and not ignore our sin but to bring attention to the fact that we all have sin more than ever before and that He and only He could help anyone with the Father's call!

This Christian for a President is actually following multiculturalism or Marxist/Leninism and now wants to take on what English and the British have taken on, and his cousins, the Germans who also cannot be trusted for whatever they say or do! He is leading our very nation into a pit of no return and is one of the worse ever to be in the White House. He is definitely not an intellectual because he does not have high morals and look where he sends his one daughter: the Harvard that hates America!. We had only one choice and that was to not vote at all We also can decide if the average American can think that far to change our government from a socialist form to an authoritarian form of government and there are so many and in fact too many young college indoctrinated students coming out to now run what they think is a democracy for all what that would incur and that would be very little. They have no say, the same as us and are not aware of what they are up against nor do they even realize that this enemy is about to take over and just the state is going to be here.

This incumbent's dad was the same as him, a New Ager, and with this means the one world government and one world religion something both these Anglophiles seem to want so much for everyone without asking anyone that is anyone who has a normal mindset what they think of Marxist/Leninism! To them they keep rolling along all of us into oblivion and we as dumb Americans play follow the leader and the Germans who are really noted for this, like it that way as well as going along with the winner!

Since we now have one party after this election and there is no doubt about it we all can breathe a sigh of relief and now know for sure the one candidate is all we now need! This ideology which is in all political parties is now the one and the only one that anyone who so chooses foolishly enough to think that their vote really meant something when all it meant was just that a delayed walk to stronger socialism and hence Communism. Islam shall not get the first shot if Red China has anything to say about the entire West and Red China has something to back themselves up with and that is good old fashioned nuclear weapons and the fact that they shall shoot first and then ask questions and that is so comforting to know that now this Anglophile holds as the royalty in England hold just a sort of kind of formality position as Commander In Chief and he shall not do what they do not want him to do. We can now thank our lucky stars that Kerry did not win because now we get a chance to move into socialism at a slightly slower rate of speed and the people in America have been indoctrinated only to know about political parties. They can only understand that since they have never really lived or even studied socialism for real or for that matter Communism or even Islam when they stet have to debate if any of these have socialism in them and they all do indeed! To Americans their utopia is in fact that it can never happen in America! Well it already has for some time and it is time to get ready for the real foundation to be built with the help of the executive, the judicial and the legislative. They would all not be there if they knew what they were now involved in and will not be so easy to get out for to do so would indeed put them at odds with what this very foundation is all about! This would leave them even if they left out in the cold once they got into the so called private world of professionals?

They run, but they cannot hide for this has encompassed all and this President means for it to stay forever which, to our nation, is not too very long. The state usually shall last not real long but just long enough to eliminate the believers and others who cannot defend themselves because now their law shall tie completely everyone's hands including the law enforcement people as well as the military and that is why this President if one can call him that refused to change the "don't ask don't tell" rule in the military because now the Nazi New Age can run its course here in America as it has in Europe and we must remember we are always part of Europe and especially England and Germany proper.

We are now being governed by not this Congress or this President even though he thinks so but by the internationalists who now control all of Europe which means America too! Islam shall pose some what of a problem but not for long and then the Communists shall takeover them or else! The Communists shall have no other religion but Marxist/Leninism! They will not share this absolute power struggle with anyone and that is why we as a national government have been helping Red China thinking that yes they would come to our aid when we needed them too and like they promised too and one can see how they came to the aid of their own peasants when Mao was in!

Their conventional army is almost 200,000,000 men strong plus they now have the nuclear know how to do what they have to do and Islam shall follow along with them since they did in the Soviet Union since they too have an innately socialistic religion with a death wish like Marxist/Leninism.

The American people are waiting for someone to defend our borders but shall wait till hell freezes over.

It would surely appear that GOD has cursed us with absolutely no leaders now, even near the top, to be President of these United States, and the ones who talk about Christianity just do that they talk! Probably the only one I could possibly think of as a President would be a Negro man by the name of Alan Keyes. The only problem would be is that he is a Catholic like Floyd Patterson was when it was not very popular to be a Negro Catholic and I am not saying that Mr. Keyes would ever do that but his wife is from India and so probably he turned Catholic later in life because he is more much more qualified than Clarence Thomas because he defends Scripture better than any Catholic I have ever heard of in my life and hence this leads one to conclude that he is a Christian for real.

He is very excitable but for the right reasons and he does not go around like this incumbent as if he were a businessman making oil deals and deals through NAFTA! He would never be nominated because first of all he is a Christian and second because he is a Negro man and in the exact order. If he would be a Jesse Jackson then he too would have been nominated for President and Mr. Jackson is what one would call a social Christian just the same that this incumbent now really appears to be. He is cold as most of the English are and has no compassion for our soldiers in harms way and continues not to bring them back because of oil and because of what could possibly occur when they came back and the stories they would have to tell their friends, family, neighbors, etc. It would surprise one to finally hear from the NCO'S and those who are down on the totem poll and not the Colin Powells and Sanchezes and Franks who are in it for the career and medals and prestige. Remember it was a captain and a lieutenant and a colonel all involved in the My Lai Massacre in Vietnam.

There are also no Scalias that this incumbent has so far picked for the Supreme Court but look like a Yugoslavian type of court or courts that he would have just to please his proclivity towards people who do not know the first thing about what America stood for (or do they care?) just the same as him and all he appears to do is to do a lot of talking like all good politicians and was a graduate from Yale business school which should tell one what influence he was brought up around. There is always some type of influence with the Anglo-Saxons and so we would have to believe that they along with the atheistic Jews and the Vatican influence here in America and now Islam has changed a once Christian nation into a heathen nation in a matter of a short time and all of us also must take the responsibility too!

Many dollars from American taxpayers which would amount at least to billions and now trillions have been taken by the Halleburtons and the Bechtel families of which the latter did business with the Arab oil sheiks in Saudi Arabia and also World Bank of Rockefeller fame as well as Robert McNamara who also was president of World Bank. The United Nations is anything but uniting the nations or the nationalities and is all about making money off of the American taxpayer and that is why the United Nations is located in New York City. We make up 5% of the entire world's population and use 25% of the entire world's resources and so even though we see bad things-the rest of the world must be a total disaster which-could in essence lead to a worldwide disaster since one part of the world lives in luxury and others are dying and being murdered and because this wealth never ever gets to the inhabitants of these foreign countries. For example electric lines in foreign countries do not get put up for the citizens there but for the big huge worldwide corporations and their industrial monstrosities that have cause great havoc in the world today such as what is going in Iraq and this incumbent knows it!

Puerto Rico for example was taken by the Rockefellers for America so that David Rockefeller could channel funds meaning taxpayers funds through there in all of Latin America such as through the bank called the American Bank Capitalism does not like water rise to its own level, but in fact it rises to such a level that this wealth becomes absolute power and rules in over all the peoples in all those nations whose government of which most are oligarchies that separate two classes the rich from the poor. When so much is in a few peoples' hands then what occurs almost like a natural metamorphosis is a turn to socialism where the elite dictate what they want and when they want and also who they want. These people make Enron look small.

Socialism's one product is pure materialism which means nothing is spiritual and that no longer does capitalism play a role in what goes on any longer because all capitalisms lead to socialism!

One can no longer say free enterprise because it is not and in fact when government also becomes involved it is socialism because these lawyers in government play along with the special interests and no longer even in America for the average American taxpayer. They are bought out before they take office or they would not be there. Absolute power corrupts absolutely! These loans that are made are so that, for instance, when they cannot be paid back the internationalists then say to that government 'sell your own oil to us at the cheapest price to make up that difference! This is the scandal everyday that occurs through the United Nations because now this becomes not only a businessman's organization but a socialistic form of world government. This is just like the USSR which had to reach out and grab for all these nations by force and here they do it behind closed doors but nonetheless it is socialism with pure materialism and shall eventually turn into something much more ugly and cruel and right now there is no coming back We are on. a collision course with destiny that shall affect the entire world and there is no getting around this and even the Halleburtons and the Bechtels shall have to be brought to their knees even though they think that they shall control even more. There is only so much they can control and then an enemy shall consume them and many billions of others worldwide who know nothing of all of this!

George Schultz and Caspar Weinberger were both part of the Bechtel Corporation As the Gentiles continue to try to destroy Israel it shall almost look hopeless for them, but then something shall occur that even these elitists shall not be able to stop but that is in the future. This is not a prognostication on my part at all, but a reality since the world if one studies it can for sure see what these internationalists really want to do but shall be stopped when they least expect it and do not now really care how far they take this to. Their own pride has blinded them to what is coming for the entire world and barring none.

Even in America because of our own ego we too shall self destruct because there is a limit to the resources on this earth and when push comes to shove the Communists shall not stop and the

Western elites shall shudder because the Communists shall indeed do what these internationalists would not do and that is nuclear holocaust and since they are alive and not even their own relatives will matter to them in the final analysis.

This is winner takes all and the billionaires also shall be eaten up just like that within due time and shall believe that they themselves are still in control when really they are not. Their arrogance shall blind them. This is also a spiritual world and that is where that this battle shall take place even though we as mortals shall see many things taking place before our very eyes. When the ice thickens enough then it shall crack The number of billionaires shall decrease one by one and soon a trillionaire shall appear that shall overcome all their inadequacies which they do not see and even the United Nations or united world elites also.

My wife finally had her gall bladder operation. Oh yes, that's right, I did not mention that GOD was with her and answered our prayers and Jesus's prayers to the Father who is always interceding for His children in the family of GOD.

As my wife was in the hospital there were many experiences that simply astounded me so much that it was hard to believe that we were in a hospital. As I was waiting for my wife in the recovery room, one male individual decided it would be time for him to go to sleep and snore at the same time while in front of others who also had come in to wait for their loved ones as well as friends and neighbors. As I was the very first one to get in the room, since my wife's surgery was for very early in the morning, I could hear the sounds of a hospital and also some of its employees who were busy at work, at least most of them. I could hear one woman worker complain that she did not have enough chairs and another woman who could have cared less. Then I heard what sounded like another woman but was a male talking as if another woman to these two above women and had these lisps as he spoke, which was very annoying to me as I sat alone at that time in the waiting room. Another woman came in and we spoke for a little while about our own loved ones and then went about reading what we had brought along. Of course I had one of my Solzhenitsyn's books with me to read since I knew I would have to wait some time for the surgery and the recovery to be over.

In the Ambulatory Services area my wife was wheeled back and she was very groggy from the anesthesia but knew who I was. Some time later another woman came in along with all of her relatives or at least most of them. She was moaning noisily (not from the surgery), that she did not get the treatment she felt she deserved, and was using profanity. Her husband (this I can only assume) continued to pursue the issue until my wife told the nurse in her rest room that she could not rest and wanted to be moved to another room. A few minutes later about 3-4 nurses came and moved my wife, knowing the reason, and were very friendly about it. As we were going out of the room, I heard what this lady next to us (who appeared well enough to swear and rant and rave) say something about my wife's move, but I just ignored it because my wife later said she had some kind of mental disturbance. I had felt that her only problem, though, was that she was again not being treated fairly yet she created the above circumstances by her profanity in GOD'S name and her relatives, her talking and annoying others constantly about the hospital personnel, and demanding this and that! They had no consideration for any of the patients or the personnel in the hospital except again that they were not being treated equal! They must have thought they were in a government building or something, and they also had something on television that looked like liquid manure.

There were many other annoyances that were permeating the hallways and the rooms all around. They were all speaking in Spanish and were very arrogant, and again this incumbent and his predecessor could be thanked for that. They also had on only the basic Hispanic channels for the not too intelligent and caring.

Then my wife was moved again to another room and this was to the orthopedic section of the hospital because my wife had requested with much concern and in an intellectual way one who has high morals that she had labile blood pressure and some pain and was afraid to take pain medicine orally by the mouth because of her ulcerated stomach which could cause severe intestinal and stomach pain and discomfort, but if left in the hospital would be treated for pain intravenously and would bypass the stomach completely and hence prevent further complications, and her surgeon approved it.

In this room was a nice woman who had been totally confused because different agencies were telling her different things about how she would get her treatment in regards to her personal physical condition and was in almost all week and we listened to her until all of her relatives had heard her story which would come in and then go and others would come in and then go until it came to the point that one could not but overhear this same story over and over again and again and my wife and I just smiled and my wife said to me, "It appears that no one comes into a hospital to rest and recuperate." I thought to myself my wife did not know just how right she was since first the hospital administration were all bureaucrats and only wanted all the patients in and out with no consideration for each and every separate case, but just so they had enough bed space for the next "customer"! As I had said before all of the hospital personnel were very professional and were constantly busy. Being understaffed again another hospital administrative decision who no one knew their names was showing its ugly and silent and nameless head!

To all the above negative things with the negativity involved with patients and hospital personnel they had all been of the civil rights' socialism ideology! This was not the squeaky wheel this time getting the oil because this was a hospital and not a government agency where one could annoy and demand whatever they thought was wrong and whatever they demanded had to be rectified immediately with no questions asked!

This is how far it had gotten with this new socialism that was now even trying to turn their equality into equivalency which had nothing whatsoever to do with medicine or the Hippocratic Oath and of which no one could or dare say but here in this hospital thank goodness they did just that! Here one had to be qualified to hold a position or else the hospital would go broke from financial law suits. It was bad enough that the trial lawyers had done what they had already done in the past and that was to legitimize whatever that they wanted legitimized no matter what just so they got the financial benefits in the end! I did wonder who their surgeons and doctors were.

Of course there would always be some no matter who would demand their equal day in "court". This, as I said before, was repeated time and time again daily all over the nation to the point that it created such confusion that now this group of people wanted anything but what was normal and decent!

How could one ever miss what this was all about but most Americans were too afraid to challenge even when it came to the point of absurdity and mental health issues! This was indeed a cancer that would eat out itself plus America if allowed to spread any longer and this false guilt and this equivalence was nothing more than the arrogance that was imbedded by government officials who could care less what happened to all of the American people and not just to some.

Usually if one went into prison with a criminal intent and were bad before they went in, then it was almost certain that when they came out they would still not reform and the recidivism rate went higher and higher and younger and younger until criminals now were at the age of 10 and 11 years of age! The state now was both their family and "father" figure who would head the household for them and they continued to go along with this now for many many years and now would lead this nation through the good reforms of socialism!

As I was saying, if one went into prison as a repeater or as one who would have done criminal acts no matter what, then releasing them with such leniency was again the idea of the judicial system's fine professional lawyers! They were making a wreck out of this nation and could care less where America ended up. This was more of capitalism's avarice and greed which now had gone to socialism pure and simple and which meant that materialism was above all things! Was that not what capitalism was all about? How much could one make in the shortest amount of time and with the least amount of work and hard labor and never having to work up a sweat or ever use the physical part of the body?

That is why Marxism spread so well worldwide because it had made most of the poor people envious as to what they did not and could not obtain no matter how hard they tried and the fact that now that they had known about it through the Halliburtons and the Bechtels socialism could rise up and also Islam could rise up since Islam itself was innately socialistic and would catch on fire since it took time for one to accomplish things and for some socialism promised now a better way then to wait and that was to go on a warpath no matter what! There would now be no turning back with this Islamic Jihad since these people who lived in poverty and destitute were dying and only now the Christians would be not affected because no matter what they would not renounce their faith for capitalism or socialism no matter what it promised or what persecution they would have to suffer in the mean time. Theirs could only be one way and that was the way of our Saviour and that would be now as before and that was through suffering!

Their faith, no matter what would happen in the flesh, would see them through and would not affect nor change them and they would not complain but would continue on in life just the same. This is what socialism had failed to take into consideration and the proponents of!

While the entire world except the Christians and the Messianic Jews would accept now what the world was offering there would now be even more persecutions and murdering of Christians throughout the world and now even in the Western part of the world because they too had latched onto this quick get rich scheme that appeared beneficial in the flesh at least for the present time. This was all too good to be true but nonetheless the world in the higher principalities was at work to convince all that this was the sure way to go!

America maybe if fate was with us maybe 5 years or so and then all would turn over to socialism completely and that would be all the state power and none to the spiritual realm with power by GOD.

Where do we as American citizens go from here when there now is so much divisiveness amongst our very own people and even more so with the direct importation of over population almost like Stalin had done with millions of people and amongst those people many Communists and Moslems that did represent socialism en masse over our nation and its survival? This incumbent was too destroying from within our own type of nationality because he himself had never ever lived amongst the average American ever! He refused to understand that only one language would ever due and that assimilation by coercive methods would never do. Now with more Communists from the Mexican side of the border we were being infiltrated each day so that all things would become legal and GOD Himself would become illegal.

Our own city was completely destroyed by drug dealers, legitimacy, abused children, homosexuality, prostitution with children and male homosexual prostitutes, and this multiculturalism that had destroyed our own city and was destroying many other cities, towns and communities across this large nation! He was totally for the underdog no matter how insane it appeared to be and was not for these United States but for the village that Hillary Clinton had established and also these HMO'S that were doing harm to many citizens in the United States. He would not be affected since he could go anywhere to get the best medical care and could care less about how the real average American and not Hispanic Jihad or civil rights' socialism lived which was anything but normal and with decency!

We had to make room for the freeloaders as had occurred in Russia with the Finns who also refused to speak Russian and also brought with them many who were loyal Communists and this was right with in Moscow itself and its surrounding areas. We in America had the Hispanics just for starts that were doing the very same thing also and who also refused to speak our mother tongue, not because they could not learn it but because they did not want to. Our government approved of this all the way and so did our own churches who were so much in the dark that they too got lost with this underdog mentality and this bilingual mentality! They too had forgotten what it was like to be an American and soon we too would be worse than a Yugoslavia but no one seemed to care as long as they could move away from it, collaborate with it, be part of it for what it really was and that was Marxist/Leninism!

We had become a totally pampered nation and look too much to politics while the spiritual realm continued to suffer daily and of course Roman Catholicism was involved with this too since they needed more recruitments into their own pyramid! The Vatican was losing many members because first of all many of them did not subscribe to the Bible not that the Vatican did but that their present stance was anti-infanticide and anti-homosexual but if one looked at the churches in America it would have been very hard to tell especially in regards to homosexuality! These new recruits would come from America by way of Mexico since now they too would substitute for sure their own faith for happiness in slavery or socialism in mysticism which Dostoyevsky had so correctly pronounced even over a century ago.

Americans no longer communicated at all and were beginning to go against GOD Himself because they liked this new land of rebellious freedom that gave them everything except liberty and that was something each individual American had to decide for themselves. Most thought that just the military and government would uphold that and this is where the lie was promoted to the fullest. As Americans, each one of us adults had to fight for what we believed in and not what someone else supposedly had told us was the truth! We Americans refused to check out anything spiritual and were deeply involved in the financial which was in the flesh!

More and more these foreign religions and nothing even appearing as the Biblical Christianity were enveloping us more and more. The Pilgrims were forgotten all about even in this time of Thanksgiving something that Roman Catholicism had nothing to do with. This was from the Old Testament which was in remembrance of The Feast of Tabernacles which said both the Jewish and the Gentile males were to celebrate and the Pilgrims made it somewhat inclusive because of Jesus' appearance on earth.

Our very own children had learned too much from my generation the 60's generation and were abusing our own grandchildren because we had failed as parents to equip them with the Bible and we gave in even to popular opinion too many times which was direct from the pit of Hell in America and that was none other than Hollywood! It now appeared that Nazism and Soviet Communism were making their move not from Europe but from here in America and that now they both would join together to become one not that they were ever different like most educated people liked to falsely believe. Our real guilt was not being dealt with but only our false guilt which GOD Himself could do nothing about!

From "we are our brother's keeper" it went to the Padré mentality that said all would be taken care of by this Church and this Government! Again too much politics and no amount of faith was involved in this debacle. Our religion like Russia had become Marxist/Leninism and someone everyday had to keep reminding us about this day after day as if we were an infant who had to be spoon fed! We did not want to be held responsible morally for anybody including ourselves and would rather enjoy the so called "good life" of" eat, drink and be merry".

There were so many criminals now out on the streets who did not even serve one day of jail time which told one immediately that our whole society had gone sour and that our morals and some which were not punishable by man's law but were against GOD Himself would go unseen and unheard of and since only crimes that were reported counted and many were not reported is all that mattered! Once a person wants to commit a crime and sometimes it is by mistake or their first mistake and not involving life or death they would most of the time not need to either serve time or little time since they did not have the mentality of a criminal before they would have even entered prison. Then there were ones who were criminals before they even entered prison and would be repeat offenders time and again and nothing would reform or change them to good citizenship! This had to be a distinguishable mark. If one had character and that in and of itself was so very important it could be seen, but if they did not then recidivism and not poverty or any amount of extremity could affect them.

When the law itself is no law and is only the socialization of society itself to blame the environment then we for sure have a problem and that problem is the lie! With no character then it would be hopeless to seek to reform and also if there was no real repentance or remorse on the part of that criminal then all was just semantics and a waste of time since this criminal would continue to repeat the crime or crimes over and over again. English law said the punishment had to meet the crime.

If we were incarcerating individuals and not because of civil rights' issues but because there was or was not character within that particular individual then and only then could justice be served in the penal code and in no other way! One cannot judge a book by its cover and hence character looked at the inside of each and every human being. Or what is a pretty package with nothing in it! We would go from one extreme to another and neither were right or near right as to how to bring justice to all individually.

As Dr. Cornfeld had witnessed to Solzhenitsyn in a hospital bed in camp one night when Solzhenitsyn and the Dr. were all alone he went on to also explain and to paraphrase if possible that we all had done things in our very own lives that came back to us in suffering and not always within a short period of time but sometime in our life. Later that night as Dr. Cornfeld who had changed from Judaism to Christianity and these were to be his last spoken words on earth ever he was murdered while sleeping before the break of dawn when usually in this particular camp it was done when many doors were un locked! So without this Jewish or Messianic believer Solzhenitsyn might have had to wait for many years later to be witnessed too and would have missed his opportunity in life this early to know GOD personally and the Russian Orthodox faith does not subscribe to this in the way that we would suppose. Since Solzhenitsyn had character and was wrongly imprisoned somehow through this very imprisonment he believed he was turned around and made to see the light. Again character showed to be the deciding factor along with suffering for something he had not really done that was immoral! He was wrongly imprisoned and as he said only ones who have been imprisoned with character can really say thank prison for my spiritual turn around! Ones who have never served in prison always say not me! Then there were those who could say, "Yes, but you are still alive."

Today in America the prisoners did not work or learn a trade but are pampered and these are the ones who have no character along with the ones who do and hence we now see what affect this has on the ones who need to work and learn a trade and the ones who shall only continue to commit crime after crime because character and the Christian faith is totally missing! A wolf sheds its fur but not its habits!

How many wolves do we now have that the courts and trial lawyers and defense attorneys knew for certain that they were guilty and intentionally lied in the courtroom and intentionally released them be cause to prosecute them then they would have to prosecute themselves? The Nuremberg Trials did a wonderful job but it forgot that some of those very same judges were Soviet judges who too should have been tried!

Was this the rule of law or was it what today we are seeing again what occurred in Russia with the same result that criminals would be running our own government and soon would be taking over by force and by lies upon lies to obtain power with no faith and character but just for absolute power?

There was one business that was local that had a Bush/Cheney sticker on its window and the peculiar thing about that was that the owners were Vietnamese/Chinese! Did that mean they knew all about John Kerry, the one who had met with the Vietcong in Paris and were they really going to vote for the Bush/Cheney ticket or was it to conceal who they were really for? No other businesses around had signs in their front windows during the election so this seemed sort of obvious one way or the other!

This EL PRESIDENTE' was pushing his Hispanic Jihad more and more and it was the first thing he did to promote his new re-election just the same as Clinton had done with homosexuality and some days later he was walking with him while this terrorist was still alive and the dedication for his own library was probably full of all Marxist/Leninist books plus some of Darwin, Mao, Ho Chi Minh, Castro, Tito, Adolf Hitler, Stalin, Lenin, etc! Yes this incumbent was walking side by side as if this was his best friend with a smile on his face instead of prosecuting this traitor for treason in 1973!

Both parties had one ideology and that was who the American people were voting for time and again and with no reservation but even most Christians thought that this incumbent was doing the right thing. He had first said with Blair that Islam and Christianity worshipped the same GOD; he executed a Christian lady while governor of Texas, but allowed criminal Mexicans into our own nation plus Mexican Communists, he promoted NAFTA because of Mexico mostly, and was ruling two nations now but as one, he would not defend our own borders, he was allowing multiculturalism to spread in America like it had spread in Yugoslavia and would not ever eliminate all homosexuals from the military, and had yet one judge to be nominated to any federal court in over 4 years! But nonetheless leads a Christian nation, yet did not understand in the slightest about what GOD now wanted him to do immediately!

Our own owner of our own local newspaper was too an Ivy Leaguer as well as this incumbent and Clinton, but Ronald Reagan was not and one could readily see the difference! They had no contact with the real world and could in no way relate to what was going on in the heart of America at all! Nothing but politics was now absorbing America and the spiritual realm was dying quickly. More concern was placed on the President then on GOD Himself because if GOD would have been first then things would have moved in a different direction to save the unborn as well as our children and our youth by investigating all the homosexual pedophile organizations that were getting to our very children.

I had just found out Arby's was supporting the homosexual organization of Big Brothers/Big Sisters! The United Way in our area had a Sodomite woman running its organization, and now it could add to its already agenda of infanticide, homosexuality with pedophilia. Big business in America had sold out to the lowest form of scum that one could now think of and were like the Nazis of World War II! America was self-destructing because the Anglo—Saxons and the atheistic ACLU lawyers of secular Jews were all working overtime to destroy the very moral fiber of America and nobody here was prosecuting them even for murder in the first degree for years and now even NAMBLA was recognized in America, which had gone to show just how sick America really was.

America would have to go through all of this to the very end because no one could now criticize what this President had said for the last 4 years even though he did not have much to say except that there should also be a Palestinian State on Abraham's land! He was okay as long as the people here and the Christians here were okay and to hell with the Jewish people in Israel since he was an Anglophile whose heart bled more for the Mexicans then the ones in Israel who were being blown up and the anti Semites he was putting on his Cabinet. What Englishman could one ever trust and now Arnold Schwarzenegger wanted a President who was not born in America to be able to run and who could he possibly have in mind for that position? He too was a wolf in sheep's clothing just like Arlen Specter was and why did Rick Santorum and this incumbent support this Senator when Pat Toomey was pro-life and only lost by 1/3 of 1%? Again every party has an ideology and only an individual has a particular point of view!

What was good enough for England was good for America too and the Anglophiles proved it time and again! Many Jewish people in Israel were going hungry as well as having lost many loved ones because of the United States' State Department that kept on saying they wanted no Israelis' state to exist and only a Palestinian State and there was no 2 ways about it.

The English had felt that first Africa was theirs and now the Middle East because of rich and wealth and could care less about the people who lived in those lands! The English had set up so many problems in Africa that they wanted to do the same against

Israel! This was a one way street for the English and in fact all of the British Isles had some kind of strange mannerisms about them for centuries including the Irish who were killing each other as well as the Scottish who were super cheap and even the Welch!

Yes, Charles Spurgeon and Alexander Solzhenitsyn were both right in their own ways as to one's salvation which is just not one prayer but first GOD the Father must call and second as Solzhenitsyn said that in all people's lives there is the line of good vs. evil meaning that even with GOD we oscillate from one extreme to another and do not ever stop sinning. Many television ministries appear as angelic as can be, but what does one know of their private lives not to mention our very own at times? This is not some kind of contract that we have with GOD but a covenant that is holy and sacred and speaks to the heart. This is an eternal vow but with each day we must be conscious of what GOD would have us do as well as have us not to do!

Too many times I personally find many Christians not in tune with Christ because monetary things are the only things that come out of their mouths and did not GOD say that He would provide for us what He felt that we really needed and not what we thought we needed. Every hour let alone everyday we must be conscious and make that effort to always be aware of who we are in Christ Jesus. We were bought with a price and always remain vigilant to that. Our lives must show that Christ is at work in our lives and it is not ourselves that can ever take any credit, but we can take credit for the sin in our lives after we become Christians which is a growing process continually. Yes, we become Christians at some point in our very lives as Jesus called His Disciples to Himself or they never would have come without that calling.

In America today most Christians had so very much and this appeared to them to be what they felt that GOD had given as a blessing! The physical financial over the purely spiritual Without suffering though what can one know of the real love of GOD and not a way of life that the Western religions have pronounced to all who would follow them. Life is a constant struggle and we as Christians cannot just allow any kind of sin to take place in our very lives and we constantly miss the mark in regards to this since we also live in such an affluent society that has too much materialism! America to me was the Second Evil Empire and yet most Christians took faith and pride in what America still stood for! One was not to ever hate their nation but they were to always be on guard so that it would not slip into the abyss and one by one we could keep watch on the spiritual heart of America by showing the character of what it was to obey GOD and stay clear of evil things as well as evil people. Remember not all people are saved nor shall they ever be! This is GOD'S own calling for his children to come into the kingdom of GOD. We are to humble ourselves before GOD and He is everywhere and be silent most of the time in our lives and learn that through suffering no matter how long that we should not complain but pray to Him so that Jesus can intercede for us to the Father and to always bring glory to the Father on the throne. Continue onto do what He wants us to do by praying in the Holy Spirit wherever we are. He is there to always to help and guide us no matter how painful it is. He does love all His children.

Yes, America had so many sins from all of us and so America had become so very evil when America should have realized, or we should have realized, that the more that GOD gives us that much more is required because we are only stewards to all the things on this earth. It is not ours to keep or hoard, but His to use as He sees fit no matter how much the world, the enemy and even our own wrongful will may oppose GOD'S will. This hoarding of time, purpose, sharing and caring means we have sinned and fallen short of the glory of GOD which is what faith is all about, this very glory of GOD. It is GOD also who gives us our faith but we must step out in faith and trust a loving and caring GOD. There is no other one that we can trust.

GOD is always perfect GOD always has been and always shall be for there is no beginning and no ending for He is eternal and there is no time whatsoever with a Holy GOD. Some of us must endure much more but then GOD is in control so let us not fight with Him and listen quietly in our very own spirits to what He is saying to us always in love and if he disciplines us that means He loves us!

There was not one person taken to heaven in the New Testament except Jesus and He was GOD in the flesh and only in the Old Testament did GOD take 2 men and they were Enoch and Elijah! This Old Testament had to do mostly with the Israelites but was preparing a way for all to come into His kingdom meaning both Jews and Gentiles. Ruth came with Naomi, Jacob crossed his arms with Joseph and Ephraim, Abraham was willing to sacrifice his son Isaac, Jonah was in the stomach of the whale for 3 days and 3 nights, the Passover in Egypt, and other stories where GOD made provision again for both Jew and Gentile.

Once we know in our own hearts the love of Jesus meaning His grace and our freewill acceptance of Him into our hearts then we have obediently followed our Father's calling.

Well when do we judge one another? Do we judge another for instance in regards to one's character or lack thereof? How about when we vote for a candidate and vote for certain individuals or at least should we not judge them also? How about when we get married and are looking for the right wife do we not judge? Or when a young man is looking for the right young lady does he not judge?

If our own judging, meaning we decided with careful thought and prayer for all believers then we have made a decision, and we have to make a decision or else how can one judge? This parity of all men is . . . keep us all to a group mentality and as such then are we really judging and just following along with the group mentality or party ideology, right?

If one is to decide or to make a decision then they must by all means judge to see that if this individual is following an ideology and not a particular point of view and must so be prudent as not to confuse the two even though that person replaces faith with ideology in this instance! I must judge in order to know who it is that I am going to have represent me. There is no other way but to reason through and also use one's spiritual heart. We are not so much judging the individual but what he believes in and what he chooses to follow and if it does not build character or follow the auspices of GOD then one would have to say shun that individual in voting because character tells a lot about someone when you do see them in public eye, but not in their private life of one!

If one believes that human life is worthless then one must say that person has no faith whatsoever and does subscribe to some type of ideology that kills in the millions. If one has murdered another one and has done so unequivocally with DNA and no shadow of a doubt then one as a jurist must again judge not only the crime but the intent of the crime and to what degree that intent was carried out. How is one not to judge by GOD'S laws if we are to remain a civilized society? It is easy to say do not judge but what should we not judge must be explained more explicitly and in much more detail and here I shall not go into that at the present time.

One must know to judge righteously especially about another brother in the Lord one must do with caution and much loving concern but nonetheless must do it! We should understand that if one is not a believer, and that is not always easy to tell and in fact only GOD knows for certain, then we are to judge very carefully but again use GOD'S law and Commandments. Did someone who was starving steal the same as one who stole to get rich or just for the heck of it? We must separate and differentiate between many things and many circumstances that occur in life almost everyday. These decisions are to make right or wrong but hopefully right as in the sense that it brings one into repentance. If one is a Communist it is this ideology that has poisoned their mind and heart and hence they feel certain that they are for this lie and are aware of this lie and it is this lie or the ideology that one must hate and not the person. (That is easy for you to say, you are still alive!)

This poisoning ideology is what is to be hated to the fullest and not the human being because GOD shall judge their unrighteousness and we can judge the ideology that they believe in and hence oppose not so much them as their ideology that has destroyed their inner spiritual life. Yes, they have freewill but remember we all travel on the road of life in different ways. Let us keep our eyes, yes, on what the ideology or false religion is that they bow down too and hence come to understand that even though with free will remember GOD must choose first, so let us judge again the ideology or false religion they have come to believe is true to them. When we call that ideology evil, we then are saying that that man is also like us the sense that we all have sinned and fallen short of the glory of GOD!

If we judge our brother because he is truly sinning then we must judge with the love of GOD and not to condemn them but to warn them. Since every man has sin, but some are believers we must judge accordingly and remember that if one is not a Christian or has not professed it or maybe they do not talk about it that does not mean that they are not a Christian for only GOD knows that, so when we judge let us judge by what he believes whether it is ideology or the Christian faith in GOD. People carry out their judgment, then what they are doing is playing GOD. There are systems within society unless that society like the Soviet Union, or Cuba with no moral code of ethics to judge by but then one in their own minds and hearts can judge as to how they themselves would react to certain situations and one situation does not necessarily make a person nor break a person for with this only faith of Christianity is a way of life each and everyday and one must be sure at all times that they give a proper witness to a dying world! If one's conscience is seared it is almost then hopeless because repeatedly they have heard the Gospel did not respond to GOD. Each time more that they continue to hear the Word of GOD and refuse to accept GOD'S free gift then one must know they come that much closer to Hell itself! If we criticize say for instance a leader in our own nation or some other nation and see that evil is being done to others whether or not they are Christians then we must speak out for these victims. We are to help all the poor in Christ first and then the unbelieving poor. The rich rely on what the world has offered them or the enemy has enticed them with for the momentary. They do not have to depend on GOD since they believe their wealth and money is that all they really need.

The poor must rely on GOD and we as fellow believers must do what GOD wants us to do to help our brothers and sisters in Christ first here in America and not by government fiat but by each and everyone of us as believers and we should want to do this in whatever way that we can to help the Christian poor and then the unbelieving poor.

Our nation has preached so much that now ones here or at least most of the ones here have heard the Gospel and have seared consciences as opposed to ones who have never even heard the Gospel one time. So we must first get our own house in order before we march like many of the European religions did to foreign countries hence abandoning their very own nation. There is always much work to do here in America for all of us believers. For we are our brothers' keepers, meaning we should encourage and share and help and not just with our excesses but with the most we can do or give because there are too many today that do not even have the basics necessities and never should it be done through guilt but always done with Christ's love and we should always be free to share what GOD has given us plenty of and that is love and needs no matter how much GOD should ask us to do or to give to that particular person or family. We must go out and help our neighbors here first. Our home community must know that we love them so very much that we would virtually give them the only shirt on our very back and again not through our own excesses that we have collected through the years or have waited in want so that we can just sit back and retire and let our money do the walking. Christianity is not 1-2-3 it is much more complicated than that, but it is so easy to give of one's last dollar if GOD so asks because for believers it all yes all belongs to Him and for others well they are of and in this world and do not know Jesus in the heart and have not been transformed to continue to do until. Jesus comes back!

This is not in anyway works' salvation but it is doing what He wants us to do after we are saved for GOD does the saving and our works do not, not one iota! Our fruit that GOD supplies is His to give!

Today I saw GOD'S little innocent children as I was walking to an appointment. From a far distance when I first saw them I was hoping that it would not be what I thought it to be and yes it was just that! There was one young lady in the front holding a rope and one at the very end holding the end of the rope. In between were little tiny children that were so precious that it broke my heart to see them tied one after the other like Eskimo dogs are tied one after the other. I had a hard time looking at their angelic faces since it was breaking my heart. As they got closer and closer I really thought about GOD and as they were upon me I waved gently and softly, but do not know if they even saw me. I smiled at them with a soft smile and watched each of their faces go by and was struck by how very cruel our own society had become that now we did not have the time to raise and nurture our very own and had them tied with rope in a straight line. I understood why they needed rope and why the two ladies had to keep a constant eye on them, but I could not for the life of me come to understand what could be more important to a mother and a father that would choose for their children that this could somehow be better for them when they were so very innocent!

I said in my own mind to GOD that why is this the way it is and not why in the sense that these children were all from poor families but the fact that they had wanted their own loved ones to take care of them and make no mistake about it these children wanted so much to be with mom and dad all the time and not tied together like animals in a circus! We had forgotten how to love GODLY and most of all our very own precious little ones who we thought were only little adults that we could push to the side and that our precious jobs were somehow more important then to be with the little children and what would these children ever know of GOD'S loving family if it was by group ideology?

Their faces and hands were so very small and again I remember them and smiled and waved gently at them with my heart broken. Such beautiful little children bundled up in their winter coats and hands and the faces, some so sad at what was occurring as if this was some sort of animal show!

We in America had been desensitized to anything that was humane and Christian, and other people just went their own selfish way and could have cared less that they too once were this small for how now had they forgotten when they were growing up? Each little angel pulled at my own heart so much I said I must get this down on paper and say it as it really was and pray that their parents' hearts would feel!

This multiculturalism was now in vogue and even Christians were following it because it too meant equal rights for all of those in America! But how could that be if there were illegals, criminals of all sorts, people who did not even know what Christianity was, so forth and so on? Everybody was entitled to do whatever their little heart pleased them to do! Government would be all for that as long as it brought more revenue and any easy form or type of life with clean hands all the time and never having to labor at all We the people were looking for the government that is us to supply our every need and were constantly rewarding ourselves with monetary funds that were free to all or at least almost to all except that if one had a family, was married one time, was indeed a Christian, spoke English clear, provided also for our grandparents, and had a wonderful support system as well such as aunts, uncles, cousins, nieces, nephews!

Whatever happened to 'we are our brothers' keepers'? We now were anything but and ones on television kept telling us just how much they had done repeatedly over and over again and were not humble enough to keep silent like most Orthodox and Ultra-Orthodox Jewish people would do. The Gentiles needed stain glass windows, recognition of some sort that was public and anything else that could be made public. Were we not to be quiet about what we gave for the Lord?

It was like a trophy day for all those involved, but yet the 2% of the Jewish people which made up the whole part of their population in America gave more than 98% of the Gentiles! What was it that the Gentiles were doing wrong constantly even with all the television ministries directed towards only the Gentiles? Where had almost 6 million Jewish people in America gone that too were supposed to be witnessing since after all they were the Old Testa-ment people and Jesus was a Jewish man?

Somehow Europeanism's major religions, which now included Islam, were growing faster and faster. At least 3 of these major religions from there were spreading worldwide while the Gospel was not really being spoken but was only providing for food, medicines and of course no miracles for those who had nothing at all and nowhere to live. Yet many were dying that is Christians who would not renounce their faith even under death threats that were carried through to the end and the United Nations was more like World Bank, and the IMF plus the Halleburtons and the Bechtels all put together.

America was in a plastic world of its own and could care less what happened to our brothers and sisters that were being murdered here and abroad now in the millions and millions! Where were these Christian soldiers who were to give up, oh no not that whatever they had in life? Most Christians I knew had so much money that one wondered what one would do with it? They were buying new cars for each family member and building new cathedrals and churches here and there and were taking trip after trip here and there! What had happened to the poor and wretched church that use to do much more than the Western church could ever do?

The Western church was dying so very quickly because once again all our needs would be met by capitalism and this ever necessary want of more and more. When would it stop and if it ever did stop would there be enough to feed others not so fortunate who also were our brothers and sisters in Christ and though they did not have fancy clothes and necklaces around their necks but their hearts were right with the Lord and they were walking in the power of the Holy Spirit?

Now many women who would not remain silent as Paul had told them too were ministers in many different churches and the excuse was our men did not want to do it and so women had to do it no matter what (St. Paul had said in quite a harsh tone for all to know that women were to hold no position of authority in the church and many men who wanted this authority also wanted a nice home and nice car plus extra money to send all their children through college).

I could see why the Jewish people saw not too much that represented what even the Old Testament said about how one should share and care first for others while taking care of their own family. There would always be orphans and in America none should have been left in foster care whatsoever but of course the trial lawyers needed to make a living!

America had missed the mark and we had assumed what we should never have assumed, and that was GOD is a mighty and awesome GOD and they were not just words, and would we too not be judged for the things and the lack of time that we always seemed to have in the sports season which now was 24-7?

America I had felt and believed would soon really be judged because up to this time we were only being warned by GOD that we had to get our own house in order here before we got involved elsewhere.

It is the things that are unseen such as Jesus in the flesh and GOD'S whole Word that are the facts. With real faith always comes opposition or suffering. No positive thinking which means things shall be, but faith is for now. Blessings can too many times be based on just feelings. What GOD is to man not what man is to GOD. We need GOD he really does not need us. I cannot stand the old man in me and not so much my sins because my sins are forgiven already not that I should want to sin. Grace is now and there is no duration. Disappointment and discouragement is unbelief and not from failure of devotion. The enemy's first tool is discouragement. We are sons to GOD and not slaves if we obey. Come to the Word for one purpose and that is to meet the Lord. Always look for the hungry and needy heart for the abiding fruit to be. The overpower of sin's conviction causes the lost to reach out for salvation. The spiritual hunger must be carried by believers with GOD'S impressions. Christ died for us but also we died with Christ hence the old man Adam is dead. We died and resurrected with Christ. The power to do is not a permanent gift. Not I, but

Christ, is a whole truth and we are a half truth by Plato is "know thyself ". It is our own reaction to failure that causes failure. We are weak in sin? No. We are dying as such? No. We are dead? Yes. To deny oneself to conquer or control the old man, confessions, new resolutions, are all no and the blood washes away all sin, but only the Cross crucifies self, yes!

Justification only through the blood and nothing to add and emancipation the old man and nothing to add to the Death. To hate self is to hate the old man till we can stand it no longer. Take GOD'S side against ourselves. Maturity is to know Him to be life itself Do not beg for GOD has already done or cannot do because of our own unbelief. Plead less and claim more on Jesus's blood. Our deliverance from sin makes us weaker and weaker and not stronger and stronger and as John the Baptist said, "I shall decrease and He shall increase." Our service is for our own spiritual growth. The servant is more important than the work. We are not saved to work or to serve only. We are first to worship the Father, and Him . . . . This is a happiness to work and not work to be happy. It takes time to know ourselves, but it takes eternity to know Christ If we do not judge our flesh then GOD will.

The ladder of grace: GOD sent His Son-1; the fullness of what He done we are justified-2; to make His acquaintance-3; we see Him in heaven and our association with Him-4; we learn the mystery of being in His Body-5; we are seated in heavenly places with Him-6; we are lost in wonder and in praise in Him. Here from the above was, in part, some of the learning yet, but some was from what I already knew. To understand and to appropriate the facts of the Cross is the most difficult for a growing believer, The grain or better yet the kernel to oneself must surely die in order for the seed to be planted. Die to oneself.

John Wesley at first made 30 pounds in England and tithed 2 pounds and spent 28 pounds and some time later he made 150 pounds and tithed 122 pounds and still spent only 28 pounds. In the free enterprise system there is too much attention only on the free and not enough on the enterprise!

The 7 laws of teaching: As Paul said, come from where the other person is, not where you are at. The teacher's true expectations of the class. Teach so that the students can use it for practical use and not just head knowledge. Give the whole picture first such as in Genesis and be logical and organized. This is the 4th law of teaching. Always meet the needs of others and not your own needs. Equip the students also to teach (a coach does not play; the players do). The 7th law is to teach about the Great Teacher or Rabboni and know Him personally!

With adults the destruction time is from 10-15 years and for adolescents it is 10-15 months. To just say no is only for none users. One must heal the whole person. The physical body, the spirit which is the intuition, His presence, one's conscience-and the soul is one's will, one's mind and one's emotions. Addiction in alcohol is a chemical imbalance which with the first drink one is addicted. So first one has to deal with the biological component and then the moral or emotion problem. One experiments, then it becomes recreational with mood swings, then preoccupational (how and where do I get my next high?), then the dependency where it becomes normal to be addicted, and then burnout where the mind cannot actually think! Do not, though, become an enabler or a knight in shining armor to come to save the day. This is a personal decision with a support system that is constructive and not destructive!

There are 9 eras from the Bible:

Creation—Adam
Patriarch—Abraham
Exodus—Moses and slavery in Egypt
Conquest—the Promised Land, Joshua;
Judges—Samson
The Kingdom—King David, and 400 years
 of being ruled by a monarch
Exile-Daniel, 70 years in Babylon
Return—Ezra, to rebuild Jerusalem
Silence—400 years between the Old Testament and its
 closing and the opening of the New Testament.

Our own United States History, which is not too well known, and its periods was something I had thought about, which included some of our famous men.

POETS AND WRITERS:

Jonathan Edwards	Thomas Paine	
Henry W. Longfellow	Walt Whitman	

COLONIAL PERIOD:

Revolutionary War	Federal Period	Civil War

PHILOSOPHERS:

Ben Franklin	Thomas Jefferson	
Henry David Thoreau	Abraham Lincoln	

POETS AND WRITERS:

Emily Dickinson	F. Scott Fitzgerald	Robert Frost

HISTORICAL PERIOD:

Gilded Age	Industrial Expansion	Modern Era

PHILOSOPHERS:

Mark Twain	William Jennings Bryan	
Martin Luther King, Jr.		

Franklin	Jefferson	Jackson	Lincoln	Cleve-land	Roosevelt	FDR
Colonial period	Revolu-tionary war	Federal period	Civil war	Gilded age	Industrial expansion	Modern era
Boston	Philadel-phia	Wash. D.C.	Gettys-buiry	The West	The North	Wash. D. C.

Creation = creation - fall - flood - tower of Babel

Patriarch = Abraham - Isaac - Jacob - 12 sons - Joseph - slavery in Egypt for 400 years.

Exodus = deliverance (Moses) - the Law (Moses at Mt. Sinai) - Kadesh Bamea and the 12 spies - 40yrs.

The Conquest Era = Jordan-Jericho - Conquest over Canaan - Dominion, 12 tribes take dominion.

The Judges Era = Judges (Deb, Gideon, Samson, Samuel) - Rebellion - Cycles(7 cycles each with 5 components. Ruth who was a Gentile.

The Kingdom Era = King Saul (kingdom is united) - division of the kingdom (Solomon civil war) - Northem Kingdom (10 tribes that are unrighteous) - Southern Kingdom (Judah and Benjamin)

The Exile Era = Prophecy, 722 BC North, 586 BC South Babylon - Prophets, Ezekiel and Daniel - Exiles Babylon, Daniel - Power Change, Persia conquers Babylon.

The Return Era = Disrepair in Jerusalem for 70 year exile - Temple, Cyrus King of Persia rebuilds the Temple - People, Ezra teaches the Law - Walls, the Book of Esther and the city wall falls.

The Silence Era = the changing guard, the Old Testament closes and Alexander the Great at 333 BC - political sects, Maccabeans and the Zealots - Religious sects, Pharisees and the Sadducees - Messianic
Hope = His coming 400 years later! This is the Old Testament.

The New Testament has 3 eras:

Gospels = life of Jesus—Church= formation of the church—Missions = missions into Roman Empire.

Jesus in Palestine—Peter in Jerusalem—Paul in the—Roman Empire.

The 4 Gospels:

Matthew—the Jewish Gospel
Mark—the oldest Gospel
Luke—the most accurate
John—the love Gospel.

The differences between Christianity and all other religions:

Different answers to the nature of man's basic problem and the answer to that problem. Most believed falsely in good works! The Hindu, the Buddha, the New Age, and of course Islam!

The conception of GOD and who GOD is:

Buddha never claimed deity. Jesus did.

Hindus are pantheists—everything is GOD.

Islam or Allah not a personal GOD. Mohammed a prophet who never claimed deity and prophet here is used in a secular manner.

Judaism no Messiah and that the Messiah who came was not GOD in the flesh. Truth is intolerant of error for if that would not be then lies would be believed!

Christianity allows all others to worship freely as long as it is not violent to others, and in some cases even then Christians endure with perseverance, but that is not a prerequisite to allow murder to go on if one can protect the innocent from murder and in turn possibly help save the one who is about to murder as in the *Switchblade And The Cross* by David Wilkerson!

These were some of the things that made America good and great and that was GOD alone for without GOD there would be no guidance from the Holy Spirit. This is why all Communists whether in the USSR, Red China, Cuba, North Korea, etc. do not allow first of all the Bible to be read since it opposes evil in a spiritual way and can defeat it without any violence or revolution!

The NBA or the National Black Association is now showing how basketball players or prima donnas are doing the very same thing that happens in Latin America at most all their soccer games and that is rioting but this time not in the stands but from the players into the stands and Mr. Stern another atheistic

Jew has given a one year suspension for this altercation the first ever that I can ever remember that has ever gotten this bad. First it started with the Charles Barkley incident in Philadelphia when this chubby boy spit on a fan to show his appreciation! These brownshirts now have gone so far that whatever they do someone from Mars shall protect their rights not to attack these overgrown and underminded prima donnas with the multi million dollar contracts which otherwise they might be working in some sanitation department for their city! It has been time to call a spade and a spade and totally throw out for good any athlete that takes drugs one time or does any infamous act such as this and be barred for life from ever participating in any professional sport in America!

Since there is no affirmative action in the NBA then one could instill one to make the game much more exciting on the floor and not in the stands! There are so many very fine athletes in colleges who are not only black but white and let us start to use those who also have no criminal records and score high in academics for after all is that not why one goes to college and that is to get a higher education and not to become a criminal without any character?

We can tell the millionaires that they will have to take their games somewhere else like Latin America if they want to contract the bottom of the academic barrel Since major corporations now own these teams that is why they can afford to pay them millions and millions of dollars for exactly doing nothing constructive in a free and democratic society. And as to the appointments that this incumbent is picking one can totally see that he is a great brown noser with the multiculturalists and does not look for quality but for the color of their skin only; hence now once again we have racial discrimination within the highest levels of government!

This incumbent is sort of like the pied piper that plays his melodious tune to the multiculturalists and now that tune has become old and worn out and it is about time he now appoints people for positions that are really qualified to hold those positions and not to look good! It appears, as I said before, there are no Scalias or Keyes who are much more qualified to date, but where are they?

The following were the Kings of Judah:

King Saul—King David—King Solomon—King Rehoboam—King Abijah—King Asa—King Jehoshaphat – King Jehoram—King Ahaziah Queen Athaliah—King Joash—King Amaziah—King Uzziah—King Jotham—King Ahaz—King Hezekiah—King Manasseh—King Amon—King Josiah—King Jehoahaz—King Jehoiakim—King Jehoiachin—King Zedekiah—Start of the Gentiles 605 B.C.

The following were the Kings of Israel:

King Jeroboam—King Nadab—King Baasha—King Elah—King Omri—King Ahab—King Ahaziah—King Joram—King Jehu—King Jehoahaz—King Jeoash—King Jeroboam II—King Zechariah—King Shallum – King Menahem—King Pekahiah—King Pekah—King Hoshea and with the last King of Israel, Israel is eliminated by GOD, but not the tribe of Judah!

These are what the Israelites had asked for and that was a king like the other nations!

<u>The 7 Dispensations:</u>

Innocence (Eden)
Conscience (world)
Human government (Noah)
The Law (Moses)
Grace (Jesus)
Tribulation (7 years)
The Kingdom (The Millennium).

The 7 churches mentioned in the Book of Revelation:

Ephesus (the beginning with the Disciples-losing their first love)

Smyrna (illegal religion by the Romans and the blood of the martyrs and also Constantine's state religion)

Pergamos (the church settled into the world and a common cause with the world)

Thyatira (rich and accepted by the world with the devil and immorality and moral subversion and the church dissipates; the time of King Ahab of Israel who married Jezebel and this is the most evil King of the line of Israel)

Sardis (the Augustian monk Martin Luther and the German Reformation which ran on money)

Philadelphia (exists at the same time as the last church and that is the church of Laodicea; Brotherly love and is taken up by the Lord that is the church or Body of Christ)

Laodicea (the voice of the people, democracy, which is consumer driven and is not authoritarian and exists at the same time as the church of Philadelphia and is the liberal church at the end times that is Laodicea is).

A brief synopsis of the 7 churches of the 7 ages or also the 7 letters to the 7 churches sent out by Christ!

Now even in our own town we find Moslem extremists who have contributed to 9/11 and yet the federal government has done absolutely nothing about it. It would again appear that they are wait ing for something to happen before they react and not act which is asinine. Our own government can—not make a simple decision since it suffers from paralysis and must seek the approval of the internationalists and in fact I myself have reported to the local authorities of license plates that had El Salvador on them plus other things and yet nothing has occurred, why?

Now it has affected, even a small town such as ours and no one is concerned in the slightest again because memories are very short indeed and no order from the Commander In Chief has been given to remove these terrorists from the United States and only more and more of these Moslems and the Marxists/Leninists are coming from south of the border plus the fact the one of the bridges in the northern border only checks trucks on our own side of the border instead of Canada and more trucks travel over this bridge than any other in the United States!

What is our government now waiting for? More profits and directions from the internationalists in the world located in Europe and having meetings in Mexico and elsewhere in Latin America? We appear to be leaderless at this present time and it again appears like a Cuban missile crisis but maybe even worse since this shall affect the entire Western Hemisphere and also the entire world in one way or another! If we are not going to enforce the immigration laws of this land than we might as well consider ourselves now part of the European Union which in essence shall now take on Latin America because of its natural resources.

We have no power to act decisively and now our soldiers who should have been by now brought back makes one to conclude that they now know as to the why and want to come home and is the opposite of Vietnam because we were fighting ALL of Communism in the world and here we are told we are fighting just a few Moslems which is a total lie! The conflict in Vietnam should have been sup ported and won and the war in Iraq should never have been at all. The two are like apples and oranges. This President must now be very careful as to what he intends to do since other factors have entered into the picture and he needs to get a real Secretary of State to hold that post or he shall for sure find himself and our very nation in dire consequences and shall be opposing Israel for some insane reason!

Many of the Biblical stories related so much to today in America that one could now see that the time was almost right for the churches of Philadelphia and Laodicea for this part of the church age of grace that was quickly coming on and that this word democracy and consumer driven was proving to be just what the church in the West had become in so many ways but there was no condemnation for the church of Philadelphia since it was one near the Advent of Messiah and that now even the 1040 Window was being now attended to by other Christians who also knew from the Holy Spirit that the time of the Hebrews was nearing more and more and their small remnant of Messianic Jews even into the Tribulation Period.

On his Thanksgiving Day I had read the first 10 Chapters of Romans as well as I Kings which described King David as turning over the kingdom to King Solomon his son and the fact that in the Book of Romans there was much to be explained in the present day affairs of man in our very own nation. King Solomon almost had his kingdom stolen but King David intervened so that the one King David would choose would be the one who would sit on the throne and build the Temple and a palace for himself and his Egyptian wife of Pharaoh. This is where some of King Solomon's problems would come from in the fact that he had married out of his faith that is of Messiah.

Early in his reign he was a good king and later he became one could say almost evil since foreign women were coming into play and in America too foreign women were coming into play also who knew absolutely nothing about the Judeo-Christian faith which could not ever be compromised no matter what! We were beginning to take on other wives also in this nation at a rapid pace with no regard for what the Bible had said about heathen nations.

America had become a land for all but the Christian person who wanted to worship as a Christian and be free to do that at all public places. Even in China they had Bibles in public places or public buildings!

We had forgotten to take care of ourselves here at home in regards to GOD and our Thanksgiving in the form of what the Pilgrims meant in the Feast of Tabernacles which was what all believers Jews and Gentiles had to celebrate even now and most Gentiles did not even know that much about Scripture and even the churches ignored it completely.

We find today in America people taking credit for whatever there appears to take credit for but what ever it is to take credit for one would indeed have to wonder as to the why? What can any of us take credit for when this nation even though having it better as far as in the flesh and in some places yet in the spirit we still have much to do that we have not done for others here and our brothers and sisters in the world such as speaking out against Red China instead of patting ourselves on the back as if we have accomplished anything with all the resources at our disposal! What credit can we take when only about 86,000 missionaries come out of the United States and we have about 300,000,000 people in this nation plus the fact we have more materialism to share to others and yet we still refuse to do that for the most part and instead we keep on saying, "Well you should see how bad the rest of the world is?" Well since that is true would it not make even more sense-to then help those poor Christians and poor unbelievers with the truth staring us in the face?

If America is the best in the world what does that say not about the rest of the world but about us in particular? Does it say that we have too much materialism and care not about others suffering just so we do not suffer? Yes, many unbelievers feel that way because this is their only time to live for eternity. There shall be no tomorrow after time for them has gone and so they say live it up and stop complaining and let the others go die! No, this is not their exact wording but it means the same thing to them. Hurray for me and the Hell with you! If we have so much, and we do, then why do we continue to hoard it here on earth for we cannot get by death no matter what and where is it going to go when one dies and is either lost in eternity and saved in eternity?

This cliché of love America or leave it does not make it because that means we should surrender to the unbelievers all that is here in America including our national soul! Let them leave America and I am sure they would return too soon because they then would see reality not just a cliché and would not wish such a horrible fate on another once they have experienced it themselves and even then they probably would soon forget! Americans love America because of sentimentality and the guilt of the affluence that they could not live without and let one catastrophe' occur and their world caves in. Even if something minor should occur or even inconvenience them, to them that is a tragedy to say the least! Yet they propose that Israel should get along with their so called neighbors whose ideology does not even want to admit or allow for that at all. They want their utopia and are callous to the real fact that this life is not their own and never was meant to be. We are spiritual beings with personalities and not robots to think only about ourselves and even our very own families because sentimentality is not agapé love or Biblical love. Christianity goes well beyond that and reaches into the realm of ones who are strangers to us but not to GOD. We must reach out for their starving spiritual hearts that want to know about GOD and this is the GOD of the Bible and not the Koran whichever god that happens to be? We want others to leave yet we ourselves do not do anything for anybody else to help them in any charitable way or any way big would help either save a soul or a life!

This is now the American mindset of don't complain while you live here and that is like saying just follow the leader mentality or the pied piper. They do not ever want to answer that it is their own materialism that they love so very much and that this is all that really matters and they could care less about their own nation but only about themselves! Why should they even care if one does not vote since they do not care if children in America are being murdered? There is no consistency there at all to say the least.

Whenever it comes to the original thought which is so very hard to find and almost virtually impossible to find at least in America, we constantly hear the same cliché as I said before and that is then go where you like it! No, that is not the answer to the world's problem of there is no GOD, or yet GOD has been so good to me and I deserve it not! This is such hypocrisy that they only can lash out because of their small minds as well as their small hearts! It is this avarice of free enterprise and where the emphasis is on free and nothing is on enterprise. Just so we live and the hell with the rest and be for the underdog or at least say that one is and then their guilt, real guilt, they believe can be erased. This is how they believe their very own lies. Who wants to confront them with this since most do not know what to say because self preservation is the ultimate in their own lives.

The rich and well educated almost always try to get the crowd from the down and out and the poor because then they can get a listening audience for their pathetic excuses that amount to absolutely zero! Can they help it that they were born so rich and well educated and so full of leadership? Is it their fault that they have to carry the football time and time again until they fumble?

Darwinism is not a science and not an academic study of anything that has to do with sanity! What it is, though, is ideology the kind that Stalin got his very insane and sick ideas from since it said man is an animal, but some have progressed a little more than others. It is also a lie from this ideology that has been as old as man himself, but has added a new wrinkle to the lie all animals are created equal! Socialism works with this very well since socialism itself is atheism and also based solely on the lie that produces violence and more violence and guess what. Even the well educated sell it to others to be swallowed with hook, line and sinker! Who has evolved more than the Communists since now they have been crawling for at least almost 2 centuries on all fours and now appear to be standing almost upright?

Of course the NEA in America has a lot to do with this ideology very much and into the educational system is where they need to be to indoctrinate our very children with the lie. Many are saying that parents need to take the responsibility for their own children which is true, but so does the NEA which has also followed this ideological lie that says to our children "See how some people have come to stand on two legs", which really also is a lie because that is exactly what they have not done and that is to stand on their own without government and the intelligentsia that says we know it all and how it started when they themselves were not here when it started!

As far as another aspect with this and that is that now not only human body parts but animal parts are being harvested for the rich and well educated so that they can live longer because once they depart they somehow know that this shall be it whether it is in their own closed state or a permanent state that says is here to stay for eternity! How far can this insanity take one and this is truly what it is and because it has absolutely nothing to do with GOD? Their belief system stops when they die and so does their eternal soul but with the believer it does not and since it does not, one would hope to believe that with this thought in mind that one would have to say that the atheist is 99% correct according to him but that 1% is what dooms him and hence since he is not a gambling man he shall go with the 99% even though out of 100% this 1% is actually all that is needed since the 99% is a lie.

If the whole is that 1% and that really represents 100% and the 99% is a figment of one's imagination . . . the equation would look something like this: the whole which is equal to 100% is 1 and since 1 is all there is, then that means there is no remainder left for them to divide 1 into any smaller unit. Since the common denominator and the common numerator are both 1, we can then only say that theory cannot be applied here for it has never been proven that there is no GOD. In fact, the existence of GOD can be proven while the non-existence of GOD can never be or we for example would not be able to reason that a whole number can not be added to an hypothetical number that does not exist and never has existed and has never been proven to exist since numbers are accurate and truthful in the sense that 1+1=2 and if that is true, and it is, then how can any whole true number which in this sense cannot be made smaller because the whole truth cannot either be reduced into any type of proper fraction since that would mean again that theory is allowed to play a part which goes against mathematics again in this sense because there are no half truths or half whole numbers but only true real whole numbers and 1 is the 100% without a doubt that one whole number which cannot be any more or any less since this truth is based not on relativity but GOD!

If one is to walk upright then one would suppose they would have to try and first stand and try it in order to find out that it is more than possible that one can walk on two legs and not four legs and hence the fact and not the assumption says that to suppose otherwise would mean that all animals cannot reason or they can reason and if the animals cannot reason, why is that they cannot?

And why is it that since they cannot would some men like for man to walk even now on all fours, which is even below slavery, but is the socialistic type of slavery that . . . Is this the illusion or lie that all animals are not created equal because not all animals walk on all fours and not all humans walk on both two's!

If the above is illogical, well that is because when one talks to the study of the lie one must always keep in mind that all things are possible and that the truth is fiction to them and the lie is truth to them so hence the world can mean to them that even now at this very time their own existence determines consciousness and not that consciousness determines existence and since animals know about how they came to be and know that they are one with man then the conclusion can only mean that either once dreamt that he was an animal on both two's or that he evolved himself without the gray area of the brain itself and from the looks of it his hypothesis was surely reflective to all those who could murder and torture not because they could not reason but because they could not find any conscience in which to remember how to reason. Now this is how all socialists deal with the problem of man's beginning on this here earth. An amoeba mass one could say but then again what came first the chicken or the egg With Stalin and Hitter they both had to think that they too were hatched from the same egg since their own special kind of "uniqueness" had come from one egg in the sense that they were "identical twin liars" of the same persuasion. No, better yet of the very same kind of evil lie!

Hollywood shall continue until who knows when to believe that the earth is flat and the moon is the sun as long as it is around! They claim that their ideology says that if man can think it he can certainly do it. This is not a compliment to them but in fact an accusation that accuses them by themselves since they do not even know the reality of life, and that part of that reality is that one must work for a living in order to live!

All play and no work makes Jack a dull boy. They have a plastic world that shields them from their own sanity since they too believe that ideology is above everything and since they believe this, one must suppose that their foundation for this belief is based once again on the lie because for them to believe otherwise would mean they would leave Hollywood and come back to the real world where people live and die and in the in between they must also find something in life that contributes to the very good in society and since a vacuum cannot possibly do that then they have no oxygen to breathe with and are in a real vacuum in outer space!

Their journey has taken them everywhere except to the truth itself and that is that man cannot neither be created nor destroyed by anyone at anytime for any reason since man is an eternal being! The clock has already stopped for them because they believe that death is later but really for them it is now and they continue to believe again the ideological lie that says insanity is the way one can only think if they are to remain a part of this world, but never mind what occurs after that! One should not suppose that they should even want to entertain such a thought as the evolution of Hollywood itself and that is that it did evolve through a metamorphosis since all the creatures there appear to want to exalt the theatre as a form of art and beauty and nothing could ever be farther from the truth! They have it backwards in the sense that they want all to have faith in their own ideology that is not really original but heaven forbid if one should have faith in His faith and the faith that He gives to His elect is original.

KINGS OF ISRAEL
From 931 B.C. to 722 B.C.

King Jeroboam	931-910 who ruled 22 years
King Nadab	910-909 who ruled 2 years
King Baasha	909-886 who ruled 24 years
King Elah	886-885 who ruled 2 years
King Zimri	885—who ruled 7 days
King Omri	885-874 who ruled 12 years

King Ahab	874-853 who ruled 22 years and married Jezebel
King Ahaziah	853-852 who ruled 2 years
King Joram (Jehoram)	852-841 who ruled 11 years
King Jehu	841-814 who ruled 28 years
King Jehoahaz	814-798 who ruled 17 years
King Jeoash (Jehoash)	798-782 who ruled 16 years
King Jeroboam II	793-753 who ruled 41 years
King Zechariah	753-752 who ruled 6 months
King Shallum	752 who ruled 1 month
King Menachem	752-742 who ruled 10 years
King Pekahiah	742-740 who ruled 2 years
King Pekah	752-732 who ruled 20 years
King Hoshea	732-722 who ruled 9 years and Samaria was destroyed in 722

KINGS OF JUDAH

King Saul	40 years he ruled
King David	40 years 33 year's in Jerusalem, and 7 years in Hebron
King Solomon	40 years
King Rehoboam	931-913 B.C. who ruled 17 years
King Abijah	913-911 B.C. who ruled 3 years
King Asa	911-870 B.C. who ruled 41 years
King Jehoshaphat	873-848 B.C. who ruled 25 years
King Jehoram	853-841 B.C. who ruled 8 years
King Ahaziah	841 B.C. who ruled 1 year
Queen Athaliah	841-835 B.C. who ruled 6 years (wicked queen, only interruption to King David's line)
King Joash	835-796 B.C. who ruled 40 years
King Amaziah	796-767 B.C. who ruled 29 years
King Uzziah (Azariah)	792-740 B.C. who ruled 52 years
King Jotham	750-732 B.C. who ruled 16 years
King Ahaz	735-716 B.C. who ruled 16 years?
King Hezekiah	716-687 B.C. who ruled 29 years
King Manasseh	697-643 B.C. who ruled 55 years

King Amon	643-641 B.C. who ruled 2 years
King Josiah	641-609 B.C. who ruled 31 years
King Jehoahaz	609 B.C. who ruled 3 months
King Jehoiakim	609-598 B.C. who ruled 11 years
King Jehoiachin	598-597 B.C. who ruled 3 months
King Zedekiah	597-586 B.C. who ruled 11 years

THE FALL OF JERUSALEM IN 586 B.C.

One would suppose that someone might just ask out of curiosity how the average American person spends their money on a weekly or on a monthly basis? The reason I ask this question is because one can see that most Americans have a severe problem of having so much money and not knowing what to do with it! For instance one can see the elderly spend their retirement money on gambling as well as 401K's that are nothing but more foolish investments so that the stock market itself is over inflated. Others use their money to buy automobiles that are monstrosities that all now look alike and the pick up truck mentality has seen so many of these shorties drive the most expensive types of play trucks for their very lack of self confidence in the form of stature. Also many children are given $50-$100 to go to the mall and this in essence is to make a 10 or 12 year old a millionaire with that amount of money in one day to spend. The fashions are depressing as well as so revealing and even vulgar and also the fact the most young girls and older women are wearing until they can stand up on their own their wonderful pair of blue jeans.

One can also see how much alcohol that is being consumed and how many fast food places are frequented in just one day! How much is spent on daycare Soviet style? How many fathers' children do not support them or even have a job or if they have a job no one at least the courts are concerned about this epidemic of negligence? How many have youth going to college and universities just to learn that that itself shall not really make one aware of what really is going on? How much money is spent for nothing to get a so called degree just to make these socialists institutions that much more corrupt? How much money is spent on cigarettes and drugs?

How much money is spent on unnecessary food items that make ones obese and can cause malnutrition? How many children do not really eat properly at all and not from lack of income but no kind of discipline set at home or in the schools? How many waste money at casinos, bars, pornography, Hollywood and other garbage as such? How many women spend money on cosmetics? How about clothing which are not really feminine or even needed but just because of boredom or ego or braggadocio? How many men buy motorcycles or any other kind of noisy contraption just for ego also?

If one continues under this correct premise, one can really see that most Americans waste their money on idiotic things and also get locked into so much interest that even if they make $100,000 or $200,000 a year they can still have bad credit or cannot obtain any credit! Credit that is good and useful and little used credit is good to have. Established credit is just that to establish credit and not run one's life to ruin and wreck by buying anything and nothing! If one has the cash then this is most of the time best unless if for say a car is purchased because once the total is paid in cash then the dealer hesitates to take care of the customer. Also some little credit also is good since it establishes one in good as a consumer with the business world but of course now anyone or almost anyone now can purchase anything with the worse kind of credit and that goes against all common sense and would lead one to believe that money is readily available since no good credit report is done and hence others follow on along who do have good credit and start to buy things that they do not really need. It is always best to do without and not even use a budget which already obligates one and doing without means most of the time that the item is not really needed but is almost a subconscious affect on the consumer to want to spend more and more and hence the more one makes the more one goes into debt and now with bankruptcy and other ways to subterfuge one's responsibility they have no credit no problem the system that allows almost everyone to buy whatever as long as the money is up front and also do not care if it is even drug money even if they the seller knew about it and most of the time they do!

Today with so much change floating around by private consumers and by the government it makes one suspicious as to why government itself would give away money that does not even belong to them at all and yet have no reservations about it and especially if it is for asinine or immoral things? Today material items are worth more than the human being and in some cases the human body. It is as if one was buying a hunk of meat off of a butcher!

It is wise to always pay off a mortgage instead of gambling one's money on the roulette' table of the Down Jones Gambling House which has all the percentages on its side. Now people can obtain ready cash just for the asking so again government has become the bank that never runs out of money and always can collect the funds to replenish those lost funds by the easy method and that is by the payroll and the real estate taxes which are now almost like levies since much of America is owned by the government or by foreign investors who are buying out all of the good farming land in America plus the service industries since now the manufacturing plants have all but been eliminated for good. One can retrain but then with that one will have to most surely retrain in the field of computers and get used to thinking like the Germanic robots.

The government cannot prosecute because for them to do so would mean that the politicians themselves would have to be incarcerated if our laws were moral and upright! When the government itself is not accountable to anyone but themselves and the IRS is not about to lose power from the United States Congress who gave them their power they do not pursue banks, big corporations, etc. because economical fascism would come into play since the taxpayer is really unaware of what he pays to promote big international business with anybody at anytime as long as they can repay at the going rate with interest!

Just consider what the interest on one billion dollars is like? Now WalMart and others have reduced their prices so low because of illegals and slave labor from Red China that these new immigrants go there because now they can pay them slave wages and even more so the average American citizen who is here legally and has not been invited here by the Ivy Leaguers. The circulation of money in legal tender is small compared to the credit with interest and that is what keeps the ball rolling on and on! Have the middle class at your mercy and make them to be willing to almost sell their very soul to the devil so that they can live at the level that they are so accustomed to living at!

Oh, it gets much uglier as one could continue to delve into this corruption of why only really hard assets are vitally important since legal tender has no value whatsoever and hence when one invests with paper work it means that someone big is backing it up and not the government since the government is so broke that only socialism can be used to disguise it like as if it was a free enterprise system and of course one can always claim that it is still a democracy and so was Russia, China, Italy and Germany!

The only course that now is being pursued is the socialistic ideological course that says all the money belongs to the state meaning that wages can be eliminated anytime and that one's wealth might just be the very shirt on one's back. That is why there is still estate taxes and that is to confiscate properties from people and lease them to others who are not too bright and used to America's value system!

One can usually get a higher amount of money than a lower amount and that is so that this ideology of socialism shall make the middle class extinct and useless and that only the poor and the rich shall be left to run this nation and for the rich and well educated it would mean much more pesos and denarii in their pockets as well as the franc as well of course as the pound!

People now buy homes and only pay the interest on it and people in their 50's take out 30-year loans!

It was so good to be around my two grandchildren that I did not want to be around adults anymore. They were so honest and caring and so very truthful that it was such a joy to be around them even though they never seemed to run out of energy. They were the center of my wife's and my own life next to Jesus, and it was Jesus who had given them to take care of for Him so they would always know who Jesus was and not just a name or when one went to church or just on a Sunday! More and more one could see the sins of America coming out publicly in regards especially to homosexual pedophiles who were growing in our area like a hidden cancer on the body of America and yet Hollywood and the media and the Democratic Socialist Party that had thought that Nazism was still in vogue.

It always made me sick to even see these homosexuals on the prowl looking for innocent young people or even children to take advantage of, and our own government (made up of mostly socialists) were involved in it too! Who said that homosexual Nazi Germany was a fascist state when there were so many homosexuals in that perverted nation? That is why so many Nazis had grown so fast and there were also so many in that culture even before Hitler came to power, but when he came to power they were all ready to take over with their degeneracy immediately!

Too many were so sorry for these homosexuals but had no feeling and did not want to hear what these perverts were doing to our own children. They had asked what if I were a homosexual, and all I could do was give them a dirty look and say to myself, "How ignorant and asinine most people seemed to be who felt that these perverts were born into this when science had proven beyond a shadow of a doubt that this was an abomination plain and simple! These were these same bleeding heart liberals who could care less what happened to the unborn in the millions and what had happened to many who had contracted AIDS because of these homosexuals who were bent, as the Nazis were, on eliminating the Jews from America and from Israel as fast as they could. That is another reason the Arabs were also part of this degeneracy that both the Old and the New Testaments condemn so strongly and with no ands, ifs or buts!

America was too educated and liberated to hear what the Bible had to say and we could see it by how civilized our own nation had become! We were on our way up to the top but to the top of a cliff with no return to any kind of normalcy whatsoever. The Roman Catholic Church was full of them and the Episcopalian church also had its full of them all over and it broke their hearts to see them not being able to see them get married and be able to adopt children and also be able to serve as Nazi clergy! What a shame it was not for their sexual perversion but for the way that they could not have their own special rights to cause mayhem and insanity just like in Nazi Germany! We were the brutes for not allowing them to molest and rape and torture and murder innocent children since many in our own courts and in government were of the same political persuasion that is of Nazism!

This cancer grew and grew and metastasized itself to unknown levels and with the Anglo-Saxons it made no difference as well as with the half breeds in America such as Michael Jackson and Dennis Rodman who both were homosexual pedophiles that Hollywood and the NBA both loved to uphold as their iconoclasts! Allen Iverson had said something about homosexuals and so they attacked him again and again in the media just the same way they attacked Anita Bryant unmercifully years ago when she had enough foresight to know what sexual deviancy was when she saw it. So do I and so did most of the Italians who were not real true Catholics!

Roman Catholicism had to be opposed and not even Dostoyevsky would have taken it that far and that is probably why along with Islam and England and Germany helped more then any other thing to destroy Russia with that special train ride that went through Switzerland and to Berlin! The Nazi Germans and the English Anglophiles had done now more to destroy millions of lives worldwide that there was no doubt that they were once again at it to destroy America and Israel, the people in these two nations, and blame it on anybody but them!

Why had Solzhenitsyn even sent his son Ignat to Harvard even though he was a world reknown mystrol? The very ones that perpetrated the evil in Russia had come out of these same type of schools that preached socialism and death to millions and millions and yet he allowed his son to have anything to do with these "seminaries of socialism"! One can always find someone's weakest since we are all human beings and have our own misinformation about the other side of the world.

Too many people were always giving in in some form, such as Alan Keyes who had gone to Harvard and was a Catholic but yet was a family man but yet defended Roman Catholicism not in what they did but in the sense that their doors should have been allowed to be opened when day after day new cases of pedophilia and homosexuals at that were coming out! Every major religion had some kind of either Anti-Semitism or was for the most immoral type of sexual pleasure and yet their leaders would not close their doors either for good or until they could admit their sin and their guilt and come clean and also be prosecuted to the fullest extent of the law with no ands, if or buts! A homosexual was not a civil rights issue which also was nothing more than superior rights and it also had nothing to do with anything human or humane and the Holocaust had already proven that without a doubt and also and most of all it was an abomination to a just and righteous GOD!

No more subterfuging the truth especially with all Christians and getting to the point about how sick and deviant period homosexuality was, is and always shall be with no excuses any more but more and more prosecution on Sodomy laws and new laws that made it illegal even to be one! No more political correctness that Lenin thought up and no more socialism of any kind no matter who promoted it Hollywood or the Ivy Leaguers! It had to be stopped now and that did not mean go back in time but to prosecute no matter whom it was for this horrible mental disorder that spread by coercion only! Too many Christian males acted if they too might be willing to join in with this crowd since their wives were the only ones speaking out and then again if one had to guess which denominations most Christians in America came from one would have to guess from Protestantism and guess where that originated from?

The authority figure in the home now could be anybody including the teen age adolescents who only knew how to describe sexual pleasures and knew absolutely nothing about the Bible and what it had to say and there was ample tune to do so in America since we did have most of the Bibles in the entire world but only used them as dust collectors and nothing more and kept changing wording to mean what GOD never ever said through all His prophets, saints and even through GOD in the flesh. What did Paul say or even Moses say about this? There was no question if it was a truth or a lie, but just the fact that it made the young what they knew best and that was to have sex and then the 60's generation which never ever stood up for anything anyways and then the elderly who had ostracized themselves by emulating the younger ones because they thought that that was the way to win favor with them and also to give their inheritance to the ones who most catered to them no matter how immoral they were themselves!

Money and materialism meant pure socialism and which lead to atheism and more deviant sexual homo-erotic insanity for these Nazi red and black uniformed pedophiles. They were spreading the AIDS virus but that was okay and then they threatened Dr. Lorraine Day and that too was okay and also Anita Bryant and were raping and murdering children and youth and now even their parents were degenerates just like they would become all because of Hollywood, our own government, the 60's radicals, the civil righters, the media, the rich and well educated, the dead beat dads, the Nazis in government and in the churches and elsewhere, Communists and Arabs, many English and Germans and the Roman Catholic church and now many protestant denominations and on and on and on!

Oh no, it was not any of the above who were abnormal or mentally disturbed but it was the ones who wanted to take away the GIVEN RIGHTS! This was how arrogant they were just like in Nazi Germany where they too thought they would get away with it and then cover it up but there would always be an odd ball in the group to spoil it for them that is all their fun and games!

If one could not beat them then they could join them in this to the very end and then the earth would spew us out! No matter they were determined, no more then determined they were 100% sure that all would be Nazis like themselves and going along with the 1 and 1/2 million Jewish children they exterminated in Nazi Germany not because of anti-Semitism but because of homosexuality which the Orthodox Jews like the Italians could not stomach and hence good old nice boy Hitler soon realized for his master race to so call "procreate" he had to eliminate what Mr. Harden and Samuel Igra had found out to be the truth and then the rest of German Orthodox Jewry picked up the ball and said Hitler and his deviants had to go right now but the Reichstag a democracy said, "Oh that is okay we are so used to this type of thing here in Germany." Who could stop a majority and is not a democracy a majority or ruled by a majority, right? That is all we hear today, "let the majority rule for they know best, yet most did not have the light of truth shed upon them nor did they even care if they did! All they knew was that they had to be whatever their leader was for and whatever would give them peace and satisfaction and that was materialism and the hell with homosexuality, infanticide and euthanasia because if Nazi Germany could do it so could we but in a more sophisticated way, right?

One had thought that the "exterminators" had eliminated this 3rd Reich after World War II but there was no stopping the stout hearted German from their persistence and effort to have it their way as long as it was on the winning side and that would be all that would matter! Once others thought this way then all would come to think and understand like a real true blue Nazi thought like! Well they did have a few obstacles now to deal with since this was not Germany and not all Germans lived here plus the fact that many other variables would pose a problem for their type of so called lifestyle! First of all the Italians would have a little to say if their children were molested by priests, homosexual pedophiles, Clintonites, etc.! Then they would have to, of course, deal with fathers and uncles and grandfathers and nephews who would stand in the way to block their civil rights or superior rights, as I had said before. That meant that now they could do almost anything they wanted and to their hearts desire! Well of course not all the people wanted their children to be tortured, murdered, raped, molested, etc. and why should they? After all, they did really love their children and not hate them, right?

This was so very hard to understand amongst the rich and well educated who really never ever raised their own children and almost always had a nice proxy for a cheap price to take good care of their most precious commodity their very own children, but then again their most precious commodity along with many other Americans was the green stuff called legal tender and what it could buy and that was materialism but then again no one could buy materialism they had to first believe in it such as socialism; and sell out the whole store including their family to be a member of this most famous "brotherhood" and that was Nazism's homosexuality that once was dormant and now this beast would once again raise his head to do the once unthinkable but never mind that it all was for a good cause or better yet for the "cause" and nation or no nation it did not matter because this brotherhood would sell out its very own nation without blinking an eye and one must remember without psychiatric help then one could only "legally" be declared what they liked to call as "normal" like in the ovens at Auschwitz and Buchenwald!

Even the ally soldiers who got there could not believe their very eyes but then again they were heterosexuals! Only a severely disturbed mind and a wicked heart could conjure up such ignominies! Did one ever just suppose that this was a part of a war and that ideology and perversion did not play a part? Who would have ever believed it was possible to exterminate people including children first having fun with them and then destroying them so that no evidence would remain such as Stalin had tried to do in the Gulag? America had become a second Nazi Germany targeted for destruction and these homosexuals had no patriotic spirit and no one ever questioned them on that part at all or on the part they played in Nazism!

One always had to give credit where credit was due even if the perpetrators did not want to take the credit and why would they not since they wanted now in America to take the credit for the very same thing that had happened in Nazi Germany with Hitler's Youth Corps which was equivalent to them such as our own Boys Scouts of America, Big Brothers and Big Sisters of America, the Girls' Scouts of America and on and on! They could be very proud of what they had accomplished and that was to try and eliminate the heterosexual and if possible the homosexual Jewish people of which the second group did not make up a big part at all but Barney Frank and Ira Glasser were certainly putting up a good effort to reestablish Nazism in the second homeland for these rejuvenated Nazis in the highest levels of government. Why even the Vice President himself was for it!

This was the shining moment for the Anglo-Saxons in the entire last century to say that they almost eliminated all the Jews in the world by covering up a lie called homosexuality but would the world buy that even if it upheld anti-Semitism? This they were not sure about and in fact they were trying to disassociate themselves for this "brotherhood", but that would certainly be hard to do now since many or at least some would still be for this kind of anti-Semitism just like the Nazis had been! Even India was deeply involved in this up to their necks also and why not if one had ever visited that New Age Soviet State that Indira Gandhi had given to Moscow before they too eliminated her! So much of this brotherhood now called civil rights brotherhood was going along with this if it meant, "Exterminate all the Jews!"

But in America the Jews were not paying attention and could care less because they were having a ball of a time enjoying their own extravagance at the very price of 6 million Jews and 7 million Gentiles not to mention 66,000,000 Russians! Why the progroms in Nazi Germany were less yes less to the American Jew because now they too realized that homosexuals could never do this sort of thing and that they could clearly see that the homosexual needed even more protection as a special class just like the

Nazis had in Nazi Germany! And what about affirmative action which said no Jew could hold a government . . . . But where was that ever written in American legal texts? It wasn't but it was in good old Nazi Germany! All in favor say aye and all of those who oppose say . . . Well anyway, it did not matter; that was old news and had nothing to do with the American Jew. After all, one can not believe everything they read but where had they read this at all in America?

Well I guess I have belabored that point and have bored most of you to death with that old news. It certainly is old news since no one ever talks or has even heard about it including the Jews in America who now have been supporting the ones who still believe that there is too much overpopulation in the Jewish community today! I guess too that when that many Jews are still alive about 17,000,000 worldwide one still has to worry or at least Barney Frank and the ACLU' S Ira Glasser both feel that way! They would never support anything that would ever be anti-Semitic just like Trotsky or Mr. Bronstein had never done?

They would always know somehow who and what to stand up or sit down for and know also the right time in which to do just that! They were convinced that the homosexual Butches were their friends for life and that those nasty horrible Christians would have to pay for what they had done it Nazi Germany but then again who did Hitler and his own group of sexual deviants worship? Oh that's right it was only the two lightning bolts which established for sure it had to be Christianity, right? But where in Scripture does it say that that is a Christian symbol? Oh well nonetheless one cannot be bothered about little things like that!

Always know who your real enemy is. As for the atheistic and Communistic ACLU they always knew who was their real enemy and who had put them into ovens to the sweet sound of music and who as I recalled as a nation never repented and probably never would but nonetheless one could trust them more then one could ever trust the Italians or even the Russian peasants!

When one thinks like this and has to convey to them that their enemy is their friend and their friend is their enemy, then one would suppose that one themselves gets confused between even the genders. Is that not right? It was Adam and Steve and not Adam and Eve but then again what would an atheist and a Communist know about something they not once had ever read and yet can render such a verdict as guilt by association, but nonetheless why should I, a Gentile, tell such a well educated and brilliant people about how one should choose its friends so very carefully after all one must always oppose the one who does something for nothing and never anyone who shall accept anything in place of nothing. But this nothingness sometimes is more than meets the eye and in fact one must have bionic vision to see what some of us have already seen but try as one may they cannot be convinced and what Gentile would want to convince the well educated and the rich amongst the Jewish people when they all know what they want.

So now we come to the intellectual which by far in today's world is the hardest to find especially in the Western world and also in the Eastern world with all its pagan religions even though there are more nonwhite Christians in the entire world than there are white Christians. The intellectual is first of all a highly moral person which is a rare find indeed. He or she usually go beyond reproach and can be trusted with GOD'S Word to the fullest and not only to know His Word but also to live it constantly day by day and almost moment by moment. Their lives are first of all not their own and they know that one must truly know who their Saviour is. They are highly aware of what a good and Biblical education requires and do not just collect facts and knowledge and then subscribe to a sinful way of life. It is this type of person such as Alexander Solzhenitsyn come under since first of all he was Christian not because of what he had done but what he knew in his heart Jesus had done for him in a loving and caring way and he then passed that love which is called agapé love which is Jesus' love.

He was an educated person but who did not allow that to determine who he shall serve in this world. His first responsibility was the truth, and that requires much of what man does not have and that is His will and not our own will. He articulated as few can what the truth is and also told in a novel form how important good must prevail over evil and if one allows Jesus into their own heart then already one has started on the right path even though it is narrow. He knew also that his spiritual freedom more important than his physical freedom but appreciated his physical freedom, since this is what most people see. Nonetheless his spiritual freedom came first and used to give glory to the Father. No, not perfect but the first one to realize that and included himself with his own country's failures and articulated from beginning to end what true history had to say about one's own nation since we all have a nation that is ours.

The intellectual follows GOD'S calling in his life and understands that even though things look hopeless and can come to the point of despair one must keep their heart, mind and their soul on Jesus. He says little and gives few speeches, but speaks through the written Word with the Bible as his guide. He also subscribes and not their religion or guilt what James in the New Testament who was Jesus' half brother about faith without works is dead which means once one knows who GOD is personally then one does what the Holy Spirit is guiding him to do. So the repentance and the change of heart comes through Jesus. He also understands as a saint in the Lord as Paul describes so many times that his con—sciousness is what determines his very own existence and not the other way around. Most people who have ever lived subscribe to the idea if one can call it that that their existence is most important and miss the most important thing in their own life and that is what is their own purpose in The only way to not just exist in this life is to truly understand through Jesus that He does have a purpose for those who know Him personally.

Socialism subscribes to this notion that one's existence which really means in the flesh is only a temporary thing while they are alive and serves only one reason and that is to live for the ego or for the I in one's self. This first of all, one must realize is a child and so it is vitally important not to stray from this as one goes through the different stages in life and with those stages the different trials and tribulations as well as joy. Materialism does not play any role in an intellectual's life because he knows that this is not his own and that this world here is to serve one's brother and to always understand one must be a servant to GOD. In the Western part of the world John Locke's philosophy is "eat, drink and be merry". This in no one way determines anything in the same way that when one looks into water to always know how very deep or shallow that water might be.

Our GOD can pick and choose but we do not know who He picks and chooses but we can at least reach out to those whose heart is looking for Him and do not know how to find Him. This is where the Gospel comes in and not just about salvation (remember James) since we are our brother's keeper. It is not our own life that is so important even though we may at—times think so but it is what Jesus had to show us and has left the Holy Spirit with us so that we would and could always know who it is we are following and be reading His Word the Bible we continue to grow and grow and also in the way we think, say and also do. Without faith it is impossible to please GOD and it is GOD who gives us our own amount of faith and it is not so much in how much but in how well we do what He wants us to do on a moment by moment basis. If we lapse from this time of moment by moment we quickly can lose our own way.

So the intellectual usually has a GODLY education but much more than that is not a crowd pleaser or a follow the leader but does follow what the Holy Spirit is saying moment by moment if one stays in tune to its teachings. Remember we do not live under law even though the law tells and shows us what we have done wrong. We are like sheep who always go astray without a shepherd who by the way knows all of his sheep by name as individual sheep. They not only get lost, but they fall down and cannot get up and also must be guided to stay with their own flock. The shepherd does this so well and that is why he is called the shepherd. We to have all gone astray and are not born to know who Jesus is even though the innocence of childhood is there but not the removal of sin in our own lives. Yes children are saints in the sense that if they are not at the age of accountability then they remain saints but then again only GOD knows this for sure and that is why in Proverbs it says, "Teach your children in the way of the Lord and as they get older they shall not go astray."

Yes there are very few intellectuals at any given time on earth and now more than ever there are fewer and fewer ones but just because we may not at this time know them they are placed in the world by a loving GOD. These intellectuals know and see things that others cannot as I said before articulate into words what for example beauty is which in essence means harmony with GOD. Usually the writer that is an artist must describe in words and not by human eyesight what it is that has occurred or is occurring. The future is always speculative but with some foresight one can see things that would admonish man he is going the wrong way. The artistic writer is given this gift, if you will to see things as they now are. Again it is in words and not drawings or any other type of physical means that the senses use except the sense to be able to read which is a sense that means one has become educated enough to understand and also interpret the things in life that are many times a mystery in and of themselves.

This is not an occupation or a position or a job in the mundane use of those words. This is purely spiritual which comes from GOD for it is He who instructs the ones who through Christ and Christ alone have become the light of the world and understand the deeper hidden meaning about life itself and not just in the living or the existence of being here on earth with no purpose that would come from GOD and GOD alone. Does anyone live for GOD alone? No, but they can be able with of course GOD'S help to come to understated that without Him everything else is meaningless and shall not be carried from this world into the next.

Love as well as marriage is a commitment and must be learned gradually in life and Jesus is always there to do that for all of those who are saints in the Lord and who hear His calling into His flock. Why would GOD throw pearls in front of swine? A dog or a swine in Scripture is one who would mock GOD'S holy and sacred Word. One can now see why one must do as Jesus told the Disciples before they went out two by two and that was if any town does not except your peace then wipe the dust off of your feet and leave that house or town right away. Not much chance there to hear it a second and a third time.

The saints in Scripture speak to no particular denomination within man's religions. It does speak to the Body of Christ which are people saved by grace and are hearing and doing what GOD wants them to do no matter how small and insignificant it may appear in the world. When Jesus confronted the Pharisees that is why He told them what they were because He was not about to throw pearls in from of swine and neither should we. He knew and understood that they were already hard hearted and would not listen. He understood that their own pride like Satan was blocking the way and hence they would be lost forever.

These saints of GOD are in the Body of Christ and not in any denomination or religion because they belong to Jesus and not to anything else and also Jesus must always come first. "If you have seen Me you have seen the Father I and the Father are One."

This Body has many different parts but all the parts are in this Body and Christ is the Head of this only type of church which is His church by grace and with grace alone the faith that He gives to all of His own. These again are the—true saints in the world all over the world who are doing many things including giving up their very own lives for Him. If our Shepherd would leave us alone we all would be lost and not know what to do. The Holy Spirit is here to guide us and instruct us and even when we cannot pray the Holy Spirit shall pray for us in words that we ourselves cannot articulate verbally.

It cost us nothing for this grace but it was paid in full once and for all. It is a free gift to all who GOD calls to Himself The Shepherd calls his sheep and they actually know his voice even though at times they do and can stray. Each and every one is known. Out of the 99 who are not lost but the one who is lost it is a wonderful joy for him to have been found!

The intellectual then has Jesus inside of him and understands what it is that gives all meaning and purpose to his own life. This is also the character that one develops through listening to Him. The old man Adam is no longer alive who was disobedient to GOD. He rebelled against what GOD told him not to do. Yes, now this intellectual has a difficult and almost an impossible road to travel but all things are possible!

So why is it that so many accuse Paul, and by the way falsely, about why all women must remain silent in the church and also hold no position of authority in the church? Let us first look at Eve who was deceived by Satan in the Garden but Adam was not!

Since then women have been trying somehow to usurp a man's, a father's, an uncle's, a grandfather's role in life and that is man is the authority figure in the home and in the church, and he must be a provider and a priest. One can see that when one allows anyone to go against the Word of GOD how it affects all of society. For example many men in America have refused to be fathers; hence with that we now see women raising male youth and boys who are confused about their own identity in their own sexual role and are turning to homosexuality because of disobedience to GOD'S holy Word which never changes.

We also see what deadbeat dads have created in this country, and that is illegitimacy and infanticide. Many feel that these children are just criminals waiting to grow up, which in essence is half true and half a lie. The truth lies in the fact that women in general were never equipped to handle boys and to have that special bond that only a loving father who marries his wife for honor and to uphold what GOD'S Word has to say about this. A most vital relationship since the family is the very backbone of Christianity and that is why all other heathen religions do not express it like the Bible does in love and consideration. When a mother is taken out of the picture and not allowed to be at home, this removes her role as a mother bonding to her daughters; but also in infancy what a man can never do in regards to an infant's necessity that has all to do with procreation.

Paul knew all this. If one reads the Book of Romans which is the Constitution of the New Testament, then one can readily see what he addresses and why. Worship is an individual thing but is recognized when the children are not bastards as our own society has found more in the pleasure then in the fulfillment of marriage to have a family with all of its trials and tribulations and also the joy knowing that this is what GOD himself intends for His church in the Second Advent And in regards to that the Jews shall be saved once all the Gentiles have come in who are going to come in according to GOD: Only a remnant shall be saved which is a small part but nonetheless GOD keeps His promises no matter how long man may think He has forgotten.

A husband and a father must love his wife as Christ loves the church and notice it is in the present tense. In America now one can also see the destruction to the family in the Roman Catholic idea that men must never get married if they are to serve what they call "The Church"! This celibacy now is showing how abnormal it is for a man not to get married and on such a large scale since it is a normal thing to get married and have a family. "Be fruitful and multiply." One cannot do that if one observes celibacy and does not ever come to know if he would have ever been married and it would have been better to have gotten married if one lusts in the flesh, and right here is where this Roman Catholicism idea has corrupted the idea that one cannot serve GOD in any capacity if one is married, but it proves the very opposite, that if this natural and human urge to get married and have children is forbidden then the outlet as we now well see, leads into sexual deviancy on a much larger scale than we had ever thought.

To obtain property centuries for this celibacy has all through the centuries allowed man not to procreate because materialism was more important then GOD'S Word. Now the women also, on the other side of this religion, have to face the same dilemma and that is they must never get married and have children and enjoy a family. Where in Scripture can one find this to uphold what GOD Himself has written through man and is that why the Bible was not adhered too for many centuries and not even allowed to be read? This form of spiritual ignorance has done so much irreparable damage that now with hindsight one can see what this European religion] has done against Scripture.

This religion is pro life but what is the underlying reason for that if not to only increase its membership into this world of ignorance and to increase the numbers to come into this religion on a larger scale with their own rule making and of course the work ethic of "not by grace alone." I have personally seen in America what this religion appears to me to be and that is all for materialism.

Very few in this religion hear the Word of GOD in the sense that they can do nothing to obtain salvation by works! Of course over many centuries and many generations this has been carried through so much that one would almost think that if the Vatican would not be there then GOD Himself would not be around which is almost like a Deist. The truth must be told before GOD closes His door to all the Gentiles and opens it for all the Hebrews.

Even Judaism belives that a man and a woman should get married and have a family and it is scorned upon not to have a wife for life and children and continue what GOD always said one should do.

We are coming to that time in the year in America when from Roman Catholicism's entourage of a somewhat unBiblical holiday known as Christ's Mass or Christmas. This is something that most Americans believe that we need in our lives as well as our children which is more and more materialism to the point that depression sets in afterwards because it is on money and stress and not peace and goodwill. Our children do not need more materialism, but need more of spiritual things that are truly Biblically correct. Their lives need to be filled with joy and not to seek happiness. This one person is Jesus in our own hearts because what can commercialism do for any child. that Jesus cannot do? One must learn from a very young age about what Jesus is all about and needs to learn that at home and not worry about what the public schools may or may not celebrate for it is the home that government cannot intervene, and so be it for the good! Parents should be raising their children at home in accordance to what they believe and the heck with what government does or does not do in their decimated public schools.

Our own home is where it should be and as long as the public school does not say that there is no GOD then it is okay to send them to public school but it starts at the grassroots level Going to Catholic school is a problem too because they try to indoctrinate one into their own religion which is far from the Bible.

They may even coerce your children into what their Vatican tradition teaches and not what the Word of GOD teaches.

Yes, our children and us do not need to make even a simple holiday to be used to desecrate the simple message that Jesus was born so that the Jewish children can hear and know why He had already come in the flesh and this can be done outside the public government buildings. I have even had a rabbi and a cantor give to me a gift for this birthday of Jesus. It is the state that one must be afraid of the most because it has no spiritual value since it is not really a part of the Christian faith. In fact it supersedes the church when the church and the Bible should supersede the state or atheism forms. And now they want to destroy the 10 Commandments. Use what you have to worship in a different kind of way by sharing with others stories from the Bible plus your time and not in gluttony and on monetary poison. There are so many distractions at this time that one has to wonder if this is a Christian or a pagan holiday and does it contribute more to atheism than to Christ Himself? If His resurrection is not included then Jesus was a man who was born and that 'would be it which is not true and helps promote the enemy's lie. This resurrection means that grace has been bestowed to all that would believe. Now for the Jew this holiday would indeed say something different in the sense that Jesus is the reason for the season which would mean that Messiah has already come. As for us Gentiles, we must know more and do since we have been allowed to hear that message and most Jews seclude their children and to follow tradition which is wonderful but not as wonderful as GOD Himself!

So it is imperative for us to include this resurrection for then the enemy cannot take away what only His birth says and that He was born from Mary. We also need to hear why He was born to this earth and chosen at a special time. It is not enough to fake it with let us not talk about it right now but enjoy what products we have bought and then to bring in one of the biggest lies and at such a young age to children which can render already their faith almost dead and carry them into a secular world all their life and then have their consciences seared for life.

Let them hear at least the whole story and not the half of a story with such ridiculous symbolism that takes away the very sacredness of the whole story of Jesus. Some would say that that is what Easter is for but only Passover is period! Easter alone is a pagan holiday because this Passover we all should be celebrating and see how the Jew wants' to do what they want and how we want to do what we want! There must be this shedding of blood and where in Christmas is there really any shedding of blood? Our children must be shown when they are small and not later when they become even more skeptical, to say the least, with now more distractions then ever to take one's eyes off of Jesus also on the cross and His death and finally His resurrection which no one had ever done before!

Let us give glory to the Father at this time of the year by at least including not Santa Claus or reindeer or whatever, but by including the resurrection power of the Lord and was giving glory to the Father and so should we since this is why He came to earth and that was to not only identify with us but to save us from our own sins which no one else could ever do no matter what!

The method of Christmas is wrong but Christmas is all right if the whole message is told from beginning to end and not just the beginning. What kind of story is it that really has no real ending or conclusion to draw from? It has no power in this instance since again the resurrection is never mentioned except for just a few people who might have a cross somewhere in their decorations!

We were indeed heading in the same direction that preceded the Russian Revolution in that now criminals were allowed to roam the streets and foreign ones at that The President was almost exactly like Nicholas II who allowed revolutionaries to do almost anything they wanted to do which included Lenin, Stalin and Trotsky! They never served any real hard time in prison and were allowed to go back and forth from Russia even though they all had criminal revolutionary pasts such as the sailor incident, publishing revolutionary newspapers, inciting the military, having underground Bolshevikism, attacking and trying to kill heads of state and yet nothing was done the same as nothing was done to the terrorists that bombed the World Trade Centers in New York City. This President too was too close to realize that a great danger was lurking behind the scenes since he was more interested in equality and the stock market.

He did not have the resolve to do what he had to do and soon it would be too late to do anything at all! He had the authority but was afraid to use it and now even Colombian drug lords were even threatening him because of his non-immigration policy and because Colombia too had oil wells that these drug lords now owned since they had murdered all the people in authority. The English were always ones to run away from a fight if they knew they were outnumbered or had no chance of winning even though they would precipitate it.

The Anglos spoke very well, but when it came to enforcing the laws they could not because as I had said they lacked the intestinal fortitude to do it and do it quickly. This administration was noted for its inability to stand firm and now they were jeopardizing our entire nation because they were paralyzed with fear! If they could not knock back the few homosexuals in this nation what could they ever possibly begin to do against the Moslems? They were in no way like the Israelis even though we had 300,000,000 people and Israel had about 2-4 million Jewish people in the state of Israel.

This President, even with all his security, failed at his most important duty and that was to be Commander In Chief and not for the Michael Moore reason who himself was a Communist but for the reason that he did not want to become unpopular and also did not want to ruin his reputation in case the economy went down hill but was not shy if we would lose our own liberty!

He was a Christian, but that did not mean that he would be a good President since he kept failing to do what any national leader was suppose to do and that was stand as Commander In Chief!

This multiculturalist in the White House was destroying America not quickly enough for these other multiculturalists who were actually Marxists/Leninists behind the scenes. Both now were out of the country so that they could not be questioned about their insanity that was occurring in America and was created by them for their own deception and ignorance as to how socialism worked and that it came in many forms and theirs was by the multinational and multicultural ideology that said any culture but the Judeo-Christian culture was okay and in fact we had to give up our liberty just so these well educated and rich ideologues could prove their point and that was that they were qualified to hold any position let alone be President and Vice President.

Where had they learned so much about Marxist/Leninism and where did they learn how to scramble a few eggs as Lenin would have said? What made them so understanding about freedom and liberty? They had for sure been well versed on how not to hold together a nation that spoke one language and must have been studying Yugoslavia on a grand scale but then after all they lived in the ivory towers always protected and never having to worry about their loved ones being murdered or raped!

There was no good vs. evil and all things came down to the bottom line and that was how could they boost their own stock market and why were they so impatient with not having enough illegals in the nation? Yes, the illegals, I suppose, voted them in and as for asylum there was nothing heard which meant that Christians coming from foreign lands would not be included in their multiculturalism. But that was no surprise since for whatever insane reason they found to import their coerced immigration only ones who were of the non-Judeo Christian faith. This was all quite normal for them and being the fact that one was an Anglophile one could understand Since they had some centuries ago brought slaves here of their own freewill since they found it easier to make a living that way and did not have to work with their hands or break out in a sweat.

Now that hunting season was open to all white American males of the middle class, especially those who were born here, these same kinds of slave owners again wanted to bring in slavery for diversity, which also was another word for socialism by the multiculturalists. America was falling fast and faster and the media was destroying public opinion because they would report only lies and hence the American people themselves had no opinion of their own so the true blue American was in deep trouble since it was what their agenda was and that Was to destroy America intentionally or not. They had no brains to think with and that is why they had become "royalty of the state" so that we could serve their every wonderful need! It was just like the royal family in England that owned one third of London! They always liked to use their slavery in some way no matter where they chose to take it. It was a wonderful life if one happened by chance to be one of the fortunates that could labor all the lives and have absolutely nothing to show for it since this President wanted us to pay for his ideas that would also cost us our own liberty but we should not get angry but only them if we did not approve of their insanity!

Now 8 white men had been shot by an oriental, but yet this fine oriental, as explained by his high priced lawyer, had shot four of these white men in the back! This made all the sense in the world to these Anglo-Saxons at the top and it was as if they had only had always just a spiritual body and not a physical one that felt pain. Satan for sure would qualify here as to that but as for them . . . Now it was hunting season for all white males because if this government could intimidate them completely then over half the battle would be over. They had to destroy the image of the white male first of all to destroy this nation because he was the one who had built it into a free society just so illegal criminals could come into the nation!

All men are created . . . except the white male for he was the evilest of all of them even though just about all the civil rights' leaders were members of the Communist Party and they still kept calling themselves as well as the media reverends so and so! I could only think of two such groups of people who thought consistently nice that and hated the Jew most of all and they were of course the Anglo-Saxons and why not Martin Luther and Mr. Churchill hated the Jews very much. We already knew what Roman Catholicism thought of the "Jew". For them it had been a most silent Holocaust with Pope Pius XII.

Now the Vietcong had come to America via the World Bank and the IMF, the New York Times, Hollywood and Jane Fonda and others, and yet these communists and internationalists did really love their money and wealth and not their very own nation even in Europe! It made the Anglo-Saxons feel smarter except that the Russians, the Italians, the Greeks, etc. were all smarter than they were! This could not be since only they could always rule and always wanted to rule directly by themselves and their Masons and also the Vatican wanted to rule also from such a, distance in such a small territory just almost like DC here in

America. People who were these illegals could be taken advantage of more quickly and would also resort to violence if they did not get their entitlements from us, the taxpayers provided by EL PRESIDENTE!

The Jewish people for the most part were sincere even though they were wrong about some things, but the Anglo-Saxons could care less if they were telling the truth or lying but just so it made their ego's fly high as hell. They had no honor for the most part and could like a sociopath lie and look one right in the eye but then again that whole British Isles were like that many times. They were also very cold and arrogant and had to play the part of always knowing what was right and doing what was wrong! Yes, this is what America now needed and that was a President who had this same kind of insincerity but as long as it met his needs and the needs of his fellow comrades in arms amongst the rich and well educated!

The Jewish people were the only ones speaking out like Michael Savage and others like the Gentiles such as Rush Limbaugh and O'Reilly were just entertainers and could care less about America with their party ideology which they always quoted time and again. G. Gordon Liddy was another phoney also in the line of these as Well as Larry King and Ted Koppel. Yes, for the most part the Jewish people were defending America now when it needed defending and not like the Anglo-Saxons who saw their so called equality as just equivalence and could care less as I said before how it affected the average white American male and it "would not be them that made history by being famous but by the average American who would either choose to do what was right and also moral or would play follow the leader. I knew of two ex Marines who would sell out their own nation for the green buck and the brutality they must have gone through must have in some way affected their minds and hearts for it was very brutal to be a United States Marine and made one cold to morals and to GOD since semper fi had meant to the Corps first and not to GOD like the South African soldiers who use to carry Bibles with them all the time. When had our soldiers ever carried Bibles? Also the English started apartheid in South Africa and not DeClerc or even Ian Smith but yet the English loved to support their Marxist/ Leninist of Nelson Mandela and Tutu. And where is Marx buried but in good old England!

Not even Israel wanted the German Jewish traitor! The Jewish were Christian in nature and now were starting to see once again what was really going on in America and there was a change to destroy them from within their own people by intermarriage that started in the 60's and their lost of even the Old Testament! The ones in Hollywood only knew the book of Marx and Lenin! Yes, this President had really appointed none except Rumsfeld who was Jewish because he knew that the war would fail and he could then blame a Jew for it and then more of his anti-Semitism could be promoted since then Israel would be brought into their so called peace process which was nothing more than suicide for Israel to ever agree to such insane terms and that is why he also picked a black anti-Semite for his Secretary of State and was now promoting Hispanics who were not the best qualified for the job as opposed to Europeans when they could not even speak Castellian Spanish but a slang form of Spanish since they were very illiterate! This is who this President could communicate with only it seemed the very illiterate and anti-Semitic. He had a vendetta out for them for some inexplicable reason except possibly that Israel itself broke up his friendship with Bin Laden's relatives in Saudi Arabia!

All his congenial appearances and all his constant now even about the election when the election was over and all his sneaky way of bringing in more illegals to catch many Americans off guard. May be he felt he owed his brother Jeb some kind of honor or dignity since he had married a Mexican woman. If it was good enough fort them then it was good enough for us. This though would not sail quite the way he thought it would no matter how much he tried unless all public opinion would be destroyed in

America and it appeared other Anglo-Saxons not only wanted homosexuality but were intermarrying with all these foreign people who resented the American very much and just played up to them all the time and now government had given them the free right to kill Christians and Jews. Sometimes the Jews were gullible when it came to being deceived and the Anglo-Saxons knew that because they were not sincere. Even Christians who were Anglo-Saxons hated Jews!

One would have definitely thought that Jesus was an Anglo-Saxon Himself by the way they wanted to rule at least for now the Western part of the world when the Eastern part of the world saw through them, and had a grudge now for all white European males and females because of what these two people had done all over the world to promote their one world government and cannot we all not just get along mentality when they knew and especially this President knew that there would be resentment and animosity from all sides? He nonetheless was determined to do what he wanted but what would happen when a Hillary would get in who was more of a man then he was and would go all the way to social justice or Communism?

When his second term would end, what condition would this country be in after all his filibustering?

What is the first tax that all governments raise, such as in America when the government needs more money and is bankrupt? It is of course the property taxes to bring down the middle class and make us come under socialism in a euphemistic way. Now even my county and school district are going to raise this tax because now they need to build wasteful stadiums and wetland idiocy, not to mention entitlements for illegals who resent and hate Americans born here! This recycling of artificial money does nothing for the middle class except make them support the poor as well as the rich through the stock market that is only for the rich and well educated and as Lou Dobbs has said many times with these illegals the middle class shall certainly disappear.

Now to compound that if the minimum wage is increased then that means that the unions shall ask for even more money for their members and at the same time become a party in and of itself with the Democratic Socialist Party and dues shall go even higher and higher to support their cronies who are all socialists!

We now can have anyone become President if this incumbent can do it with his "foreign" agenda of no asylum but plenty of illegal immigration. Even a foreigner shall be able to run and that is the reason they chose Schwarzenegger for the job (because he is a foreigner) to possibly go as high as he did. Also, he is an Austrian just like Hitler, his father was a Nazi, and he sounds like one too. He is a major part of Hollywood's socialism with his homosexuality promo and also pro infanticide and is, of course, married to a Kennedy by the name of Maria Shriver. Need one say anymore about that Nazi family?

Whenever politicians say they shall make a pledge they mean simply to raise taxes. The lawyers are our scoundrels that help destroy our nation completely and they also belong to the Internationale. Who now shall be picked that is unqualified for Homeland Security after the pro infanticide Tom Ridge?

Apparently by the cast of characters and not people of character we shall have another puppet.

When this incumbent was governor of Texas he had a white Christian woman executed, and now in Texas they have a black woman with a stay of execution for at least 120 days! And also this incumbent has gone to Canada to agitate, like he has in Mexico, where if they come here they have something to gain, but if we go there we have absolutely nothing at all to gain. Who would even want to go there since it is a socialist state controlled by the rich as in an oligarchy?

Now the socialist media wants the criminals in Guantanamo Bay to be released immediately and this in defense of the terrorists, again a reminder of Nicholas II of Russia before the Bolshevik Revolution! This incumbent is also bringing more danger to himself more than he'll ever know. Also more Hispanics who make up less then 30% of our entire population and the blacks under 13%, are again being appointed over the white European male for positions of great importance.

Now with the United Nations, which is recommending a lesser global threat, all I can say to that is close the United Nations or at least get them out of America. These businessmen turned socialists need to go to Peking; Moscow or Havana to have their meetings and not here and World Bank can also take its trillions to Berlin or Londontown!

Now the government is giving to those who own United States Savings Bonds a chance to get credit by supporting your very local college for the betterment of socialism. And as far as money goes when one takes their car to get checked then one has to know and understand that the people who check their cars are only computer technicians and not mechanics so if you have any problem with your car the best thing to do is to buy an older model car with no computers!

Now this story in Wisconsin about a Laotian who has lived in this country since he was 12 years old and is near 40 now. He just happened to shoot 8 white American males and 4 in the back, and the media and his wonderful lawyers said he was a fine outstanding citizen, but really another sort of illegal of a race other than white, who was getting his fair chance in court since the media have said he is the victim in this hunting case. In this case the 8 were hunting for deer and he was hunting for white males, the same many blacks and Hispanics do when they know they can get away with it, like O.J. Simpson, like Rodney King (a druggie who had a rap sheet as long as my arm), and like Reginald Denny who just happened to be in the wrong place at the right time, as the black racists would like to say and have said! There is also Michael Jackson, the homosexual pedophile who molests children just like the Nazis did and still do here in America! And how about the two killers in D.C. and Virginia who had to be tracked down. Once the media found out they were Moslems, guess what? They dropped the story like a hot potato since this incumbent is friends with Saudi Arabia and could be related to the ultra liberal Tony Blair from none other than Anglophilia! There was also a case where a 17-year-old woman was murdered along with a husband and two small children, and it was because he did not know what he was doing and the fact that he was black which now has become another politically correct term that Lenin started and also the fact that Lenin himself had kept his eye on the Negro in America years ago!

The Vanguard Doctrine shall only change their own guards which has to do with the television anchor men who have all of a sudden resigned because now they see that they have this incumbent who is doing everything that they believe in. except for GOD!

International soccer now has this total equality where all the continents must be represented in the play offs no matter how bad of a losing record they have! This is more political correctness that is being followed and that is why most black people say that they do not believe in political correctness or believe that anything such as that exists because they too have bought the lie and now like what they too see that they believe can only benefit the blacks here in America!

Government mediocrity continues as the state highway workers go back to work if that is what one calls it, to work on the turnpike! There are so many government workers who do absolutely nothing but stand and stare, for example, on the highways when about 15 of them are together and 2 or 3 are really working. This, of course, is government by the people. Well at least it is meant for the most lackadaisical person one could possibly find and one who is not that bright or either that very honest about how one spends their time while the taxpayers pay their usurious wages plus their 23 holidays a year plus the Blue Shield with no HMO's! What a life of Riley it must be for them to be able to retire early too and get a pension without really doing any hard physical labor except constantly move their mouths. Their shattered self esteem is really only jealously that they do not make more money with more and more taxpayer paid monies that provide them, with too much money that it destroys them in the end since they were never use to having so much money before!

Most children hardly read any books but just sit either in front of the television or the computer and do idiotic games that amount to insanity and violence. They never really learn about the real classics that, if one is smart enough, promote the good in them since they have a moral ending.

Yes, America is going down and down and now the people themselves have been dumbed down not to know their left from their right and act like robotic Germans who do all things with systems.

Today I had some interesting conversations with two or three men who were not in anyway affiliated with each other. The first was with a coworker with whom I discussed the shootings in Wisconsin that a Laotian had done to 8 white American males and one a Vietnam Veteran. I mentioned first that this individual was not a newcomer to America and the fact that this President was bringing 15,000 more of this same sect into America as illegals. It appeared that he only wanted to melt down and mix races like the English wanted to do and not for any good reason! And again this was the same thing. Then this coworker mentioned the fact that this President had to please his wealthy oil friends who were Moslems!

Then later in the evening I spoke to an NCO who had to go soon to Kosovo and head a base there in Serbia that would be in charge of chemical, biological and nuclear warfare. If he gave the order to suit up, then everyone there had to suit up including the Commander. He had mentioned that he had only a 2-week training at Fort Dix! He was 53 years old and had some sons still at home. My wife had asked if there were any young people and he had said that most the men were old and bald. I then mentioned that Bill Clinton had gotten us into that quagmire and he agreed completely. Europe could not fight its own wars. Outside the base were many landmines and so all were restricted to the base except the MP'S and some other special officers and they usually used tanks with magnets because all of the ones who placed them there were already dead and from the weather and other conditions the landmines for sure were at all different places such as mud slides that also affected where they might be.

I had already talked to one courier who said that his history professor let them read only from Reagan books and that Reagan had written most of his own speeches. I had said that Reagan did not belong to the Trilateral Commission or the Council on Foreign Relations like all the other Presidents had!

Yes, today was quite an interesting day and not one about the weather, sports or any other asinine thing. It was a relief to talk to a few intelligent people who had seen and known things that most Americans did not and could care less and hence public opinion was dying. Also Tom Brokaw left the anchor news desk and it appeared something was up since Dan Rather had also mentioned his retirement, so one now had to wonder why both of them now were retiring knowing that they both were owned by the elites in the media which was very powerful with its lies and more lies and they were a big part of that lie.

I had said to the NCO that the Serbs were Russian Orthodox for the most part where he was going and their neighbors were Bosnian who were mostly Moslems and then the Croatians who were Roman Catholics. We agreed that the Roman Catholics were nothing but materialists, that the Vatican was a pyramid, that money making was their only business, and that Dostoyevsky was right in what he had said about that institution of Roman Catholicism and their preposterous image of the Pope. The Pope, they claimed, started with St. Peter when St. Peter was not even a Gentile and would have nothing to do with that type of socialism or heathenism in the world which was part of Satan's kingdom here on earth!

The NCO had also said that Albania had mostly Moslems and that all of Islam was poison. I said that Professor Igor Shafaravich, a world famous algebraist, had studied in depth more about socialism and in its truest context and said that socialism had been here since the beginning of man. Shafaravich said Islam was innately socialistic and had a death wish for all mankind, and that it had nothing to do with Christianity which this President said it had, and here is where he knew absolutely nothing about the Bible or its context and nothing about Mohammed and his Satanic religion which was the worship of demons and nothing more!

We would be in for a rough road for the next 4 years and it would only get worse and not better as Christ had said almost

2,000 years ago when he was on earth. America was really losing its way with such incompetent leaders at the top who only saw things in color and nothing else. Even though he was now a moral man, he did not understand what the Middle East itself was all about and hence he was making mistake after mistake and doing just what England was doing since he himself was English. His father was a New Ager for sure, and these were all Ivy Leaguers with the one world government they were trying to form. These elites were sending in the wrong direction because they were doing exactly what the Bible said the church of Laodicea would do and that was to be consumer driven even though Philadelphia, the church had no harsh statement from the Lord Himself since it was the one that would go up in the twinkling of an eye and that both of these church ages would exist at the same time as written in the Book of Revelation. These were churches 6 and 7 the two lasts church ages with the age of grace leaving and the Tribulation or Daniel's 70th Week coming into fruition for the Hebrews.

I had also mentioned that Pat Robertson and Chuck Colson had signed the ECT Document which said that the Evangelical (E) and the Roman Catholic Church (C) believed in the same salvation, which was far from the truth and Dr. D. James Kennedy and Mr. Sproul, a Biblical scholar, asked the above both to remove their names from that forgery of a document and they refused to because, as it said in Revelation that the end times church would be a consumer driven church!

The Book of Revelation and Daniel went hand in hand and both described in full detail about much prophecy that was hard to understand and some had not yet been given by GOD to man to fully understand but we were coming closer and closer to that time as my wife and I both believed! The Bible was not a history book if one was a believer. It was the living word meaning now of GOD! Man was moving on schedule according to Scripture and it was in GOD'S timing that all of this was lining up with. We were stewards to His Holy Word and since that was so we had to continue what Jesus said that we should do and that was to continue until the end of the age and not the end of the world as most secular religions and other religions and some within what they liked to call themselves" Christianity"!

One could see the unbelief and doubt within the church of believers itself and Satan was working over time to get things done for he knew his time was short but did not know just when but only the Father knew that. The spirit world was moving here and there and the Holy Spirit too was bringing in more believers and so the workload for all believers should have been very busy because the time of the Gentiles as I said before was getting very short and man was becoming his very own god and in America one could see the ravages of sin everywhere and it was growing and growing into more and more heathenism and had absolutely nothing to do with Jesus at all even though it emulated to the fullest like it was Christianity but only by word mostly and not by action at all!

There were so many deceptions and false teachers now in the world one had to be constantly on the alert not to listen to them no matter how famous they were since almost the very elect would be saved. "Many are called but few are chosen." This was a deep Biblical passage that one should always think about before taking for granted that man alone depended only on freewill and nothing that GOD had to say through the Holy Spirit. Too many seminaries were already poisoned and so one had to again check real Scripture for the truth and pray in the Spirit for discernment and guidance into prophecy and salvation by grace alone! In other words grace was the only way one could enter into the kingdom of GOD and now evangelicals were including Roman Catholicism along with this which was totally off of the mark!

My next dialogue was with myself as to what GOD'S Word said about salvation and something else which most born again believers refused to really listen to but had to answer so far to suffice what Scripture said. In Scripture it says, "Many are called but few are chosen" and if I break this apart it might look some thing like this. Many are called (not all are called by GOD) and few are chosen (Paul on the road to Dsmascus)! Many believe that GOD calls all to Himself in the sense that he wants all to be saved yet all shall not be saved and the ones who get saved only GOD really knows and no one else. Unbelief? No. He does wish that not any should be lost could imply that this is how much He loves man. We again know that not all or even most probably shall be saved like Charles Spurgeon had said when he had made the comment that since the mortality rate was so high then that is why more would come into the kingdom of heaven. To be sure mentally is only mental assent but to have one's heart and soul and mind cleansed by Jesus is by His grace and grace alone and since GOD has to do the calling it is not freewill alone because it does not depend alone on man. When Jesus approached the rich young man Jesus had asked him to give up everything he had and come and follow Him and the rich young man went sadly away. This was Jesus who already knew this man's heart and respond before he would say it and hence then did Jesus only go to ones who would believe or did he go to ones who would not? This rich young man was approached but did not respond so many would say he refused grace and yet if that alone would be true than why did Jesus go to Him? The Father had called him and Jesus knew that and he witnessed to him.

When Paul says that women should not talk in church and not hold any authoritative position then what he is saying is 100% and without a doubt that women should be silent because Adam was not deceived but it was Eve who was deceived. The churches today ignore so much that one has to wonder if they believe any real parts of Scripture since they want to pick and choose and GOD does not allow that in His Word.

It says in the Bible that after the age of grace when all the Gentiles have come in that only a remnant shall be saved which means in this instance 100% of the Jews then that are left and GOD is always specific when it comes to the Jewish people only.

When were the Disciples really saved? When Jesus died, rose, and descended and ascended to the Father then the Disciples were saved and not before realistically. They had to wait like the Old Testament saints did for Messiah to resurrect in order for salvation to take place.

If no one preaches then how can one hear and if one cannot hear how can one believe? This means that it is our own responsibility to witness when the Holy Spirit leads and not when we feel like because chances are it shall be the wrong time with the truth. Then there are those who believe they are saved and are not and those who do not believe they are saved but are. Dialogues with the enemy can confuse a believer very much and it is them that the enemy wants to attack so that their own testimony is not valid to the dying world.

Who was the Bible written for, all people or just believers? Can one interpret the Bible without the Holy Spirit? Did some not search GOD out but in all the wrong places, and did that mean that He did not call them to be His own? If why? Why? The Bible says none are ignorant but all know or have this search for GOD because GOD has put it there in all men to search Him out but did GOD call them? "I have lost no not one of them . . . "

These were just some of my thoughts that I said to myself since there was some dispute amongst Christians themselves and as horrible as this sounds many today in the church were not proselytizing as they should have and what did James say that "faith without works is death", which did not mean that that works counted for anything at all in regards to salvation but it again was only GOD'S grace!

I always do what the Father tells Me to do yet Jesus was in the flesh and part of the one with the Father but the Father was a spirit always and this is truly a mystery of GOD! Only the Father knows when Jesus shall return for the Second Advent and no one else. Through Jesus though I believe he did feel since His very own Son hung on the cross and GOD could not look upon sin yet GOD took all sin for all time with Him once and for all.

There are only 2 people in the world and they are the Jewish and the Gentiles and none other and amongst those two Jesus has made a way for them to become as one but with the roots of the tree in the Jews and the Gentiles in the branches so let us always remember that the Jews must lead and no one can replace them with a Gentile religion. That was GOD'S purpose in all of this but it was to show mercy.

People were working so hard that they forgot what to live for and what life was for not to mention no family, friends, etc. They knew they "needed" more and more money, but just how much more they did not know or did they? First it was higher wages for less work because of the so called inflation which was nothing more than avarice at the very top with no morals or goodness in them at all. Then came along spending for high prices and over inflated colleges but for what? Then the multitude of status symbolism of the car itself. Then expensive eating habits at expensive restaurants. This was nothing more than ego in all the above. So it came down to sin and good vs. evil and not inflation, not to mention starvation and famine in the world, but nobody here was really concerned about that for they lived in splendor. But for sure they were concerned about the corrupt United Way, the Girls Scouts of America, Big Brothers/Big Sisters, the American Red Cross, the infamous hospitals (yes hospitals), the medical profession without Hippocrates, the infamous jurists and that was nothing new, Hollywood's Reds, the psychiatric homosexual agenda, NAMBLA, the United Nations, the March of Dimes, the NAACP, AARP, the HMO's, all of them, Senior and senor' citizens by the millions, millions of illegals, "war criminals", the Latin Kings, the Guardian Angels, Planned Parenthood, the unions, the parties all of them, the public and the Catholic schools, and even the churches! Yes, we had time for anything and everything but GOD and His poor Christians and also unbelieving poor.

Deadbeat dads came along with Soviet day care by LBJ, the redneck, the Kennedys and Nazism, Ford and socialism, Nixon and Communism, Carter and his social "Christianity", the better-red-than-dead Clintons, the New Age Bushes, and who knows what next possibly such as Hillary's "villages", which would be like another My Lai!

We were reverting to the 60's, but now the public was swayed with this lie and not just the rich and well educated along with the civil righters.

A second time might do the trick since we had murdered like Russia over 50,000,000 people and now would be the time to butcher the fatted pig in the temple! The Congress, the Court yes the Great Tribunal, the ACLU, People For The American Way, the Black Congressional Caucus made up of socialists, etc. were all moving in that direction including this Anglophile incumbent.

Marxist/Leninism went from the top to the very bottom now in our society and 80% of society and counting were hooked onto socialism for better or worse and what free handouts were there for the picking as well as for the illegals mostly and the entitlements who spoke the Heinz 57 variety kind of slang called the forked tongue of government with its lies to keep Americans not in the know and that was the real American citizen that could read, write, and spell in English and understood America was for Judeo-Christians and for only them to hold authority in government and that tribalism and multiculturalism had no place here in America since not all cultures were equal! This incumbent maybe had fetal alcohol syndrome or some other birth defect that made him think only of multiculturalism? One of its tree's roots—no all of its tree's roots were Marxist/Leninism and this EL PRESIDENTE' was for democracy? New terms meant new definitions? No, old words meant new definitions completely new and so new they were antonyms or out right lies. Evil meant now that political correctness was pure and good meant now that homosexuality and infanticide were both excellent especially for the ever growing population explosion and MR. EL PRESIDENTE' was already fulfilling our lack of taxpayers' rolls by importation of illegals because this was the quickest way to boost the artificial stock market so hard assets something he did not have nor the U.S. Senate would drop but they did not! The ceiling was falling through and not the floor since we were beneath all the rubble. He talked a good line, hook and sinker!

Now our wonderful insurance companies were making a concerted effort to insure employees without their knowledge and were in bed with the banks, to have future health care which appeared congruent to euthanasia when the time came and also properties that were being bought all at once in huge quantities by a private corporation but yet one needed a mutual, no stockholders, life insurance policy which had what to do with any kind of home? This appeared more like a catch 22 by government just as the Home stead Act did, gambling and the lottery for the so called senor' citizens and more mobster like or politician like Al Capone.

No fault car insurance started with the big bang theory of "it is not your fault", but higher much higher premiums shall be determined by geography and if done this way people would complain less since they were not being individually picked out, except the ones with excellent driving records and settlements out of court by the insurance companies which raised insurance premiums because the trial lawyers in government and in the courts were like sharks in the water. This was feminism for sure and it kept getting worse and worse for all our American families regardless if they were a husband and a wife, since society was abnormal to say the least. Most were under the control of Satan the father of all lies. The women Sodomites with their good paying jobs and positions wanted more freedom and felt their rates should be equal to their counterparts, the half male to them which was about 30% higher in premiums! In one city 40% of the people had no car insurance because the rate was so high geographically in that area, which was really unconstitutional.

Government intrusion to all the above put mediocrity in front of conscientiousness and good driving records, but it was, after all, for a good cause. Since the excuse was used for seat belts and no smoking, they then went into a more dominant place where good morals were and that was your very own home.

Their real interest (this time not the financial) was how much privacy, decent privacy, can we get into making one's private life now as one instead of two which were one's public and one's private life?

They said it was for safety and consideration, but why were they allowing Cubans first which were their criminals, Islamic Moslems, different colored racists, illegals from wherever who too had vendettas and hold it against Americans. These illegals include Haitians (remember Aristide's $30 million that our own government gave him) and the Marxists/Leninists such as Angela Davis and Khruscnev's son, who were both professors in America. The latter had to get out or else the peasants would have probably gotten him. Other illegals are the Mexican Marxists, the Romanian gypsies, the Hispanic anti-American people, Nazis and their lot with homosexuality and now AIDS, and the South African Marxists such as Mandela and Tutu. But this was the very essence of America this Marxist/Leninism. At least that is what the United States Supreme Court had said time and again not to mention their multiculturalism. That is why there were weeds growing in the White House, the same kind of dilemma when Jimmy Carter was President and there were rats around the White House! This told one that they did not even live there anymore and it was all for show. That is why this President was in Florida at the time, most likely, and seemed not in the slightest concerned, knowing his Saudi friends so very well. Did he really know? Nothing now would surprise me after what he has done to destroy America and its Judeo Christian faith!

It really appeared that certain people were probably the only real Christians following GOD'S Word to the fullest and with the gimmick such as money all the time and since they had none while the others made rule changes while this society was making a move towards its own progressive movement. Yes, even I was asked, in English in fact mind you, if I did speak any Spanish and I said, "Me know comprendi" just like that and they thought I meant" Me no comprendi "!

I knew if government had it it had to surely work well at least for a day or two. We had such a wonderful head of state that I sometimes wondered what state his head was in? Euphoria, utopia, paradise? Well at least Islam had the very latter! It was often called adventures in paradise amongst the living on this earth though some would certainly disagree that Islam itself was anything but paradise but then the incumbent had said so but then that was not for here but the hereafter if one in that condition wanted to really go there at that very moment in their lives and it appeared all of Islam certainly wanted to! But being there could mean it would be too late and too long!

Yes, I did say that with John Kerry we would get instant socialism and with Bush we would get a delayed affect but now with all his illegals and insanity of foreign demonic cultures maybe he too would be an instant believer in this wholesale. There was no other word for it since millions had come in and millions more were coming in actually to destroy and take over if possible this nation's face and soul unless there was an optimistic hope that American citizens would defend their homeland right here with the Second Amendment backing them up! No one had the right to take away one's nation without their say so and who would even say so to such insanity except of course English diplomacy?

I personally had seen enough English diplomacy(or read about it) in China around 1949 and before, in India, in South Africa, in America (their slavery which made me an accessory after the fact since I was an American and not an Englishman), and in Israel when Churchill gave up Transjordan to the Arabs which today is Jordan. One can see where now the Palestinians really belong but one sin and it continues on into today; the effigies in Israel under the British mandate with human bodies, the return of Russian peasants to Stalin by the millions to be murdered immediately, the giving away of Hungary, Poland, half of

Germany, a way into Manchuria where Kim Il Sung's Communist son was today right now reigning and now with the incumbent in America doing what he was made it too much for me to ever trust them in what they said or what they did because there was always an ulterior motive and that was self-preservation.

I noticed for some reason that certain languages in and of themselves were very arrogant sounding when one truly listened to them. The sound of the language told one especially about the nationality and culture to a great degree and also the attitude of the people who spoke those languages! Even when those very same languages are not spoken and English, for example, is spoken by those very same people, the broken dialect itself in English, as I just said, is also arrogant sounding. Some of those languages are, for example, the German language where the letter "w" is pronounced like a very hard "v". Or one can take the

English language that sounds so highly sophisticated even when the dialect is, say, from Berkshire or the Hay Market Square accent! All the many English accents sound arrogant to me with no intention by the speaker most of the time to be so. Also when one is that background and speaks perfect American English, their personality in speaking also tends to sound arrogant and sarcastic, just as if the thought came instantly and was not thought up by the speaker himself.

The Italian language and the Hebrew language both appeal to me. One sounds almost poetic and the other so hospitable that I could listen to either language for hours whether they actually spoke the language or a broken English accent. The real Spanish also flows from the mouth very smoothly, and this is the Castillian language, which most in Latin America do not even speak. The real Spanish has a melodious sound to it, so if this President wants them to speak English or Spanish, then at least promote the real Spanish and not one that is totally slang and rude and does not wait to listen to another since also in Spanish there is no word for compromise or dissent; hence one can see why they do not really listen when another is talking. It is a mindset that is there without even thinking about it and is ingrained in the culture since as I just said there are no words for compromise or dissent which in essence means whatever one says means absolutely nothing and it is all or nothing and nothing in between which we also like to call being obstinate!

French is another language that is a Latin derivative, but if one listens to it, one gets that almost better-than-thou feeling when one hears it spoken fluently. Even the music from these peoples speak to one in such a way that one can almost tell what kind of people they are. So one's own nationality means very much to all, and no one is alike. So why would religion of another nation's way of worshipping GOD?

Many people misarticulate with the words like and dislike, and by that I mean one might say, "I do not like him for President" which would say nothing in the slightest about whether or not he is first qualified and whether or not he also has, most importantly, character. For example, one can vote for a candidate and know that by hearing him speak they probably would not get along with him if they ever would have met him and knew him personally, but that does not mean since I do not like him say as one would like a friend I might vote for him because of his character even though his qualifications were to be desired and by the way I believe the incumbent for me applies in this manner and that is why I did not vote for him or the other candidate but the other candidate I should say I did not vote for was for a completely different reason. Just like Michael Moore may say he is against the war but for a completely different reason than I myself would say! Today elections are really popularity contests that go on appearances even though John Kerry was menacing looking to say the least. But in reality most candidates win on looks, money, education, and mannerisms, etc., but not for the reason one should be elected for office, and that is to uphold the truth and not one's particular pick of truth but GOD'S truth alone!

My wife and I always try to find out if the candidate is pro abortion and if they are, then automatically we do not hesitate to not vote for them at all no matter what party! Character is very important, and most Presidents ever elected, I believe, did not have the character to hold such a high position. Only one President that I did vote for was Ronald Reagan and not because he was of a certain party but because he had character and high morals, and he opposed the anti-humanity of Communism consistently time and again. He did not belong also to the Council On Foreign Affairs or also the Tri Lateral Commission which were both internationalists organizations that recognized anybody at any time as long as they had power and money, just the same as the World Bank does and has been doing for many years. In essence they were once capitalists who went over to world socialism since it paid in bigger profits and more wealth and power for them and all billionaires are about money and power and nothing else.

When a billionaire buys something, he buys the people also without their knowledge, so he has bought in essence his own slaves who work for him without their knowledge. Nonetheless, the end is the same as if they would have known since human nature tends to always go for the evil and not the good. The only real good in any man is Jesus inside of his spiritual heart and without that, man is totally corrupt.

Yes, the only way of salvation was through GOD's grace, which came at Calvary about 2,000 years ago. Y'eshua Messiah was crucified, died, buried and then rose again in fulfillment of the Scripture, and whatever any Christian or non-Christian denomination says otherwise is totally wrong. He paid it all and nothing more can be done for salvation. As far as worshipping, then each nation must come to worship as their own nationality has come to do so and not by any intrusion by any worldwide religion that says it comes in the name of the Lord. Jesus told us to spread His Gospel and not religions and denominations, but what He had done and this was GOD in the flesh speaking.

When man interprets alone what he feels should be done, it is always wrong and that is why Jesus said that He would leave the Holy Spirit here to interpret and guide us while He ascended to the Father and is sitting at the right hand of the Father interceding for us believers once we have accepted His grace and grace alone and do not be fooled by any man's trickery about how one becomes saved plus the fact then we have an awesome responsibility to do what He wants us to do. We as believers were bought with a price. It was paid in full the way the Father said He wanted it to be.

I thought about how many people had been lied to about Jesus in the so called Christmas season, which was founded under a pagan heritage and yet in America even Christians celebrated this sinful day with pagan roots. Christmas became so commercialized that the Book of Revelation was right when it described at the end of the age that the church and not of Roman Catholicism but the real church would be a consumer driven church with democracies, and so we now hear this constantly over and over again and GOD is not a democratic do-as-you-wish GOD but an authoritarian GOD meaning a monarch type of GOD. America could not understand that at all since it had always lived with democracy, which was never in search of the truth but only about party ideology! America was part of Europeanism.

If one would say a monarch that would mean nothing to most Americans because they were going on life's own experience and not what the Bible said since He was King now and before and that is what a government had to be under Him. He was our government and has always been except we had fooled ourselves to believe that we had man over us instead of a holy GOD and a King. No government by man was even near perfect to what the King was like. Either we followed Jesus and the Word or who was the Word who became flesh as it stated in the Gospel of John in the very first Chapter and in the very first paragraph probably the greatest wording that man has ever known to describe who and what Jesus was, why He came, and all the power and mystery of this one great GOD in the Trinity that too was a mystery. "If you have seen me, you have seen the Father I and the Father are One."

America had totally gone astray with too much of the Old Testament and not enough of the New Testament for the old kind of "covenant" was gone and Jesus fulfilled the new covenant which was He came and resurrected and shall RETURN for His church at the end of this church age or this age of grace that He and He alone provided and nothing else! No one or no man can give any man salvation he can only preach and hear the Word and the Word was Christ alone and what He had done at Calvary and no name should ever appear before a holy GOD.

There were institutions and organizations all over the world who tried to usurp this message because they themselves had been deceived to believe in tradition more than in Jesus or they believed even in their national religion or international religion before Jesus and that was going no where with most of the Jews in the world but when the 70th Week of Daniel and thereafter would come then a remnant would be saved which, as I said before, meant all of the Jews here on earth.

No Gentile religion or denomination would ever replace Israel or the nation of Israel and the Jewish people, no matter how much that they would say that they were the Church! The Body of Christ was GOD'S only church with all the saints saved by grace alone and nothing else in the past in the present or in the future. This was the only Body of Christ and that is why Europe was turning to Islam because now the enemy was coming for his and others who he could deceive in the flesh.

We as America came under Europe and that was not such a good thing in the sense that Europe had done some very horrible things to the Jewish people as a whole, and that meant European-ism had spread almost all over the world with its John Locke type of socialism. That was totally opposite to what the real Gospel said about salvation and that was by faith and faith alone which was the only way to please GOD!

If any kind of denomination, let alone any non Christian religion, hated the Jewish people, then one could be certain to stay away from that since they too were in essence hating Jesus who was a Jewish man.

I once again remembered what I had thought about and later discussed about how GOD always calls to His sheep because no one comes by free will alone, not that GOD has ever coerced, but He picks first ones who He shall call into His family and they hear His voice for His flock always hear His voice. Many Christians oppose this and say then GOD has predestined. Yet did they not also have to choose? So the calling and the choosing was it always 100% or did it at least mean GOD would call and maybe some would still not, with free will, respond? Hence so that none should be lost (not that none would be ever lost) and between the two, there was a difference and they were not the same even though they sounded like they were.

GOD is GOD and can any of us know for sure GOD'S thoughts because His thoughts are not our thoughts and that meant that the finite could not really go into the realm of the infinite or the Infinite! GOD was always eternal and no one else and not even the angelic host were always there, just the Father, the Son and the Holy Spirit which have always been and shall always be and that the great controversies are how does one become saved and second did Jesus come already and nothing more than these 2 questions have to be answered and also the fact the Jesus was the only one to say He was equal to GOD!

When we really listen to these 3 things we shall see, for those who have an interest and those who appear that they do, that GOD puts in all men this search for Himself. Most do not find Him and get lost because of their own sin, Adam's fall, Satan, or the world itself that pulls to the evil side and the other side that gently sways to the pure side of GOD who is the only one who is pure and good and no one else since all and that means all have sinned and fallen short of the glory of GOD, which means glory to the Father which can only be done through Christ as a believer and through the power of the Holy Spirit and nothing whatsoever!

Man likes to change what GOD has had to say but GOD has never changed His Word so that man would come into his kingdom or even obey Him in all things. GOD is the same yesterday, today and tomorrow! This is the wonderful thing about Messiah He has truly done it all for all those who would believe what He said He was and that was GOD in the flesh and no less and could be equal to GOD.

Jesus was sent to destroy also the works of the devil and hence Satan has been judged and found guilty but has not been sentenced and That needs to be repeated so people here on earth can see that Satan is here!

The cult of Roman Catholicism and the reasons why: First, they have what they call a worldwide leader who is called the vicar of Christ and is called a Pope and does not just serve for the Vatican but for this religion's worldwide membership. Second they believe erroneously that Mary had no sin whatsoever and so she had to be perfect, right? Third they believe that works and church tradition are the way of salvation. Fourth, they have a Vatican or a businessmen's organization of highly educated priests or Cardinals and from which one is always chosen to be their Pope. They believe in praying to their saints and using a rosary also for the same purpose. Fifth, they believe one must confess to another human being such as a sinful priest and not to Jesus alone. Sixth, they do not believe in marriage and having children for their very own clergy, both men (the priests) and women (the nuns). Seventh, they believe that communion is the actual body and blood of Christ and some even believe that is the way to salvation. Eighth, they believe that only a priest can read the Bible but now have changed that to all members. Ninth, they believe that they or their religion is the only way to salvation. Tenth, they believe that there is a purgatory where one can be prayed out of into heaven. Eleventh, they believe in having many statues that are molded in the image of man and woman which GOD Himself told everyone never to make anything in the image of anything. Twelfth, they believe in lighting candles for the dead. They also believe that any Catholic saved or unsaved can take communion. They believe, at least a part of them, in Liberation Theology which occurs mostly in Hispanic America when the priests and nuns become involved in revolutionary causes. They believe in refusing to give communion to one who is not a Catholic, and believe that Peter was their first Pope when he was a Jew. Some even believe that Joseph and Mary were Italian and not Jewish! They have a crucifix and not just a cross, which would appear that Jesus has not resurrected. Also, Christmas and Easter are both pagan holidays in the sense that the roots derive from pagan holidays. They also, because of All Saints Day, brought Halloween or Satan's day to America and even have this hierarchy from Pope, to Cardinal, to Bishop, to Monsignor which means my lord, to Pastor, to priest, to deacon, to sacristan to altar boys and altar girls, to nuns and lay people who teach only about Roman Catholicism, as well as principals in school. They tell one how much they should tithe, which in and of itself means 10% according to Scripture. I personally have found them very highly anti-Semitic. They believe in confirmation and receive a name from that. They indoctrinate children into their own religion and not so much as to what the Bible says. They do not believe in salvation by grace alone and are the only ones to have an Apocrypha in the middle of their Bible which is not holy inspired. They were in charge of the Crusades, and Constantine made it a state religion like Islam does. They also were behind the Spanish Inquisition which persecuted the Jewish people in Spain unless they converted to Roman Catholicism. Many would say, since they believe that Roman Catholicism believes in the Trinity, that it is not a cult but yet there are all these above mentioned things that GOD in His Word has never ever said that one should or must do in order to be a Christian or to understand anything about GOD Himself. And now they have an epidemic of homosexuality and pedophilia and of course are not the only ones, but have kept it secret and have not prosecuted their own for such an abomination. Because of celibacy, more than anything, and that one must be single, I believe it has promoted sexual deviants to enter the clergy, and not sexual deviants only but ones who should have gotten married and had a wife and children. Sex in marriage is a wonderful thing which GOD meant for almost all to enjoy and to be fruitful and multiply, and Catholics are by far the hardest to witness to that I personally have found. The higher clergy are, or appear, almost like royalty amongst their own parishioners and money and materialism is a most important thing with the Roman Catholics in America. They repeat the same prayers over and over again as the heathen do and their garbs are very expensive to say the least as well as huge cathedrals all over the world that now are mostly empty.

Only a few Catholics I believe become Christians according to Scripture and that is by grace and grace alone and there are some Protestants who hate Catholics which is a sin in itself but my observation is that one should not hate them but pray for them and witness to them since for centuries they have been mislead and misguided in regards to Scripture and salvation by grace and grace alone. The Roman Catholic church also is highly anti-Semitic and hence that is one of the most major sinful things about it and it transcends around the world. Their children then begin to see the flesh and not Jesus as being first: and materialism overtakes them suddenly.

The incident at Ruby Ridge with Randy Weaver, the Green Beret is a sad affair under the socialist Presidency of Bill Clinton and his Sodomite United States Attorney Janet Reno. When Randy Weaver's 14 year old son heard yelling and gunshots down the hill and had found out that his dog had been shot and started to yell obscenities at them and as he ran up the hill he too was murdered in cold blood. His mother was carrying a two-year-old baby in her arms and she too was murdered, but the baby survived as well as Randy Weaver. The story goes that Randy Weaver was a white supremacist, but Bill Clinton was for sure a Communist Red. The same Japanese government sniper here was also at WACO in Texas the one that precipitated Timothy McVeigh's insane bombing along with other Moslems and Terry Nichols. None of these federal agents were prosecuted to the fullest extent of the law, but why not? Janet Reno was the top law enforcement officer at that time in the United States as US Attorney General! Yes much explaining still has to be done about that whole Clinton Administration and they still must be brought to trial which would involve so many people in government even now that it would take years but nonetheless it has to be done to clean out the Communists within our own government now and this incumbent can only joke about it which shows his regard for his very own nation of America!

In America today if it does not involve the so-called "black and white" something that Lenin created years ago then it seems to be swept under the rug since there are so many lies and murders involved in this so called civil rights socialism which is nothing more than another way to usurp America's founding and undermine our Biblical foundation and it appears if color is not included than it must not be at all important at all. A constant barrage of propaganda of race, race and more race to the point of ad nauseum. Everything has to wait until this so-called issue is resolved and it has been and even beyond what others here in America have and that means that civil rights themselves are always superior rights such as affirmative action which was used in Nazi Germany to keep all Jews out of the government jobs! If one looks close enough, one can see how this cancerous civil rights issue has ruined America for good and created animosity not so much as to reparations but that now the blacks themselves have become so very arrogant since government has told them do what you want to anyone at anytime and we shall defend your right to do it and even exonerate you with our own politicians or lawyers who can change any law with a majority or a minority vote nonetheless. The American Negro has gone from one of a Christian nature and always a willingness to help all others and an agricultural people to ones who now see themselves as the ones to get even at any cost and no one dare say that because of political correctness which says if one does than they themselves must be bigoted and prejudice and must be evil! Hollywood and the media and the New York Times all support this along with big business not to mention our own government which likes to see all of this on the front burner to deflect from themselves the politicians, all the corruption they are involved in over their pretty little necks. On and on this goes and now has infiltrated all the races to emulate that African American can get away with all of that so why can I not get away with it being the fact that the black now represents almost everything that is arrogant and revolutionary and our government loves it that much more as well as the rich and well educated, the middle class, and even now the poor. Yes, some see through this very facade that the Communists have infiltrated all the civil rights programs and gotten away with it because of being first black, then red, then yellow and then mulatto and then Hispanic and then 3rd world person then Islamic Moslems and so forth and so on!

Now we have a multicultural state here in America which means that eventually the hate shall build to such a crescendo unless of course some go along with it who are Anglo-Saxons such as this incumbent and his merry group of Robin Hoods who really steal from the poor to give to the rich with his constant spending of taxpayers' dollars and seems to believe he is some kind of royalty since his ancestry comes from England! This is where we have come to where neighbor vs. neighbor since the one neighbor refuses to assimilate unless they can take over and destroy our very way of life which shall not go down so easy with all Americans since they know that this is evil and the fact that the American people do not trust now their own officials in government that is the true blue patriotic Americans who live by the Bible and want America to be a Judeo-Christian nation and the fruits should always show and not what they just say and pretend to do in front of the media cameras such as Tony Campolo who was a good friend of Bill Clinton. Our politicians associate with anybody no matter what and then rescind what they said they believed in just to take the pressure off of them and then they get out and go back to their private lives so they can live in peace and quiet and ones like Kennedy, Boxer, Feinstein, the Clintons still agitate and no one yet questions them about their treasonous activities and even one of the above who was involved in a murder and the fact that all the above are all socialists which is nothing new and want us to forget their infamous deeds and crimes and go on as if nothing has occurred and that we should also fall in love with socialism just as they have! Americans or true Americans must constantly oppose these evil leaders but to do so shall require some sacrifice and none of our leaders wants to give up their good way of life along with all its comforts and luxuries for the sake of the truth and nothing but the truth so help you GOD!

Apartments, one way streets, abbreviations, group thought and policies, categorization of people, places and things, etc. all showed that socialism had taken over in America, but still our politicians and the media called all of this a democracy to make us all feel much better about how certain groups such as theirs would decide for all of us! The apartment dilemma meant that property was just to hard to keep and now with the illegals another part of socialism itself one had felt that Stalin or Lenin had been in charge since millions and millions of foreigners would come here and millions and millions of American citizens would have to be displaced and this incumbent knew this very well but did not care and not to own any property would be better for all especially at the top! After all what was the one way streets that made a simple ride on a city street almost like a maze and made things appear to most to proceed only in one direction and never to have been able to go the other direction on that very same street at all! Then we have the abbreviations of states and names and words that meant that words and places were irrelevant which meant also that eminent domain would apply in some cases. This was how we became to now be a union like the Union of Soviet Socialists Republics since each state was so separated by multiculturalism that one would have thought one was in a different country when they crossed the state line from one state to another and this was also this village affect by Hillary which meant in essence the soviet village. The reparations had been paid by government out of our tax dollars because of the dead beat dads and their mates procreating for the purpose of sexual pleasure alone and never having to work at all for a living and so the reparations, as I just said, were paid in full by the "peasants" here in America who had no choice since of civil rights' socialism and with that came this group mentality that said one had to be first a certain color, then a certain age, then a certain sex, then a certain type of deviant sexual person and on and on! Yes socialism had grown so much that without government we would not survive or was it the other way around?

Taxation without representation which meant that voting or not voting meant absolutely the same be cause at the top they all came from the same can of worms. There were no distinguishing marks that made them different and no one could ever say that any were poor or uneducated and in fact they were too well educated for their own good if they had any of that in themselves any longer but their theatrics were very good at least to the majority and is that not what one had to fool in a democracy a majority since the truth was never an issue?

How can a rich man believe in GOD? What requests can he ask for in the flesh since materialism is usually the only request and he only wants more? He depends on ego and self-esteem and could careless about the rest of the world. For him life comes around only once so he must gather as much as fast as he can. For him also there is no after life or he has been deceived by the enemy to believe that lie! His has influenced at least the nation into a playground for childish things. There are amusement parks, fast food chains, computer games and other nonsense, metal tin cars, eat till your sick, nothing with a real purpose, spur of the moment activities, a plastic world of credit with no responsibility, etc. America is a big huge playground and amusement park of emptiness and has a huge spiritual void. Constant sermons on how good we have it, how good we shall have it and how good we are!

This facade that has inundated us is from John Locke's socialism that said, "Now with this new enlightenment from man we shall need no GOD only entertainment, industry, (German style), because now we have freed ourselves from the slave labor, and the Middle Ages unto this utopia nowhere on earth." Thank goodness for now at least John Kerry a Jew has not gotten in and not because I think he is Jewish but because he is Jewish to others! What a disaster for all Jews in Israel and America and anti-Semitism would have grown and grown? Thus he lost and as for now the borders remain open for Jews to ingress and egress. Just say the word Jew and anti-Semitism appears so quickly. Let this Anglophile do some thing wrong very wrong and most shall soon be forgotten instantly. The Anglo-Saxons run America and are running it into the ground. It is they who have the most to lose financially in the Middle East!

Much debris from Europe came to America in the form of anti-Semitism. The Reformation and the Vatican are indeed enough to make one see about the Masons, the Teutonics, the Illuminati to create fiction story about the Protoccols Of The Elders Of Zion.

Did only rich or well to do Europeans come to America since most other poor people from there never made it? America was always, except for the Pilgrims, a well to do country backed by good finances or why else could they afford slaves and have 153 Rhodes' Scholars from Oxford and Cambridge here at one time? Even today the lower class financially is nothing like the lower class around the world. There is quite a difference in our" serfdom "from their serfdom and again John Locke's socialism one can point to time and again.

Even the Jews of favor financially were welcomed here but not the Russian Jews. Since the beginning our Presidents were rich and well to do and well educated and hence others also well to do lead our country such as inventors, lawyers, bankers, generals, etc. So many of the well to do always had control of America and most were from at first England and Germany, then came other Europeans who were also well to do and promoted their capitalism to include slave labor which always is an evil as the Bible clearly states. These were not maidservants or otherwise but honest to goodness slaves.

This was, "How can I live easily without physical labor and still maintain my status quo?" Marxism spread just because of this capitalism which said some do not have to physically work while others must be made slaves. Two wrongs do not make a right.

See now today in America that this avarice has transcended to every part of America and even the poor are not really that poor as in foreign countries besides Europe, but only our children in many ways! We have come full circle almost from capitalism to now socialism and possibly now Communism except yet the Gulags for the older or the ones already born have not been set in place yet but we have murdered 50,000,000 plus unborn innocent children for John Locke's socialism or materialism.

Who actually benefited when slave labor was okay not that it ever was okay with GOD? Was it not the same ones now in office and others such as the Roman Catholic Church who only saw dollars signs when they came to America? The Protestant pastors here had to live like kings and so much for "do not muzzle the oxen when they are treading out the grain."

America has a very short history and probably shall remain that because it has relied on economic capitalism which always goes to socialism and does not an elite always like socialism? The supply can never meet their demand for more and more and hence the people themselves, we who are corrupted by the very same ideology of materialism as in slavery since we now do it with Red China's slavery!

When has any priest or pastor ever dressed as a ultra-orthodox rabbi does? This would be unheard of with the neat haircuts and close shaven beard and seersucker suits with 4 button down sleeves.

It is so very hard to worship Jesus today in any type of church since the churches have constantly been concerned by self and self esteem and being entertained with music and otherwise. It never stops!

Even people at Ellis Island had to have enough to enter to get in. That is why the refugees from the Exodus could not land here because they were quite poor and also they were of Jewish extraction and this all happened under Eisenhower.

The well educated clergy were there to serve whom? Christianity in America had the more worldly Christians like in Corinth in the Bible and the spiritual Christians never made it here hardly which meant that all the works of the unspiritual would be burned up because it was not of Christ and the elect would barely make it through the fire! Again John Locke's socialism is soon cleaning house because that age is closing and a new age is opening hopefully up for Jesus first and whatever He provides and not philosophies by man for the betterment of man. Christians are not here for the betterment of man but for spiritual findings in Jesus and this is what the Enlightenment left out!

We were poor but not ever destitute and to own land in America was very common place for most, but we did not own any but nonetheless we managed without government's interference at all and moved many times with no harm done but usually found our surroundings beyond our very means which gave me the blessing to know and to see the real blessings in life from GOD.

The blessings in America were so called monetary valued and had lost their purpose as being GOD'S real blessings. When one can get out of bed, can hear and can see, can walk and talk and think and can enjoy the sounds of nature and have their physical and mental health (and what did Jesus mostly all the time minister to?) then truly one can be filled with real joy and not in pursuit of happiness which is materialism from moment to moment!

The shallow world of America has nothing to offer to those that Christ died for their sins, no for our salvation.

There is so much here that is not there in heaven! We have been born into wealth and hence we die. What have we accomplished through . . . Not only very much sin which was intentional but even our Sabbaths were extinct, and we are too tired to give a helping hand.

Why is slavery overstressed here? Is it not because of avarice and more avarice and which capitalism followed almost naturally a path to socialism which is usually its path and now civil rights have ruined the work ethic along with the unions for so many people since avarice was placed over one's immortal soul.

Every war, it appears, was for money avarice and with that the control of power for without money power remains ever elusive. Where can an immature grown man who does no work and be paid the sum of $40,000,000 ? And this is not a playground of idiocy in sports, in good citizenship?

People function totally from their five senses instead of spiritual sense which cannot be seen at all. We are not looking with the eyes of Jesus nor are our thoughts of His also. We see as an instinctive animal would to take and plunder and not think twice about it. But animals only have instinct to rely on we have reason but reason alone can make us cold without a spirit filled heart of Jesus. Compassion, mercy and pity means servanthood by Him for others through you and the Holy Spirit.

We now transport or carry one service to another and real work has dissipated next to nothing. The body has become rendered physically useless and chronic arthritis, impotence, heart attacks, cancers, strokes, barren wombs, etc. have now become common place not to mention VD and AIDS and HIV and still we say all is well!

When a sick man has been sick so long he tends to see it as an only way of life for him. One forgets to have two arms, two legs, two ears, two hands, two eyes, etc. We become incapacitated because of our own failure to understand that a healthy hard working body helps the mind and the heart to think better about others first then ourselves and paralysis does set in from lack of labor and mental thought that go hand and hand and that is why most farmers are the best all around workers in the nation.

When any "race" meaning color fails to act like part of the human race one can only conclude that the Neanderthal man has visited upon them although evolution is only by years and decades and not ages and ions!

Evaluation is only another way of saying all men are created mutually equal or all animals are created equal and the latter applies to Darwinism! Since the English in their own private lives on the whole one could see why Darwin would come up with such an insane idea. Remember the rich and well educated are not always homo sapiens they also can be homosexuals or some other species since Darwin did not mention how they evolved or did he? This metamorphosis if one can call it that can only make one conclude that we are what Darwin says we are or Darwin was himself a mutation from his own evolutionary theory! This cross mixing of "man" without a soul as an animal or the "animal" with a soul as a man leads one to conclude that at random can this evolutionary theory ever exist and if that is the case then at random Darwin so chose his own species based just upon that at random insanity! One can see how well this applies to wolves in a pack so very well. And once the tiger can meow, then we shall know for sure that one stage at least has developed but in which direction? Is it better to be a tiger or a house cat depending on where one derives their food from? Now can the feline species understand if they are more domesticated?

In a million years, which time has never known since man himself is only here about 7,000 years and the earth 10,000 how does one suppose that man's metamorphosis took so short a time when beyond time itself cannot be counted into evolution's picture and if the human eye is perplexing to explain how about the neo-cortex in the brain of man? Consciousness determines existence hence man can reason and learn and with animals existence alone prevails which means animals have no knowledge, no memory, no ability to reason, but only retain through instinct or being programmed into as such by this very same instinct that is for them that is the animal world their way of living. So this conclusion can be drawn. No one can murder an animal ever; one can only kill one! As with human beings they can be murdered. Why? They have a neo-cortex with which to reason. So a murder affects human beings and killing affects Darwin's animal world?

If an animal cannot remember or reason as to the why or why not, one can only conclude that animals are dumb in the sense we must oversee them as Adam and Noah did. Dumb, for in their makeup their brain does not have a neo-cortex to reason or make decisions with the conscientiousness of man and the instinct and the animal is innately made and that is why dogs bite and cats scratch, but all humans talk!

So if one should by chance experience a visit to the zoo and a "Darwin" should appear on all two's and walk and not hop, but in case he does not, then we know for sure that the zoo has bars for that very reason because an animal cannot reason but only survive where he habitats, but a human being must live where he is!

If man can always worry about only money, then what is faith for? For the well to do or most of America then we appear not to need faith! Faith is to give glory to the Father first and foremost. Without faith it is impossible to please GOD hence man needs money more than GOD in this case and then he can please himself and America has certainly done that. "Babylon" now has done what almost anyone can do with money especially when one loves it so passionately. With that comes the vilest evil man has ever known but we are a "good" country comes the lie. Are we comparing ourselves to Islam, Hinduism or what or the rest of the world without materialism? That is not a true comparison. First we were given Scripture, then freedom, then wealth then much more and we used it ultimately for evil! Other countries have much much less than us and yet they supply more to GOD'S kingdom then we ever have in our entire history because we gave only of our surplus!

Our main concern is not how do I get my next meal, or provide shelter for my family, but where can I get my next drink, or fix or where can I get money for gambling, pornography, Hollywood filth, liquid manure, over eating, over spending, cosmetics, clothing, cigarettes, cars, gas, computers, trips, education. Yes, everything but what faith asks for and that is that He shall provide all of your needs. He does not need your urging as to His timing for the glory of the Father! I hear buts and more buts. "But what if.."? Yes, those buts are worries about money so why use or waste faith on things that have no use in the kingdom or for another and especially only for self? One can only eat so much, buy so much so why the worry for worry is unbelief in the flesh. Be satisfied with what GOD says and gives to you not in money necessarily but more importantly in faith itself!

The faith of a nation is important for its soul and the survival of, people as one nation under GOD and nothing else since GOD'S laws are adequate to fulfill our entire life. He could have made more and more laws so we should be thankful He made the ones and not ever being in the flesh and that is why Jesus came since He could experience what it was like to be a human being with feelings and emotions and pain and comfort! Do we want more laws so that there is no longer any law that would not exist which would mean we would not be able to live as human beings or should we be the way we are under grace or undeserved merit?

Let us be thankful to a loving GOD removing the Book of Leviticus and now we have Jesus' grace.

Artificial hair, artificial teeth, artificial breast, artificial plants, artificial hearts, artificial grass, artificial people! America has made good use of the artificial everywhere. I have observed for quite some time also there are artificial men and artificial women. Transsexuals in disguise just like where else but Nazi Germany, and this has spread now to Nazi-led America! Artificial sweeteners, artificial colorings, artificial money—now that is not a misnomer either. Since legal tender is now artificial, it is little more worth than monopoly money is it is the theory of the economic revolution that is the one world economical system. When American legal tender is no more, and it soon shall be, then the peso shall equal what our $1.00 bill shall be worth: absolutely zero. There is no gold standard to say that $1.00 has $1.00 worth of gold to back it up which FDR took us off of the Gold Standard another socialist move so that only certain ones would have all the hard assets since liquid or soft assets are only based on paper work which can buy absolutely nothing with the one world economic system. Also all the gold shall do nothing if there is no food or necessities for survival such as water, medicines, food, etc. to be able to buy. Then gold becomes actually "worthless" as a bartering tool. Probably the one who has land, water, food, some assets, shelter, clothing, and a little savings shall do well as long as he can stay out of the collectivization of one's farmland completely and as time goes on that shall become almost impossible.

What shall it take for America to economically fall? It appears it already has occurred and Islam in higher education in Europe is the main part. An atheistic continent shall pull us down plus our own love of money which means power for a while with no assets to uphold our power by only so called promissory notes to repay or for us to repay our loans to this one world economic system.

In our own housing one can see Anglo-Saxon mentality of row after row of row homes like chicken coops, mass production with 100% mass building to squeeze the life out of people and so maintain less land for each individual while the government owns everything surrounding that slum. Unable to breathe let alone move these roll homes were or had to be a Germanic invention of robotics where most all look the same hence a system.

People rent land, lease land but do not down right own land and taxes make it impossible ever to own the land free and clear. In Russia in 1990 their government said, "You can buy your home, but you must lease the land it sits on" and also in Japan they have mortgages for 90 years since 4 generations usually live together. Money tied up for 2 lifetimes at least in usurious interest without a way out and soon the state shall find a better way? Land that can never be called one's private property now because of the banks! The intricacies are in much more details but the affect is the same landless people or slaves once again the serfs or common man with no middle class! The only thing preventing that today is man's not selling out his home for $1.00 which would dissipate his savings and equity since the corrupt market would attack buying all private land. The Great Society's much lend lease land so that no property was privately owned but government built and owned all with taxpayers' dollars so hence group socialism through Community Development (banks) again our taxes had gone up now and group style living such as in high rise tenement buildings and also to get the public use to socialism in the way they would live in the future! These government officials were our own kind of "robbing hoods" who stole from the people to give to the rich which to them was an honest proposal called the "all or nothing" and the 9/10's of the law decree. Artificial play money means for example that bread use to cost about .10 a loaf and now sells for $1.00 which means that $10 is $1.00 was about 1/10 of that $1.00.

Now it would take $10.00 with of course that same .10. Ten dollars is now the same in price buying power as yesterday's $1.00 and as one can see it would take now not a real 10 cents but an over inflated .10 to now buy that loaf if we were in yesterday's time which is insane and is more insane today because the dollar is really worth 1% and taxes increase so that taxes can be paid at a higher rate equal to almost what that first 10 cents really was so hence there is no value in legal tender with the instant increase in government spending at the old dollar value. In other words the old 10 cents was 10% and the new 10 cents is 1% of what it used to be. So with more money comes less buying power for the consumer. Prices must stabilize (never with government) or else socialism must take over which shall then spend only according to a particular elite group or other groups and so the majority gets the small remainder which is soon to come starting with the unborn, the elderly, the newly married with children so forth and so on. One must now have $10.00 to buy a 10 cents loaf of bread at yesterday's fair prices and since bread is actually about $1.00 then one from yesterday must now carry $10.00 today for a loaf of bread. One needs an honest old $1.00 not $1.00 x 1-$10.00. This is what (not inflationi) but avarice and supporting socialism and lending money at 1'% interest has done and even more so with socialism since prices always rise no matter if the supply supersedes the demand which is the opposite under capitalism yet capitalism out of control such as Mobil/Exxon escalates so much again because of no set limitations and human nature so interest on say $1.00 is 6% which would equal 6 cents and on $6,000,000 at 6 would equal $360,000 and on $6,000,000,000 at 6% is $360,000,000 and should one compound daily well one can see that now money is power and power is money at this level and absolute power corrupts absolutely! This is no longer free enterprise or private entrepreneurship but an oligarch of business above democracies and even dictatorships because they too need money and wealth to sustain power plus ruthlessness.

If World Bank lends $100,000,000 at a simple 1% less than you could ever get a mortgage at in America then one can see how capitalism upholds socialism because it needs its natural resources to survive that is capitalism which is only an economic system and socialism is an ideology or a whole way of life!

Let socialism die do not support it and see what it can grow and that would be only what the earth has naturally put there! It appears America is ready to give up its way of life totally for something strangely foreign.

If I would go to my friend's house without being invited and demanded he feed and take care of me I am like an illegal into his home uninvited and enter into his home and then demand my so-called share of my friend's wealth, then one might say "what does that have to do with capitalism vs. socialism?" First I am coercing one illegally to support one and since capitalism needs not people but natural resources it must barter and in this case more people illegals for the rights to those natural resources to promote capitalism's stock market to make it financially solvent and with a socialist country hence now what does capitalism do? It upholds socialism and socialism shall then take, by force if it has to, what it was almost given for free by another nation such as America and Canada which deems no better for us either except it has more wealth, but also is a socialist state. This is this NAFTA Treaty which is nothing more than what Yalta did!

Free trade? Hardly so. Barter people for natural resources and in Mexico kidnapping is a big thing amongst the rich and well educated that they require guards everywhere that they go! Do we, too, want this kind of living socialism that is already in our own government and next would be in our very own streets and homes and neighborhoods and communities?

Yes, we appear to be heading in the same direction as Russia went before their revolution. Maybe mankind for the most part had no real interest for salvation since GOD Himself had not called them to Himself, for none can come to the Father unless He calls them unto Himself! In America even public opinion had died since people were functioning not as real human beings but almost in a sense like German robots. Was not America, for the most part, nothing like the Germans except for their ancestors that were here? We were a more compassionate people with regards for what life's purpose had in store for us at least we use to be and now . . . . America had come under the demise that maybe we were what we were now doing without ever questioning as to the reason why but only knowing that now at this very moment was what was most important even though it may have absolutely nothing to do with GOD. We went along the path to sure destruction because we had only known what the enlightenment had brought and that was materialism.

For without faith it is impossible to please GOD, and who gave or gives us our own faith if not GOD Himself? We were, as you will be, doing what did not necessarily come naturally but in fact what was very unnatural for us and that was to do what Europeanism had left to us for the 3rd and 4th generations as if we had been born into this John Locke mysticism. Whatever was important in the spiritual realm there was always so much more important in the finance and the political realm which meant we had lost our purpose as a nation in GOD'S overall plan in this thing known as time!

Big business for many years has been so corrupt and has been collaborating with our very enemy that we became immune to the devastating affects it had on all of us and with now hardly any public opinion the spiritual and moral things were blasé to us here in America. We had broken anti-trust laws which were probably the best restraints for capitalism since capitalism would always seek not a higher level but always a lower immoral level called socialism. These big businessmen did not care about the sovereignty of the United States but only for what could go into their own barns which were already full and overflowing. Our government officials were up to their necks in this also for all they saw was a way to be on top of the business world which was nothing more than socialism working its way to the very top of our own government and we knew that no government was perfect but to be atheistic would prove once and for all that GOD would not be on our side because we did not want Him to be. The Constitution is no longer a reality and is now only parchment paper which most constitutions are and do not uphold anytime for any length of time at all. We had plenty of judicial activism which had absolutely nothing to do with the rule of law or the justice system and we also had moral relativism which meant that values were all relative including the 10 Commandments! We had a combination of Communism by class warfare and now racial socialism like in Nazi Germany.

Armand Hammer in the USSR and Kissinger and Haig in Red China did not draw the line between good vs. evil but only between the rich vs. the poor and the illiterate such as in Red China where 80% of the people were peasants and just wanted bread and water and not what our own form of socialism would give to their own leaders! They called this free trade but I called it "free labor" or "free slave labor" at the price of murder and death for those who would have to sacrifice their lives for our own better way of life for cheaper prices and all one had to do was to go to any WalMart or Dollar store and find what slave labor did to prices since all the labor workers were not paid one iota and still they had the nerve to charge a price for these products!

Even today businessmen serve in the United States Congress for avarice, and doctors and lawyers and other professionals were aligning themselves not with the peasants but with the Communists since it appealed to their better taste in ideology! They only see what their predecessors have seen, and before the color red always comes the color green. They have no country and one cannot call them Americans for to do so would be saying that they believed in the pledge of allegiance and the Constitution but most of all in a holy and righteous GOD!

These are the "robbing hoods" which, in essence, explains what they are and this is they rob and steal at big levels and do it immorally and are thugs or hoods like a gang and make up this internationalist's group of well dressed mobsters. They shall not be prosecuted because our own government also is in up to their necks in pilfering trillions of dollars and that the American people were voting for the lesser of• two evils they really had no good choice to vote for any candidate that really thought about the sovereignty of America and just how free it would be for our own grandchildren and possibly children. Even our own United States Senate was in bed with the Communists and the sheiks so to them it was only natural for them to understand that only the fittest survive! Either politics or money makes America run no matter what profession and the spiritual realm has a complete void here!

Nothing is new on Wall Street. It is the same as before but much worse now since 9/11 and not because of the bombings but because now these investors became even more ruthless to get what they wanted no matter what price the American people first had to pay in the bombing and now with our young men over there who were getting killed, maimed, crippled, blinded, mentally unstable, etc. and this was not a war as that of the Vietnam conflict where we again so chose to lose before we had started, to not consider even our own men's lives on the line and plus the fact at that time we did not have the moral resolve to fight against the evil of Communism and now again and only in this sense did we once again not have the resolve to defend now our own turf and which made this even that much more worse since it told the whole world what a paper tiger we were! Our so called leaders did not know their right from their left and up from down and could care less what happened just so that they could go on living with the attitude that 'please don't bother me; just leave me alone' and we accelerated so much that now even on the mainland and here we only thought even more about self-preservation but for how long or whenever we were ready and we were ready to change our very lifestyle in regard to liberty and freedom of conscience since it appeared so convenient to do so as it had when the Soviets had taken country after country while we twiddled our thumbs back during the Cold War. What now could we sacrifice for some good peace and quiet and still be left to do at least the physical things we had always done and that was to "eat, drink and be merry".

Big business in the West shall sit down with anyone at anytime for any reason if it means for a profit. We will recognize any regime just so they had the money to repay their loans no matter how they had gotten them. It was a little like our own car dealers who sold cars to people who had no yearly income but would buy a black gold lined Mercedes for about $125,000 with no questions asked! Not enough people had given up their lives as of yet for this one world government but soon it was coming to that because nuclear arsenals were already being allowed to be developed as long as Red China could liquidate them since now Red China knew what they were really dealing with in the West. Would the West give up everything just for a peace of mind and would the West be willing to be second in the world since now that they had what they wanted and that was their total freedom from any moral restraints but nonetheless Red China did not want any of the West's offers when it could just take it soon at will! Checkmate was soon on the board and the West thought that to appease Red China the dragon would suffice since they were making so much progress in the field of human relations and humanity! Whose blood though this time would have to pay for such shortsightedness since most of the Russian peasants were no longer around? Would Israel for instance be a good down payment for at least the Moslem world, but what about Red China that did not have any missiles pointed at them but at us? Who would suffice as bait? Maybe America itself or even Europe and that would leave possibly the British

Isles and us and then maybe the Red Chinese would have their fill but a dragon has a huge appetite and much more of a one than the Soviets ever had for they would do it by economic ways even though we helped them and along came Reagan that burst their balloon but now we had a different kind of President who would do business at least with the Islamic world no matter what and England though would have to be spared first instead of the United States but then again he wanted us also to be included in that pact! Yes, the Russian peasants of about 20,000,000 paid with their very lives what Armand Hammer, FDR and Churchill had done to open up Pandora's Box! The ones to blame would be the middle class in. America for not listening to what was already privy information and highly secretive but nonetheless they would, be blamed for not listening or not knowing even if as I just said they had no idea of what was going on at the very top of society in the Western part of the world especially since the he was always being used in the West as to their real achievement and as for socialism they would tell it like it is and it would inspire and yes inspire the young in the West to pursue this social utopia and all would know what to expect with this social justice!

Yes, these Ivy Leaguers sure knew what they were doing and had felt since the Jews' hands were tied up in Israel that now they could pursue Islam and Red China with a hands down policy which was being sold to them by the finest in the business that is the business of Communism's ideology! Now we had for the 5th straight consecutive time in the White House someone who really knew how to play checkers but understood absolutely nothing about chess and treated the first one like the second and felt that they would surely win in the end because since they believed in self preservation themselves they also thought that the Red Chinese government did the same as them but Communism had always believed in the destruction of man kind which could include themselves and was nothing like the kind of self preservation with self delusion' that our Western leaders had thought or did they really think at all?

So much was done under John Locke's socialism just here in America such as David Rockefeller's ownership of most of

Latin America and his own ownership of IBM, Kodak, Exxon, K-Mart, Kresge's, Jupiter, and most of all President of World Bank which had about 100,000 business and important names in two little black books with 50,000 in each one on his whisper jet that travelled to the Vatican, the Knesset, Moscow, Peking, etc. David also spoke Spanish, German and English fluently and graduated from Harvard Business School. Then there was Mr. Hearst who owned Knight-Ridder publishing and also was a billionaire and had a museum in San Diego made out of solid gold objects and of course Patty Hearst who was a disappointment since she would have been the heiress to this large estate except that she had other plans of her very own! The Eatons of Ohio were others, the Melons of Pittsburgh, the Stoshberries of Philadelphia, etc.

Prudential, Burger King, Archer Daniels, Scott Paper, Mobil /Exxon, Chase Manhattan Bank, AT and T, Johnson and Johnson, Bayer Aspirin, Heinz Foods, Levi Strauss, and many many more were all either pro infanticide or pro homosexual and these were not some run-of-the-mill small companies but were worldwide, and these were the socialistic ideas for which they stood!

Can they get rich and powerful or be so high in public and non public policies that they forever escape prosecution completely? Apparently so since all the people I have mentioned in government or big business have never even served one day in jail for all of their crimes and treason that they committed over all of these years. Incredible? No. "Yes, the love of money was the root to all kinds of evil" and the above shows so clearly that is what has happened to the West that is this John Locke socialism but with the name of capitalism which only stood for greed and in the East the transformation of native people from their own habitat to be educated where else but at the Ivy League schools and Oxford and Cambridge in England! "How Harvard Hates America" was a must read for all Americans who wanted to really know what they taught about America itself right here in New England and even in the proper name one got the conclusion that we were the "New" England and the Old England was still in London!

Yes, a wolf sheds its fur but not its habits was a true saying in regards to certain nationalities who refused to let go of their hold of the entire West and we in America would play second fiddle even though we looked like we were out in front but then it was us who were bombed in 9/11.

So what was this freedom worth if one was afraid to leave their home or apartment for fear of being murdered and now even in one's own residence one could be done in? What had this so called freedom been when now people with money had moved into conclaves or a circle the wagons type of development with mortgages and interests for decades and homes built out of "sand"? If one was poor, then freedom meant from one day to the next to survive not only physically but spiritually from the hell of multicultural ism or Marxist/Leninism that plagued all those neighborhoods and only the strong survive really! Elderly who most assuredly had not outlived their own children but who were ostracized because of the, pain and problem they posed for others especially if they had little or no money! There was freedom to move around but that was it and that freedom was not so free in the sense that one could be taking their lives into their own hands and not because of lack of law enforcement but because of judicial reform and when wealth can do so much for the criminal!

Why were so many blacks as well as secular Jews turning to Roman Catholicism? I could remember only Floyd Patterson the boxer who had been one in the 50's. Also more and more of Roman Catholicism tried to push their Christ's Mass season along with the Jewish Hanukkah together so that one began to wonder about the Jews themselves that were going from the frying pan into the fire? One could almost see this very conception of the one world religion or the harlot spoken about in the Bible. Again the Jews were being mislead, but then again Roman Catholicism's materialism appealed to the secular and extravagant Jews in America.

Many businesses had trouble even taking orders on the phone and could not even get a name down at all or even a proper address or even a telephone number or the business name and yet this was not the U.S. Postal Service's fault for once. Computers were making people actually illiterate from not using their own brains and relying on what someone else said was the truth or the facts!

How was America staying afloat with such hodge podge of socialism when the right hand did not know what the left hand was doing? Of course if all was taken for granted that it was the gospel truth which meant anything could replace the something or this spiritual void in America. But what spiritual void? We tithed, we gave, we helped, we shared, etc but all in our own spare time which was not so spare any longer! Everyone was reaching for the brass ring!

Knowledge was more important than truth and occupied man's mind constantly. Our kind of science proved that man was from ape and that the ozone layer was depleted and that a spotted owl or a turtle or even an insect had creative worth above man himself! Our children were educated but in just what no one seemed to really know or care?

As I was saying, the elderly were orphans and had no relatives, at least not ones who wanted to attend and take care of them! They were the last to listen to, and the young were brought to the fore who appeared as experts in the field of sexual endeavors! We were making progress at least that is what we thought. We were re-inventing the wheel again but this time to be oval instead of round. We were counting all our pennies but in the value of mills. Money was printed just like one would photograph paper with no limit and was used to look good only for it bought hardly anything that was a real necessity. More was spent on filth and garbage then was spent on items such as food, water, medicine, etc. Just about every addiction was prevalent and was thought of as the norm. We had nicotine, caffeine of all kinds, cocaine, LSD, codeine, alcoholic beverages galore, marijuana 20 times as strong as before, angel dust, PCP, heroin, etc. Our own medications were also becoming habit forming especially for pain since affluence always tries to repel suffering at any price and now medicines once called that were habit forming drugs to ease our every pain.

People had so much put away for a rainy day that the sun never came out! We could not solve the most commonsense problem but could go to the moon for whatever purpose or far out reason, and yet we had babies dying in a mother's arms back here on earth! In America, though, they were dying in the arms of doctors and nurses for some strange reason.

Self discipline and gratitude were unheard of but there were plenty of human cattle willing to stampede. We had a longer life expectancy but euthanasia could always rectify that! Age was just that a number or so they said. Sometimes one plus one did equal two. But according to different ages one had to be careful what number they had gotten too or in fact no number at all. Some "families" had numbers that could increase very easily and that was without any procreation or any adoption or foster care!

Once big families were a blessing but now one child became a burden because the government did want more than what it could "raise".

"If it was moral, was it made legal?" was the question that was not being asked. That one question had almost summed it up for America's dilemma of good vs. evil. Did the question have to be asked at all? Well if one wanted to judge for oneself it was now a daily question to answer, but the answer was most assuredly it did not matter because if it met the Constitution or the Declaration of Independence or even the long list of Bill of Rights it had always to be good, right? This is where a democratic/republic would always go astray by having a majority, that is a democracy, decide on what paper or papers which were not set in granite would surely mean that all was not well in DC, or now PC!

If the actual question asked, "If it was legal was it moral seemed to best or better to describe not what the situation was coming to in America. In other words if the law okayed it, it was right! Well legally right, right? Well that now meant that whatever man could rationalize by reason alone had to be "good" for at least some one no matter what the ends, so the ends justify the means! It was how one got there that was most important and since law over morality ruled man was his own god now! This was socialism's definition that meant man could do anything at anytime regardless of what morality had to say since law by the people was not always law by GOD and elections were not a search for the truth!

In the first question the issue was morality first and legality second with law morality had to be over legality or rule of law meant absolutely nothing. That is why the judicial favored the second question because it made law rule over morality or one's notions rule over GOD' S laws and for a good reason it meant instead of chaos we would and could have an oligarchy!

The quintessential statement would be "if it was not moral then it would not be legal". Notice the statement is not a question since it is affirmed already by GOD. GOD'S law which is merciful, nature's law which was natural or physical law was harsh and deadly and then man's law which is hellish. GOD'S law reveals GOD'S grace or His love and nature's law reveals how brutal physical law really is and well man's law reveals just how evil man is!

Heathenism now was actually questioning validity, but more than that was making immorality valid. If immorality was valid then law enforcement had to be coerced at first to side for the underdog till the under dog grew oversized and was no longer under but over and above everything else when push came to shove it would then be too late to do otherwise but surrender one's freewill physically and spiritually to remain firm. That would be easier said then done.

One could be tried for the same crime or so-called crime or offense twice, such as in double jeopardy which was already tried by Mr. George Bush, Sr. when he ordered (that is the executive ordered) that the judicial retry some police officers a second time for things he felt, or the jury felt, they were thinking about and had not as of yet done! So on the second round they then found these family men guilty of the crime or so called crime even though they were apprehending a vicious criminal high on drugs that did not matter and were there to uphold the law which also did not matter in the slightest. They had to get this politically correct for all the world to see and especially in Europe but yet his own son could not bring to justice the 9/11 criminals because now that was not politically correct! This was indeed the famous Rodney King case in Los Angeles that was played again and again by Rush Limbaugh and others time and again until even the good guys agreed with this procedure because it went along with the ideology of the party and in this case it was the Republican Party or the Grand Old Party as they liked to use to call. it. This was not Abraham Lincoln's party but more like Abraham Lincoln's Brigade! This indeed had set a precedent for other cases that would fall under the so-called civil rights socialism act that went into play the day they made civil rights the all in everything that was possible and with affirmative action as in Nazi Germany they now could at anytime come back to this in the future no matter how far down the road when most people would forget what had happened to these police officers who had families to take care of and now were out of a job and a home, but political correctness as Lenin created it was still doing its job the way he would have wanted it too and the English were always good at going after someone who was not on their side or political ideology!

Yes, with these Bushes we had gotten more than we had bargained for and that meant that like father like son and that would continue since both would find it very easy to do just that that is the easy thing at least for them politically for they never wanted to commit themselves in any way to the fullest for then they would look out of place and out of style.

Image and popularity was the thing that was most important now in this democracy that was being led by ones who had others special interests on their minds and not the sovereignty of any nation but most Americans could not see that since the other candidate represented something almost from outer space!

A stake in the vampire's heart is not enough now! We must burn the entire body from the wretched smell that it has produced! This blood sucking venomous vampire that has sucked as much innocent blood, after a cessation of sorts somewhat in between but not really privately; never ending in its greed not only for wealth but for human blood. Procreation must be limited which means that conception has taken place and hence murder can only be left to describe what happens afterward!

America has sucked out the very blood that was to uphold our very nation and still now after birth, if they make it through the abortion mill they must now face Sodom and Gomorrah's vicious attack once again on their innocent lives by the all so many Nazis in our own government! Perverted and sick in mind this deviancy even by GOD is called an abomination and nothing less and yet we tempt GOD even more so with man's law vs. GOD'S eternal law. Insane? Yes it is always insane without GOD! Sick? So sick that now these Nazis want what they had in Nazi Germany and want us to approve of their own Nazism!

GOD shall not be mocked for us here in America no matter how we feel or superior we may feel which is all self delusion for the church here in America that remains constantly silent everyday and everyday we must continue the fight to oppose this sick world or subculture that no normal person could ever be involved in no matter what the American Psychiatric Association says. We shall dearly pay a dear price for this horrible mental illness and abominable sin that destroys or has destroyed and continues to do so in the millions and millions of lives just like in the Holocaust. Innocent lives that could have been helped but now those lives have grown up to do the unthinkable, pedophilia.

It was sanctioned, made legal, approved beyond their shadow of a doubt, encouraged to be as such, and now is their trophy to show the whole world and now Africa is suffering because of America's approval and with a few of the rich and well educated who apparently are not repulsed or did not want to regurgitate when they see this filth and garbage like Hollywood which is the main scoundrel and is made to look like a male prostitute like Hitler when he was young in Vienna!

What correction can be made for someone not even a man or to be called that who makes his money off of such garbage and filth? This is his contribution to our way of life in the underground now out in the open from Hollywood and is a vicious subculture of sickness which brings with it its insanity to fruition amongst many people to impregnate more minds and hearts and even souls to this sick deviancy from the very pits of Hell itself and notice I say pits and not pit!

And who are his biggest fans: homosexual pedophiles, perverts of all kinds, pimps, prostitutes, the Ted Bundys, the Jeffrey Dahmers, the John Wayne Gacys, and 6 other all time homosexual pedophile serial murderers not to mention judges, doctors, lawyers, pharmacists, drug dealers, the Hollywood crowd, Communists and the ever present Nazis! It is the who's who of the real high and low or infamous criminal world that even the ones in prison would destroy since they harm innocent children but since they shall serve no time for their horrible crimes they have absolutely nothing to worry about. What had Ted Bundy said to Dr. Dobson about what all the criminals had in common: PORNOGRAPHY!

Hugh Hefner and Hollywood and the gullible sports' world have all produced the most vicious criminals in the entire world and they are all from here in regards to destroying children's lives. Constantly this is what their sick appetites feed on, children who are innocent! Was it not pornography over and over again?' Women were never meant to be raped by thousands of men with their eyes focused on magazines or on the screen. A woman's body is her privacy with regard to this and only for her husband and no one else. There is a sacredness to the sexual role in life. It should not be the liquid manure of the pornography world!

To hell with Hollywood and its vaudevillian sickness that has never for one moment served any sort of moral purpose just like Lenin had said it would and would serve, no moral purpose from that of GOD which was for marriage for life or for any kind of real decency!

We in America for most of our lives look at the filth of those in Hollywood who themselves are mostly perverts. Hollywood has made all this as American as apple pie except with a worm in it! Now this war in Iraq is turning out as I suspected always and that was for oil and only oil. Even our soldiers are tired of dying for Bush's Islam and no longer want to fight for the Ivy Leaguers and big business. They all want to come home now and be done with it. If the Bushes want oil profits then let them buy it for themselves and if their Moslem friends in Saudi Arabia want to buy oil then let them hire their own mercenaries to do their own dirty work and not our soldiers because our own soldiers are not for sale for no one including this incumbent! American blood is too high a price to pay and since this incumbent wants to allow all our borders open then the soldiers should be relieved of the oath they took! If he wants terrorist and illegals here then let them deal with it and the United States Congress and let them send their own men and woman! This incumbent could care less what happens to our own military when it is compared to his own selfish interests and has absolutely no foresight. He could never relate to the average American in a million years since he never really has ever worked for a living.

The upper strata do not understand nor do they care too what America in the heartland is all about. All we see is multicultural faces that he appoints all the time so let them serve in the military such as the illegals from Mexico and elsewhere and draft them to fight the war plus the Moslems here in America if he prefers them over the patriotic American! He lives in a fantasy world and is always smiling because none of his family is in harm's way or in dire need! They could be no further from the truth and could care less about America's demise or for that matter Israel's survival and remember the English have always been anti-Semitic and would like to see the destruction of Israel because the Israelis stand in their path that is the Anglophiles from making even more money and wealth! That is why this incumbent is calling for a Palestinian State so that it can destroy the state of Israel and now we all have to worry what GOD will do to our very nation? Yes, the English are good at acting and this incumbent continues his play acting until . . . One cannot trust the English for whatever they might say for their record on diplomacy is horrible and they are a very cold and calculating people in general and have horrible private perverted lives!

Bring our soldiers, not your soldiers, since you have relinquished your concern for their safety and care and we shall ask Congress if they will deploy them at all of our own borders? Who the hell cares about the Islamic Moslems in Iraq that shall go on killing each other that is the Arabs just like Alexander Solzhenitsyn told his own government the Politburo years ago! Once they come back that is the soldiers then we shall see how popular this President with all of the troops and not just some few high ranking generals and politicians and most news media outlets and this shall have absolutely nothing to do with the Communists in downtown Burbank.

Tell his Ivy Leaguers and the other socialist think tanks known as colleges and universities that we are the ones who pay the taxes and not them and it is us who shall make history and not the elite.

What can the average American citizen who is loyal to America and not to an ideological party do to save his own nation and the lives of our very own sons and daughters since we have no control and this incumbent wants to play Napoleon? There is now no media for even the conservatives can only speak and do nothing else since they are paid by the rich and well educated and repeat what only they hear others say time and again over and over again like a broken record. I am not concerned about the President's prestige and could care less about any of that but I am concerned about our own liberty and the mercenary affect our soldiers that he refuses to release are being used just so that he can look good! There is not much public opinion now in America, but if the soldiers come home then we would see a different kind of public opinion and that is why this incumbent refuses to send them home and this war is nothing at all like the Vietnam conflict when the State Department and David Rockefeller of World Bank along with his buddy Robert McNamara waged a financial war against our very soldiers in the rice paddies in Vietnam and back in the states the moral fiber of America had become so weak that it would give in to Communism lock, stock and barrel!

This is no longer a decision to be discussed and America and England with their own demise and it shall be sooner than we all think what it is to come into the living hand of an Almighty and living GOD! His attack on Israel shall be his doom for his entire term and with no let up unless he backs off on this Palestinian State! Wealth and power shall not uphold against truth and strength and especially when it has to do with the state of Israel and the Jewish people! A lonely voice trying to make sense of why a President would want to side with the enemy and remember all of Islam IS the enemy to every Christian and Jew wherever they are and also to be willing to listen in his spirit the lies that the enemy has been telling him day after day?

We must now first bring the soldiers home and have them protect our own borders and drill oil in Alaska and then tell Islam they are no longer wanted here since they are a violent religion and no ands, if or buts! Then we must have a draft for all the ones who are dead weight in our own society just like Russia had done in the 19th Century when they took the peasants who only caused trouble in the villages first! Let us get our own priorities in order and let us silence the United States Supreme Court which even Scalia himself has called a kangaroo court! And this is one of their own justices!

Censor all of Hollywood and all pornography and start prosecuting them and stop worrying how much money that they shall lose and not what they say is an infringement on the First Amendment rights.

United States Supreme Court Justice Antonin Scalia himself has called the court that he serves on a kangaroo court and also has said that he did not want any homosexuals in his home, business or place of worship! These were profound statements since a majority of the Supreme Court Justices support homo sexuality and when Scalia got on the Supreme Court little did they know that they would have to contend with an Italian who would not tolerate for one minute this abominable sin and the fact that he would not collaborate with the group mentality no matter what. His father was an educated man being a professor so that in and of itself is also remarkable but then again Italians more than any other nationality abhor homosexuality and possibly also that is why the Italian underground in World War II tore Mussolini apart because he went along with the Nazis who were homosexual pedophiles themselves!

It was good to know at least for me that my own nationality for the most part would not for one minute put up with homosexuality like the English, the Germans, the Greeks, the Arabs and now the blacks did! Never when I was growing up had we ever given it any thought to be abnormal or never did I see two men or two women with each other as the Germans and the English mostly had done as I grew older. Their cultures were completely different then ours and then again they were cousins as well as the Austrians who Hitler himself was. Now we had Roman Catholics with the clergy and elsewhere with the Polish who were falling in line with homosexuality as well as the Irish and now the Americans. I always wondered why some of our own Founding Forefathers wore wigs and silk stockings with a sword hanging down their side as had been done in Europe years ago. Somewhat I would say like the French Jesuits who were on par with the Masons who both hated each other but stood for the very same ideology!

A wolf sheds its fur but not its habits and here it was apropos to say just that since again they were bringing their perverseness to America along with also a few Jewish people who themselves were probably the most ignorant because it was the homosexuals who murdered their relatives in the Holocaust and amongst them one and one half million children which told anyone with enough common sense that they that is the Nazis were homosexual pedophiles because one and one half million out of 6 million Jewish people meant that approximately 25% of the murders in the concentration camps were all children! Not to hard to figure out as to the why if 60-70% of all homosexuals were pedophiles!

The American Jew wanted more to cry than to hear the actual facts about their own grandchildren and great grandchildren. They were in love with extravagance too much here in this country of eat, drink and be merry! America had turned into a Sodom and Gomorrah and it was silent since now the English were showing just what kind of horrible private lives they had always lived for many years and since Eng land had done it we as America would follow along at least some of them would!

There were others who would never go along with this no matter what some so called Christian denominations had in their own clergy and no matter how much the media pushed it so to be! Hollywood was for anything and everything that was evil and now since a hard rock musician was killed along with his other players he was being eulogized by the Irish as some kind of good hero and not that anyone was promoting murdering anybody but to equate this with the level of sainthood was total insanity when anyone with enough knowledge knew that rock music especially this kind always dealt with the occult and Satan! So many rock groups dabbled in the occult and the head player for KISS an Israelis gone sour completely was eulogizing this group since he himself worshipped Satan and their own name went to prove that.

If this would have been a Christian choir nothing would have been heard. What can one expect when they live in a world of evil all the time'? This is a doctrine of demons and Satan was coming for his very own since he already had them. Most people in the world fit into this group but not to this extent as say the hard rock musicians who also were involved up to 85% in homosexuality which to some was some sort of civil right and maybe it was since it was superior to the degenerates in Hollywood and the media all over the United States who kept their favorite past time alive and well and the fact evil begets evil and now Nazi lead America was on par with Nazi Germany. This is the way Satan came into America and that was by its so called music! And were not all civil rights superior rights so that meant that everyone who fell under this heading had just that, superior rights like in Nazi Germany!

We were a mixed bag of marbles from many different nations and now evil religions and evil countries who saw only the death side of life and nothing else and were brought up that way all of their entire lives and America just kept enjoying the so called good times! What would wake up this nation to the evil that was being perpetrated in it day in and day out in home after home all over this nation that would be horrible to describe at all?

Now even our own leaders were like Hollywood and one could suit tell the difference between the two?

How can these Naziphile homosexuals look at themselves in the mirror each and everyday knowing what harm they have done to innocent children and the spreading of AIDS now worldwide and to all sectors in our own society including unborn children, hemophiliacs, etc? Their consciences have been seared and Satan has them in his control with this obsession with sexual deviancy with no end in sight except their immediate death and that of others! There still is no excuse for them to claim innocent lives as if they were some kind of perverse play things. "It is okay, so what it is equal rights, etc." They are responsible for committing one of the most egregious sinful crimes and that is homo-sexual pedophilia let alone the spread of AIDS outside the homosexual community plus the fact once again what is coming to light is that the 3rd Reich hierarchy were all homosexual pedophiles! Now they want all youth and children organizations to accept their vicious crimes since Nazis run this government and entertain some such as the Kennedys, Barney Frank a homosexual pedophile, the Clintons, Billy Jean King, Martina Navratilova, Liberace, Little Richard, Paul Lynne, Charles Nelson Reilly, Frank Collins a Nazi homosexual pedophile, Mr. Cordoba, Jeffery Dahmer, John Wayne Gacy, Truman Capote, Dennis Rodman, Ruth Bader Ginsburg, George Stephanopolus, Madeleine Albright, Janet Reno, Dick Cheney, Congressman Stubbs. Should I go on or do you get how sick this society with the elites also really is?

The red cross, that is the symbol, is not accepted because of the Roman Catholicism's killing of Jews during the Crusades, murdering Jews in the Spanish Inquisition. It was used on their knights' shields as an emblem. Roman Catholicism also has now liberation theology revolutionaries. This is in no way Christianity when Jesus said, "Those who live by the sword shall die by the sword." It does not believe in grace but only works or church or their Church tradition.

Every nation that comes up against Israel that is mentioned in the Old Testament and who loses are all Islamic nations. Who shall really try as a President to destroy Israel like this President is trying to do right now? Heaven help us all if he or she gets elected and continues this insanity against GOD'S Word. We are already on the road to destruction and again Israel is not to be shared with Islam or anybody else including

Gentiles. It is a Jewish state period! The New Age Nazis mentality which is worldwide is taking affect in India the land of the swastika and Germany with the Holocaust as well as its long period of homosexuality and England and America with both of their collaboration with the Moslems to destroy all of Israel?

Can the Western powers defeat a small Eastern country like Israel? Now Israel more than ever keeps its eye on our American government and with good reason and also on Western big business. Israel must soon remove Sharon because he gives into the State Department too much and entertains black rock groups which shall do nothing to uphold Israel's freedom and years back Moshe' Dayan and Menachem Begin and Ezer Weisman would never think to do such a horrible thing! Soon there shall be no more land and then possibly nuclear weapons might come into play. Deport now all Moslems to Jordan and close the Gaza Strip and the West Bank. Israel must now do what GOD has said theirs to do and not be coerced because GOD does not coerce the Jews to leave their land but is bringing them back through His absolute will and that means all of the land!

"Blessed is He who comes in the name of the Lord." Just as a Christian father can turn a son over to the Father so can, I believe, Israel be turned over to the Father also! Now absolute will come? We cannot follow our own government blindly, but must pray for the peace of Jerusalem first even though we love our own country we are still a part of the branches. GOD has put us here and now we must do, yes do, our part as He wants us to do through Him to help Israel remain as a state and not a piece of America or the Islamic world. This is more than just a piece of land this is the Father's Land!

American males and females seemed not to be able to find the right mate for life so they have endeavored to marry elsewhere in society and there became an inferiority complex and an over sensitivity as to physical traits. Most were urged by Hollywood, the media, the rich and well educated and a very few because of their faith alone. As only to the last one, could I personally see the truth in that type of marriage for life, not that it always remains, but nonetheless became as one. As one goes back to the 60's, sex was just for the thrill of sin at anytime, any place and anywhere and television and Hollywood also, till this day present it as such to all who would lessen their moral and mental skills and emulate what they saw, not always knowing why. We all have what we believe in as far as marriage goes, but GOD has laid down the law for a lifetime in regards to believers even though unbelievers have followed this path which today has become very narrow for almost all married people but especially for Christians to stay afloat.

Since some are drawn to color then the physical becomes even more predominant and to some means in their own narrow mindedness that one must entertain what they propose through what they so nicely call diversity or the stressing of one's differences! This is coercion being applied where it should not be but if they should, say be two Christians to get married we should definitely rejoice!

It is not at the top where one sees things but the foundation of a marriage where it is hidden from view where it counts. The foundation is what holds any marriage together and if not built on Christ then it means nothing at all. To base it on the aesthetic top that is the seeable part they see or we see with only what is popular or is even diverse. To look beyond and into a marriage one must spiritually see its foundation and how can one see in this way without faith? Fads do not last and are not meant to, but agapé love sustains marriage because it is not carnal lust. It has been blessed by GOD Himself that is the Christian marriage of two believers. Let no one be mistaken that popularity or physical attraction alone really has anything to do with a commitment and for a lifetime of vows to last just for that reason for life! It is like a whole person a whole marriage. The Old Testament also speaks of marriage as forever. Christ (the groom) comes for His church (the bride) or the Body of Christ! This church represents what husband and wife should correlate to.

Thomas Jefferson wanted to return all the slaves back to where they came from, yet he had an affair. Two wrongs do not make a right. It was unheard of at one time and now not to be for it is to be always bigoted because the ones who use this term are themselves the bigots! Political correctness kept most American conservatives deaf and dumb because most conservatives did in deed have plenty of money. When men of any one race and in a plebiscite of races if you will refuses to be respectful to their own

First, then that presents a major dilemma since the weaker sex should be upheld and be taken care of for life such as in holy matrimony and make no excuse whatsoever for being loyal to their own first in order to understand what it is their own women need as the Bible says.

In America most Americans have missed their apparent opportunity and their purpose in life because they failed, sometimes repeatedly, to meet the Author of Life. They have wasted so many years that now that time is almost up for them they shall not be remembered since they are not in the family of GOD. Others live much shorter lives and have contributed so much more to His kingdom. It is not one's stay here on earth that matters, but what has anyone of us done as an individual and as a believer say as to help an unbeliever to come to the Lord. Just think in part of this small action that to help bring the very Gospel to another that has never really heard it for the very first time is just so wonderful!

"Do not be unequally yoked" is a small but important verse that speaks directly to marriage of two believers and never to marry an unbeliever if one is a believer themselves. "What does good have to do with evil" meaning that one should never date or ever marry an unbeliever if one is a believer themselves. This is a powerfully strong statement not to be taken for granted as many times as it is or lightly as many times as it is! Matrimony is in front of GOD and is for a lifetime and no less! Until death do us part.

Marriage is not a popularity contest or a trophy issue but is a sacred ceremony for life between two equally yoked individuals who become one through Christ which is the only way. This is what His church the saints saved by grace alone is.

Believers are held to a much higher standard degree of sacredness, and we as believers must be the salt of the earth. We cannot lie down and say it is over but continue on as Christ has told us to do until His return and continue the good fight as soldiers in GOD'S army. As His knights we carry a sword which is His Word and our code of armor is the breastplate of righteousness, the belt of truth, the helmet of salvation, our feet are shod in the peace of good news, and His shield of faith! We fight not in flesh and blood but in the principalities. Our spirit and our souls are sinless but it is in the flesh that still holds us in sin and until we get new bodies we shall have to deal with this and avoid sin by His grace and His strength. The spirit is willing but the flesh is weak." The world was perfect in Genesis but in the Garden it was for believers only and then Satan almost at the same time as he had fallen came to Adam so he would sin and hence the entire world came into sin.

The metals in Scripture such as gold and precious metals represent believers like in the statue in Daniel. King Nebuchadnezzar was a believer and so was King David who also was saved by grace and a man after GOD'S own heart even though he had some egregious sins. His sins were covered.

The Reagan Administration had made hospitals, HMO'S and nursing homes that were non-profit if one could have ever called them that into profit business oriented organizations or companies that were competing for business but also did not the Clintons add on to that their little version of socialism where prices never go down no matter what since it is a failed system that is socialism is? Hospitals now no longer deal in the value of human life but in how to make a quick buck and the employees that they hire are ones who should be working somewhere in a fast food chain such as Wendy's. Appealing to man's human nature now and not the Hippocratic Oath any longer money and avarice at the top have definitely taken over yet the patients now more then ever in the hospitals with their very lives so easy and simply and of course the lawyers are always there to accommodate as best as they could to be of any help! Some of the most creative and intelligent people and in fact too many of those kind of people are holding down jobs that these idiots on the top should have since they see life as a shallow financial structure that serves their every need.

The inferior quality of the professionals is also derived from the fact that a police-man is watching all the time and that also tends to make one to make mistakes. Young people with no experience of life or patience for the patients is there and they only know best about how to procreate. Now even homosexuals with the HIV and the AIDS virus are working around sick people and blood and other kinds of organic materials that just with one drop one could be dead! They do not know the right hand from the left hand and sometimes many charts get lost in the shuffle and also the fact that some of the employees cannot hardly speak English let alone be able to properly and exactly read and write it and the elderly nurses have the roles of no nothings while the not too bright have the higher positions and the ones with the socialist education can never seem to answer any question that one might have for fear of . . .

Yes many followers of Allah and other insane religions are administering drugs and medications and performing surgery on people who they have nothing in common with and who do not even believe in GOD and that is the GOD of Abraham, Isaac and Jacob and also our Saviour Jesus or Messiah. This indeed is a very scary thing to say the least and now the ones who were so silent about infanticide are at the top or are in positions to do the greatest good but do the greatest harm since their best interest at heart or their own heart is one of gold.

Now we are playing follow the leader to the time of civil rights which I have already mentioned is superior rights for the other guy who could care less what happens to even their very own children! The best care sometimes goes to these people since they are already a group of politically correct people that adhere to the rule "if you're not one of us, then the hell with you."

Today's poor has a totally different meaning than when I was a young boy, when there was no freeloading by grown men and women who wanted to have sex and more sex and have the rest of society pay for them and not their children since most of those children never saw a penny because the biological parents did not care enough even to try to work for their own blood; so the Marxist ideology that "Since we are so poor you need to help me feed my sex and drug habit day and night so that I can get more rest in between to procreate and sometimes not to procreate since I cannot control myself being that I am from a culture or a race of people held so far down that now it is time to make up for lost time! But did not the last 40 years just do that? How was it that one family after another had no father for at least 2 or 3 generations at all and everyone thought how sad that must truly be but did not give it any thought that the children would or should be the ones to feel sorry for when they are only babies and toddlers and not when it is almost too late to do anything once they reach a certain age and proxy organizations only create a system for homosexual pedophiles to get their own hands on children that not even the biological parents want but only want what they can get from government from taxpayers who had given into the system for so many years and now were being questioned as to the why they wanted to be helped also when we first needed to help the dead beat dads, ones who could and would not speak English, obese people and drug dealers and drug addicts who refused to seek help except the help of a ready made life and handouts galore that was creating the rising costs in hospital care along with the trial lawyers who were eating it all up like good little PAC men! Yes, one could get at this super market certain values but not the kind that were so humane and also ones that were of course at brand name prices for inferior quality and sanctity of human life and one again must always remember that most doctors kept their mouths shut when it came to infanticide and did absolutely nothing to defend the unborn and now they are crying about the parasitical trial lawyers who would suck the blood out of one like a huge mosquito!

So if one hounds the rich too much then one can be accused of class warfare, and if one hounds the poor, the same also. The middle class is moderate, but in America the middle class leans more to the upper strata; hence even that class too in wealth if one hounds can one also be called a Marxist or accused of class warfare? We know the rich do always run any society no matter if they are a George Washington or a Lenin, but of course can there be any comparison between the two? With ones who proclaim for the unskilled laborer or are always for the poor no matter what one can run amuck as a Marxist. Hence if one does so with the rich, one can accuse a "monarch" also. One must decipher who follows Biblical law that is who has GOD as head of government. It is good vs. evil and from there the basis can be seen quite clearly. Does one or a group uphold the 10 Commandments as not ever to be changed not that any government including ours has done as such but nonetheless it should always be deciphered except for instance in a monarch which the ruler follows, in a democracy which is usually mob rule and never is in search of the truth and of course an oligarchy which is nothing more than dictatorship. These only 3 forms of government almost in and of themselves can show which only one has a chance of following Biblical Scripture since 2 follow ideology or party politics. One has the unique opportunity and with vested interest to serve or follow GOD'S Word. The other two usually run with the world or the national system which goes with what that particular civilization or system has deemed to be "original". The only original is GOD Himself so if a monarch follows GOD that civilization can last for quite some time, but all civilizations do come to an end. Sometimes only the state remains with no spiritual body then again totalitarianism which we have seen all throughout history because of sin or Adam's fall and man prefers control over chaos. A democratic/republic is a quasi democracy with a constitution that rarely lives up to what that document as in the Soviet Union or even in America now that was set out to accomplish even though both documents professed or did not profess certain things and as always ran out into a tangent of their own thereby saying, "We have found the perfect way or utopian way." This is Kingdom Dominion Theology, which is heresy because Christ's millennial kingdom shall be the perfect government on earth set by Messiah from the New Jerusalem. This too shall be a monarchy and not a tyranny or mob rule type of government.

Government always has power in order to restrain man from cannibalism and yet sometimes through government itself that is just what happens as in Russia. Whenever a group or a majority rule one can be assured power shall become the obsessive thing. Yet again without government man shall devour himself but also without a spiritual life government shall devour even itself eventually. Hence we originate to where only government can possibly work and that is through a monarch who has Jesus devoutly and applies the same principles to himself and to the people he rules. Even our incumbent now who is a Christian misses the mark by a lot! In a democracy one does not really rule but leads and hence leadership is given to ones of a political persuasion regardless if it is good vs. evil! Monarchs are trained to remain silent and composed and to listen and then evaluate with GOD first always in mind. Some quasi monarchs are no more then a sham for an oligarchy that calls itself a "monarch" such as the Arab sheiks. We have tested all methods of these 3 forms of government and have found them wanting and not because the one is bad but because man himself is innately evil. With that said though only a monarch is Biblical in its precepts and the other 2 are mundane and one being evil or another ending up as evil. In Russia Nicholas II was weak but still it was not the monarch that fell to totalitarianism, but afterwards with 8 months of democracy that fell to Communism as did Italy, the Weimar Republic and China all in the 20th century. Now into the 21st century we see an even worse scenario of democracies driven by commercialism which can only mean socialism worldwide coming together piece by piece to form a whole which one could again call a quasi monarch or an oligarchy in the sense that there shall be 3 who shall rule the entire world at that time under the auspices of total evil and even communism has not done that! There is a plan laid out by GOD but we are not privy to know it in full until the time appears as such. Much of the Gentile religions speaking in terms within Judeo-Christianity have failed time and again and by far have failed to uphold that form of Biblical government. Man has devised his own form of wisdom and since socialism has been around since man it has come to be what the Gentiles have partaken in and it was only when the Jews appeared that the only Biblical government really came into being up to this time and that was the promise of Messiah. Where else had the Gentiles gotten the idea of a king from? The Old Testament is about the Jewish people and not in a secular context and stands above any Gentile religion even if it be from Europeanism which has two main religions and they are Roman Catholicism and the German Reformation and now also Islam again!

We now see PETA another insane attempt to rationalize just that the insanity of this New Age or one big world government and yet it could just very well be that a Hebrew shall rule in the Tribulation which shall be the worse time ever on earth. Now this may appear as a paradox of some sort that all through the ages it appeared that the Jews small in numbers and who are stiff-necked would rule on and on but then again and I say again because now the Gentiles emulated what the Hebrews had done and brought to earth the weak forms of Christianity that both were anti-Semitic and extremely so! They tried to replace Messianic Jewry with a Gentile religion that stayed the course through nationalism, such as the Italian Vatican and the German Reformation, and yet both served more of themselves than the message of what the Jews meant to GOD Himself and Israel even though that would come in later ages. Few writers outside the Bible have ever even come close to what I believe was a plan to get the Hebrews in and yet fulfill a plan for the Gentiles! Did GOD hold up this process or was it man himself that allowed even Paul to believe that Messiah was coming with His kingdom? And then Gentile evasion of the Gospel procrastinated maybe what GOD had wanted earlier in time, but man, knowing better, made GOD extend His return, not that He had to.

Again, back to PETA and its New Age insanity has such concern for animals slaughtered inhumanely but none whatsoever for a child that too is butchered. But one can overlook human flesh and blood as opposed to the animal world which can reason, speak, etc! This is the same group that spoke about how thousands of chickens were just as bad as being slaughtered in the Holocaust! One can only conclude that insanity or their anti-Semitism has grown much more since this one world government is growing daily and in fact hour by hour. It would only make sense that to cut an animal's throat properly would take precedence over murdering a child viciously as a serial killer but with an MD degree! Yes certainly trained to do an expert job since death and dying is the now objective of the entire medical world.

Getting back to anti-Semitism because Satan is anti-Semitic since he could not be as the Son who was not created but always has been but as for Lucifer his was from a creation form meaning not GOD Himself in any of the 3 spots of the Trinity!

The brotherhood of abnormality is growing in the sense that the highest positions are being reached by this brotherhood with no national inclination or care for one's sovereignty. Only the fact that brotherhood first and foremost with, of course, sexual deviancy and perverseness always.

This insanity of homosexuality, pedophilia, AIDS, HIV, NAMBLA, bath houses, etc. are all a part of this sick heathenism that grows now fast amongst the elites where the authority to coerce either by artificial judicial law or coerce by raped and murder which nonetheless shall obtain many marvelous wonders of the world such as two dads with a child!

Let us promote the Jesuit French Roman Catholicism with the all inclusive German Martin Luther's private beliefs of anti-Semitism. Nazism's status quo which Hitler was seeking more deviants in other nations not for sovereignty but for the brotherhood of deviancy and with Italy he ran into a buzz saw! Who could ever be like the status quo German whose language also is as far from Italian as it is from Russian? Their system did not Work and now again this perverted system along with the English cousin is trying to promote the Anglo-Saxon homosexual brotherhood where procreation shall be by test tube tested! Which other way could it be to procreate when two identical people of the same sex living together try to procreate abnormally?

As my mentor had said, "Do not go along with what is evil." At that time I thought I understood what he meant, but now I really understand years later because now more than ever, at least in my time, no such kind of evil existed for me and now with each passing day literally I find more and more of an okay evil by the majority and it continues to have an ambience in all the facets of life until one has to either live as the "scum of the earth" or as "royalty" of some other kind! The dividing line is getting closer and closer and one can throw away race, nationality, creed, religion, etc. for the line is getting almost now to be one and not two parallel lines with a gray area in between. The Christian even is finding the loneliness of fellowship and the willingness to give one's entire will and life to Christ. No more room for being on the fence and now good vs. evil to the very bone and marrow. Compromises now mean not small choices but huge choices with sin always lurking and even Christians taking the easy or alternate route and seeing everything political and not spiritual. One has little time with GOD if they allow democracy to be their all. The room for the spiritual is almost null and void. Each day makes one or entices one to lie about something since this one world system is entirely based on the lie. If one upholds family forget it or if one upholds GOD' S precepts then it must be opposed and the crushing device shall apply even more pressure to those who oppose it.

While in the east right now even death shall not render one to give in or give up the faith since materialism plays little part nor doles food itself in their lives and death with Christ has already occurred! This is better than eternity in the burning lake of fire! With watered down sermons the Gospel with hucksters selling it shall also see their judgment at GOD'S time. Up to the time of no grace or Holy Spirit it shall get even worse after that and man shall curse the very name of GOD Himself?

Now one can see even children being controlled as soon as they walk. The evil has come upon this earth and the principalities are in constant war until the Holy Spirit shall be removed and total evil shall be in the world and one's lifelong friend shall appear as somebody you never knew in your life! Family members shall disown you and shall speak evil about you and shall he about you with no end. Even their knowing any truth shall have been gone forever and Jesus shall be not here and man shall have it his own way but with GOD'S judgments that shall come upon this earth and in the heavens and not until GOD'S time has come for his Son to rule for the millennium of 1,000 years when Satan is put away in that time period.

"Those who are first shall be last and those who are last shall be first." GOD knows who shall come into His kingdom even before the very foundation of this earth and knew of us before we were in our mother's womb!

This is soon the day of great reckoning upon this earth for all of our sins that man has caused and that includes all of us for without Christ we all would be going to the burning lake of fire forever. It is what He has already done that has completed our entire healing process of our heart, soul and our mind. We were bought for a high price but with an eternal love that only GOD can give and no other and this love is agape love that He has shown for all who belong into the family of GOD!

Yes, we all have gone astray like sheep and not one of us could have ever found our own way without the love of dear Jesus who gave His life and then resurrected and in this time of Hanukkah we can celebrate the defeat of Antiochus Epiphanes who had brought a pig into the temple to desecrate it but was defeated by the Maccabees.

We now must protect the Messianic Jews from harm since the enemy shall attack even more so the roots.

Who in America would ever believe they were part of socialism itself because this was America and socialism is some extreme foreign ideology. The word itself is also an extreme language of someone not wrapped to tightly together for them to call America socialistic!—language that is archaic and out of date since the time of the Cold War and since memories are poor. American memories dissipate quickly, too quickly. Even today's news is old because of anxiety; wanting it to already end before the day is even over. Anxiety creates much run-of-the-mill confusion such as in corporate business which only contends its employees to settle for lesser money paid out and then some and more money gotten in, no matter how illegal and unethical. In other words, if one worked 60-70 hours and if, for example, government was giving out more for investing more frivolously, then by all means buy more with the taxpayers' monies and also buy and purchase life insurance policies for people not even aware that they have an insurance policy out on them! Produce more for less until the government pays all wages and healthcare so that universal healthcare or socialism would be installed forever and everything would not be individually done but would be categorized as if need be or if not! Government or the state would control all hence no private life just a public life. The medical and teaching profession would suffer morally and ignoramuses would be installed. In capitalism even one's money or wealth bought qualifications and in socialism the party did always!

If Nazis ran big business and big government then it is conclusive to say that homosexuality would run rampant on the national and international level and as for the robed justices they are involved into this sexual deviancy of pedophilia also. The 9th Circuit Court of Appeals has a woman who is a judge whose father was a Communist! They are attacking Israel so that the Jews have no where to go in any of the Gentile nations as well as the destruction of Israel itself and homosexuality is a predominant Gentile Anglo-Saxon thing and now with civil rights many minorities have come on board and Greeks and most of all Israel's neighbors the Arabs! This is this brotherhood of evil with no national boundary and loyalty but only to Nazism's homosexuality!

Maybe one day the Red Chinese will lock in the Western businessmen and say, "It is over and time is up." No exit out of Red China and what a celebration for all free people worldwide! Now promoters of socialism and ideology will also shed to a red color of War Communism. The West will have to now cater to Israel that stands at the very center of the world. The Arabs will have been defeated by nuclear or obsolete petroleum. Then of course Europe (America) shall be part of this system but they too shall also lose!

In the West everywhere one went it was an obsession with food and eating continuously. There was no end to the insanity of overweight or obesity and fat people even at a young age. Food was plentiful and as poisonous to one's health 10 times over, but at least in America they were still getting their share and then some. With the New Age system stealing more and more food and hoarding worldwide famines already started were killing millions but now the West would soon experience a surprise of its own. Eating also is a part of materialism! This was gluttony and not at all normal. Three meals a day with food that kept most in hospitals for more surgery and pills and even early death and not always the certainty as to the why!

How would the young Westerners inexperienced deal with the experienced male Communists leaders in Red China and North Korea? Also the ones here and in Europe from the 60's who were dying off and now Islam with its proclivity for Marxist/Leninism and its death wish and destruction of mankind! There was great similarity there but the Arabs needed oil to be valuable or else . . . Without materialism or the natural resources what would the West do since they were not about to give up their gold mines?

The businessmen was the worse warrior of all since he supplied both the finances and the natural resources for totalitarianism to spread and spread which improved their own power worldwide.

The English always liked a side show or freak show as in a 3 ring circus and of course Satan loved to display through man abnormalities of all kinds and could then blame GOD for it! America and Russia also liked spectacles such as car crashes, insane scenes of drunkenness, people who have physical disorders visible to the human eye, etc. The English have a proclivity for the unusual also and are very crude to say the least.

The English have sick private lives, but the Germans have a vicious public life. What the English hide the Germans show for all the world to see except the Jewish homosexual Holocaust because the Rockefellers, the Fords, the Krupps, the Thuns, Sunoco, etc. all need the Rothchilds' banking. Israel blocks the road to what the West wants and what the East needs. One is materialism, the other is technological power. The mindsets are different and the peoples are opposing each other when the leaders should be doing that. Maybe that is why the media stresses over and over again the leaders because only a people in reality can create history? Separate the people and hence power grows with the elites. Establish hate between nations and unite the governments for evil. This is the United Governments which we know as the United Nations!

Side-shadowing in simplicity presents many possibilities which Tolstoy and Dosteyevsky agreed on. In other words it did not have to happen that way but then also to go backwards in time is impossible or as some say, "Back to the good old days." The past also might have been different from what we might have thought or now to have perceived it to be! This in turn would affect, then, even our future. Side-shadowing deals with open time or not yet what has happened or will happen but socialists try to foreshadow and make it happen and are sure this is what most or all will happen and hence their own kind of utopia! An example of this is President Kennedy's assassination, which could have had one other possibility being that a secret service agent accidentally shot the fatal shot to the back of the head that killed the President! Even though it is never mentioned as such the possibility is there and it so then sheds a light on my life time when most or all stories may have all varied but not as to an assassination which meant that possibly what was left was intentional from the socialists point of view and of course their own invested interest since the lie if intentional or not and intentions do not always proceed actions. This would mean the accidental death was totally left out! For the intrigue and more than mysterious reasons it would all make it appear as if the Soviets were involved or even the Mafia because of the Bay of Pigs and hence would diminish the well thought up story and also would make Nazism appear to be diametrically opposed to what Russia had and that also would be a lie since both were on the left and not the right and both were two forms of socialism and one was racial and one was class warfare.

As today's final thought I also wondered that the stars and celebrities and athletes all had this ego problem or least 99% of them did and hence this too contributed to their love for socialism also because it gave them a power above most others just like the businessmen in the West! Who would give up all the egoism to live a perfectly normal life and without ever having to work for a living they were in some way like the proletarian who was unskilled labor which meant that he did piece work and also with them they did not labor with any real mental insight since the theatre has always been used to promote Leninism!

The American Jew has forgotten their very roots which lie in Jerusalem, Israel. They have forsaken for the most part GOD and many will say within the Christian church that this was prophesied but nonetheless it is on the Christian church's part not to appease them in this but to bring the Gospel to them with GOD'S eternal love. Since Israel now is in such perilous times do we really want the end to be here in the way we might perceive it to be or would we at least pray to GOD that we need still more time to do what it is He wants us to do? We cannot ignore what is happening in other parts of the world such as the Sudan where Christians have already been butchered and this incumbent has ignored that for an oil war in Iraq and made up every kind of excuse not to protect our brothers and sisters in Christ and maybe he has had too many dialogues with the enemy!

He has appointed people who are diametrically opposed to what Scripture says and continues to lead us down a path of destruction. He refuses to protect our own sovereign borders so that our nation can remain Judeo-Christian. His wife is pro-infanticide and he has done absolutely nothing while in office that has remained. He has not shown the resolve to continue to do what would be the decent and respectful thing to do. He has even decided to give up Israel to our enemies and the enemies of GOD since Israel is the apple of GOD'S eye.

We the people have been also a big problem because we have refused to stand up for what is right they have continued to murder and this is first degree pre-meditated murder. There have been no, if you will, Nuremburg Trials for any of our judges or politicians or celebrities or even famous sports' athletes who have stood above GOD'S law. We all are accountable to GOD for this most grievous sin, the murder of our fellow man, not in a foreign land but right here in our very own homes and institutions. We have allowed Sodom and Gomorrah to destroy the very moral fiber, whatever was left here, to be also destroyed and so now it has become "dog eat dog".

Yes, democracies have a funny way of turning perverse and most unjust since we let it up to the majority to decide about GOD'S Law. Where in the Bible has the majority ever been for GOD'S law for any length of time? It is always the few who must stand up no matter what is at stake to defend others first and especially the innocent who have no one to defend them and not just preach self preservation for one.

We cannot know for certain if GOD has now turned to His own judgment for this nation but we can at least know that what has occurred has certainly affected all parts of the world and they no longer look at us as a free and loving nation. We have failed horribly to show that we are a peace loving nation and have abandoned even our own children for our own rights and more rights that started before I was born but that I too went along with and now we still refuse to do what is right. Our own chroniclers have said so much that they have repeated themselves blue in the face and have only talked also about self-preservation and have not begun even to realize that we now must sacrifice our own materialism for the truth and not sit in our own ivory towers preaching to others what we should have done a long time ago.

This is our responsibility (a word not commonly used these days), to do what it is we must do regardless if we are married and have children or not and we must do it according to Scripture. We are not that ignorant of Scripture that we do not know what it is that GOD really wants us to do instead of bragging as Christians how much money and wealth we have to others and remain totally silent about what is happening to our own meaning America's children, and if we cannot do that then how can we possibly think that we can help other nations to do right when we do wrong over and over again?

We are on the precipice of destruction from within and now we have invited the enemy into our nation by worshipping demons and doctrine of demons and the clergy is still silent about it and keep preaching about self-preservation which means more ego! Who has taken Christ's place on the cross or who has removed our sins? Has it been anyone else but Christ? And who was it done for? Was it not for both Jew and Gentile? So why do we pretend that we do not know what it is that GOD would have us do since His Word is very clear about it over and over again?

Why are so many criminals on television and in sports and in Hollywood and in the Congress of the U.S. government without being prosecuted for high crimes and misdemeanors? We have ignored what these criminals have done to undo America's GOD! We are all accountable for this and soon we may feel the wrath of GOD for up to now we have only been warned! Each day it is important not only to pray but to act on that prayer the way GOD wants us to and His Word tells us to.

As a very young nation we are acting the part just like a juvenile delinquent and I say this with love for my very own nation. If we do not speak out and correct our own then who shall do it besides GOD Himself which we do not really want to do since it would appear He has already told us this sin must stop! We cannot ignore GOD any longer and it cannot be stressed any stronger that now we must sacrifice what we have in order now to at least be saying to GOD that we as His children shall respond to His discipline. If we have it too easy then we are most likely running the road to destruction for this nation and we are part of this nation no matter what.

If we abandon our very own plus Israel and other nations who are our true allies then what is GOD to think of how serious we take Him? It is time for Christians in this nation to give up their love affair with money and democracy and start to understand that GOD is an authoritarian GOD and not a pick and choose GOD. This is not an election but this is the King that is ruler of all Christian nations and so He has the right to judge us even more sternly then a nation that does not know GOD as a personality!

We must put aside all things no matter what and look to GOD and no matter what the majority wants we must seek Him first and foremost and especially my own generation must put away its toys that they have been playing with for so many years and it is time to have grown up into adults. No more liquid manure, no more Hollywood, no more machines of any kind that serve no good purpose to serve GOD, no more love of money or materialism, no more lies to ourselves as well as others as to what should really come first and least of all self-preservation, etc. The 60's generation my generation must forget their own rights and think about others first and be first concerned about our own responsibilities. Hollywood has been copying what Dostoyevsky has written about and now they use his writings in a twisted way to promote their filth and garbage on the screen and to mock GOD and GOD shall not be mocked! We are a group or army of Christians here in America since we think money can solve all of our problems and we are a poor spiritual army for the Lord in that we have not given up what He wants us to give up and that is all of our own materialism plus to give up all of our very own will! Shall we do this now or shall we . . .

There is actually no law any longer in America-when people can murder innocent children and then be rewarded for that and have the Christian church remain totally silent on that issue alone not to mention the abominable sin and that is homosexuality with its deviancy for our own children also and we also have remained silent too long on that issue and have not approached our own government strongly enough.

The DaVinci Code is probably one of the most horrible books ever written and of course had to be written by an atheist. 7 million copies were sold here in America! I shall not even explain what is in the book itself. The publishing business is interested now in the one world government which owns and controls it to the fullest; hence anything that degrades the Judeo-Christian faith or adds lies here or there shall be most welcomed to be printed no matter how bad and evil the book might be! It has been thoroughly checked out to make sure that it is atheistic and heathenistic. Now there are more television ministries going along with this one world government more and more and yet come off as if they are for Christianity, but their own bottom line is money and more of it. These hucksters are appearing more and more on television and no one checks them out to see if they are true and honest except the Holy Spirit.

The Internet now is sold by Christians of which only the Messianic Jews will have nothing to do with it all since they know what it represents! The Gentile religions keep going on and inviting the one world government into their very homes by buying this Internet so the enemy has nothing to do. In Florida somewhere chips are being put into people's hands and also in Europe. AIDS is being blamed on some green monkey, whatever that means, when it was the homosexual community that started it and that is now the reason GOD had and has called it an abomination!

The reason America is called the best country now to live in in the entire world is because it has more materialism that fulfills the flesh and not because it is the most Christian. In fact, if America now would stop, most of the filth and garbage from Hollywood would stop in the world and the world would be that much better for it in the end. That's how bad this nation is in in regard to morality or should I say immorality! We have the easy but not the most blessed way of life on this planet and to even suppose we do is another lie. Comfort is not always a blessing when sin is promoted and is prevalent as much as it is here. Most of our wealth is invested in evil homosexuality, movies, pornography, infanticide, etc. and is distributed worldwide to all nations, and we even uphold the strength in totalitarian nations where Christians are being murdered and butchered left and right. Yet we say we cannot be a policeman for the world, but we could be a guardian for many Christians in the world who need our help individually and through our own government instead of building up Islam all the time, which is so shortsighted.

We have not evaded the Cold War as we think but have increased it to be now War Communism that could include even here, America itself! We have upheld for far too long the evil on the red horse and now we appear to also be on the bandwagon to help the one world government that is diametrically opposed to anything the Bible has to say. The churches have become consumer driven by taking funds from the state, which is a power. Churches also have followed what the state has said to do, and it should be the other way around in order for society to know right from wrong, not that they do not, but that it should be said to let our own government know to support anything they do since they believe in the lie! Who shall lead? One by one as individuals we must hold firm to the faith that Jesus or Messiah gave to us and stop worrying about money for television time and other things that involve materialism such as fine homes and cars and trips and educations plus personal things that have no place in the life of any Christian! We should be willing to stop begging for more money all the time and start showing some faith in GOD for through Him we can do all things!

Money is leaving the local area and is starving the spiritual world of many American communities and again consumerism and this democracy has lead us astray to believe that if we are a so—called majority that that will somehow keep us in the way of life and luxury that we love so very much and refuse to part with no matter what GOD has already said for us to do! We are in and now of the world as Christians and we refuse to stand up for our own faith that GOD has given to us. We do not want to see the handwriting on the wall GOD has shown us and had occurred in Babylon many years ago when King Nebuchadnezzar had died and his grandson took over! We have come to believe that at now the present moment we shall always have and care not about the future for anyone but ourselves and since we have this self preservation of this life and no regard for the eternal life we continue to live it up to the fullest!

Christmas alone is from pagan origins but now they want to take Jesus out of Christmas, and I say then why celebrate it in the first place and be like the Jewish people who celebrate Hanukah which is at least not a lie in the way that it is presented with the Maccabees and Antiochus Epiphanes who brought a pig into the temple. Pagan origins always have bad results since it is not from GOD Himself and so we have for all these centuries never ever challenged the validity of Easter or Christmas and have accepted it as a religious holiday when all along the Jewish people knew more than even the Christian believers about these two so called holidays which only kept the fact that Christ had come into the world and that He was crucified.

The American soldier in Vietnam was somewhat like the Soviet Red Army soldier under Stalin during World War II. In Stalin's Russia the peasants and others fought for Russia and not for Stalin but also knew that if they would win they would have to go back to that butcher and hence they would be tortured for the rest of their lives that is the ones up in the front and hence even the people back in Russia were for Stalin and his Communism. When the American soldier landed in the city by the bay (which is now known as Sodom and Gomorrah) and had many anti-war protesters in the streets as American GI's returned from Vietnam, the citizens there reacted the same way the Russian citizens in Moscow, Leningrad, and St. Petersburg did. They mocked and made fun of the American GI and called them baby killers which spread to all of our major cities while the civil rights' movement joined in with the so called hymn of praise with none other then Martin Luther King, Jr. who was by then affiliated with Pits 0' Dell who was a well known member of the American Communist Party just like Gus Hall was and DuBois! So the soldiers in both campaigns were being used by first the Communist Party to achieve a strangle hold on the Russian people and in the second case it was being used to mock the American soldier who went over there to fight against Communism, and our very own State Department and Mr. McNamara both saw to it that they would never win since it interfered with big business such as World Bank!

Even our own soldiers, when they came back were perplexed to find that Hollywood and the rich and well educated and others in America actually hated them because they themselves did not have the courage to stand up and fight for America and defeat Communism in Southeast Asia which has now spread to that entire region and then followed what happened in Cambodia in Ground Zero and then Laos and then Thailand where today children are prostituted and the Khmer Rouge were exonerated by big business for all the atrocities that they had committed against people who were civilians. Yes, man repeats himself and not history and so we have this continuation of the red horseman thanks to big business and party politics there and here with Nixon in America as well as McGovern, Jane Fonda, Tom Hayden, the Black Panthers, etc.

The moral fiber of our very nation at that time was so low that that also contributed to the loss there in Vietnam because of my generation the Baby Boomers born from 1946-1964 who did really nothing ever in their entire life to oppose this evil ideology and of course Vietnam was a poor soldiers' conflict with draft deferments for conscientious objectors such as Mohammed Ali who is a Moslem, the rich and well educated.

Hollywood crew and of course the Ivy Leaguers! These were the ones most of all who had a vested interest in us losing the conflict in Vietnam. Their love with this ideology was what they sought with their all. Many soldiers also who had gone there were breaking under the stress and had to smoke pot because their moral lives here had been anything but good. Movies in Hollywood as said "you made us go" and that was just an excuse for them being for the Communist regime in Vietnam and their treasonous attack against our own soldiers, most of whom were not that educated to know enough, like the Russian peasants who did not know enough about what Stalin and his Communist Party was really up to. It was Germany with their own ego that attacked Russia and soon found themselves frozen in the snow near Moscow and no farther. The German was no match for the Russian soldier who could withstand their extreme cold! Yet the beneficiary would be the West, and Stalin, their good old friend of

Londontown with FDR and Churchill at Yalta who sold us out too to this very day and that is why now Red China, North Korea and Cuba are all strongholds for Communism, because of so-called English diplomacy. FDR also had appointed Joseph Kennedy (a Nazi himself) as ambassador to England, and Chamberlain made his visit to Hitler; hence both the English and the German governments cut their so-called allies throats by agreeing with totalitarianism.

"Never, never, never give up," or "the only thing to fear is fear itself", were just cliches blowing in the wind and whichever way that would blow to and fro. These were the biggest chickens in all the world at that time and yet would preach to others about courage and no fear which was all hot air. We did not need Stalin in any way to defeat Nazi homosexual Germany because the American soldier was one of the most vicious fighters in all the world once he started fighting along with the Russian fighters except that we had the military arsenal with which to fight and to have defeated Stalin would have done the Russians a great favor for the entire world and not just Russia but the English had always hated the Russians so much that they would do this atrocious treaty at Yalta all for their own ego that is Churchill and FDR who could care less about the rest of the world and were so shortsighted with any decision they had made. When could a straight heterosexual army not defeat a bunch of homosexual leaders with the Nazis? All they needed to do was attack and attack and then move on to the weasel who had already left Moscow and that was the monkey face moustached Stalin!

The Reverend Schueller with his crystal cathedral always had appeared to me as a New Age religion facade and now that his music conductor has committed suicide unfortunately one has to feel sorrow for this man and now his wife and 3 children. Satan though does usually come to religions in music and even into cultures so there could have been something there that the enemy himself was attacking and this was the same Reverend Schueller who had invited Armand Hammer onto his show the man who gave soviet Communism a boost in the arm many years ago and had gotten all Western businessmen into the Soviet Union and now Henry Kissinger and Alexander Haig had gotten the Western businessmen into the even worse Red China where this President and others in government and in the media and even some ministries were saying there would be a change in Red China such as freedom and were disillusioning themselves into believing that Communism in Red China would soon phase out and that would be that while still Moscow had 10,000 warheads pointed at us at the present with the Communist and head of the KGB Vladimir Putin!

The American people had become, for the most part, as evil as its own government and we were the second evil empire now! We had murdered so many children here and yet the Vietnam Veteran had been called the baby killers by this same people who had murdered almost 55,000,000 unborn children and were now promoting here homosexual pedophilia with the help of the United Nations through NAMBLA!

We the people had become just that a majority of uncaring people who only now thought of each election as a way to get more for their money and it had nothing to do with GOD'S Word the Bible and even with believers they too were afraid to speak out because that would mean that they would have to give up the good life of eat, drink and be merry and the world of materialism!

If the church was not willing to help GOD then GOD would go somewhere else where the people were willing to stand up for the truth and for their brothers and sisters in Christ and the time had come and gone. That could not be said to any of the churches and ministries because they thought that GOD would wait and wait until we were ready to do what He wanted us to do any old time that we felt like doing it We would be the ones to suffer since we had ignored GOD'S warnings repeatedly time and again. If I knew about these warnings and I was only one person then for sure others in the Body of Christ certainly had to also know what GOD had wasted for so many years in America because GOD was slow to anger!

No one could say anything about this incumbent to other, Christians but yet he was being lead by the enemy because he was like the rich young man in the Bible Jesus had approached or he was also like King Saul who started out good and then fell to evil and this is what was going on in the Presidential Administration and the ministries on television liked it because now it meant more hucksters could advertise the Gospel that was a Jewish Gospel and so what did they have to lose except the land of Israel which was thousands of miles away from us and the farther one place was the less it affected the morality of the issue at hand as opposed to it happening right here or in one's own neighborhood!

But that would not do as to the consistency of Christianity that said all in the Body of Christ had to help one another no matter where they were or where they lived and this was not by government decree but by GOD'S HOLY WORD! If distance made the difference then that meant also whatever happened in Texas, Arizona and New Mexico would be all right with Washington DC since it was thousands of miles away for now! This is how the West had always thought in the 20th century about Russia and other lands that we would give up to Communism but now our own turn had come and we too would sell out our very own nation for a piece of meat!

America had gone into the abyss because we had forgotten about GOD and thought constantly about the flesh and what the flesh needed and that was pure materialism or socialism and we certainly had plenty of that now in America wherever one went. We no longer gave any concern for anything but just for the immediate moment to satisfy our own flesh which was always sin when it was to allow others to suffer so we could live like kings in this world for the present time! We had become so smart that we deceived even ourselves into believing Satan's own lie of eat, drink and be merry for tomorrow never comes and yet we kept storing more for a rainy day and then some and for what since America would soon have implosion on its shores from coast to coast?

We had forgotten to do without for so many years that now we thought we needed everything that we saw and that anything that came along we started to believe in and soon GOD was a thing of the past even at Christmas time when that was when they said that Jesus was born but that too would have to go if it interfered with materialism and our wants and not needs even!

Could the enemy deceive believers? It appeared so since most of them were still hung up on the 60's.

Since all these non-profit organizations were not businesses, they had to be part of government's own socialistic programs where most of them got their operational fees. How many non-profit hospitals alone in America existed since they were government sponsored, which meant a cash flow in the millions through Medicaid and Medicare as well as to the doctors and administrators?

This was part of "Constantine's" church state instead of promoting religion it would promote state power and be regulated as such. Replace as Lenin had done with the Russian Orthodox church with Marx ism and class warfare would soon appear that state would be the one to worship then as the bread winner.

Everyday in corporate business America in the offices started to appear like Siesta days along with multiculturalism. One could do as one pleased, but on most weeks one had to get 60-70 hours of work in in a 40-hour work week!

Computers now could tabulate into the trillionths of a second or millisecond when the speed of light was 186,282 miles per second.

This "free state "or socialist ruling of everyone's lives would disallow only the working family man whose wife stayed at home as a mother should to care for their children. Now the civil righters meaning always superior rights would excel for those born into it almost like a special kind of "royalty". Affirmative Action meant that reverse discrimination was in affect and that by law could be instantly reversed by the courts and was following the path of Nazi Germany before World War II against the Jews in German government who were not allowed to acquire any government position after that and now black racism was praised for the very same thing.

Government needed money and so now the middle class had to move up or down and it was most likely down and class warfare would mean the poor vs the rich or the peasants vs. the Bolsheviks. Government was proposing gambling, athletic and celebrity million dollar contracts with millions of dollars of taxes and now these illegals would make less than Puerto Ricans on welfare as well as Mexicans but cheaper paid work for all concerned and would also make Canada and Mexico two socialists states and now as one big happy family through NAFTA that included also these illegals who would be allowed to stay here for good!

Also the CD's, the IRA's, the 401K's, U.S. Savings Bonds, etc. would all be highly channeled as tax sources plus estate taxes, inheritance taxes, unpaid house taxes since many retirees would not be able to pay guess what? The property taxes that would go on forever and ever! Theirs would have to be given to whom the ones in the federal government wanted it to go to even if they were not United States citizens! We only had illegals, foreign rich people, ones who could not speak, obese people or laterally challenged people, AIDS patients, and also many illegal drug dealers that the government was hoping would become legal and that is why they wanted to call alcohol a drug because that would bring all the hard core drugs under the same tax code say as for beer and wine and liquor!

This incumbent was an excellent businessman but an atrocious President. He knew more about the stock market then he did about Israel or foreign policy. His state department was running the show. He even knew less about Christianity and that I know for sure! He was a social Christian the one that could be worse than say a socialist! He had no priorities in regards to America's sovereignty and thought wealth alone would suffice but not in the world of rogue states who could care less about the Western businessmen and Osama Ben Laden proved that! For sure they wanted only strategic offensive weapons and nothing else. This would be their plan to arm all of their soldiers and the skies, but conventional would be more practical to them. A conventional army that would soon march across Asia toward the Middle East with no one to stop them except the dam that was located in Turkey at the top of the Euphrates River!

The only fools were the Western businessmen who were ready to die anyway and leave this world in any shape and they could care less about that at all It was winner take all and if the solution was socialism then so be it since that meant less to share with the rest of the world or even the rest of the nation. There would then be no competition but only autocratic raw power!

As long as the Jews would finance Arab oil investments that meant that Islam would have more power and somebody somewhere wanted just that in order to take out Israel all together! Then they could control most of the world's trade and commerce and also hold a strategic location in the world just as Angola would be in order to wage nuclear war!

Would America perhaps the nation closest to Israel since we took on the Old Testament too in our own founding be the one to betray Israel for a piece of bread. "Man does not live by bread alone but by . . . "

The "undisciplined children" in America were inviting more of the same kind of undisciplined children into America, and they both got along just fine since both were anti-Judeo-Christian in faith and they thought all religions and faiths were the same in culture no matter what. These were the children that learned never to grow up and continued to listen to rock music, take drugs, shack up with one another, now were into homosexuality, promoted anything anti-American and were anti-Israel which meant that they had real anti-Semitism! They would often visit amusement parks and never ever seemed to grow up at all and used the new money they had never had before on gambling, drugs, sex, pornography, Hollywood, cars, clothes, boats, homes, etc. They did not know what the value of a dollar meant or what charity in hope, faith and charity meant.

These were the ones now running our very government and were making a shambles of it entirely. They thought that democracy meant freedom alone and did not understand at all what the word responsibility meant at all! My generation as well as my parent's generation did not even blink an eye when the war was over and continued to let others around the world die in misery and felt that after World War II everything would be fine and dandy and this again would be the war to end all wars whatever that meant?

They then brought their own children up not to care for others who were in need and started to follow the road to socialism under social security and continued to only think in sentimental terms about anything. They did not get too depressed because they had won the last war we would have or at least that is what they must have thought even though Communism was much much greater than Nazism ever was and today we all could really see what was going on in the entire world since they had fallen asleep and we too were brought up to ignore the rest but not to ignore what was next to us until many years later which meant now and in the present. Our own neighborhoods now did not matter because nobody left their television sets or they were always traveling to get away from reality and what life was really all about.

America had really lived the good life and never wanted to give it up and that meant that now even if someone infringed on our very own pleasures we would not let them get away with it since that was the most important things in our own lives. We grew up ignorant and naive' as to the whole world around us and had thought nothing of the Soviet Union until Kennedy got in and then it was almost too late to do anything about It. We see today now, after about one generation or 40 years that we have let ourselves go and we let ourselves go in the spiritual sense and could care less even about the person next to us let alone others in the world. There were always a few who cared but they were in the minority and the others in a democracy also had a sales pitch to listen to. Never did the majority in America since the signing of at least the important documents and a little before ever really have a close relationship with GOD in the sense that they knew Him personally. We were a nation that had grown too fast and too far and so we could not learn in the time that allotted us to learn since it was only about 3 centuries. We were like undisciplined children who appeared not to have any parents at all until the 60's generation came and then we had become orphans in the sense that we had no spiritual relationship with Jesus and we only wanted what we thought was right or wrong and wanted to do the things that we wanted to do and continued to think that there would be no day of reckoning for all of this misery. We murdered our very own children us undisciplined children and we encouraged the worse of sins and still we kept talking ourselves blue in the face and nothing any longer meant anything to anyone since the words were empty and their meanings had changed completely from what they had use to mean.

America had lost its way many years ago but no one ever wanted to say just that in so many words so we pretended to be on the road to recovery when all along we were on the road to destruction and now we ourselves were lost in this quagmire that we had created along with previous generations and we confused affluence with purity of some kind when in essence we lost our purity many many generations ago. We did not want to really work the land for the most part and since only a small portion did we saw what it was like to live in the now only and we could care less about really what had happened and most of all what would happen since this would indeed affect the future and the way our children were already abused by Hollywood, the media, affluence, pornography, materialism, socialism, atheism, etc. we continued on as if nothing in the world mattered except our very own lives and no one else's!

Our egos were so huge our heads became so heavy that we walked around with our head down to the ground oblivious to all that was going on in the world as well as in our very own nation and Hollywood most of all played the lies again and again and we thought that the world owed us a living and when it did not we rebelled in the 60's, which so far has been the worse generation to have lived in America and the 20th century and did not do anything to help our fellow man in distant shores except shared a little of our affluence and since our spiritual realm was weak we could not share too much of that at all since also in the 60's we were are own worse enemy. We could have done so very much more if we would have stayed close to the soil and had forgotten about public education and higher education which was in a major part a major problem since it brought into our very nation some pernicious kind of heresy that said GOD does not matter at all and we have all that we need and then we continued to follow England and Germany and still do today to the very end and this time we have reached our very end and there is no more real time to turn around to make up for the valuable and lost days and so we must now do that is us believers what GOD wants us to do no matter if it means that we have to give up everything that we own and possibly our very own lives and we brought all this upon ourselves and were not forced to accept the perniciousness that we had so comfortably come to know! Now it was our turn to wait on GOD and see what he would have to say about the future and not be content to even try to save what we had in materialism because this went way past the materialistic stage and now we were in the garbage heap of destruction but the aesthetic value of everything around us made us feel comfortable even though we were highly insecure about our possessions!

This Babylon now known as America could not go back but only forward into a dark unknown but as believers we knew that Jesus was there with us and it did not matter but we would uphold that small part of America that was still wholesome and pure! "Save me from the wretched body."

Just to know that we were still able to share the Gospel with other people was such a wonderful thing and knowing that Jesus was always with us was also a wonderful thing and GOD was everywhere and knew our very thoughts and we continued to pray nonetheless for the nation that we loved and now we would again have to wait on Him!

We threw away our very own freedom for a short time in our own history but we could only go forward and not backwards and could not regret what we had done or we would never get on with what GOD wanted us for today and for His kingdom. One by one we would have to do this with GOD as our guide. Our Bibles were still legal and we could worship Jesus in public still so America still had much to do!

Why do Christian television ministries always have to advertise whatever they do for charity or in the name of Jesus? The Jewish people donate millions and nothing is ever heard about it and that is the way that Scripture wants it to be. The Gentiles publicize their good works and would probably say that all this was to encourage more people to give if they saw where the money was going. Why is it then that the Jewish people do not advertise at all and yet get millions of dollars and need no encouragement when the Holy Spirit would be enough to encourage Christians to donate their offerings after they have always tithed first to their own house of worship?

This is not a Madison Avenue thing where one has to show what they do and appear to take the credit for what Christ is doing under the power of the Holy Spirit. Television ministries need to take a lesson from the Jewish people and stop showing starving children to draw the guilt of Christians because GOD does not want donations or contributions through guilt but through His Son's love only. We should be lead by the Holy Spirit which we cannot see and so we do not need to see what it is that these television ministries are giving to since they say they are true believers and are helping others in need and who are poor and desperate!

GOD is not in need of showing what He needs if one is in tune with the Holy Spirit and who cannot be lead or feel compassion and mercy for ones in special need and ones who need to hear that GOD loves them just the way they are and not to continue to advertise just how much money is involved because GOD is not about money or how much but is it given in the spirit of His love and if not then it should not be given and if given through guilt then also it should not but should again be given with the love of Jesus first and foremost and that is all one needs if they are a true believer in Christ.

Too many of our senses need to be fed in order for us to give to these television ministries who also live like kings and queens and have too much in this world and that if they continue to huckster GOD' S Word then they need to be especially careful that what they say and do is always done in a humble way and that none of the proceeds as they would say would ever be for anything but food, the Bible, medicine and other things that they really need and not air time which only feeds into this one world system of ideology.

We must test all the spirits for sure and not just because they say and others say that they are a Christian Organization and they do not need to go on begging and pleading for funds since GOD does not want people to give who need others to beg from them since this would not be from one's inner heart at all! GOD wants His people to give with a cheerful heart and not one of Roman Catholicism where guilt is played upon day after day or on television ministries and then they thank GOD for what He has done when all along it was their begging and pleading with people that made them give for even unbelievers might also give which would mean that the money is not blessed by GOD since it is His people in His family that He wants to give and continue on but again first to tithe and not through guilt but through love and always love and nothing in return and GOD so does so be it and also that with GOD a small amount can go much further than with one who feels guilty in giving. Again this is not Madison Avenue where one needs to feel that they need to buy something and in this case to give something because of the power of human suggestion that goes way beyond that of a cheerful giver and is anything but.

People who are unbelievers as I said also might give and not know why they do it but then again also one should only want believers to give to their cause because it is through them that the Body of Christ works and if unbelievers do give then let it be by GOD and not by begging!

We see men in the streets beg to a dying world and do we want to be noted for that type of begging even if it is in earnest? We need to clean up this area of ministries that continue to make GOD look like He needs us to beg in order to get something no matter if for another. Yes, let your requests be known to GOD and let that be a very personal and private thing between you and GOD.

If we are truly saved we shall be lead to give where He wants us to give and not where man thinks we should give and we need to remember that. Money is not the issue but the method is. We are our brother's keeper and so we need to always pray for others while others can pray for us and stop this constant asking for ourselves when we have plenty and some have none at all!

Be in prayer and remember the Holy Spirit shall interpret what we cannot even say in our own words so GOD is not unable to do what needs to be done and we as instruments need to be able to play only GOD' S tune of love or charity and there is plenty of this to go around if we would open truly our hearts to GOD first and not to materialism and not worry about how much or how long we have given or not given.

Again the people on television must in some way perform on the air but also must be sincere in order to have a thawing of people or else the ministry will go off of the air and most can be seen for what they are. If they are hucksters it is not to hard to find out or see since many times they will continue to ask for funds and more funds and do nothing to share Scripture with the audience. Charles Stanley also really helps and informs and he never says that for a donation of but always the price of. This is another way to tell if the ministry itself is honest and another way is to send some small cash amount and see if they send a return receipt once you have known for sure that they have received it. If they have received it, there shall be some other information always about the ministry and that is to keep your interest up.

A few of the many ministries on television do a find job but they too miss the mark when they do not address the fact and in an exact manner the moral sins of our nation. Many do not address homosexuality and will only usually do that when it is election time or maybe when financial times get real hard. If the protection of our own children are never addressed then how can one support any ministry that subterfuges the issue when it is us Christians who must always speak out no matter how many times we have to say it and it is our responsibility as one Jewish grandmother said in regard to abortion or infanticide and she meant all Christians because in Nazi Germany that is what they first started with!

Usually a good ministry in the sense that the way they present that ministry on the air has a lot to do with, the success of that ministry and one can usually tell if there are many contributors but remember that is not always a sure sign if they are the most sincere ministry that one can listen to as well as support since one will usually support something that they have an interest in and someone or somebody they believe is telling the truth to them.

Remember in today's world money is too much the prerogative and the message of the Gospel gets lost and also one can check to see how financially honest and how well they use the money that is donated and contributed to that ministry by getting a hold of the evangelical association. Never support any ministry that goes against GOD'S Word which is his will. Remember man's human nature can come between that preacher and GOD. Look to see how the stage is set and see if they ever show what type of house they live in and what type of car they drive. Their lifestyle should always be moderate to low and never exclusive.

An "I" for another "I" would mean America would take on socialism over Judeo-Christianity and that GOD would have nothing to do with America as any kind of leading nation if it ever was? We as Americans had made our decision to fight against ourselves in America for oil but as against Communism we refused to oppose that evil with such stoutheartedness and let ourselves be fooled by materialism and a lack of moral fiber from the 60's and our own heroes became the "better red than dead" iconoclasts.

It became tom foolery for us to say no more Mr. Incumbent and you can have your love for Islam and your love for anti-Semitism and we peasants would have no part in the Soviet Union's own Islamic respect that said. They are so much like ourselves in that they hate all Jews everywhere just like all the main line denominations that felt the same way and were silent with Islam when they wanted to buy out America and also establish Arabic as a language. And Spanish, the slang type, also was in favor with most American people since they could not and would not oppose a people from a heathen land that too wanted to destroy not only

America but also Israel any way they could. Louie, my mentor, was right when he said that most Americans were not too bright. How true that turned out to be!

We were a people who wanted it to end so that we could go to our graves knowing that we had gotten all we could from a mundane world! What a relief it would be to know that our children would not be anything like us but even worse than one could ever imagine just so we could live the easy life with the prevalent lie!

The rich would continue to come to America as in years passed and the poor would be left out since America for the most part wanted mostly the rich and well educated to build up capitalism but what we were really building up was socialism to the fullest and Islam would definitely see us through to the end and the end would soon be here and in fact it was already here and America did not even know it at all!

We were in favor of an easy heathen culture as opposed to a rich GOD fearing land and nation of one people under GOD and the one nation under GOD became many nationalities under Islam and heathenism.

The end of this story was coming but not the end of what was to soon happen here as well as in the world and now we would see what a nation without GOD would really be like and then know for sure the real judgment of GOD! The I now meant ego in America and nothing else and we did not even have respect for a Holy and a just GOD and we would not give up our 60's sins no matter how bad it got and yet we wondered why all these catastrophes were occurring here especially in America the land that GOD had once blessed but now would judge in order to save its soul like St. Paul had done in the Bible when a young man within the church at that time was going with his own step mother and not even this was happening in the unbelieving world as St. Paul states!

Now the I and the other I stood for ego and Islam and the violence of the lie of both from the pits of Hell and also the fact that now there were few Christians in America. Church now meant only a social gathering so people could eat, drink and be merry. This was indeed a very bad sin. Now we were doing what we once had only thought about and thought it to be no different and some did not even see any sin in this way of life and hence did not recognize let alone think about a just and mighty GOD! It was our turn now to eat, drink and be merry.

House churches would have to be worshipped at since the church buildings themselves looked and acted more like the world then the Christ! As in Red China people would have to worship GOD privately as they had in Red China and the Soviet Union in order to truly just worship and not for a social gathering of entertainment! This had become the main cause for now coming to a building known as the church and so house churches would have to be done since the government was now controlling all the church buildings but could not control the hidden house churches that were growing here and there all over America!

We had taken democracy and consumerism to such a level that now we replaced faith in GOD or in things that one cannot see with the things that one could see and there was hardly any healings or other kinds of miracles from GOD! We kept saying, "Why not?" We could not figure out what was wrong yet many of our saints who had spoken out were now starting to die in our very own nation and next would come many of us as Peter had said, "Judgment begins with the household of GOD." The household of GOD . . .

And finally we come to this big big lie to our children all over America: this Germanic Santa. If we rearrange the letters to this felonious name, we come up with none other than Satan! How coincidental that these 5 letters would make up another one's lie of lies and that was the master of the lie Satan himself! Yes, as we hear many say, "Santa or Satan brought you these so called gifts of materialism so he could lie to you as a child." The parents went along with this lie willingly and more than willingly because it benefited them to get more materialism through what else than Roman Catholicism, another lie. So lie upon lie produces violence, not that the opposite of peace is war but is violence because Satan can also come in the form of a light.

Roman Catholicism was not anyone's brother's keeper but was this antichrist—no not the Antichrist because Satan would save the Antichrist for something even more diabolically anti-Semitic and that would be that this was "The Church" when all of these centuries it was the Jewish people themselves that GOD Himself had picked out to be the basis of the church and not another lie in this facade that they would call Roman Catholicism some kind of form of Christianity which also was a lie as this President had also called exactly the same thing as Islam and Messiah in the flesh and so much for these born again believers who said they were born again at least 100,000,000 in America which again was another lie and the billions upon billions of people since Adam had gone to Hell because of the lie that Satan devised from himself and none no not one iota ever came from GOD the everlasting GOD that would go beyond our own earth, sun and then planets which was our own solar system and then to our own Milky Way, which also was our own galaxy and then from there to millions of millions of other galaxies, and then the entire universe which was expanding more and more, and we thought that GOD was something much smaller and yet could see all of our doings and heal all of our infirmities as well as all of our iniquities!

This was an age of sure unbelief for within the church there too were many lies that were set in motion and man instead of reading the Word of GOD the Bible would believe hearsay because they knew that GOD'S Word was meant for all of us and the more we learned the more we were accountable for but little did they know that even if they would claim ignorance would still be not ignorance as far as GOD was concerned! This was an awesome GOD who came in the flesh one time and forever and ever.

So, out of all of this America had thought or we had thought that our own nation was the epitome of what GOD was looking for. But GOD had already found that in the Old and the New Jerusalem that would come down from heaven and it would be a Jewish Messiah, not a Christian Gentile messiah even though Christ was used since anti-Semitism had been so great from many centuries and ages of this earth as long as man walked this earth.

The reason the Jews would get depressed around the time of the year was because the spirit was willing but the flesh was weak; hence also the first Hanukah was on December 25th and not the first Christmas as the Roman Vatican had lied all these centuries. They did not know what even the word Messiah meant except that it was something foreign and Jewish, and as for Hanukah they only knew that the candle burned miraculously for 8 days and then they were not so sure about why that was. So they actually did not really know why they were celebrating in this Festival of Lights which meant Hanukah, which as I had already said, was in the Gospel of John.

No, the Romans had gotten it wrong and so did the Germans. Martin Luther only rediscovered what this grace was all about and that the German Reformation was never original since it had to be from GOD who was the only ORIGINAL and Messiah was that original for the entire world and not Europeanism! Even Russian Orthodoxy missed the marked in regards to Messiah but had been also blessed by the number of Jews in that nation of Russia but they too failed to perceive the usefulness of that and only saw the Pharisees!

Now the "I" in Israel was not good enough for America as the "I" in Islam and all for the love of money! We were a nation that truly had lost its bearings and had gone adrift because man the Gentile man thought that he would make history and keep his lie when it was a Jewish man Messiah who would allow the Gentile to come in which was totally opposite then what all these major denominations had thought!

"I" as in the ego, "I" as in Islam, or "I" as in Israel or Jacob who later was called Israel because of 12 tribes and that from the tribe of Judah would come this Messiah. The Gentiles, all of us, would be included because of the disobedience of the nation of the Jews! Now where is one to go to see this Son of man? What would be the status of all the nations? Which America chose the right "I" and . . . ?